D0049197

VOWS AND HONOR

The Oathbound
Oathbreakers

MERCEDES LACKEY

GUILDAMERICA BOOKS®

Contents

VOWS AND HONOR

The Oathbound

Dedicated to
Lisa Waters
for wanting to see it
and my parents
for agreeing with her

Introduction

This is the tale of an unlikely partnership, that of the Shin'a'in swordswoman and celibate Kal'enedral, Tarma shena Tale'sedrin and the nobly-born sorceress Kethry, member of the White Winds school, whose devotees were sworn to wander the world using their talents for the greatest good. How these two met is told in the tale "Sword Sworn," published in Marion Zimmer Bradley's anthology SWORD AND SORCERESS III. A second of the accounts of their wandering life will be seen in the fourth volume of that series. But *this* story begins where that first tale left off, when they have recovered from their ordeal and are making their way back to the Dhorisha Plains and Tarma's home.

One

The sky was overcast, a solid gray sheet that seemed to hang just barely above the treetops, with no sign of a break in the clouds anywhere. The sun was no more than a dimly glowing spot near the western horizon, framed by a lattice of bare black branches. Snow lay at least half a foot thick everywhere in the forest, muffling sound. A bird flying high on the winter wind took dim notice that the forest below him extended nearly as far as he could see no matter which way he looked, but was neatly bisected by the Trade Road immediately below him. Had he flown a little higher (for the clouds were not as low as they looked), he might have seen the rooftops and smokes of a city at the southern end of the road, hard against the forest. Although the Trade Road had seen enough travelers of late that the snow covering it was packed hard, there were only two on it now. They had stopped in the clearing halfway through the forest that normally saw heavy use as an overnighting point. One was setting up camp under the shelter of a half-cave of rock and tree trunks piled together—partially the work of man, partially of nature. The other was a short distance away, in a growth-free pocket just off the main area, picketing their beasts.

The bird circled for a moment, swooping lower, eyeing the pair with dim speculation. Humans sometimes meant food—

But there was no food in sight, at least not that the bird recognized as such. And as he came lower still, the one with the beasts looked up at him suddenly, and reached for something slung at her saddlebow.

The bird had been the target of arrows often enough to recognize a

bow when he saw one. With a squawk of dismay, he veered off, flapping
his wings with all his might, and tracing a twisty, convoluted course out of
range. *He* wanted to be the eater, not the eaten!

Tarma sighed as the bird sped out of range, unstrung her bow, and
stowed it back in the saddle-quiver. She hunched her shoulder a little
beneath her heavy wool coat to keep her sword from shifting on her
back, and went back to her task of scraping the snow away from the grass
buried beneath it with gloved hands. Somewhere off in the far distance
she could hear a pair of ravens calling to each other, but otherwise the
only sounds were the sough of wind in branches and the blowing of her
horse and Kethry's mule. The Shin'a'in place of eternal punishment was
purported to be cold; now she had an idea *why*.

She tried to ignore the ice-edged wind that seemed to cut right
through the worn places in her nondescript brown clothing. This was no
place for a Shin'a'in of the Plains, this frozen northern forest. She had no
business being here. Her garments, more than adequate to the milder
winters in the south, were just not up to the rigors of the cold season
here.

Her eyes stung, and not from the icy wind. Home—Warrior Dark, she
wanted to be home! Home, away from these alien forests with their
unfriendly weather, away from outClansmen with no understanding and
no manners . . . home. . . .

Her little mare whickered at her, and strained against her lead rope,
her breath steaming and her muzzle edged with frost. *She* was no fonder
of this chilled wilderness than Tarma was. Even the Shin'a'in winter pastures never got this cold, and what little snow fell on them was soon
melted. The mare's sense of what was "right" was deeply offended by all
this frigid white stuff.

"Kathal, dester'edra," Tarma said to the ears that pricked forward at
the first sound of her harsh voice. "Gently, windborn-sister. I'm nearly
finished here."

Kessira snorted back at her, and Tarma's usually solemn expression
lightened with an affectionate smile.

"Li'ha'eer, it is ice-demons that dwell in this place, and nothing else."

When she figured that she had enough of the grass cleared off to at
least help to satisfy her mare's hunger, she heaped the rest of her forag-
ings into the center of the area, topping the heap with a carefully measured portion of mixed grains and a little salt. What she'd managed to
find was poor enough, and not at all what her training would have preferred—some dead seed grasses with the heads still on them, the tender

tips from the branches of those trees and bushes she recognized as being nourishing, even some dormant cress and cattail roots from the stream. It was scarcely enough to keep the mare from starving, and not anywhere near enough to provide her with the energy she needed to carry Tarma on at the pace she and her partner Kethry had been making up until now.

She loosed little Kessira from her tethering and picketed her in the middle of the space she'd cleared. It showed the measure of the mare's hunger that she tore eagerly into the fodder, poor as it was. There had been a time when Kessira would have turned up her nose in disdain at being offered such inferior provender.

"Ai, we've come on strange times, haven't we, you and I," Tarma sighed. She tucked a stray lock of crow-wing-black hair back under her hood, and put her right arm over Kessira's shoulder, resting against the warm bulk of her. "Me with no Clan but one weirdling outlander, you so far from the Plains and your sibs."

Not that long ago they'd been just as any other youngling of the nomadic Shin'a'in and her saddle mare; Tarma learning the mastery of sword, song, and steed, Kessira running free except when the lessoning involved her. Both of them had been safe and contented in the heart of Clan Tale'sedrin—true, free Children of the Hawk.

Tarma rubbed her cheek against Kessira's furry shoulder, breathing in the familiar smell of clean horse that was so much a part of what had been home. Oh, but they'd been happy; Tarma had been the pet of the Clan, with her flute-clear voice and her perfect memory for song and tale, and Kessira had been so well-matched for her rider that she almost seemed the "four-footed sister" that Tarma frequently named her. Their lives had been so close to perfect—in all ways. The king-stallion of the herd had begun courting Kessira that spring, and Tarma had had Dharin; nothing could have spoiled what seemed to be their secure future.

Then the raiders had come upon the Clan; and all that carefree life was gone in an instant beneath their swords.

Tarma's eyes stung again. Even full revenge couldn't take away the ache of losing them, all, all—

In one candlemark all that Tarma had ever known or cared about had been wiped from the face of the earth.

"What price your blood, my people? A few pounds of silver? Goddess, the dishonor that your people were counted so *cheaply!*"

The slaughter of Tale'sedrin had been the more vicious because they'd taken the entire Clan unawares and unarmed in the midst of celebration; totally unarmed, as Shin'a'in seldom were. They had trusted to the vigilance of their sentries.

But the cleverest sentry cannot defeat foul magic that creeps upon him out of the dark and smothers the breath in his throat ere he can cry out.

The brigands had not so much as a drop of honorable blood among them; they knew had the Clan been alerted they'd have had stood the robbers off, even outnumbered as they were, so the bandits' hired mage had cloaked their approach and stifled the guards. And so the Clan had fought an unequal battle, and so they had died; adults, oldsters, children, all. . . .

"Goddess, hold them—" she whispered, as she did at least once each day. Every last member of Tale'sedrin had died; most had died horribly. Except Tarma. She *should* have died; and unaccountably been left alive.

If you could call it living to have survived with everything gone that had made life worth having. Yes, she had been left alive—and utterly, utterly alone. Left to live with a ruined voice that had once been the pride of the Clans, with a ravaged body, and most of all, a shattered heart and mind. There had been nothing left to sustain her but a driving will to wreak vengeance on those who had left her Clanless.

She pulled a brush from an inside pocket of her coat, and began needlessly grooming Kessira while the mare ate. The firm strokes across the familiar chestnut coat were soothing to both of them. She had been left Clanless, and a Shin'a'in Clanless is one without purpose in living. Clan is everything to a Shin'a'in. Only one thing kept her from seeking oblivion and death-willing herself, that burning need to revenge her people.

But vengeance and blood-feud were denied the Shin'a'in—the ordinary Shin'a'in. Else too many of the people would have gone down on the knives of their own folk, and to little purpose, for the Goddess knew Her people and knew their tempers to be short. Hence, Her law. Only those who were the Kal'enedral of the Warrior—the Sword Sworn, out-Clansmen called them, although the name *meant* both "Children of Her Sword" and "Her Sword-Brothers"—could cry blood-feud and take the trail of vengeance. That was because of the nature of their Oath to Her —*first* to the service of the Goddess of the New Moon and South Wind, *then* to the Clans as a whole, and only after those two to their own particular Clan. Blood-feud did not serve the Clans if the feud was between Shin'a'in and Shin'a'in; keeping the privilege of calling for blood-price in the hands of those by their very nature devoted to the welfare of the Shin'a'in as a whole kept interClan strife to a minimum.

"If it had been you, what would you have chosen, hmm?" she asked the mare. "Her Oath isn't a light one." Nor was it without cost—a cost some might think far too high. Once Sworn, the Kal'enedral became weapons in Her hand, and not unlike the sexless, cold steel they wore.

Hard, somewhat aloof, and totally asexual were the Sword Sworn—and this, too, ensured that their interests remained Hers and kept them from becoming involved in interClan rivalry. So it was not the kind of Oath one involved in a simple feud was likely to even consider taking.

But the slaughter of the Tale'sedrin was not a matter of private feud or Clan against Clan—this was a matter of more, even, than personal vengeance. Had the brigands been allowed to escape unpunished, would that not have told other wolfheads that the Clans were not invulnerable—would there not have been another repetition of the slaughter? That may have been Her reasoning; Tarma had only known that she was able to find no other purpose in living, so she had offered her Oath to the Star-Eyed so that she could pledge her life to revenge her Clan. An insane plan—sprung out of a mind that might be going mad with grief.

There were those who thought she was *already* mad, who were certain She would accept no such Oath given by one whose reason was gone. But much to the amazement of nearly everyone in the Clan Liha'irden who had succored, healed, and protected her, that Oath had been accepted. Only the shamans had been unsurprised.

She had never in her wildest dreaming guessed what would come of that Oath and that quest for justice.

Kessira finished the pile of provender, and moved on to tear hungrily at the lank, sere grasses. Beneath the thick coat of winter hair she had grown, her bones were beginning to show in a way that Tarma did not in the least like. She left off brushing, and stroked the warm shoulder, and the mare abandoned her feeding long enough to nuzzle her rider's arm affectionately.

"Patient one, we shall do better by you, and soon," Tarma pledged her. She left the mare to her grazing and went to check on Kethry's mule. That sturdy beast was capable of getting nourishment from much coarser material than Kessira, so Tarma had left him tethered amid a thicket of sweetbark bushes. He had stripped all within reach of last year's growth, and was straining against his halter with his tongue stretched out as far as it would reach for a tasty morsel just out of his range.

"Greedy pig," she said with a chuckle, and moved him again, giving him a bit more rope this time, and leaving his own share of grain and foraged weeds within reach. Like all his kind he was a clever beast; smarter than any horse save one Shin'a'in-bred. It was safe enough to give him plenty of lead; if he tangled himself he'd untangle himself just as readily. Nor would he eat to foundering, not that there was enough browse here to do that. A good, sturdy, gentle animal, and even-tempered, well suited to an inexperienced rider like Kethry. She'd been lucky to find him.

His tearing at the branches shook snow down on her; with a shiver she brushed it off as her thoughts turned back to the past. No, she would never have guessed at the changes wrought in her life-path by that Oath and her vow of vengeance.

"Jel'enedra, you think too much. It makes you melancholy."

She recognized the faintly hollow-sounding tenor at the first word; it was her chief sword-teacher. This was the first time he'd come to her since the last bandit had fallen beneath her sword. She had begun to wonder if her teachers would ever come back again.

All of them were unforgiving of mistakes, and quick to chastise—this one more than all the rest put together. So though he had startled her, though she had hardly expected his appearance, she took care not to display it.

"Ah?" she replied, turning slowly to face him. Unfair that he had used his other-worldly powers to come on her unawares, but he himself would have been the first to tell her that life—as she well knew—was unfair. She would not reveal that she had not detected his presence until he spoke.

He had called her "younger sister," though, which was an indication that he was pleased with her for some reason. "Mostly you tell me I don't think enough."

Standing in a clear spot amid the bushes was a man, garbed in fighter's gear of deepest black, and veiled. The ice-blue eyes, the sable hair, and the cut of his close-wrapped clothing would have told most folk that he was, like Tarma, Shin'a'in. The color of the clothing would have told the more knowledgeable—since most Shin'a'in preferred a carnival brightness in their garments—that he, too, was Sword Sworn; Sword Sworn by custom wore only stark black or dark brown. But only one very sharp-eyed would have noticed that while he stood amid the snow, he made no imprint upon it. It seemed that he weighed hardly more than a shadow.

That was scarcely surprising since he had died long before Tarma was born.

"Thinking to plan is one case; thinking to brood is another," he replied. "You accomplish nothing but to increase your sadness. You should be devising a means of filling your bellies and those of your *jel'suthro'edrin.* You cannot reach the Plains if you do not eat."

He had used the Shin'a'in term for riding beasts that meant "forever-younger-Clanschildren." Tarma was dead certain he had picked that term with utmost precision, to impress upon her that the welfare of Kessira and Kethry's mule Rodi were as important as her own—more so, since they could not fend for themselves in this inhospitable place.

"With all respect, teacher, I am . . . at a loss. Once I had a purpose. Now?" She shook her head. "Now I am certain of nothing. As you once told me—"

"Li'sa'eer! Turn my own words against me, will you?" he chided gently. "And have you *nothing?"*

"My *she'enedra.* But she is outClan, and strange to me, for all that the Goddess blessed our oath-binding with Her own fire. I know her but little. I—only—"

"What, bright blade?"

"I wish—I wish to go home—" The longing she felt rose in her throat and made it hard to speak.

"And so? What is there to hinder you?"

"There is," she replied, willing her eyes to stop stinging, "the matter of money. Ours is nearly gone. It is a long way to the Plains."

"So? Are you not now of the mercenary calling?"

"Well, unless there be some need for blades hereabouts—the which I have seen *no* evidence for, the only way to reprovision ourselves will be if my *she'enedra* can turn her skill in magic to an honorable profit. For though I have masters of the best," she bowed her head in the little nod of homage a Shin'a'in gave to a respected elder, "sent by the Star-Eyed herself, what measure of attainment I have acquired matters not if there is no market for it."

"Hai'she'li! You should market that silver tongue, *jel'enedra!"* he laughed. "Well, and well. Three things I have come to tell you, which is why I arrive out-of-time and not at moonrise. First, that there will be storm tonight, and you should all shelter, mounts and riders together. Second, that because of the storm, we shall not teach you *this* night, though you may expect our coming from this day on, every night that you are not within walls."

He turned as if to leave, and she called out, "And third?"

"Third?" he replied, looking back at her over his shoulder. "Third—is that everyone has a past. Ere you brood over your own, consider an-other's."

Before she had a chance to respond, he vanished, melting into the wind.

Wrinkling her nose over that last, cryptic remark, she went to find her *she'enedra* and partner.

Kethry was hovering over a tiny, nearly smokeless fire, skinning a pair of rabbits. Tarma almost smiled at the frown of concentration she wore;

she was going at the task as if she were being rated on the results! They were a study in contrasts, she and her outClan blood-sister. Kethry was sweet-faced and curvaceous, with masses of curling amber hair and startling green eyes; she would have looked far more at home in someone's court circle as a pampered palace mage than she did here, at their primitive hearth. Or even more to the point, she would not have looked *out* of place as someone's spoiled, indulged wife or concubine; she really looked nothing at all like any mage Tarma had ever seen. Tarma, on the other hand, with her hawklike face, forbidding ice-blue eyes and nearly sexless body, was hardly the sort of person one would expect a mage *or* woman like Kethry to choose as a partner, much less as a friend. As a hireling, perhaps—in which case it should have been *Tarma* skinning the rabbits, for *she* looked to have been specifically designed to endure hardship.

Oddly enough, it was Kethry who had taken to this trip as if she were the born nomad, and Tarma who was the one suffering the most from their circumstances, although that was mainly due to the unfamiliar weather.

Well, if she had not foreseen that becoming Kal'enedral meant suddenly acquiring a bevy of long-dead instructors, this partnership had come as even more of a surprise. The more so as Tarma had really not expected to survive the initial confrontation with those who had destroyed her Clan.

"Do not reject aid unlooked-for," her instructor had said the night before she set foot in the bandits' town. And unlooked-for aid had materialized, in the form of this unlikely sorceress. Kethry, too, had her interests in seeing the murderers brought low, so they had teamed together for the purpose of doing just that. Together they had accomplished what neither could have done alone—they had utterly destroyed the brigands to the last man.

And so Tarma had lost her purpose. Now—now there was only the driving need to get back to the Plains; to return before the Tale'sedrin were deemed a dead Clan. Farther than that she could not, would not think or plan.

Kethry must have sensed Tarma's brooding eyes on her, for she looked up and beckoned with her skinning knife.

"Fairly good hunting," Tarma hunched as close the fire as she could, wishing they dared build something larger.

"Yes and no. I had to use magic to attract them, poor things." Kethry shook her head regretfully as she bundled the offal in the skins and buried the remains in the snow to freeze hard. Once frozen, she'd dispose of them away from the camp, to avoid attracting scavengers. "I felt so guilty, but what else was I to do? We ate the last of the bread yester-day, and I didn't want to chance on the hunting luck of just one of us."

"You do what you have to, Keth. Well, *we're* able to live off the land, but Kessira and Rodi can't," Tarma replied. "Our grain is almost gone, and we've still a long way to go to get to the Plains. Keth, we need money."

"I know."

"And you're the one of us best suited to earning it. This land is too peaceful for the likes of me to find a job—except for something involving at least a one-year contract, and that's something we can't afford to take the time for. I need to get back to the Plains as soon as I can if I'm to raise Tale'sedrin's banner again."

"I know that, too." Kethry's eyes had become shadowed, the lines around her mouth showed strain. "And I know that the only city close enough to serve us is Mornedealth."

And there was no doubt in Tarma's mind that Kethry would rather have died than set foot in that city, though she hadn't the vaguest notion why. Well, this didn't look to be the proper moment to ask—

"Storm coming; a bad one," she said, changing the subject. "I'll let the hooved ones forage for as long as I dare, but by sunset I'll have to bring them into camp. Our best bet is going to be to shelter all together be-cause I don't think a fire is going to survive the blow."

"I wish I knew where you get your information," Kethry replied, frown smoothing into a wry half-smile. "You certainly have *me* beat at weather-witching."

"Call it Shin'a'in intuition," Tarma shrugged, wishing she knew whether it was permitted to an outland *she'enedra*—who was a magician to boot—to know of the veiled ones. Would they object? Tarma had no notion, and wasn't prepared to risk it. "Think you can get our dinner cooked before the storm gets here?"

"I may be able to do better than that, if I can remember the spells." The mage disjointed the rabbits, and spitted the carcasses on twigs over the fire. She stripped off her leather gloves, flexed her bare fingers, then held her hands over the tiny fire and began whispering under her breath. Her eyes were half-slitted with concentration and there was a faint line between her eyebrows. As Tarma watched, fascinated, the fire and their dinner were enclosed in a transparent shell of glowing gold mist.

"Very pretty; what's it good for?" Tarma asked when she took her hands away.

"Well, for one thing, I've cut off the wind; for another, the shield is concentrating the heat and the meat will cook faster now."

"And what's it costing you?" Tarma had been in Kethry's company long enough now to know that magic always had a price. And in Kethry's case, that price was usually taken out of the resources of the spell-caster.

Kethry smiled at her accusing tone. "Nowhere near so much as you might think; this clearing has been used for overnighting a great deal, and a good many of those camping here have celebrated in one way or another. There's lots of residual energy here, energy only another mage could tap. Mages don't take the Trade Road often, they take the Couriers' Road when they have to travel at all."

"So?"

"So there's more than enough energy here not only to cook dinner but to give us a little more protection from the weather than our bit of canvas."

Tarma nodded, momentarily satisfied that her blood-sister wasn't exhausting herself just so they could eat a little sooner. "Well, while I was scrounging for the hooved ones, I found a bit for us, too—"

She began pulling cattail roots, mallow-pith, a few nuts, and other edibles from the outer pockets of her coat. "Not a lot there, but enough to supplement dinner, and make a bit of breakfast besides."

"Bless you! These bunnies were a bit young and small, and rather on the lean side—should this stuff be cooked?"

"They're better raw, actually."

"Good enough; want to help with the shelter, since we're expecting a blow?"

"Only if you tell me what to do. I've got no notion of what these winter storms of yours are like."

Kethry had already stretched their canvas tent across the top and open side of the enclosure of rocks and logs, stuffed brush and moss into the chinks on the inside, packed snow into the chinks from the outside, and layered the floor with pine boughs to keep their own bodies off the snow. Tarma helped her lash the canvas down tighter, then weighted all the loose edges with packed-down snow and what rocks they could find.

As they worked, the promised storm began to give warning of its approach. The wind picked up noticeably, and the northern horizon began to darken. Tarma cast a wary eye at the darkening clouds. "I hope you're done cooking because it doesn't look like we have too much time left to get under cover."

"I think it's cooked through."

"And if not, it won't be the first time we've eaten raw meat on this trip. I'd better get the grazers."

Tarma got the beasts one at a time; first the mule, then her mare. She backed them right inside the shelter, coaxing them to lie down inside, one on either side of it, with their heads to the door-flap just in case something should panic them. With the two humans in the space in the middle, they should all stay as close to warm as was possible. Once again she breathed a little prayer of thankfulness for the quality of mule she'd been able to find for Kethry; with a balky beast or anything other than another Shin'a'in-bred horse this arrangement would have been impossible.

Kethry followed, grilled rabbit bundled into a piece of leather. The rich odor made Tarma's mouth water and reminded her that she hadn't eaten since this morning. While Kethry wormed her way in past her partner, Tarma lashed the door closed.

"Hold this, and find a comfortable spot," the mage told her. While Tarma snuggled up against Kessira's shoulder, Kethry knelt in the space remaining. She held her hands just at chin height, palms facing outward, her eyes completely closed and her face utterly vacant. By this Tarma knew she was attempting a much more difficult bit of magery than she had with their dinner.

She began an odd, singsong chant, swaying a little in time to it. Tarma began to see a thin streak of weak yellow light, like a watered-down sunbeam, dancing before her. In fact, that was what she probably would have taken it for—except that the sun was nearly down, not overhead.

As Kethry chanted, the light-beam increased in strength and brightness. Then, at a sharp word from her, it split into six. The six beams remained where the one had been for a moment, perhaps a little longer. Kethry began chanting again, a different rhythm this time, and the six beams leapt to the walls of their shelter, taking up positions spaced equally apart.

When they moved so suddenly, Tarma had nearly jumped out of her skin—especially since one of them had actually passed *through* her. But when she could feel no strangeness—and certainly no harm from the encounter—she relaxed again. The animals appeared to be ignoring the things, whatever they were.

Now little tendrils of light were spinning out from each of the beams, reaching out until they met in a kind of latticework. When this had spread to the canvas overhead, Tarma began to notice that the wind, which had been howling and tugging at the canvas, had been cut off, and that the shelter was noticeably warmer as a result.

Kethry sagged then, and allowed herself to half-collapse against Rodi's bulk.

"Took less than I might think, hmm?"

"Any more comments like that and I'll make *you* stay outside."

"First you'd have to fight Kessira. Have some dinner." Tarma passed her half the rabbit; it was still warm and amazingly juicy and both of them wolfed down their portions with good appetite, nibbling the bones clean, then cracking them and sucking out the last bit of marrow. With the bones licked bare, they finished with the roots of Tarma's gleaning, though more than half of Tarma's share went surreptitiously to Kessira.

When they had finished, the sun was gone and the storm building to full force. Tarma peeked out the curtain of tent-canvas at the front of the shelter; the fire was already smothered. Tarma noticed then that the light-web gave off a faint illumination; not enough to read by, but enough to see by.

"What is—all this?" she asked, waving a hand at the light-lattice. "Where'd it come from?"

"It's a variation of the fire-shield I raised; it's magical energy manifesting itself in a physical fashion. Part of that energy came from me, part of it was here already and I just reshaped it. In essence, I told it I thought it was a wall, and it believed me. So now we have a 'wall' between us and the storm."

"Uh, right. You told that glowing thing you thought it was a wall, and it believed you—"

Kethry managed a tired giggle at her partner's expression. "That's why the most important tool a magician has is his will; it has to be strong in order to convince energy to be something else."

"Is that how you sorcerers work?"

"All sorcerers, or White Winds sorcerers?"

"There's more than one kind?"

"Where'd you think magicians came from anyway? Left in the reeds for their patrons to find?" Kethry giggled again.

"No, but the only 'magicians' the Clans have are the shamans, and they don't do magic, much. Healing, acting as advisors, keepers of outClan knowledge—that's mostly what they do. When we need magic, we ask Her for it."

"And She answers?" Kethry's eyes widened in fascination.

"Unless She has a damn good reason not to. She's very close to us—closer than most deities are to their people, from what I've been able to judge. But that may be because we don't ask Her for much, or very often. There's a story—" Tarma half smiled. "—there was a hunter who'd been very lucky and had come to depend on that luck. When his luck left him, his skills had gotten very rusty, and he couldn't manage to make a kill. Finally he went to the shaman, and asked him if he thought She would listen to a plea for help. The shaman looked him up and down, and finally said, 'You're not dead yet.' "

"Which means he hadn't been trying hard enough by himself?"

"Exactly. She is the very last resort—and you had damned well better be careful what you ask Her for—She'll give it to you, but in Her own way, especially if you haven't been honest with Her or with yourself. So mostly we don't ask." Tarma warmed to Kethry's interest, and continued when that interest didn't flag. This was the first chance she'd had to explain her beliefs to Kethry; before this, Kethry had either been otherwise occupied or there hadn't been enough privacy. "The easiest of Her faces to deal with are the Maiden and the Mother, they're gentler, more forgiving; the hardest are the Warrior and the Crone. Maiden and Mother don't take Oathbound to themselves, Warrior and Crone do. Crone's Oathbound—no, I won't tell you—you *guess* what they do."

"Uh," Kethry's brow furrowed in thought, and she nibbled a hangnail. "Shamans?"

"Right! And Healers and the two Elders in each Clan, who may or may not also be Healers or shamans. Those the Crone Binds are Bound, like the Kal'enedral, to the Clans as a whole, serving with their minds and talents instead of their hands. Now—you were saying about magicians?" She was as curious to know about Kethry's teaching as Keth seemed to be about her own.

"There's more than one school; mine is White Winds. Um, let me go to the very basics. Magic has three sources. The first is power from within the sorcerer himself, and you have to have the Talent to use that source —and even then it isn't fully trained by anyone I know of. I've heard that up north a good ways they use *pure* mind-magic, rather than using the mind to find other sources of power."

"That would be—Valdemar, no?"

"Yes!" Kethry looked surprised at Tarma's knowledge. "Well, the second is power created by living things, rather like a fire creates light just by being a fire. You have to have the Talent to *sense* that power, but not to use it so long as you know it's there. Death releases a lot of that energy in one burst; that's why an unTalented sorcerer can turn to dark wizardry; he knows the power will be there when he kills something. The third source is from creatures that live in places that *aren't* this world, but *touch* this world—like pages in a book. Page one isn't page two, but they touch all along each other. Other Planes, we call them. There's one for each element, one for what we call 'demons,' and one for very powerful creatures that aren't quite gods, but do seem kindly inclined to humans. There may be more, but that's all anyone has ever discovered that *I* know

of. The creatures of the four Elemental Planes can be bargained with—
you can build up credit with them by doing them little favors, or you can
promise them something they want from this Plane."

"Was that what I saw fighting beside you when you took out that
wizard back in Brether's Crossroads? Other-whatsit creatures?"

"Exactly—and that fight is why my magic is so limited at the moment
—I used up all the credit I had built with them in return for that help.
Fortunately I *didn't* have to go into debt to them, or we'd probably be off
trying to find snow-roses for the Ethereal Varirs right now. There *is*
another way of dealing with them. You can coerce them with magical
bindings or with your will. The creatures from the Abyssal Plane can be
bought with pain-energy and death-energy—they feed off those—or coerced if your will is strong enough, although the only way you can 'bind'
them magically is to hold them to this Plane; you can't force them to do
anything if your own will isn't stronger than theirs. The creatures of the
Sixth Plane—we call it the 'Empyreal Plane'—*can't* be coerced in any
way, and they'll only respond to a call if they feel like it. Any magician
can contact the Other-Planar creatures, it's just a matter of knowing the
spells that open the boundaries between us and them. The thing that
makes schools of magic different is their ethics, really. How they feel
about the different kinds of power and using them."

"So what does yours teach?" Tarma lay back with her arms stretched
along Kessira's back and neck; she scratched gently behind the mare's
ears while Kessira nodded her head in drowsy contentment. This was the
most she'd gotten out of Kethry in the past six months.

"We don't coerce; not ever. We don't deal at all with the entities of the
Abyssal Planes except to send them back—or destroy them if we can. We
don't deliberately gain use of energy by killing or causing pain. We hold
that our Talents have been given us for a purpose; that purpose is to use
them for the greatest good. That's why we are wanderers, why we don't
take up positions under permanent patrons."

"Why you're dirt-poor and why there're so few of you," Tarma interrupted genially.

" 'Fraid so," Kethry smiled. "No worldly sense, that's us. But that's
probably why Need picked me."

"She'enedra, why don't you want to go to Mornedealth?"

"I—"

"And why haven't you ever told me about *your* home and kin?" Tarma
had been letting her spirit-teacher's last remark stew in the back of her
mind, and when Kethry had begun giving her the "lesson" in the ways of
magic had realized she knew next to nothing about her partner's ante-

cedents. She'd been brooding on her own sad memories, but Kethry's avoidance of the subject of the past could only mean that hers were as sorry. And Tarma would be willing to bet the coin she didn't have that the mystery was tied into Mornedealth.

Kethry's mouth had tightened with an emotion Tarma recognized only too well. Pain.

"I'll have to know sooner or later, *she'enedra*. We have no choice but to pass through Mornedealth, and no choice but to try and raise money there, or we'll starve. And if it's something I can do anything about— well, I want doubly to know about it! You're my Clan, and nobody hurts my Clan and gets away with it!"

"It—it isn't anything you can deal with—"

"Let me be the judge of that, hmm?"

Kethry sighed, and visibly took herself in hand. "I—I guess it's only fair. You know next to nothing about me, but accepted me anyway."

"Not true," Tarma interrupted her, *"She* accepted you when you oathbound yourself to me as blood-sib. That's all I needed to know then. She wouldn't bind two who didn't belong together."

"But circumstances change, I know, and it isn't fair for me to keep making a big secret out of where I come from. All right." Kethry nodded, as if making up her mind to grasp the thorns. "The reason I haven't told you anything is this; I'm a fugitive. I grew up in Mornedealth; I'm a member of one of the Fifty Noble Houses. My real name is Kethryveris of House Pheregrul."

Tarma raised one eyebrow, but only said, "Do I bow, or can I get by with just kissing your hand?"

Kethry almost smiled. "It's a pretty empty title—or it was when I ran away. The House estates had dwindled to nothing more than a decaying mansion in the Old City by my father's time, and the House prerequisites to little more than an invitation to all Court functions—which we generally declined graciously—and permission to hunt the Royal Forests— which kept us fed most of the year. Father married mother for love, and it was a disaster. Her family disowned her, she became ill and wouldn't tell him. It was one of those long declining things, she just faded bit by bit, so gradually that he, being absentminded at best, really didn't notice. She died three years after I was born. That left just the three of us."

"Three?"

Kethry hadn't ever mentioned any sibs before.

"Father, my brother Kavin—that's Kavinestral—and me. Kavin was eight years older than me, and from what everyone said, the very image of Father in his youth. Handsome—the word just isn't adequate to describe Kavin. He looks like a god."

"And you worshiped him." Tarma had no trouble reading *that* between the lines.

It wasn't just the dim light that was making Kethry look pale. "How could I not? Father died when I was ten, and Kavin was all I had left, and when he exerted himself he could charm the moss off the wall. We were fine until Father died; he'd had some income or other that kept the house going, well, that dried up when he was gone. That left Kavin and me with no income and nowhere to go but a falling-down monstrosity that we couldn't even sell, because it's against the law for the Fifty Families to sell the ancestral homes. We let the few servants we had go—all but one, my old nurse Tildy. She wouldn't leave me. So Tildy and I struggled to run the household and keep us all clothed and fed. Kavin hunted the Royal Forests when he got hungry enough, and spent the rest of his time being Kavin. Which, to me, meant being perfection."

"Until you got fed up and ran away?" Tarma hazarded, when Kethry's silence had gone too long. She knew it it wasn't the right answer, but she hoped it would prod Kethry back into speaking.

"Hardly." Kethry's eyes and mouth were bitter. "He had me neatly twined 'round his finger. No, things went on like that until I was twelve, and just barely pubescent. Two things happened then that I had no knowledge of. The first was that Kavin himself became fed up with life on the edge, and looked around for something to make him a lot of money quickly. The second was that on one of his dips in the stews with his friends, he accidentally encountered the richest banker in Mornedealth and found out exactly what his secret vice was. Kavin may have been lazy, but he wasn't stupid. He was fully able to put facts together. He also knew that Wethes Goldmarchant, like all the other New Money moguls, wanted the one thing that all his money couldn't buy him—he wanted inside the Fifty Families. He *wanted* those Court invitations we declined; wanted them so badly it made him ache. And he'd never get them—not unless he somehow saved the realm single-handedly, which wasn't bloody likely."

Kethry's hands were clenched tightly in her lap, she stared at them as if they were the most fascinating things in the universe. "I knew nothing of all this, of course, mewed up in the house all day and daydreaming about finding a hidden cache of gold and gems and being able to pour them in Kavin's lap and make him smile at me. Then one day he *did* smile at me; he told me he had a surprise for me. I went with him, trusting as a lamb. Next thing I knew, he was handing me over to Wethes; the marriage ceremony had already taken place by proxy. You see, Wethes' secret vice was little girls—and with me, he got both his ambition *and* his lust satisfied. It was a bargain too good for either of them to resist—"

Kethry's voice broke in something like a sob; Tarma leaned forward and put one hard, long hand on the pair clenched white-knuckled in her partner's lap.

"So your brother sold you, hmm? Well, give him a little credit, *she'enedra;* he might have thought he was doing you a favor. The merchant would give you every luxury, after all; you'd be a valued and precious possession."

"I'd like to believe that, but I can't. Kavin saw some of those little girls Wethes was in the habit of despoiling. He *knew* what he was selling me into, and he didn't care, he plainly did not care. The only difference between them and me was that the chains and manacles he used on me were solid gold, and I was raped on silk sheets instead of linen. And it was rape, nothing else! I wanted to die; I prayed I would die. I didn't understand anything of what had happened to me. I only knew that the brother I worshiped had betrayed me." Her voice wavered a moment, and faded against the howl of the storm-winds outside their shelter. Tarma had to strain to hear her.

Then she seemed to recover, and her voice strengthened again. "But although I had been betrayed, I hadn't been forgotten. My old nurse managed to sneak her way into the house on the strength of the fact that she *was* my nurse; nobody thought to deny her entry. When Wethes was finished with me, she waited until he had left and went inquiring for me. When she found me, she freed me and smuggled me out."

Kethry finally brought her eyes up to meet her partner's; there was pain there, but also a hint of ironic humor. "You'd probably like her; she also stole every bit of gold and jewelry she found with me and carried them off, too."

"A practical woman; you're right, I think I *would* like her. I take it she had somewhere to hide you?"

"Her brother's farm—it's east of here. Well, I wasn't exactly in my right mind for a while, but she managed to help with that for a bit. But then—then I started having nightmares, and when I did, every movable thing in my room would go flying about. Mind you, I never broke anything—"

"Since I gather this was a 'flying about' without benefit of hands, I would think it would be rather unnerving."

"Tildy knew she hadn't any way of coping with me then, so she took me to the nearest mage-school she knew, which was White Winds. It only took one nightmare to convince them that I needed help—and that I was going to be a pretty good mage after I got that help. That's where I got Need."

Kethry's hands unclenched, and one of them strayed to the hilt of a plain short-sword wedged in among the supplies tucked into the shelter.

"Now that's another tale you never told me."

"Not for any reason, just because there isn't much to tell. We had a guard there, an old mercenary who'd been hired on to give us a bit of protection, and to give her a kind of semiretirement. Baryl Longarm was her name. When I was ready to take the roads, she called me into her rooms."

"That must have had you puzzled."

"Since she didn't have a reputation for chasing other females, it certainly did. Thank goodness she didn't leave me wondering for long. 'You're the first wench we've had going out for a dog's age,' she said, 'and there's something I want you to have. It's time it went out again, anyway, and you'll probably have to use it before you're gone a month.' She took down this sword from the wall, unsheathed it, and laid it in my hands. And the runes appeared on the blade."

"I remember when you showed me. 'Woman's Need calls me, as Woman's Need made me. Her Need I will answer as my maker bade me.' " Tarma glanced at Kethry's hand on the hilt. "Gave me a fair turn, I can tell you. I always thought magic blades were gold-hilted and jewel-bedecked."

"Then she told me what little she knew—that the sword's name was Need, that she was indestructible so far as Baryl had been able to tell. That she only served women. And that her service was such that she only gave what you yourself did not already have. That to her, a fighter, Need gave a virtual immunity to all magic, but didn't add so much as a fillip to her fighting skills—but that for me, a mage, if I let it take control when it needed to, it would make me a master swordswoman, though it wouldn't make the least difference to any spell I cast. And that it would help Heal anything short of a death-wound."

"Rather like one of Her gifts, you know?" Tarma interrupted. "Makes you do your utmost, to the best of your abilities, but bails you out when you're out of your depth."

"I never thought about it that way, but you're right. Is there any way Need could be Shin'a'in?"

"Huh-uh. We've few metal-workers, and none of them mages—and we don't go in for short-swords, anyway. Now, what's the problem with you going back to Mornedealth? Changing the subject isn't going to change my wanting to know."

"Well, you can't blame me for trying—*she'enedra,* I have angered a very powerful man, my husband—"

"Crap! He's no more your husband than I am, no matter what charade he went through."

"—and a very ruthless one, my brother. I don't know what either of them would do if they learned I was within their reach again." Kethry shuddered, and Tarma reached forward and clasped both her hands in her own.

"I have only one question, my sister and my friend," she said, so earnestly that Kethry came out of her own fear and looked deeply into the shadowed eyes that met hers. "And that is this; which way do you want them sliced—lengthwise, or widthwise?"

"Tarma!" The sober question struck Kethry as so absurd that she actually began laughing weakly.

"In all seriousness, I much doubt that either of them is going to recognize you; think about it, you're a woman grown now, not a half-starved child. But if they do, that's what I'm here for. If they try anything, I'll ask you that question again, and you'd best have a quick answer for me. Now, are you satisfied?"

"You are insane!"

"I am Shin'a'in; some say there is little difference. I am also Kal'enedral, and most say there is *no* difference. So believe me; no one is going to touch you with impunity. I am just crazed enough to cut the city apart in revenge."

"And this is supposed to make me feel better?"

"You're smiling, aren't you?"

"Well," Kethry admitted reluctantly, "I guess I am."

"When a child of the Clans falls off her horse, we make her get right back on again. *She'enedra,* don't you think it's time you remounted this one?"

"I—"

"Or do you prefer to live your life with *them* dictating that you shall not return to your own city?"

Her chin came up; a stubborn and angry light smoldered in her eyes. "No."

"Then we face this city of yours and we face it together. For now, make a mattress of Rodi, *she'enedra;* and sleep peacefully. I intend to do the same. Tomorrow we go to Mornedealth and make it deal with us on *our* terms. *Hai?*"

Kethry nodded, convinced almost against her will, and beginning to view the inevitable encounter with something a little more like confidence.

"Hai," she agreed.

Two

Kethry envied her partner's ability to drop immediately into sleep under almost any circumstances. Her own thoughts were enough to keep her wakeful; add to them the snoring of her mule and the wailing of the wind outside their shelter, and Kethry had a foolproof recipe for insomnia.

She wanted to avoid Mornedealth no matter *what* the cost. Just the thought that she might encounter Wethes was enough to make her shudder almost uncontrollably. In no way was she prepared to deal with him, and she wondered now if she would ever be. . . .

And yet, Tarma was right. She would never truly be "free" unless she dealt with her fear. She would never truly be her own woman if she allowed fear and old memories to dictate where she would or would not go.

The disciplines of the Order of White Winds mandated self-knowledge and self-mastery. She had deceived herself into thinking she had achieved that mastery of self; Tarma had just shown her how wrong she was.

It's been seven years, she thought bitterly. *Seven long years—and those bastards still have power over me. And I'll never be an adept until I break that power.*

For that, after all, was the heart of the White Winds discipline; that no negative tie be permitted to bind the sorcerer in any way. Positive ties— like the oath of *she'enedran* she had sworn with Tarma, like the bond of lover to lover or parent to child—were encouraged to flourish, for the sorcerer could draw confidence and strength from them. But the negative bonds of fear, hatred, or greed must be rooted out and destroyed, for they would actually drain the magician of needed energy.

Sometimes Tarma can be so surprising, see things so clearly. And yet she has such peculiar blind spots. Or does *she? Does she realize that she's driving us both to the Plains as if she was geas-bound? She's like a messenger-bird, unable to travel in any direction but the one appointed.*

Kethry hadn't much cared where she wandered; this was her time of journey, she wouldn't settle in any one place until she reached the proficiency of an Adept. *Then* she would either found a school of her own, or find a place in an established White Winds enclave. So Tarma's overwhelming need to return home had suited her as well as anything else.

Until she had realized that the road they were on led directly to Mornedealth.

It all comes back to that, doesn't it? And until I face it, I'm stalemated. Dammit, Tarma's right. I'm a full sorceress, I'm a full adult, and I have one damned fine swordswoman for a partner. What in Teslat's name am I afraid of? There is nothing *under the law that they can really do to me—I've been separated from Wethes for seven years, and three is enough to unmake the marriage, assuming there really was one. I'm not going in under my full name, and I've changed so much. How are they even going to recognize me?*

Across the shelter Tarma stirred, and curled herself into a tighter ball. Kethry smiled and shook her head, thinking about her partner's words on the subject.

"Do you want them sliced lengthwise or widthwise"—Windborn, she is such a bundle of contradictions. We have got to start talking; we hardly know anything about one another. Up until now, we've had our hands full of bandit-extermination, then there just wasn't the privacy. But if I'd had all the world to choose a sister from, I would have picked her over any other. Goddess-oath and all, I would have chosen her. Though that Warrior of hers certainly took the decision right out of our hands.

Kethry contemplated the sleeping face of her partner. In repose she lost a great deal of the cold harshness her expression carried when she was awake. She looked, in fact, a great deal younger than Kethry was.

When she sleeps, she's the child she was before she lost her Clan. When she's awake—I'm not sure what she is. She eats, drinks and breathes the Warrior, that's for certain, yet she hasn't made any move to convert me. I know it would please her if I did, and it wouldn't be any great change to do so; her Goddess just seems to me to be one more face of the Windborn Soulshaper. She seems like any other mercenary hire-sword—insisting on simple solutions to complicated problems, mostly involving the application of steel to offending party. Then she turns around and hits me with a sophisticated proverb, or some really esoteric knowledge—like knowing that mind-magic is used in Valdemar. And she's hiding something from me; something to do with that Goddess of hers, I think. And not because she doesn't trust me . . . maybe because I don't share her faith. Her people—nobody really knows too much about the Shin'a'in; they keep pretty much to themselves. Of course that shouldn't be too surprising; anyone who knew the Dhorisha Plains the way they do could dive into the grass and never be seen again, if that's what he wanted to do. You could hide the armies of a dozen nations out there, and they'd likely never run into each other. Assuming the Shin'a'in would let them past the Border. I suspect if Tale'sedrin had been on the Plains instead of camped on the road to the Great Horse Fair the bandits would be dead and the Hawk's Children still riding. And I would be out a sister.

Kethry shook her head. *Well, what happened, happened. Now I have to think about riding into Mornedealth tomorrow. Under a glamour?*

She considered the notion for a moment, then discarded it. *No. I'll go in wearing my own face, dammit! Besides, the first sorcerer who sees I'm wearing a glamour is likely to want to know why—and likely to try to find out. If I'm lucky, he'll come to us with his hand out. If I'm not, he'll go to Wethes or Kavin. No, a glamour would only cause trouble, not avoid it. I think Tarma's right; we'll go in as a mercenary team, no more, no less, and under her Clanname. We'll stay quiet, draw no attention to ourselves, and maybe avoid trouble altogether. The more complicated a plan is, the more likely it is to go wrong. . . .*

Kethry began formulating some simple story for her putative background, but the very act of having faced and made the decision to go in had freed her of the tension that was keeping her sleepless. She had hardly begun, when her weariness claimed her.

The blizzard cleared by morning. Dawn brought cloudless skies, brilliant sun, and still, cold air that made everything look sharp-edged and brightly-painted. They cleared camp and rode off into a world that seemed completely new-made.

Tarma was taken totally by surprise by the changeling forest; she forgot her homesickness, forgot her worry over Kethry, even temporarily forgot how cold she was.

Birdcalls echoed for miles through the forest, as did the steady, muffled clop of their mounts' hooves. The storm had brought a fine, powder like snow, snow that frosted every branch and coated the underbrush, so that the whole forest reflected the sunlight and glowed so that they were surrounded by a haze of pearly light. Best of all, at least to Tarma's mind, the soft snow was easy for the beasts to move through, so they made good time. Just past midafternoon, glimpses of the buildings and walls of Mornedealth could be seen above and through the trees.

It was a city made of the wood that was its staple in trade; weathered, silver-gray wooden palisades, wooden walls, wooden buildings; only the foundations of a building were ever made of stone. The outer wall that encircled it was a monument to man's ingenuity and Mornedealth's woodworkers; it was two stories tall, and as strong as any corresponding wall of stone. Granted, it would never survive being set afire, as would inevitably happen in a siege, but the wall had never been built with sieges in mind. It was intended to keep the beasts of the forest out of the city when the hardships of winter made their fear of man less than their hunger, and to keep the comings and goings of strangers limited to specific checkpoints. If an enemy penetrated this realm so far as to threaten Mornedealth, all was lost anyway, and there would be nothing for it but surrender.

Since the only city Tarma had ever spent any length of time in was Brether's Crossroads—less than half the size of Mornedealth—the Shin'a'in confessed to Kethry that she was suitably impressed by it long before they ever entered the gates.

"But you spent more than a year hunting down Gregoth and his band. Surely you—"

"Don't remember much of that, *she'enedra*. It was a bit like being in a drug haze. I only really came awake when I was tr—" she suddenly recalled that Kethry knew nothing of her faceless trainers and what they were, and decided that discretion was in order. "When I had to. To question someone, or to read a trail. The rest of the time, I might just as well not have been there, and I surely wasn't in any kind of mood for seeing sights."

"No—you wouldn't be. I'm sorry; I wasn't thinking at all."

"Nothing to apologize for. Just tell me what I'm getting into here. You're the native; where are we going?"

Kethry reined in, a startled look on her face. "I—I've spent so much time thinking about Kavin and Wethes . . ."

"Li'sa'eer!" Tarma exclaimed in exasperation, pulling Kessira up beside her. "Well, think about it *now,* dammit!" She kneed her mare slightly; Kessira obeyed the subtle signal and shouldered Rodi to one side until both of the beasts had gotten off onto the shoulder of the road, out of the way of traffic. There wasn't anybody in sight, but Tarma had had *yuthi'so'coro*—road-courtesy—hammered into her from the time she was

old enough to sit a horse unaided. No Shin'a'in omitted road-courtesy while journeying, not even when among deadly enemies. And road-courtesy dictated that if you were going to sit and chat, you didn't block the progress of others while you were doing it.

"We'll have to use the Stranger's Gate," Kethry said after long thought, staring at the point where the walls of Mornedealth began paralleling the road. "That's no hardship, it's right on the Trade Road. But we'll have to register with the Gate Guard, give him our names, where we're from, where we're going, and our business here."

"Warrior's Oath! What do they want, to write a book about us?" Tarma replied with impatience.

"Look, this is as much for our sakes as theirs. Would *you* want total strangers loose in your Clan territory?"

"*Sa-hai.* You're right. Not that strangers ever get past the Border, but you're right."

"The trouble is, I daren't tell them what I really am, but I don't want to get caught in a complicated falsehood."

"Now *that's* no problem," Tarma nodded. "We just tell him a careful mixture of the truth with enough lie in it to keep your enemies off the track. Then?"

"There are specific inns for travelers; we'll have to use one of them. They won't ask us to pay straight off, we'll have three days to find work and get our reckoning taken care of. After that, they confiscate everything we own except what we're wearing."

Tarma snorted a little with contempt, which obviously surprised Kethry.

"I thought you'd throw a fit over the notion of someone taking Kessira."

"I'd rather like to see them try. You've never seen her with a stranger. She's not a battle-steed, but *nobody* lays a finger on her without my permission. Let a stranger put one hand on her rein and he'll come away with a bloody stump. And while he's opening his mouth to yell about it, she'll be off down the street, headed for the nearest gate. If I were hurt and gave her the command to run for it, she'd carry me to the closest exit she could remember without any direction from me. And if she couldn't find one, she might well *make* one. No, I've no fear of anyone confiscating her. One touch, and they wouldn't *want* her. Besides, I have something I can leave in pledge—I'd rather not lose it, but it's better than causing a scene."

Tarma took off her leather glove, reached into the bottom of her saddlebag and felt for a knobby, silk-wrapped bundle. She brought the palm-sized package out and unwrapped it carefully, uncovering to the brilliant sunlight an amber necklace. It was made of round beads alternating with carved claws or teeth; it glowed on the brown silk draped over her hand like an ornament of hardened sunbeams.

"Osberg wore that!"

"He stole it from me. I took it back off his dead body. It was the last thing Dharin gave me. Our pledge-gift. I never found the knife I gave him."

Kethry said nothing; Tarma regarded the necklace with a stony-cold expression that belied the ache in her heart, then rewrapped it and stowed it away. "As I said, I'd rather not lose it, but losing it's better than causing a riot. Now how do we find work?"

"We'd be safest going to a Hiring Hall. They charge employers a fee to find people with special talents."

"Well, that's us."

"Of course, that's money we won't see. We could get better fees if we went out looking on our own, but it would probably take longer."

"Hiring Hall; better the safe course."

"I agree, but they're sure to notice at the gate that my accent is native. Would you mind doing the talking?"

Tarma managed a quirk of the lips that approximated a half-smile. "All right, I'll do all the talking at the gate. Look stupid and sweet, and let them think you're my lover. Unless that could get us in trouble."

Kethry shook her head. "No, there's enough of that in Mornedealth. Virtually anything is allowed provided you're ready to pay for it."

"And they call this civilization! *Vai datha;* let's get on with it."

They turned their beasts once more onto the road, and within a candlemark were under scrutiny of the sentries on the walls. Tarma allowed a lazy, sardonic smile to cross her face. One thing she had to give them; these guards were well disciplined. No catcalls, no hails, no propositions to Kethry—just a steady, measuring regard that weighed them and judged them unthreatening for the moment. These "soft, city-bred" guards were quite impressive.

The Stranger's Gate was wide enough for three wagons to pass within, side by side, and had an ironwork portcullis as well as a pair of massive bleached-wood doors, all three now standing open. They clattered under the wall, through a wooden-walled tunnel about three horse-lengths deep. When they reached the other entrance, they found themselves stopped by a chain stretched across the inner side of the gate. One of the men standing sentry approached them and asked them (with short words, but courteous) to follow him to a tiny office built right into the wall.

There was always a Gate Guard on duty here; the man behind the desk was, by the insignia pinned to his brown leather tunic, a captain. Kethry had told her partner as they approached the walls that those posted as Gate Guards tended to be high-ranking, and above the general cut of mercenary, because they had to be able to read and write. Their escort squeezed them inside the door, and returned to his own post. The Gate Guard was a middle-aged, lean, saturnine man who glanced up at them from behind his tiny desk, and without a word, pulled a ledger, quill and ink from underneath it.

The Gate Guard was of the same cut as the men on the walls; Tarma wondered if Kethry would be able to pass his careful scrutiny. It didn't look like he missed much. Certainly Kethry looked nothing like a Shin'a'in, so she'd have to be one damn convincing actress to get away with claiming a Shin'a'in Clanname.

Tarma stole a glance sideways at her partner and had to refrain from a hoarse chuckle. Kethry wore a bright, vapid smile, and was continuously fussing with the way her cloak draped and smoothing down her hair. She looked like a complete featherhead. No problem. The Guard would have very little doubt why the partner of a rather mannish swordswoman was claiming her Clanname!

At the Guard's brusque inquiry as to their names and business, Tarma replied as shortly, "We're Shin'a'in mercenaries. Tarma shena Tale'sedrin, Kethry shena Tale'sedrin. We're on our way back to the Dhorisha Plains; I've got inheritance coming from my Clan I need to claim. But we've run out of provisions; we're going to have to take some temporary work to restock."

"Not much call for your kind on a temporary basis, Swordlady," he replied with a certain gruff respect. "Year contract or more, sure; Shin'a'in have a helluva reputation. You'd be able to get top wage as any kind of guard, guard-captain or trainer; but not temporary. Your pretty friend's in mage-robes; that just for show, or can she light a candle?"

"Ah, Keth's all right. Good enough to earn us some coin, just no horse-sense, *he shala?* She's worth the trouble taking care of, and for more reasons than one, bless her."

"Eyah, and without you to keep the wolves away, a pretty bit like that'd get eaten alive in a week," the Guard answered with a certain gleam of sympathy in his eyes. "Had a shieldmate like that in my younger days, fancied himself a poet; didn't have sense enough to come in out of a storm. Caught himself a fever standing out in a blizzard, admiring it; died of it eventually—well, that's the way of things. You being short of coin; tell you what, one professional to another—you go find the Broken

Sword, tell 'em Jervac sent you. And I hear tell the Hiring Hall over by the animal market was on the lookout for a mage on temp."

"Will do—luck on your blade, captain."

"And on yours. Ah—don't mount up; lead your beasts, that's the law inside the gates."

As they led their mounts in the direction the Gate Guard had indicated, Kethry whispered, "How much of that was good advice?"

"We'll find out when we find this inn; chances are he's getting some kickback, but he could be doing us a good turn at the same time. Thanks for the help with the ruse of being your protector; that should warn off anybody that might be thinking your services other than magery are for hire. We couldn't have done better for a sympathizer if we'd planned this, you know, that's why I played it a bit thick. He had the feeling of a *she'chorne;* that bit about a 'shieldmate' clinched it. If you're not lovers, you call your partner 'shieldbrother,' not 'shieldmate.' How are you doing?"

Kethry looked a bit strained, but it was something likely only someone who knew her would have noticed. "Holding up; I'll manage. The more time I spend with nobody jumping me out of the shadows, the easier it'll get. I can handle it."

"Vai datha." If Kethry said she'd be able to handle her understandable strain, Tarma was willing to believe her. Tarma took the chance to look around, and was impressed in spite of herself. "Damn, Greeneyes, you never told me this place was so *big!"*

"I'm used to it," Kethry shrugged.

"Well, I'm not," Tarma shook her head in amazement. The street they led their beasts on was fully wide enough for two carts with plenty of space for them to pass. It was actually paved with bricks, something Tarma didn't ever remember seeing before, and had a channel down the middle and a gutter on either side for garbage and animal droppings. There were more people than she ever recalled seeing in one place in her life; she and Kethry were elbow to elbow in the crush. Kessira snorted, not liking so many strangers so close. "Why isn't anyone riding? Why'd the Guard say riding was counter the law?" Tarma asked, noticing that while there were beasts and carts in plenty, all were being led, like theirs —just as the guard had told them.

"No one but a member of one of the Fifty is allowed to ride within the walls, and for good reason. Think what would happen if somebody lost control of his beast in this crush!"

"Reasonable. Look, there's our inn—"

The sign was plain enough—the pieces of an actual blade nailed up to a shingle suspended above the road. They turned their mounts' heads into a narrow passage that led into a square courtyard. The inn itself was built entirely around this yard. It was two-storied, of the ubiquitous wood stained a dark brown; old, but in excellent repair. The courtyard itself was newly swept. The stabling was to the rear of the square, the rest of the inn forming the other three sides.

"Stay here, I want to have a look at the stabling. That will tell me everything I need to know." Tarma handed over her mare's reins to Kethry, and strode purposefully toward the stable door. She was intercepted by a gray-haired, scar-faced man in a leather apron.

"Swordlady, welcome," he said. "How may we serve you?"

"Bed, food and stabling for two—if I like what I see. And I'd like to see the stables first."

He grinned with the half of his mouth not puckered with a scar. "Shin'a'in? Thought so—this way, lady."

He himself led the way into the stables, and Tarma made up her mind then and there. It was clean and swept, there was no smell of stale dung or urine. The mangers were filled with fresh hay, the buckets with clean water, and the only beasts tied were those few whose wild or crafty eyes and laid-back ears told Tarma that they were safer tied than loose.

"Well, I *do* like what I see. Now if you aren't going to charge us like we were gold-dripping palace fatheads, I think you've got a pair of boarders. Oh, and Jervac sent us."

The man looked pleased. "I'm Hadell; served with Jervac until a brawl got me a cut tendon and mustering-out pay. About the charges; two trade-silver a day for both of you and your beasts, if you and the mage are willing to share a bed. Room isn't big, I'll warn you, but it's private. That two pieces gets you bed and breakfast and supper; dinner you manage on your own. Food is guard-fare; it's plain, but there's plenty of it and my cook's a good one. I'll go the standard three days' grace; more, if you've got something to leave with me as a pledge. Suits?"

"Suits," Tarma replied, pleased. "I do have a pledge, but I'd rather save it until I need it. Where's your stableboy? I don't want my mare to get a mouthful of him."

"Her," Hadell corrected her. "My daughter. We're a family business here. I married the cook, my girl works the stables, my boys wait tables."

"Safer than the other way 'round, hey? Especially as she gets to the toothsome age." Tarma shared a crooked grin with him, as he gave a piercing whistle. A shaggy-haired urchin popped out of the door of what probably was the grain room, and trotted up, favoring Tarma with an utterly fearless grin.

"This is—" he cocked his head inquiringly.

"Tarma shena Tale'sedrin. Shin'a'in, as you said."

"She and her partner are biding here for a bit, and she wants to make sure her mount doesn't eat you."

"Laeka, Swordlady." The urchin bobbed her head. "At your service. You're Shin'a'in?" Her eyes widened and became eager. "You got a battlesteed?"

"Not yet, Laeka. If I can make it back to the Plains in one piece, though, I'll be getting one. Kessira is a saddle-mare; she fights, but she hasn't the weight or the training of a battlesteed."

"Well, Da says what the Shin'a'in keep for thesselves is ten times the worth o' what they sells us."

The innmaster cuffed the girl—gently, Tarma noticed. "Laeka! Manners!" Laeka rubbed her ear and grinned, not in the least discomfited.

Tarma laughed. "No insult taken, Keeper, it's true. We sell you out-Clan folk our culls. Come with me, Laeka, and I'll introduce you to what we keep."

With the child trotting at her side and the innkeeper following, Tarma strolled back to Kethry. "This's a good place, *she'enedra,* and they aren't altogether outrageous in what they're charging. We'll be staying. This is Laeka, she's our Keeper's daughter, and his chief stableman."

Laeka beamed at the elevation in her station Tarma granted her.

"Now, hold out your hand to Kessira, little lady; let her get your measure." She placed her own hand on Kessira's neck and spoke a single command word under her breath. That told Kessira that the child was not to be harmed, and was to be obeyed—though she would only obey *some* commands if they were given in Shin'a'in, and it wasn't likely the child knew *that* tongue. Just as well, they didn't truly need a new back door to their stabling.

The mare lowered her head with grave dignity and snuffled the child's hand once, for politeness' sake, while the girl's eyes widened in delight. Then when Tarma put the reins in Laeka's hands, Kessira followed her with gentle docility, taking careful, dainty steps on the unfamiliar surface. Kethry handed her the reins to the mule as well; Rodi, of course, would follow *anyone* to food and stabling.

Hadell showed them their room; on the first floor, it was barely big enough to contain the bed. But it did have a window, and the walls were freshly whitewashed. There were plenty of blankets—again, well-worn but scrupulously clean—and a feather comforter. Tarma had stayed in far worse places, and said as much.

"So have I," Kethry replied, sitting on the edge of the bed and pulling off her riding boots with a grimace of pain. "The place where I met you, for one. I think we've gotten a bargain, personally."

"Makes me wonder, but I may get the answer when I see the rest of the guests. Well, what's next?" Tarma handed her a pair of soft leather half-boots meant for indoor wear.

"Dinner and bed. It's far too late to go to the Hiring Hall; that'll be for first thing in the morning? I wonder if we could manage a bath out of Hadell? I do *not* like smelling like a mule!"

As if to answer that question, there came a gentle rap on the door. "Lady-guests?" a boy's soprano said carefully, "Would ye wish th' use o' the steamhouse? If ye be quick, Da says ye'll have it t' yerselves fer a candlemark or so."

Tarma opened the door to him; a sturdy, dark child, he looked very like his father. "And the charge, lad?" she asked, "Though if it's in line with the rest of the bill, I'm thinking we'll be taking you up on it."

"Copper for steamhouse and bath, copper for soap and towels," he said, holding out the last. "It's at the end of the hallway."

"Done and done, and point us the way." Kethry took possession of what he carried so fast he was left gaping. "Pay the lad, Tarma; if I don't get clean soon, I'm going to rot of my own stink."

Tarma laughed, and tossed the boy four coppers. "And here I was thinking you were more trail-hardened than me," she chuckled, following Kethry down the hall in the direction the boy pointed. "Now you turn out to be another soft sybarite."

"I didn't notice *you* saying no."

"We have a saying—"

"Not another one!"

" 'An enemy's nose is always keener than your own.' "

"When I want a proverb, I'll consult a cleric. Here we are," Kethry opened the door to the bathhouse, which had been annexed to the very end of the inn. "Oh, heaven!"

This was, beyond a doubt, a well managed place. There were actually three rooms to the bathing area; the first held buckets and shallow tubs, and hot water bubbled from a wooden pipe in the floor into a channel running through it, while against the wall were pumps. This room was evidently for actual bathing; the bather mixed hot water from the channel with cold from the pumps, then poured the dirty water down the refuse channel. The hot-water channel ran into the room beside this one, which contained one enormous tub sunk into the floor, for soaking out aches and bruises. Beyond this room was what was obviously a steamroom. Although it was empty now, there were heated rocks in a pit in the center of the floor, buckets with dippers in them to pour water on the rocks, and benches around the pit. The walls were plain, varnished wood; the windows of something white and opaque that let light in without making a mockery of privacy.

"Heaven, in very deed," Tarma was losing no time in shedding her clothing. "I think I'm finally going to be warm again!"

One candlemark later, as they were blissfully soaking in hot mineral water—"This is a hot spring," Kethry remarked after sniffing the faint tang of copper in the air. "That's why he can afford to give his baths away"—a bright grin surmounted by a thatch of tousled brown hair appeared out of the steam and handed them their towels.

"Guard-shift's changin', miladies; men as stays here'll be lookin' fer their baths in a bit. You wants quiet, ye'd best come t' dinner. You wants a bit o' summat else—you jest stays here, they'll gie' ye that!"

"No doubt," Tarma said wryly, taking the towel Laeka held out to her and emerging reluctantly from the hot tub, thinking that in some ways a child being raised in an inn grew up even faster than a child of the Clans. "We'll take the quiet, thanks. What's wrong?"

The child was staring at her torso with stricken eyes. "Lady—you—how did—who did—"

Tarma glanced down at her own hard, tawny-gold body, that was liberally latticed with a network of paler scars and realized that the child had been startled and shocked by the evidence of so many old wounds on one so relatively young. She also thought about the adulation that had been in Laeka's eyes, and the concern in her father's when the man had seen it there. This might be a chance to do the man a good turn, maybe earn enough gratitude that he'd exert himself for them.

"A lot of people did that to me, child," she said quietly. "And if you've ever thought to go adventuring, think of these marks on me first. It isn't like the tales, where people go to battle one candlemark and go feast the next, with never a scratch on them. I was months healing from the last fight I had, and the best that those I fought for could give me was a mule, provisions, and a handful of coin as reward. The life of a mercenary is far from profitable most of the time."

Laeka gulped, and looked away. "I like horses," she ventured, finally. "I be good with 'em."

"Then by all means, become a horse-trainer," Tarma answered the unspoken question. "Train 'em well, and sell 'em to fools like me who earn their bread with swords instead of brains. Tell you what—you decide to do that, you send word to the Clans in my name. I'll leave orders you're to get a better choice than we give most outlanders. Hmm?"

"Aye!" The girl's eyes lighted at the promise, and she relaxed a little as Tarma donned her close-fitting breeches, shirt, and wrapped Shin'a'in jacket, covering the terrible scars. "Da says t' tell you supper be stew, bread 'n' honey, an' ale."

"Sounds fine—Keth?"

"Wonderful."

"Tell him we'll be there right behind you."

The child scampered out, and Kethry lifted an eyebrow. "Rather overdoing it, weren't you?"

"Huh! You didn't see the hero-worship in the kid's eyes, earlier, or the worry in her Da's. Not too many female mercenaries ride through here, I'd guess; the kid's seen just enough to make it look glamorous. Well, now she knows better, and I'm thinking it's just as well."

"You knew better, but you took this road anyway."

"Aye, I did," Tarma laced her boots slowly, her harsh voice dropping down to a whisper. "And the only reason I left the Plains was to revenge my Clan. All Shin'a'in learn the sword, but that doesn't mean we plan to live by it. We—we don't live to fight, we fight when we have to, to live. Sometimes we don't manage the last. As for me, I had no choice in taking up the blade, in becoming a mercenary; no more than did you."

Kethry winced, and touched Tarma's arm lightly. "Put my foot in it, didn't I? *She'enedra*, I'm sorry—I meant no offense—"

Tarma shook off her gloom with a shake of her head. "I know that. None taken. Let's get that food. I could eat this towel, I'm that hungry."

The whitewashed common room was quite empty, although the boy who brought them their supper (older than the other two children, darker, and quieter) told them it would be filling shortly. And so it proved; men of all ages and descriptions slowly trickling in to take their places at table and bench, being served promptly by Hadell's two sons. The room could easily hold at least fifty; the current crowd was less than half that number. Most of the men looked to be of early middle-age with a sprinkling of youngsters; all wore the unconsciously competent air of a good professional soldier. Tarma liked what she saw of them. None of these men would ever be officers, but the officers they did serve would be glad to have them.

The talk was muted; the men were plainly weary with the day's work. Listening without seeming to, the women soon gleaned the reason why.

As Tarma had already guessed, these men were foreign mercenaries, like themselves. This would be Hadell's lean season—one reason, per-

haps, that his prices were reasonable, and that he was so glad to see
them. The other reason was that he was that rare creature, an honest
man, and one who chose to give the men he had served beside a decent
break. Right now, only those hire-swords with contracts for a year or
more—or those one or two so prosperous that they could afford to bide
out the mercenary's lean season in an inn—were staying at the Broken
Sword. Normally a year-contract included room and board, but these
men were a special case. All of them were hired on with the City Guard,
which had no barracks for them. The result was that their pay included a
stipend for board, and a good many of them stayed at inns like the
Broken Sword. The job was never the easy one it might appear to the
unknowing to be; and today had been the occasion of a riot over bread
prices. The Guard had been ordered to put down the riot; no few of
these men had been of two minds about their orders. On the one hand,
they weren't suffering; but on the other, most of them were of the same
lower-classes as those that were rioting, and could remember winters
when they *had* gone hungry. And the inflated grain prices, so rumor had
it, had no basis for being so high. The harvest had been good, the grana-
ries full. Rumor said that shortages were being created. Rumor said, by
Wethes Goldmarchant.

Both Tarma and her partner took to their bed with more than a bel-
lyful of good stew to digest.

"Are you certain you want to come with me, even knowing there probably won't be work for you? You deserved a chance to sleep in for a
change."

Kethry, standing in the light from the window, gave her sorcerer's robe
a good brushing and slipped it on over her shirt and breeches—and
belted on her blade as well.

"Eyah. I want to be lurking in the background looking protective and
menacing. I want to start rumors about how it's best to approach my
partner with respect. You put on whatever act you think will reinforce
mine. And I don't think you should be wearing *that.*"

Kethry glanced down at Need and pursed her lips. "You're probably
right, but I feel rather naked without her."

"We don't want to attract any attention, right? You know damn well
mages don't bear steel other than eating knives and ritual daggers."
Tarma lounged fully-clothed—except for her boots—on the bed, since
there wasn't enough room for two people to be standing beside it at the
same time.

"Right," Kethry sighed, removing the blade and stowing it under the bed with the rest of their goods. "All right, let's go."

The Hiring Hall was no more than a short stroll from the inn; an interesting walk from Tarma's point of view. Even at this early an hour the streets were full of people, from ragged beggars to well-dressed merchants, and *not* all from around here—Tarma recognized the regional dress of more than a dozen other areas, and might have spotted more had she known what to look for. This might be the lean season, but it was evident that Mornedealth always had a certain amount of trade going.

At the Hiring Hall—just that, a hall lined with benches on both sides, and a desk at the end, all of the ubiquitous varnished wood—they gave essentially the same story they'd given the guard. Their tale differed only in that Kethry was being more of herself; it wouldn't do to look an idiot when she was trying to get work. As they had been told, the steward of the hall shook his blond head regretfully when Tarma informed him that she was only interested in short-term assignments.

"I'm sorry, Swordlady," he told her, "Very sorry. I could get you your pick of a round dozen one-to-five-year contracts. But this is the lean season, and there just isn't anything for a hire-sword but long-term. But your friend—yes."

"Oh?" Kethry contrived to look eager.

"There's a fellow from a cadet branch of one of the Fifty; he just came into a nice fat Royal grant. He's getting the revenue from Upvale wine taxes, and he's bent on showing the City how a *real* aristo does things when he gets the cash to work with. He's starting a full stable; hunters, racers, carriage beasts and pleasure beasts. He knows his horseflesh; what he *doesn't* know is how to tell if there's been a glamour put on 'em. Doesn't trust City mages, as who could blame him. They're all in the pay of somebody, and it's hard to say who might owe whom a favor or three. So he's had me on the lookout for an independent, and strictly temporary. Does that suit your talents?"

"You couldn't have suited me better!" Kethry exclaimed with delight. "Mage-sight's one of my strongest skills."

"Right then," the steward said with satisfaction. "Here's your address; here's your contract—sign here—"

Kethry scrutinized the brief document, nodded, and made her mage-glyph where he indicated.

"—and off you go; and good luck to you."

They left together; at the door, Tarma asked, "Want me with you?"

"No, I know the client, but he won't know me. He's not one of Kavin's crowd, which is all I was worried about. I'll be safe enough on my own."

"All right then; I'll get back to the inn. Maybe Hadell has a connection to something."

Hadell poured Tarma a mug of ale, sat down beside her at the bench, and shook his head with regret. "Not a thing, Swordlady. I'm—"

"Afraid this is the lean season, I know. Well look, I'm half mad with boredom, is there at least somewhere I can practice?" Her trainers would not come to her while she was within city boundaries, so it was up to her to stay in shape. If she neglected to—woe betide her the next time they *did* come to her!

"There's a practice ground with pells set up behind the stable, if you don't mind that it's outside and a simple dirt ring."

"I think I'll survive," she laughed, and went to fetch her blades.

The practice ground was easy enough to find; Tarma was pleased to find it deserted as well. There was a broom leaning against the fence to clear off the light snow; she used it to sweep the entire fenced enclosure clean. The air was crisp and still, the sun weak but bright, and close enough to the zenith that there would be no "bad" sides to face. She stood silently for a moment or two, eyes closed; shaking off the "now" and entering that timeless state that was both complete concentration and complete detachment. She began with the warmup exercises; a series of slow, deliberate movement patterns that blurred, each into the next. When she had finished with them, she did not stop, but proceeded to the next stage, drawing the sword at her back and executing another movement series, this time a little faster. With each subsequent stage her moves became more intricate, and a bit more speed was added, until her blade was a shining blur and an onlooker could almost see the invisible opponent she dueled with.

She ended exactly where she had begun, slowing her movements down again to end with the resheathing of her blade, as smooth and graceful as a leaf falling. As it went home in the scabbard with a metallic click, the applause began.

Startled, Tarma glanced in the direction of the noise; she'd been so absorbed in her exercises that she hadn't noticed her watchers. There were three of them—Hadell, and two fur-cloaked middle-aged men who had *not* been part of the Guard contingent last night.

She half-bowed (with a wry grin), and let them approach her.

"I'd heard Shin'a'in were good—Swordlady, you've just proved to me that sometimes rumor speaks truth," said the larger of the two, a weathered-looking blond with short hair and a gold clasp to his cloak. "Lady, I'm Justin Twoblade, this is my shieldbrother Ikan Dryvale."

"Tarma shena Tale'sedrin," she supplied, "And my thanks. A compliment comes sweeter from a brother in the trade."

"We'd like to offer you more than compliments, if you're willing," said the second, amber-haired, like Kethry, but with blue eyes; and homely, with a plowboy's ingenuous expression.

"Well, since I doubt it's a bid for bed-services, I'll at least hear you out."

"Lessons. We'll pay your reckoning and your partner's in return for lessons."

Tarma leaned on the top bar of the practice-enclosure and gave the notion serious thought. "Hmm, I'll admit I like the proposition," she replied, squinting into the sunlight. "Question is, why, and for how long? I'd hate to miss a chance at the only short-term job for months and then have you two vanish on me."

Hadell interceded for them. "They'll not vanish, Swordlady," he assured her. "Justin and Ikan are wintering here, waiting for the caravans to start up again in spring. They're highly valued men to the Jewel Merchants' Guild—valued enough that the merchants pay for 'em to stay here idle during the lean season."

"Aye, valued and bored!" Ikan exclaimed. "That's one reason for you. Few enough are those willing to spar with either of us—fewer still with the leisure for it. And though I've seen your style before, I've never had a chance to learn it—or how to counter it. If you wouldn't mind our learning how to counter it, that is."

"Mind? Hardly. Honest guards like you won't see Clan facing your blades, and anyone else who's learned our style thinking he'll have an easy time against hirelings deserves to meet someone with the counters. Done, then; for however long it takes Keth to earn us the coin to reprovision, I'll be your teacher."

"And we'll take care of the reckoning," Justin said, with a sly grin. "We'll just add it to our charges on the Guild. Odds are they'll think we've just taken to drinking and wenching away the winter nights!"

"Justin, I think I'm going to like you two," Tarma laughed. "You think a lot like me!"

Three

Yellow lamplight made warm pools around the common room of the Broken Sword, illuminating a scene far more relaxed than that of the night before. The other residents of the inn were much more cheerful, and certainly less weary, for there had been no repetition of yesterday's riot.

The two women had taken a table to themselves at the back of the room, in the corner. It was quieter there, and easier for them to hear each other. A lamp just over the table gave plenty of light, and Kethry could see that Tarma was quite well pleased with herself.

". . . so I've got a pair of pupils. Never thought I'd care for teaching, but I'm having a rare good time of it," Tarma concluded over fish stew and fried potatoes. "Of course it helps that Ikan and Justin are good-tempered about their mistakes, and they've got the proper attitude about learning swordwork."

"Which is?" Kethry asked, cheered to see a smile on Tarma's face for a change. A real smile, one of pleasure, not of irony.

"That inside that enclosure, I'm the only authority there is."

Kethry sniffed in derision; it was quiet enough in the back-wall corner they'd chosen that Tarma heard the sniff and grinned. "Modest, aren't you?" the mage teased.

She was feeling considerably better herself. No spies of Wethes or Kavin had leapt upon her during the day, and nothing that had occurred had brought back any bad memories. In point of fact she had frequently forgotten that she was in Mornedealth at all. All her apprehension now seemed rather pointless.

"No, seriously," Tarma replied to her japing. "That's the way it is; no matter what your relationship is outside the lessons, inside the lesson the master is The Master. The Master's word is law, and don't argue about the way you learned something before." Tarma wiped her plate clean with a last bit of bread, and settled back against the wall. "A lot of hire-swords don't understand that relationship—especially if it's a woman standing in the Master's place—but Ikan and Justin have had good teaching, and got it early enough to do some good. They're able, and they're serious, and they're going to come along fast."

"What if you wanted to learn something from one of them?" Kethry asked, idly turning a ring on her finger. "Wouldn't all this Master business cause problems?"

"No, because when I become the pupil, my teacher becomes the Master—actually that's already happened. Just before we wrapped up for the day, I asked Justin to show me a desperation-counter he'd used on me earlier." Tarma sighed regretfully. "Wish you knew something of swordwork, Greeneyes—that was a clever move he showed me. If you knew enough to appreciate it, I could go on about it for a candlemark. Could get you killed if you tried it without timing it exactly right, but if you did, it could save your getting spitted in a situation I couldn't see any way out of."

Kethry shook her head. "I don't see how you keep things straight. Back at the School, we only had *one* Master for each pupil, so we didn't get mixed up in trying to learn two different styles of magery."

"But half of your weaponry as a hire-sword is flexibility. You've got to be able to learn anything from anybody," Tarma replied. "If you can't be flexible enough mentally to accept any number of Masters, you've no business trying to make your living with a blade, and that's all there is to say. How did your day go?"

"Enlightening." Kethry wore a fairly wry smile. She raised her voice slightly so as to be heard above the hum of conversation that filled the room. "I never quite realized the extent to which polite feuding among the Fifty goes before I took this little job."

"Ah?" Tarma cocked an inquiring eyebrow and washed down the last bite of bread and butter with a long pull on her mug.

"Well, I thought that business the fellow at the Hiring Hall told us was rather an exaggeration—until I started using mage-sight on some of the animals my client had picked out as possibles. A good half of them had been beglamoured, and I recognized the feel of the kind of glamour that's generally used by House mages around here. Some of what was being covered was kind of funny, in a nasty-brat sort of way—like the pair of matched grays that turned out to be fine animals, just a particularly hideous shade of muddy yellow."

"What would that have accomplished? A horse is a horse, no matter the color."

"Well, just imagine the young man's chagrin to be driving these beasts hitched to his maroon rig; in a procession, perhaps—and then the glamour is lifted, with all eyes watching and tongues ready to flap."

Tarma chuckled. "He'd lose a bit of face over it, not that I can feel too sorry for any idiot that would drive a maroon rig."

"You're heartless, you are. Maroon and blue are his House colors, and he hasn't much choice but to display them. He'd lose more than a little face over it; he wouldn't dare show himself with his rig in public until he got something so spectacular to pull it that his embarrassment would be forgotten, and for a trick like that, he'd practically have to have hitched trained griffins to overcome his loss of pride. By the way, that's *my* client you're calling an idiot, and he's paying quite well."

"In that case, I forgive him the rig. How long do you think you'll be at this?"

"About a week, maybe two."

"Good; that will give my pupils their money's worth and get us back on the road in good time."

"I hope so," Kethry looked over her shoulder a little, feeling a stirring of her previous uneasiness. "The longer I stay here, the more likely it is I'll be found out."

"I doubt it," Tarma took another long pull at her mug. "Who'd think to look for you here?"

"She's *where?*" The incredulous voice echoed in the high vaulting and bounced from the walls of the expensively appointed, blackwood paneled office.

"At one of the foreigners' inns; the Broken Sword. It's used mostly by mercenaries," Kavin replied, leaning back in his chair and dangling his nearly-empty wineglass from careless fingers. He half-closed his gray eyes in lazy pleasure to see Wethes squirming and fretting for his heirloom carpet and fragile furniture. "She isn't using her full name, and is claiming to be foreign herself."

"What's she doing there?" Wethes ran nervous fingers through his carefully oiled black locks, then played with the gold letter opener from his desk set. "Has she any allies? I don't like the notion of going after her in an inn full of hire-swords. There could be trouble, and more than money would cover."

"She wears the robes of a sorceress, and from all I could tell, has earned the right to—"

"That's trouble enough right there," Wethes interrupted.

Kavin's eyes narrowed in barely-concealed anger at the banker's rudeness. *"That* is what you have a house mage to take care of, my gilded friend. *Use* him. Besides, I strongly doubt she could be his equal, else she'd have a patron, and be spending the winter in a cozy little mage-tower. Instead of that, she's wandering about as an itinerant, doing nothing more taxing than checking horses for beglamouring. As to her allies, there's only one that matters. A Shin'a'in swordswoman."

"Shin'a'in? One of the sword-dancers? I don't like the sound of that."

"They seem," he continued, toying with a lock of his curly, pale gold hair, "to be lovers."

"I like that even less."

"Wethes, for all your bold maneuvering in the marketplace, you are a singularly cowardly man." Kavin put his imperiled glass safely on one of Wethes' highly-polished wooden tables, and smiled to himself when Wethes winced in anticipation of the ring its moist bottom would cause. He stood up and stretched lazily, consciously mirroring one of the banker's priceless marbles behind him; then smoothed his silk-velvet tunic back into its proper position. He smiled to himself again at the flash of greed in Wethes' eyes; the banker valued him as much for his decorative value as for his lineage. With Kavin as a guest, any party Wethes held was certain to attract a high number of Mornedealth's acknowledged beauties as well as the younger members of the Fifty. It was probably time again to grace one of the fat fool's parties with his presence, after all, he did owe him something. His forbearance in not negating their bargain when Kavin's brat-sister vanished deserved some reward.

Of course, their arrangement was not all one-sided. Wethes would have lost all he'd gained by the marriage and more had it become known that his child-bride had fled him before the union was a day old. And now that she'd been gone more than three years—by law, she was no longer his wife at all. That would have been infinitely worse. It had been Kavin who had suggested that they pretend that Kethry had gone to stay on Wethes' country estate. Kethry was unused to dealing with people in any numbers, and found her new position as Wethes' helpmeet somewhat overwhelming—so they told the curious. She was happier away from the city and the confusion of society. Kavin was only too pleased to represent her interests with Wethes, and play substitute for her at formal occasions.

They'd kept up the fiction for so long that even Kavin was starting to half-believe in Wethes' "shy" spouse.

"The Shin'a'in will be no problem," Kavin said soothingly, "She's a stranger in this city; she doesn't know it, she has no friends. All we need do is take your wayward wife when she's out from under the swords-woman's eye, and the Shin'a'in will be helpless to find her. She wouldn't even begin to know where to look. Although why you're bothering with this is beyond me. Kethry's hardly of an age to interest you anymore. And you have the connections you want without the burden of a real wife."

"She's mine," Wethes said, and the expression in his eyes was cold and acquisitive. "What's mine, I keep. No one robs me or tricks me with impunity. I'll keep her in chains for the insult she's done me—chains of her own body. She'll do to breed a dozen heirs, and they tell me no pregnant mage can work her tricks while so burdened."

Kavin raised a sardonic eyebrow, but made no further comment except to say, "I wouldn't believe that particular peasants' tale if I were you—I've had friends thought the same and didn't live to admit they were wrong. Now, I suspect your next question was going to be whether or not the Shin'a'in might be able to get a hearing with the Council. It might be possible—but who would believe a foreigner's tale of abduction against the word of the wealthiest man in Mornedealth?"

"Put that way, I see no risk of any kind to us," Wethes put down the gold paper knife. "And certainly I wish above all to have this accomplished at no risk of exposure. There are enough stories about why I mew my wife up in the country as it is. I'd rather no one ever discovered she's never been in my possession at all. But how do we get her away from her lover?"

"Just leave that—" Kavin smiled, well aware that his slow smile was not particularly pleasant to look on, "—to me."

Kethry woke with an aching head and a vile taste in her mouth; lying on her side, tied hand and foot, in total darkness. It hurt even to think, but she forced herself to attempt to discipline her thoughts and martial them into coherency, despite their tendency to shred like spiderwebs in a high wind. What had happened to her—where was she?

Think—it was so hard to think—it was like swimming through treacle to put one thought after another. Everything was fogged, and her only real desire was to relax and pass back into oblivion.

Which meant she'd been drugged.

That made her angry; anger burned some of the befuddlement away.

And the resulting temporary surge in control gave her enough to remember a cleansing ritual.

Something like a candlemark later, she was still tied hand and foot and lying in total darkness. But the rest of the drug had been purged from her body and she was at last clearheaded and ready to think—and act. Now, what had happened?

She thought back to her last clear memory—parting with her client for the day. It had been a particularly fruitless session, but he had voiced hopes for the morrow. There were supposed to be two horse tamers from the North arriving in time for beast-market day. Her client had been optimistic, particularly over the rumored forest-hunters they were said to be bringing. They had parted, she with her day's wages safely in the hidden pocket of her robe, he accompanied by his grooms.

And she'd started back to the inn by the usual route.

But—now she had it!—there'd been a tangle of carts blocking the Street of the Chandlers. The carters had been swearing and brawling, laughingly goaded on by a velvet-clad youth on his high-bred palfrey who'd probably been the cause of the accident in the first place. She'd given up on seeing the street cleared before supper, and had ducked into an alley.

Then had come the sound of running behind her. Before she could turn to see who it was, she was shoved face-first against the rough wood of the wall, and a sack was flung over her head. A dozen hands pinned her against the alley wall while a sickly-sweet smelling cloth was forced over her mouth and nose. She had no chance to glimpse the faces of her assailants, and oblivion had followed with the first breath of whatever-it-was that had saturated the cloth.

But for who had done this to her—oh, that she knew without seeing their faces. It could only be Kavin and his gang of ennobled toughs—and to pay for it all, Wethes.

As if her thought had conjured him, the door to her prison opened, and Wethes stood silhouetted against the glare of light from the torch on the wall of the hallway beyond him.

Terror overwhelmed her, terror so strong as to take the place of the drug in befuddling her. She could no longer think, only feel, and all she felt was fear. He seemed to be five hundred feet tall, and even more menacing than her nightmares painted him.

"So," he laughed, looking down at her as she tried to squirm farther away from him, "My little bride returns at last to her loving husband."

* * *

"Damn, damn, damn!" Tarma cursed, and paced the icy street outside the door of the Broken Sword; exactly twenty paces east, then twenty west, then twenty east again. It was past sunset: Kethry wasn't back yet; she'd sent no word that she'd be late, and that wasn't like her. And—

She suddenly went cold, then hot, then her head spun dizzily. She clutched the lintel for support while the street spun before her eyes. The door of the inn opened, but she dared not try and move. Her ears told her of booted feet approaching, yet she was too giddy to even turn to see who it was.

"I'd ask if you had too much wine, except that I didn't see you drink more than a mouthful or two before you left the room," Justin spoke quietly, for her ears alone, as he added his support to that of the lintel. "Something's wrong?"

"Keth—something's happened to Keth—" Tarma gasped for air.

"I know she's late, but—"

"The—bond, the *she'enedran*-oath we swore to each other—it was Goddess-blessed. So if anything happens to one of us—"

"Ah—the other knows. Ikan and I have something of the kind, but we're spell-bound and we had it done a-purpose; useful when scouting. Sit. Put your head between your knees. I'll get Ikan. He knows a bit more about leechcraft and magery than I."

Tarma let him ease her down to the ice-covered doorstep, and did as she was told. The frosted stone was very cold beneath her rump, but the cold seemed to shake some of the dizziness away, getting her head down did a bit more. Just as her head began to clear, there were returning footsteps, and two pairs of booted feet appeared beside her.

"Drink this—" Ikan hunched on his heels beside her as she cautiously raised her head; he was holding out a small wooden bottle, and his whole posture showed concern. "Just a swallow; it's only for emergencies."

She took a gingerly mouthful, and was glad she'd been cautious. The stuff burned all the way down her gullet, but left a clear head and renewed energy behind it.

"Goddess—oh, Goddess, I have to—" she started to rise, but Justin's hands on her shoulders prevented her.

"You have to stay right where you are. You want to get yourself killed?" Ikan asked soberly. "You're a professional, Shin'a'in—act like one."

"All right," Justin said calmly, as she sank back to the stone. "Something's happened to your oath-sister. Any clue as to what—"

"—or who?" Ikan finished. "Or why? You're not rich enough to ransom, and too new in Mornedealth to have acquired enemies."

"Why and who—I've got a damn good idea," Tarma replied grimly, and told them, in brief, Kethry's history.

"Gods, how am I to get her away from them? I don't know where to look, and even if I did, what's one sword against what Wethes can hire?" she finished in despair. "Why, oh why didn't I listen to her?"

"Kavin—Kavinestral—hmm," Justin mused. "Now that sounds familiar."

"It bloody well should," Ikan replied, stoppering his precious bottle tightly and tucking it inside his tunic. "He heads the Blue faction."

"The—what?" Tarma blinked at him in bewilderment.

"There are five factions among the wilder offspring of the Fifty; Blue, Green, Red, Yellow, and Black. They started out as racing clubs, but it's gotten down to a nastier level than that within the last few years," Ikan told her. "Duels in plenty, one or two deaths. Right now only two factions are strong enough to matter; Blue and Green. Kavin heads the Blues; a fellow called Helansevrith heads Green. They've been eyeblinks away from each other's throats for years, and the only thing that has kept them from taking each other on, is that Kavin is essentially a coward. He'd rather get his followers to do his dirty work for him. He makes a big pose of being a tough, but he's never personally taken anyone out. Mostly that doesn't matter, since he's got his followers convinced."

He stood up, offering his hand to Tarma. "I can give you a quick guess who could find out where Kethry is, because I know where Wethes won't take her. He won't dare take her to his home, his servants would see and gossip. He won't risk that, because the tale he's given out all these years is that Kethry is very shy and has been staying in seclusion on his country estate. No, he'll take her to his private brothel; I know he has one, I just don't know where. But Justin's got a friend who could tell us."

"That she could—and be happy to. Any harm she could bring that man would make her right glad." Even in the dim light from the torch over the door Tarma could see that Justin looked grim.

"How do you know all this about Wethes and Kavin?" Tarma looked from one to the other of them.

"Because, Swordlady," Ikan's mouth stretched in something that bore very little resemblance to a smile, "my name wasn't always Dryvale."

Kethry had wedged herself back into a corner of her barren, stone-floored cell. Wethes stood over her, candle-lantern in one hand, gloating. It was the very worst of her nightmares come true.

"What's mine remains mine, dear wife," he crowed. "You won't be given a second chance to escape me. I bought you, and I intend to keep you." He was enjoying every moment, was taking pleasure in her fright, just as he had taken pleasure in her pain when he'd raped her.

Kethry was paralyzed with fear, her skin crawling at the bare presence of him in the same room with her. What would she do if he touched her? Her heart was pounding as if she'd been running for miles. And she thought wildly that if he did touch her, perhaps her heart would give out.

He bent and darted his hand forward suddenly, as if intending to catch one of her arms, and she gave a little mew of terror and involuntarily kicked out at him with her bound feet.

His startled reaction took her completely by surprise.

He jumped backward, eyes widening, hands shaking so that the candle flame wavered. Fear was a mask over *his* features—absolute and utter fear of *her.* For one long moment he stared at her, and she at him, hardly able to believe what her own eyes were telling her.

He was *afraid* of her. For all his puffing and threatening, he was *afraid* of her!

And in that moment she saw him for what he was—an aging, paunchy, greedy coward. Any sign of resistance in an *adult* woman obviously terrified *him.*

She kicked out again, experimentally, and he jumped back another pace.

Probably the only females he *could* dominate were helpless children; probably that was why he chose them for his pleasures. At this moment he was as terrified of her as she had been of him.

And the nightmare-monster of her childhood revealed itself to be a thing of old clothes stuffed with straw.

Her fear of him evaporated, like a thing spun of mist. Anger quickly replaced the fear; and while fear paralyzed her magecraft, anger *fed* her powers. That she had been held in thrall for seven long years by fear of *this!*

He saw the change from terror to rage on her face; she could see his realization that she was no longer cowed mirrored on his. He bit his lip and stepped backward another three or four paces.

With three barked words she burned through the ropes on her hands and feet. She rose swiftly to her feet, shaking the bits off her wrists as she did so, her eyes never once leaving his face.

"Kidnap me, will you?" she hissed at him, eyes narrowed. "Drug me and leave me tied up, and think you can use me as you did before—well, I've grown up, even if you haven't. I've learned how to deal with slime like you."

Wethes gulped, and backed up again.

"I'll teach *you* to mend your ways, you fat, slobbering bastard! I'll show *you* what it feels like to be a victim!"

She pointed a finger at him, and miniature lightning leapt from it to his feet.

Wethes yelped, hopping from one foot to the other. Kethry aimed her finger a bit higher.

"Let's see how *you* like being hurt."

He screeched, turned, and fled, slamming the door behind him. Kethry was at it in an eyeblink, clawing at it in frustration, for there was no handle on this side. She screamed curses at him; in her own tongue, then in Shin'a'in when that failed her, pounding on the obdurate portal with both fists.

"Come back here, you half-breed son of a pig and an ape! I'll wither your manhood like a fifty-year-old sausage! Coward! Baby-raper! If I ever get my hands on your neck, I'll wrap a rope around it and spin you like a top! I'll peel your skull like a chestnut! *Come back here!*"

Finally her bruised fists recalled her to her senses. She stopped beating senselessly on the thick wood of the door, and rested for a moment, eyes closed as she reined in her temper. Anger did feed her power, but uncontrolled anger kept her from using it. She considered the door, considered her options, then acted.

A half-dozen spells later, her magic energies were becoming exhausted; the wood of the door was blackened and splintered, and the floor before it warped, but the door remained closed. It had been warded, and by a mage who was her equal at the very least. She used the last of her power to fuel a feeble mage-light; it hovered over her head, illuminating the barren cell in a soft blue radiance. She leaned her back against the far wall and allowed herself to slide down it, wearily. Wrapping her arms around her tucked-up knees, she regarded the warded door and planned her next move.

If Wethes could have seen the expression on her face, he'd have died of fright on the spot.

Tarma had been expecting Justin's "friend" to be a whore. Certainly she lived on a street where every other door housed one or more who practiced that trade—and the other doors led to shops that catered to their needs or those of their customers. They stopped midway down the block to tap lightly at one of those portals that plainly led to a small apartment, and Tarma expected it to be opened by another of the painted, bright-eyed trollops who bestowed themselves on doorways and windows all up and down this thoroughfare. She was shivering at the sight of most of them, not from dislike, but from sympathy. *She* was half-frozen (as usual), and could not imagine for a moment how they managed to stay warm in the scarves and shreds of silk they wore for bodices and skirts.

She didn't hold them in low esteem for selling themselves to earn their bread. After all, wasn't that exactly what she and Keth were doing? It was too bad that they had no other commodity to offer, but that was what fate had dealt them.

But the dark-eyed creature who opened her door at Justin's coded knock was no whore, and was unlikely to ever be mistaken for one, no matter how murky the night or intoxicated the customer.

In some ways she was almost a caricature of Tarma herself; practically sexless. Nothing other than Justin's word showed she was female—her sable hair cut so short it was hardly more than a smooth dark cap covering her skull; the thin, half-starved-looking body of an acrobat. She wore midnight blue; the only relief of that color came from the dozens of knives she wore, gleaming in the light that streamed from the room behind her, the torches of the street, and the lantern over the door, which Tarma noticed belatedly was of blue glass, not red. Two bandoliers were strapped across her slim chest, and both housed at least eight or nine matched throwing daggers. More were in sheaths strapped to her arms and legs; two longer knives, almost short swords, resided on each hip. Her face was as hard as marble, with deeply etched lines of pain.

"Justin, it's late," she said in a soft voice, frowning a little. "I take my shift soon."

"Cat-child, I know," Justin replied; Tarma realized in that instant that the hard lines of the girl's face had deceived her; she couldn't have been more than fifteen or sixteen. "But we have a chance to get at Wethes Goldmarchant and—"

The girl's face blazed with an unholy light. "When? *How?* I'll have somebody else sub for me; Gesta owes me a favor—"

"Easy, girl," Ikan cautioned. "We're not sure what we're going to be doing yet, or how much we're going to be able to hurt him, if at all."

She gave Ikan a sidelong look, then fixed her attention again on Justin. "Him—who?" she asked, shortly, jerking her head at Ikan.

"My shieldbrother; you've heard me talk about him often enough," he replied, interpreting the brief query, "And this swordlady is Tarma shena Tale'sedrin, Shin'a'in mercenary. Wethes has her oathsister, a sorceress—it's rather too long a tale to go into, but we know he took her, he's got his reasons for wanting her and we know he won't be taking her to his house in the District."

"And you want to know if I know where his latest pleasure-house is.

Oh, aye; I do that. But unless you swear to let me in on this, I won't tell you."

"Cat, you don't know what you're asking—"

"Let her buy in," Tarma interrupted, and spoke to the girl directly. "I'm guessing you're one of Wethes' discards."

"You're not wrong. I hate his littlest nail-paring. I want a piece of him —somehow, some way—preferably the piece he prizes the most."

"That's a reasonable request, and one I'm inclined to give you a chance at. Just so long as you remember that our primary goal is the rescue of my oathsister, and you don't jeopardize getting Keth out in one piece."

"Let me roust out Gesta."

The girl darted between Tarma and Justin; ran up the staircase to the second floor to knock on another nondescript door. The ugliest man Tarma had ever seen in her life answered it; Cat whispered something inaudible. He grinned, pulled a savage-looking half-ax from somewhere just inside the door, and sauntered down the stairs with it, whistling tunefully. He gave all three of them a wink as he passed them, said shortly, "Good hunting," and passed out of sight around a corner. The girl returned with a thoughtful look in her eyes.

"Come on in. Let's sit and plan this over. Being too hasty to look before I acted got me *into* Wethes' hands."

"And you won't be making that mistake a second time, will you, my girl?" Justin finished for her.

They filed into the tiny room; it held a few cushions and a pallet, a small clothes chest, more knives mounted on the wall, and a lantern, nothing more.

"You say your friend's a sorceress? The old bastard probably has her under binding from his house mage," she mused as she dropped down cross-legged on the pallet, leaving them to choose cushions. "Think she could break herself free if we gave him something else to think about?"

"Probably; Keth's pretty good—"

"The mage isn't all we have to worry about. Kavinestral's crowd is bound to be hanging around," Ikan interrupted.

"Damn—there's only four of us, and that lot is nearly thirty strong." The girl swore under her breath. "Where in *sheva* are we going to get enough bodies to throw at them?"

Whatever had been in that drink Ikan had given her seemed to be making Tarma's mind work at high speed. " 'Find your enemy's enemy.' That's what my people would say."

Ikan stared at her, then began to grin.

*   *   *

The last explosion from the sealed room below made the whole house rattle. Wethes turned to Kavin with stark panic in his face. "What have you gotten me into?" he choked hysterically, grabbing Kavin by the front of his tunic and shaking him. *"What kind of monster has she become?"*

Kavin struck the banker's hands away, a touch of panic in his own eyes. Kethry wasn't going to be any happier with him than she was with Wethes—and if she got loose— "How was I to know? Magecraft doesn't breed true in my family! Mages don't show up oftener than one in every ten births in my House! She never gave any indication she had that much power when I was watching her! Can't your mage contain her?"

"Barely—and *then* what do I do? She'll kill me if I try and let her go, and may the gods help us if Regyl has to contend with more than simply containing her."

He might have purposefully called the sounds of conflict from the yard beyond the house. Shouts and cries of pain, and the sound of steel on steel penetrated the door to the courtyard; mingled in those shouts was the rally cry of the Greens. That galvanized Kavin into action; he started for the door to the rear of the house and the only other exit, drawing his sword as he ran, obviously hoping to escape before the fracas penetrated into the building.

But he stopped dead in his tracks as the door burst inward, and narrowly missed being knocked off his feet by the force that blew it off its hinges. His blade dropped from numb fingers, clattering on the slate-paved floor. His eyes grew round, and he made a tiny sound as if he were choking. Behind him, Wethes was doing the same.

There were five people standing in the doorway; whether Wethes knew all of them, he didn't know, but Kavin recognized only two.

First in line stood Kethry. Her robes were slightly torn and scorched in one place; she was disheveled, smoke-stained, and dirty. But she was very clearly in control of the situation—and Kavin found himself completely cowed by her blazing eyes.

Behind her was the Shin'a'in Tarma; a sword in one hand, a dagger in the other, and the look of an angry wolf about her. Should Kethry leave anything of him, he had no doubt that his chances of surviving a single candlemark with her were nil.

Next to Tarma stood a young girl in midnight blue festooned with throwing daggers and with a long knife in either hand. She was the only one of the lot not dividing her attention between himself and Wethes. Kavin looked sideways over his shoulder at the banker, and concluded that he would rather not be in Wethes' shoes if that girl were given her way with him; Wethes looked as if he were as frightened of her as of the rest combined.

Behind those three stood a pair of men, one of whom looked vaguely familiar, although Kavin couldn't place him. They took one look at the situation, grinned at each other, sheathed their own weapons, and left, closing what remained of the door behind the three women.

Kavin backed up, feet scuffling on the floor, until he ran into Wethes.

"Surprise, kinsmen," Kethry said. "I am *so* glad to find you both at home."

The Broken Sword was the scene of general celebration; Hadell had proclaimed that the ale was on the house, in honor of the victory the five had just won. It was a double victory, for not only had they rescued Kethry, but Ikan had that very day gotten them a hearing and a highly favorable verdict from the Council. Wethes was, insofar as his ambitions went, a ruined man. Worse, he was now a laughing-stock to the entire city.

"Cat-child, I expected you at least to want him cut up into collops." Justin lounged back precariously in his chair on the hearth, balancing it on two legs. "I can't fathom why you went along with this."

"I wanted to *hurt* him," the girl replied, trimming her nails with one of her knives. "And I knew after all these years of watching him that there's only two ways to hurt that bastard; to hit his pride or his moneybags. Revenge, they say, is a dish best eaten cold, and I've had three years of cooling."

"And here's to Kethry, who figured how to get both at the same time," Ikan raised his mug in a toast.

Kethry reciprocated. "And to you, who convinced the Council I was worth heeding."

Ikan smiled. "Just calling in a few old debts, that's all. You're the one who did the talking."

"Oh, really? I was under the impression that you did at least half of it."

"Some, maybe. Force of habit, I'm afraid. Too many years of listening to my father. You may know him—Jonis Revelath—"

"Gods, yes, I remember him!" Kethry exclaimed. "He's the legal counsel for half the Fifty!"

"Slightly more than half."

"That must be why you're the one who remembered it's against the law to force any female of the Fifty into *any* marriage without her consent," Kethry said admiringly. "Ikan, listening to you in there—I was truly impressed. You're clever, you're persuasive, you're a good speaker. Why aren't you . . ."

"Following in my father's footsteps? Because he's unable to fathom why I am more interested in justice than seeing that every client who hires me gets off without more than a reprimand."

"Which is why the old stick wouldn't defend Wethes for all the gold that bastard threw at him," Justin chuckled, seeing if he could balance the chair on *one* leg. "Couldn't bear to face his son with Ikan on the side of Good, Truth, and Justice. Well, shieldbrother, going to give up the sword and Fight for Right?" The irony in his voice was so strong it could have been spread on bread and eaten.

"Idiot!" Ikan grinned. "What do you think I am, a dunderhead like you? Swords are safer and usually fairer than the law courts any day!"

"Well, I think you were wonderful," Kethry began.

"I couldn't have done it without you and Cat being so calm and clear. You had an answer for everything they could throw at you."

"Enough!" Tarma growled, throwing apples at all of them. "You were all brilliant. So now Wethes is poorer by a good sum; Cat has enough to set herself up as anything she chooses, we have enough to see us to the Plains, and the entire town knows Wethes isn't potent with anything over the age of twelve. He's been the butt of three dozen jokes that I've heard so far; there are gangs of little boys chanting rude things in front of his house at this moment."

"I've heard three songs about him out on the street, too," Cat interrupted with an evil grin.

"And last of all, Keth's so-called marriage has been declared null. What's left?"

"Kavin?" Justin hazarded. "Are we likely to see any more trouble from him?"

"Well, I saw to it that he's been declared disinherited by the Council for selling his sister. Keth didn't want the name or the old hulk of a house that goes with it, so it's gone to a cadet branch of her family."

"With my blessings; they're very religious, and I think they intend to set up a monastic school in it. As for my brother, when last seen, Kavin was fleeing for his life through the stews with the leader of the Greens in hot pursuit," Kethry replied with a certain amount of satisfaction. "I saw him waiting for Kavin outside the Council door, and I was kind enough to pinpoint my brother for him with a ball of mage-light. I believe his intention was to paint Kavin a bright emerald when he caught him."

Justin burst into hearty guffaws—and his chair promptly capsized.

The rest of them collapsed into helpless laughter at the sight of him, looking surprised and indignant, amid the ruins of his chair.

"Well!" he said, crossing his arms and snorting. "There's gratitude for you! That's the last time I *ever* do any of you a fav—"

Whatever else he was going to say ended in a splutter as Ikan dumped his mug over his head.

"Still set on getting back to the Plains?" Kethry asked into the darkness.

A sigh to her right told her that Tarma wasn't asleep yet. "I have to," came the reluctant answer. "I can't help it. I have to. If you want to stay . . ."

Kethry heard the unspoken plea behind the words and answered it. "I'm your *she'enedra*, am I not?"

"But do you really understand what that means?"

"Understand—no. Beginning to understand, yes. You forget, I'm a mage; I'm used to taking internal inventory on a regular basis. I've never had a Talent for Empathy, but now I find myself knowing what you're feeling, even when you're trying to hide it. And you knew the instant I'd been taken, didn't you?"

"Yes."

"And now you're being driven home by something you really don't understand."

"Yes."

"Does it have anything to do with that Goddess of yours, do you think?"

"It might; I don't know. We Sworn Ones move mostly to Her will, and it may be She has some reason to want me home. I *know* She wants Tale'sedrin back as a living Clan."

"And She wants me as part of it."

"She must, or She wouldn't have marked the oathtaking."

Kethry stretched tired muscles, and put her hands under her head. "How much time do you have before you *have* to be back?"

"Before Tale'sedrin is declared dead? Four years, maybe five. Kethry . . ."

"It's all right, I told you, I can feel some of what you're feeling now, I understand."

"You're—you're better. I'm—I'm feeling some of what you're feeling, too."

"This whole mess was worth it," Kethry replied slowly, only now beginning to articulate what she'd only sensed. "It really was. My ghosts have been laid to rest. And revenge—great Goddess, I couldn't have hoped for a better revenge! Kavin is terrified of me; he kept expecting me to turn him into a toad, or something. And Wethes is utterly ruined. He's still got his money, but it will never buy him back his reputation. Indirectly, you got me that, Tarma. I finally realized that I would *never* reach Adept without coming to terms with my past. You forced me into the confrontation I'd never have tried on my own. For that alone I would be indebted to you."

"She'enedran don't have debts."

"I rather figured that. But—I want you to know, I'm going with you because I want to, not because I think that I owe you. I didn't understand what this oath meant at first, but I do now, and I would repeat it any time you asked."

A long silence. Then, *"Gestena, she'enedra."*

That meant "thank you," Kethry knew—thanks, and a great deal more than thanks.

"Yai se corthu," she replied uncertainly. "Two are one." For she suddenly felt all Tarma's loneliness and her own as well, and in the darkness of the night it is sometimes possible to say things that are too intense and too true for daylight.

"Yai se corthu." And a hand came from the darkness to take hers.

It was enough.

Four

"Tarma, we've been riding for weeks, and I still haven't seen any sign that this country is going to turn into grass-plains," Kethry complained, shifting uncomfortably in Rodi's saddle. "Brush-hills, yes. Near-desert, certainly. Forest, ye gods! I've seen more trees than I ever want to see again!"

"What's wrong with forest, other than that you can't do a straight-line gallop or get a clear shot at anything, that is?"

Kethry gazed in all directions, and then glanced up to where branches cut off every scrap of sky overhead. Huge evergreens loomed wherever she looked; the only sunlight came from those few beams that managed to penetrate the canopy of needles. It seemed as if she'd been breathing resin forever, the smell clung to everything; clothing, hair—it even got into the food. It wasn't unpleasant; the opposite, in fact, especially after they'd first penetrated the edges of the forest after days of fighting a dusty wind. But after days of eating, drinking, and breathing the everlasting odor of pine, she was heartily tired of it.

It was chilly and damp on the forest floor, and lonely. Kethry hadn't seen a bird in days, for they were all up where the sun was. She could hear them calling, but the echoes of their far-off singing only made the empty corridors between the tree trunks seem more desolate. This forest had to be incredibly ancient, the oldest living thing she'd ever seen, perhaps. Certainly the trees were larger than any she was familiar with. They towered for yards before branching out, and in the case of a few giants she had noticed, their trunks were so large that several adults could have circled the biggest of them with their arms without touching hand to hand. The road they followed now was hardly more than a goat track; the last person they had seen had been two weeks ago, and since that time they'd only had each other's voices to listen to.

At first it had been pleasurable to ride beneath these branches, especially since they had spent weeks skirting that near-desert she had mentioned, riding through furlong after furlong of stony, brush-covered hills with never anything taller than a man growing on them. While the spring sun had nowhere near the power it would boast in a mere month, it had been more than hot enough for Kethry during the height of the day. She couldn't imagine how Tarma, dressed in her dark Sword Sworn costume, could bear it. When the hills began to grow into something a bit more impressive, and the brush gave way to real trees, it was a genuine relief to spend all day in their cool shade. But now . . .

"It's like they're—watching. I haven't sensed anything, either with mage-senses or without, so I know it must be my imagination, but . . ."

"It's not your imagination; something is watching," Tarma interrupted calmly. "Or rather, some*one*. I thought I'd not mention it unless you saw or felt something yourself, since they're harmless to *us*. Hadn't you ever wondered why I haven't taken any shots at birds since we entered the trees?"

"But—"

"Oh, the watchers themselves aren't within sensing distance, and not within the scope of your mage-senses either—just their feathered friends. Hawks, falcons, ravens and crows by day, owls and nighthawks by dark. *Tale'edras,* my people call them—the Hawkbrothers. We really don't know what they call themselves. We don't see them much, though they've been known to trade with us."

"Will we see any of them?"

"Why, do you want to?" Tarma asked, with a half-grin at Kethry's nod. "You mages must be curiosity incarnate, I swear! Well, I might be able to do something about that. As I said, we're in no danger from them, but if you really want to meet one—let's see if I still have my knack for identifying myself."

She reined in Kessira, threw back her head, and gave an ear-piercing cry—not like the battle shriek of a hawk, but a bit like the mating cry, or the cry that identifies mate to mate. Rodi started, and backed a few steps, fighting his bit, until Kethry got him back into control. A second cry echoed hers, and at first Kethry thought it *was* an echo, but it was followed by a winged streak of gold lightning that swooped down out of the highest branches to land on Tarma's outstretched arm.

It braked its descent with a thunder of wings, wings that seemed to Kethry to belong to something at least the size of an eagle. Talons like ivory knives bit into the leather of Tarma's vambrace; the wings fanned the air for a heartbeat more, then the bird settled on Tarma's forearm, regal and gilded.

"Well if I'd wanted a good omen, I couldn't have asked for a better," Tarma said in astonishment. "This is a vorcel-hawk; you see them more on the plains than in the forests—it's my Clan's standard."

The bird was half-again larger than any hawk Kethry had ever seen; its feathers glistened with an almost metallic gold sheen, no more than a shade darker than the bird's golden eyes. It cocked its head to one side and regarded Kethry with an intelligent air she found rather disturbing. Rodi snorted at the alien creature, but Kessira stood calmly when one wing flipped a hair's-breadth from her ear, apparently used to having huge birds swoop down at her rider from out of nowhere.

"Now, who speaks for you, winged one?" Tarma turned her attention fully to the bird on her arm, stroking his breast feathers soothingly until he settled, then running her hand down to his right leg and examining it. Kethry edged closer, cautiously; wary of the power in that beak and those sharp talons. She saw that what Tarma was examining was a wide band on its leg, a band of some shiny stuff that wasn't metal and wasn't leather.

"Moonsong k'Vala, hmm? Don't know the name. Well, let's send the invitation to talk. I really should at least pay my respects before leaving the trees, if anyone wants to take them, so . . ."

Tarma lowered her arm a little, and the hawk responded by moving up it until he perched on her shoulder. His beak was in what Kethry considered to be uncomfortably close proximity to Tarma's face, but Tarma didn't seem at all concerned. Thinking about the uncertain temperament of all the raptors *she'd* ever had anything to do with, Kethry shivered at Tarma's casualness.

When the bird was safely on her shoulder, Tarma leaned over a little and rummaged in her saddlebag, finally coming up with a cluster of three small medallions. Kethry could see that they were light copper disks, beautifully enameled with the image of the bird that sat her shoulder.

She selected one, dropped the other two back in her bag; then with great care, took a thong from a collection of them looped to a ring on her belt, passed the thong through the hole in the top of the medallion and knotted it securely. She offered the result to the bird, who looked at it with a surprising amount of intelligence before opening his beak slowly and accepting the thong. He bobbed his head twice, the medallion bouncing below his head, and Tarma raised her arm again. He sidled along it until he reached her wrist, and she launched him into the air. His huge wings beat five or six times, raising a wind that fanned their hair, then he was lost to sight among the branches.

"What was that all about?"

"Politeness, more than anything. The Hawkbrothers have known we were here from the moment we entered the forest, and they knew I was Shin'a'in Kal'enedral when they came to look at us in person—that would have been the first night we camped. Since then they've just been making sure we didn't wander off the track, or get ambushed by something we couldn't handle. We'll be leaving the forest soon."

"Soon? When?"

"Keep your breeches on, girl! Tomorrow afternoon at the latest. Anyway, you wanted to see one of the Hawkbrothers, and it's only polite for me to acknowledge the fact that they've been guarding us."

"I thought you said they were watching us."

"Since I'm Shin'a'in and we're allies, it amounts to the same thing. *Sahai;* I just sent my Clan token off to our current guardian, whoever it is. If he or she chooses, we'll get a response before we leave."

"Moonsong sounds like a female name to me," Kethry replied.

"Maybeso, maybeno. The Hawkbrothers are v-e-r-y different—well, you'll see if we get a visitor. Keep your eyes busy looking for a good campsite; stick to the road. As Shin'a'in I have certain privileges here, and I'm tired of dried beef. I'm going hunting."

She swung Kessira off under the trees, following the path the hawk had taken, leaving Kethry alone on the track. With a shrug, Kethry urged Rodi back into a walk and did as she'd been told.

Still homing in on the Plains; she's been easier than she was before Mornedealth, but still—home is drawing her with a power even I can feel. I wonder if it's because she hasn't a real purpose *anymore, not since she accomplished her revenge.*

Kethry kept Rodi to a walk, listening with half her attention for the sound of water. Running surface water was somewhat scarce in the forest; finding it meant they made a campsite then and there.

I don't really have a purpose either, except to learn and grow stronger in magic—but I expected that. I knew that's the way my life would be once I left the school until I could found my own. But Tarma—she needs *a purpose, and this home-seeking is only a substitute for one. I wonder if she realizes that.*

When Tarma caught up with her, it was a candlemark or so before sunset, but it was already dark under the trees. Kethry had found a site that looked perfect, with a tiny, clear stream nearby and a cleared area where one of the giant trees had fallen and taken out a wide swath of seedlings with it. That had left a hole in the green canopy above where sunlight could penetrate, and there were enough grasses and plants growing that there was browse for their animals. The tree had been down for at least a season, so the wood was dry and gathering enough firewood for the evening had been the task of less than a candlemark.

Kethry discovered when she was sweeping out the area for stones to line a firepit that others had found the site just as perfect, for many of the stones bore scorch marks. Now their camp was set up, and the tiny fire burning brightly in the stone-lined pit. When they had entered this forest, Tarma had emphasized the importance of keeping their fires small and under strict control. Now that Kethry knew about the Hawkbrothers, she could guess why. This tree-filled land was theirs, and they doubtless had laws that a visitor to it had better keep, especially with winged watchers all about.

She heard Tarma approaching long before she saw her; a dark shape looming back along the trail, visible only because it was moving.

"Ho, the camp!" Tarma's hoarse voice called cheerfully.

"Ho, yourself—what was your luck?"

"Good enough. From *this* place you take no more than you need, ally or not. Got browse?"

Tarma appeared in the firelight, leading Kessira, something dangling from her hand.

"Behind me about forty paces; Rodi's already tethered there, along a downed tree. If you'll give me what you've got, I'll clean it."

"Skinning is all you need to do, I field-gutted 'em." Tarma tossed two odd creatures at Kethry's feet, the size and shape of plump rabbits, but with short, tufted ears, long claws, and bushy, flexible tails.

"I'll go take care of Rodi and my baby, and I'll be right back." Tarma disappeared into the darkness again, and sounds from behind her told Kethry that she was unsaddling her mare and grooming both the animals. She had unsaddled Rodi but had left the rest to Tarma, knowing the Shin'a'in could tend a saddlebeast in the dark and half asleep. Rodi, while well-mannered for a mule, was too ticklish about being groomed for Kethry to do it in uncertain light.

When Tarma returned, she brought with her their little copper traveling-kettle filled with water. "We'll have to stew those devils; they're tough as old boots after the winter," she said; then, so softly Kethry could hardly hear her, "I got a reply to my invitation. We'll have a visitor in a bit. Chances are he'll pop in out of nowhere; try not to look startled, or we'll lose face. I can guarantee he'll look very strange; in this case, the stranger the better—if he really looks odd it will mean he's giving us full honors."

Just at the moment the stewed meat seemed ready, their visitor appeared.

Even though she'd been forewarned, Kethry *still* nearly jumped out of her skin. One moment the opposite side of the fire was empty—the next, it was not.

He was tall; like Tarma, golden-skinned and blue-eyed. Unlike Tarma, his hair was a pure silver-white; it hung to his waist, two braids framing his face, part of the rest formed into a topknot, the remainder streaming unconfined down his back. Feathers had been woven into it—a tiny owlet nestled at the base of the topknot, a nestling Kethry thought to be a clever carving, until it moved its head and blinked.

His eyes were large and slightly slanted, his features sharp, with no trace of facial hair. His eyebrows had a slight, upward sweep to them, like wings. His clothing was green, all colors of green—Kethry thought it at first to be rags, until she saw how carefully those seeming rags were cut to resemble foliage. In a tree, except for that hair, he'd be nearly invisible, even with a wind blowing. He wore delicate jewelry of woven and braided silver wire and crystals.

He carried in his right hand a strange weapon; a spearlike thing with a wicked, curving point that seemed very like a hawk's talon at one end and a smooth, round hook at the other. In his left he carried Tarma's medallion.

Tarma rose to her feet, gracefully. "Peace, Moonsong."

"And upon you, Child of the Hawk." Both of them were speaking Shin'a'in—after months of tutoring Kethry was following their words with relative ease.

"Tarma," the Shin'a'in replied, "and Kethry. My *she'enedra*. You will share hearth and meal? It is tree-hare, taken as is the law; rejected suitors, no mates, no young, and older than this season's birthing."

"Then I share, and with thanks." He sank to the ground beside the fire with a smoothness, an ease, that Kethry envied; gracefully and soundlessly as a falling leaf. She saw then that besides the feathers he had also braided strings of tiny crystals into his hair, crystals that reflected back the firelight, as did the staring eyes of the tiny owlet. She remembered what Tarma had told her, and concluded they were being given high honor.

He accepted the bowl of stewed meat and dried vegetables with a nod of thanks, and began to eat with his fingers and a strange, crystalline knife hardly longer than his hand. When Tarma calmly began her own portion, Kethry did the same, but couldn't help glancing at their visitor under cover of eating.

He impressed her, that was certain. There was an air of great calm and patience about him, like that of an ancient tree, but she sensed he could be a formidable and implacable enemy if his anger was ever aroused. His silver hair had made her think of him as ancient, but now she wasn't so certain of his age. His face was smooth and unlined; he could have been almost any age at all, from stripling to oldster.

Then she discovered something that truly frightened her; when she looked for him with mage-sight, he wasn't there.

It wasn't a shielding, either—a shield either left an impression of a blank wall or of an absolute nothingness. No, it was as if there was no one across the fire from them at all, nothing but the plants and stones of the clearing, the woods beyond, and the owlet sitting in a young tree.

The owlet sitting in a young tree!

It was then she realized that he was somehow appearing to her mage-sight as a part of the forest, perfectly blended in with the rest. She switched back to normal vision and smiled to herself. And as if he had known all along that she had been scanning him—in fact, if he were practiced enough to pull off what he was doing, he probably *did*—he looked up from his dinner and nodded at her.

"The banner of the Hawk's Children has not been seen for seasons," he said breaking the silence. "We heard ill tales. Tales of ambush on the road to the Horse Fair; tales of death come to their very tents."

"True tales," Tarma replied, the pain in her voice audible to Kethry . . . and probably to Moonsong. "I am the last."

"Ah. Then the blood-price—"

"Has been paid. I go to raise the banner again; this, my *she'enedra,* goes with me."

"Who holds herds for Tale'sedrin?"

"Liha'irden. You have knowledge of the camps this spring?"

"Liha'irden . . ." he brooded a moment. "At Ka'tesik on the border of their territory and yours. So you go to them. And after?"

"I have given no thought to it." Tarma smiled suddenly, but it was with a wry twist to her mouth. "Indeed, the returning has been sufficient to hold my attention."

"You may find," he said slowly, "that the Plains are no longer the home to you that they were."

Tarma looked startled. "Has aught changed?"

"Only yourself, Lone Hawk. Only yourself. The hatched chick cannot go back to the shell, the falcon who has found the sky does not willingly sit the nest. When a task is completed, it is meet to find another task—and you may well serve the Lady by serving outlanders."

Tarma looked startled and pale, but nodded.

"OutClan Shin'a'in—" He turned his attention abruptly to Kethry. "You bear a sword—"

"Aye, Elder."

He chuckled. "Not so old as you think me, nor so young either. Three winters is age to a polekit, but fifty is youth to a tree. You bear a sword, yet you touched me with mage-sight. Strange to see a mage with steel. Stranger still to see steel with a soul."

"What?" Kethry was too startled to respond politely.

"Hear me, mate of steel and magic," he said, leaning forward so that he and the owlet transfixed her with unblinking stares. "What you bear will bind you to herself, more and more tightly with each hour you carry her. It is writ that Need is her name—you shall come to need her, as she needs you, as both of you answer need. This is the price of bearing her, and some of this you knew already. I tell you that you have not yet reached the limit to which she can—and will—bind you to herself, to her goals. It is a heavy price, yet the price is worth her service; you know she can fight for you, you know she can heal you. I tell you now that her powers will extend to aid those you love, so long as they return your care. Remember this in future times—"

His blue eyes bored into hers with an intensity that would have been frightening had he not held her beyond fear with the power he now showed himself to possess. She knew then that she was face-to-face with a true Adept, though of a discipline alien to hers; that he was one such as she hardly dared dream of becoming. Finally he leaned back, and Kethry shook off the near-trance he had laid on her, coming to herself with a start.

"How did you—"

He silenced her with a wave of his hand.

"I read what is written for me to see, nothing more," he replied, rising with the same swift grace he had shown before. "Remember what I have read, both of you. As you are two-made-one, so your task will be one. First the binding, then the finding. For the hearth, for the meal, my thanks. For the future, my blessing. Lady light thy road—"

And as abruptly as he had appeared, he was gone.

Kethry started to say something, but the odd look of puzzlement on Tarma's face stopped her.

"Well," she said at last, "I have only one thing to say. I've passed through this forest twenty times, at least. In all that time, I must have met Hawkbrothers ten out of the twenty, and that was extraordinary. But this—" she shook her head. "That's more words at once from one of them than any of my people has ever reported before. Either we much impressed him—"

"Or?"

"Or," she smiled crookedly, "we are in deep trouble."

Kethry wasn't quite sure what it was that woke her; the cry of a bird, perhaps; or one of the riding beasts waking out of a dream with a snort, and so waking her in turn.

The air was full of gray mist that hung at waist height above the nee-dle-strewn forest floor. It glowed in the dim blue light that signaled dawn, and the treetops were lost beyond thought within it. It was chill and thick in the back of her throat; she felt almost as if she were drinking it rather than breathing it.

The fire was carefully banked coals; it was Tarma's watch. Kethry sighed and prepared to go back to another hour of sleep—then stiffened. There were no sounds beyond what she and the two saddlebeasts were making. Tarma was gone.

Then, muffled by the fog, came the sound of blade on blade; unmistak-able if heard once. And Kethry had heard that peculiar *shing* more times than she cared to think.

Kethry had lain down fully-clothed against the damp; now she sprang to her feet, seizing her blade as she rose. Barefooted, she followed the sound through the echoing trunks, doing her own best to make no sound.

For why, if this had been an attack, had Tarma not awakened her? An ambush then? But why hadn't Tarma called out to her? Why wasn't she calling for help now? What of the Hawkbrothers that were *supposed* to be watching out for them?

She slipped around tree trunks, the thick carpet of needles soft be-neath her feet, following the noise of metal scissoring and clashing. Away from the little cup where they had camped the fog began to wisp and rise, winding around the trunks in wooly festoons, though still thick as a storm cloud an arm's length above her head. The sounds of blades came clearer now, and she began using the tree trunks to hide behind as she crept up upon the scene of conflict.

She rounded yet another tree, and shrank again behind it; the fog had deceived her, and she had almost stumbled into the midst of combat.

The fog ringed this place, moving as if alive, a thick tendril of it wind-ing out, now and again, to interpose itself between Tarma and her foe. It glowed—it glowed with more than the predawn light. To mage-sight it glowed with power, power bright and pure, power strong, true, and— strange. It was out of her experience—and it barred her from the charmed circle where the combatants fenced.

Tarma's eyes were bright with utter concentration, her face expressionless as a sheet of polished marble. Kethry had never seen her quite like this, except when in the half-trance she induced when practicing or meditating. She was using both sword and dagger to defend herself—

Against another Shin'a'in.

This man was unmistakably of Tarma's race. The tawny gold skin of hands and what little Kethry could see of his face showed his kinship to her. So did the strands of raven hair that had been bound out of his face by an equally black headband, and ice-blue eyes that glinted above his veil.

For he *was* veiled; this was something Tarma never had worn for as long as Kethry had known her. Kethry hadn't even known till this moment that a veil could be part of a Shin'a'in costume, but the man's face was obscured by one, and it did not have the feeling of a makeshift. He was veiled *and* garbed entirely in black, the black Tarma had worn when on the trail of those who had slaughtered her Clan. Black was for blood-feud—but Tarma had sworn that there was *never* blood-feud between Shin'a'in and Shin'a'in. And black was for Kal'enedral—three times barred from internecine strife.

There was less in their measured counter and riposte of battle than of dance. Kethry held her breath, transfixed by more than the power of the mist. She was caught by the deadly beauty of the weaving blades, caught and held entranced, drawn out of her hiding place to stand in the open.

Tarma did not even notice she was there—but the other did.

He stepped back, breaking the pattern, and motioned slightly with his left hand. Tarma instantly broke off her advance, and seemed to wake just as instantly from her trance, staring at Kethry with the startled eyes of a wild thing broken from hiding.

The other turned, for his back had been to Kethry. He saluted the sorceress in slow, deliberate ceremony with his own blade. Then he winked slowly and gravely over his veil, and—vanished, taking the power in the magic fog with him.

Released from her entrancement, Kethry stared at her partner, not certain whether to be frightened, angry or both.

"What—was—that—" she managed at last.

"My trainer; my guide," Tarma replied sheepishly. "One of them, anyway." She sheathed her sword and stood, to all appearances feeling awkward and at a curious loss for words. "I . . . never told you about them before, because I wasn't sure it was permitted. They train me every night we aren't within walls . . . one of them takes my watch to see you safe. I . . . I guess they decided I was taking too long to tell you about them; I suppose they figured it was time you knew about them."

"You said your people didn't *use* magic—but he—he was alive with it! Only your Goddess—"

"He's Hers. In life, was Kal'enedral; and now—" she lifted up her hand, "—as you saw. His magic *is* Hers—"

"What do you mean, 'in life'?" Kethry asked, an edge of hysteria in her voice.

"You mean—you couldn't tell?"

"Tell *what?*"

"He's a spirit. He's been dead at least a hundred years, like all the rest of my teachers."

It took Tarma the better part of an hour to calm her partner down.

They broke out of the trees, as Tarma had promised, just past midafternoon.

Kethry stared; Tarma sat easily in Kessira's saddle, and grinned happily. "Well?" she asked, finally.

Kethry sought for words, and failed to find them.

They had come out on the edge of a sheer drop-off; the mighty trees grew to the very edge of it, save for the narrow path on which they stood. Below them, furlongs, it seemed, lay the Dhorisha Plains.

Kethry had pictured acres of grassland, a sea of green, as featureless as the sea itself, and as flat.

Instead she saw beneath her a rolling country of gentle, swelling rises; like waves. Green grass there was in plenty—as many shades of green as Kethry had ever seen, and more—and golden grass, and a faint heathered purple. And flowers—it must have been flowers that splashed the green with irregular pools of bright blue and red, white and sunny yellow, orange and pink. Kethry took an experimental sniff and yes, the breeze rising up the cliff carried with it the commingled scents of growing grass and a hundred thousand spring blossoms.

There were dark masses, like clouds come to earth, running in lines along the bottoms of some of the swells. After a long moment Kethry realized that they must be trees, far-off trees, lining the water-courses.

"How—" she turned to Tarma with wonder in her eyes, "how could you ever bear to leave this?"

"It wasn't easy, *she'enedra,*" Tarma sighed, deep and abiding hunger

stirring beneath the smooth surface of the mask she habitually wore.
"Ah, but you're seeing it at its best. The Plains have their hard moments,
and more of them than the soft. Winter—aye, that's the coldest face of
all, with all you see out there sere and brown, and so barren all the life
but the Clans and the herds sleeps beneath the surface in safe burrows.
High summer is nearly as cruel, when the sun burns everything, when the
watercourses shrink to tiny trickles, when you long for a handsbreadth of
shade, and there is none to be found. But spring—oh, the Plains are
lovely then, as lovely as She is when She is Maiden—and as welcoming."

Tarma gazed out at the blowing grasslands with a faint smile beginning
to touch her thin lips.

"Ah, I swear I am as sentimental as an old granny with a mouthful of
tales of how golden the world was when *she* was young," she laughed,
finally, "and none of this gets us down to the Plains. Follow me, and keep
Rodi exactly in Kessira's footsteps. It's a long way down from here if you
slip."

They followed a narrow trail along the face of the drop-off, a trail that
switched back and forth constantly as it dropped, so that there was never
more than a length or two from one level of the trail to the next below it.
This was no bad idea, since it meant that if a mount and rider *were* to
slide off the trail, they would have a fighting chance of saving themselves
one or two levels down. But it made for a long ride, and all of it in the
full sun, with nowhere to rest and no shade anywhere. Kethry and her
mule were tired and sweat-streaked by the time they reached the bottom,
and she could see that Tarma and Kessira were in no better shape.

But there was immediate relief at the bottom of the cliff, in the form of
a grove of alders and willows with a cool spring leaping out of the base of
the escarpment right where the trail ended. They watered the animals
first, then plunged their own heads and hands into the tinglingly cold
water, washing themselves clean of the itch of sweat and dust.

Tarma looked at the lowering sun, slicking back wet hair. "Well," she
said finally, "We have a choice. We can go on, or we can overnight here.
Which would you rather?"

"You want the truth? I'd rather overnight here. I'm tired, and I ache;
I'd like the chance to rinse all of me off. But I know how anxious you are
to get back to your people."

"Some," Tarma admitted, "But . . . well, if we quit now, then made
an early start of it in the morning, we wouldn't lose too much time."

"I won't beg you, but—"

"All right, I yield!" Tarma laughed, giving in to Kethry's pleading eyes.

Camp was quickly made; Tarma went out with bow and arrow and returned with a young hare and a pair of grass-quail.

"This—this is strange country," Kethry commented sleepily over the crackle of the fire. "These grasslands shouldn't be here, and I could swear that cliff wasn't cut by nature."

"The gods alone know," Tarma replied, stirring the fire with a stick. "It's possible, though. My people determined long ago that the Plains are the bowl of a huge valley that is almost perfectly circular, even though it takes weeks to ride across the diameter of it. This is the only place where the rim is that steep, though. Everywhere else it's been eroded down, though you can still see the boundaries if you know what to look for."

"Perfectly circular—that hardly seems possible."

"You're a fine one to say 'hardly possible,' " Tarma teased. "Especially since you've just crossed through the lowest reaches of the Pelagir Hills."

"I *what?*" Kethry sat bolt upright, no longer sleepy.

"The forest we just passed through—didn't you know it was called the Pelgiris Forest? Didn't the name sound awfully familiar to you?"

"I looked at it on the map—I guess I just never made the connection."

"Well, keep going north long enough and you're in the Pelagirs. My people have a suspicion that the Tale'edras are Shin'a'in originally, Shin'a'in who went a bit too far north and got themselves changed. They've never said anything, though, so we keep our suspicions to ourselves."

"The Pelagirs . . ." Kethry mused.

"And just what are you thinking of? You surely don't want to go in there, do you?"

"Maybe."

"Warrior's Oath! Are you *mad?* Do you know the kind of things that live up there? Griffins, firebirds, colddrakes—things without names 'cause no one who's seen 'em has lived long enough to give them any name besides 'AAAARG!' "

Kethry had to laugh at that. "Oh, I know," she replied, "Better than you. But I also know how to keep us relatively safe in there—"

"What do you mean, 'us'?"

"—because one of my order came from the heart of the Pelagirs. The wizard Gervase."

"Gervase?" Tarma's jaw dropped. "The Lizard Wizard? You mean that silly song about the Wizard Lizard is true?"

"Truer than many that are taken for pure fact. Gervase was a White Winds adept, because the mage that gifted him was White Winds—and it was a good day for the order when he made that gift. Gervase, being a reptile, and being a Pelagir changeling as well, lived three times the span of a normal sorcerer, and we are notoriously long-lived. He became the High Adept of the order, and managed to guide it into the place it holds today."

"Total obscurity," Tarma taunted.

"Oh, no—protective obscurity. Those who need us know how to find us. Those we'd rather couldn't find us can't believe anyone who holds the power a White Winds Adept holds would *ever* be found ankle-deep in mud and manure, tending his own onions. Let other mages waste their time in politics and sorcerer's duels for the sake of proving that one of them is better—or at least more devious—than the other. We save our resources for those who are in need of them. There's this, too—*we* can sleep sound of nights, knowing nobody is likely to conjure an adder into one of *our* sleeping rolls."

"Always provided he could ever find the place where you've laid that sleeping roll," Tarma laughed. "All right, you've convinced me."

"When we find your people—"

"Hmm?"

"Well, then what?"

"I'll have to go before a Council of the Elders of three Clans, and present myself. They'll give me back the Clan banner, and—" Tarma stopped, nonplussed.

"And—" Kethry prompted.

"I don't know; I hadn't thought about it. Liha'irden has been taking care of the herds; they'll get first choice of yearlings for their help. But—I don't know, *she'enedra;* the herds of an entire Clan are an awful lot for just two women to tend. My teacher told me I should turn mercenary . . . and I'm not sure now that he meant it to be temporary."

"That *is* how we've been living."

"I suppose we could let Liha'irden continue as caretakers, at least until we're ready to settle down, but—I don't want to leave yet."

"I don't blame you," Kethry teased, "After all, you just got here!"

"Well, look—if we're going to really try and become mercenaries, and not just play at it to get enough money to live on, we're both going to have to get battlesteeds—and *you* are going to have to learn how to manage one."

Kethry paled. "A battlesteed?" she faltered. "Me? I've never ridden anything livelier than a pony!"

"I don't want you at my side in a fight on anything *less* than a Shin'a'in-bred and trained battlesteed," Tarma said in a tone that brooked no argument.

Kethry swallowed, and bit her lip a little.

Tarma grinned suddenly. "Don't go lathering yourself, *she'enedra,* we may decide to stay here, after all, and you can confine yourself to ponies and mules or your own two feet if that's what you want."

"That prospect," Kethry replied, "sounds more attractive every time you mention battlesteeds!"

Kethry had no idea how she did it, but Tarma led them straight into the Liha'irden camp without a single false turning.

"Practice," she shrugged, when Kethry finally asked, "I know it looks all the same to you, but I know every copse and spring and hill of this end of the Plains. The Clans are nomadic, but we each have territories; Liha'irden's was next to Tale'sedrin's. I expected with two Clans' worth of herds they would be camped by one of the springs that divided the two, and pasturing in both territories. When the Hawkbrother told me which spring, I knew I was right."

Tarma in her costume of Kal'enedral created quite a stir—but Kethry was a wonder, especially to the children. When they first approached the camp, Tarma signaled a sentry who had then ridden in ahead of them. As they got nearer, more and more adolescents and older children came out on their saddlebeasts, forming a polite but intensely curious escort. When they entered the camp itself, the youngest came running out to see the visitors, voluble and quite audible in their surprise at the sight of Kethry.

"She has grass-eyes!"

"And sunset-hair!"

"Mata, how come she's riding a mule? She doesn't *look* old or sick!"

"Is she Sworn, too? Then why is she wearing dust-colors?" That from a tiny girl in blazing scarlet and bright blue.

"Is she staying?" "Is she outClan?" "Is she from the magic place?"

Tarma swung down off Kessira and took in the mob of children with a mock-stern expression. "What is this clamor? Is this the behavior of Shin'a'in?"

The babble cut off abruptly, the children keeping complete silence.

"Better. Who will take my mare and my *she'enedra's* mule?"

One of the adolescents handed his reins to a friend and presented himself. "I will, Sworn One."

"My thanks," she said, giving him a slight bow. He returned a deeper bow, and took both animals as soon as Kethry had dismounted.

"Now, will someone bring us to the Elders?"

"No need," said a strong, vigorous voice from the rear of the crowd. "The Elders are here."

The gathering parted immediately to allow a collection of four Shin'a'in through. One was a woman of middle years, with a square (for a Shin'a'in) face, gray-threaded hair, and a look of determination about her. She wore bright harvest-gold breeches, soft, knee-high, fringed leather boots, a cream-colored shirt with embroidered sleeves, and a scarlet-and-black embroidered vest that laced closed in the front. By the headdress of two tiny antelope horns she wore, Kethry knew she was the Shaman of Liha'irden.

The second was a very old man, his face wrinkled so that his eyes twinkled from out of the depths of deep seams, his hair pure white. He wore blue felt boots, embroidered in green; dark blue breeches, a lighter blue shirt, and a bright green vest embroidered with a pattern to match the boots, but in blue. The purely ornamental riding crop he wore at his belt meant he was the Clan Chief. He was far from being feeble; he walked fully erect with never a hint of a limp or a stoop, and though his steps were slow, they were firm.

Third was a woman whose age lay somewhere between the Clan Chief and the Shaman. She wore scarlet; nothing but shades of red. That alone told Kethry that this was the woman in whose charge lay both the duties of warleader and of instructing the young in the use of arms.

Last was a young man in muted greens, who smiled widely on seeing Tarma. Kethry knew this one from Tarma's descriptions; he was Liha'irden's Healer and the fourth Elder.

"Either news travels on the wings of the birds, or you've had scouts out I didn't see," Tarma said, giving them the greeting of respect.

"In part, it did travel with birds. The Hawkbrothers told us of your return," the Healer said. "They gave us time enough to bring together a Council."

The crowd parted a second time to let five more people through, all elderly. Tarma raised one eyebrow in surprise.

"I had not expected to be met by a full Council," she said, cautiously. "And I find myself wondering if this is honor, or something else."

"Kal'enedra, I wish you to know that this was nothing of my doing," the Clan Chief of Liha'irden replied, his voice heavy with disapproval. "Nor will my vote be cast against you."

"Cast against me? *Me?* For why?" Tarma flushed, then blanched.

"Tale'sedrin is a dead Clan," one of the other five answered her, an old woman with a stubborn set to her mouth. "It only lacks a Council's pronouncement to make history what is already fact."

"*I* still live! And while I live, Tale'sedrin lives!"

"A Clan is more than a single individual, it is a living, growing thing," she replied, "You are Kal'enedral; you are barren seed by vow and by the Warrior's touch. How can Tale'sedrin be alive in you, when you cannot give it life?"

"Kal'enedra, Tarma, we have no wish to take from you what is yours by right of inheritance," the Warleader of Liha'irden said placatingly. "The herds, the goods, they are still yours. But the Children of the Hawk are no more; you are vowed to the Shin'a'in, not to any single Clan. Let the banner be buried with the rest of the dead."

"*No!*" Tarma's left hand closed convulsively on the hilt of her dagger, and her face was as white as marble. "Sooner than that I would die with them! Tale'sedrin *lives!*"

"It lives in *me.*" Kethry laid one restraining hand on Tarma's left and then stepped between her and the Council. "I am *she'enedra* to the Sworn One—does this not make me Shin'a'in also? *I* have taken no vows of celibacy; more, I am a White Winds sorceress, and by my arts I can prolong the period of my own fertility. Through *me* Tale'sedrin is a living, growing thing!"

"How do we know the bond is a true one?" One of the group of five, a wizened old man, asked querulously.

Kethry held up her right hand, palm out, and reached behind her to take Tarma's right by the wrist and display it as well. Both bore silvered, crescent-shaped scars.

"By the fact that She blessed it with Her own fire, it can be nothing but a true bond—" Tarma began, finding her tongue again.

"*Sheka!*" the old man spat, interrupting her. "She says openly she is a sorceress. She could have produced a seeming sign—could have tricked even you!"

"For what *purpose?*"

"To steal what outClan have always wanted; our battlesteeds!"

Tarma pulled her hand away from Kethry's and drew her sword at that venomous accusation.

"Kethry has saved my life; she has bled at my side to help me avenge Tale'sedrin," Tarma spat, holding her blade before her in both hands, taking a wide-legged, defensive stance. "How *dare* you doubt the word of Kal'enedral? She is my true *she'enedra* by a Goddess-blessed vow, and you will retract your damned lie or die on my blade!"

Whatever tragedy might have happened next was forestalled by the battle scream of a hawk high in the sky above Kethry. For some reason—

she never could afterward say why—she flung up her arm as Tarma had
to receive the hawk in the forest.

A second scream split the air, and a golden meteor plummeted down
from the sun to land on Kethry's wrist. The vorcel-hawk was even larger
than Moonsong's had been, and its talons bit into Kethry's arm as it
flailed the air with its wings, mantling angrily at the Council. Pain raced
up her arm and blood sprang out where the talons pierced her, for she
had no vambrace such as Tarma wore. Blood was dying the sleeve of her
robe a deep crimson, but Kethry had endured worse in her training as a
sorceress. She bit her lip to keep from crying out and kept her wrist and
arm steady.

The members of the Council—with the exception of the Clan Chief,
the Shaman and the Healer of Liha'irden—stepped back an involuntary
pace or two, murmuring.

Tarma held out her arm, still gripping her blade in her right hand; the
hawk lifted itself to the proffered perch, allowing Kethry to lower her
wounded arm and clutch it to her chest in a futile effort to ease the pain.
Need would not heal wounds like these; they were painful, but hardly
life-threatening. She would have to heal them herself when this confrontation was over; for now, she would have to endure the agony in silence,
lest showing weakness spoil Tarma's bid for the attention of the Council.

"Is *this* omen enough for you?" Tarma asked, in mingled triumph and
anger. "The emblem of Tale'sedrin has come, the spirit of Tale'sedrin
shows itself—and it comes to Kethry, whom you call outClan and de-
ceiver! *To me, she'enedra!*"

Again, without pausing for second or third thoughts, Kethry reached
out her wounded right hand and caught Tarma's blade-hand; the hawk
screamed once more, and mantled violently. It hopped along Tarma's
arm until it came to their joined hands, hands that together held Tarma's
blade outstretched, pointing at the members of the Council. There it
settled for one moment, one foot on each wrist.

Then it screamed a final time, the sound of its voice not of battle, but
of triumph, and it launched itself upward to be lost in the sun.

Kethry scarcely had time to notice that the pain of her arm was gone,
before the young Healer of Liha'irden was at her side with a cry of
triumph of his own.

"You doubt—you dare to doubt still?" he cried, pulling back a sleeve
that was so soaked with blood that beneath it the flesh was surely pierced
to the bone. "Look here, all of you—*look!*"

For beneath Kethry's sleeve her arm was smooth and unwounded,
without so much as a scar.

Five

The gathering-tent was completely full; crowded with gaudily garbed Shin'a'in as it was, it would have been difficult to find space for even a small child. Tarma and Kethry had places of honor near the center and the firepit. Since the confrontation with the Council and their subsequent vindication, their credit had been very high with the Liha'irden.

"Keth—" Tarma's elbow connected gently with Kethry's ribs.

"Huh?" Kethry started; she'd been staring at the fire, more than half mesmerized by the hypnotic music three of her Liha'irden "cousins" had been playing. Except for her hair and eyes she looked as Shin'a'in as Tarma; weeks in the sun this summer had turned her skin almost the same golden color as her partner's, and she was dressed in the same costume of soft boots, breeches, vest and shirt, all brightly colored and heavily embroidered, that the Shin'a'in themselves wore. If anything, it was Tarma who stood out in her sober brown.

It had been a good time, this past spring and summer; a peaceful time. And yet, Kethry was feeling a restlessness. Part of it *had* to be Need's fault; the sword wanted her about and doing. But part of it—part of it came from within her. And Tarma was often unhappy, too. She hadn't said anything, but Kethry could feel it.

"It's your turn. What's it going to be; magic, or tale?"

The children, who had been lulled by the music, woke completely at that. Their young voices rose above the murmuring of their elders, all of them trying to have some say in the choice of entertainment. Half of them were clamoring for magic, half for a story.

These autumn gatherings were anticipated all year; in spring there were the young of the herds to guard at night, in summer night was the time of moving the herds, and in winter it was too cold and windy to put up the huge gathering-tent. Children were greatly prized among the Clans, but normally were not petted or indulged—except here. During the gatherings, they were allowed to be a little noisy; to beg shamelessly for a particular treat.

This was the first time Tarma had included her *she'enedra* in the circle of entertainment, and the Liha'irden were as curious about her as young cats.

"Does it have to be one or the other?" Kethry asked.

"Well, no . . ."

"All right then," Kethry said, raising her voice to include all of them. "In that case, I'll tell you *and* show you a tale I learned when I was an apprentice with Melania of the White Winds Adepts." She settled herself carefully and spun out some of her own internal energy into an illusion-form. She held out her hands, which began to glow, then the thin thread of the illusion-form spun up away from them like a wisp of rising smoke. The tendril rose until it was just above the heads of the watching Shin'a'in, then the end thickened and began to rotate, drawing the rest of the glow up into itself until it was a fat globe dancing weightlessly up near the centerpole.

"This is the tale as it was told me," Kethry began, just as the Shin'a'in storytellers had begun, while the children oohed and whispered and the adults tried to pretend they weren't just as fascinated as the children. "Once in a hollow tree on the top of a hill, there lived a lizard."

Within the globe the light faded and then brightened, and a scene came into focus; a stony, vetch-covered hill surmounted by a lightning-blasted tree of great girth, a tree that glowed ever so faintly. As the Clansfolk watched, a green and brown scaled lizard poked his head cautiously out of a crevice at the base of it; the lizard looked around, and apparently saw nothing, for the rest of him followed. Now even the adults gasped, for this lizard walked erect, like a man, and had a head more manlike than lizardlike.

"The lizard's name was Gervase, and he was one of the *hertasi* folk that live still in the Pelagir Hills. *Hertasi* once were tree-lizards long, long ago, until magic changed them. Like humans, they can be of any nature; good or bad, kind or cruel, giving or selfish. But they all have one thing in common. All are just as intelligent as we are, and all were made that way long ago by magic wars. Now this Gervase knew a great deal about magic; it was the cause of him being the way he was, after all, and there was so much of it in the place where he lived that his very tree-home glowed at night with it. So it isn't too surprising that he should daydream about it, now, is it?"

The scene changed; the children giggled, for the lizard Gervase was playing at being a wizard, just as they had often done, with a hat of rolled-up birch bark and a "wand" of a twisted branch.

"He wanted very badly to *be* a wizard; he used to dream about how he would help those in trouble, how he would heal the sick and the wounded, how he would be so powerful he could stop wars with a single wave of his wand. You see, he had a very kind heart, and all he ever really wanted to do was to make the world a little better. But of course, he knew he couldn't; after all, he was nothing but a lizard."

The lizard grew sad-looking (odd how body-language could convey dejection when the creature's facial expressions were nil), put aside his hat and wand, and crawled up onto a branch to sit in the sun and sigh.

"Then one day while he was sunning himself, he heard a noise of hound and horse in the distance."

Now the lizard jumped to his feet, balancing himself on the branch with his tail while he craned his neck to see as far as he could.

"While he was trying to see what all the fuss was about, a man stumbled into his clearing."

A tattered and bloody human of early middle age fell through the bushes, catching himself barely in time to keep from cracking his head open on the rocks. There was a gasp from the assembled Clansfolk, for the man had plainly been tortured. Kethry had not toned the illusion-narrative down much from the one she'd been shown; firstly, the children of the Clans were used to bloodshed, secondly, it brought the fact home to all of them that this was a *true* tale.

The man in the illusion was dark-haired and bearded; bruised and beaten-looking. And if one looked very carefully, it was possible to see that the rags he wore had once been a wizard's robe.

"Gervase didn't stop to wonder about who the man was or why he was being chased; he only knew that no thinking creature should hunt another down like a rabbit with dogs and horses. He ran to the man—"

The lizard slid down the tree trunk and scampered to the fallen wizard. Now it was possible to see, as he helped the man to his feet, that he was very close to being man-sized himself, certainly the size of a young adolescent. At first the man was plainly too dazed to realize what it was that was helping him, then he came to himself and did a double take. The shock and startlement on his face made the children giggle again—and not just the children.

" 'Come, human,' Gervase said. 'You must hide in my tree, it's the only place where you can be safe. I will keep the dogs away from you.' The wizard—for that was what he was—did not waste any breath in arguing with him, for he could clearly hear the dogs baying on his track."

The lizard half-carried the man to the crevice in the tree; the man crawled inside. Gervase then ran over to a rock in the sun and arranged himself on it, for all the world like an ordinary (if overly-large) lizard basking himself.

"When the dogs came over the hill, with the hunters close behind them, Gervase was ready."

As the dogs and the horses burst through the underbrush, Gervase jumped high in the air, as if startled out of his wits. He dashed back and forth on all fours for a moment, then shot into the crack in the tree. There he remained, with his head sticking out, obviously hissing at the dogs that came to bark and snap at him and the man he was protecting. When one or two got too close, Gervase bit their noses. The dogs yelped and scuttled to the rear of the pack, tails between their legs, while the entire tent roared with laughter.

"Then the man who had been hunting the wizard arrived, and he was not pleased. He had wanted the wizard to serve him; he had waited until the wizard's magics were either exhausted or nullified by his own magicians, then he had taken him prisoner and tortured him. But our wizard had pretended to be unconscious and had escaped into the Pelagirs. The lord was so angry he had escaped that he had taken every hunter and dog he had and pursued him—but thanks to Gervase, he thought now that he had lost the trail."

The plump and oily man who rode up on a sweating horse bore no small resemblance to Wethes. Tarma smiled at that, as the "lord" whipped off his hounds and laid the crop across the shoulders of his fearful huntsman, all the while turning purple with rage. At length he wrenched his horse's head around, spurring it savagely, and led the lot out of the clearing. Gervase came out of hiding; so did the wizard.

"The wizard was very grateful. 'There is a great deal of magical energy stored in your home,' he said. 'I can grant you nearly anything you want, little friend, if you'll let me use it. What way can I reward you?' Gervase didn't even have to think about it. 'Make me a man like you!' he said, 'I want to be a man like you!' 'Think carefully on what you're asking,' the mage said. 'Do you want to be human, or do you want to be a magician? You have the potential within you to be a great mage, but it will take all the magic of your tree to unlock it, and even then it will take years of study before you can make use of your abilities. Or would you rather have the form of a human? That, too, will take all the magic of your tree. So think carefully, and choose.' "

The little lizard was plainly in a quandary; he twitched and paced, and looked up at the sky and down at the ground for help.

"Gervase had a terrible decision, you see? If he became a human, people would listen to him, but he wouldn't have the magic to do what he wanted to do. But if he chose to have his Gifts unlocked, where would he find someone who would teach the use of them to a lizard? But finally, he chose. 'I will be a mage,' he said, 'and somewhere I will find someone willing to teach me, someone who believes that good inside is more important than the way I look on the outside.' "

The wizard in the vision smiled and raised his hands over Gervase. The tree began to glow brightly; then the glow flowed off the tree and over the little lizard, enveloping him and sinking into him.

" 'You need look no further, little friend,' said the mage, when he'd done. 'For I myself will teach you, if you wish to be my apprentice.' "

Gervase plainly went half-mad with joy; he danced comically about for a good several minutes, then dashed into the now-dark tree and emerged again with a few belongings tied into a cloth. Together he and the mage trudged down the path and disappeared into the forest. The glowing globe went dark then, and vanished slowly, dissolving like smoke.

"And that is the tale of how Gervase became an apprentice to Cinsley of White Winds. What happened to him after that—is another tale."

The applause Kethry received was as hearty as ever Tarma had gotten back in the days when her voice was the pride of the Clans.

"Well done," Tarma whispered, when the attentions of those gathered had turned to the next to entertain.

"I was wondering if my doing magic would offend anyone—" Kethry began, then looked up, suddenly apprehensive, seeing one of the Clansfolk approaching them.

And not just any Shin'a'in, but the Shaman.

The grave and imposing woman was dressed in earthy yellows this evening; she smiled as she approached them, as if she sensed Kethry's apprehension. "Peace, *jel'enedra*," she said quietly, voice barely audible to the pair of them over the noise of the musicians behind her. "That was well done."

She seated herself on the carpeted floor beside them. "Then—you didn't mind my working magic?" Kethry replied, tension leaving her.

"Mind? *Li'sa'eer!* Anything but! Our people seldom see outClan magic. It's well to remind them that it can be benign—"

"As well as being used to aid the slaughter of an entire Clan?" Tarma finished. "It's well to remind them that it exists, period. It was that for-getfulness that lost Tale'sedrin."

"*Hai,* you have the right of it. *Jel'enedra,* I sense a restlessness in you. More, I sense an unhappiness in both you and your oathkin."

"Is it that obvious?" Kethry asked wryly. "I'm sorry if it is."

"Do not apologize; as I said, I sense it in your *she'enedra* as well."

"Tarma?" Kethry's eyebrows rose in surprise.

"Look, I don't think this is where we should be discussing this," Tarma said uncomfortably.

"Will you come to my tent, then, Kal'enedra; you and your oath-sister?" The request was more than half command, and they felt almost compelled to follow her out of the tent, picking their way carefully among the crowded Clansfolk.

Tarma was curious to see what the Shaman's dome-shaped tent looked like within; she was vaguely disappointed to see that it differed very little from her own inside. There was the usual sleeping pad of sheepskins and closely-woven woolen blankets, the mule-boxes containing personal be-longings and clothing, two oil-lamps, and bright rugs and hangings in profusion. It was only when Tarma took a closer look at the hangings that she realized that they were something out of the ordinary.

They seemed to be figured in random patterns, yet there was a sense of rhythm in the pattern—like writing.

The Shaman seemed uncannily aware of what Tarma was thinking. "*Hai,* they *are* a written history of our people; written in a language all their own. It is a language so concise that one hundred years of history can be contained in a single hanging."

Tarma looked around the tent, and realized that there must be close to fifty of these hangings, layered one upon the other. But—that meant *five thousand years!*

Again the Shaman seemed to sense Tarma's thoughts. "Not so many years as you may think. Some of these deal with the history of peoples other than our own, peoples whose lives impinge upon ours. But we are not here to speak of that," the Shaman seated herself on her pallet, allowing Kethry and Tarma to find places for themselves on her floor. "I think the Plains grow too small for both of you, *he shala?*"

"There's just no real need for me here," Kethry replied. "My order—well, we just can't stay where there's nothing for us to do. If some of the Clansfolk had magic gifts, or wanted to learn the magics that don't re-quire a Gift, it would be different; I'd gladly teach them here. But no one seems interested, and frankly, I'm bored. Actually, it's a bit worse than being bored. I'm not *learning* anything. I'll never reach Adept status if I stay here."

"I . . . don't fit here," Tarma sighed, "And I never thought I'd say that. Like Keth, I'd be happy to teach the children swordwork, but that would be usurping Shelana's position. I thought I could keep busy working with *her,* but—"

"I venture to guess you found her scarcely more challenging than her pupils? Don't look so surprised, my child; I of all people should know what your Oath entails. Liha'irden has not had Kal'enedral in its midst for a generation, but I know what your skill is likely to be—and how it was acquired."

There was silence for a moment, then Tarma said wryly, "Well, I wish you'd told *me!* The first time one of Them showed up, it was enough to stop my heart!"

"We were a trifle short of time to be telling you anything, even had you been in condition to hear it. So—tell me more of your troubles."

"I love my people, I love the Plains, but I have no *purpose* here. I am totally useless. I'd be of more use raising income for Tale'sedrin than I am now."

"Ah—you have seen the problem with raising the banner?"

"We're only two; we can't tend the herds ourselves. We could bring in orphans and third and fourth children from Clans with far too many to feed, but we have no income yet to feed them ourselves. And frankly, we have no Name. We aren't likely to attract the kind of young men and women that would be my first choice without a Name."

"Would you mind telling me what you two are talking about?" Kethry demanded, bewilderment written plainly on her face.

"Goddess—I'm sorry, Keth. You've fallen in with us so well, I forget you aren't one of us."

"Allow me," the Shaman interrupted gently. *"Jel'enedra,* when you pledged yourself to providing children for Tale'sedrin, you actually pledged only to provide the Clan core—unless you know some magic to cause you to litter like a grass-runner!" The Shaman's smile was warm, and invited Tarma as well as Kethry to share the joke. "So; what will be, is that when you do find a mate and raise up your children, they must spend six months of the year here, shifting by one season each year so that they see our life in harsh times as well as easy. When they come of age, they will choose—to be Shin'a'in always, or to take up a life off of the Plains. Meanwhile, we will be sending out the call, and unmated *jel'asadra* of both sexes are free to come to your banner to make it their own. Orphans, also. Until you and your *she'enedra* declare the Clan closed. Do you see?"

"I think so. Now what was the business about a Name?"

"The caliber of youngling you will attract will depend on the reputation you and Tarma have among the Clans. And right now—to be frank, you will only attract those with little to lose. Not the kind of youngling I would hope to rebuild a Clan with, if *I* were rebuilding Tale'sedrin."

"The part about income was clear enough," Kethry said after a long moment of brooding. "We—we'd either have to sell some of the herd at a loss, or starve."

"Are you in condition to hear advice, the pair of you?"

"I think so," said Tarma.

"Leave the Clans; leave the Plains. There is nothing for you here, you are wasting your abilities and you are wasting away of boredom. I think there is something that both of you wish to do—and I also think that neither of you has broached the subject for fear of hurting the other's feelings."

"I . . ." Kethry faltered. "Well, there's two things, really. Since I've vowed myself to rebuilding Tale'sedrin—that needs a man, I'm afraid. I'll grant you that I could just go about taking lovers but . . . I want something more than that, I want to care for the father of any children I might have. And frankly, most of the men here are terribly alien to me."

"Understandable," the Shaman nodded. "Laudable, in fact. The Clan law holds that you, your *she'enedra,* and your children would comprise a true Clan-seed, but I think everyone would be happier if you chose a man as a long-term partner-mate, and one with whom you have more in common than one of us. And the other?"

"If I ever manage to get myself to the stage of Adept, it's more-or-less expected of a White Winds sorceress that she start a branch of the school. But to do that, to attract pupils, I'd need two things. A reputation, and money."

"So again, we come to those two things, as important to you as to the Clan."

"Well that's odd, that you've been thinking of starting a school, because I've been playing with the same notion," Tarma said in surprise. "I've been thinking I enjoyed teaching Justin and Ikan so much that it would be no bad thing to have a school of my own, one that teaches something besides swordwork."

"Teach the heart as well as the mind and body?" the Shaman smiled. "Those are praiseworthy goals, children, and not incompatible with rebuilding Tale'sedrin. Let me make you this proposition; for a fee,

Liha'irden will continue to raise and tend your herds—I think a tithe of the yearlings would be sufficient. Do you go out before the snows close us in and see if you cannot raise both the reputation and the gold to build your schools and your Clan. If you do not succeed, you may always return here, and we will rebuild the harder way, but if you do, well, the Clan is where the people are; there is no reason why Tale'sedrin should not first ride in outClan lands until the children are old enough to come raise the banner themselves. Will that satisfy your hungers?"

"Aye, and then some!" Tarma spoke for both of them, while Kethry nodded, more excitement in her eyes than had been there for weeks.

Kessira and Rodi remained behind with the herds when they left two weeks later. Now that they were to pursue their avocation of mercenary in earnest, they rode a matched pair of the famed Shin'a'in battlesteeds; horses they had picked out and had been training with since spring.

Battlesteeds were the result of a breeding program that had been going on for as long as the Shin'a'in had existed as nomadic horsebreeders. Unlike most horsebreeding programs, the Shin'a'in had not been interested in looks, speed, or conformation. They had bred for intelligence, above all else—and after intelligence, agility, strength, and endurance. The battlesteeds were the highly successful result.

Both horses they now rode were mottled gray; they had thick necks and huge, ugly heads with broad foreheads. They looked like unpolished statues of rough granite, and were nearly as tough. They could live very handily on forage even a mule would reject; they could travel sunrise to sunset at a ground-devouring lope that was something like a wolf's tireless tracking-pace. They could be trusted with an infant, but would kill on signal *or* on a perceived threat. They were more intelligent than any horse Kethry had ever seen—more intelligent than a mule, even. In their ability to obey and to reason they more resembled a highly trained dog than a horse, for they could actually work out a simple problem on their own.

This was why Shin'a'in battlesteeds were so famed—and why the Clansfolk guarded them with their very lives. Between their intelligence and the training they received, battlesteeds were nearly the equal partners of those who rode them in a fight. It was in no small part due to the battlesteeds that the Shin'a'in had remained free and the Dhorisha Plains unconquered.

But they were rare; a mare would drop no more than four or five foals in a lifetime. So no matter how tempting the price offered, no battlesteed would ever be found in the hands of anyone but a Shin'a'in—or one who was pledged blood-sib to a Shin'a'in.

These horses had been undergoing a strenuous course of training for the past four years, and had just been ready this spring to accept permanent riders. They were trained to fight either on their own or with a rider —something Kethry was grateful for, since she was *nothing* like the kind of rider Tarma was. Tarma could stick to Hellsbane's back like a burr on a sheep; Kethry usually lost her seat within the first few minutes of a fight. But no matter; Ironheart would defend her quite as readily on the ground—and on the ground Kethry could work her magics without distraction.

Both battlesteeds were mares; mares could be depended on to keep their heads no matter what the provocation, and besides, it was a peculiarity of battlesteeds that they tended to throw ten or fifteen fillies to every colt. That meant colts were never gelded—and never left the Plains.

This time when Tarma left the Liha'irden encampment, it was with every living soul in it outside to bid her farewell. The weather was perfect; crisp and cool without being too cold. The sky was cloudless, and there was a light frost on the ground.

"No regrets?" Kethry said in an undertone as she tightened Ironheart's girth.

"Not many," Tarma replied, squinting into the thin sunlight, then mounting with an absentminded ease Kethry envied. "Certainly not enough to worry about."

Kethry scrambled into her own saddle—Ironheart was nearly sixteen hands high, the tallest beast she'd ever ridden—and settled her robes about herself.

"You have some, though?" she persisted.

"I just wish I knew this was the right course we're taking . . . I guess," Tarma laughed at herself, "I guess I'm looking for another omen."

"Lady Bright, haven't you had *enough*—" Kethry was interrupted by a scream from overhead.

The Shin'a'in about them murmured in excitement and pointed—for there, overhead, was a vorcel-hawk. It might have been the same one that had landed on Kethry's arm when Tarma had been challenged; it was certainly big enough. This time, however, it showed no inclination to land. Instead, it circled the encampment overhead, three times. Then it sailed majestically away northward, the very direction they had been intending to take.

As it vanished into the ice-blue sky, Kethry tugged her partner's sleeve to get her attention.

"Do me a favor, hmm?" she said in a voice that shook a trifle. *"Stop asking for bloody omens!"*

"Why I ever let you talk me into this—" Tarma stared about them uneasily. "This place is even weirder than they claim!"

They were deep into the Pelagir Hills—the *true* Pelagirs. There was a track they were following; dry-paved, it rang under their mares' hooves, and it led ever deeper into the thickly forested hills and was arrow-flight straight. To either side of them lay the landscape of dreams . . . or maybe nightmare.

The grass was the wrong color for fall. It should have been frost-seared and browning; instead it was a lush and juicy green. The air was warm; this was fall, it should have been cool, but it felt like summer, it smelled like summer. There were even flowers. Tarma disliked and distrusted this false, magic-born summer. It just wasn't *right*.

The other plants besides the grass—well, some were normal (or at least they seemed normal), but others were not. Tarma had seen plants whose leaves had snapped shut on unwary insects, flowers whose blooms glowed when the moon rose, and thorny vines whose thorns dripped some unnamable liquid. She didn't know if they were hazardous, but she wasn't about to take a chance; not after she saw the bones and skulls of small animals littering the ground beneath a dead tree laden with such vines.

The trees didn't bear thinking about, much. The least odd of them were as twisted and deformed as if they'd grown in a place of constant heavy winds. The others . . .

Well, there was the grove they'd passed of lacy things that sang softly to themselves in childlike voices. And the ones that pulled away from them as they passed, or worse, actually reached out to touch them, feeling them like blind and curious old women. And the sapling that had torn up its roots and shuffled away last night when Tarma thought about how nice a fire would feel . . .

And by no means least, the ones like they'd spent the night in (though only after Kethry repeatedly assured her nervous partner that it was perfectly harmless). It had been hut-sized and hut-shaped, with only a thatch of green on the "roof"—and hollow. And inside had been odd protrusions that resembled stools, a table, and bed-platforms to a degree that was positively frightening. A lovely little trap it would have made— Tarma slept restlessly that night, dreaming about the "door" growing closed and trapping them inside, like those poor bugs the flowers had trapped.

"I'm at the stage where I could use a familiar," Kethry replied, "I've explained all this before. Besides, a familiar will be able to take some of the burden of night-watch off both of us, particularly if I can manage to call a *kyree*."

Tarma sighed.

"It's only fair. *I* came with you to the Plains. I took a battlesteed at your insistence."

"Agreed. But I don't have to like this place. Are you sure there's anything here you can call? We haven't seen so much as a mouse or a sparrow since things started looking weird."

"That's because they don't want you to see them. Relax, we're going to stop soon; we're almost where I wanted to go."

"How can you tell, if you've never been here?"

"You'll see."

Sure enough, Tarma *did* see. The paved road came to a dead end; at the end it widened out into a flat, featureless circle some fifty paces in diameter.

The paved area was surrounded by yet another kind of tree, some sort of evergreen with thin, tangled branches that started a bit less than knee-high and continued straight up so that the trees were like green columns reaching to the sky. They had grown so closely together that it would have been nearly impossible for anything to force its way between them. That meant there was only one way for anything to get into the circle—via the road.

"Now what?"

"Find someplace comfortable and make yourself a camp wherever you feel safest—although I can guarantee that as long as you stay inside the trees you'll be perfectly safe."

"Myself? What about you?"

"Oh, I'll be here, but I'll be busy. The process of calling a familiar is rather involved and takes a long time." Kethry dismounted in the exact center of the pavement and began unloading her saddlebags from Ironheart's back.

"How long is 'a long time'?" The paved area really took up only about half of the circular clearing. The rest was grass and scattered boulders, a green and lumpy rim surrounding the smooth gray pavement. There was plenty of windfall lying around the grassy area, most of it probably good and dry, dry enough to make a fire. And there was a nice little nook at the back of the circle, a cluster of boulders that would make a good firepit. Somehow Tarma didn't want even the slightest chance of fire escaping from her. Not here. Not after that walking sapling; no telling what its mother might think about fire, or the makers of fire.

"Until sunset tomorrow night."

"What?"

"I told you, it's very complicated. Surely you can find something to do with yourself . . ."

"Well, I'm going to have to, aren't I? I'm certainly not going to leave you alone out here."

Kethry didn't bother to reply with anything more than an amused smile, and began setting up her spell-casting equipment. Tarma, grumbling, took both mares over to the side of the paved area and gave them the command to stay on the grass, unsaddled and unharnessed them, and began grooming them to within an inch of their lives.

When she slipped a look over at her partner, Kethry was already seated within a sketched-in circle, a tiny brazier emitting a spicy-scented smoke beside her. Her eyes were closed and from the way her lips were moving she was chanting. Tarma sighed with resignation, and hauled the tack over to the area where she intended to camp.

It had lacked about a candlemark to sunset when they'd reached this place; by the time Tarma finished setting up camp to her liking, the sun was down and she was heartily glad of the fire she'd lit. It wasn't that it was cold . . .

No, it was the things outside that circle of trees that made her glad of the warm glow of the flames. The warm *earthly* glow of the flames. There were noises out there, sounds like she'd never heard before. The mares moved over to the fireside of their own volition, and were not really interested in the handfuls of grain Tarma offered them. They stood, one on either side of her, in defensive posture, ears twitching nervously.

It sounded like *things* were gathering just on the other side of the trees. There was a murmuring that was very like something speaking, except that no human throat ever made burbling and trilling sounds quite like those Tarma heard. There were soft little whoops, and watery chuckles. Every now and then, a chorus of whistlers exchanged responses. And as if that weren't enough—

Through the branches Tarma could see amorphous patches of glow, patches that moved about. As the moon rose above the trees, she unsheathed her sword and dagger, and held them across her lap.

"Child—"

Tarma screeched and jumped nearly out of her skin.

She was on her feet without even thinking about rising, and whipped around to face—

Her instructor, who had come with the first moonlight.

"You—you—*sadist!*" she gasped, trying to get her heart down out of her throat. "You nearly frightened me to death!"

"There is nothing for you to fear. What is outside the trees is curious, no more."

"And I'm the Queen of Valdemar."

"I tell you truly. This is a place where no evil can bear to tread; look about you—and look to your *she'enedra.*"

Tarma looked again, and saw that the mares had settled, their heads down, nosing out the last of the grain she'd given them. She saw that the area of the pavement was glowing—that what she'd mistaken for a soft silver reflection of the moonlight was in fact coming from within the paving material. Nor was that all—the radiance was brighter where Kethry sat oblivious within her circle, and blended from the silver of the pavement into a pale blue that surrounded her like an aura. And the trees themselves were glowing—something she hadn't noticed, being intent on the lights on the other side—a healthy, verdant green. All three colors she knew from Kethry's chance-made comments were associated with life-magic, positive magic.

And now the strange sounds from outside their enclosure no longer seemed so sinister, but rather like the giggling and murmuring of a crowd of curious small children.

Tarma relaxed, and shrugged. "Well, I still don't exactly like this place . . ."

"But you can see it is not holding a threat, *hai?*"

"*Hai.*" She placed the point of her blade on the pavement and cocked her head at him. "Well, I haven't much to do, and since you're here . . ."

"You are sadly in need of practice," he mocked.

"*Shesti!*" she scoffed back, bringing her sword up into guard position. "I'm not *that* badly off!"

By day the circle of trees no longer seemed quite so sinister, especially after Tarma's instructor had worked her into sweat-dripping exhaustion. When dawn came—and he left—she was ready to drop where she stood and sleep on the hard pavement itself.

But the mares needed more than browse and grain, they needed water. There was no water here save what they'd brought with them. And Tarma dared not truly sleep while Kethry remained enwrapped in spell-casting.

So when the first hint of the sun reddened the sky, she took Hellsbane with her and cautiously poked her nose out of the sheltered area, looking for a hint of water.

There was nothing stirring outside the circle of trees; the eerie landscape remained quiet. But when Tarma looked at the dirt at the foot of the trees she saw tracks, many tracks, and few of them were even remotely identifiable.

"Kulath etaven," she said softly to her mare, "Find water."

Hellsbane raised her head and sniffed; then took two or three paces to the right. Tarma placed one hand on the mare's shoulder; Hellsbane snorted, rubbed her nose briefly against Tarma's arm, then proceeded forward with more confidence.

She headed for a tangle of vines—none of which moved, or had bones beneath them—and high, rank bushes, all of which showed the familiar summery verdancy. As the pair forced their way in past the tangle, breaking twigs and bruising leaves, Tarma found herself breathing in an astringent, mossy scent with a great deal of pleasure. The mare seemed to enjoy the odor too, though she made no move to nibble the leaves.

There was a tiny spring at the heart of the tangle, and Tarma doubted she'd have been able to locate it without the mare's help. It was hardly more than a trickle, welling up from a cup of moss-covered stone, and running a few feet, only to vanish again into the thirsty soil. The mare slurped up the entire contents of the cup in a few swallows, and had to wait for it to fill again several times before she'd satisfied her thirst.

It was while she was awaiting Hellsbane's satiation that Tarma noticed the decided scarcity of insects within this patch of growth. Flies and the like had plagued them since they entered the Pelagirs; as a horsewoman, Tarma generally took them for granted.

There were no flies in here. Nor any other insects. Curious . . .

When the mare was finished, Tarma guided her out backward, there being no room to turn her around; it seemed almost as if the bushes and vines were willing to let them inflict a limited amount of damage in order to reach the water, but resisted any more than that. And as soon as they were clear of the scent of the crushed vegetation, the flies descended on Hellsbane again.

An idea occurred to her; she backtracked to the bushes, and got a handful of the trampled leaves and rubbed them on the back of her hand. She waited for some sort of reaction; rash, burning, itching—nothing happened. Satisfied that the vegetation at least wasn't harmful, she rubbed it into the mare's shaggy hide. It turned her a rather odd shade of gray-green, but the flies wouldn't even land on her.

Very pleased with herself, Tarma watered Ironheart and repeated the process on her. By the time she'd finished, the sun was well up, and she was having a hard time keeping her eyes open. She was going to have to get *some* rest, at least.

But that was another advantage of having battlesteeds.

She loosed Hellsbane and took her to the entrance of the circle. "Guard," she said, shortly. The mare immediately went into sentry-mode —and it would take a determined attacker indeed to get past those iron-shod hooves and wicked teeth. Now all she needed to keep alert for was attack from above.

She propped herself up with their packs and saddles, and allowed herself to fall into a half-doze. It wasn't as restful as real sleep, but it would do.

When hunger finally made further rest impossible, it was getting on to sunset—and Kethry was showing signs of breaking out of trance.

She'd carefully briefed Tarma on what she'd need to do; Tarma shook herself into full alertness, and rummaged in Kethry's pack for high-energy rations. Taking those and her waterskin, she sat on her heels just outside of the inscribed circle, and waited.

She didn't have to wait long; Kethry's eyes opened almost immediately, and she sagged forward with exhaustion, scarcely able to make the little dismissing motion that broke the magic shield about her. Tarma was across the circle the instant she'd done so, and supported her with one arm while she drank. Kethry looked totally exhausted; mentally as well as physically. She was pale as new milk, and scarcely had the energy to drink, must less speak. Tarma helped her to her feet, then half-carried her to the tiny campsite and her bedroll.

Kethry had no more than touched her head to her blankets than she was asleep. She slept for several hours, well past moonrise, then awoke again with the first appearance of the lights and noises that had so disturbed Tarma the night before.

"They seem to be harmless," Tarma began.

"They are. That's not what woke me," Kethry croaked from a raw throat. "It's coming—what I called—"

"What *did* you call, anyway?"

After a swallow or two of water, Kethry was better able to speak. "A *kyree*—they're a little like wolves, only bigger; they also have some of the physical characteristics of the big grass-cats, retractile claws, that sort of thing. They're also like Gervase's folk; they're human-smart and have some gift for magic. They'd probably do quite well for themselves if they had hands instead of paws—well, that's one reason why some of them are willing to become mage-familiars. Another is gender. Or lack of."

"*Get'ke?*"

"*Kyree* throw three kinds of cubs—male, female, and neuter. The neuters really don't have much to do in pack-life, so they're more inclined to wander off and see the world."

Kethry broke off, staring over Tarma's shoulder. Tarma turned.

In the opening of the tree-circle where the road turned into the paved "court" was—something. It looked lupine—it had a wolf-type head, anyway. But it was so damn *big!*

Kethry pulled herself to her feet and half-stumbled to the entrance. "If you come in the Name of the Powers of Light, enter freely," she croaked, "If not, be you gone."

The thing bowed its head gravely, and padded into the circle. There it stood, looking first at Kethry, then at Tarma; deliberately, measuringly.

I bond to you, said a deep voice in the back of Tarma's head.

Once again she nearly jumped out of her skin.

"*Li'sa'eer!*" she choked, backing a few paces away from the thing. "What?"

I bond to you, warrior. We are alike, we two; both warriors for the Light, both—celibate— The voice in her head had a feeling of amusement about the choice of the last word. *It is fit we be soul-bonded. Besides, Lady of Power—*he turned to look at Kethry,—*you do not need me. You have the spirit-sword. But you—*he turned his huge eyes back to Tarma,—*YOU need me.*

"*She'enedra,*" Tarma said tightly, keeping a firm grip on her nerves, "What in hell am I supposed to do? He says he wants *me!*"

"Oh, my Lady Bright—what a bloody mess! It could only happen to me! Give in," Kethry staggered to her bedroll and half-collapsed into it, laughing weakly. "A day and a night of spell-casting, and what happens? My familiar decides he'd rather bond to my partner! Lady Bright—if it weren't so damned funny I think I'd kill you both!"

"But what am I supposed to *do?*"

You could try talking to me.

Tarma gulped, and approached the beast cautiously. It sat at its ease, tongue lolling out in a kind of grin. She could sense his amusement at her apprehension in the back of her mind. Curiously, that seemed to make her fear vanish.

"Well," she said at last, after several long moments of trying to think of something appropriate. "I'm Tarma."

And I—am Warrl. The creature lay down on the pavement, and cocked its head to one side. Its—no, his; it might have been a "neuter" but there was a distinctly masculine feeling to him—his eyes caught the moonlight and reflected greenishly.

"I'm not quite sure what I should do about you," she confessed. "I mean I'm no mage—what's the next move?"

You might start by offering me something to eat, Warrl said, *I've come a long way, and I'm hungry. Do I smell meat-bars?* There was something in his mental sending that was so like a child begging for a sweet that Tarma had to laugh.

"You do, my friend," she replied, rising to get one for him. "And if you like them as much as I *dislike* them, I have the feeling we're going to suit each other very well indeed!"

Six

They were fortunate; almost as soon as they emerged from the Pelagirs, they were able to find a short-term job as escorts. A scrawny, middle-aged man sought them at their inn within hours of when they had posted themselves at the Mercenaries' Guild and paid their fees.

"You'll be providing protection for my new bride," their employer, an hereditary knight who didn't look capable of lifting his ancestral blade, much less using it, told Tarma. "I will be remaining here for a month or more to consolidate my interests with Darthela's father, but I wish her to make the journey to Fromish now, before winter weather sets in."

"Are we to be the only guards?" Tarma asked, a little doubtfully. She shifted on the wooden bench uncomfortably, and wished Kethry was here instead of visiting the tiny White Winds enclave she'd ferreted out. She could have used the sorceress' quick wits right now.

"I'm afraid so," he replied with a sheepish smile. "To be brutally frank, Swordlady, my house is in rather impoverished condition at the moment. I couldn't afford to take any of my servants away from the harvesting to serve as guards for her, and I can't afford to hire more than the two of you. And before you ask, my bride's retinue is confined to one handmaiden. Her dower is to be in things less tangible, but ultimately more profitable, than immediate cash."

Tarma decided that she liked him. The smile had been genuine, and his frankness with a pair of hirelings rather touching.

Of course, she thought wryly, *that could just be to convince us that the fair Darthela won't have much with her worth stealing.*

"I'll tell you what we can do to narrow the odds against us a bit," Tarma offered. "I can arrange to set out a little later than you asked us, so that we're about half a day behind that spice-trader. Anybody looking for booty is likely to go for him and miss us."

"But what about wild beasts?" he asked, looking concerned. "Won't they have been attracted to the campsites by the trader's leavings?"

Tarma's estimation of him rose a notch. She *had* been picturing him as so likely to have his nose in a book all the time that he had little notion of the realities of the road.

"Wild beasts are the one problem we *won't* have," she replied. "You're getting a bargain, you know—you aren't actually getting two guards, you're getting three."

At her unspoken call, Warrl inched out from under the bar where he'd been drowsing, stretched lazily, and opened enormous jaws in a yawn big enough to take in a whole melon. Sir Skolte regarded the *kyree* with astonishment and a little alarm.

"Bright Lord of Hosts!" he exclaimed, inching away a little. "What *is* that?"

"My partner calls him a *kyree,* and his name is Warrl."

"A Pelagir Hills *kyree?* No wonder you aren't worried about beasts!" The knight rubbed a hand across his balding pate, and looked relieved. "I am favored by your acquaintance, Sirrah Warrl. And grateful for your services."

Warrl nodded graciously and returned to his resting place beneath the bar. This close to the Hills, the innmaster and his help were fairly familiar with the *kyree* kind—and when Warrl had helped to break up a barfight within moments of the trio's arrival, he had earned their gratitude and a place of honor. And no few spiced sausages while he rested there.

Tarma was pleased with the knight's ready acceptance of her companion, and finalized the transaction with him then and there. By the time Kethry returned, she had already taken care of supplies for the next day.

They appeared at the house of the bride's father precisely at noon the next day, ready to go. Sir Skolte met them at the gate—which was something of a surprise to Kethry.

"I—rather expected you would send a servant to wait for us," Kethry told him, covering her confusion quickly, but not so quickly that Tarma didn't spot it.

"Darthela has been insisting that I 'properly introduce' you," he replied, a rather wry smile on his thin lips. "That isn't the sort of thing one leaves to a servant. I confess that she has been *most* eager to meet you."

Tarma caught her partner's quizzical glance and shrugged.

The odd comment was explained when they finally met the fair young bride; she entered the room all flutters and coquettishness, which affectations she dropped as soon as she saw that her escorts were female. She made no effort to hide her disappointment, and left "to pack" within moments.

"Now I see why you hired us instead of that pair of Barengians," Tarma couldn't help but say, stifling laughter.

Sir Skolte shrugged eloquently. "I won't deny I'm a bit of a disappointment for her," he replied cynically. "But beggars can't be choosers. She's the sixth in a set of seven daughters, and her father was so pleased at being able to make trade bargains with me in lieu of dower that he almost threw her at me. Fortunately, my servants are all uglier than I am."

The look in his eye told Tarma that Darthela was going to have to be a great deal cleverer than she appeared to be if she intended to cuckold *this* fellow.

But then again . . .

"Tell me, are folk around here acquainted with the tale of 'Bloody Carthar's Fourteen Wives?' Or 'Meralis and the Werebeast?' "

He shook his head. "I would say I know most of the tales we hear in these parts by heart, and those don't sound familiar."

"Then we'll see if we can't incline Darthela's mind a bit more in an appropriate direction," Kethry said, taking her cue from the two stories Tarma had mentioned. "We'll be a week in traveling, and stories around the campfire are always welcome, no?"

"What—oh, I see!" Sir Skolte began to laugh heartily. "Now, more than ever, I am *very* glad to have met you! Ladies, if you are ever looking for work again, I shall give you the *highest* recommendations—especially to aging men with pretty young wives!"

That took them from Lythecare to Fromish, on the eastbound roads. In Fromish they ran into old friends—Ikan and Justin.

"Hey-la! Look who we have here!" Tarma would have known that voice in a mob; in the half-empty tavern it was as welcome as a word from the tents.

She leapt up from her seat to catch Justin's forearm in a welcoming clasp. And not more than a pace behind *him* came Ikan.

They got themselves sorted out, and the two newcomers gave their orders to the serving boy before settling at Tarma's table.

"Well, what brings you ladies to these benighted parts?" Ikan asked, shaking hair out of his guileless eyes. "Last we saw, you were headed south."

"Looking for work," Tarma replied shortly. "We *did* get home but . . . well, we decided, what with one thing and another, to go professional. Even got our Guild tags." She pulled the thong holding the little copper medal out of her tunic to display it for them.

"I thought you two didn't work in winter," Kethry said in puzzlement.

"It isn't winter *yet,* at least not according to our employers. Last caravan of the season. Say—we might be able to do each other a favor, though." Justin eyed the two women with speculation. "You say you're Guild members now? Lord and Lady, the Luck is with us, for certain!"

"Why?"

"We've got two guards down with flux—and it does not look good. *We* want out of here before the snows close in, but we daren't go shorthanded and *I* don't trust the scum that's been turning up, hoping to get hired on in their places. But you two—"

"Three," Tarma corrected, as Warrl shambled out of the kitchen where he'd been enjoying meat scraps and the antics of the innkeeper's two children.

"Hey-la! A *kyree!*" Ikan exclaimed in delight. "Even better!"

"Shieldbrother," Justin lounged back in his chair with an air of complete satisfaction, "I will never doubt your conjuring of the Luck again. And tonight the drink's on me!"

The nervous jewel merchants were only too pleased to find replacements that could be vouched for by their most trusted guard-chiefs. They were even happier when they learned that one of the two was Shin'a'in and the other a mage. Kethry more than earned her pay on that trip, preventing a thief-mage from substituting bespelled glass for the rubies and sapphires they had just traded for.

They left the merchants before they returned to Mornedealth, Kethry not particularly wanting to revisit quite yet. Ikan and Justin did their best to persuade them otherwise, but to no avail.

"You could stay at the Broken Sword. Tarma could keep drilling us like she did last year," Justin coaxed. "And Cat would dearly love to see you. She's set herself up as a weapons merchant."

"No . . . I want things to cool down a little more," Kethry said. "And frankly, we need to earn ourselves a reputation and a pretty good stake, and we won't do that sitting around in Mornedealth all winter."

"You," Ikan put in, a speculative gleam in his eyes, "have got more in mind than earning the kind of cozy docket we have. Am I right, or no?"

"You're right," Tarma admitted.

"So? What've you got in mind?"

"Schools—or rather *a* school, with both of us teaching what we're best at."

"You'll need more than a good stake and a rep—you'll need property. Some kind of big building, stables, maybe a real indoor training area— and a good library, warded research areas, and neighbors who aren't too fussy about what you conjure."

"Gods, I hadn't thought that far, but you're right," Tarma said with chagrin. "Sounds as if what we want is on the order of a manor house."

"Which means you'd better start thinking in terms of working for a noble with property to grant once you get that rep. A crowned head would be best." Justin looked at both of them soberly. "That's not as unlikely as you might think; a combination like you two is rare even among men; sword and magic in concert are worth any ten straight swordsmen, however good. Add to it that you're female—think about it. Say you've got a monarch needing bodyguards; who'd check out his doxy and her servant? There's a lot of ways you could parlay yourself into becoming landed, and Keth's already ennobled."

"But for now . . ." Kethry said.

"For now you've got to *earn* that rep. Just bear in mind that what you're going after is far from impossible."

"Can we—ask you for advice now and again?" Kethry asked. "Justin, you sound to me as if you've figured some of this out for yourselves."

"He did," his partner grinned. "Or rather, *we* did. But we decided that it was too big a field for the two of us to hope to plow. So we settled for making ourselves indispensable to the Jewel Merchants' Guild. Fact is, we've also been keeping our eyes out for somebody like you two. We aren't going to be young forever, and we figured on talking somebody into taking us on at their new school as instructors before we got so old our bones creaked every time we lunged." He winked at Kethry.

Tarma stared. "You really think we have a chance of pulling this off?"

"More than a chance, nomad—I'd lay money on it. I'm sure enough that I haven't even *tried* luring your lovely little partner into my bed—I don't make love to prospective employers."

"Well!" Tarma was plainly startled. "I will be damned . . ."

"I hope not," Justin chuckled, "or I'll have to find another set of prospects!"

They got a commission with another caravan to act as guards—courtesy of their friends. On their way they detoured briefly when Need called

them to rid a town of a monster, a singularly fruitless effort, for the
monster was slain by a would-be "hero" the very day they arrived.

After that they skirmished with banditti and a magician's half-trained
ex-apprentice who thought robbing caravans was an easier task than
memorizing spells. Kethry "slapped his hands," as she put it, and left him
with a geas to build walls for the temple of Sun-Lord Resoden until he
should learn better.

When the caravan was safely gotten home, they found an elderly mage
of the Blue Mountains school who wanted some physical protection as he
returned to his patron, and was delighted with the bonus of having a
sorceress of a different discipline to converse with.

During these journeys Tarma and Warrl were learning to integrate
themselves as a fighting team; somewhat to Tarma's amazement, her
other-worldly teachers were inclined to include him whenever he chose.
After her initial shock—and, to some extent, dismay—she had discovered that they *did* have a great deal in common, especially in attitudes.
He was, perhaps, a bit more cynical than she was, but he was also older.
He never would admit exactly how old he was; when Tarma persisted, he
seized one of her hands in his powerful jaws and mindsent, *My years are
enough, mindmate, to suffice.* She never asked again.

But now they had fallen on dry times; they had wound up on the estate
of Viscount Hathkel, with no one needing their particular talents and no
cities nearby. The money they had earned must now be at least partially
spent in provisioning them to someplace where they were likelier to find
work.

That was the plan, anyway—until Need woke from her apparent slum-
bers with a vengeance.

Tarma goaded her gray Shin'a'in warsteed into another burst of speed,
urging her on with hand and voice (though not spur—*never* spur; that
would have been an insult the battlesteed would not tolerate) as if she
were pursued by the Jackals of Darkness. It had been more than long
enough since she had first become Kal'enedral for her hair to have
regrown—now her long, ebony braids streamed behind her; close enough
to catch one of them rode Kethry. Kethry's own mare was a scant half a
length after her herd-sister.

Need had left Kethry almost completely alone save for that one prod
almost from the time they'd left the Liha'irden camp. Both of them had
nearly forgotten just what bearing her could mean. They had been reminded this morning, when Need had woken Kethry almost before the
sun rose, and had been driving the sorceress (and so her blood-oath

sister as well) in this direction all day. At first it had been a simple pull, as she had often felt before Tarma had teased, and Kethry had grumbled; then they had packed up their camp and headed for the source. Kethry had even had time enough to summon a creature of the Ethereal Plane to scout and serve as a set of clairvoyant "eyes" for them. But the call had grown more urgent as the hours passed, not less so—increasing to the point where by midafternoon it was actually causing Kethry severe mental pain, pain that even Tarma was subject to, through the oath-bond. That was when they got Warrl up onto the special carry-pad they'd rigged for him behind Tarma's saddle, and prepared to make some speed. They urged their horses first into a fast walk, then a trot, then as sunset neared, into a full gallop. By then Kethry was near-blind with mental anguish, and no longer capable of even directing their Ethereal ally, much less questioning it.

Need *would* not be denied in this; Moonsong k'Vala, the Hawkbrother Adept they had met, had told them nothing less than the truth. Kethry was soul-bonded to the sword, just as surely as Tarma was bonded to her Goddess or Warrl to Tarma. Kethry was recalling now with some misgiving that Moonsong had also said that she had not yet found the limit to which it would bind itself to her—and if this experience was any indication of the future, she wasn't sure she *wanted* to.

All that was of any importance at the moment was that there was a woman within Need's sensing range in grave peril—peril of her life, by the way the blade was driving Kethry. And they had no choice but to answer the call.

Tarma continued to urge Hellsbane on; they were coming to a cultivated area, and surely their goal couldn't be far. Ahead of them on the road they were following loomed a walled village; part and parcel of a manor-keep, a common arrangement in these parts. The gates were open; the fields around empty of workers. That was odd—very odd. It was high summer, and there should have been folk out in the fields, weeding and tending the irrigation ditches. There was no immediate sign of trouble, but as they neared the gates, it was plain just who the woman they sought was—

Bound to a scaffold high enough to be visible through the open gates, they could see a young, dark-haired woman dressed in white, almost like a sacrificial victim. The last rays of the setting sun touched her with color —touched also the heaped wood beneath the platform on which she stood, making it seem as if her pyre already blazed up. Lining the mud-plastered walls of the keep and crowding the square inside the gate were scores of folk of every class and station, all silent, all waiting.

Tarma really didn't give a fat damn about what they were waiting for, though it was a good bet that they were there for the show of the burning. She coaxed a final burst of speed out of her tired mount, sending her shooting ahead of Kethry's as they passed the gates, and bringing her close in to the platform. Once there, she swung Hellsbane around in a tight circle and drew her sword, placing herself between the woman on the scaffold and the men with the torches to set it alight.

She knew she was an imposing sight, even covered with sweat and the dust of the road; hawk-faced, intimidating, ice-blue eyes glaring. Her clothing alone should tell them she was nothing to fool with—it was obviously that of a fighting mercenary; plain brown leathers and brigandine armor. Her sword reflected the dying sunlight so that she might have been holding a living flame in her hand. She said nothing; her pose said it all for her.

Nevertheless, one of the men started forward, torch in hand.

"I wouldn't," Kethry was framed in the arch of the gate, silhouetted against the fiery sky; her mount rock-still, her hands glowing with sorcerous energy. "If Tarma doesn't get you, *I* will."

"Peace," a tired, gray-haired man in plain, dusty-black robes stepped forward from the crowd, holding his arms out placatingly, and motioned the torch-bearer to give way. "Istan, go back to your place. Strangers, what brings you here at this time of all times?"

Kethry pointed—a thin strand of glow shot from her finger and touched the ropes binding the captive on the platform. The bindings loosed and fell from her, sliding down her body to lie in a heap at her feet. The woman swayed and nearly fell, catching herself at the last moment with one hand on the stake she had been bound to. A small segment of the crowd—mostly women—stepped forward as if to help, but fell back again as Tarma swiveled to face them.

"I know not what crime you accuse this woman of, but she is innocent of it," Kethry said to him, ignoring the presence of anyone else. *"That* is what brings us here."

A collective sigh rose from the crowd at her words. Tarma watched warily to either side, but it appeared to be a sigh of relief rather than a gasp of arousal. She relaxed the white-knuckled grip she had on her sword-hilt by the merest trifle.

"The Lady Myria is accused of the slaying of her lord," the robed man said quietly. "She called upon her ancient right to summon a champion to her defense when the evidence against her became overwhelming. I, who am priest of Felwether, do ask you—strangers, will you champion the Lady and defend her in trial-by-combat?"

Kethry began to answer in the affirmative, but the priest shook his head negatively. "No, lady-mage, by ancient law *you* are bound from the field; neither sorcery nor sorcerous weapons such as I see you bear may be permitted in trial-by-combat."

"Then—"

"He wants to know if I'll do it, *she'enedra,*" Tarma croaked, taking a fiendish pleasure in the start the priest gave at the sound of her harsh voice. "I know your laws, priest, I've passed this way before. I ask you in my turn—if my partner, by her skills, can prove to you the lady's innocence, will you set her free and call off the combat, no matter how far it has gotten?"

"I so pledge, by the Names and the Powers," the priest nodded—almost eagerly.

"Then I will champion this lady."

About half the spectators cheered and rushed forward. Three older women edged past Tarma to bear the fainting woman back into the keep. The rest, except for the priest, moved off slowly and reluctantly, casting thoughtful and measuring looks back at Tarma. Some of them seemed friendly; most did not.

"What—"

"Was that all about?" That was as far as Tarma got before the priest interposed himself between the partners.

"Your pardon, mage-lady, but you may not speak with the champion from this moment forward. Any message you may have must pass through me."

"Oh, no, not yet, priest." Tarma urged Hellsbane forward and passed his outstretched hand. "I told you I know your laws—and the ban starts at sundown—Greeneyes, pay attention, I have to talk fast. You're going to have to figure out just who the real culprit is, the best I can possibly do is buy you time. This business is combat to the death for the champion. I can choose just to defeat my challengers, but they *have* to kill me. And the longer you take, the more likely that is."

"Tarma, you're better than anybody here!"

"But not better than any twenty—or thirty." Tarma smiled crookedly. "The rules of the game, *she'enedra,* are that I keep fighting until nobody is willing to challenge me. Sooner or later they'll wear me out and I'll go down."

"What?"

"Shush, I knew what I was getting into. You're as good at your craft as

I am at mine—I've just given you a bit of incentive. Take Warrl." The tall, lupine creature jumped to the ground from behind Tarma where he'd been clinging to the special pad with his retractile claws. "He might well be of some use. Do your best, *veshta'cha;* there're two lives depending on you."

The priest interposed himself again. "Sunset, champion," he said firmly, putting his hand on her reins.

Tarma bowed her head, and allowed him to lead her and her horse away, Kethry staring dumbfounded after them.

"All right, let's take this from the very beginning."

Kethry was in the Lady Myria's bower, a soft and colorful little corner of an otherwise drab fortress. There were no windows—no drafts stirred the bright tapestries on the walls, or caused the flames of the beeswax candles to flicker. The walls were thick stone covered with plaster, warm by winter, cool by summer. The furnishings were of light yellow wood, padded with plump feather cushions. In one corner stood a cradle, watched over broodingly by the lady herself. The air was pleasantly scented with herbs and flowers. Kethry wondered how so pampered a creature could have gotten herself into such a pass.

"It was two days ago. I came here to lie down in the afternoon. I—was tired; I tire easily since Syrtin was born. I fell asleep."

Close up, the Lady proved to be several years Kethry's junior; scarcely past her midteens. Her dark hair was lank and without luster, her skin pale. Kethry frowned at that, and wove a tiny spell with a gesture and two whispered words while Myria was speaking. The creature of the Ethereal Plane who'd agreed to serve as their scout was still with her—it would have taken a far wilder ride than they had made to lose it. And now that they were doing something about the lady's plight, Need was quiescent; leaving Kethry able to think and work again.

The answer to her question came quickly as a thin voice breathed whispered words into her ear.

Kethry grimaced angrily. "Lady's eyes, child, I shouldn't wonder that you tire—you're still torn up from the birthing! What kind of a miserable excuse for a Healer have you got here, anyway?"

"We have *no* Healer, lady," one of the three older women who had borne Myria back into the keep rose from her seat behind Kethry and stood between them, challenge written in her stance. She had a kind, but careworn face; her gray and buff gown was of good stuff, but old-fashioned in cut. Kethry guessed that she must be Myria's companion, an older relative, perhaps. "The Healer died before my dove came to child-bed and her lord did not see fit to replace him. We had no use for a Healer, or so he claimed. After all, he kept no great number of men-at-arms; he warred with no one. He felt that birthing was a perfectly normal procedure and surely didn't require the expensive services of a Healer."

"Now, Katran—"

"It is no more than the truth! He cared more for his horses than for you! He replaced the farrier quickly enough when *he* left!"

"His horses were of more use to him," the girl said bitterly, then bit her lip. "There, you see, *that* is what brought me to this pass—one too many careless remarks let fall among the wrong ears."

Kethry nodded, liking the girl; the child was *not* the pampered pretty she had first thought. No windows to this chamber, only the one entrance; a good bit more like a cell than a bower, it occurred to her. A comfortable cell, but a cell still. She stood, smoothed her buff-colored robe with an unconscious gesture, and unsheathed the sword that seldom left her side.

"Lady, what—" Katran stood, startled by the gesture.

"Peace; I mean no ill. Here," Kethry said, bending over Myria and placing the blade in the startled girl's hands, "hold this for a bit."

Myria took the blade, eyes wide, a puzzled expression bringing a bit more life to her face. "But—"

"Women's magic, child. For all that blades are a man's weapon, Need here is strong in the magic of women. She serves women only—it was her power that called me here to aid you—and given an hour of your holding her, she'll Heal you. Now, go on. You fall asleep."

Myria accepted the blade gingerly, then settled the sword somewhat awkwardly across her knees and took a deep breath. "Something woke me, a sound of something falling, I think. You can see that this room connects with my Lord's chamber, that in fact the only way in or out is through his chamber. I saw a candle burning, so I rose to see if he needed anything. He—he was slumped over his desk. I thought perhaps he had fallen asleep."

"You thought he was drunk, you mean," the older woman said wryly.

"Does it *matter* what I thought? I didn't see anything out of the ordinary, because he wore dark colors always. I reached out my hand to shake him—and it came away bloody!"

"And she screamed fit to rouse the household," Katran finished.

"And when we came, she had to unlock the door for us," said the second woman, silent till now. "Both doors into that chamber were locked—hallside with the lord's key, seneschal's side barred from within this room. And the bloody dagger that had killed him was under her bed."

"Whose was it?"

"Mine, of course," Myria answered. "And before you ask, there was only one key to the hallside door; it could only be opened with the key, and the key was under his hand. It's an ensorcelled lock; even if you made a copy of the key the copy would never unlock the door."

"Warrl?" The huge beast rose from the shadows where he'd been lying and padded to Kethry's side. Myria and her women shrank away a little at the sight of him.

"You can detect what I'd need a spell for. See if the bar was bespelled into place on the other door, would you? Then see if the spell on the lock's been tampered with."

The dark gray, nearly black beast trotted out of the room on silent paws, and Myria shivered.

"I can see where the evidence against you is overwhelming, even without misheard remarks."

"I had no choice in this wedding," Myria replied, her chin rising defiantly, "but I have been a true and loyal wife to my lord."

"Loyal past his deserts, if you ask me," Katran grumbled. "Well, that's the problem, lady-mage. My Lady came to this marriage reluctant, and it's well known. It's well known that he didn't much value her. And there's been more than a few heard to say they thought Myria reckoned to set herself up as Keep-ruler with the Lord gone."

Warrl padded back into the room, and flopped down at Kethry's feet.

"Well, fur-brother?"

He shook his head negatively, and the women stared at this evidence of like-human intelligence.

"Not the bar nor the lock, hmm? And how do you get into a locked room without a key? Still . . . Lady, is all as it was in the other room?"

"Yes, the priest was one of the first in the door, and would not let anyone change so much as a dust mote. He only let them take the body away."

"Thank the Goddess!" Kethry gave the exclamation something of a prayerful cast. She started to rise herself, then stared curiously at the girl. "Lady, *why* did you choose to prove yourself as you did?"

"Lady-mage—"

Kethry was surprised at the true expression of guilt and sorrow the child wore.

"If I had guessed strangers would be caught in this web I never would have. I—I thought that my kin would come to my defense. I came to this marriage of their will, I thought at least one of them might—at least try. I don't think anyone here would dare the family's anger by killing one of the sons, even if the daughter is thought worthless by most of them." A slow tear slid down one cheek, and she whispered her last words. "My youngest brother, I thought at least was fond of me. . . ."

The spell Kethry had set in motion was still active; she whispered another question to the tiny air-entity she had summoned. This time the answer made her smile, albeit sadly.

"Your youngest brother, child, is making his way here afoot, having ridden his horse into foundering trying to reach you in time. He is swearing by every god that if you have been harmed he will not leave stone on stone here."

Myria gave a tiny cry and buried her face in her hands; Katran moved to comfort her as her shoulders shook with silent sobs. Kethry stood, and made her way into the other room. Need's magic was such that the girl would hold the blade until she no longer required its power. While it gave Kethry an expertise in swordwork a master would envy, it would do nothing to augment her magical abilities, so it was fine where it was. Right now there was a mystery to solve, and two lives hung in the balance until Kethry could puzzle it out.

As she surveyed the outer room, she wondered how Tarma was faring.

Tarma sat quietly beneath the window of a tiny, bare, rock-walled cell. In a few moments the light of the rising moon would penetrate it, first through the eastern window, then the skylight overhead. For now, the only light in the room was that of the oil-fed flame burning on the low table before her. There was something else on that table—the long, coarse braids of Tarma's hair.

She had shorn those braids off herself at shoulder-length, then tied a silky black headband around her forehead to confine what remained. That had been the final touch to the costume she'd donned with an air of robing herself for some ceremony—clothing that had long stayed untouched, carefully folded in the bottom of her pack. Black clothing; from low, soft boots to chainmail shirt, from headband to hose—the stark, unrelieved black of a Shin'a'in Sword Sworn about to engage in ritual combat or on the trail of blood-feud.

Now she waited, patiently, seated cross-legged before the makeshift altar, to see if her preparations received an answer.

The moon rose behind her, the square of dim white light creeping slowly down the blank stone wall opposite her, until, at last, it touched the flame on the altar.

And without warning, without fanfare, *She* was there, standing between Tarma and the altar-place. Shin'a'in by Her golden skin and sharp features, clad identically to Tarma, only Her eyes revealed Her as something not human. Those eyes—the spangled darkness of the sky at midnight, without white, iris or pupil—could belong to only one being; the Shin'a'in Goddess of the South Wind, known only as the Star-Eyed, or the Warrior.

"Child, I answer." Her voice was melodious.

"Lady." Tarma bowed her head in homage.

"You have questions, child? No requests?"

"No requests, Star-Eyed. My fate—does not interest me. I will live or die by my own skills. But Kethry's fate—*that* I would know."

"The future is not easy to map, child, not even for a goddess. I must tell you that tomorrow might bring your life *or* your death; both are equally likely."

Tarma sighed. "Then what of my *she'enedra* should it be the second path?"

The Warrior smiled, Tarma felt the smile like a caress. "You are worthy, child; hear, then. If you fall tomorrow, your *she'enedra,* who is perhaps a bit more pragmatic than you, will work a spell that lifts both herself and the Lady Myria to a place leagues distant from here, while Warrl releases Hellsbane and Ironheart and drives them out the gates. I fear she allows you this combat only because she knows you regard it as touching your honor to hold by these outClan customs. If the choice were in her hands, you would all be far from here by now; you, she, the lady and her child and all—well; she will abide by your choices. For the rest, when Kethry recovers from that spell they shall go to our people, to the Liha'irden; Lady Myria will find a mate to her liking there. Then, with some orphans of other Clans, they shall go forth and Tale'sedrin will ride the plains again, as Kethry promised you. The blade will release her, and pass to another's hands."

Tarma sighed, and nodded. "Then, Lady, I am content, whatever my fate tomorrow. I thank you."

The Warrior smiled again; then between one heartbeat and the next, was gone.

Tarma left the flame to burn itself out, lay down upon the pallet that was the room's only other furnishing, and slept.

Sleep was the last thing on Kethry's mind.

She surveyed the room that had been Lord Corbie's; plain stone walls, three entrances, no windows. One of the entrances still had the bar across the door, the other two led to Myria's bower and to the hall outside. Plain stone floor, no hidden entrances there. She knew the blank wall held nothing either; the other side was the courtyard of the manor. Furnishings; one table, one chair, one ornate bedstead against the blank wall, one bookcase, half filled, four lamps. A few bright rugs. Her mind felt as blank as the walls.

Start at the beginning—she told herself. *Follow what happened. The girl came in here alone, the man followed after she was asleep, then what?*

He was found at his desk, said a voice in her mind, startling her. *He probably walked straight in and sat down. What's on the desk that he might have been doing?*

Every time Warrl spoke to her mind-to-mind it surprised her. She still couldn't imagine how he managed to make himself heard when she hadn't a scrap of that particular Gift. Tarma seemed to accept it unquestioningly; how she'd ever gotten used to it, the sorceress couldn't imagine.

Tarma—time was wasting.

On the desk stood a wineglass with a sticky residue in the bottom, an inkwell and quill, and several stacked ledgers. The top two looked disturbed.

Kethry picked them up, and began leafing through the last few pages, whispering a command to the invisible presence at her shoulder. The answer was prompt. The ink on the last three pages of both ledgers was fresh enough to still be giving off fumes detectable only by a creature of the air. The figures were written no more than two days ago.

She leafed back several pages worth, noting that the handwriting changed from time to time.

"Who else kept the accounts besides your lord?" she called into the next room.

"The seneschal; that was why his room has an entrance on this one," the woman Katran replied, entering the lord's room herself. "I can't imagine why the door was barred. Lord Corbie almost never left it that way."

"That's a lot of trust to place in a hireling."

"Oh, the seneschal isn't a hireling, he's Lord Corbie's bastard brother. He's been the lord's right hand since he inherited the lordship of Felwether."

The sun rose; Tarma was awake long before.

If the priest was surprised to see her change of outfit, he didn't show it. He had brought a simple meal of bread and cheese, and watered wine;

he waited patiently while she ate and drank, then indicated she should follow him.

Tarma checked all her weapons. She secured all the fastenings of her clothing (how many had died because they had forgotten to tie something tightly enough?), and stepped into place behind him, as silent as his shadow.

He conducted her to a small tent that had been erected in one corner of the keep's practice ground, against the keep walls. The walls of the keep formed two sides, the outer wall the third; the fourth side was open. The practice ground was of hard-packed clay, and relatively free of dust. A groundskeeper was sprinkling water over the dirt to settle it.

Once they were in front of the little pavilion, the priest finally spoke.

"The first challenger will be here within a few minutes; between fights you may retire here to rest for as long as it takes for the next to ready himself, or one candlemark, whichever is longer. You will be brought food at noon and again at sunset." His expression plainly said that he did not think she would be needing the latter, "and there will be fresh water within the tent at all times. I will be staying with you."

Now his expression was apologetic.

"To keep my partner from slipping me any magical aid?" Tarma asked wryly. "Hellfire, priest, *you* know what I am, even if these dirt-grubbers here don't!"

"I know, Sword Sworn. This is for your protection as well. There are those here who would not hesitate to tip the hand of the gods somewhat."

Tarma's eyes hardened. "Priest, I'll spare who I can, but it's only fair to tell you that if I catch anyone trying an underhanded trick, I won't hesitate to kill him."

"I would not ask you to do otherwise."

She looked at him askance. "There's more going on here than meets the eye, isn't there?"

He shook his head, and indicated that she should take her seat in the champion's chair beside the tent-flap. There was a bustling on the opposite side of the practice ground, and a dark, heavily bearded man followed by several boys carrying arms and armor appeared only to vanish within another, identical tent on that side. Spectators began gathering along the open side and the tops of the walls.

"I fear I can tell you nothing, Sword Sworn. I have only speculations, nothing more. But I pray your little partner is wiser than I."

"Or I'm going to be cold meat by nightfall," Tarma finished for him, watching as her first opponent emerged from the challenger's pavilion.

The priest winced at her choice of words, but did not contradict her. Circles within circles. . . .

Kethry had not been idle.

The sticky residue in the wineglass had been more than just the dregs of drink; there had been a powerful narcotic in it. Unfortunately, this just pointed back to Myria; she'd been using just such a potion to help her sleep since the birth of her son. Still, it wouldn't have been all that difficult to obtain, and Kethry had a trick up her sleeve, one the average mage wouldn't have known; one she would use *if* they could find the other bottle of potion.

More encouraging was what she had found perusing the ledgers. The seneschal had been siphoning off revenues; never much at a time, but steadily. By now it must amount to a tidy sum. What if he suspected Lord Corbie was likely to catch him at it?

Or even more—what if Lady Myria *was* found guilty and executed? The estate would go to her infant son, and who would be the child's most likely guardian but his half-uncle, the seneschal?

And children die so very easily, and from so many natural causes.

Now that she had a likely suspect, Kethry decided it was time to begin investigating him.

The first place she checked was the barred door. And on the bar itself she found an odd little scratch, obvious in the paint. It looked new, her air-spirit confirmed that it was. She lifted the bar after examining it even more carefully, finding no other marks on it but those worn places where it rubbed against the brackets that held it.

She opened the door, and began examining every inch of the door and frame. And found, near the top, a tiny piece of hemp that looked as if it might have come from a piece of twine, caught in the wood of the door itself.

Further examination of the door yielded nothing, so she turned her attention to the room beyond.

It looked a great deal like the lord's room, with more books and a less ostentatious bedstead—and a wooden floor, rather than one of stone. She called Warrl in and sent him sniffing about for any trace of magic. That potion required a tiny bit of magicking to have full potency, and if there were another bottle of it anywhere about, Warrl would find it.

She turned her own attention to the desk.

Tarma's first opponent had been good, and an honest fighter. It was with a great deal of relief—especially after she'd seen an anxious-faced woman with three small children clinging to her skirt watching every move he made—that she was able to disarm him and knock him flat on his rump without seriously injuring him.

The second had been a mere boy; he had no business being out here at all. Tarma had the shrewd notion he'd been talked into it just so she'd have one more live body to wear her out. Instead of exerting herself in any way, she lazed about, letting him wear *himself* into exhaustion, before giving him a little tap on the skull with the pommel of her knife that stretched him flat on his back, seeing stars.

The third opponent was another creature altogether.

He was slim and sleek, and Tarma smelled "assassin" on him as plainly as if she'd had Warrl's clever nose. When he closed with her, his first few moves confirmed her guess. His fighting style was all feint and rush, never getting in too close. This was a real problem. If she stood her ground, she'd open herself to the poisoned dart or whatever other tricks he had secreted on his person. If she let him drive her all over the bloody practice ground he'd wear her down. Either way, she lost.

Of course, she might be able to outfox him—

So far she'd played an entirely defensive game, both with him and her first two opponents. If she took the offense when he least expected it, she might be able to catch him off his guard.

She let him begin to drive her, and saw at once that he was trying to work her around so that the sun was in her eyes. She snarled inwardly, let him think he was having his way, then turned the tables on him.

She came at him in a two-handed pattern-dance, one that took her back to her days on the Plains and her first instructor; an old man she'd never *dreamed* could have moved as fast as he did. She hadn't learned that pattern then; hadn't learned it until the old man and her Clan were two years dead and she'd been Kethry's partner for more than a year. She'd learned it from one of Her Kal'enedral, a woman who'd died a hundred years before Tarma had ever been born.

It took her opponent off-balance; he back-pedaled furiously to get out the the way of the shining circles of steel, great and lesser, that were her sword and dagger. And when he stopped running, he found *himself* facing into the sun.

Tarma saw him make a slight movement with his left hand; when he came in with his sword in an over-and-under cut, she paid his sword-hand only scant attention. It was the other she was watching for.

Under the cover of his overt attack he made a strike for her upper arm with his gloved left. She avoided it barely in time; a circumstance that made her sweat when she thought about it later, and executed a spin-

and-cut that took his hand off at the wrist at the end of the move. While he stared in shock at the spurting stump, she carried her blade back along the arc to take his head as well.

The onlookers were motionless, silent with shock. What they'd seen from her up until now had not prepared them for this swift slaughter. While they remained still, she stalked to where the gloved hand lay and picked it up with great care. Embedded in the fingertips of the gloves, retracted or released by a bit of pressure to the center of the palm, were four deadly little needles. Poisoned, no doubt.

She decided to make a grandstand move out of this. She stalked to the challenger's pavilion, where more of her would-be opponents had gathered, and cast the hand down at their feet.

"Assassin's tricks, 'noble lords'?" she spat, oozing contempt. "Is this the honor of Felwether? I'd rather fight jackals. At least they're honest in their treachery! Have you no trust in the judgment of the gods—and their champion?"

That should put a little doubt in the minds of the honest ones—and a little fear in the hearts of the ones that weren't.

Tarma stalked stiff-legged back to her own pavilion, where she threw herself down on the little cot inside it, and hoped *she'd* get her wind back before *they* got their courage up.

In the very back of one of the drawers Kethry found a very curious contrivance. It was a coil of hempen twine, two cords, really, at the end of which was tied a barbless, heavy fishhook, the kind sea-fishers used to take shark and the great sea-salmon. But the coast was weeks from here. What on earth could the seneschal have possibly wanted with such a curious souvenir?

Just then Warrl barked sharply; Kethry turned to see his tail sticking out from under the bedstead.

There's a hidden compartment under the boards here, he said eagerly in her mind. *I smell gold, and magic—and fresh blood.*

She tried to move the bed aside, but it was far too heavy, something the seneschal probably counted on. So she squeezed in beside Warrl, who pawed at the place on the board floor where he smelled strangeness.

Sneezing several times from the dust beneath the bed, she felt along the boards—carefully, carefully; it could be booby-trapped. She found the catch, and a whole section of the board floor lifted away. And inside . . .

Gold, yes; packed carefully into the bottom of it—but on top, a wadded-up tunic, and an empty bottle.

She left the gold, but brought out the other things. The tunic was bloodstained; the bottle, by the smell, had held the narcotic potion she was seeking.

"Hey-la," she whispered in satisfaction.

Now if she just had some notion how he could have gotten into a locked room without the proper key. There was no hint or residue of any kind of magic. And no key to the door with the bar across it.

How *could* you get into a locked room?

Go before the door is locked, Warrl said in her mind.

And suddenly she realized what the fishhook was for.

Kethry wriggled out from under the bed, replacing tunic and bottle and leaving the gold in the hidden compartment untouched.

"Katran!" she called. A moment later Myria's companion appeared; quite nonplussed to see the sorceress covered with dust beside the seneschal's bed.

"Get the priest," Kethry told her, before she had a chance to ask any question. "I know who the murderer is—and I know how he did it, and why."

Tarma was facing her first real opponent of the day; a lean, saturnine fellow who used twin swords like extensions of himself. He was just as fast on his feet as she was—and he was fresher. The priest had vanished just before the beginning of this bout, and Tarma was fervently hoping this meant Kethry had found something. Otherwise, this fight bid fair to be her last.

Thank the Goddess this one was an honest warrior; if she went down, it would be to an honorable opponent. Not too bad, really, if it came to it. Not even many Sword Sworn could boast to having defeated twelve opponents in a single morning.

Even if some of them had been mere babes.

She had a stitch in her side that she was doing her best to ignore, and her breath was coming in harsh pants. The sun was punishing-hard on someone wearing head-to-toe black; sweat was trickling down her back and sides. She danced aside, avoiding a blur of sword, only to find she was moving right into the path of his second blade.

Damn!

At the last second she managed to drop and roll, and came up to find him practically on top of her again. She managed to get to one knee and trap his first blade between dagger and sword—but the second was coming in—

From the side of the field, came a voice like a trumpet call.

"Hold!"

And miracle of miracles, the blade stopped mere inches from her unprotected neck.

The priest strode onto the field, robes flapping. "The sorceress has found the true murderer of our lord and proved it to my satisfaction," he announced to the waiting crowd. "She wishes to prove it to yours."

Then he began naming off interested parties as Tarma sagged to her knees in the dirt, limp with relief, and just about ready to pass out with exhaustion. Her opponent dropped both his blades in the dust at her side, and ran off to his side of the field, returning in a moment with a cup of water.

And before handing it to her, he smiled sardonically, saluted her with it and took a tiny sip himself.

She shook sweat-sodden hair out of her eyes, and accepted the cup with a nod of thanks. She downed the lukewarm water, and sagged back onto her heels with a sigh.

"Sword Sworn, shall I find someone to take you to your pavilion?"

The priest was bending over her in concern. Tarma managed to find one tiny bit of unexpended energy.

"Not on your life, priest. I want to see this myself!"

There were perhaps a dozen nobles in the group that the priest escorted to the lord's chamber. Foremost among them was the seneschal; the priest most attentive on him. Tarma was too tired to wonder about that; she saved what little energy she had to get her into the room and safely leaning up against the wall within.

"I trust you all will forgive me if I am a bit dramatic, but I wanted you all to see exactly how this deed was done."

Kethry was standing behind the chair that was placed next to the desk; in that chair was an older woman in buff and gray. "Katran has kindly agreed to play the part of Lord Corbie; I am the murderer. The lord has just come into this chamber; in the next is his lady. She has taken a potion to relieve pain, and the accustomed sound of his footstep is not likely to awaken her."

She held up a wineglass. "Some of that same potion was mixed in with the wine that was in this glass, but it did not come from the batch Lady Myria was using. Here is Myria's bottle," she placed the wineglass on the desk, and Myria brought a bottle to stand beside it. "Here," she produced a second bottle, "is the bottle I found. The priest knows where, and can vouch for the fact that until he came, no hand but the owner's and mine touched it."

The priest nodded. Tarma noticed with a preternatural sensitivity that made it seem as if her every nerve was on the alert that the seneschal was beginning to sweat.

"The spell I am going to cast now—as your priest can vouch, since he is no mean student of magic himself—will cause the wineglass and the bottle that contained the potion that was poured into it glow."

Kethry dusted something over the glass and the two bottles. As they watched, the residue in the glass and the fraction of potion in Kethry's bottle began to glow with an odd, greenish light.

"Is this a true casting, priest?" Tarma heard one of the nobles ask in an undertone.

He nodded. "As true as ever I've seen."

"Huh," the man replied, frowning with thoughts he kept to himself.

"Now—Lord Corbie has just come in; he is working on the ledgers. I give him a glass of wine," Kethry handed the glass to Katran. "He is grateful; he thinks nothing of the courtesy, I am an old and trusted friend. He drinks it, I leave the room, presently he is asleep."

Katran allowed her head to sag down on her arms.

"I take the key from beneath his hand, and quietly lock the door to the hall. I replace the key. I know he will not stir, not even cry out, because of the strength of the potion. I take Lady Myria's dagger, which I obtained earlier. I stab him." Kethry mimed the murder; Katran did not move, though Tarma could see she was smiling sardonically. "I take the dagger and plant it beneath Lady Myria's bed—and I know that because of the potion *she* has been taking—and which I recommended, since we have no Healer—she will not wake either."

Kethry went into Myria's chamber, and returned empty-handed.

"I've been careless—got some blood on my tunic, I've never killed a man before and I didn't know that the wound would spurt. No matter, I will hide it where I plan to hide the bottle. By the way, the priest has that bloody tunic, and he knows that his hands alone removed it from its hiding place, just like the bottle. Now comes the important part—"

She took an enormous fishhook on a double length of twine out of her beltpouch.

"The priest knows where I found this—rest assured that it was *not* in Myria's possession. Now, on the top of this door, caught on a rough place in the wood, is another scrap of hemp. I am going to get it now. Then I shall cast another spell—and if that bit of hemp came from this twine, it shall return to the place it came from."

She went to the door and jerked loose a bit of fiber, taking it back to the desk. Once again she dusted something over the twine on the hook and the scrap, this time she also chanted as well. A golden glow drifted down from her hands to touch first the twine, then the scrap.

And the bit of fiber shot across to the twine like an arrow loosed from a bow.

"Now you will see the key to entering a locked room, now that I have proved that this was the mechanism by which the trick was accomplished."

She went over to the door to the seneschal's chamber. She wedged the hook under the bar on the door, and lowered the bar so that it was only held in place by the hook; the hook was kept where it was by the length of twine going over the door itself. The other length of twine Kethry threaded *under* the door. Then she closed the door.

The second piece of twine jerked; the hook came free, and the bar thudded into place. And the whole contrivance was pulled up over the door and through the upper crack by the first piece.

All eyes turned toward the seneschal—whose white face was confession enough.

"Lady Myria was certainly grateful enough."

"If we'd let her, she'd have stripped the treasury bare," Kethry replied, waving at the distant figures on the keep wall. "I'm glad you talked her out of it."

"Greeneyes, they don't have it to spare, and we both know it. As it is, she'll have to spend most of the seneschal's hoard in making up for the shortfalls among the hirelings that his skimmings caused in the first place."

"Will she be all right, do you think?"

"Now that her brother's here I don't think she has a thing to worry about. She's gotten back all the loyalty of her lord's people and more besides. All she needed was a strong right arm to beat off unwelcome suitors, and she's got that now! Warrior's Oath, I'm glad *that* young monster wasn't one of the challengers. I'd never have lasted past the first round!"

"Tarma—"

The swordswoman raised an eyebrow at Kethry's unwontedly serious tone.

"If you—did all that because you think you owe me—"

"I 'did all that' because we're *she'enedran,"* she replied, a slight smile warming her otherwise forbidding expression. "No other reason is needed."

"But—"

"No 'buts,' Greeneyes." Tarma looked back at the waving motes on the wall. "Hell, we've just accomplished something we really needed to do. This little job is going to give us a real boost on our reputation. Besides, you know I'd do whatever I needed to do to keep you safe."

Kethry did not reply to that last; not that she wasn't dead certain that it was true. That was the problem.

Tarma had been stepping between Kethry and possible danger on a regular basis, often when such intercession wasn't needed. At all other times, she treated Kethry as a strict equal, but when danger threatened—

She tried to keep the sorceress wrapped in a protective cocoon spun of herself and her blades.

She probably doesn't even realize she's doing it—but she's keeping me *so safe, she's putting* herself *in more risk than she needs to. She knows I can take care of myself—*

Then the answer occurred to her.

Without me, there will never be a Tale'sedrin. She's protecting, not just me, but her hopes for a new Clan! But she's stifling me—and she's going to get herself killed!

She glanced over at Tarma, at the distant, brooding expression she wore.

I can't tell her. She might not believe me. Or worse, she might believe, and choke when she needs to act. I wonder if Warrl has figured out what she's doing? I hope so—

She glanced again at her partner.

—or she's going to end up killing all three of us. Or driving me mad.

Seven

The sorcerer was young, thin, and sweating nervously, despite the cold of the musty cellar chamber that served as his living area and workroom. His secondhand robe was clammy with chill and soaked through with his own perspiration.

He had every reason to be nervous. This was the first time he and his apprentice (who was now huddled out of the way in the corner) had ever attempted to bind an imp to his service. The summoning of a spirit from the Abyssal Planes is no small task, even if the spirit one hopes to summon is of the very least and lowliest of the demonic varietals. Demons and their ilk are always watching for a chance misstep—and some are more eager to take advantage of a mistake than others.

The torches on the walls wavered and smoked, their odor of hot pitch nearly overwhelming the acrid tang of the incense he was burning. Mice squeaked and scuttled along the rafters overhead. Perhaps they were the cause of his distraction, for he *was* distracted for a crucial moment. And one of those that watched and waited seized the unhoped-for opportunity when the sorcerer thrice chanted, not the name "Talhkarsh"—the true-name of the imp he meant to bind—but *"Thalhkarsh."*

Incandescent ruby smoke rose and filled the interior of the diagram the mage had so carefully chalked upon the floor of his cluttered, dank, high-ceilinged stone chamber. It completely hid whatever was forming within the bespelled hexacle.

But there *was* something there; he could see shadows moving within the veiling smoke. He waited, dry-mouthed in anticipation, for the smoke to clear, so that he could intone his second incantation, one that would coerce the imp he'd summoned into the bottle that waited within the exact center of the hexacle.

Then the smoke vanished as quickly as it had been conjured—and the young mage nearly fainted, as he looked *up* at what stood there. And looked higher. And his sallow, bearded visage assumed the same lack of color as his chalk when the occupant, head just brushing the rafters, calmly stepped across the spell-bound lines, bent slightly at the waist, and seized him none-too-gently by the throat.

Thinking quickly, he summoned everything he knew in the way of arcane protections, spending magical energy with what in other circumstances might have been reckless wastefulness. There was a brief flare of light around him, and the demon dropped him as a human would something that had unexpectedly scorched his hand. The mage cringed where he had fallen, squeezing his eyes shut.

"Oh, fool," the voice was like brazen gongs just slightly out of tune with each other, and held no trace of pity. "Look at me."

The mage opened one eye, well aware of the duplicity of demons, yet unable to resist the command. His knowledge did him little good; his face went slack-jawed with bemusement at the serpentine beauty of the creature that stood over him. It had shrunk to the size of a very tall human and its—*his*—eyes glowed from within, a rich ruby color reminiscent of wine catching sunlight. He was—wonderful.

He was the very image of everything the mage had ever dreamed of in a lover. The face was that of a fallen angel, the nude body that of a god. The ruby eyes promised and beckoned, and were filled with an overwhelming and terribly masculine power.

The magician's shields did not include those meant to ward off beglamoring. He threw every pitiful protection he'd erected to the four winds in an onslaught of delirious devotion.

The demon laughed, and took him into his arms.

When he was finished amusing himself, he tore the whimpering creature that remained to shreds . . . slowly.

It was only then, only after he'd destroyed the mage past any hope of resurrection, and when he was sated with the emanations of the mage's torment and death, that he paused to think—and, thinking, to regret his hasty action.

There had been opportunity there, opportunity to be free forever of the Abyssal Planes, and more, a potential for an unlimited supply of those delights he'd just indulged in. If only he'd *thought* before he'd acted!

But even as he was mentally cursing his own impulsiveness, his attention was caught by a hint of movement in the far corner.

He grew to his full size, and reached out lazily with one bloodsmeared claw to pull the shivering, wretched creature that cowered there into the torchlight. It had soiled itself with fear, but by the torque around its throat and the cabalistic signs on its shabby robe, this pitiful thing must have been the departed mage's apprentice.

Thalhkarsh chuckled, and the apprentice tried to shrink into insignificance. All was not yet lost. In fact, this terror-stricken youth was an even better candidate for what he had in mind than his master would have been.

Thalhkarsh bent his will upon the boy's mind; it was easy to read. The defenses his master had placed about him were few and weak, and fading with the master's death. Satisfied by what he read there, the demon assumed his most attractive aspect and spoke.

"Boy, would you live? More, would you prosper?"

The apprentice trembled and nodded slightly, his eyes glazed with horror, a fear that was rapidly being subsumed by the power the demon was exerting on his mind.

"See you this?" the demon hefted the imp-bottle that had been in the diagram with him. Plain, reddish glass before, it now glowed from within like the demon's eyes. "Do you know what it is?"

"The—imp-bottle," the boy whispered, after two attempts to get words out that failed. "The one Leland meant to—to—"

"To confine me in—or rather, the imp he meant to call. It is a worthless bottle no more; thanks to having been within the magic confines of the diagram when I was summoned instead of the imp, it has become my focus. Did your master tell you what a demonic focus is?"

"It—" the boy stared in petrified fascination at the bottle in the demon's hand, "it lets you keep yourself here of your own will. If you have enough power."

The demon smiled. "But I want more than freedom, boy. I want more than power. I have greater ambitions. And if you want to live, you'll help me achieve them."

It was plain from the boy's eyes that he was more than willing to do just about anything to ensure his continued survival. "How—what do you want?"

Thalhkarsh laughed, and his eyes narrowed. "Never mind, child. I have plans—and if you succeed in what I set out for you, you will have a life

privileged beyond anything you can now imagine. You will become great
—and I, I will become—greater than your poor mind can dream. For
now, child, *this* is how you can serve me. . . ."

"Here?" Tarma asked her mage-partner. "You're sure?"

The sunset bathed her in a blood-red glow as they approached the
trade-gate of the city of Delton, and a warm spring breeze stirred a lock
of coarse black hair that had escaped the confines of her short braids; her
hair had grown almost magically the past few months, as if it had re-
sented being shorn. The last light dyed her brown leather tunic and
breeches a red that was nearly black.

Kethry's softly attractive face wore lines of strain, and there was worry
in her emerald eyes. "I'm sure. It's here—and it's bad, whatever it is.
This is the worst Need's ever pulled on me that I can remember. It's
worse than that business with Lady Myria, even." She pushed the hood
of her traveling robe back from an aching forehead and rubbed her
temples a little.

"Huh. Well, I hope that damn blade of yours hasn't managed to get us
knee-deep into more than we can handle. Only one way to find out,
though."

The swordswoman kneed her horse into the lead, and the pair rode in
through the gates after passing the cursory inspection of a somewhat
nervous Gate Guard. He seemed oddly disinclined to climb down from
his gatehouse post, being content to pass them through after a scant few
moment's scrutiny.

Tarma's ice-blue eyes scanned the area just inside the gate for signs of
trouble, and found none. Her brow puckered in puzzlement. *"She'enedra,*
I find it hard to believe you're wrong, but this is the quietest town I've
ever seen. I was expecting blood and rapine in the streets."

"I'm not mistaken," Kethry replied in a low, tense voice. "And there's
something *very* wrong here—the very quiet is wrong. It's *too* quiet.
There's no one at all on the streets—no beggars, no whores, no nothing."

Tarma looked about her with increased alertness. Now that Keth had
mentioned it, this looked like an empty town. There were no loiterers to
be seen in the vicinity of the trade gate or the inns that clustered about
the square just inside it, and that was very odd indeed. No beggars, no
thieves, no whores, no strollers, no street musicians—just the few stablehands and inn servants that *had* to be outside, leading in the beasts of
fellow travelers, lighting lanterns and torches. And those few betook
themselves back inside as quickly as was possible. The square of the
trade inns was ominously deserted.

"Warrior's Oath! This is blamed *spooky!* I don't like the look of this, not one bit."

"Neither do I. Pick us an inn, *she'enedra;* pick one fast. If the locals don't want to be out-of-doors after sunset, they must have a reason, and I'd rather not be out here either."

Tarma chose an inn with the sign of a black sheep hanging above the door, and the words (for the benefit of those that could read) "The Blacke Ewe" painted on the wall beside the door. It looked to be about the right sort for the state of their purses, which were getting a bit on the lean side. They'd been riding the Trade Road north to Valdemar, once again looking for work, when Kethry's geas-forged blade Need had drawn them eastward until they ended up here. The sword had left them pretty much alone except for a twinge or two—and the incident with the feckless priestess, that had wound up being far more complicated than it had needed to be thanks to the Imp of the Perverse and Tarma's own big mouth. Tarma was beginning to hope that it had settled down.

And then this afternoon, Kethry had nearly fainted when it "called" with all of its old urgency. They'd obeyed its summons, until it led them at last to Delton.

Tarma saw to the stabling of their beasts; Kethry to bargaining for a room. The innkeeper looked askance at a mage wearing a sword, for those who trafficked in magic seldom carried physical weaponry, but he was openly alarmed by the sight of what trotted at Tarma's heels—a huge, black, wolflike creature whose shoulders came nearly as high as the swordswoman's waist.

Kethry saw the alarm in his eyes, realized that he had never seen a *kyree* before, and decided to use his fear as a factor in her bargaining. "My familiar," she said nonchalantly, "and he knows when I'm being cheated."

The price of their room took a mysterious plunge.

After installing their gear and settling Warrl in their room, they returned to the taproom for supper and information.

If the streets were deserted, the taproom was crowded far past its intended capacity.

Tarma wrinkled her nose at the effluvia of cheap perfume, unwashed bodies, stale food odors and fish-oil lanterns. Kethry appeared not to notice.

Tarma's harsh, hawklike features could be made into a veritable mask of intimidation when she chose to scowl; she did so now. Her ice-cold stare got them two stools and a tiny, round table to themselves. Her harsh voice summoned a harried servant as easily as Kethry could summon a creature of magic. A hand to her knife-hilt and the ostentatious shrugging of the sword slung on her back into a more comfortable position got her speedy service, cleaning her fingernails with her knife got them decent portions and scrubbed plates.

Kethry's frown of worry softened a bit. "Life has been ever so much easier since I teamed with you, *she'enedra,*" she chuckled quietly, moving the sides of her robe out of the way so that she could sit comfortably.

"No doubt," the swordswoman replied with a lifted eyebrow and a quirk to one corner of her mouth. "Sometimes I wonder how you managed without me."

"Poorly." The green eyes winked with mischief.

Their food arrived, and they ate in silence, furtively scanning the crowded room for a likely source of information. When they'd nearly finished, Kethry nodded slightly in the direction of a grizzled mercenary sitting just underneath one of the smoking lanterns. Tarma looked him over carefully; he looked almost drunk enough to talk, but not drunk enough to make trouble, and his companions had just deserted him, leaving seats open on the bench opposite his. He wore a badge, so he was mastered, and so was less likely to pick a fight. They picked up their tankards and moved to take those vacant seats beside him.

He nodded as they sat; warily at Tarma, appreciatively at Kethry.

He wasn't much for idle chatter, though. "Evening," was all he said.

"It is that," Tarma replied, "Though 'tis a strange enough evening and more than a bit early for folk to be closing themselves indoors, especially with the weather so pleasant."

"These are strange times," he countered, "And strange things happen in the nights around here."

"Oh?" Kethry looked flatteringly interested. "What sort of strange things? And can we take care of your thirst?"

He warmed to the admiration—and the offer.

"Folk been going missing; whores, street trash, such as won't be looked for by the watch," he told them, wiping his mouth on his sleeve, while Tarma signaled the serving wench. He took an enormous bite of the spiced sausage that was the Blacke Ewe's specialty; grease ran into his beard. He washed the bite down by draining his tankard dry. "There's rumors—" His eyes took on a certain wariness. He cast an uneasy glance around the dim, hot and odorous taproom.

"Rumors?" Tarma prompted, pouring his tankard full again, and sliding a silver piece under it. "Well, *we* little care for rumors, eh? What's rumor to a fighter but ale-talk?"

"Plague take rumors!" he agreed, but his face was strained. "What've magickers and demons got to do with us, so long as they leave our masters in peace?" He drained the vessel and pocketed the coin. "So long as he leaves a few for me, this Thalhkarsh can have his *fill* of whores!"

"Thalhkarsh? What might that be? Some great lecher, that he has need of so many lightskirts?" Tarma filled the tankard for the third time, and kept her tone carefully casual.

"Sh!" the mercenary paled, and made a cautionary wave with his hand. " 'Tisn't wise to bandy that name about lightly—them as does often aren't to be seen again. That—one I mentioned—well, some say he's a god, some a demon summoned by a mighty powerful magicker. All *I* know is that he has a temple on the Row—one that sprang up overnight, seemingly, and one with statues an' such that could make *me* blush, were I to go view 'em. The which I won't. 'Tisn't safe to go near there—"

"So?" Tarma raised one eyebrow.

"They sent the city guard trooping in there after the first trollops went missing. There were tales spread of blood-worship, so the city council reckoned somebody'd better check. Nobody ever saw so much as a scrap of bootleather of that guard-squad ever again."

"So folk huddle behind their doors at night, and hope that they'll be left in peace, hmm?" Kethry mused aloud, taking her turn at replenishing his drink. "But are they?"

"Rumor says not—not unless they take care to stay in company at night. Odd thing though, 'cept for the city guard, most of the ones taken by night have been women. I'd watch meself, were I you twain."

He drained his tankard yet again. This proved to be one tankard too many, as he slowly slid off the bench to lie beneath the table, a bemused smile on his face.

They took the god-sent opportunity to escape to their room.

"Well," Tarma said, once the door had been bolted, "we know *why,* and now we know *what.* Bloody Hell! I wish for once that that damned sword of yours would steer us toward something that pays!"

Kethry worked a minor magic that sent the vermin sharing their accommodations skittering under the door and out the open window. Warrl surveyed her handiwork, sniffed the room over carefully, then lay down at the foot of the double pallet with a heavy sigh.

"That's not quite true—we don't really know *what* we're dealing with. Is it a god, truly? If it is, I don't stand much chance of making a dent in its hide. Is it a demon, controlled by this magician, that has been set up as a god so that its master can acquire power by blood-magic? Or is it worse than either?"

"What could possibly be worse?"

"A demon loose, uncontrolled—a demon with ambition," Kethry said, flopping down beside Warrl and staring up at nothing, deep in thought.

Their lantern (more fish-oil) smoked and danced, and made strange shadows on the wall and ceiling.

"Worst case would be just that: a demon that knows exactly how to achieve godhood, and one with nothing standing in the way of his intended path. If it is a god—a real god—well, all gods have their enemies; it's simply a matter of finding the sworn enemy, locating a nest of his clerics, and bringing them all together. And a demon under the control of a mage can be sent back to the Abyssal Planes by discovering the summoning spell and breaking it. But an uncontrolled demon—the *only* way to get rid of it that I know of is to find its focus-object and break it. Even that may not work if it has achieved enough power. With enough accumulated power, or enough worshipers believing in his godhood, even breaking his focus wouldn't send him back to the Abyssal Planes. If that happens—well, you *first* have to find a demon-killing weapon, *then* you have to get close enough to strike a killing blow. And you hope that he isn't strong enough to have gone beyond needing a physical form. Or you damage him enough to break the power he gets from his followers' belief —but that's even harder to do than finding a demon-killing blade."

"And, needless to say, demon-killing weapons are few and far between."

"And it isn't terribly likely that you're going to get past a demon's reach to get that killing blow in, once he's taken his normal form."

Tarma pulled off her boots, and inspected the soles with a melancholy air. "How likely is that—an uncontrolled demon?"

"Not really likely," Kethry admitted. "I'm just being careful—giving you worst-case first. It's a lot more likely that he's under the control of a mage that's using him to build a power base for himself. That's the scenario I'd bet on. I've seen this trick pulled more than once before I met you. It works quite well, provided you can keep giving your congregation what they want."

"So what's next?"

"Well, I'd suggest we wait until morning, and see what I can find out among the mages while you see if you can get any more mercenaries to talk."

"Somehow I was afraid you'd say that."

They met back at the inn at noon; Tarma was empty-handed, but Kethry had met with a certain amount of success. At least she had a name, an address, and a price—a fat skin of strong wine taken with her, with a promise of more to come.

The address was in the scummiest section of the town, hard by the communal refuse heap. Both women kept their hands on the hilts of their blades while making their way down the rank and odorous alleyway; there were flickers of movement at various holes in the walls (you could hardly call them "doors" or "windows") but they were left unmolested. More than one of the piles of what seemed to be rotting refuse that dotted the alley proved to be a human, though it was difficult to tell for certain if they were living humans or corpses. Kethry again seemed blithely unaware of the stench; Tarma fought her stomach and tried to breathe as little as possible, and that little through her mouth.

At length they came to a wall that boasted a proper door; Kethry rapped on it. A mumbled voice answered her; she whispered something Tarma couldn't make out. Evidently it was the proper response, as the door swung open long enough for them to squeeze through, then shut hurriedly behind them.

Tarma blinked in surprise at what lay beyond the alleyside door. The fetid aroma of the air outside was gone. There was a faint ghost of wine, and an even fainter ghost of incense. The walls were covered with soft, colorful rugs; more rugs covered the floor. On top of the rugs were huge, plush cushions. The room was a rainbow of subtle reds and oranges and yellows. Tarma was struck with a sudden closing of the throat, and she blinked to clear misting eyes. This place reminded her forcibly of a Shin'a'in tent.

Fortunately the woman who turned from locking the door to greet them was not a Clanswoman, or Tarma might have had difficulty in ridding her eyes of that traitorous mist. She was draped head to toe with a veritable marketplace-full of veils, so that only her eyes showed. The voluminous covering, which rivaled the room for color and variety of pattern, was not, however, enough to hide the fact that she was wraith-thin. And above the veils, the black eyes were gray-ringed, bloodshot, and haggard.

"You know my price?" came a thin whisper.

Kethry let the heavy wineskin slide to her feet, and she nudged it over to the woman with one toe. "Three more follow, one every two days, from the master of the Blacke Ewe."

"What do you wish to know?"

"How comes this thing they call Thalhkarsh here—and why?"

The woman laughed crazily; Tarma loosened one of her knives in its hidden arm-sheath. What in the name of the Warrior had Kethry gotten them into?

"For that I need not even scry! Oh, no, to my sorrow, that is something I know only too well!"

The eyes leaked tears; Tarma averted her gaze, embarrassed.

"A curse on my own pride, and another on my curiosity! For now *he* knows my aura, knows it well—and calls me—and only the wine can stop my feet from taking me to him—" the thin voice whined to a halt, and the eyes closed, as if in a sudden spasm of pain.

For a long moment the woman stood, still as a thing made of wood, and Tarma feared they'd get nothing more out of her. Then the eyes opened again, and fixed Kethry with a stillettolike glare.

"Hear then the tale of my folly—'tis short enough. When Thalhkarsh raised his temple, all in a single night, I thought to scry it and determine what sort of creature was master of it. My soul-self was trapped by him, like a cruel child traps a mouse, and like cruel children, he and his priest tormented it—for how long, I cannot say. Then they seemed to forget me; let me go again, to crawl back to myself. But they had *not* forgotten me. I soon learned that each night he would call me back to his side. Each night I drink until I can no longer hear the call, but each night it takes more wine to close my ears. One night it will not be enough, and I shall join his other—brides."

The veils shook and trembled.

"This much only did I learn. Thalhkarsh is a demon; summoned by mistake instead of an imp. He bides here by virtue of his focus, the bottle that was meant to contain the imp. He is powerful; his priest is a mage as well, and has his own abilities augmented by the demon's. No sane person would bide in this town with them rising to prominence here."

The woman turned back to the door in a flutter of thin fabric and cracked it open again. One sticklike arm and hand pointed the way out. "That is my rede; take it if you are not fools."

Tarma was only too pleased to escape the chamber, which seemed rather too confining of a sudden. Kethry paused, concern on her face, to reach a tentative hand toward the veiled mystery. The woman made a repudiating motion. "Do not pity me!" she whispered harshly. "You cannot know! He is terrible—but he is also glorious—so—glorious—"

Her eyes glazed for a moment, then focused again, and she slammed the door shut behind them.

*   *   *

Kethry laced herself into the only dress she owned, a sensuous thing of forest green silk, a scowl twisting her forehead. "Why do *I* have to be the one pawed at and drooled over?"

Tarma chuckled. "You were the one who decreed against using any more magic than we had to," she pointed out.

"Well, I don't want to chance that mage detecting it and getting curious!"

"And you were the one who didn't want to chance using illusion."

"What if something should break it?"

"Then don't complain if I can't take your place. *You* happen to be the one of us that is lovely, amber-haired, and toothsome, not I. And you are the one with the manner-born. No merchant-lord or minor noble is going to open his doors to a nomad mercenary, and no decadent stripling is going to whisper secrets into the ear of one with a face like an ill-tempered hawk and a body like a swordblade. Now hurry up, or the market will be closed and we'll have to wait until the morrow."

Kethry grumbled under her breath, but put more speed into her preparations. They sallied forth into the late afternoon, playing parts they had often taken before, Kethry assuming the manners of the rank she actually was entitled to, playing the minor noblewoman on a journey to relatives with Tarma as her bodyguard.

As was very often the case, the marketplace was also the gathering-place for the offspring of what passed for aristocracy in this borderland trade-town. Within no great span of time Kethry had garnered invitations to dine with half a dozen would-be gallants. She chose the most dissipated of them, but persuaded him to make a party of the occasion, and invite his friends.

A bit miffed by the spoiling of his plans (which had not included having any competition for Kethry's assets), he agreed. As with the common folk, the well-born had taken to closing themselves behind sturdy doors at the setting of the sun, and with it already low in the west, he hastened to send a servant around to collect his chosen companions.

The young man's father was not at home, being off on a trading expedition. This had figured very largely in his plans, for he had purloined the key to his father's plushly appointed gazebo for his entertainment. The place was as well furnished as many homes: full of soft divans and wide couches, and boasting seven little alcoves off the main room, and two further rooms for intimate entertainment besides. Tarma's acting abilities were strained to the uttermost by the evening's events; she was hard-put to keep from laughing aloud at Kethry's performance and the reactions of the young men to her. To anyone who did not know her, Kethry embodied the very epitome of light-minded, light-skirted, capricious demi-nobility. No one watching her would have guessed she ever had a thought in her head besides her own pleasuring.

To the extreme displeasure of those few female companions that had been brought to the festivities, she monopolized all the male attention in the room. It wasn't long before she had sorted out which of them had actually been to one of the infamous "Rites of Dark Desires" and which had only heard rumors. Those who had not been bold enough to attend discovered themselves subtly dismissed from the inner circle, and soon repaired to the gardens or semi-private alcoves to enjoy the attentions of the females they had brought, but ignored. Kethry lured the three favored swains into one of the private rooms, motioning Tarma to remain on guard at the door. She eventually emerged; hot-eyed, contemptuous, and disheveled. Snores echoed from the room behind her.

"Let's get out of here before I lose my temper and go back to wring their necks," she snarled, while Tarma choked back a chuckle. "Puppies! They should still be in diapers, every one of them! Not anything resembling a real adult among them! I swear to you—ah, never mind. I'd just like to see them get some of the treatment they've earned. Like a good spanking and a long stint in a hermitage—preferably one in the middle of a desert, stocked with nothing but hard bread, water, and boring religious texts!"

No one followed them out into the night, which was not overly surprising, given the fears of the populace.

"I hope it was worth it," Tarma said, as casually as she could.

"It was," Kethry replied, a little cooler. "They were all very impressed with the whole ritual, and remembered everything they saw in quite lurid detail. It seems that it *is* the High Priest who is the one truly in command; from the sound of it, my guess was right about his plans. He conducts every aspect of the ritual; he calls the 'god' up, and he sends him back again. The god selects those of the females brought to him that he wants, the male followers get what's left, or share the few female followers he has. It's a rather unpleasant combination of human sacrifice and orgy. The High Priest must be the magician that summoned the demon in the first place. He's almost certainly having the demon transform himself, since the god is almost unbearably attractive, and the females he selects go to him willingly—at least at first. After his initial attentions, they're no longer in any condition to object to much of anything. Those three back there were positively obscene. They gloated over all the details of what Thalhkarsh does to his 'brides,' all the while doing their best to get me out of my clothing so they could demonstrate the 'rites.' It was all I could do to keep from throwing up on them."

"You sleep-spelled them?"

"Better, I dream-spelled them, just like I did with our 'customers' when I was posing as a whore back when we first met. It's as easy as sleep-spelling them, it's a very localized magic that isn't likely to be detected, and it will keep our disguises intact. They'll have the best time their imaginations can possibly provide."

Kethry looked suddenly weary as they approached their inn. "Bespeak me a bath, would you, dearheart? I feel filthy—inside *and* out."

The next night was the night of moon-dark, the night of one of the more important of the new deity's rituals, and there was a pair of spies watching the streets that led to Temple Row with particular care. Those two pairs of eyes paid particularly close attention to two women making their cautious way through the darkened and deserted streets, muffled head-to-toe in cloaks. Though faint squeals and curses showed that neither of them could see well enough to avoid the rocks and fetid heaps of refuse that dotted the street, they seemed not to wish any kind of light to brighten their path. Gold peeked out from the hoods; the half-seen faces were old before their time; their eyelids drooped with boredom that had become habit, but their eyes revealed a kind of fearful anticipation. Their destination was the Temple of Thalhkarsh. They were intercepted a block away, by two swiftly moving figures who neatly knocked them unconscious and spirited them into a nearby alleyway.

Tarma spat out several unintelligible oaths. The dim light of a heavily shuttered dark-lantern fell on the two bodies at her feet. Beneath the cloaks, the now unconscious women had worn little more than heavy jewelry and a strategically placed veil or two.

"We'll be searched, you can bet on it," she said in disgust. "And where the bloody Hell are we going to hide weapons in these outfits?"

In truth, there wasn't enough cover among the chains and medallions to have concealed even the smallest of her daggers.

"We can't," Kethry replied flatly. "So that leaves—Warrl?"

Tarma pursed her lips. "Hmm. That's a thought. Fur-face, could you carry two swords?"

The *kyree* cocked his head to one side, and experimentally mouthed Need's sheath. Kethry took the blade off and held it for him to take. He swung his head from side to side a little, then dropped the blade.

Not that way, Tarma heard in her mind. *Too clumsy. Won't balance right;*

couldn't run or jump—might get stuck in a tight doorway. I want to be able to bite—these teeth aren't just for decoration, you know! And anyway, I can't carry two blades at the same time in my mouth.

"Could we strap them to you, somehow?"

If you do, I can try how it feels.

Using their belts they managed to strap the blades along his flanks, one on either side, to Warrl's satisfaction. He ran from one end of the alley to the other, then shook himself carefully without dislodging them or getting tangled by them.

It'll work, he said with satisfaction. *Let's go.*

They left their victims sleeping in a dead-end alley; they'd be rather embarrassed when they woke stark-naked in the morning. They'd come to no harm; thanks to Thalhkarsh not even criminals moved about the city by night, and the evening was warm enough that they wouldn't suffer from exposure. Whether or not they'd die of mortification remained to be seen.

The partners left their own clothing hidden in another alley farther on. Muffled in the stolen cloaks, they approached the temple, Warrl a shadow flitting behind them.

On seeing the entrance, Tarma gave a snort of disgust. It was gaudy and decadent in the extreme, with carvings and statuary depicting every vice imaginable (and some she'd never dreamed existed) encrusting the entire front face.

The single guard was a fat, homely man who moved slowly and clumsily, as if he were under the influence of a drug. He seemed little interested in the men who passed him by, other than seeing that they dropped their cloaks and giving them a cursory search for weaponry. The women were another case altogether. Between the preoccupation he was likely to have once he'd seen Kethry and the shadows cast by the carvings in the torchlight, Warrl should have no difficulty in slipping past him.

Kethry touched the swordswoman's arm slightly as they stood in line and nodded toward the guard, giving a little wiggle as she did so. Tarma knew what that meant—Kethry was going to make certain the guard's attention stayed on her. The Shin'a'in dropped her eyelids briefly in assent. When their turn came and they dropped their cloaks, Kethry posed and postured provocatively beneath the guard's searching hands. He was so busy filling his eyes—and greasy paws—with her that he paid scant attention to either Tarma or the shadow that slipped inside behind her.

When he'd delayed long enough that there was considerable grumbling from those waiting their turn behind the two women, he finally let

Kethry pass with real reluctance. They slipped inside the smoke-wreathed portal and found themselves walking down a dark corridor, heavy with the scent of cloying incense. When the corridor ended, they passed through a curtain of some heavy material that moved of itself, as if it sensed their presence, and had a slippery feel and a sour smell to it. Once past that last obstruction, they found themselves blinking in the light of the temple proper.

The interior was almost austere compared with the exterior. The walls were totally bare of ornamentation; the pillars upholding the roof were simple columns and not debauched caryatids. That simplicity left the eye only one place to go—the altar, a massive black slab with manacles at each corner and what could only be blood-grooves carved into its surface.

There was no sign of any bottle.

There *were* huge lanterns suspended from the ceiling and torches in brackets on the pillars, but the walls themselves were in shadow. There were braziers sending plumes of incense into the air on either side of the door. Beneath the too-sweet odor Tarma recognized the taint of *tran*-dust. This was where and how the guard had acquired his dreamy clumsiness. She nudged Kethry and they moved hastily along the wall to a spot where a draft carried fresher air to them. *Tran*-dust was dangerous at best, and could be fatal to them, for it slowed reactions and blurred the senses. They would need both at full sharpness tonight.

There was a drumming and an odd, wild music that was almost more felt than heard. From a doorway behind the altar emerged the High Priest, at this distance, little more than a vague shape in elaborate robes of crimson and gold. Behind him came an acolyte, carrying an object that made Kethry's eyes widen with satisfaction; it was a bottle, red, that glowed dimly from within. The acolyte fitted this into a niche in the foot of the altar near the edge; the place all the blood-grooves drained into.

They worked their way closer, moving carefully along the wall. When they were close enough to make out the High Priest's features, Kethry became aware of his intensely sexual attraction. As if to underscore this, she saw eager devotion written plainly on the face of a woman standing near to the altar-place. She tightened her lips; evidently this was one aspect of domination that both high priest and demon-deity shared. She warded her own mind against beglamorment. Tarma she knew she need not protect; by her very nature as Sword Sworn she would be immune to *this* kind of deception.

A gong began sounding; slowly, insistently. The music increased in tempo; built to a crescendo—a blood-red brightness behind the altar intensified, echoing the rising music. At the climax of both, when the altar was almost too bright to look at, something appeared, pulling all the light and sound into itself.

He was truly beautiful; poisonously beautiful. Compared to him, the priest's attraction was insignificant. The line of women being brought in by two more acolytes ceased their fearful trembling, sighed, and yearned toward him.

He beckoned to one, who literally ran to him, eagerly.

Tarma turned her eyes resolutely away from the spectacle being presented at the altar-place. There was nothing either of them could do to help the intended sacrifice; she was thanking her Goddess that Need was not at Kethry's hand just now. The sorceress had been known once or twice to become a berserker under the blade's influence, and she was not altogether sure how much the sword was capable of in the way of thought. It wasn't mindless—but in a situation like this it was moot whether or not it would prefer the long term goal of destroying the demon as opposed to the short term goal of ending the sacrifice's torment.

At least the rest of the devotees were so preoccupied with the victim and her suffering that they scarcely noticed the two women slowly making their way closer to the altar. Tarma looked closely into one face, and quickly looked away, nauseated. Those glazed eyes—swollen lips—the panting—it would have been obvious even to a child that the man was erotically enraptured by what he was watching. Tarma caught Kethry's eyes a moment; the other nodded, lips tightly compressed. The Shin'a'in swordswoman was past hoping to end this quietly. She had begun to devoutly wish for a chance to cleave a few skulls around here, and she had a shrewd suspicion that Kethry felt the same.

The young High Priest looked up from his work, and saw the anomalous —two women, dressed as devotees, but paying no attention to the rites, and seemingly immune to the magical charisma of Thalhkarsh. They had worked their way nearly to the altar itself.

He looked sharply at them—and noted the fighter's muscles and the faint aura of the god-touched about the thin one, then the unmistakable presence of a warding-spell on the other.

His mind flared with sudden alarm.

He stepped forward once—

He was given no time to act on his suspicions. Tarma saw his alerted glance, and whistled shrilly for Warrl.

From the crowd to the left of her came shouts—then screeches, and the sound of panic. Warrl was covering the distance between himself and Tarma with huge leaps, and was slashing out with his teeth as he did so. The worshipers scrambled to get out of the way of those awful jaws, clearing the last few feet for him. He skidded to a halt beside her; with one hand she snatched Need from her sheath and tossed her to Kethry, with the other she unsheathed her own blade, turning the operation into an expert stroke that took out the two men nearest her. Warrl took his stand, guarding Tarma's back.

Need had sailed sweetly into Kethry's hand, hilt first; she turned her catch into a slash that mirrored Tarma's and cleared space for herself. Then she found herself forced to defend against two sorts of attack; the physical, by the temple guards, and the magical, by the High Priest.

While the demon unaccountably watched, but *did* nothing, the priest forced Kethry back against the wall. As bolts of force crashed against the shield she'd hastily thrown up, Kethry had firsthand proof that his magics had been augmented by the demon. Even so, she was the more powerful magician—but she was being forced to divide her attentions.

Warrl solved the problem; the priest-mage was not expecting a physical attack. Warrl's charge from the side brought him down, and in moments the *kyree* had torn out his throat. That left Kethry free to erect a magical barrier between themselves and reinforcements for the guards they were cutting down. She breathed a prayer of thanks to whatever power might be listening as she did so—thanks that the past few months had required so little of her talents that her arcane armaments and energy reserves were at their height.

Tarma grinned maliciously as a wall of fire sprang up at Kethry's command, cutting them off from the rest of the temple. Now there were only two acolytes, the remaining handful of guards, and the oddly inactive demon to face.

"Hold."

The voice was quiet, yet stirred uneasiness in Tarma's stomach. She tried to move—and found that she couldn't. The guards were utterly motionless, as lifeless as statues. Only the acolytes were able to move, and all *their* attention was on the demon.

His gaze was bent on Kethry.

Tarma heard a rumbling snarl from behind the altar. Before she could try to prevent him, Warrl leaped from the body of the high priest in a suicidal attack on the demon.

Thalkarsh did not even glance in the *kyree's* direction; he intercepted

Warrl's attack with a seemingly negligent backhanded slap. The *kyree* yelped as the hand caught him and sent him crashing into the wall behind Tarma, limp and silent.

"Woman, I could use you." The demon's voice was low and persuasive. "Your knowledge is great, the power you command formidable, and you have infinitely more sense than that poor fool your familiar killed. I could make you a queen among magicians. I would make you *my* consort."

Tarma fumed in impotence as the demon reached for her oathkin.

Kethry's mind bent beneath the weight of the demon's attentions. It was incredibly difficult to think clearly; all her thoughts seemed washed out in the red glare of his gaze. Her enchantments to counter beguilement seemed as thin as silk veils, and about as protective.

"You think me cruel, evil. Yet what ever have I done save to give each of these people what he wants? The women have but to see me to desire me; the men lust for what women I do not care to take—all my worshipers want power. All these things I have given in exchange for worship. Surely that is fair, is it not? It would be cruelty to withhold these things, not cruelty to bestow them."

His voice was reasoned and persuasive. Kethry found herself wavering from what she had until now thought to be the truth.

"Is it the bonds with that scrap of steel that trouble you? Fear not—it would be the work of a single thought to break them. And think of the knowledge that would be yours in the place at my side! Think of the power . . ."

His eyes glowed yet more brightly and seductively, and they filled her vision.

"Think of the pleasure . . ."

Pain lancing across her thoughts woke her from the dreams called up by those eyes. She looked down at the blood trickling along her right hand—she'd clenched it around the bare blade of her sword with enough force to cut her palm. And with the pain came the return of independent thought. Even if everything he said were true, and not the usual truth-twisting demons found so easy, she was not free to follow her own will.

There were other, older promises that bound her. There was the geas she had willingly taken with the fighting-gifts bestowed by Need, and the pledge she had made as a White Winds sorceress to use her powers for the greater good of mankind. And by no means least, there was the vow she had made before all of Liha'irden; pledging Tarma that one day she would take a mate (or mates) and raise a clutch of children to bear the banner and name of Tarma's lost Clan. Only death itself could keep her from fulfilling that vow. And it would kill Tarma should she violate it.

She stared back at the demon's inhuman eyes, defiance written in every fiber.

He flared with anger. "You are the more foolish, then!" he growled—and backhanded her into the wall as casually as he had Warrl.

She was halfway expecting such a move, and managed to relax enough to take the blow limply. It felt rather like being hit with a battering ram, but the semiconsciousness she displayed as she slid into a heap was mostly feigned.

"You will find you have ample leisure to regret your defiance later!" he snarled in the same petulant tones as a thwarted spoiled child.

Now he turned his attentions to Tarma.

"So—the nomad—"

Tarma did her best to simulate a fascination with the demon that she did not in the least feel.

"It seems that I must needs petition the swordswoman. Well enough, it may be that you are even more suitable than your foolish companion."

The heat of his gaze was easily dissipated by the cool armoring of her Goddess that sheathed Tarma's heart and soul. There simply was *nothing* there for the demon to work on; the sensual, emotional parts of her nature had been subsumed into devotion to the Warrior when Tarma had Sworn Sword-Oath. But he couldn't know that—or could he?

At any rate her attempt to counterfeit the same bemused rapture his brides had shown was apparently successful.

"You are no beauty; well, then—look into my eyes, and see the face and body that might be yours as my priestess."

Tarma looked—she dared not look away. His eyes turned mirrorlike; she saw herself reflected in them, then she saw herself change.

The lovely, lithe creature that gazed back at her was still recognizably Tarma—but oh, the differences that a few simple changes made! This was a beauty that was a match for Thalhkarsh's own. For a scant second, Tarma allowed herself to be truly caught by that vision.

The demon felt her waver—and in that moment of weakness, exerted *his* power on the bond that made her Kal'enedral.

And Tarma realized at that instant that Thalhkarsh was truly on the verge of attaining godlike powers, for she felt the bond weaken—

Thalhkarsh frowned at the unexpected resistance he encountered, then turned his full attention to breaking the stubborn strength of the bond.

And that changing of the focus of his attention in turn released Tarma from her entrapment. Not much—but enough for her to act.

Tarma had resisted the demon with every ounce of stubbornness in her soul, augmenting the strength of the bond, but she wasn't blind to what was going on around her.

And to her horror she saw Kethry creeping up on the demon's back, a fierce and stubborn anger in her eyes.

Tarma knew that no blow the sorceress struck would do more than anger Thalhkarsh. She decided to yield the tiniest bit, timing her moment of weakness with care, waiting until the instant Need was poised to strike at the demon's unprotected back.

And as Thalhkarsh's magical grip loosened, her own blade-hand snapped out, hilt foremost, to strike and break the demon's focus-bottle.

At the exact moment Tarma moved, Kethry buried Need to the hilt in the demon's back, as the sound of breaking glass echoed and re-echoed the length and breadth of the temple.

Any one of those actions, by itself, might not have been sufficient to defeat him; but combined—

Thalhkarsh screamed in pain, unanticipated, unexpected, and all the worse for that. He felt at the same moment a good half of his stored power flowing out of him like water from a broken bottle—

—*a broken bottle!*

His focus—was gone!

And pain like a red-hot iron seared through him, shaking him to the roots of his being.

He lost his carefully cultivated control.

His focus was destroyed, and with it, the power he had been using to hold his followers in thrall. And the pain—it could not destroy him, but he was not used to being the recipient of pain. It took him by surprise, and broke his concentration and cost him yet more power.

He lost mastery of his form. He took on his true demonic aspect—as horrifying as he had been beautiful.

And now his followers saw for the first time the true appearance of what they had been calling a god. Their faith had been shaken when he did nothing to save the life of his High Priest. Now it was destroyed by the panic they felt on seeing what he was.

They screamed, turned mindlessly, and attempted to flee.

His storehouse of power was gone. His other power-source was fleeing madly in fear. His focus was destroyed, and he was racked with pain, he who had never felt so much as a tiny pinprick before. Every spell he had woven fell to ruins about him.

Thalhkarsh gave a howling screech that rose until the sound was nearly unbearable; he again slapped Kethry into the wall. Somehow she managed to take her blade with her, but this time her limp unconsciousness as she slid down the wall was not feigned.

He howled again, burst into a tower of red and green flame, and the walls began to shift.

Tarma dodged past him and dragged Kethry under the heavy marble slab of the altar, then made a second trip to drag Warrl under its dubious shelter.

The ground shook, and the remaining devotees rushed in panic-stricken confusion from one hoped-for exit to another. The ceiling groaned with a living voice, and the air was beginning to cloud with a sulfurous fog. Then cracks appeared in the roof, and the trapped worshipers screeched hopelessly as it began to crumble and fall in on them.

Tarma crouched beneath the altar stone, protecting the bodies of Kethry and Warrl with her own—and hoped the altar was strong enough to shelter them as the temple began falling to ruins around them.

It seemed like an eternity, but it couldn't have been more than an hour or two before dawn that they crawled out from under the battered slab, pushing and digging rubble out of the way with hands that were soon cut and bleeding. Warrl did his best to help, but his claws and paws were meant for climbing and clinging, not digging; and besides that, he was suffering from more than one cracked rib. Eventually Tarma made him stop trying to help before he lamed himself.

"Feh," she said distastefully, when they emerged. The stone—or whatever it was—that the building had been made of was rotting away, and the odor was overpowering. She heaved herself wearily up onto the cleaner marble of the altar and surveyed the wreckage about them.

"Gods—to think I wanted to do this quietly! Well, is it gone, I wonder, or did we just chase it away for a while?"

Kethry crawled up beside her, wincing. "I can't tell; there's too many factors involved. I don't *think* Need is a demon-killer, but I don't know everything there is to know about her. Did we get rid of him because he lost the faith of his devotees, because you broke the focus, because of the wound I gave him, or all three? And does it matter? He won't be able to return unless he's called, and I can't imagine anyone wanting to call him, not for a long, long time." She paused, then continued. "You had me frightened, *she'enedra.*"

"Whyfor?"

"I didn't know what he was offering you in return for your services. I was afraid if he could see your heart—"

"He didn't offer me anything I really wanted, dearling. I was never in any danger. All he wanted to give me was a face and figure to match his own."

"But if he'd offered you your Clan and your voice back—" Kethry replied soberly.

"I still wouldn't have been in any danger," Tarma replied with a little more force than she intended. "My people are dead, and no demon could bring them back to life. They've gone on elsewhere and he could never touch them. And without them—" she made a tiny, tired shrug, "—without them, what use is my voice—or for that matter, the most glorious face and body, and all the power in the universe?"

"I thought he had you for a moment—"

"So did he. He was trying to break my bond with the Star-Eyed. What he didn't know was all he was arousing was my disgust. I'd die before I'd give in to something that uses people as casually as *that* thing did."

Kethry got her belt and sheath off Warrl and slung Need in her accustomed place on her hip. Tarma suppressed the urge to giggle, despite pain and weariness. Kethry, in the sorceress' robes she usually wore, and belted with a blade looked odd enough. Kethry, dressed in three spangles and a scrap of cloth and wearing the sword looked totally absurd.

Nevertheless Tarma copied her example. "Well, that damn goatsticker of yours got us into another one we won't get paid for," she said in more normal tones, fastening the buckle so that her sword hung properly on her back. "Bloody Hell! If you count in the ale we had to pour and the bribes we had to pay, we *lost* money on this one."

"Don't be so certain of that, *she'enedra.*" Kethry's face was exhausted and bloodstreaked, one of her eyes was blackened and swelling shut and she had livid bruises all over her body. On top of that she was covered in dust, and filthy, sweat-lank locks of hair were straggling into her face. But despite all of that, her eyes still held a certain amusement. "In case you hadn't noticed, these little costumes of ours are real gold and gems. We happen to be wearing a small fortune in jewelry."

"Warrior's Truth!" Tarma looked a good deal more closely at her scanty attire, and discovered her partner was right. She grinned with real satisfaction. "I guess I owe that damn blade of yours an apology."

"Only," Kethry grinned back, "If we get back into our own clothing before dawn."

"Why dawn?"

"Because that's when the rightful owners of these trinkets are likely to wake up. I don't think they'd let us keep them when we're found here if they know we have them."

"Good point—but why should we want anyone to know *we're* responsible for this mess?"

"Because when the rest of the population scrapes up enough nerve to find out what happened, we're going to be heroines—or at least we will until they find out how many of their fathers and brothers and husbands were trapped here tonight. By then, we'll be long gone. Even if they don't reward us—and they might, for delivering the town from a demon—our reputation has just been made!"

Tarma's jaw dropped as she realized the truth of that. *"Shek,"* she said. "Turn me into a sheep! You're right!" She threw back her head and laughed into the morning sky. *"Now* all we need is the fortune and a king's blessing!"

"Don't laugh, oathkin," Kethry replied with a grin. "We just might get those, and sooner than you think. After all, aren't we demon-slayers?"

Eight

Someone wrote a song about it—but that was later. Much later—when the dust and dirt were gone from the legend. When the sweat and blood were only memories, and the pain was less than that. And when the dead were all but forgotten except to their own.

> "Deep into the stony hills
> Miles from keep or hold,
> A troupe of guards comes riding
> With a lady and her gold.
> Riding in the center,
> Shrouded in her cloak of fur
> Companioned by a maiden
> And a toothless, aged cur."

"And every packtrain we've sent out for the past two months has vanished without a trace—and without survivors," the silk merchant Grumio concluded, twisting an old iron ring on one finger. "Yet the decoy trains were allowed to reach their destinations unmolested. It's uncanny—and if it goes on much longer, we'll be ruined."

In the silence that followed his words, he studied the odd pair of mercenaries before him. He knew very well that *they* knew he was doing so. Eventually there would be no secrets in this room—eventually. But he would parcel his out as if they were bits of his heart—and he knew they would do the same. It was all part of the bargaining process.

Neither of the two women seemed in any great hurry to reply to his speech. The crackle of the fire behind him in this tiny private eating room sounded unnaturally loud in the absence of conversation. Equally loud were the steady whisking of a whetstone on blade-edge, and the muted murmur of voices from the common room of the inn beyond their closed door.

The whetstone was being wielded by the swordswoman, Tarma by name, who was keeping to her self-appointed task with an indifference to Grumio's words that might—or might not—be feigned. She sat across the table from him, straddling her bench in a position that left him mostly with a view of her back and the back of her head. What little he might have been able to see of her face was screened by her unruly shock of coarse black hair. He was just as glad of that; there was something about her cold, expressionless, hawklike face with its wintry blue eyes that sent shivers up his spine. "The eyes of a killer," whispered one part of him. "Or a fanatic."

The other partner cleared her throat and he gratefully turned his attention to her. Now *there* was a face a man could easily rest his eyes on! She faced him squarely, this sorceress called Kethry, leaning slightly forward on her folded arms, placing her weight on the table between them. The light from the fire and the oil lamp on their table fell fully on her. A less canny man than Grumio might be tempted to dismiss her as being very much the weaker, the less intelligent of the two; she was always soft of speech, her demeanor refined and gentle. She was very attractive; sweet-faced and quite conventionally pretty, with hair like the finest amber and eyes of beryl-green. It would have been very easy to assume that she was no more than the swordswoman's vapid tagalong. A lover perhaps—maybe one with the right to those magerobes she wore, but surely of no account in the decision-making.

That would have been the assessment of most men. But as he'd spoken, Grumio had now and then caught a disquieting glimmer in those calm green eyes. She had been listening quite carefully, and analyzing what she heard. He had not missed the fact that she, too, bore a sword. And not for the show of it, either—that blade had a well-worn scabbard that spoke of frequent use. More than that, what he could see of the blade showed that it was well-cared-for.

The presence of that blade in itself was an anomaly; most sorcerers never wore more than an eating knife. They simply hadn't the time—or the inclination—to attempt studying the arts of the swordsman. To Grumio's eyes the sword looked very odd and quite out-of-place, slung over the plain, buff-colored, calf-length robe of a wandering sorceress.

A puzzlement; altogether a puzzlement.

*   *   *

"I presume," Kethry said when he turned to face her, "that the road patrols have been unable to find your bandits."

She had in turn been studying the merchant; he interested her. In his own way he was as much of an anomaly as she and Tarma were. There was muscle beneath the fat of good living, and old sword-calluses on his hands. This was no born-and-bred merchant, not when he looked to be as much retired mercenary as trader. And unless she was wildly mistaken, there was also a sharp mind beneath that balding skull. He knew they didn't come cheaply; since the demon-god affair their reputation had spread, and their fees had become quite respectable. They were even able—like Ikan and Justin—to pick and choose to some extent. On the surface this business appeared far too simple a task—one would simply gather a short-term army and clean these brigands out. *On the surface,* this was no job for a specialized team like theirs—and Grumio surely knew that. It followed then that there was something more to this tale of banditry than he was telling.

Kethry studied him further. Certain signs seemed to confirm this surmise; he looked as though he had not slept well of late, and there seemed to be a shadow of deeper sorrow upon him than the loss of mere goods would account for.

She wondered how much he really knew of them, and she paid close attention to what his answer to her question would be.

Grumio snorted his contempt for the road patrols. "They rode up and down for a few days, never venturing off the Trade Road, and naturally found nothing. Over-dressed, over-paid, under-worked arrogant idiots!"

Kethry toyed with a fruit left from their supper, and glanced up at the hound-faced merchant through long lashes that veiled her eyes and her thoughts. The next move would be Tarma's.

Tarma heard her cue, and made her move. "Then guard your packtrains, merchant, if guards keep these vermin hidden."

He started; her voice was as harsh as a raven's, and startled those not used to hearing it. One corner of Tarma's mouth twitched slightly at his reaction. She took a perverse pleasure in using that harshness as a kind of weapon. A Shin'a'in learned to fight with many weapons, words among them. Kal'enedral learned the finer use of those weapons.

Grumio saw at once the negotiating ploy these two had evidently planned to use with him. The swordswoman was to be the antagonizer, the sorceress the sympathizer. His respect for them rose another notch. Most freelance mercenaries hadn't the brains to count their pay, much less use subtle bargaining tricks. Their reputation was plainly well-founded. He just wished he knew more of them than their reputation; he was woefully short a full hand in this game. Why, he didn't even know where the sorceress hailed from, or what her School was!

Be that as it may, once he saw the trick, he had no intention of falling for it.

"Swordlady," he said patiently, as though to a child, "to hire sufficient force requires we raise the price of goods above what people are willing to pay."

As he studied them further, he noticed something else about them that was distinctly odd. There was a current of communication and understanding running between these two that had him thoroughly puzzled. He dismissed without a second thought the notion that they might be lovers, the signals between them were all wrong for that. No, it was something else, something more complicated than that. Something that you wouldn't expect between a Shin'a'in swordswoman and an out-Clansman—something perhaps, that only someone like he was, with experience in dealing with Shin'a'in, would notice in the first place.

Tarma shook her head impatiently at his reply. "Then cease your inter-house rivalries, *kadessa*, and send all your trains together under a single large force."

A new ploy—now she was trying to anger him a little—to get him off-guard by insulting him. She had called him a *kadessa*, a little grasslands beast that only the Shin'a'in ever saw, a rodent so notoriously greedy that it would, given food enough, eat itself to death; and one that was known for hoarding anything and everything it came across in its nest-tunnels.

Well it wasn't going to work. He refused to allow the insult to distract him. There was too much at stake here. "Respect, Swordlady," he replied with a hint of reproachfulness, "but we tried that, too. The beasts of the train were driven off in the night, and the guards and traders were forced to return afoot. This is desert country, most of it, and all they dared burden themselves with was food and drink."

"Leaving the goods behind to be scavenged. Huh. Your bandits are clever, merchant," the swordswoman replied thoughtfully. Grumio thought he could sense her indifference lifting.

"You mentioned decoy trains?" Kethry interjected.

"Yes, lady." Grumio's mind was still worrying away at the puzzle these two presented. "Only I and the men in the train knew which were the decoys and which were not, yet the bandits were never deceived, not once. We had taken extra care that all the men in the train were known to us, too."

A glint of gold on the smallest finger of Kethry's left hand finally gave him the clue he needed, and the crescent scar on the palm of that hand confirmed his surmise. He knew without looking that that swordswoman would have an identical scar and ring. These two had sworn Shin'a'in blood-oath, the oath of *she'enedran;* the strongest bond known to that notoriously kin-conscious race. The blood-oath made them closer than sisters, closer than lovers—so close they sometimes would think as one. In fact, the word *she'enedran* was sometimes translated as "two-made-one."

"So who was it that passed judgment on your estimable guards?" Tarma's voice was heavy with sarcasm.

"I did, or my fellow merchants, or our own personal guards. No one was allowed on the trains but those who had served us in the past or were known to those who had."

He waited in silence for them to make reply.

Tarma held her blade up to catch the firelight and examined her work with a critical eye. Evidently satisfied, she drove it home in the scabbard slung across her back with a fluid, unthinking grace, then swung one leg back over the bench to face him as her partner did. Grumio found the unflinching chill of her eyes disconcertingly hard to meet for long.

In an effort to find something else to look at, he found his gaze caught by the pendant she wore, a thin silver crescent surrounding a tiny amber flame. That gave him the last bit of information he needed to make everything fall into place—although now he realized that her plain brown clothing should have tipped him off as well, since most Shin'a'in favored wildly-colored garments heavy with bright embroideries. Tarma was a Sworn One, Kal'enedral, pledged to the service of the Shin'a'in Warrior, the Goddess of the New Moon and the South Wind. Only three things were of any import to her at all—her Goddess, her people, and her Clan (which, of course, would include her "sister" by blood-oath). The Sword Sworn were just as sexless and deadly as the weapons they wore.

"So why come to us?" Tarma's expression indicated she thought their time was being wasted. "What makes you think that we can solve your bandit problem?"

"You—have a certain reputation," he replied guardedly.

A single bark of contemptuous laughter was Tarma's only reply.

"If you know our reputation, then you also know that we only take those assignments that—shall we say—interest us," Kethry said, looking wide-eyed and innocent. "What is there about your problem that could possibly be of any interest to *us?*"

Good—they were intrigued, at least a little. Now, for the sake of poor little Lena, was the time to hook them and bring them in. His eyes stung a little with tears he would not shed—not now—not in front of them. Not until she was avenged.

"We have a custom, we small merchant houses. Our sons must remain with their fathers to learn the trade, and since there are seldom more than two or three houses in any town, there is little in the way of choice for them when it comes time for marriage. For that reason, we are given to exchanging daughters of the proper age with our trade allies in other towns, so that our young people can hopefully find mates to their liking." His voice almost broke at the memory of watching Lena waving good-bye from the back of her little mare, but he regained control quickly. It was a poor merchant that could not school his emotions. "There were no less than a dozen sheltered, gently-reared maidens in the very first packtrain they took. One of them was my niece. My only heir, and all that was left of my brother's family after the plague six years ago." He could continue no further.

Kethry's breath hissed softly, and Tarma swallowed an oath.

"Your knowledge of what interests us is very accurate, merchant," Tarma said after a long pause. "I congratulate you."

"You—you accept?" Discipline could not keep hope out of his voice.

"I pray you are not expecting us to rescue your lost ones," Kethry said as gently as she could. "Even supposing that the bandits were more interested in slaves to be sold than their own pleasure—which in my experience is *not* likely—there is very, very little chance that any of them still live. The sheltered, the gentle, well, they do not survive—shock—successfully."

"When we knew that the packtrain had been taken, we sent agents to comb the slave markets. They returned empty-handed," he replied with as much stoicism as he could muster. "We will not ask the impossible of you; we knew when we sent for you there was no hope for them. No, we ask only that you wipe out this vipers' den, to insure that this can *never* happen to us again—that you make such an example of them that no one dares try this again—and that you grant us revenge for what they have done to us!" There—that was his full hand. Would it be enough?

His words—and more, the tight control of his voice—struck echoes from Tarma's own heart. And she did not need to see her partner to know *her* feelings in the matter.

"You will have that, merchant-lord," she grated, giving him the title of respect. "We accept your job—but there are conditions."

"Swordlady, any conditions you would set, I would gladly meet. Who am I to contest the judgment of those who destroyed Tha—"

"Hush!" Kethry interrupted him swiftly, and cast a wary glance over her shoulder. "The less that is said on *that* subject, the better. I am still not altogether certain that what you were about to name was truly destroyed. It may have been merely banished, and perhaps for no great span of time. It is hardly wise if the second case is true to call attention to oneself by speaking Its name."

"Our conditions, merchant, are simple," Tarma continued, outwardly unperturbed. Inwardly she had uneasy feelings about Thalhkarsh, feelings that had her ready to throw herself between Kethry and anything that even *looked* like a demon. "We will, to all appearances, leave on the morrow. You will tell all, including your fellow merchants, that you could not convince us to remain. Tomorrow night, you—and you *alone,* mind— will bring us, at a meeting place of your choosing, a cart and horse. . . ."

Now she raised an inquiring eyebrow at Kethry.

"And the kind of clothing and gear a lady of wealth and blood would be likely to have when traveling. The clothing should fit me. I will be weaving some complicated illusions, and anything I do not have to counterfeit will be of aid to me and make the rest stronger. You might include lots of empty bags and boxes," Kethry finished thoughtfully.

Tarma continued, "The following morning a fine lady will ride in and order you to include her with your next packtrain. You, naturally, will do your best to dissuade her, as loudly and publicly as possible. Now your next scheduled trip was—?"

"Coincidentally enough, for the day after tomorrow." Grumio was plainly impressed. It looked as though he'd decided that Tarma and her partner were even cleverer than he'd thought.

"Good. The less time we lose, the better off we are. Remember, only *you* are to be aware that the lady and the packtrain are not exactly what they seem to be. If you say one word otherwise to anyone—"

The merchant suddenly found himself staring at the tip of a very sharp dagger held a scant inch away from his nose.

"—I will *personally* remove enough of your hide to make both of us slippers." The dagger disappeared from Tarma's hand as mysteriously as it had appeared.

Grumio had been startled, but had not been particularly intimidated; Tarma gave him high marks for that.

"I do not instruct the weaver in her trade," he replied with a certain dignity, "nor do I dictate the setting of a horseshoe to a smith. There is no reason why I should presume to instruct you in your trade either."

"Then you are a rare beast indeed, merchant," Tarma graced him with one of her infrequent smiles. "Most men—oh, not fellow mercenaries, they know better; but most men we deal with—seem to think they know our business better than we simply by virtue of their sex."

The smile softened her harsh expression, and made it less intimidating, and the merchant found himself smiling back. "You are not the only female hire-swords I have dealt with," he replied. "Many of my trade allies have them as personal retainers. It has often seemed to me that many of those I met have had to be twice as skilled as their male counter- parts to receive half the credit."

"A hit, merchant-lord," Kethry acknowledged with open amusement. "And a shrewd one at that. Now, where are we to meet you tomorrow night?"

Grumio paused to think. "I have a farmstead. It's deserted now that the harvest is in. It's just outside of town, at the first lane past the cross- road at the South Trade Road. No one would think it odd for me to pay a visit to it, and the barn is a good place to hide horses and gear."

"Well enough," Tarma replied.

All three rose as one, and Grumio caught the faint clink of brigandine mail from Tarma's direction, though there was no outward sign that she wore any such thing beneath her worn leather tunic, brown shirt and darker breeches.

"Merchant—" Tarma said, suddenly.

He paused halfway through the door.

"I, too, have known loss. You *will* have your revenge."

He shivered at the look in her eyes, and left.

"Well?" Tarma asked, shutting the door behind him and leaning her back up against it.

"Magic's afoot here. It's the only answer to what's been going on. I don't think it's easy to deceive this merchant—he caught on to our 'di- vide and conquer' trick right away. He's no soft money-counter, either."

"I saw the sword-calluses." Tarma balanced herself on one foot, set the other against the door, and folded her arms. "Did he tell us all he knew?"

"I think so. I don't think he held anything back after he played his high card."

"The niece? He also didn't want us to know how much he valued her. Damn. This is a bad piece of business. Poor bastard."

"He'd rather we thought the loss of goods and trade meant more to him," Kethry replied. "They're a secretive lot in many ways, these traders."

"Almost as secretive as sorceresses, no?" One corner of Tarma's thin lips quirked up in a half-smile. The smile vanished as she thought of something else.

"Is there any chance that any of the women survived?"

"Not to put too fine a point upon it, no. *This—"* Kethry patted the hilt of her sword "—would have told me if any of them had. The pull is there, but without the urgency there'd be if there was anyone needing rescue. Still, we need more information, so I might as well add that to the set of questions I intend to ask."

Concern flickered briefly in Tarma's eyes. "An unprepared summoning? Are you sure you want to risk it? If nothing else, it will wear you down, and you have all those illusions to cast."

"I think it's worth it. There aren't that many hostile entities to guard against in this area, and I'll have all night to rest afterward—most of tomorrow as well, once we reach that farmstead. And my 'arsenal' is full, my nonpersonal energies are completely charged, and my other-Planar alliances doing well. It won't be any problem."

"You're the magic-worker," Tarma sighed. "Since we've hired this room for the whole evening, want to make use of it for your magicking? It's bigger than our sleeping room."

At Kethry's nod, Tarma pushed the table into a corner, stacking the benches on top of it, while Kethry set the oil lamp on the mantlepiece. Most of the floorspace was now cleared.

"I'll keep watch on the door." Tarma sat on the floor with her back firmly braced against it. Since it opened inward, the entrance was now solidly guarded against all but the most stubborn of intruders.

Kethry inscribed a circle on the floor with powders from her belt-pouch, chanting under her breath. She used no dramatic or spectacular ceremonies for she had learned her art in a gentler school than the other sorcerers Tarma had seen. Her powers came from the voluntary cooperation of other-Planar entities and she never coerced them into doing her bidding.

There were advantages and disadvantages to this. She need not safeguard herself against the deceptions and treacheries of these creatures, but the cost to her in terms of her own energies expended was correspondingly higher. This was particularly true at times when she had no chance to prepare herself for a summoning. It took a great deal of power to attract a being of benign intent—particularly one that did not have a previous alliance with her—and more to convince it that her intent was good. Hence, the circle—meant not to protect her, but to protect what she would call, so that it would know itself unthreatened.

As she seated herself within the circle, Tarma shifted her own position until she, too, was quite comfortable, removed one of her hidden daggers, and began honing it with her sharpening-stone.

After some time, there was a stirring in the circle Kethry had inscribed, and Tarma pulled her attention away from her task. Something was beginning to form mistily in front of the seated sorceress.

The mist began to revolve into a miniature whirlpool, coalescing into a figure as it did so. As it solidified, Tarma could see what seemed to be a jewel-bright desert lizard, but one that stood erect, like a man. It was as tall as a man's arm is long, and had a cranium far larger than any lizard Tarma had ever seen—except perhaps the image of Gervase that Kethry had used to entertain Liha'irden. Firelight winked from its scales in bands of shining colors, topaz and ruby predominating. It was regarding Kethry with intelligence and wary curiosity.

"Sa-asartha, n'hellan?" it said, tilting its head to one side and fidgeting from one foot to the other. Its voice was shrill, like that of a very young child.

"Vede, sa-asarth," Kethry replied in the same tongue—whatever the tongue was.

The little creature relaxed, and stopped fretting. It appeared to be quite eager to answer all of Kethry's questions. Now that the initial effort of calling it was done with, she had no trouble in obtaining all the information she wanted. Finally she gave the little creature the fruit she'd been toying with after supper. It snatched the gift greedily, trilled what Tarma presumed to be thanks, and vanished into mist again.

When it was completely gone, Kethry rose stiffly and began to scuff the circle into random piles of dirt with the toe of her boot. "It's about what I expected," she said. "Someone—someone with 'a smell of magic about him' according to the *khamsin*—has organized what used to be several small bands of marauders into one large one of rather formidable proportions. They have no set camp, so we can't arrange for their base to be attacked while they're ambushing us, I'm sorry to say. They have no favored ambush point, so we won't know when to expect them. And none of the women—girls, really—survived for more than a day."

"Oh, hell." Tarma's eyes were shadowed. "Well, we didn't really expect anything different."

"No, but you know damn well we both hoped," Kethry's voice was rough with weariness. "It's up to you now, *she'enedra*. You're the tactician."

"Then as the tactician, I counsel rest for you." Tarma caught Kethry's shoulders to steady her as she stumbled a little from fatigue. The reaction to spell-casting was setting in fast, now. Kethry had once described summoning as being "like balancing on a rooftree while screaming an epic poem in a foreign language at the top of your lungs." Small wonder she was exhausted afterward.

The sorceress leaned on Tarma's supporting shoulder with silent gratitude as her partner guided her up the stairs to their rented sleeping room.

"It's us, Warrl," Tarma called softly at the door. A muted growl answered her, and they could hear the sound of the bolt being shoved back. Tarma pushed the door open with one foot, and picked up one of the unlit tallow candles that waited on a shelf just inside with her free hand. She lit it at the one in the bracket outside their door, and the light from it fell on Warrl's head and shoulders. He stood, tongue lolling out in a lupine grin, just inside the room. He sniffed inquisitively at them, making a questioning whine deep in his throat.

"Yes, we took the job—that's our employer you smell, so don't mangle him when he shows up tomorrow night. And Kethry's been summoning, of course, so as usual she's half dead. Close the door behind us while I put her to bed."

By now Kethry was nearly asleep on her feet; after some summonings Tarma had seen her pass into unconsciousness while still walking. Tarma undressed her with the gentle and practiced hands of a nursemaid, and got her safely into bed before she had the chance to fall over. The *kyree,* meanwhile, had butted the door shut with his head and pushed the bolt home with his nose.

"Any trouble?" Tarma asked him.

He snorted with derision.

"Well, I didn't really expect any, either. This is the *quietest* inn I've been in for a long time. The job is bandits, hairy one, and we're all going to have to go disguised. That includes you."

He whined in protest, ears down.

"I know you don't like it, but there's no choice. There isn't enough cover along the road to hide a bird, and I want you close at hand, within a few feet of us at all times, not wandering out in the desert somewhere."

The *kyree* sighed heavily, padded over to her, and laid his heavy head in her lap to be scratched.

"I know. I know," she said, obliging him. "I don't like it any more than you do. Just be grateful that all we'll be wearing is illusions, even if they do make the backs of our eyes itch. Poor Kethry's going to have to ride muffled head-to-toe like a fine lady."

Warrl obviously didn't care about poor Kethry.

"You're being very unfair to her, you know. And you're *supposed* to have been her familiar, not mine. You're a magic beast; born out of magic. You belong with a spell-caster, not some clod with a sword."

Warrl was not impressed with Tarma's logic.

She doesn't need me, he spoke mind-to-mind with the swordswoman. *She has the spirit-sword. You need me, I've told you that before.* And that, so far as Warrl was concerned, was that.

"Well, I'm not going to argue with you. I never argue with anyone with as many sharp teeth as you've got. Maybe being Kal'enedral counts as being magic."

She pushed Warrl's head off her lap and went to open the shutters to the room's one window. Moonlight flooded the room; she seated herself on the floor where it would fall on her, just as she did every night when there was a moon and she wasn't ill or injured. Since they were within the walls of a town and not camped, she would not train this night, but the Moonpaths were there, as always, waiting to be walked. She closed her eyes and found them. Walking them was, as she'd often told Kethry, impossible to describe.

When she returned to her body, Warrl was lying patiently at her back, waiting for her. She ruffled his fur with a grin, stood, stretched stiffened muscles, then stripped to a shift and climbed in beside Kethry. Warrl sighed with gratitude and took his usual spot at her feet.

> "Three things see no end—
> A flower blighted ere it bloomed,
> A message that was wasted
> And a journey that was doomed."

The two mercenaries rode out of town in the morning, obviously eager to be gone. Grumio watched them leave, gazing sadly at the cloud of dust they raised, his houndlike face clearly displaying his disappointment. His fellow merchants were equally disappointed when he told them of his failure to persuade them; they had all hoped the women would be the solution to their problem.

After sundown Grumio took a cart and horse out to his farmstead, a saddled riding beast tied to the rear of it. After making certain that no one had followed him, he drove directly into the barn, and peered around in the hay-scented gloom. A fear crossed his mind that the women had tricked him, and had *truly* left that morning.

"Don't fret yourself, merchant," said a gravelly voice just above his head. He jumped, his heart racing. "We're here."

A vague figure swung down from the loft; when it came close enough for him to make out features, he started at the sight of a buxom blonde wearing the swordswoman's clothing.

She grinned at his reaction. "Which one am I? She didn't tell me. Blonde?"

He nodded, amazed.

"Malebait again. Good choice, no one would ever think I knew what a blade was for. Or that I ever thought of anything but men and clothing, not necessarily in that order. You don't want to see my partner." Her voice was still in Tarma's gravelly tones; Grumio assumed that *that* was only so he'd recognize her. "We don't want you to have to strain your acting ability tomorrow. Did you bring everything we asked for?"

"It's all here," he replied, still not believing what his eyes were telling him. "I weighted the boxes with sand and stones so that they won't seem empty."

"You've got a good head on you, merchant," Tarma saluted him as she unharnessed the horse. "That's something I didn't think of. Best you leave now, though, before somebody comes looking for you."

He jumped down off the wagon, taking the reins of his riding beast.

"And merchant—" she called as he rode off into the night, "—wish us luck."

He didn't have to act the next morning, when a delicate and aristocratically frail lady of obvious noble birth accosted him in his shop, and ordered him (although it was framed as a request) to include her in his packtrain. In point of fact, had he not recognized the dress and fur cloak she was wearing, he would have taken her for a *real* aristo, one who, by some impossible coincidence, had taken the same notion into her head that the swordswoman had proposed as a ruse. This sylphlike, sleepy-eyed creature with her elaborately coiffed hair of platinum silk bore no resemblance at all to the very vibrant and earthy sorceress he'd hired.

And though he was partially prepared by having seen her briefly the night before, Tarma (posing as milady's maid) still gave him a shock. He saw why she called the disguise "malebait"—this amply-endowed blonde was a walking invitation to impropriety, and nothing like the sexless Sworn One. All that remained of Tarma were the blue eyes, one of which winked cheerfully at him, to bring him out of his shock.

* * *

Grumio argued vehemently with the highborn dame for the better part of an hour, and all to no avail. Undaunted, he carried his expostulations out into the street, still trying to persuade her to change her mind even as the packtrain formed up in front of his shop. The entire town was privy to the argument by that time.

"Lady, I beg you—reconsider!" he was saying anxiously. "Wait for the King's Patrol. They have promised to return soon and in force, since the bandits have not ceased raiding us, and I'm morally certain they'll be willing to escort you."

"My thanks for your concern, merchant," she replied with a gentle and bored haughtiness, "but I fear my business cannot wait till their return. Besides, what is there about me that could possibly tempt a bandit?"

Those whose ears were stretched to catch this conversation could easily sympathize with Grumio's silent—but obvious—plea to the gods for patience, as they noted the lady's jewels, fine garments, the weight of the cart holding her possessions, and the well-bred mares she and her maid rode.

The lady turned away from him before he could continue; a clear gesture of dismissal, so he held his tongue. In stony silence he watched the train form up, with the lady and her maid in the center. Since they had no driver for the cart—though he'd offered to supply one—the lead-rein of the carthorse had been fastened to the rear packhorse's harness. Surmounting the chests and boxes in the cart was a toothless old dog, apparently supposed to be guarding her possessions and plainly incapable of guarding anything anymore. The leader of the train's six guards took his final instructions from his master, and the train lurched off down the Trade Road. As Grumio watched them disappear into the distance, he could be seen to shake his head in disapproval.

Had anyone been watching very closely—though no one was—they might have noticed the lady's fingers moving in a complicated pattern. Had there been any mages present—which wasn't the case—said mage might have recognized the pattern as belonging to the Spell of True Sight. If illusion was involved, it would not be blinding Kethry.

> "One among the guardsmen
> Has a shifting, restless eye
> And as they ride, he scans the hills
> That rise against the sky.
> He wears a sword and bracelet
> Worth more than he can afford

And hidden in his baggage
Is a heavy, secret hoard."

One of the guards was contemplating the lady's assets with a glee and greed that equaled his master's dismay. His expression, carefully controlled, seemed to be remote and impassive; only his rapidly shifting gaze and the nervous flicker of his tongue over dry lips gave any clue to his thoughts. Behind those remote eyes, a treacherous mind was making a careful inventory of every jewel and visible possession and calculating their probable values.

When the lady's skirt lifted briefly to display a tantalizing glimpse of white leg, his control broke enough that he bit his lip. *She* was one prize he intended to reserve for himself; he'd never been this close to a high-born woman before, and he intended to find out if certain things he'd heard about bedding them were true. The others were going to have to be content with the ample charms of the serving maid, at least until he'd tired of the mistress. At least there wouldn't be all that caterwauling and screeching there'd been with the merchant wenches. That maid looked as if she'd had a man betwixt her legs plenty of times before, and enjoyed it, too. She'd probably thank him for livening up her life when he turned her over to the men!

He had thought at first that this was going to be another trap, especially after he'd heard that old Grumio had tried to hire a pair of highly-touted mercenary women to rid him of the bandits. One look at the lady and her maid, however, had convinced him that not only was it absurd to think that they could be wary hire-swords in disguise, but that they probably didn't even know which end of a blade to hold. The wench flirted and teased each of the men in turn. Her mind was obviously on something other than ambushes and weaponry—unless those ambushes were amorous, and the weaponry of flesh. The lady herself seemed to ride in a half-aware dream, and her maid often had to break off a flirtation in order to ride forward and steady her in the saddle.

Perhaps she was a *tran*-dust sniffer, or there was *faldis*-juice mixed in with the water in the skin on her saddle-bow. That would be an unexpected bonus; she was bound to have a good supply of it among her belongings, and drugs were worth more than jewels. And it would be distinctly interesting—his eyes glinted cruelly—to have her begging him on her knees for her drugs as withdrawal set in. Assuming, of course, that she survived that long. He passed his tongue over lips gone dry with anticipation. Tomorrow he would give the scouts trailing the packtrain the signal to attack.

"Of three things be wary—
Of a feather on a cat,
The shepherd eating mutton
And the guardsman that is fat."

The lady and her companion made camp a discreet distance from the rest of the caravan, as was only to be expected. She would hardly have a taste for sharing their rough camp, rude talk or coarse food.

Kethry's shoulders sagged with fatigue beneath the weight of her heavy cloak, and she was chilled to the bone in spite of its fur lining.

"Are you all right?" Tarma whispered sharply when she hadn't spoken for several minutes.

"Just tired. I never thought that holding up five illusions would be so *hard*. Three aren't half so difficult to keep intact." She leaned her forehead on one hand, rubbing her temples with cold fingers. "I wish it was over."

Tarma pressed a bowl into her other hand. Dutifully, she tried to eat, but the sand and dust that had plagued their progress all day had crept into the food as well. It was too dry and gritty to swallow easily, and after one attempt, Kethry felt too weary to make any further effort. She laid the bowl aside, unobtrusively—or so she hoped.

Faint hope.

"Sweeting, if you don't eat by yourself, I'm going to pry your mouth open and *pour* your dinner down your throat." Tarma's expression was cloyingly sweet, and the tone of her shifted voice dulcet. Kethry was roused enough to smile a little. When she was this wearied with the exercise of her magics, she had to be bullied into caring for herself. When she'd been on her own, she'd sometimes had to spend days recovering from the damages she'd inflicted on her body by neglecting it. Tarma had her badly worried lately with all the cosseting she'd been doing—like she was trying to keep Kethry wrapped safely in lambswool all the time—but at this moment Kethry was rather glad to have the cosseting. In fact, it was at moments like this that she valued Tarma's untiring affection and aid the most.

"What, and ruin our disguises?" she retorted with a little more life.

"There's nothing at all out of the ordinary in an attentive maid helping her poor, sick mistress to eat. They already think there's something wrong with you. Half of them think you're ill, the other half think you're in a drug-daze," Tarma replied. "They *all* think you've got nothing between your ears but air."

Kethry capitulated, picked up her dinner, and forced it down, grit and all.

"Now," Tarma said, when they'd both finished eating. "I know *you've* spotted a suspect, I can tell by the way you're watching the guards. Tell me which one it is; I'd be very interested to see if it's the same one I've got *my* eye on."

"It's the one with the mouse-brown hair and ratty face that rode tail-guard this morning."

Tarma's eyes widened a little, but she gave no other sign of surprise. "Did you say *brown* hair? And a ratty face? Tailguard this morning had *black* hair and a pouty, babyish look to him."

Kethry revived a bit more. "Really? Are you talking about the one walking between us and their fire right now? The one with all the jewelry? And does he seem to be someone you know very vaguely?"

"Yes. One of the hired swords with the horse-traders my Clan used to deal with—I think his name was Tedric. Why?"

Kethry unbuckled a small ornamental dagger from her belt and passed it to Tarma with exaggerated care. Tarma claimed it with the same caution, caution that was quite justified, since the "dagger" was in reality Kethry's sword Need, no matter what shape it wore at the moment. Beneath the illusion, it still retained its original mass and weight.

"Now look at him."

Tarma cast a surreptitious glance at the guard again, and her lips tightened. Even when it was done by magic, she didn't like being tricked. "Mouse-brown hair and a ratty face," she said. "He changed." She returned the blade to Kethry.

"And now?" Kethry asked, when Need was safely back on her belt.

"Now *that's* odd," Tarma said thoughtfully. "If he's using an illusion, he should have gone back to the way he looked before, but he didn't. He's still mousy and ratty, but my eyes feel funny—like something's pulling at them—and he's blurred a bit around the edges. It's almost as if his face was trying to look different from what I'm seeing."

"Uh-huh. Mind-magic," Kethry said, with satisfaction. "So that's why I wasn't able to detect any spells! It's not a true illusion like I'm holding on us. They practice mind-magic a lot more up north in Valdemar—I think I must have told you about it at some time or other. I'm only marginally familiar with the way it works, since it doesn't operate quite like what I've learned. If what I've been told is true, his mind is telling your mind that you know him, and letting your memory supply an acceptable face. He could very well look like a different person to everyone in the caravan, but since he always looks familiar, any of them would be willing to vouch for him."

"Which is how he keeps sneaking into the pack-trains. He looks different each time, since no one is likely to 'see' a man they know is dead. Very clever. You say this isn't a spell?"

"Mind-magic depends on inborn abilities to work; if you haven't got them, you can't learn it. It's unlike *my* magic, where it's useful to have the Gift, but not necessary. Was he the same one you were watching?"

"He is, indeed. So your True Sight spell works on this 'mind-magic' too?"

"Yes, thank the gods. I'm glad now I didn't rely on mage-sight; he would have fooled that. What tipped you off to him?"

"Nothing terribly obvious, just a lot of little things that weren't quite right for the ordinary guard he's pretending to be. His sword is a shade too expensive. His horse has been badly misused, but he's a gelding of very good lines; he's of much better breeding than a common guard should own. And lastly, he's wearing jewelry he can't afford."

Kethry looked puzzled. "Several of the other guards are wearing just as much. I thought most hired swords wore their savings."

"So they do. Thing is, of the others, the only ones with as much or more are either the guard-chief, or ones wearing mostly brass and glass; showy, meant to impress village tarts, but worthless. His is all real, and the quality is high. Too damned high for the likes of him."

"Now that we know who to watch, what do we do?"

"We wait," Tarma replied with a certain grim satisfaction. "He'll have to signal the rest of his troupe to attack us sooner or later, and one of us should be able to spot him at it. With luck and the Warrior on our side, we'll have enough warning to be ready for them."

"I hope it's sooner." Kethry sipped at the well-watered wine which was all she'd allow herself when holding spells in place. Her eyes were heavy, dry, and sore. "I'm not sure how much longer I can hold up my end."

"Then go to sleep, dearling," Tarma's voice held an unusual gentleness, a gentleness only Kethry, Warrl, and small children ever saw. "Furface and I can take turns on nightwatch; you needn't take a turn at all."

Kethry did not need further urging, but wrapped herself up in her cloak and a blanket, pillowed her head on her arm and fell asleep with the suddenness of a tired puppy. The illusions she'd woven would remain intact even while she slept. Only three things could cause them to fail. They'd break if she broke them herself, if the pressure of spells from a greater sorcerer than she were brought to bear on them, or if she died.

Her training had been arduous, and quite thorough; as complete in its way as Tarma's sword training had been.

Seeing her shiver in her sleep, Tarma built up the fire with a bit more dried dung (the leavings of previous caravans were all the fuel to be found out here) and covered her with the rest of the spare blankets. The illusions were draining energy from Kethry, and she got easily chilled; Tarma didn't expect to need the other coverings. She knew *she'd* be quite comfortable with one blanket and her cloak; and if that didn't suffice, Warrl made an excellent "bedwarmer."

Warrior, guard her back, she prayed, as she had every night lately. *I can guard my own—but keep her safe.*

But the night passed uneventfully, despite Tarma's vague worries.

Morning saw them riding deeper into the stony hills that ringed the desert basin they'd spent the day before passing through. The road was considerably less dusty now, but the air held more of a chill. Both Tarma and Kethry tried to keep an eye on their suspect guard, and shortly before noon their vigilance was rewarded. Both of them saw him flashing the sunlight off his armband in what could only be a deliberate series of signals.

> "From ambush, bandits screaming
> Charge the packtrain and its prize
> And all but four within the train
> Are taken by surprise
> And all but four are cut down
> Like a woodsman fells a log
> The guardsman, and the lady,
> And the maiden and the dog.
> Three things know a secret—
> First; the lady in a dream;
> The dog that barks no warning
> And the maid that does not scream."

Even with advance warning, they hadn't much time to ready themselves.

Bandits charged the packtrain from both sides of the road, screaming at the tops of their lungs. The guards were taken completely by surprise. The three apprentice traders accompanying the train flung themselves down on their faces as their master Grumio had ordered them to do in hopes that they'd be overlooked. To the bandit master at the rear of the train, it seemed that once again all had gone completely according to plan.

Until Kethry broke her illusions.

> "Then off the lady pulls her cloak—
> In armor she is clad
> Her sword is out and ready
> And her eyes are fierce and glad
> The maiden gestures briefly
> And the dog's a cur no more.
> A wolf, sword-maid, and sorceress
> Now face the bandit corps!
> Three things never anger,
> Or you will not live for long—
> A wolf with cubs, a man with power,
> And a woman's sense of wrong."

The brigands at the forefront of the pack found themselves facing something they hadn't remotely expected. Gone were the helpless, frightened women on high-bred steeds too fearful to run. In their place sat a pair of well-armed, grim-faced mercenaries on schooled warbeasts. With them was an oversized and very hungry-looking *kyree.*

The pack of bandits milled, brought to a halt by this unexpected development.

Finally one of the bigger ones growled a challenge at Tarma, who only grinned evilly at him. Kethry saluted them with mocking gallantry—and the pair moved into action explosively.

They split up and charged the marauders, giving them no time to adjust to the altered situation. The bandits had hardly expected the fight to be carried to *them,* and reacted too late to stop them. Their momentum carried them through the pack and up onto the hillsides on either side of the road. Now *they* had the high ground.

Kethry had drawn Need, whose magic was enabling her to keep herself intact long enough to find a massive boulder to put her back against. The long odds were actually favoring the two of them for the moment, since the bandits were mostly succeeding only in getting in each other's way. Obviously they had not been trained to fight together, and had done well so far largely because of the surprise with which they'd attacked and their sheer numbers. Once Kethry had gained her chosen spot, she slid off her horse, and sent it off with a slap to its rump. The mottled, huge-headed beast was as ugly as a piece of rough granite, and twice as tough, but she was a Shin'a'in-bred and trained warsteed, and worth the weight in silver of the high-bred mare she'd been spelled to resemble. Now that Kethry was on the ground, she'd attack anything whose scent she didn't recognize—and quite probably kill it.

Warrl came to her side long enough to give her the time she needed to transfer her sword to her left hand and begin calling up her more arcane offensive weaponry.

In the meantime, Tarma was in her element, cutting a bloody swath through the bandit horde with a fiercely joyous gleam in her eyes. She clenched her mare's belly with viselike legs; only one trained in Shin'a'in-style horse-warfare from childhood could possibly have stayed with the beast. The mare was laying all about her with iron-shod hooves and enormous yellow teeth; neither animal nor man was likely to escape her once she'd targeted him. She had an uncanny sense for anyone trying to get to her rider by disabling her; once she twisted and bucked like a cat on hot metal to simultaneously crush the bandit in front of her while kicking in the teeth of the one that had thought to hamstring her from the rear. She accounted for at least as many of the bandits as Tarma did.

Tarma saw Kethry's mare rear and slash out of the corner of her eye; the saddle was empty—

She sent a brief, worried thought at Warrl.

Guard yourself, foolish child; she's doing better than you are! came the mental rebuke. Tarma grimaced, realizing she should have known better. The bond of *she'enedran* made them bound by spirit, and she'd have *known* if anything was wrong. Since the mare was fighting on her own, Kethry must have found someplace high enough to see over the heads of those around her.

As if to confirm this, things like ball-lightning began appearing and exploding, knocking bandits from their horses, clouds of red mist began to wreath the heads of others (who clutched their throats and turned interesting colors), and oddly formed creatures joined Warrl at harrying and biting at those on foot.

When *that* began, especially after one spectacular fireball left a pile of smoking ash in place of the bandit's second-in-command, it was more than the remainder of the band could stand up to. Their easy prey had turned into hellspawn, and there was *nothing* that could make them stay to face anything more. The ones that were still mounted turned their horses out of the melee and fled for their lives. Tarma and the three surviving guards took care of the rest.

As for the bandit chief, who had sat his horse in stupified amazement from the moment the fight turned against them, he suddenly realized his own peril and tried to escape with the rest. Kethry, however, had never once forgotten him. Her bolt of power—intended this time to stun, not kill—took him squarely in the back of the head.

> "The bandits growl a challenge,
> But the lady only grins.
> The sorceress bows mockingly,
> And then the fight begins
> When it ends there are but four
> Left standing from that horde—
> The witch, the wolf, the traitor,
> And the woman with the sword.
> Three things never trust in—
> The maiden sworn as pure,
> The vows a king has given
> And the ambush that is 'sure.' "

By late afternoon the heads of the bandits had been piled in a grisly cairn by the side of the road as a mute reminder to their fellows of the eventual reward of banditry. Their bodies had been dragged off into the hills for the scavengers to quarrel over. Tarma had supervised the cleanup, the three apprentices serving as her workforce. There had been a good deal of stomach-purging on their part at first—especially after the way Tarma had casually lopped off the heads of the dead or wounded bandits—but they'd obeyed her without question. Tarma had had to hide her snickering behind her hand, for they looked at her whenever she gave them a command as though they feared that *their* heads might well adorn the cairn if they lagged or slacked.

She herself had seen to the wounds of the surviving guards, and the burial of the two dead ones.

One of the guards could still ride; the other two were loaded into the now-useless cart after the empty boxes had been thrown out of it. Tarma ordered the whole caravan back to town; she and Kethry planned to catch up with them later, after some unfinished business had been taken care of.

Part of that unfinished business was the filling and marking of the dead guards' graves.

Kethry brought her a rag to wipe her hands with when she'd finished. "Damn. I wish—oh, hellspawn; they were just honest hired swords," she said, looking at the stone cairns she'd built with remote regret. "It wasn't *their* fault we didn't have a chance to warn them. Maybe they shouldn't have let themselves be surprised like that, not with what's been happening to the packtrains lately—but still, your life's a pretty heavy price to pay for a little carelessness. . . ."

Kethry, her energy back to normal now that she was no longer being drained by her illusions, slipped a sympathetic arm around Tarma's shoulders. "Come on, *she'enedra*. I want to show you something that might make you feel a little better."

While Tarma had gone to direct the cleanup, Kethry had been engaged in stripping the bandit chief down to his skin and readying his unconscious body for some sort of involved sorcery. Tarma knew she'd had some sort of specific punishment in mind from the time she'd heard about the stolen girls, but she'd had no idea of what it was.

> "They've stripped the traitor naked
> And they've whipped him on his way
> Into the barren hillsides,
> Like the folk he used to slay.
> They take a thorough vengeance
> For the women he's cut down
> And then they mount their horses
> And they journey back to town.
> Three things trust and cherish well—
> The horse on which you ride,
> The beast that guards and watches
> And your sister at your side!"

Now before her was a bizarre sight. Tied to the back of one of the bandit's abandoned horses was—apparently—the unconscious body of the highborn lady Kethry had spelled herself to resemble. She was clad only in a few rags, and had a bruise on one temple, but otherwise looked to be unharmed.

Tarma circled the tableau slowly. There was no flaw in the illusion, if indeed it was an illusion.

"Unbelievable," she said at last. "That *is* him, isn't it?"

"Oh, yes, indeed. One of my best pieces of work."

"Will it hold without you around to maintain it?"

"It'll hold all right," Kethry replied with deep satisfaction. "That's part of the beauty and the justice of the thing. The illusion is irretrievably melded with his own mind-magic. He'll never be able to break it himself, and no reputable sorcerer will break it for him. And I promise you, the only sorcerers for weeks in any direction are quite reputable."

"Why wouldn't he be able to get one to break it for him?"

"Because I've signed it." Kethry made a small gesture, and two symbols appeared for a moment above the bandit's head. One was the symbol Tarma knew to be Kethry's sigil, the other was the glyph for "Justice." "Any attempt to probe the spell will make *those* appear. I doubt that anyone will ignore the judgment sign, and even if they were inclined to, I think my reputation is good enough to make most sorcerers think twice about undoing what I've done."

"You really didn't change him, did you?" Tarma asked, a horrible thought occurring to her. "I mean, if he's *really* a woman now . . ."

"Bright Lady, what an awful paradox we'd have!" Kethry laughed, easing Tarma's mind considerably. "We punish him for what he's done to women by turning him into a woman—but as a woman, we'd now be honor-bound to protect him! No, don't worry. Under the illusion—and it's a *very* complete illusion, by the way, it extends to all senses—he's still quite male."

She gave the horse's rump a whack, breaking the light enchantment that had held it quiet, and it bucked a little, scrabbling off into the barren hills.

"The last of the band went that way," she said, pointing after the beast, "And the horse he's on will follow their scent back to where they've made their camp. Of course, none of his former followers will have any notion that he's anything other than what he appears to be."

A wicked smile crept across Tarma's face. It matched the one already curving Kethry's lips.

"I wish I could be there when he arrives," Tarma said with a note of viciousness in her harsh voice. "It's *bound* to be interesting."

"He'll certainly get *exactly* what he deserves." Kethry watched the horse vanish over the crest of the hill. "I wonder how he'll like being on the receiving end?"

"I know somebody who *will* like this—and I can't wait to see his face when you tell him."

"Grumio?"

"Mm-hmm."

"You know," Kethry replied thoughtfully, "this was almost worth doing for free."

"*She'enedra!*" Tarma exclaimed in mock horror. "Your misplaced honor will have us starving yet! We're *supposed* to be mercenaries!"

"I said *almost.*" Kethry joined in her partner's gravelly laughter. "Come on. We've got pay to collect. You know—this just might end up as some bard's song."

"It might at that," Tarma chuckled. "And what will you bet me that he gets the tale all wrong?"

"Not only that—but given bards, I can almost guarantee that it will only get worse with age."

Nine

The aged, half-blind mage blinked confused, rheumy eyes at his visitor. The man—or was it woman?—looked as awful as the mage felt. Bloodshot and dark-circled eyes glared at him from under the concealing shelter of a moth-eaten hood and several scarves. A straggle of hair that looked first to be dirty mouse-brown, then silver-blond, then brown again, strayed into those staring eyes. Nor did the eyes stay the same from one moment to the next; they turned blue, then hazel, then back to amethyst-blue. Try as he would, the mage could not make his own eyes focus properly, and light from a lanthorn held high in one of the visitor's hands was doing nothing to alleviate his befuddlement. The mage had never seen a human that presented such a contradictory appearance. She (he?) was a shapeless bundle of filthy, lice-ridden rags; what flesh there was to be seen displayed the yellow-green of healing bruises. Yet he had clearly seen gold pass to the hands of his landlord when that particular piece of human offal had unlocked the mage's door. Gold didn't come often to this part of town—and it came far less often borne by a hand clothed in rags.

He (she?) had forced his (her?) way into the verminous garret hole that was all the mage could call home now without so much as a by-your-leave, shouldering the landlord aside and closing the door firmly afterward. So this stranger was far more interested in privacy than in having the landlord there as a possible backup in case the senile wizard proved recalcitrant. That was quite enough to bewilder the mage, but the way his visitor kept shifting from male to female and back again was bidding fair to dizzy what few wits still remained to him and was nearly leaving him too muddled to speak.

Besides that, the shapeshifting was giving him one gods-awful headache.

"Go 'way—" he groaned feelingly, shadowing his eyes both from the unsettling sight and from the too-bright glare of the lanthorn his visitor still held aloft. "—leave an old man alone! I haven't got a thing left to steal—"

He was all too aware of his pitiful state; his robe stained and frayed, his long gray beard snarled and unkempt, his eyes so bloodshot and yellowed that no one could tell their color anymore. He was housed in an equally pitiful manner; this garret room had been rejected by everyone, no matter how poor, except himself; it was scarcely better than sleeping in the street. It leaked when it rained, turned into an oven in summer and a meat-locker in winter, and the wind whistled through cracks in the walls big enough to stick a finger in. His only furnishings were a pile of rags that served as a bed, and a rickety stool. Beneath him he could feel the ramshackle building swaying in the wind, and the movement was contributing to his headache. The boards of the walls creaked and complained, each in a different key. He knew he should have been used to it by now, but he wasn't; the crying wood rasped his nerves raw and added mightily to his disorientation. The multiple drafts made the lanthorn flame flicker, even inside its glass chimney. The resulting dancing shadows didn't help his befuddlement.

"I'm not here to *steal,* old fraud."

Even the voice of the visitor was a confusing amalgam of male and female.

"I've brought you something."

The other hand emerged from the rags, bearing an unmistakable emerald-green bottle. The hand jiggled the bottle a little, and the contents sloshed enticingly. The rags slipped, and a trifle more of his visitor's face was revealed.

But the mage was only interested now in the bottle. Lethe! He forgot his perplexity, his befogged mind, and his headache as he hunched forward on his pallet of decaying rags, reaching eagerly for the bottle of drug-wine that had been his downfall. Every cell ached for the blessed/damned touch of it—

"Oh, no." The visitor backed out of reach, and the mage felt the shame of weak tears spilling down his cheeks. "*First* you give me what I want, *then* I give you this."

The mage sagged back into his pile of rags. "I have nothing."

"It's not what you have, old fraud, it's what you *were.*"

"What . . . I . . . was. . . ."

"You *were* a mage, and a good one—or so they claim. That was before you let *this* stuff rob you of your wits until they cast you out of the Guild to rot. But there damn well ought to be enough left of you for my purposes."

By steadfastly looking, not at the visitor, but at the bottle, the mage was managing to collect his scattering thoughts. "What purpose?"

The visitor all but screamed his answer. *"To take off this curse, old fool! Are your wits so far gone you can't even see what's in front of you?"*

A curse—of course! No wonder his visitor kept shifting and changing! It wasn't the person that was shifting, but his *own* sight, switching erratically between normal vision and mage-sight. Normal vision showed him the woman; when the rags slipped a little more, she seemed to be a battered, but still lovely little toy of a creature—amethyst-eyed and platinum-haired—

Mage-sight showed him an equally abused but far from lovely man; sallow and thin, battered, but by no means beaten—a man wearing the kind of smoldering scowl that showed he was holding in rage by the thinnest of bonds.

So the "curse" could only be illusion, but a very powerful and carefully cast illusion. There was something magic-smelling about the man-woman, too; the illusion was linked to and being fueled by that magic. The mage furrowed his brow, then tested the weave of the magic that formed the illusion. It was a more than competent piece of work; and it was complete to all senses. It was far superior to anything the mage had produced even in his best days. In his present condition—to duplicate it so that he could lay new illusion over old would be impossible; to turn it or transfer it beyond even his former level of skill. He never even considered trying to take it off. To break it was beyond the best mage in Oberdorn, much less the broken-down wreck he had become.

Eyeing the bottle with passionate longing and despair, he said as much.

To his surprise the man accepted the bad news with a nod. "That's what they told me," he said. "But they told me something else. What a human mage couldn't break, a demon might."

"A . . . demon?" The mage licked his lips; the bottle of Lethe was again within his grasp. "I used to be able to summon demons. I still could, I think. But it wouldn't be easy." That was untrue; the summoning of demons had been one of his lesser skills. It was still easily within his capabilities. But it required specialized tools and ingredients he no longer had the means to procure. And it was proscribed by the Guild. . . .

He'd tried to raise a minor impling to steal him Lethe-wine when his money had run out; that was when the Guild had discovered what he'd fallen prey to. That was the main reason they'd cast him out, destroying his tools and books; a mage brought so low as to use his skills for personal theft was no longer trustworthy. Especially not one that could summon demons. Demons were clever and had the minds of sharp lawyers when it came to wriggling out of the bonds that had been set on them; that was why raising them was proscribed for any single mage of the Guild, and doubly proscribed for one who might have doubts as to his own mental competence at the time of the conjuration.

Of course, he was no longer bound by Guild laws since he was outcaste. And if this stranger could provide the wherewithal, the tools and the supplies, it could be easily done.

"Just tell me what you need, old man—I'll get it for you." The haggard, grimy face was avid, eager. "You bring me a demon to break this curse, and the bottle's yours."

Two days later, they stood in the cellar of the old, rotten mansion whose garret the mage called home. The cellar was in no better repair than the rest of the house; it was moldy and stank, and water-marks on the walls showed why no one cared to live there. Not only did the place flood every time it rained, but moisture was constantly seeping through the walls, and water trickled down from the roof-cisterns to drip from the beams overhead. Bright sparks of light glinted just beyond the circle of illumination cast by the lanthorn, the gleaming eyes of starveling rats and mice, perched curiously on the decaying shelves that clung to the walls. The scratching of their claws seemed to echo the scratching of the mage's chalks on the cracked slate floor.

The man-woman sat impatiently on the remains of a cask off to one side, careful not to disturb the work at hand. It had already cost him dearly—in gold and blood. Some of the things the mage had demanded had been bought, but most had been stolen. The former owners were often no longer in a condition to object to the disposition of their property.

From time to time the mage would glance searchingly up at him, make a tiny motion with his hand, frown with concentration, then return to his drawing.

After the fourth time this had happened, the stranger wet his lips with

a nervous tongue, and asked, "Why do you keep doing that? Looking at me, I mean."

The mage blinked and stood up slowly, his back aching from the strain of staying bent over for so long. His red-rimmed, teary eyes focused to one side of the man, for he still found it difficult to look directly at him.

"It's the spell that's on you," he replied after a moment to collect his thoughts. "I don't know of a demon strong enough to break a spell that well made."

The man jumped to his feet, reaching for a sword he had left back in the mage's room because the old man had warned him against bearing cold steel into a demon's presence. "You old bastard!" he snarled. "You told me—"

"I told you I could call one—and I can. I just don't *know* one. Your best chance is if I can call a demon with a specific grudge against the maker of the spell—"

"What if there isn't one?"

"There will be," the mage shrugged. "Anyone who goes about laying curses like yours and leaving justice-glyphs behind to seal them is bound to have angered either a demon or someone who commands one. At any rate, since you want to know, I've been testing the edges of your curse to make the magerune appear. I'm working that into the summoning. Since I don't know *which* demon to call, the summoning will take longer than usual to bear fruit, but the results will be the same. The demon will appear, one with a reason to help you, and you'll bargain with it for the breaking of your curse."

"Me?" The stranger was briefly taken aback. "Why me? Why not you?"

"Because it isn't my curse. *I* don't give a damn whether it's broken or not. I told you I'd summon a demon—I didn't say I'd bind him. That takes more skill—and certainly more *will*—than I possess anymore. My bargain with you was simple—one demon, one bottle of Lethe. Once it's here, you can do your own haggling."

The man smiled; it was far more of a grimace than an expression of pleasure. "All right, old fraud. Work your spell. I'd sooner trust *my* wits than yours anyway."

The mage returned to his scribbling, filling the entire area lit by the lanthorn suspended overhead with odd little drawings and scrawls that first pulled, then repelled the eyes. Finally he seemed satisfied, gathered his stained, ragged robes about him with care, and picked a dainty path through the maze of chalk. He stood up straight just on the border of the

inscriptions, raised his arms high, and intoned a peculiarly resonant chant.

At that moment, he bordered on the impressive—though the effect was somewhat spoiled by the water dripping off the beams of the ceiling, falling onto his balding head and running off the end of his long nose.

The last syllable echoed from the dank walls. The man-woman waited in anticipation.

Nothing happened.

"Well?" the stranger said with slipping patience, "Is that all there is to it?"

"I told you it would take time—perhaps as much as an hour. Don't fret yourself, you'll have your demon."

The mage cast longing glances at the shadow-shrouded bottle on the floor beside his visitor as he mopped his head with one begrimed, stained sleeve.

The woman-man noted the direction his attention was laid, thought for a moment, weighing the mage's efforts, and smiled mirthlessly. "All right, old fraud—I guess you've earned it. Come and get it."

The mage didn't wait for a second invitation, or give the man-woman a chance to take the reluctant consent back. He scrambled forward, tripping over the tattered edges of his robes, and sagged to his knees as he snatched the bottle greedily.

He had it open in a trice, and began sucking at the neck like a calf at the udder, eyes closing and face slackening in mindless ecstasy. Within moments he was near-collapsing to the floor, half-empty bottle cradled in his arms, oblivion in his eyes.

His visitor walked over with a softly sinister tread and prodded him with a toe. "You'd better have worked this right, you old bastard," he muttered, "Or you won't be waking—"

His last words were swallowed in the sudden roar, like the howl of a tornado, that rose without warning behind him. As he spun to face the area of inscriptions, that whole section of floor burst into sickening blood-red and hellish green flame; flame that scorched his face, though it did nothing to harm the beams of the ceiling. He jumped back, frightened in spite of his bold resolutions to fear nothing.

But before he touched the ground again, a monstrous, clawed hand formed itself out of the flame and slapped him back against the rear wall of the cellar. A second hand, the color of molten bronze, reached for the oblivious mage.

A face worse than anything from the realm of nightmare materialized from the flame between the two hands. A neck, arms, and torso followed.

The hands brought the mage within the fire—the visitor coughed on the stench of the old man's robes and beard scorching. There was no doubt that the fire was *real,* no matter that it left the ceiling intact. The mage woke from his drugged trance, screaming in mindless pain and terror. The smell of his flesh and garments burning was spreading through the cellar, and reached even to where the man-woman lay huddled against the dank wall; he choked and gagged at the horrible reek.

And the thing in the flames calmly bit the mage's head off, like a child with a gingerbread mannikin.

It was too much for even the man-woman to endure. He rolled to one side and puked up the entire contents of his stomach. When he looked up again, eyes watering and the taste of bile in his mouth, the thing was staring at him, licking the blood off its hands.

He swallowed as his gorge rose again, and waited for the thing to take him for dessert.

"You smell of magic." The thing's voice was like a dozen bells ringing; bells just slightly out-of-tune with one another. It made the man-woman nauseous and disoriented, but he swallowed again and tried to answer.

"I . . . have a curse."

"So I see. I assume that was why I was summoned here. Well, unless we enter into an agreement, I have no choice but to remain here or return to the Abyssal Planes. Talk to me, puny one; I do not desire the latter."

"How—why did you—the old man—"

"I dislike being coerced, and your friend made the mistake of remaining within reach of the circle. But I have, as yet, no quarrel with you. I take it you wish to be rid of what you bear. Will you bargain to have your curse broken? What can you offer me?"

"Gold?"

The demon laughed, molten-gold eyes slitted. "I have more than that in mind."

"Sacrifice? Death?"

"I can have those intangibles readily enough on my own—starting with yours. *You* are within my reach also."

The man-woman thought frantically. "The curse was cast by one you have reason to hate."

"This should make me love *you?*"

"It should make us allies, at least. I could offer revenge—"

"Now you interest me." The demon's eyes slitted. "Come closer, little man."

The man-woman clutched his rags about himself and ventured nearer, step by cautious step.

"A quaint curse. Why?"

"To make me a victim. It succeeded. It was not intended that I survive the experience."

"I can imagine." A cruel smile parted the demon's lips. "A pretty thing you are; didn't care for being raped, hmm?"

The man-woman's face flamed. He felt the demon inside of his mind, picking over all of his memories of the past year, lingering painfully over several he'd rather have died than seen revealed. Anger and shame almost replaced his fear.

The demon's smile grew wider. "Or did you begin to care for it after all?"

"Get out of my mind, you bastard!" He stifled whatever else he had been about to scream, wondering if he'd just written his own death-glyph.

"I think I like you, little man. How can you give me revenge?"

He took a deep breath, and tried to clear his mind. "I know where they are, the sorceress and her partner. I know how to lure them here—and I have a plan to take them when they come—"

"I have *many* such plans—but I did not know how to bring them within my grasp. Good." The demon nodded. "I think perhaps we have a bargain. I shall give you the form you need to make you powerful against them, and I shall let you bring them here. Come, and I will work the magic to change you, and free myself with the sealing of our bargain. I must touch you—"

The man-woman approached the very edge of the flames, cautious and apprehensive in spite of the demon's assurance that he would bargain. He still did not entirely trust this creature—and he more than certainly still feared its power. The demon reached out with one long, molten-bronze talon, and briefly caressed the side of his face.

The stranger screamed in agony, for it felt as if that single touch had set every nerve afire. He wrapped his arms over his head and face, folded slowly at the waist and knees, still crying out; and finally collapsed to the floor, huddled in his rags, quivering. Had there been anything left in his stomach, he would have lost it then.

The demon waited, as patient as a snake, drinking in the tingles of power and the heady aura of agony that the man was exuding. He bent over the shaking pile of rags in avid curiosity, waiting for the moment when the pain of transformation would pass. His expression was oddly human—the same expression to be seen on the face of a cruel child watching the gyrations of a beetle from which it has pulled all the legs but one.

The huddled, trembling creature at the edge of his flames slowly regained control of itself. The quivering ceased; rags rose a little, then moved again with more purpose. Long, delicate arms appeared from the huddle, and pushed away from the floor. The rags fell away, and the rest of the stranger was revealed.

The visitor raised one hand to her face, then froze at the sight of that hand. She pushed herself into a more upright position, frowning and shaking her head; she examined the other hand and felt of her face as her expression changed to one of total disbelief. Frantic now, she tore away the rags that shrouded her chest and stared in horror at two lovely, lily-white—and very female—breasts.

"No—" she whispered, "—it's not possible—"

"Not for a human perhaps," the demon replied with faint irony, "But I am not subject to a human's limitations."

"What have you *done* to me?" she shrieked, even her voice having changed to a thin soprano.

"I told you, I would give you a form that would make you powerful against them. The sorceress' geas prevents her from allowing any harm to befall a woman—so I merely made you woman in reality, to match the woman you were in illusion. They will be powerless against you now, your enemies and mine—"

"But I am *not* a woman! I *can't* be a woman!" She looked around her for something to throw at the demon's laughing face, and finding nothing, hurled curses instead. "Make me a man again, damn you! Make me a *man!*"

"Perhaps. Later, perhaps. When you have earned a boon from me. You still retain your strength and your weapon's expertise. Only the swordswoman could be any danger to you now, and the sorceress will be bound to see that she cannot touch you. *My* bargain now, bandit." The demon smiled still wider. "Serve me, and it may well be I shall make you a man again. But your new body serves me far better than your old would have. And meanwhile—"

He drew a swirl of flame about himself. When he emerged from it, he had assumed the shape of a handsome human man, quite naked; one whose beauty repulsed even as it attracted. He was still larger than a normal human in every regard, but he no longer filled a quarter of the cellar. He stepped confidently across the boundaries of the circle, reached forward and gathered the frozen woman to him. She struggled wildly; he delighted in her struggles.

"Oh, you make a charming wench, little toy; you play the part as if you had been born to it! A man would have sought to slay me, but you think only to flee. And I do not think a man would have guessed my intentions, but *you* have, haven't you, little one. I think I can teach you some of the pleasures of being a female, as well as the fears, hmm? Perhaps I can make you forget you ever were anything else—"

His laughter echoed through the entire house—but the rest of the inhabitants did no more than check the fastenings of their doors and return to the safety of their beds, hoping that whatever it was that was laughing would overlook *them.*

With another gesture, the demon transformed the bleak basement into a setting from a whore's nightmare; with his other hand he held his victim crushed against his chest while he reached into her mind with his.

She gasped in shock and dismay, feeling her will crumble before his, feeling him take over her senses, and feeling those senses rousing as he wished them to. He ran his hands over her body, stripping away the rags until she was as nude as he, and in the wake of his hands her skin burned with fever she could not repress.

As the last remains of her will fell to dust before his onslaught, her body, too, betrayed her; responding as the demon desired.

And at the end, she did, indeed, forget for that one moment what it had been like to be a man.

Kethry twined a lock of amber hair around her fingers, leaned over her cup and hid a smile. She found the side of herself that her swordswoman-partner was revealing disarming, and quite delightful—but she doubted Tarma would appreciate her amusement.

The common room of their inn was far from being crowded, and the atmosphere was relaxed and convivial. This was really the best such place they'd stayed in for months; it was well-lit, the food was excellent, the beds comfortable and free of vermin, the prices not outrageously extortionate. And Tarma was certainly enjoying the company.

As she had been every night for the past three, Tarma was embroiled in a religious discussion—a discussion, not an argument; although the two participants often waxed passionate, neither ever found offense or became angered during their disagreements.

Her fellow scholar was a plump little priest of Anathei of the Purifying Flame. He was certainly a full priest, and might even (from his cultured accent) be a higher prelate, yet he wore only the same soft, dark brown, unornamented robes of the least of his order's acolytes. He was clean-shaven and quite bald, and his cheerful brown eyes seemed to regard everything and everyone with the open-hearted joy of an unspoiled child. No straitlaced ascetic, he—he and Tarma had been trading rounds of good wine; tonight reds, last night whites.

Tarma looked even more out of place seated across from him than she did with her sorceress-partner. She towered over him by a head, her every movement proclaiming she knew very well how to manage that sword slung on her back, her hawklike face and ice-blue eyes holding a controlled intensity that could easily have been frightening or intimidating to a stranger. With every article of her weaponry and earth-brown clothing so precisely arranged that what she wore might almost have been some kind of uniform, and her coarse black hair braided and coiled with militant neatness, she looked as much the priest or more than he— half-barbarian priest of some warlike order, that is. She hardly looked as if she could have anything in common with the scholarly little priest.

She hardly looked literate. Certainly no one would expect erudite philosophy from her lips, not with the warlike accoutrements she bore; yet she had been quoting fully as many learned tomes as the priest—to his evident delight and Kethry's mild surprise. It would appear that service as a Sworn One did not exclude knowledge as a possible arena of combat. Kethry had long known that Tarma *was* literate, and in more than one language, but she had never before guessed that her partner was so erudite.

Kethry herself was staying out of the conversation for the moment. This evening she and her partner had had an argument, the first serious disagreement of their association. She wanted to give Tarma a chance to cool down—and to mull over what she'd said.

Because while it had been unpleasant, it was also, unfortunately, nothing less than the truth.

"You're not going out there alone, are you?" Tarma had asked doubtfully, when Kethry had voiced her intention to prowl the rather dubious quarter that housed the gypsy-mages. Kethry had heard that one of her old classmates had taken up with the wanderers, and was looking for news of him.

"Why not?" she asked, a little more sharply than she had intended.

"Because it's no place for a woman alone."

"Dammit, Tarma, I'm *not* just any woman! I'm perfectly capable of taking care of myself!"

"Look—even *I* can get taken out by a gang of street toughs."

"In the name of the gods, Tarma, leave me alone for once! You're

smothering me! I can't go anywhere or do anything without you rushing
to wrap me in gauze, like a piece of china—"

She'd stopped then, appalled by the stricken look on her partner's
face.

Then, like lightning, the expression changed. "You're imagining
things," Tarma replied flatly.

"All right—have it your way." Kethry was too tired to fight with her.
"You will anyway. Any time you hear something you don't like, you deny
it and shut down on me—just like you're doing now."

And she had turned on her heel and led the way into the inn's common room, ignoring the fact that Tarma looked as if the sorceress had
just slapped her.

The voice of the little priest penetrated her musing.

"Nay," he said. "Nay, I cannot agree. Our teaching is that evil is not a
thing of itself; it is simply good that has not been brought to see the
truth. We hold that even a demon can be redeemed—that even the most
vile of such creatures could become a blessed spirit if someone with time
and patience were to give him the proper redirection."

"Always supposing your proselytizer managed to keep from being devoured or ripped to shreds before he got a single word out," Tarma
croaked wryly, draping herself more comfortably over the edge of the
worn wooden table. "He'd better be either agile or one *damned* powerful
mage! No, I can't agree with you, my friend. Aside from what Magister
Tenavril has to say about them, I've dealt with a few demons up close and
on a quite personal basis. I have to side with the Twin Suns school; the
demonic beings must have been created purely of evil forces. It isn't just
the Abyssal dwellers that are bad clear through, either; I've known a few
humans who could pass for demons. Evil is real and a reality in and of
itself. It *likes* being that way. It wouldn't choose to be anything else. And
it has to be destroyed whenever a body gets the chance, or it'll spread.
Evil is easier to follow than good, and we humans like the easy path."

"I cannot agree. Those who are evil simply don't know what good is."

"Oh, they know, all right; and they reject it to follow pure selfishness."

"I—" the little priest blinked in the candlelight.

"Can you give me even *one* instance of great evil turned to good once
good has been pointed out to it?"

"Uh—" he thought hard for a moment, then smiled triumphantly.
"The Great Demon-Wolf of Hastandell!"

"Oh, that's *too* easy. Warrl!"

A shadow in a corner of the hearth uncoiled itself, and proved to be no shadow at all, but the *kyree,* whose shoulder came nearly as high as Tarma's waist. Closer inspection would reveal that Warrl's body was more like that of one of the great hunting-cats of the plains than a lupine, built for climbing and short bursts of high speed, not the endurance of a true wolf. But the fur and head and tail were sufficiently wolflike that this was how Tarma generally thought of him.

He padded over to the table and benches shared by the ill-assorted trio. The conversation of all the other occupants of the inn died for a moment as he moved, but soon picked back up again. After three days, the patrons of the inn were growing a little more accustomed to the monster beast in their midst. Tarma had helped that along by coaxing him to demean himself with a few tricks to entertain them the first night of their stay. Now, while the sight of him still unsettled a few of them, they had come to regard him as harmless. They had no notion of his true nature; Tarma and Kethry had tactfully refrained from revealing that he was just as intelligent as any of them—and quite probably could beat any one of them at chess.

"Here's your Demon-Wolf—one of his kin, rather." Tarma cocked her head to one side, her eyes far away as if she was listening. *"Kyree* is what they call themselves; they come from the Pelagir Hills. Warrl says to tell you that he knows that story—that Ourra didn't know the sheep he'd been feeding on belonged to anyone; when he prowled the village at night he was just being curious. Warrl says Ourra had never seen humans before that lot moved in and settled; he thought they were just odd beasts and that the houses were some kind of dead growths—believe me, I have seen some of what grows naturally in the Pelagirs—it isn't stretching the imagination to think that huts could grow of themselves once you've seen some of the bushes and trees. Well, Warrl wants you to know that when the priestess went out and gave Ourra a royal tongue-lashing for eating the stock, Ourra was quite embarrassed. Without there being someone like me or Kethry, with the kind of mind that he could talk to, there wasn't much he could do by way of apology, but he did his best to make it up to the village. His people have a very high sense of honor. Sorry, little man—Ourra is disqualified."

"He talks to you?" the little priest said, momentarily diverted. "That creature truly talks? I thought him just a well-trained beast!"

"Oh, after all our conversation, I figured you to be open-minded enough to let in on the 'secret.' *Kyree* have a lot of talents—they're as bright as you or me. Brighter, maybe—I have no doubt he could give you a good battle at taroc, and that's one game I have no gift for. As for talking—Warrior's Oath—sometimes I wish I could get him to stop! Oh, yes, he talks to me all right—gives me no few pieces of unsolicited advice and criticism, and usually with an 'I told you so' appended." She ruffled the great beast's fur affectionately as he grinned a toothy, tongue-lolling grin. Kethry tossed him one of the bones left from their dinner; he caught it neatly on the fly, and settled down beside her to enjoy it. Behind them, the hum of voices continued.

"Now I'll give *you* one—evil that served only itself. Thalhkarsh. We had firsthand experience of that one. He had plenty of opportunity to see good—it wasn't just the trollops he had stolen for his rites. Or are you not familiar with that tale?"

"Not the whole of it. Certainly not from one of the participants!"

"Right enough then—this is a long and thirsty story. Oskar?" Tarma signaled the host, a plump, shortsighted man who hurried to answer her summons. "Another round—no, make it a pitcher, this may take a while. Here—" she tossed him a coin, as it was her turn to pay; the innkeeper trotted off and returned with a brimming earthen vessel. Kethry was amused to see that he did not return to his station behind the counter after placing it on the table between Tarma and the priest. Instead he hovered just within earshot, polishing the tables next to them with studious care. Well, she didn't blame him, this was a tale Tarma didn't tell often, and it wasn't likely anyone in Oberdorn had ever heard a firsthand account of it. Oskar would be attracting folk to his tables for months after they'd gone with repetitions of the story.

"From all we could put together afterward, Thalhkarsh was a demon that had been summoned purely by mistake. It was a mistake the mage who called him paid for—well, that's usually the case when something like that happens. This time though, things were evidently a little different," she nodded at Kethry, who took up the thread of the story while Tarma took a sip of wine.

"Thalhkarsh had ambition. He didn't want to live in his own Abyssal Planes anymore, he wanted to escape them. More than that, he wanted far more power than he had already; he wanted to become a god, or a godling, at least. He knew that the quickest ways of gaining power are by worship, pain, and death. The second two he already had a taste of, and he craved more. The first—well, he calculated that he knew ways of gaining that, too. He transformed himself into a very potently sexual and pleasing shape, built himself a temple with a human pawn as his High Priest, and set up a religion.

"It was a religion tailored to his peculiar tastes. From what I know most of the demonic types wouldn't think of copulating with a human anymore than you or I would with a dog; Thalhkarsh thought otherwise."

Tarma grimaced. "Of course a part of that is simply because of the amount of pain he could cause while engaging in his recreations—but it may be he also discovered that sex is another very potent way of raising power. Whatever the reason, that was what the whole religion was founded on. The rituals always culminated with Thalhkarsh taking a half-dozen women, torturing and killing them when he'd done with them, in the full view of his worshipers. There's a kind of mind that finds that stimulating; before too long, he had a full congregation and was well on his way to achieving his purpose. That was where *we* came in."

"You know our reputation for helping women?" Kethry put in.

"You have a geas?" ventured the little priest.

"Something like that. Well, since Thalhkarsh's chosen victims were almost exclusively female, we found ourselves involved. We slipped into the temple in disguise and went for the High Priest—figuring if he was the one in charge, that might solve the problem. We didn't know he was a puppet, though I had guessed he might be, and then dismissed the idea." Kethry sighed. "Then we found our troubles had only begun. He had used this as a kind of impromptu test of the mettle of his servant; when the servant failed, he offered *me* the position. I was tempted with anything I might want; nearly unlimited power, beauty, wealth—and him. He was incredibly seductive, I can't begin to tell you how much. To try and give you a notion of his power, every one of his victims *ran* to him willingly when he called her, even though they *knew* what their fate would be. Well, I guess I resisted him a little too long; he became impatient with me and knocked me into a wall—unconscious, or so he thought."

"Then he made me the same offer," Tarma continued. "Only with me he demonstrated his power rather than just promising things. He totally transformed me—when he was done kings would have paid money for the privilege of laying their crowns at my feet. He also came damned close to breaking my bond with the Star-Eyed; I swear to you, I was within inches of letting him seduce me—except that the more he roused my body, the more he roused my anger. That was his mistake; I pretended to give in when I saw Kethry sneaking up behind him. Then I broke his focus just as she stabbed him; he lost control over his form and his worshipers' minds. When they saw what he really was, they deserted him—that broke his power, and it was all over."

"*She'enedra,* you were in no danger of breaking; your will is too strong, he'd have needed either more time to work on you *or* power to equal the Warrior's."

"Maybe. It was a damn near thing; too near for my liking. Well he was absolute evil for the sake of it—and I should well know, I had that evil crawling around in my mind. Besides that, there were other things that came out afterward. We know he took a few innocent girls who just had the bad luck to be in the wrong place; we *think* some clerics went in to try and exorcise him. It's hard to say for certain since they were hedge-priests; wanderers with no set temple. We do know they disappeared between one night and the next; that they did not leave town by the gates, and that they had been talking about dealing with Thalhkarsh before they vanished."

She trailed off, the set of her mouth grim, her eyes bleak. "We can only assume they went the way of all of his victims, since they were never seen or heard from again. So Thalhkarsh had plenty of opportunity to see good and the Light—and he apparently saw it only as another thing to crush."

The little priest said nothing; there seemed nothing appropriate to say. Instead, he took a sip of his wine; from the distant look in his eyes he was evidently thinking hard.

"We of Anathei are not fools, Sworn One," he said finally, "Even though we may not deal with evil as if it were our deadly enemy. No, to throw one's life away in the foolish and prideful notion that one's own sanctity is enough to protect one from everything is something very like a sin. The arrow that strikes a friend in battle instead of a foe is no less deadly because it is misdirected. Let me tell you this; when dealing with the greater evils, we do nothing blindly. We study carefully, we take no chances; we know everything there is to be known about an opponent before we face him to show him the Light. And we take very great care that he is unable to do us harm in his misguided state."

Tarma's eyes glinted with amusement in the shifting light. "Then it may well be your folk have the right of it—and in any case, you're going about your conversions in a practical manner, which is more than I can say for many. Once again we will have to agree to disagree."

"With that, lady, I rest content." He bowed to her a little, and the bench creaked under his moving weight. "But we still have not settled the point of contention. Even if I were willing to concede that you are right about Thalhkarsh—which I am not—he was still a demon. Not a man. And—"

"Well if you want irredeemable evil in a human, we can give you that, too! Kethry, remember that bastard Lastel Longknife?"

"Lady Bright! Now *there* was an unredeemable soul if ever there was one!"

Kethry saw out of the corner of her eye that Oskar had not moved since the tale-telling had begun, and was in a fair way to polish a hole right through the table. She wondered, as she smothered a smile, if *that* was the secret behind the scrupulously clean furniture of his inn.

"Lastel Longknife?" the priest said curiously.

"I doubt you'd have heard of that one. He was a bandit that had set up a band out in the waste between here and—"

"Wait—I think I *do* know that story!" the priest exclaimed. "Isn't there a song about it? One that goes 'Deep into the stony hills, miles from keep or hold'?"

"Lady's Blade, is that nonsense going to follow us *everywhere?*" Tarma grimaced in distaste while Kethry gave up on trying to control her giggles. "Damned impudent rhymester! I should never have agreed to talk to him, never! And if I *ever* get my hands on Leslac again, I'll kill him *twice!* Bad enough he got the tale all backward, but that manure about 'Three things never anger or you will not live for long; a wolf with cubs, a man with power and a woman's sense of wrong' came damn close to ruining business for a while! We weren't geas-pressed that time, or being altruistic—we were in it for the money, dammit! And—" she turned to scowl at Kethry. "What are *you* laughing about?"

"Nothing—" One look at Tarma's face set her off again.

"No respect; I don't get it from stupid minstrels, I don't get it from my partner, I don't even get it from *you,* Fur-face!"

Warrl put his head down on his paws and contrived to look innocent.

"Well, if my partner can contrive to control herself, this is what really happened. Longknife had managed to unite all the little bandit groups into one single band with the promise that they would be able—under his leadership—to take even the most heavily guarded packtrains. He made good on his boast. Before a few months passed it wasn't possible for a mouse to travel the Trade Road unmolested."

"But surely they sent out decoy trains."

"Oh, they did; Longknife had an extra factor in his favor," Kethry had managed to get herself back into control again, and answered him. "He had a talent for mind-magic, like they practice in Valdemar. It wasn't terribly strong, but it was very specific. Anyone who saw Longknife thought that he was someone they had known for a long time *but* not someone anywhere within riding distance. That way he avoided the pitfall of having his 'double' show up. He looked to be a different person to everyone, but he always looked like someone they trusted, so he managed to get himself included as a guard on each and every genuine packtrain going out. When the time was right, he'd signal his men and they'd ambush the train. If it was too well guarded, he'd wait until it was his turn on night-watch and drive away the horses and packbeasts; there's no water in the waste, and the guards and traders would have to abandon their goods and make for home afoot."

"That's almost diabolically clever."

"You do well to use that word; he was diabolic, all right. One of the first trains he and his men took was also conveying a half-dozen or so young girls to fosterage—daughters of the traders in town—the idea being that they were more likely to find young men to their liking in a bigger city. Longknife and his men *could* have ransomed them unharmed; could even have sold them. He didn't. He took his pleasure of each of them in turn until he tired of them, then turned them over to his men to be gang-raped to death without a second thought."

The priest thought that if the minstrel Leslac could have seen the expression in Tarma's eyes at this moment, he'd have used stronger words in his song than he had.

"The uncle of one of the girls found out we were in a town nearby and sent for us," Kethry picked up when Tarma seemed lost in her own grim thoughts. "We agreed to take the job, and disguised ourselves to go out with the next train. That's where the song is worst wrong—*I* was the lady, Tarma was the maidservant. When the bandits attacked, I broke the illusions; surprise gave us enough of an advantage that we managed to rout them."

"We didn't kill them all, really didn't even get most of them, just the important ones, the leaders." Tarma came back to herself and resumed the tale. "And we got Longknife; the key to the whole business."

"What—what was the 'thorough vengeance'?" the priest asked. "I have been eaten up with curiosity ever since I heard the song, but I hardly know if I dare ask—"

Tarma's harsh laugh rang as she tossed back her head. "We managed to keep *one* thing from that songster, anyway! All right, I'll let you in on the secret. Kethry put an all-senses illusion on him and bound it to his own mind-magic so that he couldn't be rid of it. She made him look like a very attractive, helpless woman. We made sure he was unconscious, then we tied him to his horse and sent him into the waste following the track of what was left of his band. I've no doubt he knew *exactly* what his victims had felt like before he finally died."

"Remind me never to anger you, Sworn One." The priest shook his head ruefully. "I'm not sure I care for your idea of justice."

"Turnabout is fair play—and it's no worse that what he'd have gotten at the hands of the relatives of the girls he murdered," Kethry pointed out. "Tarma's Lady does not teach that evildoers should remain unpunished; nor does mine. And Longknife is another bit of scum who had ample opportunity to do good—or at least no harm—and chose instead to deliberately inflict the most harm he could. I think he got his just desserts, personally."

"If you, too, are going to enter the affray, I fear I am outnumbered." The priest smiled. "But I shall retire with dignity, allowing the justice of your assertions, but not conceding you the victory. Though it is rather strange that you should mention the demon Thalhkarsh just now."

Both Tarma and Kethry came instantly alert; they changed their positions not so much as a hair (Tarma leaning on both arms that rested on the table, Kethry lounging a little against the wall) but now they both had dropped the veneer of careless ease they had worn, and beneath that thin skin the wary vigilance of the predator and hunter showed plain.

"Why?" Tarma asked carefully.

"Because I have heard rumors in the beggar's quarter that some ill-directed soul is trying to reestablish the worship of Thalhkarsh in the old Temple of Duross there. More than that, we have had reports of the same from a young woman who apparently dwells there."

"Have you?" Kethry pushed back the hood of her buff-colored robe. "Worshiping Thalhkarsh—that's a bit injudicious, considering what happened at Delton, isn't it?"

"Injudicious to say the least," the priest replied, "Since they must know what will happen to them if they are discovered. The Prince is not minded to have light women slaughtered on altars instead of paying his venery taxes. I heard that after Thalhkarsh's depredations, his income from Delton was halved for the better part of three years. He took care to alter or tighten the laws concerning religious practice after that. Human sacrifice in any form is punishable by enslavement; if the perpetrator has murdered taxpayers, he goes to the Prince's mages for their experiments."

Kethry lifted an eyebrow; Tarma took a largish mouthful of wine. They'd both heard about how Prince Lothar's mages produced his monstrous mindless bodyguards. They'd also heard that the process from normal man to twelve-foot-tall brute was far from pleasant—or painless. Lothar was sometimes called "the Looney"—but *never* to his face.

The little priest met blue and green eyes in turn, and nodded. "Besides that," he continued, "There are several sects, mine included, who would wish to deal with the demon on other levels. We all want him bound, at the least. But so far it's all rumor. The temple has been empty every time anyone's checked."

"So you *did* check?"

"In all conscience, yes—although the woman didn't seem terribly trust-worthy or terribly bright. Pretty, yes—rather remarkably pretty under the dirt, but she seemed to be in a half-daze all the time. Brother Thoser was the one who questioned her, not I, or I could tell you more. My guess would be that she was of breeding, but had taken to the street to supply an addiction of some sort."

Tarma nodded thoughtfully.

"Where is this temple?" Kethry's husky alto almost made the little priest regret his vow of chastity; and when she had moved into the light, and he saw that the sweet face beneath the hood matched the voice, he sighed a little for days long lost.

"Do you know the beggars' quarter? Well then, it's on the river, just downwind of the slaughter-house and the tannery. It's been deserted since the last acolyte died of old age—oh, nearly fifteen years ago. It's beginning to fall apart a bit; the last time I looked at it, there didn't *seem* to be any signs that anyone had entered it in all that time."

"Is it kept locked up?"

"Oh, yes; not that there's anything to steal—mostly it's to keep chil-dren from playing where they might be hurt by falling masonry. The beggars used it for a bit as one of their meeting halls, before the acolyte died, but," he chuckled, "One-Eye Tham told me it was 'too perishin' cold and damp' and they moved to more comfortable surroundings."

Tarma exchanged a look with her partner; *We need to talk,* she hand-signed.

Kethry nodded, ever so slightly. *We could be in trouble,* she signed back.

Tarma's grimace evidenced agreement.

"Well, if you will allow me," the little priest finished the last of his wine, and shoved the bench back with a scrape, "I fear I have morning devotions to attend to. As always, Sworn One, the conversation and com-pany have been delightful, if argumentative—"

Tarma managed a smile; it transformed her face, even if it didn't quite reach her eyes. "My friend, we have a saying—it translates something like 'there is room in the universe for every Way.' You travel yours; should you need it, my sword will protect you as I travel mine."

"That is all anyone could reasonably ask of one who does not share his faith," he replied, "And so, good night."

The two mercenary women finished their own wine and headed for their room shortly after his departure. With Warrl padding after, Kethry took one of the candles from the little table standing by the entrance to the hall, lit it at the lantern above the table, and led the way down the corridor. The wooden walls were polished enough that their light was reflected; they'd been tended to recently and Tarma could still smell the ferris-oil that had been used. The sounds of snoring behind closed doors, the homelike scents of hot wax and ferris-oil, the buzz of conversation from the inn behind them—all contrasted vividly with the horror that had been resurrected in both their minds at the mention of Thalhkarsh.

Their room held two narrow beds, a rag rug, and a table; all worn, but scrupulously clean. They had specified a room with a window, so Warrl could come and go as he pleased; no one in his right mind would break into the room with any of the three of them in it, and their valuables were in the stable, well-guarded by their well-named warsteeds, Hellsbane and Ironheart.

When the door was closed and bolted behind them, Kethry put the candle in its wall sconce and turned to face her partner with a swish of robes.

"If he's there, if it's really Thalhkarsh, he'll be after us."

Tarma paced the narrow confines of the room. "Seems obvious. If I were a demon, *I'd* want revenge. Well, we knew this might happen someday. I take it that your sword hasn't given you any indication that there's anything wrong?"

"No. At least, nothing more than what you'd expect in a city this size. I wish Need would be a little more discriminating." Kethry sighed, and one hand caressed the hilt of the blade she wore at her side over her sorceress' robes in an unconscious gesture of habit. "I absolutely refuse to go sticking my nose into every lover's-quarrel in this town! And—"

"Warrior's Oath—remember the first time you tried?" Tarma's grim face lightened into a grin with the recollection.

"Oh, laugh, go ahead! *You* were no help!"

"Here you thought the shrew was in danger of her life—you went flying in the door and knocked her man out cold—and you expected her to throw herself at your feet in gratitude—" Tarma was taking full revenge for Kethry's earlier hilarity at her expense. "And what did she do? Began hurling crockery at you, shrieking you'd killed her beloved! Lady's Eyes, I thought I was going to die!"

"I wanted to take her over my knee and beat her with the flat of my blade."

"And to add insult to injury, Need wouldn't let you lay so much as a finger on her! I had to go in with a serving dish for a shield and rescue you before she tore you to shreds!"

"She could have done that with her tongue alone," Kethry grimaced. "Well, that's not solving our problem here. . . ."

"True," Tarma conceded, sobering. She threw herself down on her bed,

Warrl jumping up next to her and pushing his head under her hand. "Back to the subject. Let's assume that the rumor is true; we can't afford not to. If somebody has brought that particular demon back, we know he's going to want our hides."

"Or worse."

"Or worse. Now he can't have gotten too powerful, or everybody in town would know about him. Remember Delton."

Kethry shifted restlessly from foot to foot, finally going over to the window to open the shutters with a creak of hinges and stare out into the night. "I remember. And I remember that we'd better do something about him *while* he's in that state."

"This isn't a job for us, *she'enedra*. It's a job for priests. *Powerful* priests. I remember what he almost did to me. He came perilously close to breaking my bond with the Star-Eyed. And he boasted he could snap your tie to Need just as easily. I think we ought to ride up to the capital as fast as Hellsbane and Ironheart can carry us, and fetch us some priests."

"And come back to an empty town and a demon transformed to a godling?" Kethry turned away from the window to shake her head at her partner, her amber hair like a sunset cloud around her face, and a shadow of anger in her eyes. "What if we're wrong? We'll have some very powerful people very angry at us for wasting their time. And if we're right—we have to act fast. We have to take him while he's still weak or we'll never send him back to the Abyssal Planes at all. He is no stupid imp—he's learned from what we did to him, you can bet on it. If he's not taken down now, we'll never be able to take him at all."

"That's *not* our job!"

"Whose is it then?" Kethry dug her fingers into the wood of the windowframe behind her, as tense and worried as she'd ever been. "We'd better make it our job if we're going to survive! And I told you earlier—I *don't* want you cosseting me! I *know* what I'm doing, and I can protect myself!"

Tarma sighed, and there was a shadow of guilt on her face as she rolled over to lie flat on her back, staring at the ceiling; her hands clasped under her head, one leg crossed over the other. "All right, then. I don't know a damn thing about magic, and all I care to know about demons outside of a book is that they scare me witless. I still would rather go for help, but if you don't think we'd have the time—and if you are sure you're not getting into more than you can handle—"

"I know we wouldn't have the time; he's not going to waste time building up a power base," Kethry replied, sitting down on the edge of Tarma's bed, making the frame creak.

"And he may not be there at all; it might just be a wild rumor."

"It might; I don't think I'd care to bet my life on waiting to see, though."

"So we need information; reliable information."

"The question is how to get it. Should I try scrying?"

"Absolutely *not!*" Tarma flipped back over onto her side, her hand chopping at the pillow for emphasis. Warrl winced away and looked at her reproachfully. "He caught that poor witch back in Delton that way, remember? That much even *I* know. If you scry, he'll have you on *his* ground. I promise I won't cosset you any more, but I *will not* allow you to put yourself in jeopardy when there are any other alternatives!"

"Well, how then?"

"Me." Tarma stabbed at her own chest with an emphatic thumb. "Granted, I'm not a thief—but I *am* a skilled scout. I can slip into and out of that temple without anyone knowing I've been there, and if it's being used for anything, I'll be able to tell."

"No."

"Yes. No choice, *she'enedra.*"

"All right, then—but you won't be going without me. If he and any followers he may have gathered *are* there and they're using magic to mask their presence, you won't see anything, but I can invoke mage-sight and see through any illusions."

Tarma began to protest, but this time Kethry cut her short. "You haven't a choice either; you need my skill and I won't let you go in there without me. Dammit Tarma, I am your partner—your *full* partner. If I have to, I'll follow you on my own."

"You would, wouldn't you?"

"You can bet on it." Kethry scowled, then smiled as Tarma's resigned expression told her she'd won the argument. Warrl nudged Tarma's hand again, and she began scratching absentmindedly behind his ears. A scowl creased her forehead, but her mouth, too, was quirked in an almost-smile.

"Warrior's Oath! I *would* tie myself to a headstrong, stubborn, foolish, reckless, crazed mage—"

"Who loves her bond-sister and won't allow her to throw her life away."

"—who is dearer to me than my own life."

Kethry reached out at almost the same moment as Tarma did. They touched hands briefly, crescent-scarred palm to crescent-scarred palm, and exchanged rueful smiles.

"Argument over?"

"It's over."

"All right then," Tarma said after poignant silence, "Let's get to it now, while we've still got the guts for it."

Ten

Tarma led the way, as soft- and sure-footed in these dark city streets as she would have been scouting a forest or creeping through grass on an open plain.

The *kyree* Warrl served as their scout and their eyes in the darkness. The uninformed would have thought it impossible to hide a lupine creature the size of Warrl in an open street—a creature whose shoulder nearly came as high as Tarma's waist; but Warrl, although somewhere close at hand, was presently invisible. Tarma could sense him, though—now behind them, now in front. From time to time he would speak a single word (or perhaps as many as three) in her mind, to tell her of the results of his scouting.

There was little moonlight; the moon was in her last quarter. This was one of the poorest streets in the city, and there were no cressets and no torches to spare to light the way by night—and if anyone put one up, it would be stolen within the hour. The buildings to either side were shut up tight; not with shutters, for they were in far too poor a state of repair to have working shutters, but with whatever bits of wood and cloth or rubbish came to hand. What little light there was leaked through the cracks in these makeshift curtainings. The street itself was rutted mud; no wasting of paving bricks on this side of the river. Both the mercenaries wore thin-soled boots, the better to feel their way in the darkness. Kethry had abandoned her usual buff-colored, calf-length robe; she wore a dark, sleeved tunic over her breeches. Kethry's ensorcelled blade Need was slung at her side; Tarma's nonmagical weapon carried in its usual spot on her back. They had left cloaks behind; cloaks had a tendency to get tangled at the most inopportune moments. Better to bear with the chill.

They had slipped out the window of their room at the inn, wanting no one to guess where they were going—or even that they were going out at all. They had made their way down back alleys with occasional detours through fenced yards or even across roofs. Although Kethry was no match for Tarma in strength and agility, she was quite capable of keeping up with her on a trek like this one.

Finally the fences had begun to boast more holes than entire boards; the houses leaned to one side or the other, almost as though they huddled together to support their sagging bones. The streets, when they had ventured out onto them, were either deserted or populated by one or two furtively scurrying shadows. *This* dubious quarter where the abandoned temple that their priestly friend had told them of stood—this was hardly a place either of them would have chosen to roam in daylight, much less darkness. Tarma was already beginning to regret the impulse that had led her here—the stubbornness that had forced her to prove that she was not trying to shelter her partner unduly. Except that . . . maybe Kethry was right. Maybe she was putting a stranglehold on the mage. But Keth was all the Clan she had. . . .

Tarma's nose told her where they were; downwind of the stockyards, the slaughterhouse, and the tannery. The reek of tannic acid, offal, half-tanned hides and manure was a little short of unbreathable. From far off there came the intermittent lowing and bleating of the miserable animals awaiting the doom that would come in the morning.

"Something just occurred to me," Kethry whispered as they waited, hidden in shadows, for a single passerby to clear the street.

"What?"

"This close to the stockyard and slaughterhouse, Thalhkarsh wouldn't necessarily *need* sacrifices to build a power base."

"You mean—he could use the deaths of the beasts?"

"Death-energy is the same for man and beast. Man just has more of it, and of higher quality."

"Like you can get just as drunk on cheap beer as on distilled spirits?"

"Something of the sort."

"Lady's Blade! *And* he feeds on fear and pain as well—"

"There's plenty of that at the slaughterhouse."

"Great. That's *just* what I needed to hear." Tarma brooded for a moment. "Tell me something; why's he taking on human shape if he wants to terrify? His own would be better for that purpose."

"Well—this is just a guess—you have to remember he wants worship and devotion as well, and he won't get that in his real shape. That might be one reason. A second would be because what *seems* to be familiar and proves to be otherwise is a lot more fear-inducing than the openly alien. Lastly is Thalhkarsh himself—most demons *like* the Abyssal Planes, and their anger at being summoned is because they've been taken from home. They look on us as a lower form of life, a species of animal. But Thalhkarsh is perverse; he wants to stay here, he wants to rule over people, and I suspect he enjoys physically coupling with humans. The Lady only knows why."

"I . . . don't suppose he can breed, can he?"

"Windborn! Thank your Lady, no. Thank *all* the gods that demons even in human form are sterile with humans, or we might have more than Thalhkarsh to worry about—he *might* be willing to produce a malleable infant. But the only way he can reproduce is to bud—and he's too jealous of his powers here to bud and create another on this Plane with like powers and a mind of its own. He won't go creating a rival, that much I'm sure of."

"Forgive me if I don't break out into carols of relief."

They peered down the dark, shadow-lined street in glum silence. The effluvium of the stockyards and tannery washed over them, causing Tarma to stifle a cough as an acrid breath seared the back of her throat a little.

The street is clear, a voice rang in Tarma's head.

"Warrl says it's safe to go," Tarma passed the word on, then, crouching low, crossed the street like one of the scudding shadows cast on the street by high clouds against the moon.

She moved so surely and so silently from the shadows of their own building to the shadows below the one across the street that even Kethry, who *knew* she was there, hardly saw her. Kethry was an instant behind her, not quite so sure or silent, but furtive enough. Warrl was already waiting for them, and snorted a greeting before slipping farther ahead of them in the direction of the temple.

Hugging the rough wood and stone of the walls, they inched their way down the street, trying not to wince when their feet encountered unidentifiable piles of something soft and mushy. The reek of tannery and stockyard overwhelmed any other taint. From within the buildings occasionally came sounds of revelry or conflict; hoarse, drunken singing, shouting, weeping, the splintering of wood, the crash of crockery. None

of this was carried into the streets; only fools and the mad walked the
streets of the beggars' quarter at night.

Fools, the mad, or the desperate. Right now Kethry had both of them
figured for being all three.

Finally the walls of buildings gave way to a single stone wall, half again
as tall as Tarma. This, by the descriptions she'd gotten, would be the wall
of the temple. Beyond it, bulking black against the stars, Kethry could
see the temple itself.

Tarma surveyed the wall, deciding it would be no great feat to scale it.

You go over first, Fur-face, she thought.

My pleasure, Warrl sent back to her, overtones of irony so strong Tarma
could almost taste the metallic emotional flavoring. He backed up six or
seven paces, then flung himself at the wall. His forepaws caught the top
of it; caught, and held, and with a scrambling of hindclaws that sounded
hideously loud to Tarma's nervous ears, he was over and leaping down on
the other side.

Now it was her turn.

She backed up a little, then ran at the wall, leaping and catching the
top effortlessly, pulling herself up onto the stones that were set into the
top with ease. She crouched there for a moment, peering through the
darkness into the courtyard beyond, identifying the odd-shaped shadows
by what she'd been told to expect there.

In the middle there stood a dried-out fountain, its basin broken, its
statuary mostly missing limbs and heads. To the right were three stone
boxes containing earth and dead trees. To the left had been a shrine, now
a heap of rubble, that had been meant for those faithful who felt unwor-
thy to enter the temple proper. All was as it should be; nothing moved.

I'd tell you if anything was here, wouldn't I? Warrl grumbled at her lack
of trust.

She felt one corner of her mouth twitch at his reply. *I can take it that
all's well?*

Nothing out of the ordinary outside.

It's inside I'm worried about.

She saluted Kethry briefly, seeing the strained, anxious face peering
whitely up at her in the moon-shadows, then slipped over the top to land
on cat-quiet feet in the temple courtyard.

She slid carefully along the wall, left foot testing the ground at the base
of it for loose pebbles that might slip underfoot or be kicked away by
accident. The moon was behind her; so her side of the wall was entirely
in shadow so long as she stayed close to it. Five steps—twenty—fifty—

her outstretched hand encountered a hinge, and wood. She'd come to the gate.

She felt for the bar and eased it along its sockets until one half of the gate was freed. That gave Kethry her way in; now she would scout ahead.

She waited for another of those scudding cloud-shadows; joining it as it raced across the courtyard. Cobblestones were hard and a trifle slippery beneath her thin-soled boots; she was glad that the first sole was of tough, abrasive sharkskin. Dew was already beginning to collect on the cold stones, making them slick, but the sharkskin leather gave her traction.

She reached the shelter of the temple entrance without incident; Warrl was waiting for her there, a slightly darker shadow in the shadows of the doorway.

Ready? she asked him. She felt his assent.

She reached for the door, prepared to find it locked, and was pleasantly surprised when it wasn't. She nudged it open a crack; when nothing happened, she opened it enough to peer carefully inside.

She saw nothing but a barren antechamber. Warrl stuck his nose inside, and sniffed cautiously.

Nothing here—but something on the other side of the door beyond; people for sure—and, I think, blood and incense. And magic, lots of magic.

Tarma sighed; it would have been nice if this had been a false alarm. *Sounds like we've come to the right place.*

Shouldn't we wait for Kethry?

You go after her; I want to make sure there isn't anyone on guard in there.

Not yet. I want to know you aren't biting off more than you can swallow. Warrl waited for her to move on, one shadow among many.

She slipped in through the crack in the door, Warrl a hairsbreadth behind her. Moonlight shone down through a skylight above. The door on the other side of the antechamber stood open; between it and the door she had entered through was nothing but untracked dust.

She hugged the wall, easing carefully around the doorpost. Once inside the sanctuary she could barely see her own hands; she continued to hug the wall, making her way by feel alone. She came to a corner, paused for a moment, and tried to see, but could only make out dim shapes in the small amount of light that came from various holes in the ceiling of the sanctuary. It was impossible to tell if those sources of light were more skylights, or the evidence of neglect. Dust filled the air, making her nose itch; other than that, lacking Warrl's senses, she could only smell damp and mildew. The stones beneath her hands were cold and slightly moist.

Beneath the film of moisture they were smooth and felt a little like polished granite.

She went on, coming at last around behind the statue of the rain-god that stood at the far end of the room. The shadows were even deeper here; she slowed her pace to inch along the stuccoed wall, one hand feeling before her.

Then her hand encountered emptiness.

A door.

I can tell that! A door to where?

To where the blood-smell is.

Then we take it. I'm going on ahead; you go back and fetch Kethry.

Now she was alone in pitchy darkness, with only the rough brick wall of the corridor as a guide, and the faint sound of her footsteps bouncing off the walls to tell her that it *was* a corridor. She held back impatience and continued to feel her way with extreme caution—until once again her hand encountered open air.

She was suddenly awash with light, frozen by it, surrounded by it on all sides. She would have been prepared for any attack but this, which left her blind and helpless, with tears of pain blurring what little vision she had. She went automatically into a defensive crouch, pulling her blade over her head with both hands from the sheath on her back; only to hear a laugh like a dozen brass bells from some point above her head.

"Little warrior," the voice said caressingly. "I have so longed for the day when we might meet again."

"I can't say I feel the same about you," Tarma replied after a bit, trying to locate the demon by sound alone. "I suppose it's too much to expect you to stand and fight me honorably?" She could see nothing but angry red light, like flame, but without the heat; perhaps the light was a little brighter above and just in front of her. She tried to will her eyes to work, but they remained dazzled, with lances of pain shooting into her skull every time she blinked. There was a smell of blood and sex and something more that she couldn't quite identify. Her heart was racing wildly with fear, but she was determined not to let *him* see how helpless she felt.

"Honor is for fools—and I may have been a fool in the past, but I am no longer quite so gullible. No, little warrior, I shall not stand and fight you. I shall not fight you at all. I shall simply—put you to sleep."

A sickly sweet aroma began to weave around her, and Tarma recognized it after a moment as black *tran*-dust; the most powerful narcotic she knew of. She had only that moment of recognition before she felt her control over herself suddenly melt away; her entire body went numb in a single breath, and she fell face down on the floor, mind and body alike paralyzed, sword falling from a hand that could no longer hold it.

And now that you cannot fight me, said a silky voice in her mind, *I shall make of you what I will . . . and somewhat more to my taste than the ice-creature you are now. And this time your Goddess shall not be able to help you. I am nearly a god now myself, and the gods are forbidden to war upon other gods.*

The last thing she heard was his laughter, like bronze bells slightly out of tune with one another.

Kethry fretted inwardly, counting down the moments until she was supposed to try the gate. This was the hardest part, for certain; the waiting. Anything else she could manage with equanimity. Waiting brought out the worst fears, roused her imagination to a fever pitch. The plan was for Tarma and Warrl to check the courtyard, then unlock the gates for her. They would precede her into the temple as well. They were to meet in the sanctuary, after Tarma had declared it free of physical hazards.

It was a plan Kethry found herself misliking more with every passing moment. They were a team; it went against the grain to work separately. Granted, Warrl was with Tarma; granted that she was something of a handicap in a skulk-and-hide situation like this—still, Kethry couldn't help thinking that *she'd* be able to detect dangers neither of the other two would notice. More than that—her place was *with* Tarma, not waiting in the wings. Now she began to wish she hadn't told the Shin'a'in that she intended to investigate this place. If she'd kept her mouth shut, she could have done this properly, by daylight, perhaps. Finally her impatience became too much; she felt her way along the wall to the wooden gates, and pushed very slightly on one of them.

It moved.

Tarma had succeeded in this much, anyway; the gates were now unbarred.

She pushed a little harder, slowly, carefully. The gate swung open just enough for her to squeeze herself through, scraping herself on the wooden bulwarks both fore and aft as she did so.

Before her lay the courtyard, mostly open ground.

Remembering all Tarma had taught her, she crouched as low as she could, waited until the moon passed behind a cloud, and sprinted for the shelter of the dried-up fountain.

Under the rim, in shadows, she looked around; watching not for objects, but for movement, any movement. But there was no movement, anomalous or otherwise. She crawled under the rim until she lay hidden on the side facing the temple doors.

She watched, but saw nothing; she listened, but heard only crickets and toads. She waited, aching from the strain of holding herself still in such an awkward position, until the moon again went behind a cloud.

She sprinted for the temple doors, flinging herself against the wall of the temple behind a pillar as soon as she reached them. It was then that she realized that there had been something very anomalous at the gate.

The aged gates, allegedly locked for fifteen years, had opened smoothly and without a sound—as if they had been oiled and put into working order within the past several days.

Something was very wrong.

A shadow bulked in front of her, and she started with alarm; she pulled the sword in a defensive move before she realized that her "enemy" was Warrl.

He reached for her arm and his teeth closed gently on her tunic; he tugged at her sleeve. That meant Tarma wanted her.

"You didn't meet with anything?" Kethry whispered.

Warrl snorted. *I think that they are all asleep or blind. A cub could have penetrated this place.*

This was too easy; all her instincts were in an uproar. Too easy by far. She suddenly realized what their easy access to this place meant. This was a trap!

And now Kethry felt a shrill alarm course through her every nerve—a double alarm. Need was alerting her to a woman in the deadliest danger, and very nearby—

—and the bond of *she'enedran* was resonating with soul-deep threat to her blood-sister. Tarma was in trouble.

As if to confirm her fears, Warrl threw up his head and voiced his battle-cry, and charged within, leaving Kethry behind.

And given the urgency of Need's pull, that could only mean one thing.

Thalhkarsh *was* here—and he had the Sworn One at his nonexistent mercy.

The time for subterfuge was over.

Kethry pulled her ensorcelled blade with her left hand, and caused a blue-green witchlight to dance before her with a gesture from her right; then kicked open the doors of the temple and flung herself frantically through them. She landed hard against the dingy white-plastered wall of a tiny, cobwebbed anteroom, bruising her shoulder; and found herself staring foolishly at an empty chamber.

Another door stood in the opposite wall, slightly ajar. She inched along the wall and eased it open with the tip of her blade. The witchlight showed nothing beyond it but a brick-walled tunnel that led deeper into the temple proper. Warrl must already have run down this way.

She moved stealthily through the door, and into the corridor, praying to find Tarma, and soon. The internal alerts of both her blade and her blood-bond were nigh-unbearable, and she hardly dared contemplate what that meant to Tarma's well-being.

But the corridor twisted and turned like a *kadessa*-run, seemingly without end. With every new corner she expected to find *something*—but every time she rounded a corner she saw only another long, dust-choked extension of the corridor behind her. The dust showed no tracks at all, not even Warrl's. Could she have somehow come the wrong way? But there were only two directions to choose—forward, or back the way she had come. Back she would never go; that left only forward. And forward was yard after yard of blank-walled corridor, with never a door or a break of any kind. She slunk on and on in a kind of nightmarish entrancement in which she lost all track of time; there was only the endlessly turning corridor before her and the cry for help within her. Nothing else seemed of any import at all. As the urgings of her geas-blade Need and the bond that tied her to Tarma grew more and more frantic, she was close to being driven nearly mad with fear and frustration. She was being distracted; so successfully in fact, that it wasn't until she'd wasted far too much precious time trying to thread the maze that she realized what it must be—

—a magical construct, meant to delay her, augmented by spells of befuddlement.

"You *bastard!*" she screamed at the invisible Thalhkarsh, enraged by his duplicity. He had made a serious mistake in doing something that caused her to become angry; that rage was useful, it fueled her power. She gathered it to her, made a force of it instead of allowing it to fade uselessly; sought and found the weak point of the spell. She sheathed Need, and spreading her arms wide over her head, palms facing each other, blasted with the white-heat of her anger.

Mage-energies formed a glowing blue-white arc between her upraised hands; a sorcerer's wind began to stir around her, forming a miniature whirlwind with herself as the eye. With a flick of her wrists she reversed her hands to hold them palm-outward and brought her arms down fully extended to shoulder height; the mage-light poured from them to form a wall around her, then the wall expanded outward. The brick corridor walls about her flared with scarlet as the glowing wall of energy touched them; they shivered beneath the wrath-fired mage-blast, wavered and warped like the mirages they were. There was a moment of resistance; then, soundlessly, they vanished.

She saw she was standing in what had been the outer, common sanctuary; an enormous room, supported by two rows of pillars whose tops were lost in the shadows of the ceiling. Tracks in the dust showed she had been tracing the same circling path all the time she had thought she was traversing the corridor. Her anger brightened the witchlight; the green-blue glow revealed the far end of the sanctuary—the forgotten god stood there, behind his altar. The statue of the gentle god of rains had a forlorn look; he and his altar were covered with a blanket of dust and cobwebs. Dust lay undisturbed nearly everywhere.

Nearly everywhere—she was not the expert tracker Tarma was, but it did not take an expert to read the trail that passed from the front doors to somewhere behind the god's statue. And in those dust tracks were paw prints.

Desperate to waste no more time, she pulled her blade again and broke into a run, her blue-green witchlight bobbing before her, intent on following that trail to wherever it led. She passed by the neglected altar with never a second glance, and found the priests' door at the end of the trace in the dust; it lay just behind and beneath the statue. It had never been intended to be concealed, and besides stood wide open. She sent the witchlight shooting ahead of her and sprinted inside, panting a little.

But the echoes of running feet ahead of her as she passed into another brick-walled corridor told her that her spell-breaking had not gone unnoticed.

Common sense and logic said she should find a corner to put her back against and make a stand.

Therefore she did nothing of the kind.

As the first of four armed mercenaries came pounding into view around a corner ahead, she took Need in both hands and charged him, shrieking at the top of her lungs. Her berserk attack took the demon-hireling by surprise; he stopped dead in his tracks, staring, and belatedly raised his own weapon. His hesitation sealed his doom. Kethry let the eldritch power of Need control her body, and the bespelled blade responded to the freedom by moving her in a lightning blow at his unprotected side. Screaming in pain, the fighter fell, arm sheared off at the shoulder.

The second hired thug was a little quicker to defend himself, but he, too, was no match for Need's spell-imparted skill. Kethry cracked his wooden shield in half with a strength far exceeding what she alone possessed, and swatted his blade out of his hands after only two exchanges, sending it clattering against the wall. She ran him through before he could flee her.

The third and fourth sought to take her while—they presumed—Kethry's blade was still held fast in the collapsing body. They presumed too much; Need freed itself and spun Kethry around to meet and counter both their strokes in a display of swordsmanship a master would envy. They saw death staring at them from the witchlight reflected on the blood-dripping blade, from the hate-filled green eyes.

It was more than they had the stomach to face—and their lives were worth far more to them than their pay. They turned and fled back down the way they had come, with Kethry in hot pursuit, too filled with berserk anger now to think that a charge into unknown danger might not be a wise notion.

There was light ahead, Kethry noticed absently, allowing her rage to speed her feet. That might mean there were others there—and perhaps the demon.

The hirelings ran to the light as to sanctuary; Kethry followed—

She stumbled to a halt, at first half-blinded by the light; then when her eyes adjusted, tripped on nothing and nearly fell to her knees, her mind and heart going numb at what she saw.

This had once been the inner temple; Thalhkarsh had transformed it into his own perverted place of unholiness. It had the red-lit look of a seraglio in hell. It had been decorated with the same sort of carvings that had ornamented the demon's temple back in Delton. The subject was sexual; every perversion possible was depicted, provided that it included pain and suffering.

The far end of the room had been made into a kind of platform, covered in silk and velvet cushions, plushly upholstered. It was a clichéd setting; an overdone backdrop for an orgy. The demon certainly enjoyed invoking pain, but it appeared that he himself preferred not to suffer the slightest discomfort while he was amusing himself. The platform was occupied by a clutch of writhing nude and partially clothed bodies. Only now were some of those on the platform beginning to disengage and take notice of the hirelings fleeing for the door on the opposite side. Evidently not even the demon foresaw that Kethry would be able to get this far on her own.

The demon and his followers had been interrupted by her entrance at the height of their pleasures. And it was the sight of the demon's partner that had stricken Kethry to the heart—for the one being used by the demon himself was Tarma.

But it was Tarma transformed; she wore the face and body the demon had given her when he had first tried to seduce her to his cause. Though smaller and far frailer, she was still recognizably herself—but with all her angularities softened, her harshness made silken, her flaws turned to beauty. Her clothing was in rags, and she had the bruises and the look of a woman who has been passed from one brutal rape to another. That was bad enough, but that was not what had struck Kethry like a dagger to the heart; it was the absence of any mind or sense in Tarma's blank blue eyes.

Tarma had survived rape before; were she still aware and in charge of herself, she would still be fighting. Mere brutal use would not have forced her mind from her, not when the slaughter of her entire Clan as well as her own abuse had failed to do that when she was a young woman and far more innocent than she was now. No—this *had* to be the work of the demon. Knowing he would be unable to break her spirit, Thalhkarsh had stolen Tarma's mind; stolen her mind or somehow forced her soul out of her body.

The demon, wearing his form of a tall, beautiful human male, was the first to recover from surprise at the interruption.

"Amusing," he said, not appearing at all amused. "I had thought the skill of those I had paid would more than equal yours, even with that puny blade to augment it. It appears that I was mistaken."

Before Kethry could make a move, he had seized Tarma, and pulled her before him—not as a shield, but with evident threat.

"Put up your blade, sorceress," he purred brazenly, "or I tear her limb from limb."

Kethry knew he was not bluffing, and Need clattered to the floor from her nerveless hand.

He laughed, a hideous howl of triumph. "You disappoint me, my enemy! You have made my conquest too easy!" He stood up and tossed Tarma aside; she fell to the pile of cushions with the limpness of a lifeless doll, not even attempting to break her own fall. "Come forth, my little toy—" he continued, turning his back on his fallen victim and beckoning to someone lurking behind the platform.

From out of the shadows among the hangings came a woman, and when she stepped far enough into the light that Kethry was able to get a good look at her, the sorceress reeled as if she had been struck. It couldn't be—

The woman was the twin of an image she herself had once worn—and that she had placed on the unconscious form of the marauding bandit Lastel Longknife by way of appropriate punishment for the women and girls he had used and murdered. It was an image she had never expected to see again; she had assumed the bandit would have been treated with brutality equaling his own by what was left of his fellows. By all rights, he should have been dead—long dead.

"I think the bitch recognizes me, *my lord,*" the dulcet voice said, heavy irony in the title of subservience. Platinum hair was pushed back from amethyst eyes with a graceful but impatient hand.

"You never expected to see me again, did you?" Her eyes blazed with helpless anger. "May every god damn you for what you did to me, woman. Death would have been better than the misery this *shape* put me through! If it hadn't been for a forgotten sword and an untied horse—"

She came closer, hands crooked into claws. "I've dreamed of having you in my hands every night since, gods—but *not like this.*" Her eyes betrayed that she was walking a very thin thread of sanity. "What you did to me was bad enough—but being trapped in this prison of a whore's carcass is more than I can bear—it's worse than Hell, it's—"

She turned away, clenching her hands so tightly that the knuckles popped. After a moment of internal struggle she regained control over herself, and turned to the demon. "Well, since it was my tales to the priests that lured them here, the time has come for you to keep *your* side of the bargain."

"You wish to lose your current form? A pity—I had thought you had come to enjoy my attentions."

The woman colored; Kethry was baffled. She had only placed the *illusion* of being female on the bandit, but this—this was a real woman! Mage-sight showed only exactly what stood before her in normal-sight, not the bandit of the desert hills!

"Damn you," she snarled. "Oh, gods, for a demon-slaying blade! Yes, you *bastard,* I enjoy it! As you very well know, squirming like a vile snake inside my head! You've made me your slave as well as your puppet; you've addicted me to you, and you revel in my misery—you cursed me far worse than ever she did. And now, damn you, I want free of it and you and all else besides! I've paid my part of the bargain. Now you live up to your side!"

Thalhkarsh smiled cruelly. "Very well, my pretty little toy—go and take her lovely throat in both your hands, and I shall free you of that body with her death."

One of the acolytes scuttled around behind Kethry and seized her arms, pinioning them behind her back. He needn't have bothered; she was so in shock she couldn't have moved if the ceiling had begun to fall in on them. The slender beauty approached, stark, bitter hatred in her eyes, and seized Kethry's throat.

A howl echoed from behind her; a hurtling black shape leaped over her straight at the demon. It was Warrl—who evidently had met the same kind of delaying tactics as Kethry had. Now he had broken free of them, and he was in a killing rage. *This* time Thalhkarsh took no chances with Warrl; from his upraised hands came double bolts of crimson lightning. Warrl was hit squarely in midair by both of them. He shrieked horribly, transfixed six feet above the floor, caught and held in midleap. He writhed once, shrieked again—then went limp. The aura of the demon's magic faded; the body of the *kyree* dropped to the ground like a shot bird, and did not move again.

Lastel was not in the least distracted by this; she tightened her hands around Kethry's neck. Kethry struggled belatedly to free herself, managing to bring her heel down on the foot of the acolyte behind her, catching him squarely in the instep so that he yowled and dropped to the floor, clutching his ruined foot.

But even when her arms were free, she was powerless against the bandit; she scratched at Lastel's hands and reached for her eyes with crooked fingers—uselessly. Her own hands would not respond; her lungs screamed for air, and she began to black out.

The demon laughed, and again raised his hands; Kethry felt as if she'd been plunged into the heart of a fire. Crackling energies surrounded both of them; her legs gave beneath her and it was only when a new acolyte caught her arms and held her up that she remained erect. With narrowing vision she stared into Lastel's pale eyes, unable to look away—

And suddenly she found herself staring down into her own face, with her own neck between her hands! Kethry released her grip with a cry of disbelief; stared down at her hands, at herself, horror written plain on her own face. Lastel stared up at her out of her own eyes, hatred and black despair making a twisted mask of her face.

The demon laughed at both of them, cruel enjoyment plain in his tone. He eased off the monstrous pile of silks and stalked proudly toward them, sweeping the bandit up onto her feet and into his arms as he came to stand over Kethry, who had sagged to her knees in shock.

"I promised to change your form, fool—I did *not* promise into what image!" he chortled. "And you, witch—I have your rightful body in my keeping now—and you will never, never reverse a spell to which I and I alone hold the key!"

He gestured at his acolyte, who dropped his hold on Kethry-now-Lastel and seized Lastel-now-Kethry's arms instead, hauling her roughly to her feet.

"My foolish sorceress, my equally foolish toy, how easy it is to manipulate you! Little toy, did you truly think that I would release you when you take such delight in my attentions? That I would allow such a potent source of misery out of my possession? As for you, dear enemy—I have only begun to take my revenge upon you. I shall leave you alive, and in full possession of your senses—unlike your sword-sister. No doubt you wonder what I have done with her? I have wiped her mind clean; in time I shall implant my teachings in her, so that I shall have an acolyte of complete obedience and complete devotion. It was a pity that I could not force her to suffer as you shall, but her will combined with her link to her chosen goddess was far too strong to trifle with. But now that her mind is gone, the link has gone with it, and she will be mine for so long as I care to keep her."

Kethry was overwhelmed with agony and despair; she stifled a moan with difficulty. She felt tears burning her eyes and coursing down her cheeks; her vision was blurred by them. The demon smiled at the sight.

"As for you, you will be as potent a source of pain as my little toy is; know that you will feed my power with your grief and anguish. Know that your blood-sister will be my plaything, willingly suffering because I order it. Know all this, and know that you are helpless to prevent any of it! As for this—"

He prodded the body of Warrl with one toe. His smile spread even wider as she tried involuntarily to reach out, only to have the acolytes hold her arms back.

"I think that I shall find something suitable to use it for. Shall I have it mounted, or—yes. The fur is quite good; quite soft and unusual. I think I shall have it tanned—and it shall be your only bed, my enemy!"

He laughed, as Kethry struggled in the arms of his acolytes, stomach twisted and mind torn nearly in shreds by her grief and hatred of him. She subsided only when they threatened to wrench her arms out of their sockets, and hung limply in their grasp, panting with frustrated rage and weeping soundlessly.

"Take her, and take her friend. Put them in the place I prepared for them," Thalhkarsh ordered with a lift of one eyebrow. "And take *that* and *that* as well," he indicated the body of Warrl and Kethry's sword Need. "Put them where she can see them until I decide what to do with them. Perhaps, little toy, I shall give the blade to you."

Lastel's hands clenched and unclenched as he attempted to control himself. "Do it, damn you! If you do, I'll use it on you, you *bastard!*"

"How kind of you to warn me, then. But come—you wear a new body now, and I wish to see how it differs from the old—don't you?"

Kethry's last sight of the demon was as he swept Lastel up onto the platform, then she and Tarma were hustled down another brick-lined corridor, and shoved roughly into a makeshift cage that took up the back half of a stone-lined storage room. Warrl's carcass and Need were both dumped unceremoniously on the slate table in front of the cage door.

The room lacked windows entirely, and had only the one door now shut and (from the sounds that had come after her guards had shut it), locked. Light came from a single torch in a holder near the door. The cage was made of crudely-forged iron bars welded across the entire room, with an equally crude door of similar bars that had been padlocked closed. There was nothing whatsoever in the cage; she and Tarma had only what they were wearing, which in Tarma's case was little more than rags, and in hers, the simple shift and breeches Lastel had been wearing. Though she searched, she found no weapons at all.

Tarma sat blank-eyed in the corner of the cage where she'd been left, rocking back and forth and humming tunelessly to herself. The only thing that the demon hadn't changed was her voice; still the ruined parody of what it had been before the slaughter of her Clan.

Kethry went to her and knelt on the cold stone at her side. "Tarma?" she asked, taking her *she'enedra*'s hand in hers and staring into those blank blue eyes.

She got no response for a moment, then the eyes seemed to see her. One hand crept up, and Tarma inserted the tip of her index finger into her mouth.

"Tarma?" the Shin'a'in echoed ingenuously. And that was all of intelligence that Kethry could coax from her; within moments her eyes had gone blank again, and she was back to her rocking and tuneless humming.

Kethry looked from the mindless Tarma to the body of the *kyree* and back again, slow tears etching their way down her cheeks.

"My god, my god—" she wept, "Oh, Tarma, you were right! We should have gone for help."

She tried to take her oathkin in her arms, but it was like holding a stiff, wooden doll.

"If I hadn't been so *damned* sure of myself—if I hadn't been so determined to prove you were smothering me—it's all my fault, it's *all* my fault! What have I done? What has my pride done to you?"

And Tarma rocked and crooned, oblivious to everything around her, while she wept with absolute despair.

Eleven

Y ou lied to me, you bastard!" Green eyes blazed passionately with anger.

"You didn't listen carefully enough," Thalhkarsh replied to the amber-haired hellion whom he had backed into a corner of his "couch." "I said I would change your form; I never said *what* I would change it into."

"You never had any intention of changing me back to a man!" Lastel choked, sagging to the padded platform, almost incoherent with rage.

"Quite right." The demon grinned maliciously as he sat himself cross-legged on the padded platform, carefully positioning himself so as to make escape impossible. "Your emotions are strong; you are a potent source of power for me, and an ever-renewable source. I had no intention of letting you free of me while I still need you." He arranged himself more comfortably with the aid of a cushion or two; he had Lastel neatly pinned, and his otherworldly strength and speed would enable him to counter any move the woman made.

"Then *when?*"

"When shall I release you? Fool, don't you *ever* think past the immediate moment?" For once the molten-bronze face lost its mocking expression; the glowing red-gold eyes looked frustrated. "Why should you *want* release? What would you do if I gave you back your previous form—where would you go? Back to your wastelands, back to misery, back to petty theft? Back to a life with every man's hand against you, having to hide like a desert rat? Is that what you *want?*"

"I—"

"Fool; blind, stupid fool! Your lust for power is nearly as great as my own, yet you could accomplish *nothing* by yourself and *everything* with my aid!" the demon rose to his feet, gesticulating. "Think—for one moment, think! You are in a mage-Talented body now; one in which the currents of arcane power flow strongly. You could have me as a patron. You could have all the advantages of being my own High Prelate when I am made a god! And you wish to throw this all away? Simply because you do not care for the responses of a perfectly healthy and attractive body?"

"But it isn't *mine!* It's a woman!" Lastel shrank back into the corner, wailing. "I don't *want* this body—"

"But I want you in it. I desire you, creature I have made; I want you in a form attractive to me." The demon came closer and placed his hands on the walls to either side of Lastel, effectively rendering her immobile. "Your emotions run so high, and taste so sweetly to me that I sometimes think I shall never release you."

"Why?" Lastel whispered. "Why me, why this? And why *here?* I thought all your kind hated this world."

"Not I." The demon's eyes smoldered as his expression turned thoughtful. "Your world is beautiful in my eyes; your people have aroused more than my hunger, they have aroused my desire. I want this world, and I want the people in it! And I *will* have it! Just as I shall have you."

"No—" Lastel whimpered.

"Then I ask in turn, why? Or why not? What have I done save rouse your own passions? You are well fed, well clothed, well housed—nor have I ever harmed you physically."

"You're *killing* me!" Lastel cried, his voice breaking. "You're destroying my identity! Every time you look at me, every time you touch me, I forget what it was ever like, being a man! All I want is to be *your* shadow, your servant; I want to exist only for you! I never come back to myself until after you've gone, and it takes longer to remember what I was afterward—longer every time you do this to me."

The demon smiled again with his former cruelty, and brought his lips in to brush her neck. "Then, little toy," he murmured, "perhaps it is something best forgotten?"

Tarma was lost; without sight, without hearing, without senses of any kind. Held there, and drained weak past any hope of fighting back. So tired—too tired to fight. Too tired to hope, or even care. Emptied of every passion—
Wake UP!

The thin voice in her mind was the first sign that there was any life at all in the vast emptiness where she abode, alone. She strained to hear it again, feeling . . . something. Something besides the apathy that had claimed her.

Mind-mate, wake!

It was familiar. If only she could remember, remember anything at all.

Wake, wake, wake!

The voice was stronger, and had the feel of teeth in it. As if something large and powerful was closing fangs on her and shaking her. Teeth—

In the name of the Star-Eyed! the voice said, frantically. *You MUST wake!*

Teeth. Star-Eyed. Those things had meant something, before she had become nothing. Had meant something, when she was—

Tarma.

She was Tarma. She *was* Tarma still, Sworn One, *kyree*-friend, *she'enedra.*

Every bit of her identity that she regained brought more tiny pieces back with it, and more strength. She fought off the gray fog that threatened to steal those bits away, fought and held them, and put more and more of herself together, fighting back inch by inch. She was Shin'a'in, of the free folk of the open plains—she would not be held and prisoned! She—would—not—be—held!

Now she felt pain, and welcomed it, for it was one more bridge to reality. Salvation lay in pain, not in the gray fog that sucked the pain and everything else away from her. She held the pain to her, cherished it, and reached for the voice in her mind.

She found that, too, and held to it, while it rejoiced fiercely that she had found it.

No—not *it. He.* The *kyree*, the mage-beast. Warrl. The friend of her soul, as Kethry was of her heart.

As if that recognition had broken the last strand of foul magic holding her in the gray place, she suddenly found herself possessed again of a body—a body that ached in a way that was only too familiar. A body stiff and chilled, and sitting—from the feel of the air on her skin—nearly naked and on a cold stone floor. She could hear nothing but the sound of someone crying softly—and cautiously cracked her eyes open the merest slit to see where she was.

She was in a cage; she could see the iron bars before her, but unless she changed position and moved, she couldn't see much else. She closed her eyes again in an attempt to remember what could have brought her to this pass. Her memories tumbled together, confused, as she tried with an aching skull to sort them out.

But after a moment, it all came back to her, and with it, a rush of anger and hatred.

Thalhkarsh!

The demon—he'd tricked her, trapped her—then overpowered her, changed her, and done—something to her to send her into that gray place. But if Thalhkarsh had taken her, then where were Warrl and Kethry?

I'm lying on the table, mind-mate, said the voice, *The demon thinks he killed me; he nearly did. His magic sent me into little-death, and I decided to continue the trance until we were all alone; it seemed safer that way. There was nothing I could do for you. Your she'enedra is in the same cage as you. It would be nice to let her know the demon hasn't destroyed your mind after all. She thinks that you're worse than dead, and blames herself entirely for what was both your folly.*

Tarma moved her head cautiously; her muscles all ached. There *was* someone in the cage with her, crumpled in a heap in the corner; by the shaking of her shoulders, the source of the weeping—but—

That's not Kethry!

Not her body, but her spirit. The demon gave her body to the bandit.

What bandit?

The *kyree* gave a mental growl. *It's too hard to explain; I'm going to break the trance. Tend to your she'enedra.*

Tarma licked lips that were swollen and bruised. She'd felt this badly used once before, a time she preferred not to think about.

There was something missing; something missing—

"No," she whispered, eyes opening wide with shock, all thought driven from her in that instant by her realization of *what* was missing. "Oh, *no!*"

The stranger's head snapped up; swollen and red-rimmed amethyst eyes turned toward her. "T-t-tarma?"

"It's gone," she choked, unable to comprehend her loss. "The *vysaka* —the Goddess-bond—it's *gone!*" She could feel her sanity slipping; feel herself going over the edge. Without the Goddess-bond—

Take hold of yourself! the voice in her mind snapped. *It's probably all that damn demon's fault; break his spells and it will come back! And anyway, you're alive and I'm alive and Kethry's alive; I want us all to STAY that way!*

Warrl's annoyance was like a slap in the face; it brought her back to a precarious sanity. And with his reminder that Kethry was still alive, she turned back toward the stranger whose tear-streaked face peered through the gloom at her.

"Keth? Is that you?"

"You're back! Oh, Goddess bless, you're back!" The platinum-haired beauty flung herself into Tarma's arms, and clung there. "I thought he'd destroyed you, and it was all my fault for insisting that we do this ourselves instead of going for help like you wanted."

"Here, now." Tarma gulped back tears of her own, and pushed Kethry away with hands that shook. "We're not out of this yet."

"T-tarma—Warrl—he's—"

Very much alive, thank you. The great furry shape on the table outside their cage rose slowly to its four feet, and shook itself painfully. *I hurt. If you hurt like I hurt, we are all in very sad condition.*

Tarma sympathized with Kethry's bewilderment. "He pulled a *kyree* trick on us all, *she'enedra*. He told me that when the demon's magic hit him, it sent him into little-death—a kind of trance. He figured it was better to stay that way until we were alone." She examined the confused countenance before her. "He also said something about you trading bodies with a bandit . . . and don't I know that face?"

"Lastel Longknife," she replied shakily. "He lived; he's the one that had Thalhkarsh conjured up, and I guess he got more than he bargained for, because the demon turned him into a real woman. He was the one spreading the rumors to lure us in here, I'll bet. Now he's got *my* body—"

"I have the sinking feeling that you're going to tell me you can't work magic in this one."

"Not very well," she admitted. "Though I haven't tried any of the power magics that need more training than Talent."

"All right then; we can't magic our way out of this cage, let's see if we can think our way out."

Tarma did her best to ignore the aching void within her and took careful stock of the situation. Their prison consisted of the back half of a stone-walled room; crude iron bars welded across the middle made their half into a cage. It had an equally crude door, padlocked shut. There was only one door to the room itself, in the front half, and there were no windows; the floor was of slate. In half of the room beyond their cage was a table on which Warrl—and something else—lay.

"Fur-face, is that Need next to you?"

The same.

"Then Thalhkarsh just made one big mistake," she said, narrowing her eyes with grim satisfaction. "Get your tail over here, and bring the blade with you."

Warrl snorted, picked up the hilt of the blade gingerly in his mouth, and jumped down off the table with it. He dragged it across the floor, complaining mentally to Tarma the entire time.

"All right, Keth. I saw that thing shear clean through armor and more than once. Have a crack at the latch. It'll have to be you, she won't answer physically to me."

"But—" Kethry looked doubtfully at the frail arms of her new body, then told herself sternly to remember that Need was a *magical* weapon, that it responded (as the runes on its blade said) to woman's need. And they certainly needed out of this prison—

She raised the sword high over her head, and brought it down on the latch-bar with all of her strength.

With a shriek like a dying thing, the metal sheared neatly in two, and the door swung open.

"You are bold, priest," the demon rumbled.

"I am curious; perhaps foolish—but never bold," responded the plump, balding priest of Anathei. "I was curious when I first heard the rumors of your return. I was even more curious when the two who were responsible for your defeat before were missing this morning. I will confess to being quite confused to find one of them here."

He cast a meaningful glance at the demon's companion, curled sullenly on the velvet beside him. The sorceress did not appear to be happy, but she also did not appear coerced in any way. Come to that, there was something oddly different about her. . . .

"I repeat, you are bold; but you amuse me. Why are you here?" Thalhkarsh settled back onto his cushions, and with a flicker of thought increased the intensity of the light coming from his crimson lanterns. The musky incense he favored wafted upward toward the ceiling from a brazier at the edge of the padded platform where he reclined. This priest had presented himself at the door and simply asked to be taken to the demon; Thalhkarsh's followers had been so nonplussed by his quiet air of authority that they had done as he asked. Now he stood before Thalhkarsh, an unimpressive figure in a plain brown cassock, plump and aging, with his hands tucked into the sleeves of his robe. And he, in his turn, did not seem the least afraid of the demon; nor did it appear that anything, from the obscene carvings to the orgy still in progress on the platform behind the demon, was bothering him the slightest bit.

And that had the demon thoroughly puzzled.

"I am here to try to convince you that what you are doing is wrong."

"Wrong? *Wrong?*" The demon laughed heartily. "I could break you with one finger, and you wish to tell me that I am guilty of doing wrong?"

"Since you seem to wish to live in this world, you must live by some of its rules—and one of those is that to cause harm or pain to another is wrong."

"And who will punish me, priest?" The demon's eyes glowed redly, his lips thinning in anger. "You?"

"You yourself will cause your own punishment," the priest replied earnestly. "For by your actions you will drive away what even you must need—admiration, trust, friendship, love—"

He was interrupted by the sound of shouting and of clashing blades; he stared in surprise to see Tarma—a transformed Tarma—wearing an acolyte's tunic and nothing else, charging into the room driving several guards ahead of her. And with her was the platinum-haired child he had last seen at his own temple, telling his brothers of the rumors of Thalhkarsh.

But the blade in her hands was the one he had last seen in the sorceress' hands.

The woman at the demon's side made a tight little sound of smothered rage as the demon's guards moved to bar the exits or interpose themselves between the women and their target.

"Your anger is strong, little toy," Thalhkarsh laughed, looking down at her. "Use it, then. Become the instrument of my revenge. Kill her, and this time I promise you that I shall give you your man's body back." He plucked a sword from the hand of the guard next to him and handed it to his amber-tressed companion.

And the priest stared in complete bewilderment.

Given the weapon, the bandit needed no further urging, and flung himself at Kethry's throat.

Kethry, now no longer the tough, fit creature she had been, but a frail, delicate wraith, went down before him. Tarma tried to get to her, knowing that she was going to be too late—

But Warrl intervened, bursting from behind the crimson velvet hangings, flinging himself between the combatants long enough for Kethry to regain her footing and recover Need. She fumbled it up into a pathetic semblance of guard position; then stared at her own hands, wearing a stupified expression. After a moment Tarma realized why. Need was not responding to her—because Need could not act against a woman, not even *for* a woman.

And between Tarma and her *she'enedra* were a dozen or so followers of the demon.

But some of them were the ones who had so lately been sharing her own body with their master.

She let herself, for the first time since her awakening, truly *realize* what had been done to her—physically and mentally. Within an eyeblink she had roused herself to a killing battle-frenzy, a state in which all her senses were heightened, her reactions quickened, her strength nearly doubled. She would pay for this energized state later—if there *was* a later.

She gathered herself carefully, and sprang at the nearest, taking with her one of the heavy silken hangings that had been nearest her. She managed, despite the handicap of no longer having *her* rightful, battle-trained body, to catch him by surprise and tangle him in the folds of it. The only weapon the Shin'a'in had been able to find had been a heavy dagger; before the others had a chance to react to her first rush, she stabbed down at him, taking a fierce pleasure in plunging it into him again and again, until the silk was dyed scarlet with his blood—

Kethry was defending herself as best she could; only the fact that the bandit was once again not in a body that was his own was giving her any chance at all. Warrl's appearance had given her a brief moment of aid when she most needed it. Now Warrl was busy with one of the other acolytes. And it was apparent that Tarma, too, had her hands full, though she was showing a good portion of her old speed and skill. At least she wasn't in that shocked and bereft half-daze she'd fallen into when she first came back to herself.

But Kethry had enough to think about; she could only spare a scant second to rejoice at Tarma's recovery. She was doing more dodging than anything else; the bandit was plainly out for her death. As had occurred once before, the demon was merely watching, content to let his pawns play out their moves before making any of his own.

Tarma had taken a torch and set the trapped acolyte aflame, laughing wildly when he tried to free himself of the entangling folds of the silk coverlet and succeeding only in getting in the way of those that remained. Warrl had disposed of one, and was heading off a second. Kethry was facing a terrible dilemma—Need *was* responding sluggishly now, but only in pure defense. She knew she dared not kill the former bandit. If she did, there would be no chance of ever getting her own body back. There was no way of telling what would happen if she killed what was, essentially, *her* body. She might survive, trapped in this helpless form that lacked the stamina and strength and mage-Talents of her own—or she might die along with her body.

Nor did she have any notion of what *Need* might do to her if she killed another woman. Possibly nothing—or the magical backlash of breaking the geas might well leave her a burned-out husk, a fate far worse than simply dying.

Now Tarma had laid hands on another sword—one lighter than the broadsword she was used to, and with an odd curve to it. She had never used a weapon quite like this before, but a blade was a blade. The rest of the acolytes made a rush for her, forgetting for the moment—if, indeed, they had ever known—that they were not dealing with an essentially helpless woman, given momentary strength by hysteria, but a highly trained martial artist. Tarma's anger and hysteria were as carefully channeled as a powerful stream diverted to turn a mill. As they rushed her, evidently intending to overpower her by sheer numbers, she took the hilt in both hands, rose and pivoted in one motion, and made a powerful, sweeping cut at waist level that literally sliced four of them in half.

Somewhere, far in the back of her mind, a normally calm, analytical part of her went wild with joy. This strange sword was better than any blade she'd ever used before; the curve kept it from lodging, the edge was as keen as the breath of the North Wind, and the grip, with a place for her to curl her forefinger around it, made it almost an extension of her hand. It was perfectly balanced for use by either one hand or two. Her eyes lit with a kind of fire, and it wasn't all the reflection of torch-flames.

Her remaining opponents stumbled over the bleeding, disemboweled bodies of their erstwhile comrades, shocked and numb by the turn in fortunes. Just last night this woman had been their plaything. Now she stood, blood-spattered and half-naked as she was, over the prone bodies of five of them. They hesitated, confused.

Warrl leapt on two from the rear, breaking the neck of one and driving the other onto Tarma's waiting blade.

Eight down, seven standing.

Seven? There were only six—

Tarma felt, more than saw, the approach of one from the rear. She pivoted, slashing behind her with the marvelously liquid blade as she did so, and caught him across the throat. Even as he went down, another, braver than the rest, lunged for her. Her kick caught him in the temple; his head snapped to one side and he fell, eyes glazing with more than unconsciousness; Warrl made sure of him with a single snap of his massive jaws, then dashed away again to vanish somewhere.

Five.

I come from behind you.

Tarma held her ground, and Warrl ran in from under the hangings. The man he jumped had both a short sword and shield, but failed to bring either up in time. Warrl tore his throat out and leapt away, leaving him to drown in his own blood.

Four.

Tarma charged between two of those remaining, slashing with a figure-eight motion, knowing they would hesitate to strike at her with the swords they'd snatched from their sheaths for fear of striking each other. She caught the first across the eyes, the second across the gut. The one she'd blinded stumbled toward her with blood pouring between his fingers, and she finished him as she whirled around at the end of her rush.

Two.

Kethry tried to simply defend herself, but the bandit wasn't holding back.

So she did the only thing she could; she cast Need away from her, and backed off far enough to raise her hands over her head, preparatory to blasting the bandit with a bolt of arcane power.

Warrl leaped on the right-hand man; tore at his thigh and brought him down, then ripped out his gut. Tarma's final opponent was the first that showed any real ability or forethought; he was crouching where Warrl couldn't come at him from the rear, with a sword in one hand and a dagger in the other. His posture showed he was no stranger to the blade. She knew after a feint or two that he was very good, which was probably why he'd survived his other companions. Now she had a problem. There was no one to get in his way, and the unfamiliar feel of her transformed body was a distraction and a handicap. Then she saw his eyes narrow as she moved her new sword slightly—and knew she had a psychological weapon to use against him. This was *his* blade she held, and he wanted it back. Very badly.

She made her plan, and moved.

She pretended to make a short rush, then pretended to stumble, dropping the sword. When he grabbed for it, dropping his own blade, Tarma snatched a torch from the wall beside her and thrust it at his face, and when he winced away from it, grabbed a dagger from the litter of weapons on the floor and flung it straight for his throat, knowing that marksmanship was not a thing that depended on weight and balance, but on the coordination of hand and eye—things that wouldn't change even though her body had shifted form considerably. As he went down, gurgling and choking, to drown in his own blood like one of the men Warrl had taken out, she saw that Kethry was being forced to take the offensive —and saw the look of smug satisfaction on the demon's face as she did so.

And she realized with a sudden flash of insight that they had played right into his hands.

"Why do you do nothing?" the little priest asked in pure confusion.

"Because this is a test, human," the demon replied, watching with legs stretched out comfortably along the platform. "I have planned for this, though I shall admit candidly to you that I did not expect this moment to come quite so soon, nor did I expect that the beast should regain its life and the swordswoman her mind. But these are minor flaws in my plan; however it comes out, I shall win. As you may have guessed, it is the sorceress' spirit that inhabits my servant's body; should he slay her, I shall be well rid of her, and my servant in possession of a mage-Talented form. Should the swordswoman die, I shall be equally well rid of her; should she live, I shall simply deal with her as I did before. Should my servant die, I shall still have the sorceress, and her geas-blade will blast her for harming a woman, even though she does not hold it in her hand —for she has been soul-bonded to it. And that will render her useful to me. Or should it kill her, she may well be damned to *my* realm, for the breaking of the oaths she swore. So you see, no matter the outcome, I win—and *I* am in no danger, for only my own magics could touch me in any way."

"I . . . see," the priest replied, staring at the bloody combat before them, mesmerized by the sight.

Tarma realized that they were once again playing right into the demon's hands. For if Kethry killed the one wearing her form, she would damn herself irrevocably, once by committing a kind of suicide, and twice by breaking the geas and the vow her bond with Need had set upon her— never to raise her hand against a woman—three times by breaking her oath to her *she'enedra*.

And by such a betrayal she would probably die, for surely Thalhkarsh had warded his creature against magics. Or Need would blast her into death or mindlessness. Should she die, she could damn herself forever to Thalhkarsh's particular corner of the Abyssal Plane, putting herself eternally in his power. It was a good bet he had planned that she must slay the bandit by magic, since Need would not serve against a woman—and certainly he had woven a spell that would backlash all her unleashed power on the caster. Kethry would be worse than dead—for she would be his for the rest of time, to wreak revenge on until even he should grow weary of it.

Unless Tarma could stop her before she committed such self-damnation. And with time running out, there was only one way to save her.

With an aching heart she cried out in her mind to Warrl, and Warrl responded with the lightning-fast reactions of the *kyree* kind, born in magic and bred of it.

He leapt upon the unsuspecting Kethry from the rear, and with one crunch of his jaws, broke her neck and collapsed her windpipe.

Both Kethry and the bandit collapsed—

Tarma scrambled after the discarded mage-blade, conscious now only of a dim urge to keep Kethry's treasured weapon out of profane hands, and to use the thing against the creature that had forced her to kill the only human she cared for. Need had hurt the demon before—

But she had forgotten one thing.

She wasn't a mage, so Need's other gift came into play; the gift that protected a woman *warrior* from magic, no matter how powerful. No magic not cast with the consent of the bearer could survive Need entering its field.

The spell binding Tarma was broken, and she found herself in a body that had regained its normal proportions.

This was just such a moment that the priest had been praying for. The spell-energy binding Kethry into Lastel's body was released explosively with the death-blow. The priest took full control of that energy, and snatched her spirit before death had truly occurred. Using the potent energies released, he sent Lastel's spirit and Kethry's back to their proper containers.

There were still other energies being released; those binding Lastel's form into a woman's shape, and those altering Tarma. Quicker than thought the priest gained hold of those as well. With half of his attention he erected a shield over the swordswoman and her partner; with the other he sent those demon-born magics hurtling back to their caster.

Kethry had been stunned by Warrl's apparent treachery; had actually felt herself dying—

—and now suddenly found herself very much alive, and back in her proper body. She sat up, blinking in surprise.

Beside her on the marble floor was a dead man, wearing the garments she herself had worn as Lastel. Warrl stood over him, growling, every hair on end. But her mage-sense for energy told her that the tale had not yet seen its end. As if to confirm this, a howl of anguish rose behind her.

"*Noooooooooooo.* . . ."

The voice began a brazen bass, and spiraled up to a fragile soprano.

Kethry twisted around, staring in astonishment. Behind her was Thalhkarsh—

A demon no longer. A *male* no longer. Instead, from out of the amethystine eyes of the delicate mortal creature he had mockingly called his toy stared Thalhkarsh's hellspawn spirit—dumbfounded, glassy-eyed with shock, hardly able to comprehend what had happened to him. Powerless now—and as female and fragile as either of the two he had thought to take revenge upon—and a great deal more helpless.

"This—cannot—be—" she whispered, staring at her thin hands. "I cannot have failed—"

"My poor friend."

The little priest, whom Kethry had overlooked in the fight, having eyes only for the demon, his servants, and Lastel, reached for one of the demon's hands with true and courageous sympathy.

"I fear you have worked to wreak only your own downfall—as I warned you would happen."

"No—"

"And you have wrought far too well, I fear—for if I read this spell correctly, it was meant to be permanent unto death. And as a demon, except that you be slain by a specific blade, you cannot die. Am I not correct?"

The demon's only response was a whimper, as she sank into a heap of loose limbs among the cushions of what once had been her throne, her eyes fogging as she retreated from the reality she herself had unwittingly created.

Tarma let her long legs fold under her and sat where she had stood, trembling from head to toe, saying nothing at all, a look of glazed pain in her eyes.

Kethry dragged herself to Tarma's side, and sat down with a thump.

"Now what?" Tarma asked in a voice dulled by emotional and physical exhaustion, rubbing her eyes with one hand. "*Now* what are we going to do with him?"

"I—I don't know."

"I shall take charge of her," the priest said, "She is in no state to be a threat to us, and we can easily keep her in a place from which she shall find escape impossible until she has a true change of heart. My child," he addressed himself to Tarma, concern in his eyes, "what is amiss?"

"My bond—it's gone—" she looked up at the priest's round, anxious face, and the look in her eyes was of one completely lost.

"Would you fetch my fellows from the temple?" he asked Kethry. *"That* one is locked within herself, but I may have need of them."

"Gladly," Kethry replied, "but can you help *her?"*

"I will know better when you return."

She ran—or tried to—to fetch the little priest's fellow devotees. She all but forced herself past a skeptical novice left to guard the door by night; the noise she made when she finally was driven to lose her temper and shout at him brought the High Prelate of Anathei to the door himself. He was more than half asleep, wrapped in a blanket, but he came awake soon enough when she'd begun to relate the night's adventures. He snapped out a series of orders that were obeyed with such prompt alacrity that Kethry's suspicions as to their friend's true rankings were confirmed long before three novices brought her his robes—those of an arch-priest—and half the members of the order, new-roused from their beds.

Though simple, hardly more ornate than what he had worn to the inn, the robes radiated power that Kethry could feel even without invoking mage-senses.

A half-dozen other members of his order scurried away from the convocation at the cloister door and came back wearing ceremonial garments and carrying various arcane implements. Kethry led the procession of cowled, laden priest-mages through the predawn streets at a fast trot. The night-watch took one look at the parade and respectfully stepped aside, not even bothering with hailing them.

When she got them as far as the open door of the temple, her own strength gave out, and she stopped to rest, half-collapsed against the smiling image of the rain-god. By the time she reached the inner sanctum, they had the situation well in hand. The bodies had been carried off somewhere, the obscene carvings shrouded, a good deal of the blood cleaned up, and—most importantly—Thalhkarsh placed under such tight arcane bindings that not even a demi-god could have escaped.

"I believe I can restore what was lost to your friend," the priest said when Kethry finally gathered up enough courage to approach him. "But I shall need the assistance of both yourself and the *kyree."*

"Certainly, anything—but why? It will help if I know what I'm supposed to be doing."

"You are familiar with her goddess, and as Shin'a'in adopted, She shall hear you where she might not hear me. You might think of yourself as the arrow, and myself as the bow. I can lend your wish the power to reach the Star-Eyed, but only *you* of all of us know Her well enough to pick Her aspect from all the other aspects of the Lady."

"Logical—what do I do? Warrl says—'whatever you want he'll do'—"

"Just try to tell her Warrior that the bond has been broken and needs to be restored—or Tarma may well—"

"Die. Or go mad, which is the same thing for a Shin'a'in."

Kethry knelt at the priest's feet on the cold marble of the desecrated temple floor, Warrl at her side. Tarma remained where she was, sunk in misery and loss so deep that she was as lost to the world around her as Thalhkarsh was.

Kethry concentrated with all her soul as the priest murmured three words and placed his hand on her head and Tarma's in blessing.

Please Lady—please hear me, she thought in despair, watching Tarma's dead eyes. *I've—I've been less understanding than I could have been. I forgot—because I wanted to—that I'm all the Clan she has left. I only thought of the freedom I thought I was losing. I don't know You, but maybe You know me—*

There was no answer, and Kethry shut her eyes in mental agony. *Please, hear us! Even if You don't give a damn about us, she pledged herself to You—*

Foolish child.

The voice in her mind startled her; it was more like music than a voice.

I am nothing but another face of your own Lady Windborn—how could I not know you? Both of you have been wrong—but you have wrought your own punishment. Now forgive yourselves as you forgive each other—and truly be the two-made-one—

Kethry nearly fainted at the rush of pure power that passed through her; when it ebbed, she steadied herself and glanced up in surprise.

The little priest was just removing his hand from Tarma's bowed head; his brow was damp with sweat, but relief showed in the smiling line of his mouth. As Tarma looked up, Kethry saw her expression change from one of pathetic bereavement to the utter relief of one who has regained something thought gone forevermore.

A heavy burden of fear passed from Kethry's heart at the change. She closed her eyes and breathed her own prayer of thanks.

So profound was her relief that it was several moments before she realized Tarma was speaking to the priest.

"I don't know how to—"

"Then don't thank me," he interrupted. "I simply re-opened what the demon had closed; my pleasure and my duty. Just as tending to the demon as she is now is my duty."

"You're certain you people can keep him—or should I say her?—from any more trouble?" she asked doubtfully of her erstwhile debating partner as Kethry shook off her weariness and looked up at them. To the sorceress' profound gratitude, Tarma looked to be most of the way back to normal—a rapid recovery, but Kethry was used to rapid recoveries from the Shin'a'in. The face she turned to Kethry was calm and sane once again, with a hint of her old sense of humor. She reached out a hand, and Tarma caught it and squeezed it once, without taking her attention from the priest.

"Sworn One, we are placing every safeguard known to mortal man upon her and the place where we shall keep her," the little priest said soberly. "The being Thalhkarsh shall have no opportunity for escape. Her only chance will be to truly *change,* for the spells we shall use will not hold against an angelic spirit, only one of evil intent. Truly you have given us the opportunity we have long dreamed of."

"Well," Tarma actually grinned, though it was weakly. "After all, it isn't every day someone can present you with a captive demon to preach to. Not to put too fine a point on it, we're giving you folk a chance to prove yourselves." She managed a ghost of a chuckle. "Though I'll admit I had no notion you were capable of restraining demons so handily."

"As you yourself pointed out, Sworn One, when one goes to preach to demons, the preacher had best be either agile or a very fine magician." The balding priest's brown eyes vanished in smile wrinkles. "And as your partner has rightly told me, while Thalhkarsh seems helpless *now,* there is no guarantee that she will remain so. We prefer to take no chance. As you say, this is our unlooked-for opportunity to prove the truth of our way to the entire world, and as such, we are grateful to you beyond telling."

With that, the little priest bowed to both of them, and his train of underlings brought the once-demon to her feet, bound by spells that at the moment were scarcely needed. She was numbly submissive, and they guided her out the way they had come, bound for their own temple.

Kethry got to her feet and silently held out her hand to Tarma, who took it once again with no sign of resentment, and pulled herself to her feet by it. They left the scene of slaughter without a backward glance, moving as quickly as their aching bodies would allow, eager to get out into the clean air.

"Warrior's Oath—how long have we been in there?" Tarma exclaimed on seeing the thin sliver of moon and the positions of the stars.

"About twenty-four candlemarks. It's tomorrow morning. Is—*that's* not your sword, is it?" Kethry, lagging a little behind, saw that the shape strapped to Tarma's back was all wrong.

" 'No disaster without some benefit,' *she'enedra,*" Tarma lifted a hand to caress the unfamiliar hilt. "I've never in my life had a weapon like this one. There's no magic to it beyond exquisite balance, fantastic design, and the finest steel I've ever seen, but it is without a doubt the best blade I've ever used. It acted like part of my arm—and you're going to have to cut off that arm to get it away from me!"

Briefly alarmed by her vehemence, Kethry stretched weary mage-senses one more time, fearing to find that the blade was some kind of ensorcelled trap, or bore a curse.

She found nothing, and sighed with relief. Tarma was right, there was no hint of magic about the blade, and her partner's reaction was nothing more than that of any warrior who has just discovered her ideal dreamed-of weapon.

They limped painfully back to their inn with Warrl trailing behind as guard against night-thugs, stopping now and then to rest against a handy wall or building. The night-watch recognized Kethry and waved them on. The cool, clean air was heavenly after the incense and perfume-laden choke of the temple. When they finally reached their inn, they used the latchstring on their window to let themselves back inside and felt their way into their room with only the banked embers of the hearth-fire for light. Kethry expended a last bit of mage-power and lit a candle, while Tarma dropped her weapons wearily. Beds had never looked so inviting before.

And yet, neither was quite ready to sleep.

"This time we've really done it, haven't we?" Tarma ventured, easing her "borrowed" boots off her feet and pitching them out the open window for whoever should find them in the morning to carry away. She stripped as quickly as her cuts and bruises would permit, and the clothing followed the boots as the Shin'a'in grimaced in distaste; Kethry handed her clean breeches and an undertunic from her pack and Tarma eased herself into them with a sigh and numerous winces.

"You mean, we've locked him up for good? I think so; at least insofar as I can ever be sure of anything. And we aren't going to make the mistake of forgetting about him again."

"Lady Bright, not bloody likely!" Tarma shuddered. "We'll be getting messages from the Temple every two months, like clockwork; that was part of the agreement I made with little Nemor. Huh, think of him as archpriest—seems logical now, but he sure doesn't look the part."

"Until he puts on the authority. I could almost feel sorry for old Thalhkarsh. I can't imagine a worse punishment for a demon than to have sweetness-and-light preached at him for as long as he lives—which might well be forever."

"And besides—" Tarma smiled, getting up with a muffled groan and another grimace, and walking over to the window. She leaned out, letting the breeze lift her hair and cool her face. "Who knows? They might succeed in redeeming him. . . ."

"Tarma—all this—we both nearly died. I would have died with a broken promise to you on my soul."

Kethry paused for a long moment, so long that Tarma was afraid she wasn't going to finish what she had begun to say.

She turned from looking out the window to regard her partner soberly, knowing that Kethry had something troubling her gravely. Even Warrl looked up from where he lay on Tarma's bed, ears pricked and eyes unfathomable. Finally Kethry sighed and continued.

"I guess what I want to ask you is this. Do you *want* me—us—to stop this wandering? To go back to the Plains? After all, it's me that's been keeping us on the road, not you. I—haven't found any man I'd care to spend more than a night or two with, but that really doesn't matter to my promise. It doesn't take liking to get children. Oh, hell, there's always Justin and Ikan, I *do* like them well enough to share a bed with them for a bit. And once we had some children, I could keep myself in practice easily enough. I could establish a White Winds school even without the cash—I'm getting close enough to Adept to do that now. I'd rather have better circumstances to do that than we have right now, but I could scrape along. We certainly have the reputation now to attract good pupils."

Tarma turned back to gaze up at the waning moon, troubled. It was true that the most important thing in the world to *her* was the re-founding of her slaughtered Clan—and they *had* nearly died without being any closer to that goal.

There were times when she longed for the tents of her people and the open Plains with all her soul. And there were other negatives to this life they were leading. There was no guarantee something like this couldn't happen again. Being gang-raped, or so she suspected, had been the least of the unspeakable things she'd suffered unaware in Thalhkarsh's hands.

Far worse was the absence of the Star-Eyed's presence in her soul when she'd returned to herself. And when her goddess had not returned to her with Thalhkarsh's transformation, she'd been afraid for a moment that the Warrior would not take her back with her celibacy violated.

That had turned out to be a foolish fear, as her priest-friend had proved to her. No sooner had he cleansed her of the last of Thalhkarsh's magic-bindings, then she felt the Warrior's cool and supportive presence once again in her heart; the asexual psychic armor of the Sword Sworn closed around her again, and she could regard the whole experience as something to learn and benefit from. She was heart-whole and healed again—in spirit if not in body.

Still, none of this would have happened if they'd returned to the Plains; in the very home of the Goddess of the Four Winds the demon would have been powerless, no matter what he had claimed; the bandit would never have made his way past the Outer Clans. And—Warrior's Oath, how Tarma longed to see the Tale'sedrin banner flying above a full encampment, with bright-faced children within and fat herds without. Kethry's wandering feet had nearly caused their deaths this time, and Tale'sedrin had nearly died with them. And her Clan, as for any Shin'a'in, was the most important thing in Tarma's life.

But no, it *wasn't* the most important thing, not anymore. Not if Kethry was going to be made a captive to see that dream achieved. A willing captive she would be, perhaps, but still a captive.

Kethry had been right—she *had* been stifling her friend, and with the best of intentions. She had been putting invisible hobbles on her, or trying to.

Her Shin'a'in soul rebelled at the notion—"You do not hobble your hound, your horse, your hawk, your lover, or your *she'enedren*," went the saying, "love must live free." A prisoner was a prisoner, no matter how willingly the bonds were taken. And how truly Shin'a'in could Kethry be, bound? And if she were not Shin'a'in in her heart, how could her children follow the Clan-ways with whole spirits?

And yet—and yet—there remained Kethry's oath, and her dream. If Kethry died . . .

She closed her eyes and emptied her heart, and hoped for an answer.

And miraculously, one came.

A tiny breath of chill wind wafted out of the north, and coiled around her body, enclosing her in silence. And in that silence, an ageless voice spoke deep in her soul.

What is your Clan but your sister? Trust in her as your left-hand blade, as she trusts in you, and you shall keep each other safe.

Tarma's heart lifted and she turned back to face her partner with a genuine smile.

"What, and turn you into 'another Shin'a'in brood mare'? Come now, *she'enedra,* we treat our stock better than that! A warsteed mates when *she* is ready, and not before. Surely you don't reckon yourself as less than Hellsbane!" Tarma's smile turned wicked. "Or should I start catching handsome young men and parading them before you to tempt your appetite . . . ?"

Kethry laughed with mingled chagrin and relief, blushing hotly.

"Perhaps I ought to begin a collection, hmm? That's what we do for our warsteeds, you know, present them with a whole line of stallions until one catches their fancy. Shall I start a picket line for you? Or would you rather I acquired a house of pleasure and stocked the rooms so that you could try their paces at your leisure before choosing?"

Kethry rolled up into the covers to hide her blushes, still laughing.

Tarma joined the laughter, and limped back to her own bed, blowing out their candle and falling into the eiderdowns to find a dreamless and healing sleep.

For there *were* going to be tomorrows, she was sure of that now—and they'd better be in shape to be ready for them.

Oathbreakers

Dedicated to:
Betsy, Don and Elsie

The real *magic-makers*

Thanks, folks.

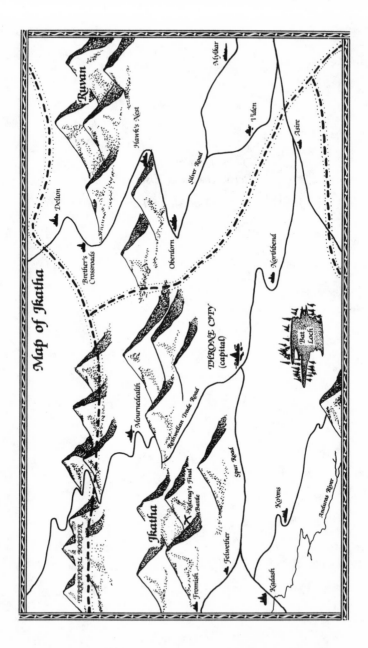

Map of Jkatha

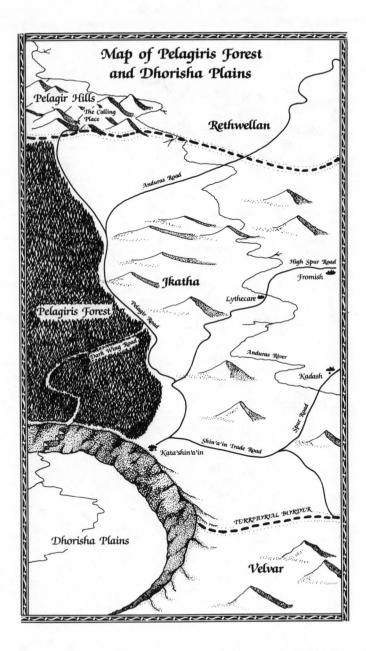

Map of Pelagiris Forest
and Dhorisha Plains

Pelagir Hills

The Calling
Place

Rethwellan

Anduras Road

High Spur Road
Fromish

Ikatha

Lythecare

Pelagiris Forest

Pelagir Road

Anduras River

Dark Wing Road

Kadash

Spur Road

Shin'a'in Trade Road

Kata'shin'a'in

TERRITORIAL BORDER

Dhorisha Plains

Velvar

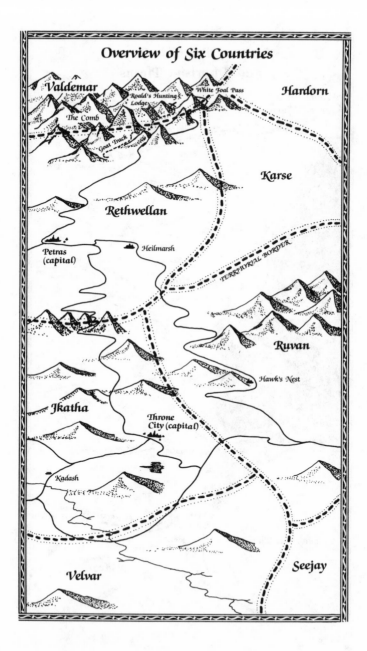

Overview of Six Countries

Valdemar

Hardorn

Roald's Hunting Lodge

White Foal Pass

The Comb

Karse

Goat Track

Rethwellan

Petras (capital)

Heilmarsh

TERRITORIAL BORDER

Ruvan

Hawk's Nest

Ikatha

Throne City (capital)

Kadash

Velvar

Seejay

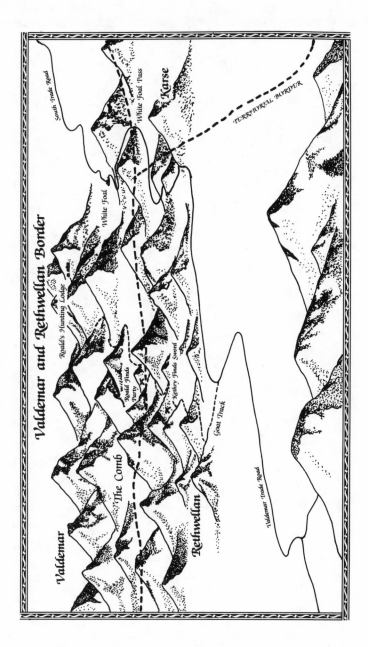

One

*I*t *was a dark and stormy night. . . .*
    :Pah!: Warrl said with disgust so thick Tarma could taste it. *:Must you even* think *in cliches?:*

Tarma took her bearings during another flash of lightning, tried and failed to make out Warrl's shaggy bulk against watery blackness, then thought back at him, *Well it* is, *dammit!*

Tarma shena Tale'sedrin, who was Shin'a'in nomad, Kal'enedral (or, to outClansmen, a "Sword-sworn"), and most currently Scoutmaster for the mercenary company called "Idra's Sunhawks" was *not* particularly happy at this moment. She was sleet-drenched, cold and numb, and mired to her armpits; as was her companion, the lupine *kyree* Warrl. The Sunhawks' camp was black as the inside of a box at midnight, for all it was scarcely an hour past sunset. Her hair was plastered flat to her skull, and trickles of icy water kept running into her eyes. She couldn't even feel the ends of her fingers anymore. Her feet hurt, her joints ached, her nose felt so frozen it was like to fall off, and her teeth were chattering hard enough to splinter. She was not pleased, having to stumble around in the dark and freezing rain to find the tent she shared with her partner and oathbound sister, the White Winds sorceress, Kethry.

The camp was dark out of necessity; even in a downpour sheltered fires would normally burn in the firepits in front of each tent, or a slow-burning torch would be staked out in the lee of every fourth, but that was impossible tonight. You simply couldn't keep a fire lit when the wind howled at you from directions that changed moment by moment, driving

the rain before it; and torches under canvas were a danger even the most
foolhardy would forgo. A few of the Sunhawks had lanterns or candles
going in their tents; but the weather was foul enough that most preferred
to go straight to sleep when not on duty. It was too plaguey cold and wet
to be sociable. For heat, most stuck to the tiny charcoal braziers Idra had
insisted they each pack at the beginning of this campaign. The Sunhawks
had known their Captain too well to argue about (what had seemed at
the time) a silly burden; now they were grateful for her foresight.

But with the rain coming down first in cascades, then in water*walls,*
Tarma couldn't see the faint glow of candles or lanterns shining through
the canvas walls that would have told her where the tents were. So she
slogged her way through the camp mostly by memory and was herself
grateful to Idra for insisting on an *orderly* camp, laid out neatly, in proper
rows, and not the hugger-mugger arrangement some of the other merc
officers were allowing. At least she wasn't tripping over tent ropes or
falling into firepits.

:I can smell Keth and magic,: Warrl said into her mind. *:You should see
the mage-light soon.:*

"Thanks, Furball," Tarma replied, a little more mollified; she knew he
wouldn't *hear* her over the howl of the wind, but he'd read the words in
her mind. She kept straining her eyes through the tempest for a sight of
the witchlight Keth had promised to leave at the front—to distinguish
their tent from the two hundred odd just like it.

They were practically on top of it before she saw the light, a blue glow
outlining the door flap and brightening the fastenings. She wrestled with
the balky rawhide ties (the cold made her fingers stiff) and it took so long
to get them unfastened that she was swearing enough to warm the whole
camp before she had the tent flaps open. Having Warrl pressed up
against her like a sodden, unhappy cat did not help.

The wind practically threw Tarma into the tent, and half the sleet that
was knifing down on their camp tried to come in with her. Warrl remained plastered against her side, not at all helpful, smelling in the
pungent, penetrating way only a wet wolf can smell—even if Warrl only
resembled a wolf superficially. The *kyree* was not averse to reminding
Tarma several times a day (as, in fact, he was doing now) that they *could*
have been curled up in a cozy inn if they hadn't signed on with this
mercenary company.

She turned her back to the occupant of the tent as soon as she got past
the tent flaps; she needed all her attention to get them laced shut against
the perverse pull of the wind. "Gods of damnation!" she spat through
stiff lips, "Why did I *ever* think this was a good idea?"

* * *

Kethry, only just now waking from a light doze, refrained from replying; she just waited until Tarma got the tent closed up again. Then she spoke three guttural words, activating the spell she'd set there before drowsing off—and a warm yellow glow raced around the tent walls, meeting and spreading upward until the canvas was bathed in mellow light and the temperature within suddenly rose to that of a balmy spring day. Tarma sighed and sagged a little.

"Let me take that," Kethry said then, unwinding herself from the thick wool blankets of her bedroll, rising, and pulling the woolen coat, stiff with ice, from Tarma's angular shoulders. "Get out of those soaked clothes."

The swordswoman shook water out of her short-cropped black hair, and only just prevented Warrl from trying the same maneuver.

"Don't you dare, you flea-bitten cur! Gods above and below, you'll soak every damned thing in the tent!"

Warrl hung his head and looked sheepish, and waited for his mindmate to throw an old thread-bare horse blanket over him. Tarma enveloped him in it, head to tail, held it in place while he shook himself, then used it to towel off his coarse gray-black fur.

"Glad to see you, Greeneyes," Tarma continued, stripping herself down to the skin, occasionally wincing as she moved. She rummaged in her pack, finding new underclothing, and finally pulling on dry breeches, thick leggings and shirt of a dark brown lambswool. "I thought you'd still be with your crew—"

Kethry gave an involuntary shudder of sympathy at the sight of her partner's nearly-emaciated frame. Tarma was always thin, but as this campaign had stretched on and on, she'd become nothing but whipcord over bone. She hadn't an ounce of flesh to spare; no wonder she complained of being cold so much! And the scars lacing her golden skin only gave a faint indication of the places where she'd taken deeper damage— places that would ache demonically in foul weather. Kethry gave her spell another little mental nudge, sending the temperature of the tent a notch upward.

I should have been doing this on a regular basis, she told herself guiltily. *Well—that's soon mended.*

"—so there's not much more I can do." The sweet-faced sorceress gathered strands of hair like suntouched amber into both hands, twisting her curly mane into a knot at the back of her neck. The light from the shaded lantern which hung on the tent's crossbar, augmented by the light of the shielding spell, was strong enough that Tarma noted the dark circles under her cloudy green eyes. "Tresti is accomplishing more than I can at this point. You know my magic isn't really the Healing kind, and on top of that, right now we have more wounded men than women."

"And Need'll do a man about as much good as a stick of wood."

Kethry glanced at the plain shortsword slung on the tent's centerpole, and nodded. "To tell you the truth, lately she won't heal anybody but you or me of anything but *major* wounds, so she isn't really useful at all at this point. I wonder sometimes if maybe she's saving herself—Anyway, the last badly injured woman was your scout Mala this morning."

"We got her to you in time? Gods be thanked!" Tarma felt the harpwire-taut muscles of her shoulders go lax with relief. Mala had intercepted an arrow when the scouts had been surprised by an enemy ambush; Tarma had felt personally responsible, since she'd sent Warrl off in the opposite direction only moments before. The scout had been barely conscious by the time they'd pounded up to the Sunhawk camp.

"Only just; an arrow in the gut is not something even for a Master-Healer to trifle with, and all we have is a Journeyman."

"Teach me to steal eggs, why don't you? Tell me something I *don't* know," Tarma snapped, ice-blue eyes narrowed in irritation, harsh voice and craggy-featured scowl making her look more like a hawk than ever.

Oops. A little too near the bone, I think.

"Temper," Kethry cautioned; it had taken years of partnership for them to be able to say the right thing at the right time to each other, but these days they seldom fouled the relationship. "Whatever happened, you can't undo it; you'd tell me that if the case were reversed. And Mala's all right, so there's no permanent harm done."

"Gah—" Tarma shook her head again, then continued the shake right down to her bare feet, loosening all the muscles that had been tensed against cold and anger and frustration. "Sorry. My nerves have gone all to hell. Finish about Mala so I can tell the others."

"Nothing much to tell; I had Need unsheathed and in her hands when they brought her inside the camp. The arrow's out, the wound's purified and stitched and half-healed, or better. She'll be back dodging arrows—with a little more success, I hope!—in about a week. After that all I could do that was at all useful was to set up a *jesto-vath* around the infirmary tent—that's a shielding spell like the one I just put on ours. After that I was useless, so I came back here. It was bad enough out there I figured a *jesto-vath* on *our* tent was worth the energy expense, and I waited for you to get in before putting it in place so I wouldn't have to cut it. Can't have the Scoutmaster coming down with a fever." She smiled, and her wide green eyes sparkled with mischief. "Listen to you, though—two years ago, you wouldn't have touched a command position, and now you're fretting over your scouts exactly the way Idra fusses over the rest of us."

Tarma chuckled, feeling the tense muscles all over her body relaxing. "You know the saying."

"Only too well—'That was then, this is now; the moment is never the same twice.' "

"You're learning. Gods, having a mage as a partner is useful."

Tarma threw herself onto her bedroll, rolling over onto her back and putting her hands behind her head. She stared at the canvas of the tent roof, bright with yellow mage-light, and basked in the heat.

"I pity the rest of the Hawks, with nobody to weatherproof their tents, and nothing but an itty-bitty brazier to keep it warm. Unless they're twoing, in which case I wish them well."

"Me too," Kethry replied with a tired smile, sitting crosslegged on her own bedroll to fasten the knot of hair more securely, "though there's only a handful really twoing it. I rather suspect even the ones that aren't will bundle together for warmth, though, the way we used to when I wasn't capable of putting up a *jesto-vath.*"

"You must be about Master-grade yourself by now, no?"

Tarma cracked her left eye open enough to see Kethry's face. The question obviously caught the mage by surprise.

"Uh—"

"Beyond it?"

"I—"

"Thought so." Tarma closed her eyes again in satisfaction. "This job should do it, then. Through Idra we'll have contacts right up into the Royal ranks. If we can't wangle the property, students and wherewithal for our schools after this, we'll never get it."

"We'd have had it before this if it hadn't been for that damned minstrel!" Now it was Kethry's turn to snap with irritation.

"*Must* you remind me?" Tarma groaned, burying her face in the crook of her arm. "Leslac, Leslac, if it weren't for Bardic immunity I'd have killed you five times over!"

"You'd have had to stand in line," Kethry countered with grim humor. "I'd have beat you to it. Bad enough that he sings songs about us, *worse* that he gets the salient points all bass-ackwards, but—"

"To give us the reputation that we're shining warriors of the Light is *too damned much!*"

They had discovered some four or five years ago that there was a particular Bard, one Leslac by name, who was making a specialty of creating ballads about their exploits. That would have been all to the good, for it was certainly spreading their name and reputation far and wide—except that he was *also* leaving the impression that the pair of them were less interested in money than in Just Causes.

Leslac had stressed and overstressed their habit of succoring women in distress and avenging those who were past distress. So now anyone who had an ax to grind came looking for them—most particularly, women. And usually they came with empty pockets, or damned little in the way of payment to offer, while the paying jobs they would *rather* have taken had been trickling away to others—because those who might have offered those jobs couldn't believe they'd be interested in "mere money."

And to add true insult to injury, a good half of the time Kethry's geas-blade Need would force them into *taking* those worthless Just Causes. For Need's geas was, as written on her blade, "Woman's Need calls me/ As Woman's Need made me./Her Need will I answer/As my maker bade me." By now Kethry was so soul-bonded to the sword that it would have taken a god to free her from it. Most of the time it was worth it; the blade imparted absolute weapons expertise to Kethry, and would Heal anything short of a death wound on any woman holding it. And after the debacle with the demon-godling Thalhkarsh, Need *had* seemed to quiet down in her demands, unless *directly* presented with a woman in dire trouble. But with all those Just Causes showing up, Need had been rapidly turning into something more than a bit expensive to be associated with, thanks to Leslac.

They'd been at their wits' ends, and finally had gone to another couple of mercenaries, old friends of theirs, Justin Twoblade and Ikan Dryvale, for advice. They hadn't really hoped the pair would have any notions, but they were the last resort.

And, somewhat to Tarma's surprise, they'd *had* advice.

It was the off-season for the Jewel Merchants' Guild, Justin and Ikan's employers; that meant no caravans. And *that* meant that the paired mercenary guards were cosily holed up in their private quarters at the Broken Sword, with the winter months to while away. They certainly weren't stinting themselves; they had a pair of very decent rooms, the Broken Sword's excellent ale—and, as Tarma discovered when she tapped at their door, no lack of female companionship. But the current pair of bright-eyed lovelies was sent pouting away when straw-haired Ikan answered their knock and discovered just who it was that had chosen to descend upon himself and his partner.

One of the innkeeper's quick-footed offspring was summoned then, and sent off for food and ale—for neither Justin nor his shieldbrother would hear a word of serious talk until everyone was settled and comfortable at their hearth, meat and drink at their elbows. Justin and Ikan took their hospitality very seriously.

"I've figured this was coming," Justin had said, somewhat to Tarma's shock, "And not just because of that idiot songster. You two have very unique and specialized skills—not like me and Ikan. You've gotten about as far as you can as an independent pairing. Now me and Ikan, we had the opposite problem. We're just ordinary fighting types; a bit better than most, but that's all that distinguishes us. We had to join a company to *get* a reputation; then we could live off that reputation as a pair. But you— you've *got* a reputation that will get you high fees from the right mercenary company."

Tarma had shaken her head doubtfully at that, but Justin had fixed her with his mournful houndlike eyes, and she'd held her peace.

"You, Tarma," he'd continued, "need much wider experience, especially experience in commanding others—and only a company will give you that. Kethry, you need to exercise skills and spells you wouldn't use in a partnership, and to learn how to delegate if your school is ever going to be successful, and again, you'll learn that in a company."

"Long speech," Tarma had commented sardonically.

"Well, I've got one, too," Ikan had said, winking a guileless blue eye at her. "You also need exposure to highborns, so that they know your reputation *isn't* just minstrelsy and moonshine. You haven't a choice; you truly need to join a company, one with a reputation of their own, one good enough that the highborns come to *them* for their contract. Then, once you *are* ready to hang up your blades and start your schools, you'll have noble patrons and noble pupils panting in anticipation of your teaching—and two not-so-noble aging fighters panting in anticipation of easy teaching jobs."

Kethry had laughed at Ikan's comic half-bow in their direction. "I take it that you already have a company in mind?"

"Idra's Sunhawks," Justin had replied blandly.

"The *Sunhawks?* Warrior's Oath—you'd aim us bloody damned *high,* wouldn't you?" Tarma had been well taken aback. For all that they were composed of specialist-troops—skirmishers, horse-archers and trackers —the Sunhawks' repute was so high that kings and queens *had* been known to negotiate their contracts with Idra in person. "Good gods, I should bloody well think highborns negotiate with them; their leader's of the damned Royal House of Rethwellan! And just how are we supposed to get a hearing with Captain Idra?"

"Us," Ikan had replied, stabbing a thumb at his chest. "We're ex-Hawks; we started with her, and probably would still be with her, but Idra was going more and more over to horse-archers, and we were getting less useful, so we decided to light out on our own. But we left on good terms; if we recommend that she give you a hearing, Idra will take our word on it."

"And once she sees that you're what you claim to be, you'll be in, never fear." Justin had finished for him. "Shin'a'in Kal'enedral—gods, you'd fit in like a sword in a sheath, Hawkface. And you, Keth—Idra's always got use for another mage, 'specially one nearly Masterclass. The best she's got now is a couple of self-taught hedge-wizards. Add in Furball there—you'll be a combination she won't be able to resist."

So it had proved. With letters in their pouches from both Ikan and his partner (both could read and write, a rarity among highborn, much less mercenaries) they had headed for the Sunhawks' winter quarters, a tiny hill town called Hawksnest. The name was not an accident; the town owed its existence to the Sunhawks, who wintered there and kept their dependents there, those dependents that weren't permanent parts of the Company bivouac. Hawksnest was nestled in a mountain valley, sheltered from the worst of the mountaintop weather, and the fortified barracks complex of the Sunhawks stood between it and the valley entrance. When the Hawks rode out, a solid garrison *and* all the Hawks-in-training remained behind. Idra believed in creating an environment for her fighters in which the only worries they needed to have on campaign were associated *with* the campaign.

Signing with Idra was unlike signing with any other Company; most Hawks stayed with Idra for years—she had led the Company for nearly twenty years. She'd willingly renounced her position as third in line to the throne of Rethwellan twenty-five years earlier, preferring freedom over luxury. She'd hired on with a mercenary company herself, then after five years of experience accompanied by her own steady rise within the ranks, had formed the Hawks.

Tarma had been impressed with the quarters and the town; the inhabitants were easy, cheerful and friendly—which spoke of good behavior on the part of the mercs. The Hawks' winter quarters were better than those of many standing armies, and Tarma had especially approved of the tall wooden palisade that stretched across the entrance to Hawksnest, a palisade guarded by *both* Hawks and townsmen. And the Hawks themselves —as rumor had painted them—were a tight and disciplined group; drilling even in the slack season, and showing no sign of winter-born softness.

Idra had sent for them herself after reading their letters; they found her in her office within the Hawks' barracks. She was a muscular, athletic looking woman, with the body of a born horsewoman, mouse-gray hair, a strong face that could have been used as the model for a heroic monument, and the direct and challenging gaze of the professional soldier.

"So," she'd said, when they took their seats across the scratched, worn table that served as her desk, "if I'm to trust Twoblade and Dryvale, it should be me begging *you* to sign on."

Kethry had blushed; Tarma had met that direct regard with an unwavering gaze of her own. "I'm Kal'enedral," Tarma said shortly. "If you know Shin'a'in, that should tell you something."

"Swordsworn, hmm?" The quick gray eyes took in Tarma's brown clothing. "Not on bloodfeud—"

"That was ended some time ago," Tarma told her, levelly. *"We* ended it, we two working together. That was how we met."

"Shin'a'in Kal'enedral and outClansman. Unlikely pairing—even given a common cause. So why are you still together?"

For answer they both turned up their right palms so that she could see the silver crescent-scars that decorated them. One eyebrow lifted, ever so slightly.

"Sa. *She'enedran.* That explains a bit. Seems I've heard of a pair like you."

"If it was in songs," Tarma winced, "let's just say the stories are true in the main, but false in the details. And the author constantly left out the fact that we've always done our proper planning before we ever took on the main event. Luck plays wondrous small part in what we do, if we've got any say in the matter. And besides all that—we're a lot more interested in making a living than being somebody's savior."

Idra had nodded; her expression had settled into something very like satisfaction. "One last question for each of you—what's your specialty, Shin'a'in—and what's your rank and school, mage?"

"Horseback skirmishing, as you probably figured, knowing me for Shin'a'in." Tarma had replied first. "I'm a damned good archer—probably as good as any you've got. I can fight afoot, but I'd rather not. We've both got battlesteeds, and I'm sure you know what *that* means. My secondary skill is tracking."

"I'm White Winds, Journeyman; I'd say I lack a year or two of being Masterclass." Kethry had given her answer hard on the heels of Tarma's. "One other thing I think Ikan and Justin may have forgotten—Tarma is mindmate to a *kyree,* and I've got a bespelled blade I'm soul-bonded to. It gives me weapons expertise, so I'm pretty good at keeping myself in one piece on a battlefield; that's damned useful in a fight, you won't have to spare anybody to look after me. And besides that, it will Heal most wounds for a woman—and that's any woman, not just me."

Idra had not missed the implication. "But not a man, eh? Peculiar, but —well, I'm no mage, can't fathom your ways. About half my force is female, so that would come in pretty useful, regardless. But White Winds —that's no Healing school."

"No, it's not," Kethry agreed, "I haven't the greater Healing magics, just a few of the lesser. But I've got the battle-magics, and the defensive magics. I'm not one to stand in the back of a fight, shriek, and look appalled—"

For the first time Idra smiled. "No, I would guess not, for all that you look better suited to a bower than a battlefield. About the *kyree*—we're talking Pelagir Hills changeling, here? Standard wolf-shape?"

"*Hai*—overall he's built like a predator cat, but he's got the coat and head of a wolf. Shoulder comes to about my waist, he runs like a Plains grasscat; no stamina for a long march, but he's used to riding pillion with me." Tarma's description made Idra nod, eyes narrowed in *definite* satisfaction. "He's got a certain ability at smelling out magic, and a certain immunity to it; given he's from the Pelagirs he might have other tricks, but he hasn't used them around me yet. Mindspeaks, too, mostly to me, but he could probably make himself heard to anyone with a touch of the Gift. Useful scout, even more useful as an infiltrator. But be aware that he eats a lot, and if he can't hunt, he'll be wanting fresh meat daily. That'll have to be part of any contract we sign."

"Well, from what my boys say, what I knew by reputation, and what you've told me, I don't think I need any more information. Only one thing I don't reckon—" Idra had said, broad brow creased with honest puzzlement. "If you don't mind my asking what's none of my business even if I *do* sign you, why's the *kyree* mindmate to the fighter and not the mage's familiar?"

Tarma groaned, then, and Kethry laughed. "Oh, Warrl has a mind of his own," the mage had answered, "I *had* been the one doing the calling, but he made the decision. He decided that I didn't need him, and Tarma did."

"So besides your formidable talents, I get three recruits, not two; three used to teamworking. No commander in her right mind would argue with that." Idra then stood up, and pushed papers across her desk to them. "Sign those, my friends, if you're still so minded, and you'll be Sunhawks before the ink dries."

*   *   *

So it had been. Now Tarma was subcommander of the scouts, and Keth was in charge of the motley crew concerned with Healing and magery—two hedge-mages, a field-surgeon and herbalist and his two apprentices, and a Healing Priest of Shayana. "Priestess" would have been a more accurate title, but the Shayana's devotees did not make any gender differences in their rankings, which ofttimes confused someone who expected one sex and got the opposite. Tresti was handfasted to Sewen, Idra's Second, a weathered, big-boned, former trooper; that sometimes caused Keth sleepless nights. She wondered what would happen if it was ever Sewen carried in through the door flap of the infirmary, but the possibility never seemed to bother Tresti.

Tarma and Kethry had fought in two intense campaigns, each lasting barely a season; this was their third, and it had been brutal from the start. But then, that was often the case with civil war and rebellion.

Ten moons ago, the King of Jkatha had died, declaring his Queen, Sursha, to be his successor and Regent for their three children. Eight moons ago Sursha's brother-in-law, Declin Lord Kelcrag, had made a bid for the throne with his own armed might.

Lord Kelcrag was initially successful in his attempt, actually driving Sursha and her allies out of the Throne City and into the provinces. But he could not eliminate them, and he had made the mistake of assuming that defeat meant that they would vanish.

Queen Sursha had talent and wisdom—the talent to attract both loyal and *capable* people to her cause, and the wisdom to know when to stand back and let *them* do what was needful, however distasteful that might be to her gentle sensibilities. That talent won half the kingdom to her side; that wisdom allowed her to pick an otherwise rough-hewn provincial noble, Havak Lord Leamount, as her General-In-Chief and led her to give *him* her full and open support even when his decisions were personally repugnant to her.

General Lord Leamount levied or begged troops from every source he could—and then hired specialists to fill in the skill gaps his levies didn't have.

And one of the first mercenary Captains he had approached was Idra. His troops were mostly foot, with a generous leavening of heavy horse—no skirmishers, no scouts, no light horse at all, other than his own personal levy of hill-clansmen. The hillmen were mounted on rugged little ponies; good in rough country but slow in open areas, and useless as strike-and-run skirmishers.

And by now Idra's troops were second to none, thanks in no small part to Tarma. The Shin'a'in had seen no reason why she could not benefit her

presumptive clan's coffers, and her new comrades as well; she'd arranged
for the Sunhawks to get first pick of the sale-horses of Tale'sedrin. These
weren't battlesteeds, which were *never* let out of Shin'a'in hands, but they
weren't culls either, which was what the Sunhawks had been seeing. And
when the Hawks had snapped up every beast she offered, she arranged
for four more clans to bring in their first-pick horses as well.

So now the Hawks were better mounted than most nobles, on horses
that could be counted as extra weapons in a close-in fight.

That fact was not lost on Lord Leamount, nor was he blind to Idra's
canny grasp of strategy. Idra was made part of the High Command, and
pretty much allowed to dictate *how* her Hawks were used.

As a result, although the fighting had been vicious, the Hawks were
still at something like four-fifths strength; their ranks were nowhere near
as decimated as they might have been under a commander who threw
them recklessly at the enemy, rather than using them to their best advantage.

At Midsummer, Lord Leamount's combined forces had fallen on the
Throne City and driven Lord Kelcrag out. Every move Kelcrag had made
since then had been one of retreat. His retreat had been hard fought, and
each acre of ground had been bitterly contested, but it had been an
inexorable series of losses.

But now autumn was half over; he had made a break-and-run, and at
this point everyone in Leamount's armies knew why. He was choosing to
make a last stand on ground *he* had picked.

Both sides knew this next battle would *have* to bring the war to a
conclusion. In winter it would be impossible to continue any kind of real
fight—the best outcome would be stalemate as troops of both sides
floundered through winter storms and prayed that ill-luck and hardship
would keep from thinning their ranks *too* much. If Kelcrag retreated to
his own lands, he'd come under seige, and ultimately lose if the besieging
troops could be supplied and rotated. If he fled into exile, the Queen
would have to mount an ever-present vigil against his return—an expensive proposition. She and Leamount had both wanted to invoke the Mercenary Code ritual of Oathbreaking and Outcasting on him—but while
he *was* undeniably a rebel, he had actually broken no vows; nor could
Sursha find the requisite triad for the full ceremony of priest, mage and
honest man, all of whom *must* have suffered personal, irreparable harm
at his hands as a result of violation of sworn oaths. So technically, he
could have been seen by some to be the injured party.

And as for Kelcrag in such a situation, exile would mean impoverish-
ment and hardship, circumstances he was not ready to face; further, it

would bring the uncertainty of when or even *if* he could muster enough troops and allies to make a second try.

Kelcrag had chosen his ground with care, Tarma had to give him that. He had shale cliffs (impossible to scale) to his left, scrub forest and rough, broken ground to his right (keeping Leamount from charging from that direction); his troops were on the high ground, occupying a wide pass between the hills, with a gradual rising slope between the loyalists and his army—

It was as close to being an ideal situation for the rebels as Tarma could imagine. There was no way to come at him except straight on, and no way he could be flanked. And now the autumnal rains were beginning.

Of all of Idra's folk, only the scouts had been deployed, seeking (in vain) holes or weaknesses in Kelcrag's defenses. For the rest, it had been Set up camp, Dig in, and Wait. Wait for better weather, better information, better luck.

"Gah—" Tarma groaned again. "I hope Kelcrag's as miserable on his damned hill as we are down here. Anything out of the mages?"

"Mine, or in general?"

"Both."

"Mine have been too busy fending off nuisance-spells to bother with trying to see what's going on across the way. I've been setting up wards on the camp, protections on our commanders, and things like the *jestovath* on the Healer's tent. I haven't heard anything directly from Leamount's greater mages, but I've got some guesses."

"Which are?" Tarma stretched, then turned on her side.

"The Great Battle Magics were exhausted early on for *both* sides in this mess, and none of the mages have had time to regather power. That leaves the Lesser—which means they're dueling like a pair of tired but equally-matched bladesmen. Neither can see what the other is doing; neither can get anything through that's more than an annoyance. And neither wants to let down their guards and their shields enough to recharge in a power circle or open up enough to try one of the Greater Magics they might have left. So your people will be pretty much left alone except for physical, material attacks."

"Well, that's a blessing, any—"

"Scoutmaster?" came a plaintive call from outside the tent. "Be ye awake yet?"

"Who the bloody—" Tarma scrambled for the lacings of the door flaps as Kethry hastily cut the spell about the door with two slashes of her hands and a muttered word.

"Get in here, child, before you turn into an ice lump!" Tarma hauled

the half-frozen scout into their tent; the girl's brown eyes went round at
the sight of the spell energy in the tent walls, wide and no little frightened. She looked like what she was, a mountain peasant; short, stocky
and brown, round of face and eye. But she could stick to the back of her
horse like a burr on a sheep, she was shrewd and quick, and nobody's
fool. She was one of the Hawks Tarma had been thinking of when she'd
mentioned other ways of keeping warm; Kyra was shieldmated to Rild, a
mountain of a man who somehow managed to sit a horse as lightly as
thin Tarma.

"Keth, this is Kyra, she's one of the new ones. Replaced Pawell when
he went down." Tarma pushed the girl down onto her bedroll and
stripped the sodden black cloak from her shoulders, hanging it to dry
beside her own coat. "Kyra, don't look so green; you've seen Keth in the
Healer's tent; this is just a bit of magic so we sleep more comfortable.
Keth's better than a brazier, and I don't have to worry about her tipping
over in the night!"

The girl swallowed hard, but looked a little less frightened. "Beg pardon, but I ain't seen much magery."

"I should think not, out in these hills. Not much call for it, nor money
to pay for it. So—spit it out; what brings you here, instead of curled up
with that monster you call a shieldmate?"

The girl blushed brilliant red. "Na, Scoutmaster—"

"Don't 'na' me, my girl. I may not play the game anymore, but I know
the rules—and before the Warrior put her Oath on me, I had my moments, though you children probably wouldn't think it to look at me, old
stick that I am. Out with it—something gone wrong with the pairing?"

"Eh, no! Naught like that—I just been thinking. Couldn't get a look
round before today; now seems I know this pass, like. Got kin a ways
west, useta summer wi' 'em. Cousins. If I'm aright, 'bout a day's ride west
o' here. And there was always this rumor, see, there was this path up
their way—"

Tarma didn't bother to hide her excitement; she leaned forward on her
elbows, feeling a growing internal certainty that what Kyra was about to
reveal was vital.

"—there was this story abaht the path, d'ye ken? The wild ones, the
ponies, they used it. At weanin' time we'd go for 'em t' harvest the foals,
but some on 'em would allus get away—well, tales said they used that
path, that it went all the way through t'other side. D'ye take my meaning?"

"Warrior Bright, you *bet* I do, my girl!" Tarma jumped lithely to her
feet, and pulled Kyra up after her. "Keth?"

"Right." Kethry made the slashing motions again, and the magic parted from the door flaps. "Wait a hair—I don't want you two finding our answer and then catching your deaths."

Another pass of hands and a muttered verse sent water steaming up out of coat and cloak—when Tarma pulled both off the centerpole they were dry to the touch.

Tarma flashed her partner a grin. "Thanks, milady. If you get sleepy, leave the door open for me, hey?"

Kethry gave a most unladylike snort. "As if I could sleep after this bit of news! I haven't been working with you for this long not to see what you saw—"

"The end to the stalemate."

"You've said it. I'll be awake for hours on this one." Kethry settled herself with her blankets around her, then dismissed the magic altogether. The tent went dark and cold again, and Kethry relit her brazier with another muttered word. "I'll put that *jesto-vath* back up when you get back—and make it fast! Or I may die of nerves instead of freezing to death!"

Two

Back out into the cold and wet and dark they went, Kyra trailing along behind Tarma. She stayed right at Tarma's elbow, more a presence felt than anything seen, as Warrl, in mindtouch with Tarma, led both of them around washouts and the worst of the mud. Tarma's goal was the Captain's tent.

She knew full well it would be hours before Sewen and Idra saw *their* bedrolls; she'd given them the reports of her scouts just before fumbling her way to her own rest, and she knew they would still be trying to extract some bit of advantage out of the bleak word she'd left with them.

So Warrl led them to Idra's quarters; even in the storm-black *it* was the only tent *not* hard to find. Idra had her connections for some out-of-the-ordinary items, and after twenty years of leading the Hawks, there was no argument but that she had more than earned her little luxuries. There was a bright yellow mage-light shining like a miniature moon atop each of the poles that held up a canvas flap that served as a kind of sheltered porch for the sentry guarding the tent. Unlike Keth's dim little witchlight, these were bright enough to be seen for several feet even through the rain. If it had been reasonable weather, and if there had been any likelihood that the camp would be attacked, or that the commanders of the army would be sought out as targets, Idra's quarters would be indistinguishable from the rest of the Hawks'. But in weather like this—Idra felt that being able to *find* her, quickly, took precedence over her own personal safety.

Idra's tent was about the size of two of the bivouac tents. The door flap was fastened down, but Tarma could see the front half of the tent glowing from more mage-lights within, and the yellow light cast shadows of Idra and Sewen against the canvas as they bent over the map-table, just as she'd left them.

Warrl was already moving into the wavering glow of the mage-lights. He was a good couple of horse-lengths in front of them, which was far enough that the sentry under that bit of sheltering canvas couldn't see Kyra and Tarma to challenge them—at least not yet. No matter—and no matter that Warrl's black fur couldn't be seen in the rain even with the glow of the mage-lights on him. Warrl barked three times out of the storm, paused, then barked twice more. That was *his* password. Every man, woman, and noncombatant in the Hawks knew Warrl and Warrl's signal—and knew that where Warrl was, Tarma was following after.

So by the time Tarma and Kyra had slogged the last few feet to the tent, the sentry was standing at ease, the door flap was unlaced, and Sewen was ready to hold it open for them against the wind. His muddy gray eyes were worried as he watched the two of them ease by him. Tarma knew what he was thinking; at this hour, any caller probably meant more trouble.

"I trust this isn't a social call," Idra said dryly, as they squeezed themselves inside and stood, dripping and blinking, in the glow of her mage-lights. The mage-lights only made her plain leather armor and breeches look the more worn and mundane. "And I hope it isn't a disciplinary problem—"

Kyra's autumnal eyes were even rounder than before; Tarma suppressed a chuckle. Kyra hadn't seen the Captain except to sign with her, and was patently in awe of her. "Captain, this is my new scout, Kyra—"

"Replaced Pawell, didn't she?"

"Aye—to make it short, she thinks she knows a way to come in behind Kelcrag."

"Great good gods!" Idra half rose off of her tall stool, then sank down again, with a look as though she'd been startled out of a doze.

Well, that *certainly got their attention,* Tarma thought, watching both Idra and her Second go from weary and discouraged to alert in the time it took to say the words.

"C'mere, kid," Sewen rumbled. He took Kyra's wool-clad elbow with a hard and callused hand that looked fit to crush the bones of her arm, and which Tarma knew from experience could safely keep a day-old chick sheltered across a furlong of rough ground. He pulled her over to the table in the center of the tent. "Y'read maps, no? Good. Here's us. Here's him. Report—"

Kyra plainly forgot her awe and fear of magic, and the diffidence with which she had regarded her leaders, and became the professional scout beneath Sewen's prodding. The tall, bony Second was Idra's right hand and more—where her aristocratic bearing sometimes overawed her own people, particularly new recruits, Sewen was as plain as a clod of earth and awed no one. Not that anyone ever thought of insubordination around him; he was just as respected as Idra—it was just that he looked and sounded exactly like what he was; a common fighter who'd come up through the ranks on brains and ability. He still dressed, by preference, in the same boiled-leather armor and homespun he'd always worn, though he could more than afford the kind of expensive riveted brigandine and doeskin Idra and Tarma had chosen. He understood everything about the Hawks from the ground up—because he'd served the Hawks since Idra's fifth year of commanding them. Idra and Tarma just leaned over the maptable with him and let him handle the young scout.

"So—on the face of it, it bears checking. That's a task for the scouts," Idra said at last, when Kyra had finished her report. She braced both hands on the table and turned to her Scoutmaster. "Tarma, what's your plan?"

"That I take out Kyra and—hmm—Garth, Beaker and Jodi," Tarma replied after a moment of thought. "We leave before dawn tomorrow and see what we can see. If this trail still exists, we'll follow it in and find out if the locals are right. I'll have Beaker bring a pair of his birds; one to let you know if we find the trail at all, and one to tell you yea or nay on whether it's usable. That way you'll have full information for Lord Leamount without waiting for us to get back."

"Good." Idra nodded in satisfaction, as a bit of gray-brown hair escaped to get into her eyes. "Sewen?"

"What I'd do," Sewen affirmed, pushing away from the table and sitting back onto his stool. "Them birds don't like water, but that's likely to make 'em want their coops more, maybe fly a bit faster, hey? Don' wanta send a mage-message, or Kelcrag's magickers might track it."

"Uh-huh; that was my thought," Tarma agreed, nodding. "That, and the sad fact that other than Keth, *our* magickers might not be able to boost a mage-message that far."

"I need Keth here," Idra stated, "and none of Leamount's mages are fit enough to travel over that kind of territory."

Sewen emitted a bark of laughter, weathered face crinkling up for a moment. "Gah, that lot's as miserable as a buncha wet chickens in a leaky hennery right now. They don' know this weather, an' ev'ry time they gotta move from their tent, y'd think it was gonna be a trip t' th' end of th' earth!"

Idra looked thoughtful for a moment, and rubbed the side of her nose with her finger. "This isn't wizard weather, is it, do you suppose?"

Both Tarma and her scout shook their heads vigorously. "Na, Cap'n," Kyra said, cheerful light brightening her round face. "Na, is just a bit of a gentle fall storm. Y'should see a *bad* one, now—"

Idra's eyebrows shot upward; she straightened and looked seriously alarmed until Sewen's guffaw told her she'd been played for an ignorant flatlander.

"Seriously, no," Tarma seconded, "I asked Keth. She says the only sign of wizard weather would be if this *stopped*—that it's got too much weight behind it, whatever that means."

Sewen lifted his own eyebrow and supplied the answer. "She meant it's somethin' comin' in the proper season—got all the weight of time an' *what should be* behind it." He grinned at Tarma's loose jaw, showing teeth a horse could envy. "Useta study wizardry as a lad, hadn't 'nough Gift t' be more'n half a hedge-wizard, so gave't up."

"Good, then, we're all agreed." Idra straightened her shoulders, gave her head an unconscious toss to get that bit of her hair out of her face. "Tarma, see to it. Who will you put in to replace you tomorrow?"

"Tamar. Next to Garth and Jodi, he's my best, and he's come in from the skirmishers."

"Good. And tell him to tell the rest of your scouts not to give the enemy any slack tomorrow, but not to get in as close as they did today. I don't want them thinking we've maybe found something else to concentrate on, but I don't want any more gutwounds, either."

It was dawn, or nearly, and the rain had slackened some. There was still lightning and growling thunder, but at least you could *see* through the murk, and it was finally possible to keep the shielded torches at the entrance to the guarded camp alight.

Tarma saw her scouts assembled beneath one of those torches as she rode up to the sentry. She felt like yawning, but wouldn't; she wouldn't be a bad example. *Cold, ye gods, I'm half-frozen and we haven't even gotten out of the camp yet,* she thought with resignation. *I haven't been warm since summer.*

:And then you were complaining about heat,: Warrl replied sardonically.

"I was not. That was Keth," she retorted. "I *like* the heat."

Warrl did not deign to reply.

Tarma was already feeling grateful for Kethry's parting gift, the water-repelling cape Keth had insisted on throwing over her coat. *It's not magic,* Keth had said, *I don't want a mage smelling you out. Just tight-woven, oiled silk, and bloody damned expensive. I swapped a* jesto-vath *on his tent to Gerrold for it, for as long as the rains last. I hope you don't mind the fact that it's looted goods—*

Not likely, she'd replied.

So today it was Keth looking out for and worrying about her. They seemed to take it turn and turn about these days, being mother-hen. Well, that was what being partners was all about.

:Took you long enough to come to that conclusion,: Warrl laughed. *:Now if you'd just start mother-henning me—:*

"You'd bite me, you fur-covered fiend."

:Oh, probably.:

"Ah—you're hopeless," Tarma chided him, smothering a grin. "Let's look serious here; this is business."

:Yes, oh mistress.:

Tarma bit back another retort. She never won in a contest of sharp tongues with the *kyree.* Instead of answering him, she pondered her choice of scouts again, and was satisfied, all things considered, that she'd picked the best ones for the job.

First, Garth: a tiny man, and dark, he looked like a dwarfish shadow on his tall Shin'a'in gelding. He was one of Tarma's first choices for close-in night work, since his dusky skin made it unnecessary for him to smear ash on himself, but his most outstanding talents were that he could ride like a Shin'a'in and track like a hound. His one fault was that he couldn't hit a haystack with more than two arrows out of ten. He was walking his bay gelding back and forth between the two sentries at the sally-point, since his beast was the most nervous of the five that would be going out, and the thunder was making it lay its ears back and show the whites of its eyes.

Beaker: average was the word for Beaker; size, coloring, habits—average in everything except his nose—*that* raptor's bill rivaled Tarma's. His chestnut mare was as placid of disposition as Garth's beast was nervous, and Beaker's temperament matched his mare's. As Tarma rode up, they both appeared to be dozing, despite the cold rain coming down on their heads. Fastened to the cantle of Beaker's saddle were two cages, each the size of two fists put together, each holding a black bird with a green head. Beaker was a good tracker, almost as good as Garth, but *this* was his specialty; the training and deployment of his messenger birds.

Jodi: sleepy-eyed and deceptively quiet, this pale, ice-blonde child with evident aristocratic blood in her veins was their mapmaker. Besides that skill, she was a vicious knife fighter and as good with a bow as Garth was poor with one. She rode a gray mare with battlesteed blood in her; a beast impossible for anyone but her or Tarma to ride, who would only allow a select few to handle her. Jodi sat her as casually as some gentle palfrey—and with Jodi in her saddle, the mare acted like one. Her only fault was that she avoided situations where she would have to command the way she would have avoided fouled water.

And Kyra: peasant blood and peasant stock, she'd trained herself in tracking, bow and knife, and hard riding, intending to be something other than some stodgy farmer's stolid wife. When the war came grinding over her parents' fields and her family had fled for their lives, she'd stayed. She'd coolly sized up both sides and chosen Sursha's—then sized up the mercenary Companies attached to Sursha's army and decided which ones she wanted to approach.

She'd started first with the Hawks, though she hadn't really thought she'd get in—or so she had confessed to Tarma after being signed on. Little had she guessed that Scout Pawell had coughed out his life pinned to a tree three days earlier—and that the Hawks had been down by two scouts *before* that had happened. Tarma had interviewed her and sent her to Sewen, who'd sent her to Idra—who'd sent her back to Tarma with the curt order—"Try her. If she survives, hire her." Tarma had sent her on the same errand that had killed Pawell. *Kyra* had returned. Since Pawell had had no relatives, no leman and no shieldmate to claim his belongings, Tarma gave her Pawell's dun horse, Pawell's gear, and Pawell's tentmate. Kyra had quickly acquired something Pawell hadn't—tentmate had turned to shieldmate and lover.

The Scouts altogether approved, as Pawell had been standoffish and his replacement was anything but. The romance had amused and touched them. Kyra had begun to bloom under the approval, to think for herself, to make judgment calls. The Kyra that had joined them would never have come to Tarma with an old tale and a rumor; Kyra of "now" had experience enough to *know* how important that rumor could be, and enough guts to present the information herself. She was Tarma's personal pick to become a subcommander herself in a few years.

It was false dawn; one hour to real dawn, and there was a hint that the sky was getting lighter. No words were needed; they all knew what they had to do. When Tarma rode gray Ironheart into the waiting knot of Scouts and horses, those dismounted swung back up into their saddles. Tarma didn't even slacken her pace; all five of them left the camp in proper diamond formation, as if they'd rehearsed the whole maneuver. Tarma had point (since as commander she was the only one of the five

with all the current passwords), Garth tail, Jodi right and Kyra left—
Beaker and his precious birds rode protected in the middle.

They rode along the back of the string of encampments; dark tents
against slowly graying sky to their right, scrub forest and hills stark black
against the sky to their left. The camps were totally dark, since just about
everyone had encountered the same troubles as the Hawks had with
lights and fires in the pouring rain.

They were challenged almost as soon as they left their own camp; a
foot-sentry, sodden, but alert. He belonged to Staferd's Cold-drakes; this
was the edge of *their* camp. Tarma nodded to herself with satisfaction at
his readiness, and gave him the countersign.

Then came a heavy encampment of regular infantry, whose sentry
hailed Warrl, who was trotting at Ironheart's flank, by name, and called
out; "You're recognized, Sunhawks. Pass on." Tarma felt a little twitchy
about that one, but couldn't fault him. You challenged those whom you
didn't recognize; you could let known quantities by. And there were no
kyree in Kelcrag's forces.

At the next encampment—Duke Greyhame's levy—they were physically challenged; a fully-armed youth with an arrogant sneer on his lips,
mounted on a heavy, wild-eyed warhorse. He blocked their path until
Tarma gave an elaborate countersign. Even then, he wouldn't clear the
path entirely. He left only enough room for them to ride past in single
file, unless they wanted to desert the firm ground and ride on the mushy
banks. And he backed off with some show of reluctance, and much induced rearing and prancing of his gelding.

"Scoutmaster—"

Garth eased his horse alongside Tarma's and whispered angrily to her:
"I'd like to feed that little son of a bitch his own damned gauntlet!"

"Peace," Tarma said, "Let me handle this. Give me rear for long
enough to teach him a lesson."

Garth passed the word; wry grins appeared and vanished in an instant,
and the scout ranks opened and closed so that Beaker had point and
Tarma had dropped back to tail. The scouts squeezed past the arrogant
sentry, one by one, Tarma the last. She didn't move, only stared at him
for a long moment, letting Ironheart feel her ground and set her feet.

Then she dropped her hands, and signaled the battlemare with her
knees.

Black as a nightmare in the rain, the battlesteed reared up to her full
height—and stayed there, as perfectly balanced as only a Shin'a'in
trained warsteed could be. Another invisible command from Tarma, and
she hopped forward on her hind hooves, forefeet lashing out at the

stranger-gelding, who, not being the fool his rider was, cleared off the path and up onto the mucky shoulder. Then Ironheart settled to all four hooves again, but only for as long as it took to get past the arrogant sentry. As Tarma had figured he would, he spurred his beast down onto the path again as soon as they got by. Whatever he'd thought to do then didn't much matter. As soon as he was right behind them and just *out* of range of what was normally an attack move, Tarma gave her mare a final signal that sent her leaping into the air, lashing out with her rear hooves in a wicked kick as she reached the top of her arc. Had the boy *been* within range of those hooves, his face would have been smashed in. As it was (as Tarma had carefully calculated), the load of mud Ironheart had picked up flicked off her heels to splatter all over him, his fancy panoply, and his considerably cowed beast.

"Next time, boy," she called back over her shoulder, as her scouts snickered, "best *know* whose tail it is you plan to twist, and be prepared for consequences."

The edge of the camps was held by the freefighters—little clots of scum no good company would take into itself. They were one of the reasons each levy and company had its own set of sentries; politics was the other. Tarma didn't much understand politics—scum, she knew. It had been a band of this sort of flotsam that had wiped out her Clan.

But a sword was a sword, and Leamount was not above paying them so long as someone he trusted could keep an eye on them. *That, thank the Warrior, is not Idra's job,* Tarma thought to herself, wrinkling her nose at the stench of their huddle of makeshift shelters. Unwashed bodies, rotting canvas, garbage, privy pits right in the camp—the mix was hardly savory. Even the rain couldn't wash it out of the air. They rode past this lot (too sodden with drink or drug, or just too damn lazy to set one of their own to sentry duty) without a challenge, but with one hand on their knives and shortswords at all times. There'd been trouble with this lot before—and five were not too many for them to consider mobbing if they thought it worth their while.

Once out of the camps, they rearranged their order. Now it was Kyra who had point, and Tarma who took tail. This side of the mountains, danger would be coming at them from the rear—Kelcrag's scouts, sniffing around the edges of the Royalist army. All of them had taken care long ago to replace metal harness pieces with leather where they could, or even carved wood—anything that wouldn't shine and wouldn't clink. The metal they had to have was *not* brightwork; it was dulled and tarnished and left that way. Shin'a'in horses were trained to neck and knee, so all they needed was a soft halter with no bit. As for their own armor, or lack of it, their best protection would be speed on a mission like this— stay out of the way if you can, and never close for a fight unless you have no choice. So they saved themselves and their horses the few extra pounds, and dressed for the weather, not for battle. Tarma kept her short Shin'a'in horsebow strung and under her cape; if it came to a fight, she would buy the rest time to string theirs. Warrl ranged all over their backtrail, keeping in steady mindtouch with Tarma. He would buy them yet more advance warning, if there was going to be trouble.

But the trek west was quiet.

The storm gradually slackened to drizzle as the sky grew lighter; the landscape was dreary, even without the devastations of warfare all about them. The hills were dead and brown, and lifeless; the herds of sheep and gercattle that usually grazed them had gone to feed one or both armies. The scrub trees displayed black, leafless branches against the gray sky, and the silence around them intensified the impression that this area was utterly deserted. Wet, rotting leaves left their own signature on the breeze, a melancholy, bitter aroma more tasted than smelled, that lingered in the back of the throat. The track they followed was part rock, part yellow mud, a thick, claylike stuff that clung to hooves and squelched when it let go.

All five of them rode in that peculiar half-trance of the scout on his way *to* something; not looking for anything, not yet—not paying outward attention to surroundings—but should anything, however small, move—

A crow, flapping up to their right, got exactly the appropriate reaction; Tarma, ready-armed, had already sighted on him before he'd risen a foot. Jodi and Beaker had their hands on their bowcases and their eyes to left and right, wary for possible ambush. Garth had his sword out and was ready to back Tarma, and Kyra was checking the road ahead for more trouble.

They all laughed, shakily, when they realized what their "enemy" was.

"Don't think even Kelcrag's taken up with the corbies," Tarma said, shaking her head, and tucking her bow back under the oiled silk. "Still— *probably* he hasn't got anyone dedicated enough to go mucking around in this weather, but we can't count on it. Stay alert, children. At least until we get out of the war zone."

By midday they had done just that—there *were* herds on the distant hills, although the shepherds and herders quickly moved them out of sight when they saw the little band approaching. Tarma saw Garth nodding in sympathy, lips moving soundlessly in what she rather thought was a blessing. His people had been all but wiped out when some war had trampled them into *their* earth, somewhere down south.

Tarma knew everything there was to know about her "children"; she had made a point of getting drunk at least once with each of her scouts. It was damned useful to know what made them twitch. One of the reasons Garth was with Idra—he was so good a tracker he could have served with any company, or even as a pampered huntsman to royalty—was because she allowed no looting of the peasantry (nobles were another matter) and insisted on the Hawks paying in trade-silver and pure copper ingots for what they needed. Like Garth, all the Hawks tended to serve their lady-Captain for more than just coin.

By now they were all fairly well sodden except for Tarma, brown and black and gray cloaks all becoming a similar dark, indeterminant shade. Even Tarma was rather damp. Rain that was one scant point from being sleet still managed to get past her high collar to trickle down her neck, and muddy water from every puddle they splashed through had soaked through her breeches long ago. She was going numb with cold; the rest of them must be in worse case.

"Kyra," she called forward, "You in territory you know yet?"

The girl turned in her saddle, rain trickling down her nose. "Hmm—eh, I'd say so. Think this's Domery lands, they're kin of my kin—"

"I don't want to stretch anybody's hospitality or honesty, but we need to dry off a bit. There any herders' huts or caves or something around here? Something likely to be deserted this time of year?"

"I'll think on't."

A few soggy furlongs later—as Kyra scanned her memory and the land around them—

"Scoutmaster," she called back, " 'Bout three hills over there be a cave; used for lambin' and shearin' and never else. That do?"

"Room for all of us? I mean horses, too. No sense in shouting our presence by tethering them out, and plain cruel to make them endure more of this than we do."

Kyra's brow creased with thought. "If I don't misremember, aye. Be a squeeze, but aye."

Kyra had misremembered—but by *under*estimating the size of the cave. There was enough room at the back for all five horses to stand shoulder to shoulder, with enough space left over for one rider at a time to rub his beast down without getting trampled on. An overhanging shelf of limestone made it possible to build a fire at the front of the cave without all of them eating smoke. And there was wood stocked at the side, dry enough that there wasn't much of that smoke in the first place.

More to the point, where concealment was concerned, the rain dissipated what trickled past the blackened overhang.

"How much farther?" Tarma asked, chewing on a tasteless mouthful of trail-biscuit.

"Not much," Kyra replied. "We better be cuttin' overland from here if m' mem'ry be still good. Look you—"

She dipped a twig in muddy, black water and drew on a flat rock near the cave's entrance.

Tarma got down on her knees beside her and studied her crude map carefully. "One, maybe two candlemarks, depending, hmm?"

"Aye, depending." Kyra chewed on the other end of the twig for a moment. "We got to stick t' ridges—"

"What?" Beaker exclaimed. "For every gossip in the hills to see us?"

"Oh, bad to be seen, but worse to be bogged. Valleys, they go boggy this time of year, like. Stuff livin' in the bogs is bad for a beast's feet. Y' want yer laddy's hooves t' rot off 'fore we reach trail's end, y' ride the valleys."

"No middle way?" Tarma asked.

"Well. . . . We won't be goin' where there's likely many, an' most of those'd be my kin. They see me, they know what I was abaht, and they keep their tongues from clackin'."

"That'll have to do." Tarma got up from her knees, and dusted the gravel off the knees of her breeches—which were, she was happy to find, relatively dry. "All right, children, let's ride."

"I dunno—" Garth said dubiously, peering up through the drizzle at what was little better than a worn track along the shale cliffside.

Tarma studied the trail and chewed at the corner of her lip. "Kyra," she said, finally, "your beast's the weakest of the lot. Give it a try. If she can make it, we all can."

"Aye," Kyra saluted, and turned her mare's head to the trail. She let the mare take her time and pick her own places to set her feet along the track. It seemed to take forever—

But eventually they could see that she was waving from the top.

"Send the first bird, Beaker," Tarma said, heading Ironheart after the way Kyra had followed. "We're going to see if this trail is a dead end or the answer to our prayers."

*   *   *

Twice before sunset they lost the track on broad expanses of bare rock, and spent precious time trying to pick it up again, all of them combing the ground thumblength by thumblength.

Sunset was fast approaching the second time they lost, then found the trail again. Tarma scanned the sky warily, trying to judge, with the handicap of lowering clouds, how much time they had before darkness fell. They obviously weren't going to make trail's end by sunset—so the choice was whether to camp here on this windswept slant of scoured stone, or to press on in the hope of coming up with something better and maybe instead find themselves spending the night on a ledge two handspans wide.

She finally decided to press on, allowing just enough time in reserve that they could double back if they had to.

The track led on through lichen and rubble: treacherous stuff, except where the wild ponies had pounded a thin line of solidity. Jodi was mapping as they went along, and marking their backtrail with carefully inconspicuous "cairns" composed of no more than three or four pebbles. The drizzle had stopped, at least, and the exertion that was warming them had driven most of the damp out of their clothing. The pony-track led down into a barren gulley—Tarma disliked that, and kept watching for water marks on the rocks they passed. If there was a cloudburst and this *happened* to be one of the local runoff sites, they could be hock-deep in tumbling rock and fast water in the time it took to blink.

But the gulley stayed dry, the track eased a bit—and then, like a gift from the gods, just before Tarma would have signaled a turnaround point, they came upon a possible campsite.

Sometime in the not-too-recent past, part of the hill above them had come sliding down, creating a horseshoe of boulders the size of a house. There would be shelter from the wind there, their fire would be out of sight of prying eyes—and it would be easy to defend from predators.

Garth eyed the site with the same interest Tarma was feeling. "No place to get out of the rain, if it decided to come down again," he observed, "and nothing much to burn but that scrub up there on the wall. We'd have us a pot of hot tea, but a cold camp."

"Huh. The choice is this or the flat back there," Tarma told them. "Me, I'd take this. Kyra? This is your land."

"Aye, I'd take this; we've slept wet afore," Kyra agreed. "This 'un isn't a runoff, an' don't look like any more of the hill is gonna slip while we're here. I'd say 'tis safe enough."

The others nodded.

"Let's get ourselves settled then, while there's light."

*   *   *

The rain began again before dawn and they were glad enough to be on the move and getting chilled muscles stretched and warmed. They lost the track once more, this time spending a frustrating hour searching for it—but that was the last of their hardships, for noon saw them emerging from the hills and onto the plains on the other side.

Tarma allowed herself a broad grin, as the rest whooped and pounded each other's backs.

"Send up that damned bird, Beaker; we just earned ourselves one *fat* bonus from Lord Leamount."

Returning was easier, though it was plain that nothing but a goat, a donkey, a mountain pony or a Shin'a'in-bred beast was ever going to make it up or down that trail without breaking a leg. Tarma reckoned it would take the full Company about one day to traverse the trail; that, plus half a day to get to their end and half to get into striking distance of Kelcrag's forces meant two days' traveling time, in total. Not bad, really; they'd had a setup that had taken almost a week, once. Knowing Idra as she did, Tarma had a pretty good idea of what the Captain's suggested strategy was going to be. And it would involve the Hawks and no one else. No bad thing, that; the Hawks could count on their own to know what to do.

The rain had finally let up as they broke back out into the herder's country; they were dead tired and ready to drop, but at least they weren't wet anymore. Tarma saw an outrider a few furlongs beyond the camp; he, she or it was waving a scarf in the Hawks' colors of brown and golden yellow. She waved back, and the outrider vanished below the line of a hill. They all relaxed at that; they were watched for, they need not guard their path—and there would almost certainly be food and drink waiting for them in the camp. That was exactly what they'd needed and hoped for.

They hadn't expected Idra and Sewen to be waiting for them at the entrance to the camp.

"Good work, children. Things are heating up. Maps," Idra said curtly, and Jodi handed over the waterproof case with a half-salute and a tired grin. They were all achingly weary at this point; horses and humans alike were wobbly at the knees. Only Tarma and Ironheart were in any kind of shape, and Tarma wasn't too certain how much of Ironheart's apparent energy was bluff. Battlemares had a certain stubborn pride that sometimes made them as pigheaded about showing strain as—

:Certain Kal'enedral,: Warrl said in her head.

Shut up, she thought back at him, *you should talk about being pig-headed—*

"Good work. *Damned* fine work," Idra said, looking up from the maps and interrupting Tarma's train of thought. "Tarma, if you're up to a little more—"

"Captain." Tarma nodded, and sketched a salute.

"The rest of you—there's hot wine and hot food waiting in my tent, and a handful of Hawks to give your mounts the good rubdown and treat *they* deserve. Tarma, give Ironheart to Sewen and come with me. Warrl, too, if he wants. The rest of you get under shelter. We'll be seeing you all later—with news, I hope."

Tarma had been too fatigue-fogged to note where they were going, except that they were working their way deeply into the heart of the encampments. But after a while the size of the tents and the splendor of the banners outside of them began to penetrate her weariness.

What in the name—

:On your best behavior, mindmate,: Warrl said. For once his mindvoice sounded dead serious. *:This is the camp of the Lord Commander.:*

Before Tarma had a chance to react, Idra was ushering her past a pair of massive sentries and into the interior of a tent big enough to hold a half dozen of the Hawks' little two-man bivouacs.

Tarma blinked in the light and warmth, and felt her muscles going to jelly in the pleasant heat. Mage-lights everywhere, and a *jesto-vath* that made Kethry's look like a simple shieldspell.

Other than that, though, the tent was as plain as Idra's, divided, as hers was, into a front and back half. In the front half was a table, some chairs and document-boxes, a rack of wine bottles. The curtain dividing it was half open; on the other side Tarma could see what looked like a chest, some weapons and armor—and a plain camp cot, piled high with thick furs and equally thick blankets.

What I wouldn't give to climb into that right now, she was thinking, when her attention was pulled away by something more important.

"Leamount, you old warhorse, here's our miracle-maker," Idra was saying to a lean, grizzled man in half-armor standing by the map-table, but in the shadows, so that Tarma hadn't really noticed him at first. Tarma had seen Lord Leamount once or twice at a distance; she recognized him by his stance and his scarlet surcote with Sursha's rampant grasscat more than anything else, although once he turned in her direction she saw the two signature braids he wore in front of each ear, an affectation he'd picked up among his hillclans. "Lord Leamount, may I present Tarma shena Tale'sedrin—"

"Lo'teros, shas tella, Kal'enedral," he replied, much to Tarma's surprise; bowing, making a fist and placing it over his heart as he bowed.

"Ile se'var, Yatakar," she replied, returning his salute with intense curiosity and sharpened interest. *"Ge vede sa'kela Shin'a'in."*

"Only a smattering, I fear. I learned it mostly in self-defense—" He grinned, and Tarma found herself grinning back. "—to keep from getting culls pushed off on me by your fellow clansmen."

"Ah, well—come to me, and you'll get the kind of horses the Hawks mount."

"I'll do that. Idra has high praise for you, the *kyree,* and your *she'enedra,* Swordsworn," he said, meeting her intensely ice-blue eyes as few others had been able. "I could only wish I had a few more of your kind with us. So—the bird returned; that told us there *was* a path through. But what's the track like?"

Somehow Tarma wasn't overly surprised that he came directly to the point. "Bad," she said shortly, as Idra spread out Jodi's maps over the ones already on the table. "It'll be brutal. The only mounts that are going to be able to negotiate that terrain are the Hawks'. *Maybe* some of the ponies your mountain-clan scouts have could make it, but they'd be fair useless on the other side of those hills. No running ability, and on Kelcrag's side of the pass, that's what they'll need. Anything else would break a leg on that track, or break the path down past using."

"Terrain?"

"Big hills, baby mountains, doesn't much matter. Shale most of the way through, and sandstone. Bad footing."

"Huh." He chewed a corner of his mustache and brooded over Jodi's tracings. "That lets out plan one, then. Idra—seems it's going to be up to you."

"Hah—up to me, my rump! If you can't get old Shoveral to move his big fat arse in time, you'll get us slaughtered—"

Tarma glanced up out of the corner of her eye, alarmed at those words, only to see Idra grinning like Warrl with a particularly juicy bone.

"Shoveral knows damned well he's my hidden card; he'll move when he needs to—now, Swordsworn, how long do you reckon it will take all the Hawks to get from here—" His finger stabbed down at the location of their camp. "—to here?"

The second place he indicated was a spot about a candlemark's slow ride from the rear of Kelcrag's lines. As Tarma had figured—striking distance. "About two days, altogether."

"Huhn. Say you got to trail's start at dawn by riding half the night. Think you could get that lot of yours up over that trail, make trail's end by dark, camp cold for a bit of rest, then be within this strike distance by, say, midmorning?"

"No problem. Damn well better have the rest though. Horses'll need it or we won't be able to count on 'em."

"Idra, how do we keep the movement secret?"

Idra thought about that a while. "Loan me those hillclan levies and their bivouac; they're honest enough to guard our camp. We'll move out in groups of about twenty; you move in an equal number of the clansmen. Camp stays full to the naked eye—Kelcrag can't tell one merc from another, no more can his magickers. The people that could tell the difference between them and us won't be able to see what's going on."

"Hah!" He smacked his fist down into his palm. "Good; let me send for Shoveral. We'll plan this out with just the three of us—four, counting the Kal'enedral. Fewer that know, fewer can leak."

The Lord Commander sent one of his pages out after Lord Shoveral, then he and Idra began planning in earnest. From time to time he snapped out a question at Tarma; how far, how many, what about this or that—she answered as best she could, but she was tired, far more weary than she had guessed. She found her tongue feeling oddly clumsy, and she had to think hard about each word before she could get it out.

Finally Leamount and Idra began a low-voiced colloquy she didn't bother to listen to; she just hung on to the edge of the table and tried enforcing her alertness with Kal'enedral discipline exercises. They didn't work overly well; she was on her last wind, for certain.

Leamount caught Tarma's wavering attention. The maps on the table were beginning to go foggy to her eyes. "Swordsworn," he said, looking a little concerned, "you look half dead, but we may need you; what say you go bed down over there in the corner—" He nodded in the direction of his own cot. "If there's a point you need to clarify for us, we'll give you a shake." He raised his voice. "Jons—"

One of the two sentries poked his head in through the tent flap. "Sir?"

"Stir up my squire, would you? Have him find something for this starving warrior to eat and drink."

Tarma had stumbled to the other side of the tent and was already collapsing onto the cot, her weariness washing her under with a vengeance. The blankets felt as welcoming and warm as they looked, and she curled up in them without another thought, feeling Warrl heaving himself up to his usual position at her feet. As the tent and the voices faded, while the wave of exhaustion carried her into slumber, she heard Idra chuckling.

"You might as well not bother Jons," the Captain told Leamount, just before sleep shut Tarma's ears. "I don't think she cares."

Three

Kethry shifted her weight over her mount's shoulders, half-standing in her stirrups to ease Hellsbane's balance as the mare scrambled up the treacherous shale of another slope. They were slightly more than halfway across the hills; it was cold and damp and the lowering gray clouds looked close enough to touch, but at least it wasn't raining again. She wasn't too cold; under her wool cloak she wore her woolen sorceress' robe, the unornamented buff color showing her school was White Winds, and under *that,* woolen breeches, woolen leggings, and the leather armor Tarma had insisted she don. The only time she was uncomfortable was when the wind cut in behind the hood of the robe.

She was a member of the last party to leave the camp and make the crossing; they'd left their wounded to the care of Leamount's hillclansmen and his own personal Healer. Tresti, the Healer-Priest, had been in the second party to slip away from the camp, riding by the side of her beloved Sewen. Oreden and Jiles, the two hedge-mages, had gone two groups later; The herbalist Rethaire and his two young apprentices had left next. Kethry had stayed to the very last, her superior abilities at sensing mage-probes making her the logical choice to deflect any attempts at spying until the full exchange of personnel was complete.

She felt a little at a loss without her partner riding at her left. Tarma had preceded her more than half a day ago, leaving before midnight, as the guide with Idra and the first group. Of all the party that had made the first crossing, only Jodi had remained to ride with the tailguard group.

Jodi was somewhere behind them, checking on the backtrail. That was not as comforting to Kethry as it should have been. Kethry *knew* her fears were groundless, that the frail appearance of the scout belied a tough interior—but—

As if the thought had summoned her, a gray shadow slipped up upon Kethry's right, with so little noise it might have been a shadow in truth. Hellsbane had been joined by a second gray mare so similar in appearance that only an expert could have told that one was a Shin'a'in full-blood battlesteed and the other was not.

That lack of sound was one clue—there was mountain-pony in Light-foot's background, somewhere. Jodi's beast moved as silently as a wild goat on this shifting surface, so quietly that the scout and her mount raised the hackles on anyone who didn't know them.

Jodi wore her habitual garb of gray leather; with her pale hair and pale eyes and ghost-gray horse, she looked unnervingly like an apparition of Lady Death herself, or some mist-spirit conjured out of the patches of fog that shrouded these hills, as fragile and insubstantial as a thing of shadow and air; and once again Kethry had a twinge of misgiving.

"Any sign of probing?" the scout asked in a neutral voice.

Kethry shook her head. "None. I think we may have gotten away with it."

Jodi sighed. "Don't count your coins before they're in the coffer. There's a reason why *we* are running tail, lady, and it's not just to do with magery, though that's a good share of it."

The scout cast a doubtful look at Kethry—and for the first time Kethry realized that the woman had serious qualms about *her* abilities to handle this mission, if it came to something other than a simple trek on treacherous ground.

Kethry didn't bother to hide an ironic grin.

Jodi noted it, and cocked her head to one side, moving easily with her horse. Her saddle was hardly more than a light pad of leather; it didn't even creak when she shifted, unconsciously echoing the movements of her mare. "Something funny, lady?"

"Very. I think we've been thinking exactly the same things—about each other."

Jodi's answering slow grin proved that Kethry hadn't been wrong. "Ha. And we should know better, shouldn't we? It's a pity we didn't know each other well enough to trust without thinking and worrying—especially since neither of us look like fighters. But we should have figured that Idra knows what she's doing; neither of us are hothouse plants—or we wouldn't be Hawks."

"Exactly. So—give me the reasons this particular lot is riding tail; maybe I can do something about preventing a problem."

"Right enough—one—" The scout freed her right hand from the reins to hold up a solemn finger. "—is the trail. Shale shifts, cracks. We're riding after all the rest, and we'll be making the last few furlongs in early evening gloom. This path has been getting some hard usage, more than it usually gets. If the trail is likely to give, it'll give under *us*. You'll notice we're all of us the best riders, and the ones with the best horses in the Hawks."

Kethry considered this, as Hellsbane topped the hill and picked her cautious way down the sloping trail. "Hmm-hmm. All right, can we halt at the next ridge? There's a very tiny bit of magery I can work that might help us out with that."

Jodi pursed her lips. "Is that wise?"

Kethry nodded, slowly. "It's a very low-level piece of earth-witchery; something even a shepherd wisewoman might well know. I don't think any of Kelcrag's mages is likely to take note of it—assuming they can even see it, and I doubt they will. It's witchery, not sorcery, and Kelcrag's magickers are all courtly mages, greater and lesser. *My* school is more eclectic; we use whatever comes to hand, and that can be damned useful —somebody looking for High Magick probably won't see Low, or think it's worth investigating. After all, what does Kelcrag need to fear from a peasant granny?"

Jodi considered that for a moment, her head held slightly to one side. "Tell me, why is it that Jiles and Oreden have gotten so much better since you've been with us?"

Kethry chuckled, but it was with a hint of sadness. It had been very hard to convince the hedge-wizards that their abilities did not match their dreams. "You want the truth? Their talents are all in line with Low Magick; earth-witchery, that sort of thing. I convinced them that there's *nothing* wrong with that, asked them which they'd rather ride, a good, steady trail-horse or *your* fire-eater. They aren't stupid; they saw right away what I was getting at." She set Hellsbane at the next slope, her hooves dislodging bits of shale and sending them clattering down behind them. "So now that they aren't trying to master spells they haven't the Talent to use properly, they're doing fine. Frankly, *I* would rather have them with us than two of those courtly mages. Water-finding is a lot more use than calling lightning, and the fire-making spell does us more good than the ability to light up a ballroom."

"You won't catch me arguing. So what's this magic of yours going to do?"

"Show me the weak spots in the trail. If there's something ready to give, I'll know about it before it goes."

"And?"

"I should be able to invoke a greater magic at that point, and hold the pieces together long enough for us to get across."

"Won't *that* draw attention?"

"It would," Kethry replied slowly, "if I did what a court mage would do, and draw on powers outside myself—which causes ripples; no, I have just enough power of my own, and that's what I'll use. There won't be any stir on the other planes. . . ." *But it's going to cost me if I do things that way. Maybe high. Well, I'll handle that when the time comes.* "You said *one* reason we're riding tailmost—that implies there's more reasons."

"Two—we're tailguards in truth. We could find ourselves fighting hand to hand with Kelcrag's scouts or his mages. They haven't detected us that we know of, but there's no sense in assuming less than the worst."

"So long as they don't outnumber us—I'm not exactly as helpless in a fight as Tresti." She caught the cloud of uncertainty in Jodi's pale blue eyes, and said, surprised, "I thought everybody knew about this sword of mine."

"There's stories, but frankly, lady—"

"Keth. I, as Tarma would tell you, am no lady."

That brought a glimmer of smile. "Keth, then. Well, none of *us* have ever seen that blade do anything but heal."

"Need's better at causing wounds than curing them, at least in *my* hands," Kethry told her. "That's her gift to me; in a fight, she makes a mage the equal of any swordswoman born. If it comes to magic, though, she's pretty well useless for my purposes—it's to a fighter she gives magic immunity. But—I'll tell you what, I've got a notion. If it comes to battle by magery, I'll try and get her to you before I get involved in a duel arcane; she'll shield you from even a godling's magic. Tarma proved that, once. She may even be able to shield more than one, if you all crowd together."

There was a flash of interest at that, and a hint of relief. "Then I think I'll worry less about you. Well—there's a reason three that we're riding tail: if we find we've ridden straight into ambush at trail's end, we're the lot that's got the best chance of getting one of us back to tell Leamount."

"Gah. Grim reasons, all of them—can we stop here for a breath or two?"

They had just topped a ridge, with sufficient space between them and the next in line that a few moments spent halted wouldn't hamper his progress any. Jodi looked about her, grimaced, then nodded with reluctance. "A bit exposed to my mind, but—"

"This won't take long." Kethry gathered the threads of earth-magic, the subtlest and least detectable of all the mage-energies, and whispered a command along those particular threads that traced their path across the hills. There was an almost imperceptible shift in the energy flows, then the spell settled into place and became invisible even to the one who had set it. The difference was that Kethry was now at one with the path; she *felt* the path through the hills, from end to end, like a whisper of sand across the surface of her mental "skin." If the path was going to collapse, the backlash would alert her.

"Let's go—"

"That's all there is to it?" Jodi looked at her askance.

"Magery isn't all lightnings and thunders. The best magery is as subtle as a tripwire, and as hard to detect."

"Well." Jodi sent her mount picking a careful path down the hillside, and looked back at Kethry with an almost-smile. "I think I could get to appreciate magery."

Kethry grinned outright, remembering that Jodi's other specialty was subterfuge, infiltration, and assassination. "Take my word for it, the real difference between a Masterclass mage and an apprentice is not in the amount of power, it's in the usage. You've been over this trail already; what do you think—are we going to make trail's end by dark?"

Jodi narrowed her eyes, taking a moment. "No," she said finally, "I don't think so. That's when I'll take point, when it starts to get dark. And that's when we'll have to be most alert."

Kethry nodded, absently, and pulled her hood closer about her neck against a lick of wind. "If an attack comes, it's likely to be then. And the same goes for accident?"

"Aye."

It was growing dark, far faster than Kethry liked, and there was still no end to the trail in sight. But there had also been no sign that their movement was being followed—

Suddenly her nerves twanged like an ill-tuned harpstring. For one short, disorienting moment, she vibrated in backlash, for that heartbeat or two of time completely helpless to think or act. Then nearly fifteen years of training and practice took over, and without even being aware of it, she gathered mage-energy from the core of her very being and formed a net of it—a net to catch what was even now about to fall.

Just in time; up ahead in the darkness, she heard the slide of rock, a horse's fear-ridden shriek, and the harsh cry of a man seeing his own death looming in his face. She felt the energy-net sag, strain—then hold.

She clamped her knees around Hellsbane's barrel and dropped her reins, telling the horse mutely to "stand." The battlesteed obeyed, bracing all four hooves, far steadier than the rocks about her. Kethry firmed her concentration until it was adamantine, and closed her eyes against distraction. Since she could not see what she was doing, this would take every wisp of her attention—

Gently, this must be done as gently as handling a pennybird chick new-hatched. If she frightened the horse, and it writhed out of her energy-net —horse and rider would plummet to their doom.

She cupped her hands before her, echoing the form of the power-net, and contemplated it.

Broken lines of power showed her where the path had collapsed, and the positioning of her "net" told her without her seeing the trail ahead just where her captives were cradled.

"Keth—" Jodi's voice came from the darkness ahead, calm and steady; no sign of panic there. "We lost a very short section of the path; those of you behind us won't have any problem jumping the gap. The immediate problem is the rider that went over. It's Gerrold and Vetch; the horse is half over on his right side and Gerrold's pinned under him, but neither one of them is hurt and you caught both before they slid more than a few feet. Gerrold's got the beast barely calmed, but he's not struggling. Can you do anything more for them other than just holding them?"

Kethry eased her concentration just enough to answer. "If I get them righted, maybe raise them a bit, can he get Vetch back onto the path?"

"You can do that?"

"I can try—"

Hoof sounds going, then returning. Kethry "read" the lines of energy cradling the man and beast, slowly getting a picture of how they were lying by the shape of the energy-net.

"Gerrold's got Vetch gentled and behaving. He says if you take it slow—"

Kethry did not answer, needing all her focus on the task at hand. Slowly she moved her fingers; as she did she lessened the pressure on one side of the net, increased it on the other, until the shape within began to tilt upright. There was a lessening of tension within the net, as horse and rider lost fear; that helped.

Now, beneath the hooves of the trapped horse she firmed the net until it was as strong as the steadiest ground, taking away some of the mage-threads from the sides to do so. When nothing untoward occurred, she took more of those threads, using them to raise the level of that surface, slowly, carefully, so as not to startle the horse. One by one she rewove those threads, raising the platform thumblength by agonizing thumblength.

She was shaking and drenched with sweat by the time she got it high enough, and just about at the end of her strength. When a clatter of hooves on rock and an exultant shout told her that Gerrold had gotten his mount back onto safe ground, she had only enough energy left to cling to her saddle for the last few furlongs of the journey.

"Right now," Idra said quietly, stretched out along a hilltop next to Tarma, "The old war-horse should be giving them a good imitation of a *tired* old war-horse."

The hilltop gave them a fairly tolerable view for furlongs in any direction; they were just beyond the range of Kelcrag's sentries, and Kethry was shielding them in the way she had learned from the example of Moonsong k'Vala, the Tale'edras Adept from the Pelagiris Forest—making them seem a part of the landscape—to mage-sight, just a thicket of brinle-bushes. In the far distance was the pass; filling it was the dark blot of Kelcrag's forces.

At this moment—as he had for the last two days—Leamount was giving a convincing imitation of a commander truly interested in coming to an agreement with his enemy. Heralds had been coming and going hour by hour with offers and counteroffers—all of this false negotiation buying time for the Hawks to get into place.

"Well, it's now or never," Idra said finally, as she and Tarma abandoned their height and squirmed down their side of the hill to join her company. "Kethry?"

Kethry, on foot like all the rest, nodded and joined hands with her two mage-partners. "Shield your eyes," she warned them. "It'll go on a count of five."

Tarma and the rest of the Hawks averted their eyes and turned their horses' heads away as Kethry counted slowly. When Kethry reached five, there was a flare of light so bright that it shone redly through Tarma's eyelids even with her head turned. It was followed by a second flash, and then a third.

From a distance it would look like the lightning that flickered every day along the hillsides. But Leamount's mages were watching this particular spot for just that signal of three flickers of light, and testing for energy-auras to see if it was mage-light and not natural lightning. Now Leamount would break off his negotiations and resume his attacks on

Kelcrag's army, concentrating on the eastern edge. That would seem reasonable: Kelcrag had stationed his foot there; they might be vulnerable to a charge of heavy cavalry. Leamount's own western flank was commanded by Lord Shoveral, whose standard was a badger and whose mode of battle matched his token; he was implacable in defense, but no one had yet seen him on the attack, so Kelcrag might well believe that he had no heart for it.

He was, one hoped, about to be surprised.

One also hoped, fervently, that Kelcrag's mages had *not* noticed that it was mage-light and not lightning that had flickered to their rear.

:They've no reason to look for mage-light, mindmate,: Warrl said soberly. *:Kelcrag's wizards are all courtly types. They very seldom think about hiding what they're doing, or trying to make it seem like something natural. To them, mage-light is something to illuminate a room with, not something to use for a signal. If they wish to pass messages, they make a sending.:*

"I hope you're right, Furface," Tarma replied, mounting. "The more surprised they are, the more of us are going to survive this."

At Idra's signal, the Hawks moved into a disciplined canter; no point in trying too hard to stay undercover now.

They urged their mounts over hills covered only with scraggy bushes and dead, dry grass; they would have been hard put to find any cover if they'd needed it. But luck was with them.

They topped a final hilltop and only then encountered Kelcrag's few sentries. They were all afoot; the lead riders coldly picked them off with a few well-placed arrows before they could sound an alert. The sentries fell, either pierced with arrows or stumbling over their wounded comrades. And the fallen were trampled—for the Hawks' horses were war-trained, and a war-trained horse does not hesitate when given the signal to make certain of a fallen foe. That left no chance that Kelcrag could be warned.

Ahead of the riders, now stretching their canter into a gallop, was the baggage train.

Kethry and her two companions rode to the forefront for the moment. Each mage was haloed by one of Kethry's glowing mage-shields; a shield that blurred the edges of vision around a mage and his mount as well. It made Tarma's eyes ache to look at them, so she tried not to. The shields wouldn't deflect missiles, but not being able to look straight at your target made that target *damned* hard to hit.

The two hedge-wizards growled guttural phrases, made elaborate throwing motions—and smoking, flaming balls appeared in the air before their hands to fly at the wagons and supplies. Kethry simply locked her hands together and held them out in front of her—and each wagon or tent she stared at burst into hot blue flame seemingly of its own accord.

This was noisy; it was meant to be. The noncombatants with the baggage—drovers, cooks, personal servants, the odd whore—were screaming in fear and fleeing in all directions, adding to the noise. There didn't seem to be anyone with enough authority back here to get so much as a fire brigade organized.

The Hawks charged through the fires and the frightened, milling civilians, and headed straight for the rear of Kelcrag's lines. Now Kethry and the mages had dropped back until they rode—a bit more protected—in the midst of the Sunhawks. They would be needed now only if one of Kelcrag's mages happened to be stationed on this flank.

For the rest, it was time for bow work. Kelcrag's men—armored cavalry here, for the most part; nobles and retainers, and mostly young— were still trying to grasp the fact that they'd been hit from the rear.

The Hawks swerved just out of bowshot, riding their horses in a flanking move along the back of the lines. They didn't stop; that would make them stationary targets. They just began swirling in and out at the very edge of the enemy's range, as Tarma led the first sortie to engage.

About thirty of them peeled off from the main group, galloping forward with what must look to Kelcrag's men like utter recklessness. It wasn't; they stayed barely within their range as they shot into the enemy lines. This was what the Hawks were famous for, this horseback skirmishing. Most of them rode with reins in their teeth, a few, like Tarma and Jodi, dropped their reins altogether, relying entirely on their weight and knees to signal their mounts. Tarma loosed three arrows in the time it took most of the rest of her sortie group to launch one, her short horsebow so much a part of her that she thought of nothing consciously but picking her targets. She was aware only of Ironheart's muscles laboring beneath her legs, of the shifting smoke that stung eyes and carried a burnt flavor into the back of her throat, of the sticky feel of sweat on her back, of a kind of exultation in her skill—and it was all over in heartbeats. Arrows away, the entire group wheeled and galloped to the rear of the Hawks, already nocking more missiles—for hard on their heels came a second group, a third—it made for a continuous rain of fire that was taking its toll even of heavily armored men—and as they rode, the Hawks jeered at their enemies, and shouted Idra's rallying call. The hail of arrows that fell on the enemy wounded more horses than men—a fact Tarma was sorry about—but the fire, the hail of arrows, and the catcalls inflamed their enemy's tempers in a way that nothing else could have done.

And, as Leamount and Idra had planned, the young, headstrong nobles let those tempers loose.

They broke ranks, leaders included, and charged their mocking foes. All they thought of now was to engage the retreating Hawks, forgetful of their orders, forgetful of everything but that this lot of commoners had pricked their vanity and was not getting away.

Now the Hawks scattered, breaking into a hundred little groups, their purpose accomplished.

Tarma managed to get to Kethry's side, and the two of them plowed their way back through the burning wreckage of the baggage train.

Iron-shod hooves pounding, their mounts raced as if they'd been harnessed side by side. Kethry clung grimly to the pommel of her saddle, as her partner could see out of the corner of her eye. She was not the horsewoman that the Shin'a'in was, she well knew it, and Hellsbane was galloping erratically; moving far too unpredictably for her to draw Need. At this point she was well-nigh helpless; it would be up to Tarma and the battlemares to protect her.

An over-brave pikeman rose up out of the smoke before them, thinking to hook Tarma from her seat. She ducked beneath his pole arm, and Ironheart trampled him into the red-stained mud. Another footman made a try for Kethry, but Hellsbane snapped at him, crushed his shoulder in her strong teeth, shook him like a dog with a rag while he shrieked, then dropped him again. A rider who thought to intercept them had the trick Tarma and Ironheart had played on Duke Greyhame's sentry performed on him and his steed—only in deadly earnest. Ironheart reared, screaming challenge, and crow-hopped forward. The gelding the enemy rode backed in panic from the slashing hooves, and as they passed him, his rider's head was kicked in before they could get out of range.

The battlesteeds kited through the smoke and flames of the burning camp with no more fear of either than of the scrubby shrubbery. Three times Tarma turned in her saddle and let fly one of the lethal little arrows of the Shin'a'in—as those pursuing found to their grief, armor was of little use when an archer could find and target a helm-slit.

Then shouting began behind them; their pursuers pulled up, looked back—and began belatedly to return to their battleline. Too late—for Lord Shoveral had made his rare badger's charge—and had taken full advantage of the hole that the work of the Sunhawks had left in Kelcrag's lines. Kelcrag's forces were trapped between Shoveral and the shale cliffs, with nowhere to retreat.

Using her knees, Tarma signaled Ironheart to slow, and Hellsbane followed her stablemate's lead. Tarma couldn't make out much through the blowing smoke, but what she *could* see told her all she needed to know. Kelcrag's banner was down, and there was a milling mass of men —mostly wearing Leamount's scarlet surcoats—where it had once stood. All over the field, fighters in Kelcrag's blue were throwing down their weapons.

The civil war was over.

Kethry touched the tip of her index finger to a spot directly between the sweating fighter's eyebrows; he promptly shuddered once, his eyes rolled up into his head, and he sagged into the waiting arms of his shield-brother.

"Lay him out there—that's right—" Rethaire directed the disposition of the now-slumbering Hawk. His partner eased him down slowly, stretching him out on his back on a horseblanket, with his wounded arm practically in the herbalist's lap. Rethaire nodded. "—good. Keth—"

Kethry blinked, coughed once, and shook her head a little. "Who's next?" she asked.

"Bluecoat."

Kethry stared askance at him. A Bluecoat? One of *Kelcrag's* people?

Rethaire frowned. "No, don't look at me that way, he's under Mercenary's Truce; he's all right or I wouldn't have let him in here. He's one of Devaril's Demons."

"Ah." The Demons had a good reputation among the companies, even if most of Devaril's meetings with Idra generally ended up as shouting matches. Too bad they'd been on opposite sides in this campaign.

Rethaire finished dusting the long, oozing slash in their companion's arm with blue-green powder, and began carefully sewing it up with silk thread. "Well, are you going to sit there all day?"

"Right, I'm on it," she replied, getting herself to her feet. "Who's with him?"

"My apprentice, Dee. The short one."

Kethry pushed sweat-soaked hair out of her eyes, and tried once again to get it all confined in a tail while she glanced around the space outside the infirmary tent, looking for the green-clad, chubby figure of Rethaire's youngest apprentice. She resolutely shut out the sounds of pain and the smell of sickness and blood; she kept telling herself that this was not as bad as it could have been. The worst casualties were under cover of the tent; those out here were the ones that would be walking (or limping) back to their own quarters when they woke up from Rethaire's drugs or Kethry's spell. They were all just lucky that it was still only overcast and

not raining. Sun would have baked them all into heatstroke. Rain . . .
best not think about fever and pneumonia.

With no prospect of further combat, Kethry was no longer hoarding
her magical energies, either personal or garnered from elsewhere, but
the only useful spell she had when it came to healing wounds like these
was the one that induced instant slumber. So that was *her* job; put the
patients out, while Rethaire or his assistants sewed and splinted them
back together again.

Poor Jiles and Oreden didn't even have *that* much to do; although as
Low Magick practitioners they *did* have Healing abilities, they'd long
since exhausted their powers, and now were acting as plain, nonmagical
attendants to Tresti. That was what was bad about a late-fall campaign
for them; with most of the land going into winter slumber, there was very
little ambient energy for a user of Low Magick to pull on.

Tarma was out with Jodi and a few of Leamount's farriers, salvaging
what horses they could, and killing the ones too far gone to save. And,
sometimes, performing the same office for a human or two.

Kethry shuddered, and wiped the back of her hand across her damp
forehead, frowning when she looked at it and saw how filthy it was.

*Thank the gods that stuff of Rethaire's prevents infection, or we'd lose half
the wounded. We've lost too many as it is.* That last sortie had cost the
Sunhawks dearly; they were down to two hundred. Fifty were dead, three
times that were wounded. Virtually everyone had lost a friend; the unin-
jured were tending wounded companions.

But it could have been so much worse—so very much worse.

She finally spotted apprentice Dee, and picked her way through the
prone and sleeping bodies to get to his side.

"Great good gods! Why is he out here?" she exclaimed, seeing the
patient. He was half-propped on a saddle; stretched out before him was
his wounded leg. Kethry nearly gagged at the sight of the blood-drenched
leg of his breeches, the mangled muscles, and the tourniquet practically
at his groin.

"Looks worse than it is, Keth." Dee didn't even look up. "More torn
up than anything; didn't touch the big vein at all. He don't need Tresti,
just you and me." His clever hands were busy cutting bits of the man's
breeches away, while the mercenary bit his lip until it, too, bled; hoping
to keep from crying out.

"What in hell got *you*, friend?" Kethry asked, kneeling down at the
man's side. She had to have his attention, or the spell wouldn't work. The
man was white under his sunburn, his black beard matted with dirt and
sweat, the pupils of his eyes wide with pain.

"Some—shit!—big wolf. Had m' bow all trained on yer back, m'lady. Bastard come outa nowhere n' took out m'leg. Should'a known better'n t' sight on a Hawk; 'specially since I *knew* 'bout you havin' that beast."

Kethry started. "Warrl—Windborn, no wonder you look like hacked meat! Let me tell you, you're lucky he didn't go for your throat! I hope you'll forgive me, but I—can't say I'm sorry—"

The man actually managed a bare hint of smile, and patted her knee with a bloody hand. "That's—gah!—war, m'lady. No offense." He clenched his other hand until the knuckles were white as Dee picked pieces of fabric out of his wounds.

Kethry sighed the three syllables that began the sleep-spell, and felt her hands begin to tingle with the gathering energy. Slow, though—*she* was coming to the end of her resources.

"But why did you come to us for help?"

"Don't trust them horse-leeches, they wanted t' take the leg off. I knew yer people'd save it. Them damn highborns, they got no notion what 'is leg means to a merc."

Kethry nodded, grimacing. Without his leg, this man would be out of a job—and likely starve to death.

"And th' Demons' ain't got no Healers nor magickers. Never saw th' need for 'em."

"Oh?" That was the root and branch of Devaril's constant arguments with Idra. "Well, now you know why we have them, don't you?" She still wasn't ready. Not *quite* yet; the level wasn't high enough. Until she could touch him, she had to keep his attention.

"Yeah, well—kinda reckon ol' Horseface's right, now. Neat trick y' pulled on us, settin' the camp afire wi' the magickers. An' havin' yer own Healers beats hell outa hopin' yer contract 'members he's s'pposed t' keep ye patched up. Specially when 'e's lost. Reckon we'll be lookin' fer recruits after we get mustered out." He grimaced again, and nodded to her. " 'F yer innerested, m'lady—well, th' offer's open. 'F not, well, pass th' word, eh?"

Kethry was a little amused at the certainty in his words. "You're so high up in the Demons, then, that you can speak for them?"

He bit off a curse of pain, and grinned feebly just as she reached for his forehead. "Should say. *I'm* Devaril."

Kethry was wrung with weariness, and her mage-energies were little more than flickers when Tarma came looking for her. She looked nearly transparent with exhaustion, ready to float away on an errant wind.

The swordswoman knelt down in the dust beside where Kethry was sitting; she was obviously still trying to muster up energies all but depleted.

"Keth—"

The mage looked up at her with a face streaked with dried blood— *Thank the Warrior, none of it hers.*

"Lady Windborn. I think I hate war."

"Hai," Tarma agreed, grimly. Now that the battle-high had worn off, as always, she was sick and sickened. Such a damned waste—all for the sake of one fool too proud to be ruled by a woman. All that death, men, women, good beasts. Innocent civilians. "Hell of a way to make a living. Can you get loose?"

"If it isn't for magery. I'm tapped out."

"It isn't. Idra wants us in her tent."

Tarma rose stiffly and gave her hand to her partner, who frankly needed it to get to her feet. The camp was quiet, the quiet of utter exhaustion. Later would come the drinking bouts, the boasts, the counting of bonuses and loot. Now was just time to hurt, and to heal; to mourn the lost friends and help care for the injured; and to sleep, if one could. With the coming of dusk fires were being kindled, and torches. And, off in the distance, pyres. The Hawks, like most mercenary companies, burned their dead. Tarma had already done her share of funeral duty; she was not particularly unhappy to miss the next immolation.

Two of the Hawks not too flagged to stand watch were acting sentry on Idra's tent. Tarma nodded to both of them, and pushed her way in past the flap, Kethry at her heels.

Idra inclined her head in their direction and indicated a pile of blankets with a wave of her hand. Sewen already occupied her cot, and Geoffrey, Tamas and Lethra, his serjeants, the equipment chest, the stool, and another pile of blankets respectively. The fourth serjeant, Bevis, was currently sleeping off one of Kethry's spells.

"Where's your *kyree?"* the Captain asked, as they lowered themselves down onto the pile.

"Sentry-go. He's about the only one of us fit for it, so he volunteered."

"Bless him. I got him a young pig—I figured he'd earned it, and I figured he'd like to get the taste of man out of his mouth."

Tarma grinned. "Sounds like he's been bitching at *you.* Captain, for a pig, he'd stand sentry all bloody night!"

"Have him see the cook when he's hungry." Idra took the remaining stool, lowering herself to it with a grimace of pain. Her horse had been shot out from under her, and she'd taken a fall that left her bruised from breast to ankle.

"Well." She surveyed them all, her most trusted assistants, wearing a troubled look. "I've—well, I've had some unsettling news. It's nothing to do with the campaign—" She cut short the obvious question hurriedly. "—no, in fact Geoffrey is sitting on our mustering-out pay. Leamount's been damned generous, above what he contracted for. No, this is personal. I'm going to have to part company with you for a while."

Tarma felt her jaw go slack; the others stared at their Captain with varying expressions of stunned amazement.

Sewen was the first to recover. "Idra—what'n th' hell is *that* supposed t'mean? Part company? Why?"

Idra sighed, and rubbed her neck with one sun-browned hand. "It's duty, of a sort. You all know where I'm from—well, my father just died, gods take his soul. He and I never did agree on much, but he had the grace to let me go my own way when it was obvious he'd never keep me hobbled at home except by force. Mother's been dead, oh, twenty-odd years. That means I've got two brothers in line for the throne, since I renounced any claim I had."

"Two?" Kethry was looking a bit more alert now, Tarma noticed. "I thought the law in Rethwellan was primogeniture."

"Sort of, sort of. That's where the problem is. Father favored my younger brother. So do the priests and about half the nobles. The merchants and the rest of the nobles favor following the law. My older brother—well, he may have the law behind him, but he was a wencher and a ne'er-do-well when I left, and I haven't heard he's improved. That sums up the problem. The Noble Houses are split right down the middle and there's only one way to break the deadlock."

"You?" Geoffrey asked.

She grimaced. "Aye. It's a duty I can't renounce—and damned if I like it. I thought I'd left politics behind the day I formed the Sunhawks. I'd have avoided it if I could, but the ministers' envoys went straight to Leamount; now there's no getting out of it. And in all honesty, there's a kind of duty to your people that goes with being born into a royal house; I pretty much owe it to them to see that they get the best leader, if I can. So I'm going back to look the both of my brothers over and cast my vote; I'll be leaving within the hour."

"But—!" The panic on Sewen's face was almost funny.

"Sewen, you're in charge," she continued implacably. "I expect this won't take long; I'll meet you all in winter quarters. As I said, we've been paid; we only need to wait until our wounded are mobile before you head back there. Any questions?"

The weary resignation on her face told them all that she wasn't looking forward to this—and that she wouldn't welcome protests. What Idra wanted from her commanders was the assurance that they would take care of things for her in her absence as they had always done in her presence; with efficiency and dispatch.

It was the least they could give her.

They stood nearly as one, and gave her drillfield-perfect salutes.

"No questions, Captain," Sewen said for all of them. "We'll await you at Hawksnest, as ordered."

Four

Kethry was in trouble.

A glittering ball of blinding white hurtled straight for her eyes. Kethry ducked behind the ice-covered wall of the fortifications, then launched a missile of her own at the enemy, who was even now charging her fortress.

The leading warrior took her return volley squarely on the chest, and went down with a blood-freezing shriek of anguish.

"Tarma!" squealed the second of the enemy warriors, skidding to a stop in the snow beside the fallen Shin'a'in.

"No—onward, my brave ones!" Tarma declaimed. "I am done for— but you must regain our ancient homeland! You must fight on, and you must avenge me!" Then she writhed into a sitting position, clutched her snow-spattered tunic, pointed at the wall with an outflung arm, and pitched backward into the drift she'd used to break her fall.

The remaining fighters—all four of them—gathered their courage along with their snowballs and resumed their charge.

Kethry and her two fellow defenders drove them ruthlessly back with a steady, carefully coordinated barrage. "Stand fast, my friends," Kethry encouraged her forces, as the enemy gathered just outside their range for another charge. "Never shall we let the sacred palace of—of—Whatever-it-is fall into the hands of these barbarians!"

"Sacred, my horse's behind!" taunted Tarma, reclining at her ease in the snowbank, head propped up on one arm. "You soft city types have mush for brains; wouldn't know sacred if it walked up and bonked you with a blessing! That's *our* sacred ground you're cluttering up with your filthy city! My nomads are clear of eye and mind from all the healthy riding they do. *They* know sacred when they see it!"

"You're dead!" Kethry returned, laughing. "You can't talk if you're dead!"

"Oh, I wouldn't bet on that," Tarma replied, grinning widely.

"Well, it's not fair—" Kethry began, when one of Tarma's "nomads" launched into a speech of her own.

It was very impassioned, full of references to "our fallen leader, now with the stars," and "our duty to free our ancient homeland," and it was just a little confused, but it was a rather good speech for a twelve year old. It certainly got her fellow fighters' blood going. This time there was no stopping them; they stormed right over the walls of the snowfort and captured the flag, despite the best efforts of Kethry and her band of defenders. Kethry made a last stand on the heights next to the flag but to no avail; she was hit with three snowballs at once, and went down even more dramatically than Tarma.

The barbarians howled for joy, piled their other victims on top of Kethry, and did a victory dance around the bodies. When Tarma resurrected herself and came to join them, Kethry rose to *her* feet, protesting at the top of her lungs.

"No, you don't—dead is dead, woman!" Kethry had come up with one of her unthrown missiles in her hands; now she launched it from point-blank range and got the surprised Tarma right in the face with it.

The never-broken rule decreed loose snowballs only. Tarma enforced that rule with a hand of iron, and Kethry would never even have thought of violating it. This was a game, and injuries had no part in it. So Tarma was unhurt, but now wore a white mask covering her from forehead to chin.

Only for a moment. "AAARRRG!" she howled, scraping the snow off her face, and springing at Kethry, fingers mimicking claws. "My disguise! You've ruined my disguise!"

"Run!" Kethry cried in mock fear, dodging. "It's—it's—"

"The great and terrible Snow Demon!" Tarma supplied, making a grab at the children, who screamed in excitement and fled. "I tricked you fools into fighting for me! Now I have *all* of you at my mercy, and the city as well! *AAAAARRRG!"*

It was only when a more implacable enemy—the children's mothers—came to fetch them away that the new game came to a halt.

"Thanks for minding them, Tarma," said one of the mothers, a former Hawk herself. She was collecting two little girls who looked—and were—

the same age. Varny and her shieldmate Sania had met in the Sunhawks, and when an unlucky swordstroke had taken out Varny's left eye, they'd decided that since Varny was mustering-out anyway because of the injury, they might as well have the family they both wanted. Though how they'd managed to get pregnant almost simultaneously was a bit of a wonder. Somewhat to their disappointment, neither child was interested in following the sword. Varny's wanted to be a scrivener, and Sania's a Healer —and the latter, at least, was already showing some evidence of that Gift.

"No problem," Tarma replied, "You know I enjoy it. It's nice to be around children who don't take warfare seriously."

In point of fact, none of these children was being trained for fighting; all had indicated to their parents that they wished more peaceful occupations. So their play-battles *were* play, and not more practice.

"Well, we still appreciate having an afternoon to ourselves, so I hope you don't ever get tired of them," one of the other mothers replied with a broad smile.

"Not a chance," Tarma told her. "I'll let you know next afternoon I've got free, and I'll kidnap them again."

"Bless you!" With that, and similar expressions of gratitude, the women and their weary offspring vanished into the streets of the snow-covered town.

"Whew." Tarma supported herself on the wall of the snowfort with both arms, and looked over at Kethry, panting. Her eyes were shining, and the grin she was still wearing reached and warmed them. "Gods, did *we* have that much energy at that age?"

"Damned if I remember. I'm just pleased I managed to keep up with them. Lady bless, I'd never have believed you could get this overheated in midwinter!"

"You had it easy. *I* was the one who had to keep leading the charges."

"So *that's* why you let me take you out so easily!" Kethry teased. "Shame on you, being in that poor a shape! You know, I rather liked that Snow Demon touch—I was a little uneasy with Jininan's rhetoric."

"Can't teach a child too early that there are folks that will use him. I just about had a foal when I found out there weren't any granny-stories up here on those lines. We Shin'a'in must have at least a dozen about the youngling who takes things on face value and gets eaten for his stupidity. Come to think of it, the Snow Demon is one of them. He ate about half a Clan before he was through."

"*Nasty* story!" Kethry helped Tarma beat some of the snow out of her clothing, and the powdery stuff sparkled in the late-afternoon sunlight as it drifted down. "Was there such a creature, really? And was that what it did?"

"There was. And it did. It showed up in an unusually cold winter one year—oh, about four generations ago. A Kal'enedral finally took it out—one of my teachers, to tell the truth. Mutual kill, very dramatic—also, he tells me, *damned* painful. I'll croak you the song sometime. Tonight, if you like."

Kethry raised an eyebrow in surprise. *That* meant Tarma was in an extraordinarily good mood. While time had brought a certain amount of healing to the ruined voice that had once been the pride of her Clan, Tarma's singing was still not something she paraded in public. Her voice was still harsh, and the tonalities were peculiar. She sometimes sounded to Kethry like someone who had been breathing smoke for forty-odd years. She was very sensitive about it and didn't offer to sing very often.

"What brought this on?" Kethry asked, as they crunched through the half-trampled snow, heading back to their double room in the Hawks' barracks. "You're seeming more than usually pleased with yourself."

Tarma grinned. "Partly this afternoon."

Kethry nodded, understanding. Tarma adored children—which often surprised the boots off their parents. More, she was very good with them. And children universally loved her and her never-ending patience with them. She would play with them, tell them stories, listen to their woes—if she hadn't been Kal'enedral, she'd have made an excellent mother. As it was, she was the willing child tender for any woman in Hawksnest who had ties to the company.

When she had time. Which, between drill and teaching duties, wasn't nearly as often as she liked. Somewhere in the back of her mind, Kethry was rather looking forward to the nebulous day when she and Tarma would retire to start their schools. Because then, Tarma would have younglings of her *own*—by way of Kethry. More, she would have the children that would form the core of her resurrected Clan.

And bringing Tale'sedrin back to life would make Tarma happy enough that the smile she wore too seldom might become a permanent part of her expression.

"So—what's the other part?" Kethry asked, shaking herself out of her woolgathering when she nearly tripped on a clump of snow.

Tarma snickered, eyes narrowed against the snow-glare and the westering sunlight. Her tone and her expression were both malicious. "Leslac's cooling his heels in the jail as of last night."

"Oh, *really?*" Kethry was delighted. "What happened?"

"Let's wait till we get inside; it's a long story."

Since they were only a few steps from the entrance to their granite-walled barracks, Kethry was willing to wait. As officers, they *could* have taken more opulent quarters, but frankly, they didn't really want them. Tarma hardly had any need for privacy; Kethry had yet to find anyone in or out of the Hawks that she wanted to dally with on any regular basis. On the rare occasions where comradeship got physical, she was more than willing to rent a room in an inn overnight. So they shared the same kind of spartan quarters as the rest of the mercenaries; a plain double room on the first floor of the barracks. The walls were wood, paneled over the stone of the building, there were pegs for their weapons, and stands for their armor, a single wardrobe, two beds, one on each wall, and three chairs and a small table. That was about the extent of it. The only concession to their rank was a wood-fired stove: Tarma felt the winter cold too much otherwise. They had a few luxuries besides: thick fur coverlets and heavy wool blankets on the beds, some fine silver goblets, oil lamps and candles instead of rush-dips—but no few of the fighters had those, paid for out of their earnings. Both of them felt that since they worked as closely as they did with their underlings, there was no sense in having quarters that made subordinates uncomfortable. And, truth to tell, neither of them would truly have felt at ease in more opulent surroundings.

They pulled off their snow-caked garments and changed quickly, hanging the old on pegs by the stove to dry. Kethry noted as she pulled on a soft, comfortable brown robe and breeches, that Tarma had donned black, and frowned. It was true that Kal'enedral only wore dark, muted colors—but black was for ritual combat or bloodfeud.

Tarma didn't miss the frown, faint as it was. "Don't get your hackles up; it's all I've got left—everything else is at the launderers or wet. I'm not planning on calling anybody out—not even that damned off-key songster. Much as he deserves it—and much as I'd like to."

Warrl raised his head from the shadows of the corner he'd chosen for his own, with a contemptuous snort. The *kyree* liked the cold even less than Tarma, and spent much of his time in the warm corner by the stove curled up on a pad of old rugs.

:You two have no taste. I happen to think Leslac is a fine musician, and a very talented one.:

Tarma answered with a snort of her own. "All right then, *you* go warm his bed. I'm sure he'd appreciate it."

Warrl simply lowered his head back to his paws, and closed his glowing golden eyes with dignity.

"Tell, tell, tell!" Kethry urged, having as little love for the feckless

Leslac as did her partner. She threw herself down into her own leather-padded hearthside chair, and leaned forward in her eagerness to hear.

"All right—here's what I was told—" Tarma lounged back in her chair, and put her feet up on the black iron footrest near the stove to warm them. "Evidently his Bardship was singing *that* song in the Falcon last night."

That song was the cause for Tarma's latest grievance with the Bard. It seemed that Leslac, apparently out of willfulness or true ignorance, had not the least notion of what being Kal'enedral meant. He had decided that Tarma's celibacy was the result of her own will, not of the hand of her Goddess—

The fact was that, as Kal'enedral, Tarma was celibate because she had become, effectively, neuter. Kal'enedral *had* no sexual desire, and little sexual identity. There was a perfectly logical reason for this. Kal'enedral served first the Goddess of the South Wind, the Warrior, who was as sexless as the blade She bore—and they served next the Clans as a whole —and lastly they served their individual Clans. Being sexless allowed them to keep a certain cool perspective that kept them free of feuding and allowed them to act as interClan arbitrators and mediators. Every Shin'a'in knew the cost of becoming Kal'enedral. Some in every generation felt the price was worth it. Tarma certainly had—since she had the deaths of her entire Clan to avenge, and *only* Kal'enedral were permitted to swear to blood-feud—and Kethry was mortally certain that having been gang-raped by the brigands that slaughtered her Clan had played no little part in the decision.

Leslac didn't believe this. He was certain—without bothering to check into Tarma's background or the customs of the Shin'a'in, so far as Kethry had been able to ascertain—that Tarma's vows were as simple as those of most other celibate orders, and as easily broken. He was convinced that she had taken those vows for some girlishly romantic reason; he had just recently written a song, in fact, that hinted—*very* broadly—that the "right man" could thaw the icy Shin'a'in. *That* was the gist of "that song."

And he evidently thought *he* was the right man.

He'd certainly plagued them enough before they'd joined up with Idra, following behind them like a puppy that couldn't be discouraged.

He'd lost track of them for two years after they'd joined the Sunhawks and that had been a profound relief. But much to their disappointment, he'd found them again and tracked them to Hawksnest. There he had remained, singing in taverns to earn his keep—and occasionally rendering Tarma's nights sleepless by singing under her window.

"That song" was new; the first time Tarma had heard it was when they'd gotten back from the Surshan campaign. Kethry had needed to practically tie her down to keep her from killing the musician.

"That's not a wise place to sing that particular ballad," Kethry observed, "Seeing as that's where your scouts tend to spend their pay."

"*Hai*—but it wasn't my scouts that got him," Tarma chuckled, "which is why I'm surprised you hadn't heard. It was Tresti and Sewen."

"*What?*"

"It was lovely—or so I'm told. Tresti and Sewen sailed in just as he began the damned thing. Nobody's said—but it wouldn't amaze me much to find out that Sewen set the whole thing up, though according to my spies, Tresti's surprise looked real enough. *She* knows what Kal'enedral means. Hellfire, we're technically equals, if I wanted to claim the priestly aspects that go with the Goddess-bond. She *also* knows how you and I feel about the little warbling bastard. So she decided to have a very public and *very* priestly fit about blasphemy and sacrilegious mockery."

That was one of the few laws within Hawksnest; that *every* comrade's gods deserved respect. And to blaspheme *anyone's* gods, particularly those of a Sunhawk of notable standing, was an official offense, punishable by the town judge.

"She didn't!"

"She ruddy well did. That was *all* Sewen and my children had been waiting for. They called civil arrest on him and bundled him off to jail. And there he languishes for the next thirty days."

Kethry applauded, beaming. "That's thirty whole days we *won't* have to put up with his singing under our window!"

"And thirty whole days I can stroll into town for a drink without hiding my face!" Tarma looked *very* pleased with herself.

Warrl heaved a gigantic sigh.

"Look, Furface, if you like him so much, why don't you go keep him company?"

:Tasteless barbarians.:

Tarma's retort died unuttered, for at that moment there was a knock at their door.

"Come—" Kethry called, and the door opened to show one of the principals of Tarma's story. Sewen.

"Are you two busy?"

"Not particularly," Tarma replied, as Kethry rose from her chair to usher him in. "I was just telling Keth about your part in gagging our songbird."

"Can I have an hour or two?" Sewen was completely expressionless, which, to those that knew him, meant that something was worrying him, and badly.

"Sewen, you can have all of our time you need," Kethry said immediately, closing the door behind him. "What's the problem? Not Tresti, I hope."

"No, no—I—I have to talk to somebody, and I figured it had better be you two. I haven't heard anything from Idra in over a month."

"Bloody hell—" Tarma sat bolt upright, looking no little alarmed herself. "Pull up the spare chair, man, and give us the details." She got up, and began lighting the oil lamps standing about the room, then returned to her seat. Kethry broke out a bottle of wine and poured three generous goblets full before resuming her perch. She left the bottle on the table within easy reach, for she judged that this talk had a possibility of going on for a while.

Sewen pulled the spare chair over to the stove and collapsed into it, sitting slumped over, with his elbows on his knees and his hands loosely clasped around the goblet. "It's been a lot more than a month, really, more like two. I was getting a message about every two weeks before then—most of 'em bitching about one thing or another. Well, that was fine, that sounded like Idra. But then they started getting shorter, and—you know, how the Captain sounds when she's got her teeth on a secret?"

"*Hai.*" Tarma nodded. "Like every word had to wiggle around that secret to get out."

"Eyah, that's it. Hints was all I got, that things were more complicated than she thought. Then a message saying she'd made a vote, and would be coming home—then, right after, another saying she *wouldn't,* that she'd learned something important and had to do something—then nothing."

"*Sheka!*" Tarma spat. Kethry seconded the curse; this sounded very bad.

"It's been nothing, like I said, for about two months. Damnit, Idra knows I'd be worried after a message like that, and no matter what had happened, she'd find some way to let me know she was all right."

"*If* she could," Kethry said.

"So I'm figuring she can't. That she's either into something real deep, too deep to break cover for a message, or she's being prevented."

Kethry felt a tug on her soul-self from across the room. Need was hung on her pegs over there—

She let her inner self reach out to the blade. Sure enough, she was "calling," as she did when there were women in danger. It was very faint —but then, Idra was very far away.

"I don't dare let the rest of the Hawks know," Sewen was saying.

Tarma coughed. "You sure as hell don't. We've got enough hotheads among us that you'd likely get about a hundred charging over there, cutting right across Rethwellan and stirring up the gods only know what trouble. *Then* luck would probably have it that they'd break right in on whatever the Captain's up to and blow it all to hell."

"Sewen, she *is* in some sort of trouble. Need stirred up the moment you mentioned this; I don't think it's coincidence." Kethry shook her head a little in resignation. "If Need calls—it's got to be more than just a little difficulty. Need's muted down since she nearly got us both killed; I hardly even feel her on a battlefield, with women fighting and dying all around. I don't talk about her, much, but I think she's been changing. I think she's managed to become a little more capable of distinguishing *real* troubles that only Tarma and I can take care of. So—I think Idra requires help, I agree with you. All right, what do you want us to do? Track her down and see what's wrong? Just remember though, if we go—" She forced a smile. "—Tresti loses her baby-tender and you lose your Masterclass mage."

Sewen just looked relieved to the point of tears. "Look, I hate to roust you two out like this, and I know how Tarma feels about traveling in cold weather, but—you're the only two I'd feel safe about sending. Most of the kids are what you said, hotheads. The rest—'cept for Jodi, they're mostly like me, commonborn. Keth, you're highborn, you can deal with highborns, get stuff out of 'em I couldn't. And Tarma can give you two a reason for hauling up there."

"Which is what?"

"You know your people hauled in the fall lot of horses just before we got back from the last campaign. Well, since we weren't *here,* Ersala went ahead and bought the whole string, figuring she couldn't know how many mounts we'd lost, and figuring it would be no big job to resell the ones we didn't want. We've still got a nice string of about thirty nobody's bespoken, and I was going to go ahead and keep them here till spring, *then* sell 'em. Rethwellan don't see Shin'a'in-breds, much; those they do are crossbred to culls. I doubt they've seen purebloods, much less good purebloods."

"We play merchant princes, hmm?" Kethry asked, seeing the outlines of his plan. "It could work. With rare beasts like that, we'd be welcome in the palace itself."

"That's it. Once you *get* in, Keth, you can puff up your lineage and move around in the court, or something. You talk highborn, and you're sneaky, you could learn a lot—"

"While I see what the kitchen and stable talk is," Tarma interrupted him. *"Hai.* Good plan, 'specially if I make out like I don't know much of the lingo. I could pick up a lot that way."

"You aren't just doing this to ease your conscience, are you?" Kethry asked, knowing there would be others who would ask the same question. Sewen had been Idra's Second for years now—playing Second to a woman had let him in for a certain amount of twitting from his peers in other companies. Notwithstanding the fact that one quarter to one third of all mercenary fighters *were* female, female Company Captains were few, and of all of them, only Idra led a mixed-sex Company. And Idra had been showing no signs of retiring, nor had Sewen made any moves indicating that he was contemplating starting his own Company.

"I won't deny that I want the Hawks," he said, slowly. "But—*not like this.* I want the Company fair and square, either 'cause Idra goes down, or 'cause she hands 'em over to me. This—it's too damn iffy, that's what it is! It's eating at me. And what's worse, it's eating at me that Idra might be in something deep—"

"—and you *have* to do something to get her out of it, if you can."

"That's it, Keth. And it's for a *lot* of reasons. She's my friend, she's my Captain, she's the one who took me out of the ranks and taught me. I can't just sit here for a year, and then announce she's gone missing and I'm taking over. I *owe* her too damned much, even if she keeps tellin' me I don't owe her a thing! How can I act like nothin's wrong an' not try t' help her?"

"Sewen, if every merc had your ethics—" Tarma began.

He interrupted her with a nonlaugh. "If every merc had my ethics, there'd be a lot more work for freefighters. Face it, Swordsworn, I can *afford* to have ethics just because of what Idra built the Sunhawks into. So I'm not going to let those ethics—or her—down."

"This is an almighty cold trail you're sending us on," Kethry muttered. "By the time we get to Petras, it'll be past Midsummer. What are you and the Hawks going to do in the meantime?"

"We're on two-year retainer from Sursha; we do spring and summer patrol under old Leamount around the Borders to keep any of her neighbors from getting bright ideas. Easy work. Idra set it up before she left. I can handle it *without* making myself Captain."

"All right, I've got some ideas. *Our* people can keep their lips laced over a secret; so you wait one week after we've left, then you tell them all what's happened and that we've been sent out under the ivy bush."

"Why?" Sewen asked bluntly.

"Mostly so rumors don't start. *Then* you and Ersala concoct some story about Idra coming back, but fevered. Tresti can tell you what kind of fever would need a two-year rest cure. That gives you a straw-Idra to leave behind while you take the Hawks out to patrol. The Hawks will know the *real* story—and tell them it might cost the Captain her life if they let it slip."

"You think it might," he said, soberly.

"I don't know what to think, so I have to cover every possibility."

"Huh." He thought about that for a long time, contemplating his wine. Finally he swallowed the last of it in a single gulp. "All right; I'll go with it. Now—should I replace you two?"

"I think you'd better," Tarma said. "I suggest promoting either Garth or Jodi. Garth is my preference; I don't think Jodi would be comfortable in a command position; she's avoided being in command too many times."

"I'll do a sending; there are White Winds sorcerers everywhere. You should be getting one or more up here within a couple of months." Kethry bit her lip a bit, trying to do a rough calculation on how far her sending would reach. "I can't promise that you'll get anything higher than a Journeymanclass, but you never know. I won't tell them more than that there's a position open with you—you can let whoever you hire in on the whole thing after you take them on. Remember, White Winds school has no edicts against using magic for fighting, and I'll make it plain in the sending that this is a position with a *merc company.* That it means killing as well as healing. That should keep the squeamish away. Have Tresti look them over first, then Oreden and Jiles. Tresti will be able to sense whether they'll fit in."

"I know; she checked you two out while Idra was waiting to interview you."

Kethry nodded wryly. "Figures; I can't imagine Idra leaving anything to chance. All right, does that pretty much take care of things?"

"I think so. . . ."

"Well, as cold as the trail is going to be, there is *no* sense in stirring up a lot of rumors by having us light out of here with our tails on fire," Tarma said bluntly. "We might just as well take our time about this, say our good-byes, get equipment put together—act like this was going to be an ordinary sort of errand we're running for you. Until we've been gone for about a week, you just make out like I'm running the string out to sell, and Keth's coming with me for company."

Sewen nodded. "That sounds good to me. I'll raid the coffers for you two. You'll be needing stuff to make you look good in the court, I expect." He rose and started for the door—then turned back, and awkwardly held out his arms.

"I—I don't know what I'd have done without you two," he said stiffly, his eyes bright with what Kethry suspected might be incipient tears. "You're more than shieldbrothers, you're friends—I—thanks—"

They both embraced him, trying to give him a little comfort. Kethry knew that Idra had been in that "more than shieldbrother" category, too —and that Sewen must be thinking what *she* was thinking—that the Captain's odds weren't very good right now.

"Te'sorthene du'dera, big man," Tarma murmured. "When we come across someone special, like you, like Tresti, like Idra—well, you help your friends, that's all I can say. That's what friends are there for, *her'y?"*

"If anybody can help her out, it'll be you two."

"We'll do our best. And you know, *you* can do *us* a favor—" Kethry almost smiled at the sudden inspiration.

"What? Anything you want."

"Leslac. I want you to teach him a lesson. I don't care what you do to him, just get him off Tarma's back."

The weather-beaten countenance went quiet with thought. "That's a pretty tall ord—wait a moment—" He began to smile, the first smile he'd worn since he walked in their door. "I think I've got it. 'Course, it all hinges on whether he's really as pig-ignorant about Shin'a'in as he seems to be."

"Go on—I think after that *damned* song we can count on *that* being true."

Sewen's arms tightened about both their shoulders as he looked down at them. "There's this sect of Spider-Priestesses down south; they sort of dress like Tarma—deal is, they *didn't* start out life as girls."

Tarma nearly choked with laughter. "You mean, convince the little bastard that I'm really a eunuched boy? Sewen, that's priceless!"

"I rather like that—" Kethry grinned. "—I rather *like* that."

"I'll get on it," he promised, giving them a last hug and closing the door to their room behind him.

Tarma went immediately to her armor-stand, surveying the brigandine for any sign of weakness or strain. Kethry put another log in the stove, then approached the wall where Need hung, reaching out to touch the blade with one finger.

Yes—the call's still there. And I can't tell anything, it's so faint—but it is Idra. The call gets perceptibly stronger when I think about her.

"Get anything?" Tarma asked quietly.

"Nothing definite, other than that Idra's in trouble. How long do you think it will take us to get to Petras?"

"With a string of thirty horses—about a month to cross the passes, then another two, maybe three. Like you said, it'll be Midsummer at the earliest."

Kethry sighed. "If I were an Adept, I could get us both there in an hour."

"But *not* the horses. And how would we explain ourselves? We'd make a lot more stir than we should if we did that."

"And stir is not what we want."

"Right." Tarma stood with a sigh, and stretched, then came back to her chair and flung herself down into it. "I seem to recall one contact we might well want to make. The Captain didn't talk about her past much, but she *did* mention somebody a time or two. The Court Archivist—" Her brows knitted in thought. "Javreck? Jervase? No—Jadrek, that's it. Jadrek. Seems like his father used to keep Idra and her older brother in tales; paid attention to them when nobody else had time for them. Jadrek was evidently a little copy of him. She'd mention him when something happened to bring one of those tales to her mind. And more important—" Tarma pointed a long finger at Kethry. "—she *also* never failed to preface those recollections by calling him 'the only completely honest man in the Court, just as his father was.' "

"That sounds promising."

"If he's still there. Seems to me she said something about him being at odds with her father and her younger brother when he took over the Archivist position. He did that pretty young, since he was younger than Idra or her brother, and she left the Court before she was twenty. She also said something about his being crippled, which could cut down on the amount he sees."

"Yes and no," Kethry replied, more than grateful for Tarma's remarkable memory. "People who are overlooked often see more that way. Need I tell you that I'm glad you have a mind like a trap?"

"What, shut?" Tarma jibed. "Now you *know* I've got a Singer's memory; if I'd forgotten *one* verse of any of the most obscure ballads, I'd have been laughed out of camp. Keth, you're worrying yourself, I can tell. You're wasting energy."

"I know, I know—"

"Take it one week at a time. Worry about getting us through the passes safely. I'll get you the avalanche map tomorrow; see what you can scry out with it. And speaking of snow, do you still want to hear that business about the Snow Demon?"

"Well . . . yes!" she replied, surprised. "But I hardly thought you'd be in the mood for it now."

"I'm just taking some of my own prescribed medicine." Tarma grinned crookedly, and went to fetch the battered little hand-drum she used on those rare occasions when she chanted—you couldn't call it singing anymore—one of the Shin'a'in history-songs. "Trying to remember all fifty-two verses will keep *me* from fretting into a sweat. And hoping," she looked down at her black sleeve, the black of vengeance-taking, "that this outfit doesn't turn out to be an omen."

Five

"*Hai'vetha! Kele, kele, kele!*"
Tarma wheeled Ironheart about on the mare's heels in a piece of horsemanship that drew a spattering of impromptu applause from those watching, and chivied the last of the tired horses into the corral assigned to them by the master of the Petras stock market. She controlled them with voice only—not hand, nor whip. She didn't even call for any encouraging nips at their heels from Warrl, another fact which impressed the spectators no end.

They were already impressed by the horses. They were not the kind of beasts that the inhabitants of Petras were used to seeing. These were Shin'a'in purebreds, and the only reason any of them had been passed over by the Sunhawks was that they were mostly saddlebreds, not trailbreds. The Shin'a'in horses bred for trail work were a little rougher looking, and a bit hardier than the saddlebreds, in the main. There were always exceptions, like Tarma's beloved Kessira, but the Shin'a'in kept the exceptions for their own use and further breeding—as Kessira was being bred, pampered queen mare of the Tale'sedrin herds.

No, these horses were *not* what the inhabitants of Petras were used to seeing in their beast-market. Their heads, broad in the forehead, small in the muzzle, and with large, doe-soft eyes were carried high and proudly on their long, elegant necks; pride showed in every line of them, despite their weariness. Their bodies were compact and muscular, the hindquarters being a trifle higher than these people were accustomed to. Their legs were well-muscled and slim; they were no longer shaggy with winter growth as they had been when the trek started. Now their coats were silky despite the dust—and their manes and tails, the pride of a Shin'a'in mount, were flowing in the wind like many-colored waterfalls. And they moved like dancers, like birds on the wind, like music made visible.

In short, they were beautiful.

"Good enough to suit a king, eh, *she'enedra?*" Tarma asked in her own tongue, feeling rather proud of her charges.

"I should think—" Kethry began, when one of the onlookers, a man possessed of more than a little wealth, by the cut of his gray and green clothing, interrupted her.

"What *are* these beauties?" he asked, in tones that bordered on veneration. "Where on earth did they spring from? Valdemar? I'd heard Companions were magnificent, but I'd never heard of anyone other than Heralds owning them, and I'd never heard that Companions were anything but white."

"No, m'lord," Kethry replied, as Tarma privately wondered what on earth a Companion could be. "These are Shin'a'in purebred saddlemares and geldings from the Dhorisha Plains."

"Shin'a'in!" The man stepped back a pace. "Lord and Lady—how did you ever get Shin'a'in to part with them? I'd have thought they'd have shown you their sword-edge rather than their horses."

"Easily enough—I'm blood-sister to the handler, there. I thought to bring a string up here and try our luck."

"She's—Shin'a'in—?" The man gulped, and eased another footstep or two away, putting Kethry between himself and Tarma. Tarma wasn't certain whether to laugh or continue to look as if she didn't understand. The man acted like she was some kind of demon!

"Oh yes," Kethry answered, "and Kal'enedral." She must have noted his look of blank nonrecognition, because she added, "Swordsworn."

He turned completely white. "I—hope—excuse me, lady, but I trust she's—under control."

"Warrior's Oath, *she'enedra,* what in Hell have they heard about us?" Tarma kept to her own tongue, as per the plan, and was keeping her face utterly still and impassive, but she knew Kethry could hear the suppressed laughter in her voice.

"Probably that you eat raw meat for breakfast and raw babies for dinner," Kethry replied, and Tarma could see the struggle to keep *her* expression guileless in the laughter sparkling in her eyes.

"Pardon—but—what's she saying?" The man eyed Tarma as if he expected her to unsheathe her blade and behead him at any moment.

"That she noticed how much you admire the horses, and thanks you for the compliment of your attention."

Tarma took care to nod graciously at him, and he relaxed visibly. She then turned her attention back to the horses. The corral seemed sizable enough to hold them comfortably; she'd been a little worried about that. *Let's see—pump or well for the watering trough? And where would it be— ah!* She spotted a pump, after a bit of looking. *Good. One good thing about so-called civilization: pumps. Think maybe I might see if the Clans would agree to having a couple installed on the artesian wells. . . .*

"Stand," she told Ironheart. The battlemare obediently locked her legs in position; it would take an earthquake to move her now. Tarma unslung the sword from her back and looped the baldric over the pommel of the saddle. "Guard," she ordered. That blade was a sweet one, and had been dearly paid for in her own blood; she didn't intend to lose it. Ironheart would see that she didn't.

"You'd better tell your friend to stay clear of 'Heart or he'll lose a hand," she called to Kethry, then dismounted and vaulted over the fence into the stockade to water her other charges. That bit of bravado cost, too, but it was worth a bit of strain to put on a proper show. Tarma meant to leave these folks with their mouths gaping—for that meant that the highborns would hear of them that much sooner.

:You're going to hurt in the morning,: Warrl observed. Thus far, the crowd's attention had been so taken up with the horses that they hadn't paid much heed to him. He'd stayed in the shadow of Ironheart, who was so tall that he didn't stand out as the monster he truly was.

And—*she* couldn't tell, but he might well be exercising a bit of his own magic to look more like an ordinary herd dog. He'd hinted that he could do just that on the way here. Which was no bad idea.

Tarma felt the strain of the muscles she'd used, and privately agreed with his critical remark about hurting. For every scar she bore on her hide, there was twice the scar tissue under it, where it didn't show—but it certainly made itself felt. Particularly when she started showing off.

But they were drawing a bigger crowd by the moment; the onlookers murmured as the loose horses crowded around her, shoving their heads under her hands for a scratch, or lipping playfully at her hair. She laughed at them, pushed them out of the way, and got to the pump. As she began to fill the trough, they pushed in to get at the water, and she rebuked them with a single sharp *"Nes!"* They shied and danced a bit, then behaved themselves.

Tarma had been doing some serious training with them on the trail— knowing that once they were in Rethwellan she would *have* to be able to command them by voice, for if they spooked, she, Kethry, and Warrl would not be enough to keep them under control. Her ability to keep them in line seemed to impress their audience no end. She decided to go all out to impress them.

She picked out one of the herd mares she'd been working with far more than the others, and called her. The chestnut mare pricked her ears, and came to the summons eagerly—she knew what this meant; first a trick from *her,* and then a treat was in store. Tarma ordered the others out of her way, then raised her hand high over her head. The mare stepped out away from her about fifteen paces, then as Tarma began to turn, followed her turn as if she was being lunged.

Except there was no lunging-rein on her.

At a command from Tarma she picked up to a trot, then a canter; after traveling all day, Tarma was *not* going to ask her to gallop. At a third command she stopped dead in her tracks. At the fourth, she reared—

The fifth command was "Come—" and meant a piece of dried apple and a good scratch behind the ears. She obeyed *that* one with eager promptitude.

The spectators, now thick on the fence, applauded. The horses flickered their ears nervously, but when nothing came of the noise, went back to watching Tarma, hoping for treats themselves.

Tarma was pleased—*more* than pleased. *Everything* was going according to the plan they'd mapped out. "Patience, children," she told the rest. "Dinner should be here soon."

Their ears flickered forward nearly as one at that welcome word, and they continued to watch her with expectation in their soft, sweet eyes.

And within moments, the beast-market attendants did appear, with the hay and sweet-feed Tarma had told Kethry to order—and more than that—

She saw carrots poking out of more than one pocket. Hmm. This was gratifying, if it was evidence of the fact that the attendants were taken with the looks of the string—but it *could* also be an attempt on the part of some other horsebreeder to poison her stock.

:*I'm checking, mindmate.*: the voice in her head told her.

"Keth, tell the younglings over there to hold *absolutely still.* I think they just want to treat the children, but Warrl's going to check for drugging, just in case."

Kethry called out the warning, and the attendants froze; the whole *crowd* froze when they saw Warrl's great gray body moving toward them. *Now* they could see just how huge he was—his shoulder came nearly to Tarma's waist—and how much like a wolf he looked. Tarma took advantage of the situation to vault the fence again, and begin relieving the attendants of their burdens. Warrl sniffed the feed over, then checked the youngsters themselves and the treats they'd brought.

:They're fine, mindmate,: Warrl told her, cheerfully. *:And about ready to soil themselves if I sneeze.:*

Tarma laughed, and patted the one next to her on the head as she took his bale of hay away from him. "They're all right, Keth. Um—tell them to wait until I've finished, then they can give the children their treats so long as they stay out of the corral. I don't want anybody in there; they get spooked, and it'll take half a day to calm them down again. And tell them we won't need any nightwatchers, that Warrl will be guarding them when I'm not here—that should prevent anybody even *thinking* about drugging them."

Warrl sprang over the fence with a single, graceful leap. The horses, of course, were so used to his presence that they totally ignored him, being far more interested in their dinner. With a fence between themselves and Warrl, the attendants calmed down a bit.

Tarma completed her task, and (with an inward wince) vaulted the fence a third time, to return to where Ironheart still stood, statue-firm.

"Rest," she said, and the battlemare unlocked her legs, and reached around to nuzzle at her rider's arm. The others were getting fed; she wanted *her* dinner.

"Hungry, *jel'enedra?*" Tarma murmured, letting her have the handful of sweet-feed she'd brought with her. "Patience, we'll be at the inn soon enough."

She cast a glance over at Kethry's companion. His eyes were taking up half of his head.

"Warrl, would you mind staying—"

:If you send me a nice haunch of pig as soon as you get there.:

"*And* a half-dozen marrowbones already cracked; you deserve it." She swung up into her saddle, and turned to Kethry, who was smiling broadly enough to split her face in two. "So much for the barbarian dog and pony show, *she'enedra,*" she said, stifling a chuckle. "Tell these nice people they can go home, and let's find our inn, shall we?"

"So how barbarian do you want me to look?" Tarma asked her partner, as they strolled down the creaking wooden stairs of the inn to the dimly lit common room. "And what kind? The aloof desert princeling, the snarling beast-thing, what?"

"Better stick with the aloof desert princeling; we don't want these people afraid to have you near the Court," Kethry chuckled. Tarma was plainly enjoying herself, willing to act any part to the hilt. "Brood—that always looks impressive, and you've certainly got the face for it."

"Oh, have I now!" They were continuing to speak in Shin'a'in between themselves; it was better than a code. The likelihood of anyone knowing Tarma's tongue, here in a country where tales of Shin'a'in were obviously so outlandish that they *feared* the Swordsworn, was nil.

The common room went absolutely silent as they entered. Tarma stepped in first, looking around sharply, as if she expected enemies to emerge from beneath the tables. Finally she gave a quick nod as if to herself, stepped aside, and motioned Kethry to precede her. She kept a casual hand on the hilt of the larger of her daggers the entire time. She'd wanted to wear her sword, but Kethry had argued against the idea; now she was glad she'd won. If Tarma *had* worn anything larger than a dagger, she *might* well have caused a panicked exodus! As it was, the impression she left was a complicated one; that she was very dangerous and suspicious of everyone and everything, that she and Kethry were equal, but that she also considered herself in charge of Kethry's safety.

It was a masterful performance, carefully planned and choreographed to avoid a problem before it could come up. The people of the primary religious sect of Rethwellan took a dim view of same-sex lovers, and the partners were doing their best to make *that* notion, which was inevitably going to occur to *someone,* seem a total absurdity. This touch-me-not bodyguarding act Tarma was putting on was hopefully going to do just that—among other things.

They took a table with seats for two in a far corner. Tarma motioned for Kethry to take the seat actually *in* the corner, then took the outer seat so that *she* would stand (or rather, sit) between Kethry and The Rest Of The World. Kethry signaled the waiter while her partner turned her own chair so that the back was up against the wall, and finally sat down. Tarma continued to watch the room from that vantage, broodingly, while Kethry placed orders for both of them. Conversation started back up again once they were seated, but Kethry noted that it was a trifle uneasy, and most of the diners kept one eye on Tarma at all times.

"They think you're going to start a holy war any second, *she'enedra,"* Kethry said, finally.

"Good," her partner replied, folding her arms, leaning back against the wall beside their table, and continuing to watch the room with icy, hooded eyes. "I hope this act of mine gets us prompt service; I'm about to eat the candle."

"Now, now, I thought you were being princely."

"I am—but I'm a *hungry* prince."

At just that moment, a serving wench, shaking in her shoes, brought their orders. Tarma looked at the cutlery, sniffed disdainfully, and drew the smaller of her daggers, cutting neat bits with it and eating them off the point. After a look of her own at the state of the implements they'd been given, Kethry rather wished the part she was playing allowed her to do the same.

They were nearly finished when the innkeeper himself, sidling carefully *around* Tarma, came to stand obsequiously at Kethry's elbow. She allowed him to wait a moment before deigning to notice his presence. This was in keeping with the rest of the parts they were playing—

For although they had *arrived* in dusty, well-worn traveling leathers— Tarma's being all-too-plainly armor, Kethry's bearing no hint of her mage-status—they were now dressed in silks. Kethry wore a knee-length robe, of an exotic cut and a deep green, and breeches of a deeper green; Tarma wore Shin'a'in-style wrapped jacket, shirt, and breeches—in black. With them, she wore a black sweatband of matching silk confining her short-cropped hair, and a wrapped sash holding her two daggers of differing sizes, a black silk baldric for the sword that she had left in the room above, and black quilted silk boots. Her choice of outfitting had stirred uneasy feelings in Kethry, but Tarma had pointed out with irrefutable logic that if the Captain was to hear of two strangers in Petras, and have *that* outfit described to her, she would *know* who those strangers were. And she would know by the sable hue that Tarma was expecting her Captain to be in trouble—possibly in need of avenging.

Their clothing was clearly the most costly (and certainly the most outre) in the room, and this was (dubious eating utensils notwithstanding) *not* an inexpensive inn. They *wanted* their presence to be known and commented on; they *wanted* word to spread. Ideally it would spread to Idra, wherever she was; if not, to the ear of the King.

"My lady," the innkeeper said, in tones both frightened and fawning, tones that made Kethry long for their old friend Hadell of the Broken Sword, or plain, genial Oskar of the Bottomless Barrel. "My lady, there is a gentleman who wishes to speak with you."

"So?" she raised an elegant eyebrow. "On what subject?"

"He did not confide in me, my lady, but—he wears the livery of the King."

"Does he, then? Well, I'll hear him out—if you have somewhere a bit more—private—than this."

"Of a certainty, if my lady would follow—" He bowed, and groveled, and at length brought them to a small but comfortably appointed chamber, equipped with one table, four chairs, and a door that shut quite

firmly. He bowed himself out; wine appeared, in cleaner vessels than they had been favored with before this, and finally, the visitor himself.

Kethry chose to receive him seated; Tarma stood, leaning against the wall with her arms folded, in the shadows at her right hand. Their visitor gave the Shin'a'in a fairly nervous glance before accosting Kethry.

"My lady," he said, bowing over her hand.

Kethry was having a hard time keeping from laughing herself sick. The right corner of Tarma's mouth kept twitching, sure sign that she was holding herself in only by the exertion of a formidable amount of will-power. This liveried fop was precisely the degree of lackey they had hoped to lure in; personal servant to the King, and probably a minor noble himself. He was languishing, and vapid, and quite thoroughly full of himself. His absurd court dress of pale yellow and green with the scarlet and gold badge of the King's Household on the right shoulder was exceedingly expensive as well as in appallingly bad taste. There was more than a little trace of a more careful toilette than Kethry *ever* bothered with in his appearance. His carefully pointed mouse-brown mustaches alone must have taken him an hour to tease into shape.

"My lord wishes to know the identity of two such—fascinating— strangers to our realm," he said, when he'd completed his oozing over Kethry's hand. "And what brings them here."

"I shall answer the second question first, my lord," Kethry replied, with just a hint of cool hauteur. "What brings us, is trade, purely and simply. But not just *any* trade, I do assure you; no, what we have are the mounts of princes, princes of the Shin'a'in—and we intend them to grace the stables of the princes of other realms. The horses we have brought are princes and princesses themselves—as I am certain you are aware."

"Word—*had* reached my noble lord that your beasts were extraordi-nary—"

"They are creatures whose like no one here has ever seen. It is only through my friendship with the noble Tarma shena Tale'sedrin, *the* Tale'sedrin of Tale'sedrin, that I was able to obtain them."

His glance lit again upon Tarma, who was still standing in the shadows behind Kethry. She moved forward into the light, inclined her head gra-ciously at the sound of her name, and said in Shin'a'in, "I also happen to be the *only* Tale'sedrin other than you, but we won't go into that, will we?"

"My companion tells me she is pleased to make the acquaintance of so goodly a gentleman," Kethry said smoothly, as Tarma allowed the shad-ows to obscure her again. "As for myself, I am Kethryveris, scion of

House Pheregul of Mournedealth, a House of ancient and honorable lineage."

From the blankness of his gaze, Kethry knew he'd never even heard of Mournedealth, much less her House—which, so far as she was concerned, was all to the good.

"A House of renown, indeed," he said, covering his ignorance. "Then, let me now tender my lord's words. I come from King Raschar himself." He paused, to allow Kethry to voice the expected murmurs of amazement and gratification. "He heard of your wondrous beasts, and wishes to have his Master of Horse view them himself—more than view them, if what rumor says of them is even half the truth. And since you prove to be more than merely common merchants, he would like to tender you an invitation to extend your visit to Petras in his Court, that he may learn of you, and you of him."

"And you may end up in the bastard's bed, if he likes your looks," murmured Tarma from the darkness.

"Tell your lord that we are gratified—and that we shall await his Master of Horse with eagerness, and will be more than pleased to take advantage of the hospitality of his Court."

More smooth nonsense was exchanged, and finally the man bowed himself out.

They waited, holding their breaths, until they were certain he was out of earshot—then collapsed into each other's arms, helpless with stifled laughter.

"Goddess! 'Tale'sedrin of Tale'sedrin' indeed! That great booby didn't even know it was a clan name and not a title!" Tarma choked. *"Isda so'tre-koth!* You know what my people say, don't you? 'Proud is the Clanchief. Prideful is the Clanchief of a two-member clan!' "

"Laid it on good and thick, didn't I?" Kethry replied, wiping tears out of her eyes. "Goddess bless, I didn't know I had that much manure in me!"

"Oh, you could have fertilized half a farm, 'my *la*-dy,' " Tarma gasped, imitating his obsequious bow. "Bright Star-Eyed! Here—" she handed Kethry one of the goblets and poured it full of wine, then took a second for herself. "We'd better get ourselves under control if we're going to get from here to our room without giving the game away."

"You're right," Kethry said, taking a long sip, and exerting control to sober herself. "There's more at stake than just this little game."

"Hai'she'li. This is just the tail of the beastie. We're going to have to get into its lair to see if it's a grasscat or a treehare—and if it's got Idra in its mouth."

"And I just realized something," Kethry told her, all thought of laughter gone. "We know the new King's name, but we don't know *which* of the brothers he is. And *that* could make a deal of difference."

"Indeed, *ves'tacha,*" Tarma replied, her eyes gone brooding in truth. "In very deed."

At dawn Tarma relieved Warrl of his watch on the horses, and amused herself by first going through a few sword drills, then working them, much to the titillation of the gawkers. Toward noon, Kethry (who had been playing the aristo, rising late, and demanding breakfast in bed) put in her appearance. With her was a pale stranger, as expensively dressed as their visitor of the previous evening, but in *much* better taste. He, too, wore the badge of the King's Household on his right shoulder. By his walk Tarma would have known him for a horseman. By the clothing and the badge, she knew him for the Master of the King's Horse.

And by the appreciation in his eyes, Tarma knew him for a man who knew his business. She heaved a mental sigh of relief at that; she'd half feared he might turn out to be as big a booby as the courtier of the night before. It would have cut her to the heart to sell these lovelies to an ignoramus—but if she refused to sell, they'd lose their cover story.

She had been taking the horses out of the corral, one at a time, and working them in a smaller pen. Most of them she *did* work on a lunge—there were only a handful among the thirty she could work loose, the way she had the chestnut. She had a particularly skittish young buckskin gelding out when Kethry and her escort arrived, one she needed to devote most of her attention to. So after taking a few mental notes on the man, she went back to work.

He spent a long time looking over the herd as a whole, and all in complete silence.

:This is a good one, mindmate,: Warrl said, from his resting place under the horse trough. *:He smells of soap and leather, not perfume. And there's no fear in him, nor on him.:*

"*Kathal, dester'edre,*" she told the buckskin, who kept wanting to break into a canter. "What else can you pick up from him?"

:Lots of horse-scent, and not a trace of horse-fear.:

"*For'shava.*"

After a time the Master of Horse left his post at the corral, and took up a nearly identical stance at the fence of the pen where she was working the buckskin. She watched him out of the corner of her eye, appraisingly. He was older than she'd first thought. Medium height, dark eyes, dark hair, beard and mustache—his complexion would be very white if not for his suntan—muscles in his shoulders that made his tunic leather stretch when he moved. His sole vanity seemed to be a set of matching silver jewelry: fillet, torque, bracelets, all inset with a single moonstone apiece. He leaned comfortably on the fence, missing nothing she did. Finally, he spoke to Kethry, who was standing at his side, dressed for the day in a cleaner and far more expensive set of the leathers she'd worn to ride in yesterday. Sewen had not spared the Company coffers when it had come time to outfit them for their ruse.

"I understood that your companion was working the horses yesterday without a lunge. . . ."

"Only a few of the horses are schooled enough to work that way at the moment," Kethry said smoothly, "although eventually *all* of them could be trained so. Do you wish to see her work one of them now?"

"If you would both be so kind."

Kethry leaned over the fence. "You heard him, *she'enedra;* is Master Flutterby there ready to pause?"

The buckskin was obeying now, having tried to fret himself into a froth. Tarma halted him, then gave him a quick rubdown, and led him out. This time she called up a gentle dappled gelding—one she was rather glad hadn't been chosen by a Sunhawk. He was so good-natured— he really wasn't suited to a battlefield, but he was so earnest he'd have broken his heart or a leg trying to do what was asked of him.

She didn't even bother to take him into the pen; she worked him in the open, then mounted him bareback, and put him through a bit of easy dressage. When she slid off, the Horsemaster approached; she kept one hand on the dapple's neck and watched as he examined the animal almost exactly as she would have. The dapple, curious, craned his head around and whuffed the man's hair as he ran his hands gently down the horse's legs, rear, then front, then picked up a forefoot. At that, the man grinned—a most unexpected expression on so solemn a face—and held out his hand for the dapple to smell, then rubbed his nose, gently.

"Lady," he spoke directly to Tarma, though he must have been told she didn't speak the language—a courtesy as delicate as any she'd ever been given, "I would cheerfully sell the Palace to purchase these horses. For once, rumor has understated fact."

"I think he's rather well hooked, *she'enedra,*" Kethry said, pretending to translate. "How is he as a horseman? Can you feel happy letting them go to his care?"

Tarma gave that slight bow of respect to him, and allowed a hint of a smile to cross her face. "I'm pleased, Warrl's pleased, and have a look at Dust, if you would."

The dapple's eyes were half-closed in pleasure as the Horsemaster continued to scratch under his loose halter.

"I think it's safe to say that they'll be in good hands. See if you can wangle a deal with him that will include me as a temporary trainer; that will give us another excuse to linger."

"My companion is gratified by your praise, my lord," Kethry said to him, "and impressed with your knowledge; she says she believes she could not find one to whose care she would be more willing to entrust her beasts."

Again, that unexpected smile. "Then, if you would care to return with me, I believe we can agree to something mutually pleasing. Since you will be selling into the King's household, there will be no merchant taxes. And I think—" He gave the dapple's forehead a last scratch. "—I think perhaps that I shall keep *this* one out of his Majesty's sight. I have my pick of the King's stables, but only after he has taken his choice. It is a pity a mount this intelligent is also so beautiful."

"Do you suppose you can come up with a distractor, Tarma?"

"*Do* I? I think so!" She led the dapple back into the pen, and walked into the center of the herd to bring out the one horse of the lot that was mostly show and little substance—a lovely gelding with a coat of gold, a mane and tail of molten silver, and without a jot of brains in that beautiful head. Fortunately, he was reasonably even of temper as well as being utterly gentle, or there'd have been no handling him.

He'd been included in the lot sent to the Sunhawks although if he'd had a bit less in the way of good looks he'd have been counted a cull. Tarma had gotten the notion that Idra might like a parade-mount, and had asked her people to be on the lookout for a truly impressive beast of good temper; for parade, brains didn't matter. You couldn't have told his beauty though, except by his lines and the way he carried himself. That was because he was filthy from rolling in the dust—which he *insisted* on doing when any opportunity presented itself.

Tarma went to work on him with brushes, as he sighed and leaned into the strokes. He was dreadfully vain, and he loved being groomed. Tarma almost suspected him of dust-rolling on purpose, just so he'd get groomed more often. As the silver and gold began to emerge from under the dirt, the Horsemaster exclaimed in surprise. When Tarma was done, and paraded the horse before him, he smacked his fist into his palm in glee.

"By the gods! One look at *him* and his Majesty won't give a bean for the gray! I thank you, my ladies," he bowed slightly to both Kethry and her partner, "and let us conclude this business as quickly as may be! I won't be easy until these beauties are safely in the Royal Stables."

As he and Kethry returned the way they had come, Tarma turned the gold loose in the stockade—where he promptly went to his knees and wallowed in the dirt.

"You," she laughed at him, "are hopeless!"

By twilight they were installed, bag and baggage, in the Palace, in one of the suites reserved for minor foreign dignitaries.

It had all happened so fast that Tarma was still looking a little bemused. Kethry, who knew just how quickly high-ranking courtiers could get things accomplished when they wanted to exert themselves, had been a bit less surprised.

She and the Master of Horse had concluded their bargain in fairly short order—and to her satisfaction, it had been at *his* suggestion that Tarma was retained for continued training. No sooner had a price been settled on and a writ made out to a reputable goldsmith, than a stream of thirty grooms and stable hands had been sent to walk the horses from the corral at the stockyard to the Royal Stables, each horse to have its own handler. The Horsemaster was taking no chances on accident or injury.

When Kethry returned to the inn, there were already three porters waiting for her orders, all in the Royal livery. They were none too sure of themselves; Tarma (still in her barbarian persona) had refused them entrance to the suite, and was guarding the door as much with her scowl as her drawn sword.

They allowed the porters to carry away most of their belongings, the ones that didn't matter, like some of that elaborate clothing. Tarma's armor and weaponry (including a few nasty little surprises she definitely did not want anyone to know about), Need, their trail gear, and the few physical supplies Kethry needed for her magecraft they brought themselves, in sealed saddlebags. They rode Hellsbane and Ironheart; Kethry had no intention of chancing accidents with a trained battlemare. "Accidents" involving a Shin'a'in warsteed generally ended up in broken bones —and *not* the horse's.

More obsequious servants met them once the mares were safely stabled, and again, Kethry made it plain to the stable crew that *only* Tarma was to handle their personal horses. To enforce that, they left Warrl with the mounts, provided with his own stall between the ones supplied to the two mares. One look at the *kyree* was all it took to convince the stablehands that they did *not* wish to rouse the beast's ire. That was where Tarma and Kethry left their *real* gear, the things they would truly need if they had to cut and run, and between Warrl and the horses, it would be worth a person's life to touch it.

But as they crossed the threshold of the Palace, a curious chill had settled over Kethry, a chill that had nothing to do with temperature. Her good humor and faint amusement had vanished. The Palace seemed built of secrets—dark secrets. Their mission suddenly took on an ominous feeling.

The suite, consisting of a private bathing room, two bedrooms, and an outer public room, all opulently furnished in dark wood and amber velvet, had been a good indication that their putative status was fairly high. The two personal servants assigned to them, in addition to the regular staff, had told them that they ranked somewhere in the "minor envoy" range. This was close to perfect: Kethry would be able to move about the Court fairly freely.

Now Tarma was immersed to her neck in a hot bath; Kethry had already had hers, and was dressing in her most impressive outfit, for there would be a formal reception for them in an hour.

Tarma did not look at all relaxed. Kethry didn't blame her; she'd been increasingly uneasy herself.

"There was no sign of Gray in the stables, and I looked for him," Tarma called abruptly from the bathing room. Gray was Idra's gelding; a palfrey, and not the Shin'a'in stallion she rode on campaign. "No sign of Hawk tack, either. It's like she's been long gone, or was never here at all."

Kethry heard splashing as her partner stood; and shortly thereafter the Shin'a'in emerged from the bathing room with a huge towel wrapped about herself. They'd turned down an offer of bath attendants; after one look at Tarma's arsenal, the attendants had seemed just as glad.

"If she's been here, we should find out about it tonight. Especially after the wine begins to flow. Do I look impressive, or seducible?" Kethry glided into Tarma's room, and turned so that her partner could survey her from all angles.

"Impressive," Tarma judged, vigorously toweling her hair.

"Good; I don't want to have to slap Royal fingers and get strung up for my pains."

Kethry's loose robes were of dark amber silk, about three shades darker than her hair, and high-necked, bound at the waist with a silk-and-gold cord. At her throat she wore a cabochon piece of amber the size of an egg; she had confined her hair into a severe knot, only allowing two decorous tendrils in front of her ears. The robes had full, scalloped-edged sleeves that were bound with gold thread. She looked beautiful, and incredibly dignified.

Tarma was dressing in a more elaborate version of her black silk outfit, this one piped at every seam and hem with silver; she had a silver mesh belt instead of a silk sash, and a silver fillet with a black moonstone instead of a headband confining her midnight hair.

"You look fairly impressive, yourself."

"I don't like the feel of this place, I'll tell you that now," Tarma replied bluntly. "I've got my Kal'enedral chainmail on under my shirt, and I'm bloody well armed to the teeth. I'm going to *stay* that way until we're out of here."

Kethry rubbed her neck, nervously. "You, too?"

"Me, too."

"You know the drill—"

"You talk and mingle, I lurk behind you. If I hear anything interesting, I cough twice, and we get somewhere where we can discuss it."

All their good humor had vanished into the shadows of the Palace, and all that was left them was foreboding.

"I don't suppose that Need . . ."

"Not a hint. Just the same as back at Hawksnest. Which could mean about anything; most likely is that the Captain is out of the edge of her range."

"I hope you're right," Tarma sighed. "Well, shall we get on with it?"

Closing the door on the dubious shelter of their suite, they moved, side by side, deeper into the web of intrigue.

Six

Perfume, wine, and wire-tight nerves. Musk, hot wax, and dying flowers. The air in the Great Hall was so thick with scent that Tarma felt overpowered by all the warring odors. The butter-colored marble of the very walls and floor seemed warm rather than cool. Lighted candles were everywhere, from massed groupings of thin tapers to pillars as thick as Tarma's wrist. The pale polished marble reflected the light until the Great Hall glowed, fully as bright as daylight. The hundreds of jewels, the softly gleaming gold on brow and neck and arm, the winking golden bullion weighing down hems sparkled like a panoply of stars.

It was not precisely *noisy* here—but the murmuring of dozens, hundreds of conversations, the underlying current of the music of a score of minstrels, the sound of twenty pairs of feet weaving through an intricate dance—the combination added up to an effect as dizzying as the light, heat or scent.

Carved wooden doors along one wall opened up onto a courtyard garden, also illuminated for the evening—but by magic, not candles. But few moved to take advantage of the quiet and cool garden—not when the real power in this land was *here*.

If power had possessed a scent, it would have overwhelmed all the others in the hall. The scarlet-and-gold-clad man lounging on the gilded wooden throne at the far end of the Great Hall was young, younger than Tarma, but very obviously the sole agent of control here. No matter *what* they were doing, nearly everyone in this room kept one eye on him at all times; if he leaned forward the better to listen to one of the minstrels, all conversation hushed—if he nodded to a lady, peacock-bright gallants thronged about her. But if he smiled upon her, even her escort deserted her, not to return until their monarch's interest wandered elsewhere.

He was not particularly imposing, physically. Brown hair, brown eyes; medium build; long, lantern-jawed face with a hard mouth and eyebrows like ruler-drawn lines over his eyes—his was not the body of a warrior, but not the body of a weakling, either.

Then he looks at you, Tarma thought, *and you see the predator, the king of his territory, the strongest beast of the pack. And you want to crawl to him on your belly and present your throat in submission.*

:Unless,: the thin tendril of Warrl's mind-voice insinuated itself into her preoccupation, *:just unless you happen to be a pair of rogue bitches like yourself and your sister.* You *bow to your chosen packleader, and no one else. And you never grovel.:*

The brilliantly-bedecked courtiers weren't entirely certain how to treat Kethry and her black-clad shadow—probably because the King himself hadn't been all that certain. Wherever they walked, conversation faltered and died. There was veiled fright in the courtiers' eyes—*real* fright. Tarma wondered if she hadn't overdone her act a bit.

On the other hand, King Raschar had kept his hands off the sorceress. It *had* looked for a moment as if he was considering chancing her "protector's" wrath—but one look into Tarma's coldly impassive eyes, (eyes, she'd often been told, that marked her as a born killer) seemed to make him decide that it might not be worth it.

Tarma would have laid money down on the odds she knew exactly what he was thinking when he gave her that measuring look. He could well have reckoned that she might be barbarian enough to act if she took offense—and quick enough to do him harm before his guards could do anything about her. Maybe even quick enough to kill him.

:The predator recognizes another of his kind.:

Tarma nodded to herself. Warrl wasn't far wrong.

If this was highborn life, Tarma was just as glad she'd been born a Shin'a'in nomad. The candlelight that winked from exquisite jewels also reflected from hollow, hungry eyes; voices were shrill with artificial gaiety. There was no peace to be found here, and no real enjoyment. Just a never-ending round of competition, competition in which the smallest of gestures took on worlds of meaning, and in which they, as unknown elements, were a very disturbing pair of unexpected variables.

The only members of this gathering that seemed to be enjoying themselves in any way were a scant handful of folks, who, by the look of them, were not important enough to worry the power-players; a few courting couples, some elderly nobles and merchants—and a pair of men over in one corner, conversing quietly in the shadows, garbed so as to seem almost shadows themselves, who stood together with winecups in hand. They were well out of the swirl of the main action, ignored for the most part by the players of this frenetic game. When one of the two shifted, the one wearing the darkest clothing, Tarma caught a good look at the face and recognized him for the Horsemaster. He had donned that impassive mask he'd worn when he first looked the horses over, and he was dressed more for comfort than to impress. Like Tarma he was dressed mainly in black—in his case, with touches of scarlet. His only ornaments were the silver-and-moonstone pieces he'd worn earlier.

The other man was all in gray, and Tarma could not manage to catch a glimpse of his face. Whoever he was, Tarma was beginning to wish she was with him and the Horsemaster. She was already tired to the teeth of this reception.

Although Tarma usually enjoyed warmth, the air in the Great Hall was stiflingly hot even to her. As she watched the men out of the corner of her eye, they evidently decided the same, for they began moving in the direction of one of the doors that led out into the gardens. As they began to walk, Tarma saw with a start that the second man limped markedly.

"Keth, d'you see our friend from this afternoon?" she said in a conversational tone. "Will you lay me odds that the fellow with him is that Archivist?"

"I don't think I'd care to; I believe that you'd win." Kethry nodded to one of the suddenly-tongue-tied courtiers as they passed, the very essence of gracious calm. The man nodded back, but his eyes were fixed on Tarma. "Care for a breath of fresh air?"

"I thought you'd never ask."

They made their own way across the room, without hurrying, and not directly—simply drifting gradually as the ebb and flow of the crowd permitted. They stopped once to accept fresh wine from a servant, and again to exchange words with one of the few nobles (a frail, alert-eyed old woman swathed in white fur) who didn't seem terrified of them. It seemed to take forever, and was rather like treading the measures of an intricate dance. But eventually they reached the open door with its carvings and panels of bronze, and escaped into the cool duskiness of the illuminated gardens.

Tarma had been prepared to fade into the shadows and stalk until she found their quarry, but the two men were in plain sight beside one of the mage-light decorated fountains. They were clearly silhouetted against the sparkling, blue-glowing waters. The Archivist was seated on a white marble bench, holding his winecup in both hands: the Horsemaster stood beside him, leaning over to speak to him with one booted foot on the stone slab, his own cup dangling perilously from loose fingers.

The partners strolled unhurriedly to the fountain, pretending that Kethry was admiring it. The Horsemaster saw them approaching; as Tarma watched, his mouth tightened, and he made a little negating motion with his free hand to his companion as the two women came within earshot.

But when they continued to close, he suddenly became resignedly affable. Placing his cup on the stone bench, he prepared to approach them.

"My Lady Kethryveris, I would not have recognized you," he said, leaving his associate's side, taking her hand in his, and bowing over it. "You surprise me; I would have thought you could not be more attractive than you were this afternoon. I trust the gathering pleases you?"

"A . . . remarkable assemblage," Kethry replied, allowing a hint of irony to creep into her voice. "But I do not believe anyone introduced me to your friend—?"

"Then you must allow me to rectify the mistake at once." He led her around the bench, Tarma following silently as if she truly was Kethry's shadow, so that they faced the man seated there. The fountain pattered behind them, masking their conversation from anyone outside their immediate vicinity.

"Lady Kethryveris, may I present Jadrek, the Rethwellan Archivist."

For some reason Tarma liked this man even more than she had the Horsemaster, liked him immediately. The mage-light behind them lit his features clearly. He was a man of middle years, sandy hair going slightly to silver, his face was thin and ascetic and his forehead broad. His gray eyes held an echo of pain, and there were answering lines of pain about his generous mouth. That was an odd mouth; it looked as if it had been made expressly to smile, widely and often, but something had caused it to set in an expression of permanent cynicism. His gray tunic and breeches were of soft moleskin, and it almost seemed to Tarma that he wore them with the intent to fade into the background of wherever he might be.

This is a man the Clans would hold in high esteem—in the greatest of honor. There is wisdom in him, as well as learning. So why is he unregarded and ignored here? No matter what Idra said—I find it hard to understand people who do not honor wisdom when they see it.

"I am most pleased to make your acquaintance, Master Jadrek," Kethry said, softly and sweetly, as she gave him her hand. "I am more pleased because I had heard good things of you from Captain Idra."

Tarma felt for the hilts of her knives as inconspicuously as she could, as both men jerked as if they'd been shot. This had *not* been part of the plans she and Kethry had discussed earlier!

The Archivist recovered first. "Are you then something other than you seem, Lady Kethryveris, that you call the Lady Idra 'Captain'?"

Kethry smiled, as Tarma loosened the knife hidden in her sleeve and wished she could get at the one at the nape of her neck without giving herself away.

Damn—I can't get them both—Keth, what the hell are you doing?

"In no way," her partner replied smoothly. "I am all that I claim to be. I simply have not claimed all that I am. We hoped to find the lady here, but strangely enough, we've seen no sign of her."

Keth— Tarma thought, waiting for one or both of the men to make some kind of move, *—you bloody idiot! I hope you have a reason for this!*

The Horsemaster continued to stare in taut wariness, and Tarma had a suspicion that he, too, had a blade concealed somewhere about him. Maybe in his boot? The Archivist was eyeing them with suspicion, but also as if he was trying to recall something.

"You . . . could be the chief mage of the Sunhawks. You seem to match the description," he said finally, then turned slightly to stare at Tarma. "And that would make *you* the . . . Scoutmaster? Tindel, these may well be two of Idra's fighters; they certainly correspond with what I've been told."

The Horsemaster pondered them, and Tarma noted a very slight relaxation of his muscles. "Might be . . . might be," he replied, "But there are ways to make certain. Why does Idra ride Gray rather than her warhorse when not in battle?" He spoke directly to Tarma, who gave up pretending not to understand him.

"Because Black enjoys using his teeth," she said, enjoying his start of shock at her harsh voice, "and if he can't take a piece out of anything else, he'll go for his rider's legs. She's tried kicking him from here to Valdemar for it, and still hasn't broken him of it. So she never rides him except in a fight. And if you know about Black, you'll also know that we almost lost him in the last campaign; he took a crossbow bolt and went down with Idra on his back, but he was just too damned mean to die. Now you tell me one; why won't she let me give her a Shin'a'in saddlebred to ride when she's not on Black?"

"Because she won't start negotiations with clients on a bad footing by being better-mounted than they are," the Archivist said quietly.

"*I* taught her that," the Horsemaster added. "I told her that the day she first rode out of here on her own, and wanted to take the best-looking horse in the stable. When she rode out, it was on a Karsite cob that had been rough-trained to fight; it was as ugly as a mud brick. When did she lose it?"

"Uh—long before we joined; I think when she was in Randel's Raiders," Kethry replied to the lightning-quick question after a bit of thought.

"I think perhaps we have verified each other as genuine?" Tindel asked with a twisted smile. Jadrek continued to watch them; measuringly, and warily still.

"Has Idra been here?" Kethry countered.

"Yes; been, and gone again."

"Keth, we both know there's something going on around here that nobody's talking about." Tarma glanced at the two men, and Tindel nodded slightly. "If we don't want to raise questions we'd rather not answer, I think we'd better either rejoin the rest of the world, or drift around the garden, then retire."

"Your instincts are correct; as strangers you're automatically under observation. It's safe enough to mention Idra, so long as you don't call her 'Captain,' " Tindel offered. "But I should warn you that we two are not entirely in good odor with His Majesty—Jadrek in particular. I might be in better case after tomorrow, when he sees those horses. Nevertheless it won't do *you* any good to be seen with us. I think you might do well to check with other information sources before you come to one of us again."

Tarma looked him squarely in the eyes, trying to read him. Every bit of experience she had told her he was telling the truth—and that now that the approach had been made, it would take a deal of courting before they would confide anything. She looked down at Jadrek; if eyes were the "windows of the soul" *his* had the storm shutters up. He had identified them; that didn't mean he trusted them. Finally she nodded. "We'll do that."

"Gods!" Tindel swore softly. "Of all the rabbit-brained—women!" He didn't pace, but by the clenching of his hand on his goblet, Jadrek knew that he badly wanted to. "If anybody had been close enough to hear her—"

"If they're what they say they are, they wouldn't have pulled this with anyone close enough to hear them," Jadrek retorted, closing his eyes and gritting his teeth as his left knee shot a spasm of pain up his leg. "On the other hand, *if* they aren't, they might well have wanted witnesses."

"If, if, if—Jadrek—" Tindel's face was stormy.

"I still haven't made up my mind about them," the Archivist interrupted his friend. "If they are Idra's friends, they're going about this intelligently. If they're Raschar's creatures, they're being very canny. They could be either. We haven't seen or heard of the pretty one so much as lighting a candle, but if she's really Idra's prime mage, she wouldn't. Char surely knows as much about the Hawks as we do, and having two women, one of them Shin'a'in Swordsworn, show up here after Idra's gone off into the unknown, must certainly have alerted *his* suspicions. If the other did something proving herself to be a mage, he wouldn't be suspicious anymore, he'd be certain."

"So what do we do?"

Jadrek smiled wearily at his only friend. "We do what we've been doing all along. We wait and watch. We see what *they* do. Then—maybe —we recruit them to our side."

Tindel snorted. "And meanwhile, Idra . . ."

"Idra is either perfectly safe—or beyond help. And in either case, nothing we do or don't do in the next few days is going to make any difference at all."

"Next time just stop my heart, why don't you?" Tarma asked crossly when they reached their suite. She shut the door tightly behind them and set her back against it, slumping weak-kneed at having safely attained their haven.

"I acted on a hunch. I'm sorry." Kethry paused for a fraction of a second, then headed for her bedroom, the soft soles of her shoes making scarcely a sound on the marble floor. Her partner followed, staggering just slightly as she pushed off from the door.

"You *could* have gotten us killed," Tarma continued, following the mage into the gilded splendor of her bedroom. Kethry turned; Tarma took a good look at her partner's utterly still and sober expression, then sighed. "Na, forget I yelled. I'm a wool-brain. There were signs you were reading that I couldn't see, is that it?"

Kethry nodded, eyes dark with thought. "I can't even tell you exactly what it was," she said apologetically.

"Never mind," Tarma replied, reversing a chair to sit straddle-legged on it with her arms folded over the back and her head resting on her arms, forcing her tense shoulder muscles to relax. "It's like trailreading for me; I don't even think about it anymore. First question; *can* you find other sources?"

"Maybe. Some of the older nobles, like that old lady who talked to us; the ones who weren't afraid of you. Most older courtiers love to talk, have seen *everything*, and nobody will listen to them. So—" Kethry shrugged, then glided over to the bed, slipping out of the amber robe and draping it over another chair that stood next to it. Fire and candle light glinted from her hair and softened the hard muscles of her body. "—I use a little kindness, risk being bored, and maybe learn a lot."

"I guess I'll stick to the original plan then; work the horses, play that I don't understand the local tongue, and keep my ears open." Tarma wasn't sure anymore that this was such a good plan, certainly not as certain as she had been when they first rode in. This place seemed full of invisible pitfalls.

"One other thing; there's more than a handful of mages around here, and I don't dare use my powers much. If I do, they'll know me for what I am. Some of them felt pretty strong, and *none* of them were in mage-robes."

"Is that a good sign, or a bad?"

"I don't know." Kethry unpinned her hair and shook it loose, then slipped on a wisp of shift—supplied by their host—and climbed into her bed. The mattress sighed under her weight, as she settled under the blankets in the middle: then she sat up, gazing forlornly at her partner. She looked like a child in the enormous expanse of featherbed—and she looked uncomfortable and unhappy as well.

Tarma knew that lost expression. This place was *far* too like the luxurious abode of Wethes Goldmarchant, the man to whom Kethry's brother had sold her when she was barely nubile.

Kethry plainly didn't want to be left alone in here. They also didn't dare share the bed without arousing very unwelcome gossip. But there was a third solution.

"I don't trust our host any farther than I could toss Ironheart," she said, standing up abruptly, and shoving the chair away with a grating across the stone floor. "And I'm bloody damned barbarian enough that *nothing* I do is going to surprise people, provided it's weird and warlike."

With that, she stalked into her bedroom, stripped the velvet coverlet, featherbed and downy blankets from the bedstead, and wrestled the lot into Kethry's room, cursing under her breath the whole time.

"Tarma! What—"

"I'm bedding down in here; at the foot of your bed so the servants don't gossip. They've been watching me bodyguard you all day, so this isn't going to be out of character."

She stripped to the skin, glad enough to be out of those over-fine garments, and pulled on a worn-out pair of breeches and another of those flimsy shifts, tossing her clothes on the chair next to Kethry's.

"But you don't have to make yourself miserable!" Kethry protested feebly, her gratitude for Tarma's company overpowering her misgivings.

"Great good gods, this is a damn sight better than the tent." Tarma laughed, and laid her weapons, dagger and sword, both unsheathed, on the floor next to the mattress. "Besides, when the servants come in to wake us up, I'll rise with steel in hand. *That* ought to give 'em something to talk about and distract them from who *we* were associating with last night. And—"

"And?"

"Well, I don't entirely trust Raschar's good sense if his lust's involved; for all we know, he's got hidden passages in the walls that would let him in here when I'm not around. Hmm?"

"A good point," Kethry conceded with such relief that it was obvious to Tarma that she had been thinking something along the same lines. "Are you *sure* you'll be all right?"

Tarma tried her improvised bed, and found it better than she'd expected. "Best doss I've had in my life," she replied, wriggling luxuriously into the soft blankets, and grinning. "You'd better find out what happened to Idra pretty quick, *she'enedra*. Otherwise, I may not want to leave."

Kethry sighed, reached up for the sconce beside her, and blew out the candle, leaving the room in darkness.

The following day Tarma managed to frighten the maids half to death, rising from the pile of bedding on the floor with sword in hand at the first sound of anyone stirring. The younger of the two fainted dead away at the sight of her. The other squeaked and ran for the door. They didn't see *that* maid again, so Tarma figured she had refused to go back into their suite; defying any and all punishments. The other girl vanished as soon as Kethry revived her, and they didn't see *her* again, either, so she probably had done the same. The next servants to enter the suite were a pair of haglike old crones with faces fit to frighten fish out of water; they attended to the cleaning and picking up of the suite, and took themselves out again with an admirable efficiency and haste. That was more like what Tarma wanted out of servants; the giggly girls fussing about drove her to distraction at the best of times, and now—well, now she wasn't going to take anything or anyone at face value. Those giggly girls were probably spies—maybe more.

Kethry heaved a sigh or two of relief when they saw the last of the new set of servitors.

Hell, she's an old campaigner; she knows it, too. Gods, I hate this place.

After wolfing down some bread and fruit from the over-generous breakfast the second set of servants had brought, Tarma headed off to oversee the further training of the horses, concentrating on the gold and the dapple. The gold she wanted schooled enough that he wouldn't cause his rider any problems; the dapple she wanted trained to the limits of his understanding. She hoped *that* might sweeten the Horsemaster's attitude toward them.

She kept her ears open—and as she'd hoped, the stable folk were fairly free with their tongues while they thought she couldn't understand them. Besides several unflattering comments about her own looks, she managed to pick up that Idra had gone off rather abruptly, but that her disappearance had not been entirely unexpected. Her name was coupled on more than one occasion with the words "that wild-goose quest." She learned little more than that.

Of the other brother, Prince Stefansen, she learned a bit more. He'd run off on his brother's coronation day. And he'd done something worse than just run, according to rumor, though what it was, no one really seemed to know. Whatever, it had been enough to goad the new king into declaring him an outlaw. If Raschar caught him, his head was forfeit.

And *that* was fair interesting indeed. And was more than Tarma had expected to learn.

"That doesn't much surprise me, given what *I've* heard," Kethry remarked that evening, when they settled into their suite after another one of those stifling evening gatherings. This one had been only a little less formal than their reception. It seemed this sort of thing took place *every* night—and attendance was expected, even of visitors. "I'd gathered something like that from Countess Lyris. It was about the only useful thing to come out of this evening."

"I think I may die of the boredom, provided the perfume doesn't kill me off first," Tarma yawned. She was sprawled on the floor of Kethry's room on her featherbed (which the maids had not dared move.) Her eyes were sleepy; her posture wasn't. Kethry knew from years of partnering her that no one and nothing would move inside or near the suite without her knowing it. She was operating on sentry reflexes, and it showed in a subtle tenseness of her muscles.

"The perfume may; I don't think boredom is going to be a problem," Kethry replied slowly. She leaned back into the pillows heaped at the head of the bed, and combed her hair while she spoke in tones hardly louder than a whisper. The candlelight from the sconce in the headboard behind her made a kind of amber aura around her head. "There is one *hell* of a lot more going on here than meets the eye. This is what I've gotten so far: when Idra got here, she supported Raschar over Stefansen.

The whole idea was that Stefansen was going to be allowed to exile himself off to one of the estates and indulge himself in whatever way he wanted. Presumably he was going to fade away into quiet debauchery. Raschar was crowned—and suddenly Stefansen was gone, with a price on his head. Nobody knows where he went, but the best guess is north."

Tarma looked a good deal more alert at that, and leaned up against the bedside, propping her head on her hands. "Oh, really? And what came of the original plan? Especially if Stefansen had agreed to it?"

Kethry shrugged, and frowned. It was a puzzle, and one that left a prickle between her shoulderblades, as if someone were aiming a weapon for that spot. "No one seems to know. No one knows what it was Stefansen did to warrant a death sentence. But Raschar was—and *is,* still, according to one of my sources—very nervous about proving that he is the *rightful* claimant to the throne. There's a tale that the Royal Line used to have a sword in Raschar's grandfather's time that was able to choose the rightful heir—or the best king, the stories aren't very clear on the subject, at least not the ones I heard. It was stolen forty or fifty years ago. Idra apparently volunteered to see if she could find it for Raschar, the assumption being that the sword would pick *him.* They say he was very eager for her to find it—and at the moment everyone seems convinced that she took off to go looking for it."

Tarma shook her head, slowly. Her mouth was twisted a little in a skeptical frown. "That doesn't sound much like the Captain to me. Sure, she might well *say* she was going off looking for it, but to really *do* it? Personally? Alone? When the Hawks are waiting for her to join them and it's nearly fighting season? And why not rope in one of Raschar's tame mages to help smell out the magic? It's not likely."

"Not *bloody* likely," Kethry agreed. "I could see it as an excuse to get back to us, but not anything else."

"Have you made any moves at old Jadrek?"

Kethry sighed. Jadrek had been *exceptionally* hard to get at. For a lame man, he could vanish with remarkable dexterity. "I'm courting him, cautiously. *He* doesn't seem to trust anyone except Tindel. I did find out why neither Raschar nor his father cared for Jadrek or *his.* The hereditary Archivists of Rethwellan both suffered from an overdose of honesty."

"Let's not get abstruse, shall we?"

Kethry grinned. This part, at least, *did* have a certain ironic humor to it. "Both Jadrek and his father before him insisted on putting events in the Archives exactly as they happened, instead of tailoring them to suit the monarch's sensibilities."

"So what's to stop the King from having the Archives altered at his pleasure?"

"They can't," Kethry replied, still amused in spite of her feelings that they were both treading an invisible knife edge of danger. "The Archive books are bespelled. They *have* to be kept up to date, or, and I quote, 'something nasty happens.' The Archives, once written in, are protected magically and can't be altered, and Raschar doesn't have a mage knowledgeable enough to break the spell. Once something is *in* the Archives, it's there forever."

Tarma choked on a laugh, and stuffed the back of her hand into her mouth to keep it from being overheard in the corridor outside. They had infrequent eavesdroppers out there. "Who was responsible for *this* little pickle?"

"One of the first Kings—predictably called 'the Honest'—he was also an Adept of the Leverand school, so he could easily enforce his honesty. I gather he wasn't terribly popular; I also gather that he didn't much care."

Tarma made a wry face. "Hair shirts and dry bread?"

"And weekly fasts—with the whole of his Court included. But this isn't getting *us* anywhere—"

Tarma nodded, and buried one hand in her short hair, leaning her head on it. "Too true. Ideas?"

Kethry sighed, and shook her head. "Not a one. You?"

To her mild surprise, Tarma nodded thoughtfully, biting her lip. "Maybe. Just maybe. But try the indirect approach first. My way is either going to earn us our information or scare the bird into cover so deep we'll never get him to fly."

"Him?"

Again Tarma nodded. "Uh-huh. Jadrek."

Three days later, with not much more information than they'd gotten in the first two days, Tarma decided it was time to try her plan.

It involved a fair amount of risk; although they planned to be as careful as they could, they were undoubtedly going to be seen at some point or other, since skulking about *would* raise suspicions. Tarma only hoped that no one would guess that their goal was Jadrek's rooms.

She waited for a long while with her ear pressed up against the edge of the door, listening to the sounds of servants and guests out in the hall. The hour following the mandatory evening gathering was a busy one; the nightlife of the Court of Rethwellan continued sometimes until dawn, and the hour of dismissal was followed by what Kethry called "the hour of scurrying" as nobles and notables found their own various entertainments.

Finally—"It's been quiet for a while now," Tarma said, when the last of the footsteps had faded and the last giggling servant departed. "I think this is a lull. Let's head out before we get another influx of dicers or something."

As usual, Kethry sailed through the door first, with Tarma her sinister shadow. There was no one in the gilded hallway, Tarma was pleased to note. In fact, at least half the polished bronze lamps were out, indicating that there would be no major entertainments tonight in this end of the Palace.

I hope Warrl's ready to come out of hiding, Tarma thought to herself, a little worriedly. *This whole notion of mine rests on him.*

:Must you think of me as if I couldn't hear you?: Warrl snapped in exasperation. *:Of course I'm ready. Just get the old savant's window open and I'll be in through it before you can blink.:*

Sorry, Tarma replied sheepishly. *I keep forgetting—damnit, Furface, I'm* still *not used to mind-talking with you! It's just not something Shin'a'in do.*

Warrl did not answer at once. *:I know,:* he said finally. *:And I shouldn't eavesdrop, but it's the mindmate bond. I sometimes have to force myself not to listen to you. We've got so much in common; you're Kal'enedral and I'm neuter and we're both fighters. You know—there are times when I wonder if your Lady might not take me along with you in the end—I think I'd like that.:*

Tarma was astonished; so surprised that she stopped dead for a moment. *You—you would? Really?*

:Not if you start acting like a fool about it!: he snapped, jolting her back to sense. *:Great Horned Moon—will* you *keep your mind on your work?:*

To traverse the guests' section they wore clothing that suggested they might be paying a social call; but once they got into the plainer hallways of the quarters belonging to those who were not *quite* nobility, but not exactly servants—like the Archivist and the Master of Horse—they stepped into a granite-walled alcove long enough to strip off their outer garments to reveal their well-worn traveling leathers. In the dim light of the infrequent candles they looked enough like servants that Tarma hoped no one would look at them too carefully. They covered their hair with scarves, and folded their clothing into bulky bundles; they carried those bundles conspicuously, so that they were unlikely (Tarma hoped) to be levied into some task or other as extra hands.

The corridor had changed. Gone were the soft, heavy hangings, the frequent lanterns. The passage here was bare stone, polished granite, floor and wall, and the lighting was by cheap clay lanterns or cheaper tallow candles placed in holders along the walls at long intervals. It was chilly here, and damp, and the tallow candles smoked.

"Well, this explains one thing about that sour old bastard," Tarma muttered under her breath, while Kethry counted doors.

"Seven, eight—who? What?"

"Jadrek. Why he's such a meddler-face. Man's obviously got bones as stiff as *I'm* going to have in a few years. Living in this section must make him as creaky as a pair of new boots."

"Ten—never thought of that. Remind me to stay on the right side of Royal displeasure. This should be it."

Kethry stopped at a wooden door set into the corridor wall, a door no different from any of the others, and knocked softly.

Tarma listened as hard as she could; heard limping footsteps; then the door creaked open a crack, showing a line of light at its edge—

She rammed her shoulder into it without giving Jadrek a chance to see who was on the other side of it, and shoved it open before the Archivist had time to react. Kethry was less than half a step behind her. They were inside and had the door shut tightly behind them before Jadrek had a chance to go from shock to outrage at their intrusion.

Tarma put her back to the rough wood of the door and braced herself against it; no half-cripple like Jadrek was going to be able to move her away from the door until she was good and ready. The rest was up to Kethry's silver tongue.

Jadrek glared, his whole attitude one of affronted dignity, but did not call for help or gibber in helpless anger as Tarma had half expected. Instead every word he spoke was forceful, but deadly cold, controlled— and quiet.

"What, pray, is this supposed to mean?" The gray eyes were shadowed with considerable pain at the moment; Tarma hoped it was not because of something she'd done to him in getting the door open. "I have come to expect a certain amount of cavalier treatment, but not in my own quarters!"

"My lord—" Kethry began.

"I," he said bitterly, "am no one's lord. You may abandon that pretense."

Kethry sighed. "Jadrek, I humbly beg your pardon, but we were trying to find a way to speak with you without drawing undue attention. If you want us to leave this moment, we will—but dammitall, we are *trying* to find out what's become of our Captain, and you seem to be the only source of reliable information!"

He raised one eyebrow in surprise at her outspokenness, and looked at her steadily. "And you might well be the instrument of my execution for treason."

Tarma whistled softly through her teeth, causing both of their heads to swivel in her direction. "That bad, is it?"

His jaw tightened, but he did not answer.

"Believe or not, I've got an answer for you. Look, I would assume you are probably the most well-read man in this city; that's what the Captain seemed to think," Kethry continued. "Do you know what a *kyree* is?"

He nodded warily.

"Do you know what it means to be mindmated to one?"

"A little. I also know that they are reputedly incapable of lying mind-to-mind—"

At Kethry's hand signal, Tarma stood away from the door, crossed the room at a sprint and flung open the casement window that looked out over the stableyard. She had seen Jadrek at this window the night before, which was how she and Kethry had figured out which set of rooms was his. Warrl was ready, in the yard below; Tarma could see him bulking dark in the thin moonlight. Before Jadrek could react to Tarma's sudden movement, Warrl launched himself through the open window and landed lightly in the middle of the rather small room. It seemed that much smaller for his being there.

The *kyree* looked at Jadrek—seemed to look *through* him—his eyes glowing like topaz in the sun. Then he bowed his head once in respect to the Archivist, and mindspoke to all three of them.

:*I am Warrl. We are Captain Idra's friends; we want to help her, but we cannot if we do not know what has happened to her. Wise One, you are one of the few honest men in this place. Will you not help us?:*

Jadrek stared at the *kyree,* his jaw slack with astonishment. "But—but—"

:*You wonder how I can speak with you, and how I managed to remain concealed. I have certain small powers of magic,:* the *kyree* said, nearly grinning. :*You may have heard that the barbarian brought her herd dog with her. I chose to appear somewhat smaller than I am; the stablehands think me a rather large wolf-dog cross.:*

The Archivist reached for the back of a chair beside him to steady himself. He was pale, and there was marked confusion in his eyes. "I—please, ladies, sit down, or as a gentleman, *I* cannot—and I feel the need of something other than my legs to support me—"

There were only two chairs in the room; Tarma solved the problem of who was to take them by sinking cross-legged to the floor. Warrl curled behind her as a kind of backrest, which made the room look much less crowded. While Kethry took the second chair and Jadrek the one he had obviously (by the book on the table beside it) vacated at their knock, Tarma took a quick, assessing look around her.

There were old, threadbare hangings on most of the stone walls, probably put up in a rather futile attempt to ward off the damp chill. There was a small fire on the hearth to her right, probably for the same reason. Beside the hearth was a chair—or rather, a small bench with a back to it —with shabby brown cushions. This was the seat Jadrek had resumed, his own brown robes blending with the cushions. Beside this chair stood a table with a single lamp, a book that seemed to have been put down rather hastily, and a half-empty wineglass. Across from this was a second, identical seat. To Tarma's left stood a set of shelves, full of books, odd bits of rock and pieces of statuary, and things not readily identifiable in the poor light. At the sight of the books, Tarma felt a long-suppressed desire to get one of them in her hands; she hadn't had a good read in months, and her soul thirsted for the new knowledge contained within those dusty volumes.

In the wall with the bookcase was another door, presumably to Jadrek's bedchamber. In the wall directly opposite the one they had entered was the window.

Pretty barren place. This time Tarma was thinking directly at the *kyree*.

:He has less—far less—respect than he deserves,: Warrl said with some heat. *:This man has knowledge many would die for, and he is looked upon as some kind of fool!:*

"I . . . had rather be considered a fool," Jadrek said slowly.

The *kyree* raised his head off his paws sharply, and looked at the man in total astonishment. *:You* hear *me?:*

"Yes—wasn't I supposed to?"

Tarma and the *kyree* exchanged a measured glance, and did not answer him directly. "Why would you rather be considered a fool?" Tarma asked, after a moment of consideration.

"Because a fool hears a great deal—and a fool is not worth killing."

"I think," Kethry said, leaning forward, "you had better begin at the beginning."

Some hours later they had a full picture, and it was not a pleasant one.

"So the story is that Stefansen intended some unspecified harm to his brother, and when caught, fled. In actuality, Tindel and I overheard some things that made us think Raschar might be considering assuring that there would be no other male claimants to the throne and we warned Stefansen."

"Where did he go?" Kethry asked.

"I don't know; I don't want to know. The less I know, the less I can betray." His eyes had gone shadowy and full of secrets.

"Good point. All right, what then?"

"Have you had a good look around you?"

"Raschar's pretty free with his money," Tarma observed.

"Freer than you think; he supports most of the hangers-on here. He's also indulging in some expensive habits. *Tran* dust, it's said. Certainly some very expensive liquors, dainties, and ladies."

"Nice lad. Where's the money coming from?"

Jadrek sighed. "That's the main reason why I—and my father before me—are not in favor. King Destillion began taxing the peasantry and the merchant class *far* too heavily to my mind about twenty years ago; Raschar is continuing the tradition. About half of our peasants have been turned into serfs; more follow every year. Opposing *that* was a point Stefansen agreed with me on—and one of the reasons why Destillion intended to cut him out of the succession."

"But didn't?" Kethry asked.

Jadrek shook his head. "Not for lack of trying, but the priests kept him from doing so."

"Idra," Tarma reminded them.

"She saw what Raschar was doing, and began to think that despite Stefansen's habit of hopping into bed with anything that wiggled its hips at him, he might well have been a better choice after all. He certainly had more understanding of the peasantry and how the kingdom's strength depends on them." Jadrek almost managed a smile. "Granted, he spent a great deal of time with them, and pretty much with rowdies, but I'm not certain now that his experience with the rougher classes was a bad thing. Well, Idra wanted an excuse to go after him—I unearthed the old story of the Sword that Sings. Raschar has one chink in his armor; he's desperate to *prove* he's the rightful monarch. Idra took Raschar the old Archive books and got permission to look for the Sword. Then—she vanished."

The fire crackled while they absorbed this. "But she'd intended to go after Stefansen?" Kethry asked, finally.

Jadrek nodded. "It might well be that she decided to just go, before Raschar could change his mind—"

Tarma finished the sentence. "But you aren't entirely certain that something didn't happen to her. Or that something didn't happen right after she set out."

He nodded unhappily, twisting his hands together in his lap. "She would have said good-bye. We've been good friends for a long time. We used to exchange letters as often as her commissions permitted. I . . . saw the world through her eyes. . . ."

There was a flash of longing in his face, there for only an instant, then shuttered down. But it made Tarma wonder what it must be like, to have dreams of adventuring—and be confined to the body of a half-lame scholar.

She stood up, suddenly uncomfortable with the insight. The tiny room felt far, far too confining. "Jadrek, we'll talk with you more, later. Right now you've given us plenty to think on."

"You'll try and find out what's happened to her?" He started to stand, but Kethry gently pushed him back down into his chair as Tarma turned abruptly, not wanting to see any more of this man's pain. She turned the latch silently, cracked the door open and checked for watchers in the corridor beyond.

"Looks clear—" Kethry and Warrl slipped out ahead of her, and Tarma glanced back over her shoulder soberly. The Archivist was watching them from his chair, and there was a peculiar, painful mixture of hope and fear on his face. "Jadrek, that was why we came here in the first place. And be warned—if anything *has* happened to Idra, there might not be a town here once the Hawks find out about it."

And with that she followed her partner back into the corridor.

Seven

Jadrek tried to return to his book, but it was fairly obvious that he was going to be unable to concentrate on the page in front of him. He finally gave up and sat staring at the flickering shadows on the farther wall. His left shoulder ached abominably; it had been wrenched when the door had been jerked out of his hands. This would be a night for a double-dose of medicine, or he'd never get to sleep.

Sleep would not have come easily, anyway—not after this evening's conversation. Tindel had been after him for the past several days to talk to the women, but Jadrek had been reluctant and suspicious; now Tindel would probably refrain from saying "I told you so" only by a strong exercise of will.

What did decide me, anyway? he wondered, trying to find a comfortable position as he rubbed his aching shoulder, the dull throb interfering with his train of thought. *Was it the presence of the* kyree*? No, I don't think so; I think I had made up my mind before they brought him in. I think it was the pretty one that made up my mind—Kethry. She's honest in a way I don't think could be counterfeited. I can't read the Shin'a'in, but if you know what to look for, Kethry's an open book.*

He sighed. *And let's not be fooling ourselves; it's the first time in years that a pretty woman looked at you with anything but contempt, Jadrek. You're as susceptible to that as the next man. More. . . .*

He resolutely killed half-wisps of wistful mightbe's and daydreams, and got up to find his medicines.

* * *

Tarma left Warrl watching the Archivist's door from the corridor, just in case. His positioning was not nearly as good as she'd have wished; in order to keep out of sight he'd had to lair-up in a table nook some distance away from Jadrek's rooms, and not in direct line of sight. Still, it would have to do. She had some serious misgivings about the Archivist's safety, especially if it should prove that he was being watched.

Creeping along the corridors with every sense alert was unnervingly like being back with the Hawks on a scouting mission. Kethry had hesitantly and reluctantly tendered the notion of using her powers to spy out the situation ahead of them; Tarma had vetoed the idea to her partner's obvious relief. If there was any kind of mage-talented spy keeping an eye on Jadrek, use of magic would not only put alerts on the Archivist but on *them* as well. Their own senses *must* be enough. But it was tense work; Tarma was sweating before they made it to the relative safety of the guesting section.

They slipped their more ornate outfits back on in the shelter of the same alcove where they'd doffed them, and continued on their way. Now was the likeliest time for them to be caught, but they got back to their rooms without a sign that they had been noticed—or so Tarma thought.

She was rather rudely disabused of that notion as soon as they opened the door to their suite.

Moonlight poured down through one of the windows in the right-hand wall of the outer room, making a silver puddle on a square of the pale marble floor. As Tarma closed the door and locked it, she caught movement in that moonlight out of the corner of her eye. She jerked her head around and pulled a dagger with the hand not still on the latch in the automatically defensive reaction to seeing motion where none should be. The moonlight shivered and wavered, sending erratic reflections across the room, and acting altogether unlike natural light.

Tarma snatched her other hand away from the latch, and whirled away from the door she had just locked. Her entire body tingled, from the crown of her head to the soles of her feet—with an energy she was intimately familiar with.

The *only* time she ever felt like this was when her teachers were about to manifest physically, for over the years she had grown as sensitive to the energies of the Star-Eyed as Kethry was to mage-energies. But the spirit-Kal'enedral, her teachers, *never* came to her when she was within four walls—and doubly never when she was in walls that were as alien to them as this palace was.

She sheathed her blade—little good it would do against magic and spirits—set sweating palms against the cool wood of the door. She stared dumbfounded at the evidence of all she'd been told being violated—the shadow and moonlight was hardening into a man-shaped figure; flowing before her eyes into the form of a Shin'a'in garbed and armed in black, and veiled. Only the Kal'enedral wore black and *only* the spirit-Kal'enedral went veiled—and here, where no one knew that, it was wildly unlikely that this could be an illusion, even if there were such a thing as a mage skilled enough to counterfeit the Warrior's powers well enough to fool a living Kal'enedral.

And there was another check—her partner, who had, over the years, seen Tarma's teachers manifesting at least a score of times. Beside her, Kethry stared and smothered a gasp with the back of her hand. Tarma didn't think it likely that any illusion could deceive the mage for long.

To top it all, this was not just any Shin'a'in, not just any spirit-Kal'enedral; for as the features became recognizable (what could be seen above his veil) Tarma knew him to be no less than the chief of all her teachers!

He seemed to be fighting against something; his form wavered in and out of visibility as he held out frantic, empty hands to her, and he seemed to be laboring to speak.

Kethry stared at the spirit-Kal'enedral in absolute shock. This—this *could not* be happening!

But it was, and there was no mistaking the flavor of the energy the spirit brought with him. This *was* a true *leshya'e Kal'enedral,* and he was violating every precept to manifest here and now, within sight of non-Shin'a'in. Which could only mean that he was sent directly by Tarma's own aspect of the four-faced Goddess, the Warrior.

Then she saw with mage-sight the veil of sickly white power that was encasing him like a filthy web, keeping him from full manifestation.

"There's—Goddess, there's a counterspell—" Kethry started out of her entrancement. "It's preventing *any* magic from entering this room! He can't manifest! I—I have to break it, or—"

"Don't!" Tarma hissed, catching her hands as she brought them up. "You break a counterspell and they'll *know* one of us is a mage!"

Kethry turned her head away, unable to bear the sight of the Kal'enedral struggling vainly against the evil power containing him. Tarma turned back to her teacher to see that he had given up the effort to speak—and she saw that his hands were moving, in the same Shin'a'in hand-signs she had taught Kethry and her scouts.

"Keth—his hands—"

As Kethry's eyes were again drawn to the *leshya'e*'s figure, Tarma read his message.

Death-danger, she read, and *Assassins. Wise one.*

"Warrior! It's Jadrek—he's going to be killed!" She reached behind her for the door, certain that they were never going to make it to Jadrek's rooms in time.

But Warrl had been watching her thoughts, probably alerted through the bond they shared to her agitation.

:Mindmate, I go!: rang through her head.

At the same moment, as if he had heard the *kyree*'s reply the *leshya'e Kal'enedral* made a motion of triumph, and dissolved back into moonlight and shadow.

While Kethry was still staring at the place where the spirit had stood, Tarma was clawing the door open, all thought of subterfuge gone.

She headed down the corridor at a dead run, and she could hear Kethry right behind her; this time there would be no attempt at concealment.

Warrl's "voice" was sharp in her mind; angry, and tasting of battle-hunger. *:Mindmate—one comes. He smells of seeking death.:*

Keep him away from Jadrek!

There was no answer to that, as she put on a burst of speed down the corridor—at least not an answer in words. But there was a surge of great anger, a rage such as she had seldom sensed in the *kyree,* even under battle-fire.

Then Tarma had evidence of her own of how strong the mindmate bonding between herself and the *kyree* had become—because she began to get image-flashes carried on that rage. A man, an armed man, with a long, wicked dagger in his hand, standing outside Jadrek's door. The man turning to face Warrl even as Jadrek opened the door. Jadrek stepping back a pace with fear stark across his features, then turning and stumbling back into his room. The man ignoring him, meeting the threat of Warrl, unsheathing a sword to match the knife he carried.

Tarma felt the growl the *kyree* vented rumbling in her own throat as she ran. Felt him leap—

Now they were in the older section—running down Jadrek's corridor. Kethry was scarcely a step behind her as they skidded to a halt at Jadrek's open door.

There was blood everywhere—spilling out over the doorsill, splashed on the wall of the corridor. The *kyree* stood over a body sprawled half-in, half-out of the room, growling under his breath, his eyes literally glowing with rage. Warrl had taken care of the intruder less than seconds before their arrival, for the body at his feet was still twitching, and the *kyree*'s mind was seething with aggression and the aftermath of the kill. His hackles were up, but he was unmarked; of the blood splashed so liberally everywhere, none of it seemed to be Warrl's.

"Goddess—" Tarma caught at the edge of the doorframe, and panted, her knees weak with relief that the *kyree* had gotten there in time.

"Jadrek!" Kethry snapped out of shock first; she slid past the slowly calming *kyree* into the room beyond. Tarma was right behind her, expecting to find the Archivist in a dead faint, or worse; hurt, or collapsed with shock.

She was amazed to find him still on his feet.

He had his back to the wall, standing next to the fireplace behind his chair, a dagger in one hand, a fireplace poker in the other. He was pale, and looked as if he was likely to be sick at any moment. But he also looked as if he was quite ready to protect himself as best he could, and was anything but immobilized with fear or shock.

For one moment he didn't seem to recognize them; then he shook his head a little, put the poker carefully down, sheathed the dagger at his belt, then groped for the back of his chair and pulled it toward himself, the legs grating on the stone. He all but fell into it.

"Jadrek—are you all right?" Tarma would have gone to his side, but Kethry was there before her.

Jadrek was trembling in every nerve and muscle as he collapsed into his chair. *Gods—one breath more—too close. Too close.*

Kethry took his wrist before he could wave her away and felt for his pulse.

He stared at her anxious face, so close to his own, and felt his heart skip for a reason other than fear. *Dammit, you fool, she's just worried that you're going to die on her before you can help her with the information they need!*

Then he thought, feeling a chill creep down his back; *Gods—I might. If Char has had a watcher on me all this time, it means he's suspected me of warning Stefan. And if that watcher chose to strike tonight only because I spoke to a pair of strangers—Archivist, your hours are numbered.*

Kethry checked Jadrek's heartbeat, fearing to find it fluttering erratically. To her intense relief, it was strong, though understandably racing.

"I—gods above—I think I will be all right," he managed, pressing his free hand to his forehead. "But I would be dead if not for your *kyree.*"

"Who was that?" Kethry asked urgently. "Who—"

"That . . . was a member of the King's personal guard," he replied thickly. "Brightest Goddess—I knew I was under suspicion, but I never guessed it went this far! They must have had someone watching me."

"Watching to see who you talked to, no doubt," Tarma said grimly, her lips compressed into a thin line. "And the King must have left orders what was to happen to you if you talked to strangers. Hellfire and corruption!"

"Now I'm a liability, so far as Raschar is concerned." He was pale, and with more than shock, but there was determination in the set of his jaw as he looked to Tarma. "Char has only one way of dealing with liabilities . . . as you've seen. Lord and Lady help me, I'm under a death sentence, without trial or hearing! I—I haven't got a chance unless I can escape. Woman, you've got to help me! If you want any more help with finding Idra, you've *got*—"

Kethry had angry words on her tongue, annoyed that he should think them such cowards, but Tarma beat her to them.

"What kind of gutless boobs do you think we are?" Tarma snapped. "Of *course* we'll help you! Dammit man, it was us coming to you that triggered this attack in the first place! Keth, clean up the mess. Go ahead and use magic, we're blown now, anyway."

Kethry nodded. "After the visitor, I should say so—even if there wasn't anyone 'watching,' he'll have left residue in the trap-spell."

"Did you pick up any 'eyes'?"

She let her mage-senses extend. "No . . . no. Not then, and not now. Evidently they haven't guessed *our* identity."

"Small piece of Warrior's fortune. Well, I'm getting rid of the body before somebody falls over it; it's likely this bastard was the only watcher, Archivist, or you'd have been caught out before this." She paused to think. "If I hide him, they may wait to check things out until *after* he was due to report. Hell, if they can't find him, they may wait a bit longer to see if he's gone following after one of Jadrek's visitors; that should buy us a couple more hours. Jadrek, are there any empty rooms along here?"

"Most of them are empty," he said dully, holding his hands up before his eyes and watching them shake with a kind of morbid fascination. "Nobody is quartered along here who isn't in disgrace; this is the oldest wing of the palace, and it's been poorly maintained and repaired but little."

"Gods, no wonder nobody came piling out to see what the ruckus was." Tarma's lip curled in disgust. "Bastard really gives you respect, doesn't he? Well, that's another piece of good luck we've had tonight."

And Tarma turned back to deal with the corpse as Kethry began mustering her energies for "clean-up."

Tarma bundled the body into its own cloak, giving Warrl mental congratulations over the relatively clean kill; the *kyree* had only torn the man's throat out. The man had been relatively small; she figured she could handle the corpse alone. She heaved the bundle over her shoulder with a grunt of effort, trusting to the thick cloak to absorb whatever blood remained to be spilled, and went out into the corridor, picking a room at random. The first one she chose didn't have its own fireplace, so she left that one—but the second did. It was a matter of moments and a good bit of joint-straining effort to stuff the carcass up the chimney; by the time she returned, a little judicious use of magic had cleaned up every trace of a struggle around Jadrek's quarters, and Kethry and the Archivist were in the little bedroom that lay beyond the closed door in his sitting room. The mage was helping Jadrek to make a pack of his belongings, and Jadrek was far calmer now than Tarma had dared to hope. Warrl was stretched across the doorway, still growling under his breath. He gave her a gentle warn-off as she sent him a thought; his blood-lust was up, and he didn't want her in his mind until he had quieted himself.

Jadrek had lit a half dozen candles and stuck them over every available surface. The bedroom was as sparse as the outer room had been, though smelling a little less of damp. There was just a wardrobe, a chest, and the bed.

"Jadrek, how well do you ride?" Tarma asked, taking over the bundle Kethry was making and freeing her to start a new one.

"Not well," he said shortly, folding packets of herbs into a cloth. "It's not my ability to ride, it's the pain. I used to ride very well; now I can't stand being in a saddle for more than an hour or so."

"And if we drugged you?"

He shrugged. "Drugged, aren't I likely to fall off? And you'd have to lead my beast, even if you tied me into the saddle; that would slow you considerably."

"Not if I put you on 'Heart. Or—better yet, Keth, you're light and you don't go armored. How about if I take all the packs and 'Bane carries double?"

Kethry examined the Archivist carefully. "It should be all right. Jadrek doesn't look like he weighs much. Put him up in front of me, and I can hold him on even if he's insensible."

The Archivist managed a quirk of one corner of his mouth. "Hardly the way I had hoped to begin my career of adventuring."

Tarma raised an eyebrow at him.

"You look surprised. Swordlady, I did a great deal of my studying in hopes of one day being able to aid some heroic quester. After all, what better help could a hero have than a loremaster? Then," he held out one hand and shoved the sleeve of his robe up so they could see the swollen wrists, "my body betrayed me and my dreams. So goes life."

Tarma winced in sympathy; her own bones ached in the cold these days, enough that rough camping left her stiff and limping these days for at least an hour after rising, or until she finished her warming exercises. She didn't like to think how much pain swollen joints meant.

"Have you any plan?" the Archivist continued. "Or are we just going to run for it?"

Tarma shook her head. "Don't you think it—Running off blindly is likely to run us right into a trap. We came out of the south, the Hawks are to the south and west—I'd bet the King's men'll expect us to run for familiar territory."

"So we go opposite?" Jadrek hazarded. "North? Then what?"

Tarma folded a shirt into a tight bundle and wedged it into the pack. "North is where Stefansen went. North is where Idra likely went. No? So we'll track them North, and hope to run into one or both of them."

"I know where Stefansen intended to go," Jadrek said slowly, "I *did* tell Idra before she went missing. But frankly it's some of the worst country to travel in winter in all of Rethwellan."

"All the better to shake off pursuit. Cough it up, man, where are we going?"

"Across the Comb and into Valdemar." He looked seriously worried. "And winter storm season in the Comb is deadly. If we're caught in an ice storm without shelter, well, let me just say that we probably won't be a problem for Raschar anymore."

"This is almost too easy," Tarma muttered, surveying the empty court below Jadrek's window. "Keth, is there anything you can't live without back in the room?"

The mage pursed her lips thoughtfully, then shook her head.

"Good, then we'll leave from here. Nobody's been alerted yet, and evidently Jadrek's in poor enough condition that nobody has even *considered* he might slip out his window."

"With good reason, Swordlady," Jadrek replied, coming to Tarma's side and looking down into the court himself. "I can't imagine how I *could* climb down."

"Alone, you couldn't; we'll help you," Kethry told him. "I can actually make you about half your real weight with magic, then we'll manage well enough."

The Archivist looked down again, and shuddered, but to his credit, did not protest.

They'd sent Warrl for a short coil of rope from the stables; there were always lead-ropes and lunges lying around, and any of those would be long enough. He returned just as Kethry completed her spell-casting; they tied one end around Jadrek's waist, then Kethry scrambled out of the window and down the wall to steady him from below as Tarma lowered him. Before they were finished, Tarma had a high respect for the man's courage; climbing down from the window put him in such pain that when they untied him they found he'd bitten his lip through to keep from crying out.

All their gear was still with the mares. When they'd left Hawksnest, they'd chosen to use a different kind of saddle than they normally chose, one meant for long rides and not pitched battles. Like the saddles Jodi preferred, these were little more than a pad with stirrups, although the pad extended out over the horse's rump. When Tarma carried Warrl pillion, he had a pad behind her battle-saddle to ride on; there was just enough room on the extended body of this saddle for him to do the same. So Kethry had no trouble fitting Jadrek in front of her, which was just as well—

Jadrek had mixed something with the last of his wine and gulped it down before attempting the window. He was fine, although still in pain, when they started saddling up. But by the time the mares were harnessed and all their gear was in place, he was fairly intoxicated and not at all steady.

They did manage to get him into the saddle, but it was obvious he wouldn't be staying there without Kethry's help.

Warrl? Tarma thought tentatively.

:All is well, mindmate,: came the reassuring reply. *:There is no one in sight, and I am distracting the gate guards. If you go swiftly, there will be no one to stop or question you.:*

"Let's move out now," she told her partner, "while Furface has the guards playing 'catch-me-if-you-can' with him."

Kethry nodded; they rode out of the palace grounds as quietly—they'd signaled the mares for silence, and now Hellsbane and Ironheart were moving as stealthily as only two Shin'a'in bred-and-trained warsteeds *could.* They managed to get out unchallenged, and waited outside the palace for Warrl to catch up with them, then put Ironheart and Hellsbane to as fast a pace as they dared, and by dawn were well clear of the city.

"Any sign of tracking?" Tarma asked her partner, reining Ironheart in beside her as they slowed to a brisk walk.

Kethry closed her eyes in concentration, extended a little tendril of energy along the road behind them, then shook her head. "My *guess* would be that they haven't missed the spy yet. But my guess would also be, that with all the mages I sensed in Raschar's court, they'll be sending at least one with each pursuit party."

"Anything you can do about that?"

"Some." She reformed that tendril of energy into a deception-web that *might* confuse their backtrail. "Listen, we need supplies; how about if I lay an illusion on you and 'Heart and you go buy us some at the next village we hit?"

"How about if you spell all three of us right now? Say—old woman and her daughter and son? Nobody knows Shin'a'in battlemares out here, and 'Heart and 'Bane are ugly enough to belong to peasants: you needn't spell them."

"Huh; not a bad thought. What about Warrl?"

:I can seem much smaller if I need to.:

Kethry started. "Furface, I *wish* you wouldn't just speak into my mind like that—you never used to!"

:My pardon. I grow forgetful of courtesy. How does the Wise One?:

Jadrek was three-quarters asleep, slumped forward in Kethry's hold, his head nodding to the rhythm of Hellsbane's hooves. Kethry touched his neck below his ear lightly enough not to disturb him. "All right; his pulse is strong."

:If you would have my advice?:

When the *kyree* tendered his opinion, it was worth having. "Go ahead."

:Rouse him up and make him speak with you. He will do his body more harm by riding unconscious.:

"On that subject," Tarma interrupted, "how long can you keep our illusions going? What kind of shape are *you* in?"

Kethry shrugged. "I've been mostly resting my powers so far. I can keep the spell up indefinitely. Why?"

"Because I want to stay under roofs at night for as long as we can. Rough camping is going to be hard on our friend at best—be a helluva note to save him from assassins and lose him to pneumonia."

Kethry nodded, thinking of how much pain the Archivist was already in. "What kind of roofs?"

"In order of preference—out-of-the-way barns, the occasional friendly farmer, and the cheapest inns in town."

"Sound, I think. Pull up here, I might as well cast this thing now, and I can't do it on a moving horse."

"Here" was a grove of trees beside the road; they got the horses off and allowed them to browse while Kethry concentrated.

Warrl flung himself down into the dry grass, and lay there, panting. He was not built for the long chase. Before too very long, Tarma would have to bring him up to ride pillion behind her for a rest.

Kethry got Jadrek leaning back against her, then spread her hands wide, palms facing out. A shell of faint, roseate light expanded from her hands outward, to contain them and their horses. Tarma could see her lips moving silently in the words of the spell. There was a tiny "pop" like a cork being pulled from a bottle; then Tarma felt an all-too-familiar itching at the back of her eyes, and when she looked down, she saw that she was wearing a man's garb of rough, brown homespun instead of her Kal'enedral-styled black silks. So Keth was going to disguise her as a young man; good, that should help to throw off nonmage spies.

Jadrek was now an old, gray-haired woman with a face like a wrinkled apple, and a body stooped from years of hard work. Behind him, Kethry was a chunky, fresh-faced peasant wench; brown-cheeked, brown-haired and quite unremarkable.

"Huh," Tarma said. "This's a new one for *you*. You look like you'd make some dirt-grubber a great wife."

Kethry giggled. "Good hips. Breed like cow, strong like bull, dumb like ox. Hitch to plow when horse dies." As Tarma stifled a chuckle, she turned her attention to her passenger. "Jadrek, wake up, there's a good fellow." She shook his shoulder gently. "Open your eyes slowly. I've put an illusion on us all and it may make you dizzy at first."

"Huhnn. I . . . thought I heard you saying that. . . ." The Archivist raised his head with care, and opened eyes that looked a bit dazed. "Gods. What am I?"

"A crippled-up old peasant woman. Warrl says you'll do yourself more harm than good by riding asleep; he wants you to talk to me."

"How . . . odd. I thought I heard him speaking in my head again. I seem to remember him saying just that. . . ."

The partners exchanged a startled look. Evidently Jadrek had a mage-Gift no one had ever suspected, for normally the only folk who heard Warrl's mind-voice were those he *intended* to speak to. That Talent *might* be useful—if they all lived to reach the Border.

"Let's get on with it," Tarma broke the silence before it went on too long, and glanced at the rising sun to her right. "We need to get as far as we can before they figure out we've bolted back there."

* * *

They stopped at a good-sized village; there was a market going on, and Tarma rode in alone and bought the supplies they were going to need. By mercenary's custom, they'd kept all their cash with them in moneybelts that they never let out of their sight, so they weren't short of funds, at least. Tarma did well in her bargaining; better than she'd expected. Even more encouraging, no one gave her a second glance.

Poor Jadrek had not exaggerated the amount of pain he was going to be in. By nightfall his eyes were sunken deeply into their sockets and he looked more than half dead; but they found a barn, full of new-cut hay, dry and warm and softer than many beds Tarma had slept in. The dry warmth seemed to do Jadrek a lot of good; he was moving better the next morning, and didn't take nearly as much of his drugs as he had the day before.

And oddly enough, he seemed to get better as the trip progressed. Kethry was wearing Need at her side again, after having left the ensorcelled blade with her traveling gear in the stables. Tarma was just thanking her Goddess that they *hadn't* ever brought the blade into their quarters—no telling what would have happened had it met with the counterspell on their rooms. Of a certainty Raschar would have known from that moment that they were not what they seemed.

Fall weather struck with a vengeance on the sixth morning. They ended up riding all day through rain; Rethwellan's fall and early winter rains were notorious far and wide. Jadrek was alert and conversing quietly and animatedly with Kethry; he seemed in better shape, despite the cold rain, than he'd been back at the palace. Now Tarma wondered—remembering the enigmatic words of Moonsong k'Vala, the Tale'edras Adept—if Need was working some of her magic on Jadrek because Kethry was concerned for him. It would be the first time in Tarma's knowledge that a *male* for whom Kethry cared had spent any length of time in physical contact with the mage while she was wearing the blade.

As for Kethry caring for him—they were certainly hitting it off fairly well. Tarma was growing used to the soft murmur of voices behind her as they talked for the endless hours of the day's ride. So maybe—just maybe —the sword was responding to that liking.

As the days passed: "Keth," she asked, when they'd halted for the night in the seventh of a succession of haybarns. "Do you remember what the Hawkbrother told you when we first met him—about Need?"

"You mean Moonsong, the Adept?" Kethry glanced over at Jadrek, but the witchlight she was creating showed the Archivist already rolled up in a nest of blankets and hay, and sound asleep. "He said a lot of things."

"Hai—but I'm thinking there's something that might be pertinent to Jadrek."

Kethry nodded, slowly. "About Need extending her powers to those I care for. Uh-huh; I've been wondering about that. Jadrek certainly seems to be in a lot less pain."

Tarma snuggled into the soft hay, sword and dagger within easy reach. Behind her, Warrl was keeping watch at the door, and Ironheart and Hellsbane were drowsing, having stuffed themselves with fresh hay. "He's not drugging himself as much, either. And . . ."

Kethry settled into her own bedroll and snuffed the witchlight.

"And he's not the bitter, suspicious man we met at the Court," she said quietly in the darkness. "I think we're seeing the man Idra knew."

Tarma heard the hay rustle a bit, then Kethry continued, very softly, "And I *like* that man, *she'enedra.* So much that I think your guess could be right."

"Krethes, ves'tacha?"

"Unadorned truth. I like him; he treats me as an intellectual equal, and that's rare, even among mages. That I'm his physical superior . . . doesn't seem to bother him. It's just . . . what I am. He'll never ride 'Bane the way I do, or swing a sword; I'll never be half the linguist he is, or beat him at chess."

"Sounds like—"

"Don't go matchmaking on me, woman!" Kethry softened the rebuke with a dry chuckle. "We've got enough on our plate with tracking Idra, the damned weather, and the mage we've got on our backtrail."

"So we *are* being followed."

"Nothing you can do about it; my hope is that when he hits the Comb he'll get discouraged and turn back."

Tarma nodded in the dark; this was Keth's province. She wouldn't do either of them any good by fretting about it. If it came to physical battle, *then* she'd be able to do some good.

And for whatever the reason, Jadrek was able to do with less of his drugs every day, and that was all to the good. They were making about as good a headway with him now as they would have been able to manage alone. And maybe . . .

She fell asleep before she could finish the thought.

Now they were getting into the Comb, and as Jadrek had warned, the Comb was no place to be riding through with less than full control of one's senses.

The range of hills along the Northern border called the Comb was among some of the worst terrain Tarma had ever encountered. The hills themselves weren't all that high—but they were sheer rock faces for the most part, with little more than goat tracks leading through them, and not much in the way of vegetation, just occasional stands of windwarped trees, a bit of scrub brush, rank grasses, and some moss and lichen— enough browse for the horses—barely, and Tarma was supplementing the browse with grain, just to be on the safe side.

It had been late spring, still winter in the mountains where Hawksnest lay, when they'd headed down into Rethwellan. It had been early fall by the time they'd made it to the capital. It had been late fall when they bolted. Now it was winter—the worst possible time to be traveling the Comb.

Now that they were in the hills the rains had changed to sleet and snow, and there were no friendly farmers, and no inns to take shelter in when hostile weather made camping a grim prospect. And they no longer had the luxury of pressing on; when a suitable campsite presented itself, they took it. If there wasn't anything suitable, they suffered.

They'd been three days with inadequate camps, sleeping cold and wet, and waking the same. Kethry had dropped the illusions two days ago; there wasn't anybody to *see* them anymore. And when they were on easy stretches of trail, Tarma could see Kethry frowning with her eyes closed, and knew she was doing *something* magical along the backtrail—which probably meant she needed to hoard every scrap of personal energy she could.

Jadrek, predictably, was in worst case. Tarma wasn't too far behind him in misery. And sometimes it seemed to her that their progress was measured in handspans, not furlongs. The only comfort was in knowing that their pursuers—if any—were not likely to be making any better progress.

Tarma looked up at the dead, gray sky and swore at the scent of snow on the wind.

Kethry urged Hellsbane up beside her partner when the trail they were following dropped into a hollow between two of the hills, and there was room enough to do so. The mage was bundled up in every warm garment she owned; on the saddle before her the Archivist was an equally shapeless bundle. He was nodding; only Kethry's arms clasped about him kept him in the saddle. He had had a very bad night, for they'd been forced to camp without any shelter, and he'd taken the full dosage of his drugs just so that he could mount this morning.

"Snow?" Kethry asked unhappily.

"Hai. Dammitall. How much more of this is *he* going to be able to take?"

"I don't know, *she'enedra*. I don't know how much more of this *I'm* going to be able to take. I'm about ready to fall off, myself."

Tarma scanned the terrain around her, hoping for someplace where they could get a sheltered fire going and *maybe* get warm again for the first time in four days. Nothing. Just crumbling hills, overhangs she dared not trust, and scrub. Not a tree, not a cave, not even a tumble of boulders to shelter in. And even as she watched, the first flakes of snow began.

She watched them, hoping to see them melting when they hit the ground—as so far, had always been the case. This time they didn't. "Oh hell*fire*. Keth, this stuff is going to stick, I'm afraid."

The mage sighed. "It would. I'd witch the weather, but I'd do more harm than good."

"I'd rather you conjured up a sheltered camp."

"I've tried," Kethry replied bleakly. "My energies are at absolute nadir. I spent everything I had getting that mage off our trail. I'd cast a *jesto-vath*, but I need some kind of wall and ceiling to make it work."

Tarma stifled a cough, hunched her shoulders against the cold wind, and sighed. "It's not like you had any choice; no more than we do now. Let's get on. Maybe something will turn up."

But nothing did, and the flurries turned to a full-fledged snowstorm before they'd gone another furlong.

"We've got to get a rest," Tarma said, finally, as they gave the horses a breather at the top of a hill. "Jadrek, how are you doing?"

"Poorly," he replied, rousing himself. The tone of his voice was dull. "I need to take more of my medicines, and I dare not. If I fell asleep in this cold—"

"Right. Look—there's a bit of a corner down there." Tarma pointed through the curtaining snow to a cul-de-sac visible just off the main trail. "It might be sheltered enough to let us get a bit warmer. And the horses need more than a breather."

"I won't argue," Kethry replied. "I can feel 'Bane straining now."

Unspoken was the very real danger that was in all of their minds. It was obvious that the snow was falling more thickly with every candlemark; it was equally obvious that unless they found a *good* campsite they'd be in danger of death by exposure if they fell asleep. That meant pressing on through the night if they didn't find a secure site. This little rest might be the closest to sleep that they'd get tonight.

And when they got to the cul-de-sac, they found evidence of how real the danger was.

Huddled against the boulders of the back was what was left of a man. Rags and bones, mostly. The carcass was decades old, at least. There were no marks of violence on him, except that done by scavengers, and from the way the bones lay Tarma judged he'd died of cold.

"Poor bastard," she said, picking up a sword in a half-rotten sheath, and turning it over, looking for some trace of ownership-marks. "Helluva way to die."

Kethry was tumbling stones down over the pitiful remains; Jadrek was doing his best to help. "Is there any *good* way to die?"

"In your own bed. In your own time. Here—can you make anything of this?"

Jadrek dug into his packs while the women were occupying themselves with the grisly remains they'd found. He was aching all over with pain, even through the haze of drugs. Worse, he was slowing them down.

But there was a solution, of sorts. They didn't need him now, and if the weather worsened, *his* presence—or absence—might mean the difference between life and death for the two partners.

So he was going to overdose. That would put him to sleep. If they *did* find shelter, there would be no harm done, and he would simply sleep the overdose off. But if they didn't—

If they didn't, the cold would kill him painlessly, and they'd be rid of an unwieldy burden. Without him they'd be able to take paths and chances they weren't taking now. Without him they could devote energy to saving themselves.

He swallowed the bitter herb pellets quickly, before they could catch him at it, and washed away the bitterness with a splash of icy water from his canteen. Then he pressed himself up against the sheltered side of Kethry's mount, trying to leech the heat from her body into his own.

Kethry took the sword from her partner, and turned it over. The sheath looked as if it had once had metal fittings; there were gaping sockets in the pommel and at the ends of the quillions of the sword that had undoubtedly once held gemstones. There was no evidence of either, now.

"Poor bastard. Might have been a merc, down on his luck," Tarma said. "That's when you know you're hitting the downward slide—when you're selling the decorations off your blade."

Kethry slid the sword a little out of the sheath; it resisted, with a grating sound, although there was no sign of rust on the dull gray blade. Tarma leaned over her shoulder, and scratched the exposed metal with the point of her dagger, then snorted at the shiny marks the steel left on the metal of the sword.

"Well, *I* feel a little less sorry for him," Kethry retorted. *"My* guess is that he was a thief. This was some kind of dress blade, but the precious metal and the stones have been stripped from it."

"Have to be a dress sword," the Shin'a'in said in disgust. "Nobody in their right mind would depend on *that* thing. It isn't steel or even crude-forged iron. You're right, he must have been a thief—and probably the pretties were stripped by somebody that came across the body."

Tarma turned back to her inspection of her mare's condition, and Kethry nodded, shoving the blade back into its sheath. "You're right about this thing," she agreed. "Metal that soft wouldn't hold an edge for five minutes. Damn thing is nearly useless. That pretty much confirms it. The departed wasn't dressed particularly well, I doubt he'd have much use for a dress-sword." She started to stick the thing point-down into the cairn they'd built—then, moved by some impulse she didn't quite understand, put it into her pack, instead.

There was something about that sword—something buried below the seeming of its surface, something that tasted of magic. And if there was magic involved, Kethry thought vaguely, it might be worth saving to look into later.

Neither Tarma nor Jadrek noticed; Tarma was checking Ironheart's feet, and Jadrek was pressed up against Hellsbane's side with his eyes closed, trying to absorb some of the mare's warmth into his own body.

Tarma straightened up with a groan. "Well, people, I hate to say this, but—"

Kethry and Jadrek sighed simultaneously.

"I know," Kethry replied. "Time to go."

Darkness was falling swiftly, and the snow was coming down thicker than ever. They'd given up trying to find a campsite themselves; Tarma had sent Warrl out instead. That meant they had one less set of eyes to guard them, but Warrl was the only one who stood a chance of finding shelter for them.

Tarma was leading both horses; on a trail this uncertain, she wanted it to be *her* that stumbled or fell, not the mares. She was cold to the point of numbness, and every time Hellsbane tripped on the uneven ground, she could hear Jadrek catching his breath in pain, and Kethry murmuring encouragement to him.

Tarma was no longer thinking much beyond the next step, and all her hopes were centered on the *kyree*. If they didn't find shelter by dawn, they'd be so weary that no amount of will could keep them from resting —and once resting, no amount of foreknowledge would keep them from falling asleep—

And they would die.

Tarma wondered how many ghosts haunted the Comb, fools or the desperate, lured into trying to thread the rocky hills and falling victim to no enemy but the murderous weather.

She half-listened to the wind wailing among the rocks above them. It sounded like voices. The voices of hungry ghosts, vengeful ghosts, jealous of the living. The kinds of ghosts that showed up in the songs of her people, now and again, who sought only to lure others to their deaths, so that they might have company.

How many fools—how many ghosts—

A white shape loomed up out of the dusk before them, blocking the path. A vague, ivory rider on an ethereal silver horse, appearing suddenly and soundlessly out of the snow, like a pallid harbinger of cold death.

"Li'sa'eer!" Tarma croaked, and dropped the reins of both horses, pulling the sword slung at her back in the next instant, and wondering wildly if Goddess-blessed steel could harm a hungry ghost.

:Mindmate, no!:

Warrl jumped down from the hillside to her right to interpose his bulk between her and the spirit. *:Mindmate—this is help!:*

"Peace upon you, lady." The voice of the one astride the strange white beast was *not* that of a spirit; nor, when Tarma allowed a corner of herself to test the *feel* of him, was there any of the tingle she associated with magic. The man's voice was not hollow, as a spirit's normally sounded; it was warm, deep, and held a tinge of amusement. "Your four-footed friend came looking for aid, and we heard his calling. I did not mean to startle you."

Tarma's arms shook as she resheathed the blade. "Goddess bless— *warn* a body next time! You just about ate six thumbs of steel!"

"Again, your pardon, but we could not tell exactly where you were. Your presences seem rather . . . blurred."

"Never mind that," Kethry interrupted from behind Tarma, her voice sharp. "Who are you? *What* are you? Why should we trust you?"

The man did not seem to be taken aback by her words. "You're wise not to take anything on appearance, lady. You don't know me—but I *do* know you; I've talked to your friend mind-to-mind, and I know who you are and what you wish. You can trust me on three counts." He and his horse moved in to stand nose to nose with Ironheart. Tarma saw with no little surprise that even in the fading light the beast's eyes were plainly a bright and startling *blue*. "Firstly—that you are no longer in Rethwellan; you crossed the Border some time back, and you are in Valdemar. The enemy on your backtrail will not be able to pass the Border, nor would I give you to him. Secondly, that the man you seek, Prince Stefansen, is Valdemar's most welcome guest, and I will be taking you to him as quickly as your tired beasts can manage. And thirdly, you can trust me because of my office."

"Look—we're tired, we *don't* know anything about your land, and our friend, who might, is not even half-conscious."

So *that* was what was making Keth's voice sound like she was walking on glass.

"I seem to be making a mess of this," the man replied ruefully. "I am Roald, one of the Heralds of Valdemar. And you may believe your large, hairy friend there, that any Herald is to be trusted."

:They are, mindmate,: Warrl confirmed. *:With more than life. There is no such creature as a treacherous Herald.:*

All right, Tarma thought, worn past exhaustion. *We've got no chance out here—and you've never been wrong before this, Furface.*

"Lead on, Herald Roald," she said aloud. And wearily hoped Warrl was right this time, too.

Eight

Tarma clasped her blue-gray pottery mug in both her hands and sniffed the spicy, rich aroma of the hot wine it contained a trifle warily. The stuff was too hot to drink; not that she minded. The heat of it had warmed the thick clay of the mug, and that, in turn, was warming her hands so that they no longer ached in each separate joint. And the heat gave her an excuse to be cautious about drinking it.

She blinked sleepily at the flames in the fireplace before her, trying to muster herself back up to full alertness. But she was feeling the heat seeping into her bones, and with the heat came relaxation. The fire cast dancing patterns of light and shadow up into the exposed rough-hewn beams of the square common room, and made the various trophies of horns and antlers hung on the polished wooden walls seem to move. *She* didn't want to stir, not at all, and that had the potential for danger.

She was wearing, bizarrely enough, some of Roald's spare clothing, all of her own too thoroughly soaked even to bother with. *A Kal'enedral in white—Warrior bless, now* that's *a strange thought.* Roald was the only one of them near to her size; off his horse he was scarcely more than a couple of thumblengths taller than Tarma, and was just as rangy-thin. He was exceedingly handsome in a rugged way, with a heavy shock of dark blond hair, a neat little beard, and eyes as blue as his horse's.

I thought I'd never be warm again. She settled a little more down into her chair and the eiderdown they'd given her to wrap around herself, and blinked at the *kyree* stretched out between her and the flames. Warrl was fast asleep on the red-tiled hearth at her feet, having bolted a meal of three rabbits first. *He trusts them. Especially Roald. Dare we?*

Her chair was set just to one side of the fireplace, practically on the hearthstone. Directly across from her, Kethry was curled up in a second chair, wrapped in eiderdown, looking small and unwontedly serious. She'd been summarily stripped of her wet gear, the same as Tarma, but opted for one of Lady Mertis' soft green wool gowns. Jadrek had been spirited away as well, and regarbed in Stefansen's warmest—heavy brown wool breeches and tunic and knitted shirt.

If Roald hadn't come when he did—Star-Eyed, we came perilously close to losing him. If I'd known he'd taken enough of that painkilling stuff to put him out like that—

Jadrek was pacing the floor beside the two chairs and within the arc of heat and light cast by the fire. He limped very badly—walking slowly, haltingly, trying to shake the fog of his medicines from his head so that he could talk coherently again. He was moving so stiffly that Tarma hurt just watching him.

I wonder; he knew we were in bad trouble when we stopped that last time. I wonder if he didn't dose himself on purpose, figuring that we'd either find shelter and he'd be all right, or that we wouldn't, and while he was unconscious the cold would kill him painlessly and get him out of our hair. That's something a Clansman might do. Dammit—I like this man! And he has no reservations about Stefansen and this Herald. But I do. I must.

Stefansen's wife, Mertis *(that* had come as a shock to Jadrek, that Stefansen had actually wedded), was seated in another chair a bit farther removed from the fire, nursing their month-old son. *I like her, too. That's a sweet little one—why do I have to distrust these people?*

Stefansen, who resembled Idra to a startling degree, (except that on a man's face the features that had been harsh for a woman were strong, and those that had been handsome were breathtaking) was talking quietly with Roald, the two of them sitting on a pair of chairs they'd pulled up near to Mertis. A most domestic and harmonious scene, if you could ignore the worry in everyone's eyes.

Good thing we had Jadrek to vouch for us, or Stefansen might have left us to freeze, and be damned to his Herald friend. He did not like the fact that we'd come looking for him out of Rethwellan. He's still watching me when he thinks I'm not paying any attention. We're both like wary wolves at first meeting, neither one sure the other isn't going to bite.

This turned out to be Roald's own hunting lodge, which, since it was not exactly a *small* dwelling, told Tarma that whatever else he was, the Herald was also a man of means. It was now the "humble" abode of the

Prince-in-exile, his bride of ten months, and their infant son. Valdemar had given Stefansen the sanctuary he needed, but it was a secret sanctuary; the King and Queen of Valdemar dared not compromise their country's safety, not with Rethwellan sharing borders with both themselves and their hereditary enemy, Karse.

The wine was cool enough to drink now, and Tarma had decided she couldn't detect anything dangerous in it. She sipped at it, letting it soothe her raw throat and ease the cold in the pit of her stomach. While she drank, she scrutinized Mertis again over the edge of the mug.

Tarma watched the gentle woman rocking her son in her arms, studying her with the same care she'd have spent on the reconnoitering of an enemy camp. Mertis was not homely, by any means, but not a raving beauty, either. She had a sweet, soft face; frank brown eyes that seemed to demand truth of you; wavy, sable-brown hair. *Not* the kind of woman one would expect to captivate an experienced rake like Stefansen. Which meant there was more to her than showed on the surface.

Then again—Tarma hid a smile with her mug as she thought of the moment when Roald had brought them stumbling up to the door of the lodge. Mertis had been everywhere, easing Jadrek down from his grip on Kethry's saddle, helping him to stumble into the warm, brightly lit lodge, building up the fire with her own hands, issuing crisp, no-nonsense orders to her spouse, the Herald, and the two servants of the lodge, without regard for rank. That just *might* have been her secret—that she had been the only woman to treat Stefansen like a simple man, a person, and not throw herself at his feet, panting like a bitch in heat.

Or it might have been a half dozen other things, but *one* was a certainty; Tarma knew love well enough to recognize it when those two looked at each other. And never mind that Mertis was scarcely higher in birth than Kethry.

"Jadrek?" Stefansen called softly, catching Tarma's attention. "Have you walked yourself out yet? *I'd* rather you got a night's sleep, but Roald seems to think we need to talk *now.*"

"Not just you two—all of us, the mercenaries included," the Herald corrected. "We all have bits of information that need to be put together into a whole."

Stefansen is looking wary again. I'll warrant he didn't expect us to be included in this little talk. Ah well, duty calls. "Just for the record," Tarma said, unwinding herself from the eiderdown, "I'd tend to agree. And the sooner we get to it, the less likely one of us will forget some triviality that turns out to be vital. My people say, 'plans, like eggs, are best at the freshest.' "

Kethry nodded, and got up long enough to turn her chair in a quarter-circle so that it faced the room rather than Tarma; Tarma did the same as the men pulled theirs closer, and Roald brought in a third chair for Jadrek. Mertis left hers where it was, but put the babe back in the cradle and leaned forward to catch every word.

Tarma watched the Prince, his spouse, and the Herald as covertly—but as intently—as she could. Warrl trusted them, and she'd never known the *kyree* to be wrong. He trusted them enough that he'd eaten without checking the food for tampering, and was now sleeping as soundly as if he hadn't a worry in the world. Still, there was a first time for everything, even for the *kyree* being deceived.

There's no sign of the Captain here, either. But that might not mean anything.

Jadrek spoke first, outlining what Raschar had been doing since Stefansen's abrupt departure. Tarma was surprised by the Prince's reactions; he showed a great deal more intelligence and thoughtfulness than rumor had given him credit for. He seemed deeply disturbed by the information that Raschar was continuing to tax the peasantry into serfdom. *He looks almost as if he's taking it personally—huh, for that matter, so does Mertis. And I don't think it's an act.*

Then Tarma and Kethry took up the thread, telling the little conclave what they'd observed in their week or so at the Court, and what they'd noted as they passed through the southern grainlands of Rethwellan.

The Prince asked more earnest questions of them, then, and seemed even more disturbed by the answers. He plainly did not like Kethry's report of the mages lurking in the Court—and the tale of the attack on Jadrek shocked him nearly white.

And that is not *an act,* Tarma decided. *He's more than shocked, he's angry. I wouldn't want to be Raschar and in front of him right now.*

And finally all three spoke of Idra—what Jadrek knew, and what the partners had heard before she'd vanished.

That changed the anger to doubt, and to apprehension. "If she headed here, she didn't arrive," Stefansen said, unhappily, the firelight flaring up in time to catch his expression of profound disturbance. *"Damn* it! Dree and I had our differences, not the least of which was that she voted for Char, but she's the one person in this world that I would *never* wish any harm on. Where in hell could she have gotten to if she didn't come here?"

Tarma wished at that moment that she could have Warrl's thought-reading abilities. The Prince *seemed* sincere, but it would have been so very easy for Idra to have met with an accident once she'd crossed into

Valdemar, particularly if Stefansen hadn't known about her change of heart. He could be using his surprise and dismay at learning *that* to cover his guilt.

At the same time all her instincts were saying he was speaking only truth—

If only I knew!

She turned her attention to Roald. He seemed to be both holding himself apart from the rest, and yet at the same time vitally concerned about all of them. *Goddess—even* us, *and he just met us a few hours ago,* Tarma realized with a start. And there was a knowledge coming from somewhere near where her Goddess-bond was seated that told her that this Herald was, as Warrl put it, someone to be trusted with more than one's life. *If Stefansen murdered Idra, he'd know,* she thought slowly. *I don't know how, but somehow he'd know. And I bet he wouldn't be sharing hearth and home with him. I can't see him giving hearth-rights to a murderer of any kind, much less a kin-slayer. Now I wonder—how much of his worry is for us two, and how much is about us?*

After a long silence, Jadrek said: "This is not something I ever expected to hear myself saying, but whatever has happened to Idra, I fear her fate is going to have to take second place to what is happening to the Kingdom." Jadrek turned to the Prince, slowly, and with evident pain. "Stefan, Raschar is a leech on the body of Rethwellan." Tarma could see his eyes now, and the open challenge in them. "You never retracted your oath to your people as Crown Champion. You still have the responsibility of the safety of the Kingdom. So what are you going to do about the situation?"

"Jadrek, you never were one to pull a blow, were you?" The Prince smiled thinly. "And you're still as blunt as ever you were. Well, let me put it out for us all to stare at. Do you think I should try to overthrow Char?"

"You *know* that's what I think," Jadrek replied, eyes glinting in the firelight. He looked alert and alive—and a candlemark ago Tarma would never have reckoned on his reviving so fast. "You'd be a thousand times better as a king than your brother, and I know that was the conclusion your sister came to after seeing him rule for six months."

"Roald?"

"You've matured. You've truly matured a great deal in the time you've been here," the Herald said thoughtfully. "I don't know if it was fatherhood, or my dubious example, but—you're not the witling rakehell you were, Stefan. The careless fool you were would have been a worse king than your brother, ultimately—but the man you are now could be a very good ruler."

Stefansen turned to Mertis, and stopped dead at a strange, hair-raising humming. Tarma felt the tingling of a power akin to the Warrior's along her spine; she glanced sharply at Kethry in startlement, only to see that the mage wore an equally surprised expression. The humming seemed to be coming from the heap of saddlepacks and weaponry they'd dumped just inside the door, after Mertis had extracted their soiled, soaked clothing for cleaning.

Stefansen rose as if in a dream, as the rest of them remained frozen in their seats. He walked slowly to the shadowed pile, reached down, and took something in his hands.

A long, narrow something.

Bits of enshrouding darkness began peeling from it, and light gleamed where the pieces had fallen away. The thing he held was a sword—not hers, not Kethry's—a sword in a half-decayed sheath—

As the last of the rotten sheath flaked off of it, Tarma could see from the shape of it that it was the dead man's sword that they'd found—and no longer the lifeless, dull gray thing it had been. In Stefansen's hands it was keening a wild song and glowing white-hot, lighting up the entire room.

Stefansen stood with it in both hands, as frozen for a moment as the rest of them were. Then he dropped it—and as it hit the wooden floor with a dull *thud,* the light died, and the song with it.

"Mother of the gods!" he exclaimed, staring at the blade at his feet. "What in hell is *that?"*

Jadrek shook his head. "This is just not to be believed—Idra pretends to go haring off after the Sword That Sings—then we just happen to stumble on it on a remote trail, and just *happen* to bring it with us—"

"Archivist, I hate to disagree," Tarma interrupted, "but it's not so much of a coincidence as you might think. Idra wanted an excuse to go north. If she'd wanted one to go south, I would bet you'd have found a different legend, but the Sword's legend says it was stolen and taken north, so that's the one you chose. There's only one real road through the Comb. No thief would take that, and no fugitive—well, that left this goat-track we followed. I *know* it's the closest path to the real road, and I'll bet it's one of the few that go all the way through. No great coincidence there. As for the coincidence of us finding the dead thief, and of Keth taking the sword—I'll bet he was found a good dozen times, or why were the goldwork and the gems gone from the sheath and the pommel? But nobody in their right mind would bother taking a blade that wouldn't cut butter. And we've been stopping in every likely sheltered spot, so it's small wonder that we ran across him and his booty. But I would be willing to stake Ironheart that no *mage* ever ran across the body. Mages can sense energies, even quiescent ones; right, Keth?"

"That's true," Kethry corroborated. "I knew there was *something* about it, but I didn't have the strength to spare to deal with it right then. So I did what most mages would do—I packed it up to look into it later, if there *was* a later. Besides, knowing how these mage-purposed things work, I would say that the sword might well have known where it was going. It could well have 'told' me to bring it here."

"And the sword, once it sensed you were wavering on making a bid for the throne, made itself known," Mertis concluded wryly.

"It appears," Stefansen said ruefully, "that *I* don't have any choice."

"No more than I did, my friend," Roald replied with a chuckle, and a smile. "No more than I did."

But Stefansen sagged, and his face took on an expression of despair. "This is utterly hopeless, you know," he said. "Just *how* am I supposed to get back the crown when my only allies are a baby, an outlander, three women, a—forgive me, Jadrek—half-crippled scholar, an outsized beast, and a sword that's likely to betray me by glowing and singing every time I touch it?"

"I really don't see why you're already giving up," Roald chided. "Thrones have been overturned with less. What do you really *need* for a successful rebellion?"

"For a start, you need someone who knows where each and every secret lies," Jadrek said, sitting up straighter, his eyes shining with enthusiasm. "Someone who knows which person can be bought and what his price is, which person can be blackmailed, and who will serve out of either love or duty. I haven't been sitting in the corners of the Court being ignored all these years without learning more than a few of those things."

"*We* could infiltrate the capital disguised," Kethry said, surprising her partner. "Magical disguises, if we have to. No one will know us then; Jadrek can tell me who are the ones he wants contacted; if we can get one of us into the Court itself, we could pass messages, arrange meetings. I *know* Tarma could go in as a man, with an absolute minimum of disguising, all physical."

So we've thrown in with this lot, have we, she'enedra? Is it the cause that attracts you, or the fact that it's Jadrek's cause? But, since Kethry had added herself to the little conspiracy, Tarma added her own thought, in spite of her better judgment. "Huh, yes—*if* we can figure something that would put me into the Court without suspicion."

"Challenge the current champion of the King's Guard to combat," Mertis put in, surprising Tarma considerably. "That's *anyone's* right if they want to get in the Guard. Free swords do it all the time, there's nothing out of the ordinary about it. If you do well, you've got a place; if you *beat* him, you automatically become head of the Guard. That would put you at Raschar's side every day. You couldn't get any closer to the heart of the Court than that."

Stefansen looked doubtfully at the lean swordswoman. "Challenge the champion? Has she got a chance?"

Still not sure you trust us, hmm, my lad? I can't say as I blame you. I'm still not entirely sure of you.

But Mertis smiled, and Tarma sensed that the gentle-seeming lady had a good set of claws beneath her velvet. "If half the tales I've heard about the Shin'a'in Swordsworn are true, she'll have his place before he can blink. And right at Raschar's side is the place we could best use you, Swordlady."

It became evident to Tarma that guileless Mertis was no stranger to intrigue as the evening wore on, and the plan began to look more and more as if it had a strong chance of success. In fact, it was she who turned to Roald, and asked, bluntly, "And what is Valdemar prepared to grant us besides sanctuary?"

Roald blinked once, and replied as swiftly, "What will Valdemar get in return?"

"Alliance in perpetuity if we succeed," Stefansen said, "My word on that, and you know my word—"

"Is more than good."

"Thank you for that. You know very well that you could use an ally that shares a border with Karse. You also know we've stayed neutral in that fight, and you know *damned* well that Char would never change that policy. I will; I'll ally with you, unconditionally. More—I'll pledge Valdemar favor for favor should you ever choose to call it in. And I'll swear it on the Sword—*that* will bind every legal heir to the pledge for as long as the Sword is used to choose rulers."

Roald let out his breath, slowly, and raised his eyebrows. "Well, that's a lot more than I expected. But you know we don't dare do anything openly. So that means covert help . . ." His brow wrinkled in thought for a moment. "What about this—every rebellion needs finances, and arms. Those I think I can promise."

Kethry looked rather outraged; Tarma was just perplexed. Who exactly *was* this Herald?

Kethry took the question right out of her mouth.

"Just what power is *yours* that you can fulfill those promises?" Kethry asked with angry cynicism. "It's damned easy to promise things you know *you* won't have to supply just to get us off your backs and out of your kingdom!"

Stefansen looked as if Kethry had blasphemed the gods of his House. Mertis' jaw dropped.

I think Keth just put her foot in it, Tarma thought, seeing their shocked reaction to what seemed to be a logical question. *Something tells me that "herald" means more than "royal mouthpiece" around here—*

"He—Roald—is the heir to the throne of Valdemar," Mertis managed to stammer. "Your Highness, I am sorry—"

Tarma nearly lost her own jaw, and Kethry turned pale. Insulting a member of a Royal House like that had been known to end with a summary execution. "It's *I* who should beg pardon," Kethry said, shaken. "I—I've heard too many promises that weren't fulfilled lately, and I didn't want Jad—my friends, I mean, counting on something that wouldn't ever happen. Your Highness—"

"Oh, Bright Havens—" Roald interrupted her, looking profoundly embarrassed. " 'Highness,' my eye! How could I have been insulted by honesty? Besides, we aren't all that much sticklers about rank in the Heraldic Circle. Half the time I get worse insults than that! And how were *you* to know? You don't even know what a Herald of Valdemar *is!*" He shrugged, then grinned. "And *I* don't know what a Swordsworn is, so we're even! Look, the law of Valdemar is that every Monarch must also be a Herald; our Companions Choose us, rather like that musical sword of Stefan's. Both Father and Mother are Heralds, which makes them co-consorts, so until they seek the Havens—may that take decades!—I'm not all that important, and I act pretty much as any other Herald. The *only* difference is that I have a *few* more powers, like being able to make promises in the name of the throne to my friend, and know my parents will see that those promises are met. Now, about those arms—"

Tarma was profoundly troubled; Kethry had thrown herself in with these people as if she had known them all her life, but it was the Shin'a'in's way to be rather more suspicious than her oathsister—or at least more than Kethry was evidencing at the moment. She needed to think—alone, and undisturbed. And maybe ask for some advice.

She let the folds of the eiderdown fall to her sides, and stood up. Four sets of eyes gave her startled glances, Kethry's included.

"I need to clear my head," she said, shortly. "If you'll excuse me, I think I'd like to go outside for a little."

"In the *dark?* In a snowstorm?" Jadrek blurted, astounded. "Are you—" He subsided at a sharp look from Kethry.

"Swordlady," the Herald said quietly, but looking distinctly troubled, "you and the others are guests in my home; you are free to do whatever you wish. You will find a number of cloaks hanging in the entry. And I am certain an old campaigner like you needs no admonitions to take care in a storm."

She followed the direction of his nod to the darkened end of the hall; past the door there, she found herself in an entryway lit by a single small lantern. As he had said, there were several cloaks hanging like the shadows of great wings from pegs near the outer door. She took the first one that came to her hand, one made of some kind of heavy, thick fur, and went out into the dark and cold.

Outside, the storm was dying; the snow was back to being a thin veil, and she could see the gleaming of the new moon faintly through the clouds. She was standing on some kind of sheltered, raised wooden porch; the snow had been swept from it, and there was an open clearing beyond it. She paced silently down the stairs and out into the untrampled snow, her footsteps making it creak underfoot, until she could no longer feel the lodge looming so closely at her back. Trees and bushes made black and white hummocks in front of her and to both sides; fitful moonlight on the snow and reflected through the clouds gave just enough light to see by. She felt unwatched, alone. This spot would do. And, by sheer stroke of fortune, "south" lay directly before her.

She took three deep breaths of the icy, sharp-edged air, and raised her head. Then, still with her back to the building, she lifted her eyes to the furtive glow of the moon, and throwing the cloak back over her shoulders, spread her arms wide, her hands palm upward.

She felt a little uncomfortable. This wasn't the sort of thing she usually did. She was not accustomed to making use of the side of her that, as Kal'enedral, was also priestess. But she needed answers from a source she *knew* she could trust. And the *leshya'e Kal'enedral* would not be coming to her here unless *she* called to *them.*

She fixed her gaze on that dimly gleaming spot among the clouds; seeking, but not walking, the Moonpaths. Within moments her trained will had brought her into trance. In this exalted state, all sensation of cold, of weariness, was gone. She was no longer conscious of the passing of time, nor truly of her body. And once she had found the place where the Moonpaths began, she breathed the lesser of the Warrior's true names. That murmur of meaning on the Moonpaths should bring one of her teachers in short order.

From out of the cold night before her came a wind redolent of sun-scorched grasslands, of endless, baking days and nights of breathless heat. It circled Tarma playfully, as the moonglow wavered before her eyes. The night grew lighter; she tingled from head to toe, as if lightning had taken the place of her blood. She felt, rather than heard the arrival of Someone, by the quickening of all life around her, and the sudden surge of pure power.

She lowered her hands and her eyes, expecting to see one of Her Hands, the spirit-Kal'enedral that were the teachers of all living Kal'enedral—

—to see that the radiant figure before her, glowing faintly within a nimbus of soft light, appeared to be *leshya'e Kal'enedral,* but was unveiled —her body that of a young, almost sexless woman. A woman of the Shin'a'in, with golden skin, sharp features, and raven-black hair. A swordswoman garbed and armed from head to toe in unrelieved black— and whose eyes were the featureless darkness of a starry night sky, lacking pupil or iris.

The Star-Eyed Herself had answered to Tarma's calling, and was standing on the snow not five paces from her, a faint smile on Her lips at Tarma's start of surprise.

My beloved jel'enedra, do you value yourself so little that you think I would not come to your summons? Especially when you call upon Me so seldom? Her voice was as much inside Tarma's head as falling upon her ears, and it was so musical it went beyond song.

"Lady, I—" Tarma stammered.

Peace, Sword of My forging. I know that your failure to call upon Me is not out of fear, but out of love; and out of the will to rely upon your own strength as much as you may. That is as it should be, for I desire that My children grow strong and wise and adult, and not weakly dependent upon a strength outside their own. And that is doubly true of My Kal'enedral, who serve as My Eyes and My Hands.

Tarma gazed directly into those other-worldly eyes, into the deep and fathomless blackness flecked with tiny dancing diamond-points of light, and knew that she had been judged, and not found wanting.

"Bright Star—I need advice," she said, after a pause to collect her thoughts. "As You know my mind and heart, You know I cannot weigh these strangers. I want to help them, I want to trust them—but how much of that is because my oathsister comes to *their* calling? How much do I deceive myself to please her?"

The warm wind stirred the black silk of Her hair as She turned those depthless eyes to gaze at some point beyond Tarma's shoulder for a moment. Then She smiled.

I think, jel'enedra, that your answer comes on its own feet, two and four.

Two feet could mean Kethry—but four? Warrl?

Snow crunched behind Tarma, but she did not remove her gaze from the Warrior's shining face. Only when the newcomers had arrived to stand shoulder to shoulder with her did she glance at them out of the tail of her eye.

And froze with shock.

On her right stood—or rather, knelt, since he fell immediately to one knee, and bowed his head—the Herald, Roald, his white cloak flaring behind him in Her wind like great wings of snow. On Tarma's left was the strange, blue-eyed horse.

Tarma felt her breath catch in her throat with surprise, but this was only to be the beginning of her astonishment. The horse continued to pace slowly forward, and as he did so, he almost seemed to blur and shimmer, much as Tarma's spirit-teachers sometimes did—as if he were, as they were, not entirely of *this* world. Then he stopped, and stood quietly when the Warrior laid Her hand gently upon his neck. He gleamed with all the soft radiance of the hidden moon, plainly surrounded by an aura of light that was dimmer, but not at all unlike Hers.

Rise, Chosen; it is not in Me to be pleased with subservience, She said to the Herald, who obeyed Her at once, rising to stand silently and worshipfully at Tarma's shoulder. *Vai datha—so, young princeling, your land forges white Swords that fit the same sheath as My black, eh?* She laughed, soundlessly, looking from Roald to Tarma and back again. *Such a pretty pair you make, like moon and cloud, day and night, bright and dark. How an artist would die for such a sight! Two such opposites— and yet so much the same!*

It was only then that Tarma saw that the white clothing she had been wearing had been transmuted to the Warrior's own ebony, as was proper for Kal'enedral.

And you, My gentle Child— She continued, caressing the white horse's shining neck, *—are leshya'e Kal'enedral of another sort, hmm? Like My Hands, and unlike. Perhaps to complete the set I should see if any of My Children would become as you. What think you, should there be sable Companions to match the silver?* The look the horse—no, Companion— bent upon Her was one of reproach. She laughed again. *Not? Well, it was but a thought. But this is well met, and well met again! This is a good land, yours. It deserves good servants, strong defenders—vigilant champions* *to guard it and hold it safe as My Hands hold Mine. Do we not all serve to drive back the Dark, each in his own fashion? So I cry—well met, Children of My Other Self!*

She turned that steady regard back to Tarma. *Are you answered, My cautious one?*

Tarma bowed her head briefly, filled with such relief that she was nearly dizzy with it. And filled as suddenly with an understanding of exactly what and who this Herald and his Companion were. "I am answered, Bright Star."

Then let white Sword and black serve as they are meant—to cleave the True Darkness, and not each other, as you each feared might befall.

There was another breath of hot wind, a surging of power that left Tarma's eyes dazzled, and She was gone.

The Herald closed his eyes briefly, and let out the breath he had been holding in a great sigh. As the horse returned to stand beside him, he opened his eyes again, and turned to face Tarma.

"Forgive me for doubting you, even a little," he said, his voice and the hand he extended to her trembling slightly. "But I followed you out here because—"

"For the same reason *I* would have followed *you* had our positions been reversed," Tarma interrupted, clasping the hand he stretched out. "I wasn't expecting Her when I called, but I think I know now why She came. Both of us have had our doubts settled, haven't we—brother?"

His hold on her hand was warm and steady, and his smile was unwavering and equally warm. "I think, more than settled, sister."

She caught his other hand; they stood facing each other with hands clasped in hands for a very long time, savoring the moment. There was nothing even remotely sexual about what they shared in that timeless space; just the contentment and love of soul-sib meeting soul-sib, something akin to what Tarma had for Kethry—

—and, she realized, with all the knowledge that passed to her from her Goddess in her moment of enlightenment, what this Herald shared with his Companion. For it was no horse that stood beside Roald, and she wondered now how she could have ever thought that it was. *Another soul-sib. And—how odd—even the Heralds don't know exactly what their Companions are—*

It was Roald who finally sighed, and let the moment pass. "I fear," he said, dropping her hands reluctantly, "that if we don't get back to the others soon, they'll think we've either frozen to death, or gotten lost."

"Or," Tarma laughed, giving his shoulders a quick embrace before pulling her cloak back around herself, "murdered each other out here!

By the way—" She stretched out her arm, showing him that the tunic she wore was still the black of a starless night. "—I wonder how we're going to explain what happened to the clothing I borrowed?"

He laughed, long and heartily. "Be damned if I know. Maybe they won't notice? Right—not likely. Oh well, I'll think of something. But you *owe* me, Swordlady; that *was* my second-best set of Whites before you witched it!"

Tarma joined his laughter, as snow crunched under their boots. "Come to the Dhorisha Plains when this is over, and I'll pay you in Shin'a'in horses and Shin'a'in gear! It will break their artistic hearts, but I *think* I can persuade some of my folk to make you a set of unadorned Kal'enedral *white* silks."

"Havens, lady, you tempt my wandering feet far too much to be denied! You have a bargain," he grinned, taking the porch steps two at a time and flinging open the door for her with a flourish. "I'll be at your tent flap someday when you least expect it, waiting to collect."

And, unlikely as it seemed, she somehow had the feeling that he would one day manage to do just that.

Nine

It was difficult, but by no means impossible, to pull energies from the sleeping earth in midwinter. All it took was the skill—and time and patience, and Kethry had those in abundance. And further, she had serious need of any mote of mage-energy she could harbor against the future, as well as any and all favors she could bank with the other-planar allies she had acquired in her years as a White Winds sorceress. She had not had much chance to stockpile either after the end of the Sunhawks' last commission, and the journey here had left her depleted down to her lowest ebb since she and Tarma had first met.

So *she* was not in the least averse to spending as much time in the hidden lodge with Stefansen and Mertis as the winter weather made necessary; she had a fair notion of the magnitude of the task awaiting them. She and Jadrek and Tarma might well be unequal to it—

In fact, she had come to the conclusion that they would need resources she did *not* have—yet.

On a lighter note, she was not at all displeased about being "forced" to spend so much time in Jadrek's company. Not in the least.

She was sitting cross-legged on the polished wooden floor next to the fireplace, slowly waking her body up after being in trance for most of the day. Jadrek was conversing earnestly with Roald, both of them in chairs placed where the fire could warm him, and she could study him through half-slitted eyes at her leisure.

Jadrek seemed so much happier these days—well, small wonder. Stefansen respected him, Mertis admired him, Tarma allowed him to

carry her off to interrogate in private at almost any hour. She was willing
to answer most of his questions about the "mysterious" (at least to the
folk of Rethwellan) nomad Shin'a'in. Roald did him like courtesy about
the equally "mysterious" Heralds of Valdemar. Both of them accorded
him the deference due a serious scholar. Warrl practically worshiped at
his feet (Jadrek's ability to "hear" the beast being in no wise abated), and
he seemed to share Tarma's feeling of comradeship with the *kyree*. Being
given the respect he was (in all sober truth) due had done wonders for
his state of mind. As the days passed, the lines of bitterness around his
mouth were easing into something more pleasant. He smiled, and often,
and there was no shadow of cynicism in it; he laughed, and there was no
hint of mockery.

Physically he was probably in less pain than he had been for years—
which Kethry was quite sure *was* due to Need's Healing abilities. Need
was exerting her magic for a *man* because he was important to Kethry.
For Kethry had no doubt as to how *she* felt about the Archivist. If there
was *ever* going to be one man for her, Jadrek was that man.

All the men I've known, she thought with a touch of wry humor, *and all
the men I've been courted by—it boggles the mind. Mages, fighters—some of
them damned good looking. Good lord, if you were to count Thalhkarsh,
I've even been propositioned by a godling! And who is it that attracts me like*
no one *else ever has? A scholar half again my age, who* I *could probably
break in half if I put my mind to it, with no recourse to Need required.*

". . . Like all those weirdling things out of the Pelagirs," Roald finished, "Except that this thing seems impossible to kill."

"The *Pelagirs?*" Jadrek exclaimed, perplexed. "But I thought you said
this thing was seen north of Lake Evendim?"

"It was—right in the heart of the Pelagir Hills."

"Wait a moment," Jadrek said, rummaging in the pile of clutter under
his chair, and hunting up a piece of scraped vellum and a bit of charcoal.
"All right—here's the lake—your Pelagirs are where?"

"Up here." The Herald took the charcoal from him and sketched.

"Huh." Jadrek studied the sketch thoughtfully. *"We* have a range of
hills we call the Pelagirs, too—here."

"Well! I will be dipped for a sheep—"

"Fairly obvious, now that we have the information, isn't it?" Jadrek
said with a grin. "Your Pelagirs and ours are the same; except that your
inland sea cuts off the tail of the range, leaving it isolated from the rest
up in your northwest corner. And now that I know *that's* true, I think I
know what your 'man-beast' is, assuming I've got the description right.

Four arms, twice man-height, face like a boar and taloned hands? No sign of genitals, nipples or navel, and the color of clay?"

"That's it."

"It's a *krashak*, a mage-made construct. Virtually immortal and inde-structible."

"You can name it; can you tell us how to get rid of it?" Roald pleaded.

"Oddly enough, yes; it's a funny thing, but High Magick seems curi-ously vulnerable to Earth Magick, and with all the mages hanging about Char I took to looking for spell-breakers. It will take courage, but if you can get in close to the thing without it seizing you, and throw a mixture of salt, moly and Lady's Star into its eyes and mouth, it will literally fall apart." He coughed, coloring a little with embarrassment. "I know it sounds like a peasant superstition, but it *does* work. I found a mage I could trust, and asked him. Now I—I always carry some with me. . . ."

Roald only looked impressed. "Havens, how long did you have to look before you found *that* out?"

Jadrek flushed, this time with pleasure. "Well, I got the first hint of it from a translation of Grindel's *Discourses on Unnatural History.*"

"The Orwind translation, or the Quenta?"

"The Orwind. . . ." Their voices sank again and Kethry lost the thread of their conversation. It didn't much matter; she was more inter-ested in watching Jadrek in an unguarded mood. *Oh, that* mind! *I don't think anything ever escapes him. And, for all that he's been treated badly, he so enjoys people—such a vital spirit in that flawed body. He's so* alive. *And damn it, I—Windborn, he makes me so shameless that I feel like a cat in heat around him. I want to purr and cuddle up against him—gods, I am bloody well infatuated. If he so much as raised an eyebrow in invitation at me, I'd warm his bed in a minute!*

Unfortunately, he seemed blissfully unaware of that fact, so far as she could tell. Oh well. . . .

As for Tarma, from the moment she had reentered the hall arm in arm with Roald, Stefansen and Mertis accepted her without reservation. And that meant that Mertis was only too happy to let her play nursemaid to little Megrarthon whenever she wished. Which was most of the time.

And which was precisely what she was doing at this very moment.

She's as happy as Jadrek, Kethry mused. *For that matter, so is the babe. Just look at her—*

Tarma was cuddling the happily cooing child in her black-clad arms, her expression a soft and warm one that few besides Kethry had ever seen. The hands that had killed so often, and without remorse, were holding the little one as gently as if he were made of down and spun glass. The harsh voice that had frightened many an errant fighter into instant obedience was crooning a monotonous lullaby.

She'd be happiest surrounded by a dozen small ones, or two or three dozen. And they know it; children know it, somehow. I've never seen one run from her, not even in the midst of a house-to-house battle. More often than not, they run to her. And rightly; she'd die *to protect a child. When this is over—when this is over, I swear we'll give this up. Win or lose, we'll refound her Clan for her, and to the nether hells with my school if that's what it takes. I'll spend the rest of my life as a hedgewizard and Shin'a'in horse-breeder if I have to.*

While she watched, Tarma put the now-slumbering child back in his cradle; rose, stretching like a cat, then began heading for the fire. The two men at hearthside turned at the soft sound of her footstep, and smiled as one. She saw the smiles, and returned their grins with a good-natured shake of her head.

"And what are you two smirking about?" she asked, clasping her hands behind her and detouring slightly to stroll over to them, her lithe, thin body seeming almost to move fluidly, bonelessly.

The rest has done her good, too. She's in better shape than she's been in months—years—

"Trying to imagine you as a man, Darksib," Roald teased, using the pet name he'd invented for her. "Put a youngling around you, and you'd give yourself away in a breath."

"Hah. I'm a better actor than that. But as to that," she paused before them, crossed her arms, and frowned a little, "you know, we really ought to be getting on with it. Raschar isn't sitting back, not likely. He's consolidating his power, you can bet on it. *We* had better be safely in place before he gets himself so ensconced on the throne that there'll be no dislodging him without an army."

Kethry felt the last of her muscles emerge into wakefulness, and began uncoiling from her position in the hearth-corner.

"The sleeper awakes," Roald noted.

"Not sleeper," she corrected, imitating Tarma's long stretch. "I've been listening while I was coming out of trance. And, loath though I am to leave, in agreement with Tarma. I'm at full power now; Tarma and Jadrek have recovered. It's time to go."

She half expected Jadrek to protest, but he, too, nodded. "If we don't go now," he opined, gravely, "Stefan won't have a kingdom to come back to. But I do have one excellent question—this plan of ours calls for Tarma to replace the champion, and you can bet that Char won't let a Shin'a'in within a spear's cast of him now. So to truly ensure her safety, that means a full magical disguise. With all the mages in the Court, how are you going to hide the fact that Tarma's bespelled? They won't let anyone with a smell of magic on him compete with the King's champion, you know."

Tarma raised an interrogative eyebrow at her. "The thought had occurred to me, too," she said. "Every trial-by-combat that *I've* ever seen has specifically forbidden any kind of magic taint, even lucky amulets."

"Well, I'll answer that in an hour," Kethry replied.

"Why in an hour?"

"Because that's how long it will take me to try a full Adept manifestation, and see if it succeeds or fails."

Kethry didn't want an audience, not for this. Not even Tarma. So she took one of the fur cloaks and went out into the snow-laden scrub forest until she found a little clearing that was far enough from the lodge that she couldn't see or sense the building or the people within it. The weather was beautiful; the air was utterly still, the sky a deepening blue, the sun beginning its downward journey into the west. There would be no better time than now.

A mage of the White Winds school was tested by no one except himself, with a series of spells marking the rise in ability from Apprentice to Journeyman, from Journeyman to Master, and from Master to Adept. A mage could attempt these spells whenever he chose, and as many times as he chose. They would only *work* when he was truly ready. The series was constructed so that the power granted by each was used to fuel the spell for the next.

A little like priming a pump, I suppose; and if you don't have faith that you're *ready, you can't bear to waste the power. I feel ready,* Kethry decided. *Well—*

She initiated the Journeyman spell, gathering her own, strictly personal power about her like a cloak, and calling the Lesser Wind of Fire and Earth, the Stable Elements. It chose to come out of the south, always a good omen, and whirled about her three times, leaving more power than it took to call it. She fairly glowed with energy now, even to normal eyes.

Next—the Master Spell, and the Greater Wind of Air and Water, the Mutable Elements—the Mutables were much harder to control than the Stable Elements.

She raised her hands high over her head, and whispered the words of the spell as she formed the energy left by the first with her will into the mage-shapes called the Cup and the Mill—concentrating with all her soul—calling, but not coercing.

This time the wind came from all four directions and melded into a gentle whirlwind around her, a wind that sang and sparkled with unformed power. When it, too, had circled her three times, she was surrounded by a shell of light and force that shifted and changed moment by moment, opalescing with every color that the mind could conceive.

She drew a deep breath and launched herself fearlessly into the Spell of Adept Manifestation—calling the White Wind itself—the Wind of the Five Elements.

It required the uttermost of any mage that dared it; she must take the power granted her by the first two spells and all of her own, and weave it into an intricate new shape with her will—and the power fought back, resisting the change to itself, twisting and twining in her mental "hands." Simultaneously, she must sing the words of the spell, controlling tone, tempo, and cadence to within a hairsbreadth of perfection. And she must keep her mind utterly empty of all other thought but the image of the form she strove to build. She dared not even allow a moment to contemplate failure, or fail she would. One mistake, and the power would vanish, escaping with the agility of a live thing.

She finished. She held her breath. There was one moment of utter quietude, as time and all time governed ceased—and she wondered.

Had she failed?

And then the White Wind came.

It fountained up out of the ground at her feet as she spread her arms wide, growing into a geyser of power and light and music that surrounded her and permeated her until all she could see and hear and feel was the light and the force. She felt the power fill her mind and give her soul great wings of fire—

It was sundown when she stepped back through the door; Tarma had plainly expected her to be exhausted, and was openly astonished to see that she wasn't.

"It worked," she said with quiet rapture, still held by the lingering exaltation—and just a little giddy with the intoxication of all that power flowing through her.

"It did?" Tarma asked, eyebrows arching toward her hairline, as Jadrek and Roald approached with avid curiosity plain on their faces.

"I'll prove it to you." Kethry cupped her hands together, concentrating on the space enclosed there. When the little wisp of roseate force she called into her hands had finished whirling and settled into a steady glow, she began whispering to it, telling it gently what she asked of it in the ancient language of the White Winds sorcerers.

While she chanted, Stefansen and Mertis joined the little group, surrounding Kethry on all sides. She just smiled and nodded, and continued whispering to her sorcerous "captive."

Then she let it go, with joy, as a child releases a butterfly, and no longer with the wrench of effort the illusion-spell used to cause her. She was an Adept now, and forces that she had been incapable of reaching were hers to command from this moment on. Not carelessly, no—and not casually—but never again, unless she *chose* to, would she need to exhaust her own strength to cast a spell. With such energies at her command, the illusion-spell was as easy as lighting a candle.

The faintly glowing globe floated toward Tarma, who watched it with eyes gone round in surprise. The Shin'a'in's eyes followed it, although the rest of her remained absolutely motionless, as the power-globe rose over her head.

Then it thinned into a faint, rosy mist, and settled over the swordswoman like a veil.

The veil clung to her for a moment, hiding everything but a vague shape within its glowing, cloudy interior. Then it was gone.

And where Tarma had been, there stood a young man, of no recognizable racial type. He had a harsh, stubborn, unshaven face, marked with two scars, one running from his right cheek to his chin, the other across his left cheek. His nose had been broken in several places, and had not healed straight at any time. His hair was dirty brown, shoulder-length, and curled; his eyes were muddy green. He was at least a handsbreadth taller than Tarma had been, and correspondingly broader in the shoulders. And that was a new thing indeed, for before this Kethry had never been able to change size or general shape in her illusion-spells. Even Tarma's clothing had changed, from her Shin'a'in Kal'enedral silks, to rough homespun and tattered leather. The only similarity between Tarma and this man was that both carried their swords slung across their backs.

"Bright *Havens*," breathed Roald. "How did you *do* that?"

Tarma studied her hands and arms, wonder in her un-Tarmalike eyes. Tiny scars made a lacework of white across the hands and as far up the arms as could be seen beneath the homespun sleeves. They were broad, strong hands, and as dissimilar to Tarma's fine-boned, long ones as could be imagined.

Kethry smiled. "Magic," she said.

"And how do you keep Char's mages from seeing that magic?" Stefansen asked.

Kethry just smiled a little more. "What else? *More* magic. The spell only an Adept can control, the spell that makes magic undetectable and invisible even to the best mage-sight."

Tarma was back to looking like herself again, and feeling a good deal happier as a result, as they rode out the next morning. Jadrek had his own horse now, a gentle palfrey that had belonged to Mertis, a sweet-tempered bay gelding with a gait as comfortable as any beast Tarma had ever encountered. He also had some better medicines; more effective and far less dangerous than his old, courtesy of a Valdemaren Healer Roald brought to the lodge himself after Jadrek had had a particularly bad night.

Kethry had augmented the protection of his traveling cloak with another spell she had not been able to cast until she reached Adept level. Jadrek would ride warm now no matter what the weather.

Tarma had turned down Kethry's offer to do the same for her; she wanted no spells on her that might betray her to a magic-sniffing mage if she needed to go scouting. But Roald had managed to round up enough cold-weather gear for all of them to keep them protected even without spellcasting. They were far better prepared this time for their journey as they rode away from the lodge on a clear, sparkling dawn just before Midwinter.

They felt—and to some extent, acted—like adolescents on holiday. If the weather turned sour, they simply put up their little tent, Kethry cast a *jesto-vath* on it, and they whiled away the time talking. When the weather was fair, while they never completely dropped vigilance, they tended to rely mostly on Warrl's senses while they enjoyed the view and the company. Beneath their ease was the knowledge that this "holiday" would be coming to an end once they broke out of the Comb, and there was a definite edge of "cherish the moment while you have it" to their cheer.

An ice storm had descended on them, but you'd never have known it inside their little tent. Outside the wind howled—inside it was as warm as spring sunshine. This was a far cry from the misery of their earlier journey on this same path.

Jadrek was still not capable of sitting cross-legged on the tent floor the way the two women were doing, but they'd given him more than enough room to stretch out, and the bedrolls and packs to use as cushioning and props, and he was reasonably comfortable.

Better than I've been in ages, he thought wonderingly. *Better than—than since I took that fever as a child, and started* having *trouble with my poor bones afterward. That's been twenty, almost thirty years. . . .*

He watched his quest companions through slitted, sleepy eyes, marveling how close he had come to them in the space of a few short weeks. *Tarma—the strong arm, so utterly without a conscience when it comes to certain choices. Brave, Lady bless, braver than anyone I could have imagined. As honor-bound as anyone I know. The outside, so cold—the inside, so warm, so caring. I'm not surprised, really, that once she and Roald got the measure of each other, they hit it off so well that they began calling each other "Darksib" and "Brightsib." There's a great deal about her that is like the Heralds I've known.*

The *kyree* at Tarma's back sighed, and flicked his tail.

Warrl—if for no other reason than to have come to know something about his kind, I'd treasure this quest. If all kyree *are like him, I don't wonder that they have little to do with humankind. There aren't many around like Tarma, and I can't imagine Warrl mindmating to anyone that didn't have her sense of honor* and *her profound compassion.*

Kethry was unbraiding and combing out her amber hair; it caught the light of the *jesto-vath* on the tent walls and glowed with the warmth of a young sun. Jadrek felt his heart squeeze. *Keth, Kethry, Kethryveris—lady, lady, how is it you make me feel like a stripling again? And I have no hope, no right to feel this way about you. When this mad scheme of ours is over, some stalwart young warrior will come, and your eyes and heart will kindle, and he'll carry you off. And I'll never see you again. Why should you find a mind attractive enough to put up with a crippled, aging body? I'm half again your age—why is it that when we're talking you make me feel no age at all? Or every age? How is it that you challenge my mind as well as my heart? How did you make me come alive again?*

He stifled a sigh. *Enjoy it while it lasts, old man,* he told himself, trying not to be too bitter about it. *The end is coming all too soon.*

As it happened, the end came sooner than they had anticipated.

Kethry frowned, and broke off her teasing in mid-sentence.

"Keth?" Tarma asked, giving Ironheart the signal to slow.

"There's—oh Windborn! I thought I'd thrown that bastard off!" Kethry looked angry—and frightened. A gust of wind pulled her hood off and she didn't even bother to replace it.

"The mage," Tarma guessed, as Jadrek brought his horse up alongside theirs.

"The mage. He's better than I thought. He's waiting for us, right where the path breaks out of the hills."

"Ambush?"

Kethry frowned again, and closed her eyes, searching the site with mage-senses. "No," she said finally. "No, I don't think so. He's just— waiting. In the open. And he's got all his defenses up. He's challenging me."

Tarma swore. "And no way past him, as he probably *damn* well knows."

Kethry looked at her soberly, reining in Hellsbane.

"She'enedra, you aren't going to like this—"

"Probably not; what if we charge him? You mages seem to have a problem with physical opposition to magical defenses."

"On that narrow path? He could take us all. And in no way are we going to be able to sneak past him, not with Jadrek. I'm going to have to challenge him to a duel arcane."

"What?"

"He's an Adept, I can tell that from here. If I issue Adept's challenge he'll *have* to answer it, or lose his status."

"And you've been Adept how long? He'll eat you for lunch!"

"Better he eats me alone than all of us. We can't just think of ourselves now, Stefan is depending on us. If—Tarma, he won't take me without a fight, and if I go down, it won't be alone. You can find another mage to disguise you. Once we get into Rethwellan, *I* become the superfluous member of the party."

"You're *not* going down!" Tarma choked, as Jadrek tightened his mouth into a thin line.

"I don't plan on it," Kethry said wryly. "I'm just telling you what to do if it happens. Contract, my love."

Tarma's face went cold and expressionless; her heart stopped. "This is professional, right?" They lived by the mercenary code and would die by it, probably—and by that code, you didn't argue with the terms of the contract once you'd agreed to it.

Kethry nodded. "This is the job we've contracted for. We're not being paid in money—"

"But we've got to do our jobs." Tarma nodded. "You win. I stopped trying to keep you wrapped in wool a long time ago; I'm not going to start up again. Let's do it." And she kicked Ironheart into a canter, with Kethry, Warrl and Jadrek following behind.

I've got to do this, Kethry thought, countering her fear with determination. *If I don't, he'll kill them. I might escape, but I could never shield all four of us, not even at Adept level. I haven't tapped into enough of the shielding spells to know how, yet. But* he *doesn't know I'm Adept, and there aren't that many White Winds mages around. I might well be able to surprise him with a trick or two.*

She kicked Hellsbane and sent her galloping past Tarma, up the slope of the barren hill before them, knowing that *she* would have to reach the waiting magician first and issue her challenge before he caught sight of the others. Otherwise he would blast first, and ask questions after.

Her move took both Tarma and the mage by surprise, for she was able to top the rise and send up the challenge signal before either Tarma or her foe had a chance to react.

The mage waiting below her was one of the ones she'd seen wandering about Raschar's court; a thin man, dark of hair and eye. He was clean-shaven, which made it all the easier to note his sardonic expression, and he wore his hair loose and shoulder length. *Now* he wore his mage-robes; whatever his school was, it was one Kethry didn't recognize. The robes were a dull red, and banded and embroidered in dark brown. Like hers, they were split front and back for ease in riding. The chestnut gelding he straddled appeared tired and drained, and stood quietly with head down as he sat with his reins loose.

"A challenge?" he called incredulously. "You'd challenge *me?* Why in the Names of the Seven should I even bother with you, girl?"

As answer, she called up her Adept Manifestation. From her body rose the misty golden form of a hawk, twenty feet tall, with fiery wings; a hawk that mantled at him and opened its beak in a silent screech of defiance. "I challenge you, Adept to Adept," she called coldly. "You will answer such a challenge; you have no choice."

He called up his Manifestation; a winged snake, with scales and wing membranes that glistened in shades of green and blue. Calling it was his formal answer to her formal challenge; now they were both bound to the duel. "You're a fool, you know that," he said matter-of-factly, dismounting, and letting his Manifestation fade away. "You can't have been an Adept for very long; I've been one for ten years. You can't hope to beat me."

By this time Tarma, Jadrek and Warrl had reached her on the crest of the hill. Kethry unbuckled Need, feeling strangely naked without the blade, and passed her to Tarma. "Hold her for me. Nothing's allowed in the circle but ourselves," she said, watching as the other mage took up a stand near the center of the tiny, barren, windswept valley and put up his half of the magical dome that would only be dispelled by the death or defeat of one of them. Then she allowed her Manifestation to dissipate, and leapt down from Hellsbane's saddle, striding purposefully to take her stand opposite him. "That remains to be seen," she answered him, locking all emotion down, and replying with absolute calm. "So—let it begin!"

With those words, the dome of mage-power sealed, leaving the others helpless witnesses outside.

For a long moment, the combatants stood, simply watching each other. Tarma took advantage of the lull to order Jadrek to station himself and Warrl on the dividing line between the two mages, and on the side of the dome opposite hers. "Warrl has some tricks—I expect you might, too," she said distantly, trying to think like a mage. "I don't trust this bastard not to cheat. Well, Keth won't either; I don't doubt she's expecting something. But if anything should happen—"

"I'll do what I can," Jadrek promised anxiously, taking out his little bag of herbs and salt from his pocket, then replacing it. "It—it isn't likely to be much, but—"

"Jadrek, I've seen a slung stone bring down a king." She frowned in thought. "We should split up; if something *does* go bad, you and Warrl go for Keth, *I'll* go for the mage. He can't know how Need works, he can't know that in my hands she protects from sorcery. *I'll* be safe from anything he can throw, and I'll keep him off your tail. Now, quick, before they start to *do* anything—"

He limped to the opposite side of the dome; Tarma could see him dimly through the red energy-haze. Warrl crouched beside him, ready to spring in an instant.

Tarma unsheathed the bespelled sword called Need and took her own stance; blade point down in the earth, both of her hands resting on the pommel, feet slightly apart. She was ready.

Just in time, for within the dome of hazy red, the battle was joined in earnest.

From the body of the stranger came a man-sized version of his Manifestation, flying upward to the top of the dome; Kethry's met it halfway. Serpent struck at hawk and was deflected; hawk tried to seize serpent in its talons, but the serpent wriggled free, then the snake tried to wrap itself around the hawk's body and neck. The hawk struck with beak and talon; the serpent let go. Both buffeted each other with punishing wing-blows. The battle rained glowing scales, feathers, and droplets of fluid, all of which vanished before they touched the ground.

Both Manifestations froze for an instant, then plummeted groundward; hawk with eyes glazing and fang marks in its chest, serpent with one wing ripped from its body.

Both thinned to mist and were gone before either struck the ground. *Round one: a draw,* Tarma thought to herself, shifting her weight to relieve muscles that had tensed, and feeling a tiny pebble roll out from under her foot.

Within the dome appeared two smaller domes, each covering a mage. Then all the fury of all the lightning storms Tarma had ever witnessed rolled into one broke loose within the greater dome. Lightning struck again and again on the two shields, seeking weak spots; it crawled over the surface of the little domes or rolled itself into balls that circled the perimeters without finding entrance. And all in complete silence; that was the truly frightening and eerie part. Tarma's eyes were dazzled to the point of having trouble seeing when the lightning finally died to nothing, and the lesser domes vanished. As Tarma blinked away the spots interfering with her vision, she tried to assess the condition of both Kethry and her erstwhile rival. They both seemed equally tired.

Round two; another draw.

Kethry might have looked tired, but she also looked slightly pleased. *Maybe a draw is good—Warrior bless, I hope so—*

Even more encouraging, the other mage looked slightly worried.

Kethry initiated the next round; throwing (literally) daggers of light at the red-robed sorcerer, daggers which he had to deflect, dodge, or absorb. He returned in kind, but he was not as good in this contest as Kethry; his blades tended to go awry. Hers never failed to reach their mark, and frequently hit.

Where they hit, they left real wounds, wounds that smoked and bled. The red mage managed to keep from being hit anywhere vital, but the daggers were taking a steady toll.

After being hit one too many times, he suddenly threw up his hands, and a wall of flame sprang up in front of him, a wall that devoured the daggers when they reached it.

The fire grew until it reached the top of the dome, cutting him off from Kethry. Arms of flame began to lick from the wall, reaching toward her. *Fighting fire with fire might not work, here, Keth,* Tarma thought, biting her lip a little. *You could both end up scorched by your own powers—*

But Kethry chose not to fight with fire, but with air; a whirlwind, a man-high tornado of milky white sprang up in front of her, sucking in those reaching arms of flame. And every time it ate one of those arms, it grew a little larger. Finally, it reached nearly to the top of the dome— and it began to move on the red-robed mage and his fiery protective wall.

Star-Eyed! If it got bigger just by eating a couple of licks of flame, what'll it do when it hits the fire-mother?

Evidently the same thought occurred to the mage, for his eyes had gone white-rimmed with panic. He backed into the restraining wall of the protective dome, then began shouting and waving his hands wildly.

And a twice-man-sized *thing* rose from the barren earth behind Kethry.

No—oh no—that bastard, he had that thing hidden there; he's had this planned from the start! Tarma recognized the *krakash,* the mage-construct, from Jadrek's descriptions. She started to sprint for the edge of the dome, even knowing she wouldn't be able to pass it.

Kethry turned to meet it, first making frantic motions with her hands, then groping for a blade she did not have. The thing reached for her with the two upper arms, missing, but raking her from neck to knee with its outsized talons. She collapsed, clutching herself with pain; it seized her as she fell with the lower two of its four arms. It lifted her as she fought to get free—and broke her back across its knee, as a man would break a dry branch.

"No!"

Tarma heard her own voice, crying the word in anguish, but it didn't seem to belong to her.

The whirlwind died to a stirring of dust on the ground; the dome thinned to red mist, and vanished.

Tarma's mind and heart were paralyzed, but her body was not. She reacted to the disaster as she had planned, charging the mage at a dead run, while Jadrek sprinted fearlessly for the *thing.*

The startled wizard saw her coming, and threw blasts of pure energy at her—spheres of blinding ball-lightning which traveled unerringly toward her, hit, and did *nothing,* leaving not even a tingle behind as they dissipated. The mage had just enough time to realize that she was protected before she reached him.

While part of her sobbed with anguish, another part of her coolly calculated, and brought Need about in a shining, swift arc, as she allowed her momentum to carry her past him. She saw his eyes, filled with fear, saw his hands come up in a futile attempt to deflect the sword—then felt the shock along the blade as she neatly beheaded him, a tiny trail of blood-droplets streaming behind the point of the sword as it finished its arc.

Before his body had hit the ground she whirled and made for Jadrek, cursing the fate that had placed mage and construct so many paces apart. The older man hadn't a chance.

As she ran, she could see that the Archivist had something in his hands. He ducked under the grasp of the horrid creature's upper two arms with an agility Tarma never dreamed to see in him. And with the courage she *had* known he possessed, came up in the thing's face, casting one handful of powder into its eyes and the second into its mouth.

The thing emitted a shriek that pierced Tarma's ears—

Then it crumbled into a heap of dry earth before she had made more than a dozen steps in its direction. As it disintegrated, it dropped Kethry into the brown dust like a broken, discarded toy.

Tarma flung herself down on her knees at Kethry's side, and tried to stop the blood running from the gashes the thing's talons had left. Uselessly—for Kethry was dying even as she and the Archivist knelt in the dust beside her.

Jadrek made a choking sound, and took Kethry into his arms, heedless of the blood and filth.

Tarma fumbled the hilt of Need into her hands, but it only slowed the inevitable. Need could not mend a shattered spine, nor could she Heal such ghastly wounds; all the blade could do was block the pain. It was only a matter of time—measured in moments—before the end.

"Well . . ." the mage whispered, as Jadrek supported her head and shoulders in his arms, silent tears pouring from his eyes, and sobs shaking his shoulders. "I . . . always figured . . . I'd never . . . die in bed."

Tarma clenched both of her hands around the limp ones on Need's hilt, fiercely willing the blade to do what she knew in her heart it could not. *"Damn* it, Keth—you *can't* just walk out on us this way! You *can't* just die on us! We—" she could not say more for the tears that choked her own throat.

"Keth—*please* don't; I'll do anything, take *my* life, only please don't die—" Jadrek choked out, frantically.

"Don't . . . have much choice . . ." Kethry breathed, her eyes glazing with shock, her life pumping out into the dust. "Be brave . . . *she'enedra* . . . finish the contract. Then go home . . . make Tale'sedrin live . . . without me."

"No!" Tarma cried, her eyes half-blind with tears. *"No!"* she wrenched her hands away, leaping to her feet. "It's *not* going to end this way! Not while I'm Kal'enedral! By the Warrior, I swear *NO!"*

Thrusting a blood-drenched fist at the sky, she summoned all the power that was hers as Kal'enedral, as priestess, as Swordsworn warrior —power she had never taken, never used. She flung back her head, and *screamed* a name into the uncaring, gray sky, a name that tore her throat even as her heart was torn.

The Warrior's Greater Name—

The harsh syllables of the Name echoed and reechoed, driving her several paces backward, then sending her to her knees in the dust. Then —silence. Silence as broodingly powerful as that in the eye of the hurricane. Tarma looked up, her heart cold within her. For a moment, nothing changed.

Then *everything* ceased; time *stopped.* The very tears on Jadrek's cheeks froze in their tracks. Sound died, the dust on the breeze hung suspended in little immobilized eddies.

Tarma alone could move; she got to her feet, and waited for Her—to learn what price *she* would be asked to pay for the gift of Kethry's life.

A single shaft of pure, white light lanced into the ground, practically at Tarma's feet, accompanied by an earsplitting shriek of tortured air. Tarma did *not* turn her eyes away, though the light nearly blinded her and left her able to see nothing but white mist for long moments. When the mist cleared from her vision, She was standing where the light had been, Her face utterly still and expressionless, Her eyes telling Tarma nothing.

They faced one another in silence for long moments, the Goddess and her votary. Then She spoke, Her voice still melodious; but this time, the music was a lament.

That you call My Name can mean only that you seek a life, jel'enedra, She said. *The giving of a life—not the taking.*

"As is my right as Kal'enedral,' Tarma replied, quietly.

As is your right, She agreed. *As it is My right to ask a sacrifice of you for that life.*

Now Tarma bowed her head and closed her eyes upon her tears, for she could not bear to look upon that face, nor to see the shattered wreck that had been her dearest friend lying beyond. "Anything," she whispered around the anguish.

Your own life? The future of Tale'sedrin? Would you release Kethry from her vow if I demanded it and have Tale'sedrin become a Dead Clan?

"Anything." Tarma defiantly raised her head again, and spoke directly to those star-strewn eyes, pulling each of her words out of the pain that filled her heart. "Keth—she's worth more to me than anything. Ask anything of me; take my body, make me a cripple, take my life, even make Tale'sedrin a Dead Clan, it doesn't matter. Because without Kethry to share it, none of that has any meaning for me."

She was weeping now for the first time in years; mostly when she hurt, she just swallowed the tears and the pain, and forced herself to show an impassive face to the world. Not now. The tears scalded her cheeks like hot oil; she let them.

Do you, Kal'enedral, feel so deeply, then?

Tarma could only nod.

It—is well, came the surprising answer. *And what price your obedience?*

"I put no price on obedience, I will serve You faithfully, Lady, as I always have. Only let Kethry live, and let her thrive and perhaps find love —and most of all, be free. That's worth anything You could ask of me."

The Warrior regarded her thoughtfully for an eternity, measuring, weighing.

Then—She laughed—

And as Tarma stared in benumbed shock, She held out Her hands, palm outward, one palm facing Tarma, one Kethry. Bolts of blinding white light, like Kethry's daggers of power, leaped from Her hands to Tarma, and to the mage still cradled in Jadrek's arms.

Or, possibly, to the ensorcelled blade still clasped in the mage's hands.

Tarma did not have much chance to see which, for the dagger of light hit her full in the chest, and suddenly she couldn't hear, couldn't see, couldn't breathe. She felt as if a giant hand had picked her up, and was squeezing the life out of her. She was blind, deaf, dumb, and made of nothing but excruciating pain—

Only let Keth live—only let her live—and it's worth any price, any pain—

Then she was on her hands and knees, panting with an agony that had left her in the blink of an eye—half-sprawled in the cold dust of the valley.

While beside her, a white-faced Jadrek cradled a dazed, shocked—and completely Healed—Kethry. Only the tattered wreckage of her traveling leathers and the blood pooled beneath her showed that it had not all been some kind of nightmare.

As Tarma stared, still too numb to move, she could hear the jubilant voice of the Warrior singing in her mind.

It is well that you have opened your heart to the world again, My Sword. My Kal'enedral were meant to be without desire, *not without feeling. Remember this always: to have something, sometimes you must be willing to lose it. Love must live free, jel'enedra. Love must ever live free.*

Ten

Jadrek blinked, trying to force what he had just witnessed into some semblance of sense. He was mortally confused.

One moment, Kethry is dying; *there is no chance anyone other than a god could survive her injuries. Then Tarma stands up and shrieks something in Shin'a'in—and—*

Kethry stirred groggily in his arms; he flushed, released her, and helped her to sit up, trying *not* to stare at the flesh showing through the rents in her leather riding clothing—flesh that had been lacerated a moment ago.

"What . . . happened?" she asked weakly, eyes dazed.

"I don't really know," he confessed. And thinking: *Tarma was* here, *and now she's over* there *and I didn't see her move, I know I didn't! Am I going mad?*

Tarma got slowly to her feet, wavering like a drunk, and staggered over to them; she looked drained to exhaustion, her face was lined with pain and there were purplish circles beneath her eyes. It looked to Jadrek as if she was about to collapse at any moment.

For that matter, Keth looks the same, if not worse—what am I thinking? Anything is better than being a heartbeat away from death!

Tarma fell heavily to her knees beside them, scrubbing away the tears still marking her cheeks with the back of a dirty hand, and leaving dirt smudges behind. She reached out gently with the same hand, and patted Kethry's cheek. The hand she used was shaking, and with the other arm she was bracing herself upright. "It's all right," she sighed, her voice sounding raw and worn to a thread. "It's all right. I did something—and it worked. Don't ask what. Bright Star, I am tired to death!"

She collapsed into something vaguely like a sitting position right there in the dust beside them, head hanging; she leaned on both arms, breathing as heavily as if she had just run an endurance race.

Kethry tried to move, to get to her feet, and fell right back into Jadrek's willing embrace again. She held out *her* hand, and watched with an expression of confused fascination as it shook so hard she wouldn't have been able to hold a cup of water without losing half the contents.

"I feel awful—but—" she said, looking down at the shreds of her tunic with astonishment and utter bewilderment. "How did you—"

"I *said* don't ask," Tarma replied, interrupting her. "I can't talk about it. Later, maybe—not now. It—put me through more than I expected. Jadrek, my friend—"

"Yes?"

"I'm about as much use as a week-old kitten, and Keth's worse off than I am. I'm afraid that for once you're going to get to play man of muscle."

She looked aside at him, and managed to muster up a half grin. There wasn't much of it, and it was so tired it touched his heart with pity, but it was real, and that comforted him.

Whatever has happened, she knows exactly what she's doing, and it will *be all right.*

"Tell me what you want me to do," he said, trying to sound just as confident.

:There's still myself,: Warrl's dry voice echoed in their thoughts. *:I have no hands, but I can be of* some *help.:*

"Right you are, Furface. Oh gods," Tarma groaned as she got back up to her knees, and took Kethry's chin in her hand, tilting it up into the light. Jadrek could see that Kethry's pupils were dilated, and that she wasn't truly *seeing* anything. "What I thought—Keth, you're shocky. Fight it, love. Jadrek and Warrl are going to find some place for us to hole up for a while." Tarma transferred her hold to Kethry's shoulder and shook her gently. "Answer me, Keth."

"Gods—" Kethry replied, distantly. "And sleep?"

"As soon as we can. Fight, *she'enedra.*"

"I'll . . . try."

"Warrl, get the horses over here, would you? Jadrek, you're going to have to help Keth mount. She's got no more bones right now than a sponge." He started to protest, but she cut him off with a weary wave of her hand. "Not to worry; our ladies are battlemares and they know the drill. I'll get them to lie down, you watch what I do, then give Keth a hand, and steady her as they get up. No lifting, just balancing. *Hai?*"

"As long as I'm not going to have to fling her into the saddle," he replied, relieved, "I don't see any problem."

"Good man," she approved. "Next thing—Warrl will go looking for shelter; I want something more substantial than the tent around us tonight. You'll have to stay with us, keep Keth in her seat. *I'll* be all right, I've ridden semiconscious for miles when I've had to. When Warrl finds us a hole, you'll have to help us off, and do all the usual camp duties."

"No problem there, either; I'm a lot more trail wise than I was before this trip started." *Aye, and sounder in wind and limb, too.*

Warrl appeared, the reins of Jadrek's palfrey in his mouth, the two battlemares following without needing to be led. Jadrek watched as Tarma gave her Ironheart a command in Shin'a'in, and was astounded to see the mare carefully fold her long legs beneath her and sink to the dusty ground, positioning herself so that she was lying within an arm's length of the exhausted swordswoman. Tarma managed to clamber into the saddle, winding up kneeling with her legs straddling the mare's back. She gave another command, and the mare slowly lurched to her feet, unbalanced by the weight of the rider, but managing to compensate for it. Tarma glanced over at Jadrek. "Think you can deal with that?"

"I think so."

Tarma repeated her command to Hellsbane; the second mare did exactly as her herd-sister had. Jadrek helped Kethry into the same position Tarma had taken, feeling her shaking from head to toe every time she had to move. Tarma gave the second command, and the mare staggered erect, with Jadrek holding Kethry in the saddle the whole time.

Warrl flicked his tail, and Jadrek felt a wave of approval from the *kyree*. *:I go, packmates. You go on—it were best you removed yourselves from the scene of combat.:*

"Spies?" Jadrek asked aloud.

:Possible. Also things that feed on magic, and more ordinary carrion eaters. Shall we take the enemy beast?:

Tarma looked over her shoulder at the weary gelding, which was still where the mage had left it, off to one side of the trail. "I don't think so," she replied after a moment. "It's just short of foundering. Jadrek, could you strip it? Leave the harness, bring anything useful you find in the packs, then let the poor thing run free."

He did as she asked; once free of saddle and bridle the beast seemed to take a little more interest in life and moved off at a very slow walk, heading deeper into the hills. Warrl trotted down the trail, and vanished from sight once past the place where it exited the valley. Jadrek mounted his own palfrey with a grunt of effort, and rode it in close beside Kethry, so that he could steady her from the side.

"You ready, wise brother?" Tarma asked.

"I think so. And not feeling particularly wise."

"Take lead then; my eyes keep fogging. Ironheart knows to follow her sister."

They headed out of the little valley, and the trail became much easier; the hills now rolling rather than craggy, and covered with winter-killed grass. But after a few hundred feet it became obvious that their original plan wasn't going to work. Kethry kept drifting in and out of awareness, and sliding out of her saddle as she lost her hold on the world. Every time she started to fall, Jadrek had to rein in both Hellsbane and his palfrey to keep her from falling over. The gaits and sizes of the two horses just weren't evenly matched enough that he could keep her steady while riding.

He finally pulled up and dismounted, walking stiffly back toward the drooping Shin'a'in. Tarma jerked awake at the sound of his footsteps.

"What? Jadrek?" she said, shaking her head to clear it.

He looked measuringly at her; she looked awake enough to think. "If I tethered Vega's reins to the back of your saddle, would that bother 'Heart?" he asked.

"No, not 't all," Tarma replied, slurring her words a little. "She's led b'fore. Why?"

"Because this isn't going to work; I'm going to put the packs on Vega and ride double with Keth, the way you carried me up here, only with me keeping her on."

Tarma managed a tired chuckle. "Dunno why I didn' think of that. Too . . . blamed . . . tired. . . ."

She dozed off as Jadrek made the transfer of the packs, then put a long lead-rein on Vega's halter and fastened it to the back of Tarma's saddle. He approached Hellsbane with a certain amount of trepidation, but the mare gave him a long sniff, then allowed him to mount in front of Kethry with no interference—although with his stiff joints, swinging his leg over 'Bane's neck instead of her back wasn't something he wanted to repeat if he had any choice. He would have tried to get up behind Kethry, but he wasn't sure he could get her to shift forward enough, and he wasn't certain he'd be able to stick on the battlemare's back if she broke into anything other than a walk. So instead he brought both of Kethry's arms around his waist, and loosely tied her wrists together. She sighed and settled against his shoulder as comfortably as if it were a pillow in her own bed.

He rather enjoyed the feeling of her snuggled up against his back, truth be told.

He nudged Hellsbane into motion again, and they continued on down the trail. The sky stayed gray but showed no signs of breaking into rain or sleet, and there was no hint of a change in the weather on the sterile, dusty air. The horses kept to a sedate walk, Tarma half-slept, and Kethry was so limp he was certain she was completely asleep. It was a little frightening, being the only one of the group still completely functional. He wasn't used to having people rely on *him*. It was exciting, in an uneasy sort of way, but he wasn't sure that he liked that kind of excitement.

Warrl returned from time to time, always with the disappointing news that he hadn't found anything. Jadrek began to resign himself to either riding all night—and hoping that there wasn't going to be another storm —or trying to put up the tent by himself. But about an hour before sunset, the *kyree* came trotting back with word that he'd found a shepherd's hut, currently unused. Jadrek set Hellsbane to following him off the track, and Ironheart followed her without Tarma ever waking.

She did come to herself once they'd stopped, and she seemed a bit less groggy. She got herself dismounted without his help, got their bedrolls off Vega, and carried them inside with her. She actually managed to get their bedding set up while Jadrek slid the half-conscious mage off her horse, then assisted her to stagger inside, and laid her down on the bedding. With a bit of awkwardness at the unaccustomed tasks, he got the horses bedded down in a shed at the side of the little building.

By the time he'd finished, Kethry was sound asleep in her bedroll, and Tarma was crawling into her own. "Can't . . . keep my eyes open . . ." she apologized.

"Then don't try, I can do what's left." *I think,* he added mentally.

But his trail skills *had* improved; he managed to get a fire going in the firepit, thought about making supper, and decided against it, opting for some dried beef and trail biscuit instead. With the fire dimly illuminating their shelter, he made a quick inspection of the place, thinking: *It would be my luck to come upon a nest of hibernating snakes.*

But he found nothing untoward; in fact, it was a very well built shelter, with stone walls, a clean dirt floor, and a thatched roof. It was a pity it didn't have a real fireplace—a good half of the smoke from the fire was *not* finding the smokehole in the center of the roof, and his eyes were watering a bit—but it was clean, and dry, and now growing warm from the fire.

He watched the moving shadows cast by the fire onto the wall, chewed the leathery strip of jerky, and tried to sort himself out.

Warrl came in once to tell him that he'd hunted and eaten, and was going to stand guard outside; after that, he was alone.

What kind of a fool have I shown myself to be? he thought, still confused by the events of the last few hours. *Did anyone even notice?*

He watched Kethry as she slept, feeling both pleasure and pain in the watching. *How much did Tarma see? Gods above, I'm afraid I've gone and fallen in love, like a greensick fool. At my age I should bloody well know better.*

Still—given the state they'd all been in—

Tarma probably hadn't been in a condition to notice much of anything except her oathsister's plight.

And I would give a great deal to know how she managed to bring Kethry back from Death's own arms. Because she's as much as admitted it was all her doing. And I can only wonder what it cost her besides strength and energy—maybe that's why she didn't want to talk about it. Still and all, she really isn't acting as if it cost her nearly as much as if whatever had happened shook her down to her soul. I think perhaps she learned something she didn't expect to. Whatever it was—I think perhaps the outcome is going to be a good one. She almost seems warmer somehow. More open. Would she ever have put all her safety and Keth's in my hands before? I—I don't think so.

He stretched, taking pleasure in the feel of joints that weren't popping, and bones that didn't creak. He was sore from the unaccustomed work, but not unbearably so.

Although—Lady of Light, I've been working like a porter all afternoon, and not had so much as a twinge *in the old bones! Now was that just because I was keyed up, or was it something else? Well, I'll know tomorrow. If I ache from head to toe, I'll know I was not privileged to be the recipient of a miracle!*

And meanwhile—the fire needs feeding.

So he watched Kethry, huddled in his own blankets while he fed the fire, and waited for the morning.

Carter's Lane in the capital city of Petras was living up to its name, even this close to the time for the evening meal. The street was wide enough for four wagons moving two abreast in each direction, and all four lanes were occupied by various vehicles now. The steady rumbling of wheels on cobblestones did not drown out the equally steady hum of voices coming from all sides. Carter's Lane boasted several popular taverns and drink-shops, not the least popular of which was the Pig and Potion. This establishment not only had an excellent cook and an admirable brewmaster, but in addition offered various forms of accommodation—ranging from single cubbyholes (with bed) that rented by the hour, to rooms and suites of rooms available by the week or month.

It was from the window of one of the latter sorts of lodging that a most attractive young wench was leaning, her generous figure frequently taking the eyes of the cart drivers from their proper work. She was, in fact, the inadvertent cause of several tangles of traffic. She paid this no heed, no more than she did the equally persistent calls of admiration or inquiries as to her price. She was evidently watching for something—or someone.

And to the great disappointment of her admirers, she finally spotted what she was watching for.

"Arton!" the brown-haired, laughing-eyed wench called from her second-floor window. "I've waited *days* for you, you ungrateful beast!"

"Now, Janna—" The scar-faced fighter who emerged from the crowd to stand on the narrow walkway beneath her looked to be fully capable of cutting his way out of any fracas—except, perhaps, this one.

"Don't you 'now, Janna,' *me,* you brute!" She vanished from the window only to emerge from a door beside it. The door let onto a balcony and the balcony gave onto a set of stairs that ran down the outside of the inn. Janna clattered down these stairs as fast as her feet could take her. "You leave me here *all alone,* and you *never* come to see me, and you *never* send me word, and—"

"Enough, enough!" the warrior begged, much to the amusement of the patrons of the inn. "Janna, I've been busy."

"Oh, *busy!* Indeed, I can guess how *busy!*" She confronted him with her eyes narrowed angrily, standing on the last two stairs so that her eyes were level with his. Her hands were on her hips, and she thrust her chin forward stubbornly, not at all ready to make peace.

"Give 'im a rest, lass," called another fighter lounging at an outside table, one wearing the same scarlet-and-gold livery as Arton. "King's nervy; keeps 'im on 'and most of th' time. 'E *'as* been busy."

"Oh, well then," the girl said, seeming a bit more mollified. "But you *could* have sent word."

"I'm here now, aren't I?" he grinned, with just a touch of arrogance. "And we ought to be making up for lost time, not wrangling in the street."

"Oh—*Oh!*" She squealed in surprise as he picked her up, threw her over his shoulder, and carried her up the stairs.

He pulled the door open; closed it behind him.

Silence.

One of the serving girls paused in her distribution of ale mugs, sighed, and made calf eyes at the closed door. *"Such* a man. Wisht I 'ad me one like 'im."

"Spring is aborning, and young love with it," intoned a street minstrel, hoping that the buxom server would take notice of *him.*

"Young *lust,* you mean, rhymester," laughed the second fighter. "Arton's no fool. That's a nice little piece he brought with him out of the country—and cheap at the price of a room, a bit of feeding, and a few gewgaws. One of these days I may go see if she's got a sister who wants to leave the cowflops for the city."

"If you can get any girl to look at your ugly face," sneered a third.

The mutter of good-natured wrangling carried as far as the second-floor room, where the young fighter had collapsed into a chair, groaning. The room's furnishings were simple; a bed, a table, a wardrobe and three chairs.

And an enormous wolflike creature on the hearth.

"Warrior's Oath, Keth—you *might* make yourself lighter next time!" the warrior groaned. "My poor back!"

"If I'd known you were going to play border-bridegroom, I'd have helped you out, you idiot!" the brown-haired girl retorted, closing the shutters of the room's single window, then snatching a second chair and plopping down into it. "Tarma, where the hell have you been these past few days? A note of three words does *not* suffice to keep me from having nervous prostrations."

:I told you she was all right,: the *kyree* sniffed. *:But you wouldn't believe me.:*

"Warrl's right, Keth. I figured that he'd tell you if anything was wrong, so I wasn't going to jeopardize my chances by doing something marginally out of character. And I've been busy, as I said," Tarma replied, rubbing her eyes. "Damn, can't you do something about the way these spells of yours make my eyes itch?"

"Sorry; not even an Adept can manage that."

Tarma sighed. "Char has gotten the wind up about something—maybe he's even getting some rumors about *our* work, who knows? Anyway, he's been keeping me with him day *and* night until I could find somebody he trusts as much as me to spell me out. How is the conspiracy business going?"

Kethry smiled, and ran her hands through her hair. "Better than we'd hoped, in a lot of ways. Jadrek will be giving me the signal as soon as he's done with his latest client, so why don't we save our news until we're all together?"

"Fine by me; I don't suppose you've got anything to eat around here?"

"Why? Don't they feed you at the palace?"

"Having gotten leave to go, I wasn't about to stick around and maybe get called back just so I could feed my face," Tarma retorted.

Kethry raised one eyebrow. "Char's *that* nervy?"

Tarma spotted half a loaf of bread and a chunk of cheese on the table behind Kethry and reached forward to seize both. "He's that nervy," she agreed, slicing bits off the cheese with her belt-knife and alternating those tidbits with hearty bites of bread. She would have said more, but a gentle tapping came from the wall. Kethry jumped up out of her chair and faced the wall, holding both palms at shoulder height and facing it. The wall itself blurred for a little, then the door that had been hidden by Kethry's illusion swam into view. Jadrek pushed it open and stepped into the room.

There had not been a door there when they'd taken these two rooms; Jadrek's suite opened only into the inn, and Kethry's had two doors, the exterior and one like Jadrek's, opening on the inn corridor. But what could be done by hands could also be done by magic, and within one day of Kethry's taking possession of this room, she had made, then concealed, the door in their common wall. It was a real door and not a magic portal, just in case Jadrek ever needed to make use of it when Kethry was not present, for Kethry had set the spell of concealment so that he controlled it on his side of the wall.

"And how does the Master Astrologer?" asked Tarma, genially.

"Better than when he was Master Archivist," Jadrek chuckled. "I think I shall have Stefan find a successor. Astrology is a more lucrative profession!"

"Why am I not surprised?" Tarma asked sardonically. "Gentle lies always cost more than the truth. I take it none of your 'clients' have recognized you?"

"It wouldn't be likely," he replied mildly, taking the third, unoccupied seat around the little table. "Most of my 'clients' are merchants' wives. When would any of *them* have seen the Court Archivist?"

"Or, given your notable ability to fade into the background, noticed him if they'd seen him?" added Kethry. "All right—Tarma, love, you first."

"Right. Jadrek, I managed to deliver all but one of your messages; the one to Count Wulfres I left with Tindel. Wulfres wouldn't let me get near him; I can't much blame him, since I have been building quite a formidable reputation as Char's chief bullyboy."

"Is that why he trusts you?" Kethry asked.

"Partially. Don't worry, though. That reputation is actually doing me more good than harm. If anyone notices when I take somebody aside for a little chat, it doesn't do them any benefit to tell the King, because Char assumes I'm delivering threats!" She chuckled. "Keth, that Adept we took out was the only one Char had; the rest of his mages are Master and Journeyman class. So don't worry about this disguise continuing to hold."

Kethry heaved a sigh of profound relief. "Thank the gods for that. That *did* have me nervy. How are you getting on with Char? You said far better than we'd hoped—"

"That's a good summation; he *doesn't* trust any of his native Guards, and he doesn't trust his nobles. That leaves him with me, a couple of other landless mercs, and a handful of outland emissaries. Since I'm trying to give an imitation of a freefighter with a veneer of civilization and a range of interests slightly beyond 'food, fornication and fighting,' he seems to be gravitating more and more toward me."

"And needless to say, you're encouraging him."

:*Idra taught you well,*: Warrl commented. :*You encourage familiarity with the King while never going over the line of being social inferior. That takes a delicate touch I did not suspect you had, mindmate.*:

"Having you coaching me in my head hasn't hurt, Furball. Thanks to you, I've never once been even remotely disrespectful; been pounding heads when some of the Guards go over the line, in fact. And as a result Char's slowly taking me as cup-companion as well as bodyguard."

"That's certainly *far* better than we hoped!" Jadrek exclaimed.

"Tarma, what about Idra?" Kethry asked, both elbows on the table, chin in her hands. She looked unwontedly sober.

Tarma sighed, and rubbed one temple. "Keth, we both know by now she's got to be dead."

Kethry nodded, reluctantly, as Jadrek bit his lip. "I just didn't want to be the one to say it," she replied sadly. "Need's pull just hasn't been strong enough for her to have still been alive."

:*I, too, have suspected the same.*:

Tarma sighed. "I think I realized it—I mean, really *believed* it—a couple of days after—" She stopped for a moment, and looked squarely at Jadrek. *He's an outClansman*—she thought, weighing him in her mind. *—but—why not? No reason why he shouldn't know; if Keth has her way, he won't be an outClansman for long.* "—after I called one of the *leshya'e* and got the Star-Eyed Warrior instead, that night in Valdemar. You know, the evening when Roald and I came back as best of friends? He saw Her, too—and She made it clear to both of us that we were all on the same side. D'you remember how She turned the set of his Whites I was wearing black?"

Kethry nodded slowly, then real enlightenment dawned. "Black . . . is for vengeance and blood feud. . . ."

"Right," Tarma nodded. "She could have left my clothing alone; She could have changed it to brown, if She was truly offended at me being out of Kal'enedral colors, which I think is rather unlikely. She doesn't get that petty. But She didn't leave the Whites white—and She'd already convinced me that Roald and Stefansen were on the side of the righteous. She can be very subtle when She chooses, and She was trying to give me a subtle message, that I was back on blood-trail. So who would be the logical one for me to avenge—and who would be the logical target for vengeance?"

"Idra—and Char."

"Right and right again. My only questions *now* are—was it accident or premeditated, and how he did it." She tightened her jaw, and felt very nearly murderous at that moment. "And the closer I get to him, the likelier I am to find the answers to both."

She let the sentence hang for a long moment, then coughed slightly. "Jadrek? Your turn."

"I've been approached by three of those nobles you contacted for me, via their wives," he said, visibly shaken by Tarma's assertions—and yet, unsurprised by them, as if her words had only confirmed something he had known, but had not wished to acknowledge that he knew. "They were already planning some sort of action on their own, which, given their temperaments, was something I had thought fairly likely. In addition, I have been approached by those I did *not* expect—prelates of no less than five separate orders. It seems *they* had already spoken quietly with my chosen highborn—"

"And went on to you. Logical." Tarma nodded thoughtfully. "And what prompted *their* dissatisfaction?"

"Oh, a variety of causes—from the altruistic to the realistic." He wrinkled his brow in thought. "Mind you, I don't personally know as much about the clergy as I do the Court, but they seem to be appropriate responses given the personalities of those I spoke with and the philosophies of their orders."

"Huh. When we start to get *clergy* on our side. . . ." Tarma propped her feet up on the table, ignoring Kethry's frown of disapproval, and sat in thoughtful silence for a long time. "All right," she said, when the silence had begun to seem unbreakable, "It's time for some hard choices, friends. We're getting the support, and not only are we moving a bit ahead of schedule, but we're getting some unexpected help. So which of the plans are we going to follow?"

She tilted her head at Jadrek, who pursed his lips thoughtfully. "I'd rather not run a full-scale uprising, frankly," he said. "It's too unwieldy for this situation, *I* think; your commanders really have to be in the field for it to succeed. Tarma, you are the most militant of us, and we *need* you here—so that would leave me or Kethry."

"Not me," Kethry objected. "Fighters don't like following a mage, and I don't blame them. I'm no strategist, either."

"And I am neither fighter nor strategist," Jadrek replied.

"Stalemate," Tarma observed, flexing her shoulders to try and relax the tense muscles there. "Not that I don't agree with you both. Warrl?"

:*I, also. It is too easy to lose a civil war.*:

"All right, we're agreed that rousing the countryside is out, then?"

The other two nodded, slowly.

"Assassination."

:*That, I favor,*: Warrl replied, raising his head from his paws. :*It would be an easy thing for* me. *Wait until he is in the garden with a wench—over the wall—*: He snapped his jaws together suggestively. :*It would give me great pleasure, and I could easily be gone before alarm could be effective.*:

"Not clear-cut enough," Jadrek asserted. "There will always be those wanting to make a martyr out of Char. It's amazing how saintly a tyrant becomes after he's dead. We want Stefan *firmly* on the throne, or this country will be having as many problems as it already has, just different ones."

Warrl sighed, and put his head back down.

"Sorry, mindmate—I sympathize. That leaves the small-scale uprising; here, in the city. Can we pull *that* off?"

"Maybe. By Midsummer we'll have the working people solidly behind us; those that aren't losing half their incomes to Char's taxes are losing half their incomes because the others have less to spend," Kethry said, nibbling at her thumbnail. "What I've been working with are the merchants, and they are vastly discontent with the way things are going. If there's an uprising, they will be on our side of the riot. The problem is that these are *not* people used to fighting."

"Maybe not, but I'll bet most of them have a few hired fighters each, either as guards for themselves, or for their goods," Tarma pointed out. "If there were some way that we could promise that their property would stay safe, I'll bet they'd turn those fighters over to us for—say—two days.

Assuming that they are professional enough to fight together as a force instead of a gaggle of individuals."

"I'll work on that," Kethry replied.

"I suspect we'll have most of the clergy, too, by Midsummer," Jadrek offered. "And for many of the same reasons. And I know of at least two militant orders within the city walls. *Those* warriors *will* fight as a single unit."

"Good. What about the highborn? Don't they have retinues?"

Jadrek shook his head with regret. "No, not inside the city walls. That was one of Destillion's edicts; no noble can have more than four armed retainers when at Court. And *you* know the size of Char's guard force."

"He's got a small army, not even counting his personal guard," Tarma agreed ruefully. "Still—maybe I can come up with a notion. I might be able to work a bit of subversion in Char's forces, who knows? Let's stick with the local uprising plan. I think we're all agreed it's got the best chance of success."

She swung her feet down off the table, and noticed with surprise that the light coming through the closed shutters was red. "Damn! Sunset already? I've got to be getting back. Char's got another drunken orgy he's holding tonight, and wants his back safe."

Kethry mussed herself artistically, pulling one sleeve of her blouse so far down that a generous portion of breast was exposed. She stood up at the same moment as Tarma, followed her to the door, and let her out. For the benefit of anyone watching, they gave a well-acted imitation of a passionate farewell.

When Kethry finished locking the door behind Tarma, she turned to see that Jadrek was still sitting at the table, looking broodingly at a stain in the wood. She was not at all unhappy about that, because she had just about decided that certain other things were going to have to come to a head—one way or another.

"Still worried?" she asked, returning to her seat, and reaching out to touch her index finger to the wick of the candle standing in the middle of the table. It promptly ignited.

Jadrek had looked up as she had taken her chair, and watched her light the candle with rapt fascination. "I never get tired of seeing you do things like that," he said. "It's just—so—magical."

She laughed, and dispelled the illusion on herself. He relaxed visibly.

She raised an eyebrow, and he shrugged.

"I like you better this way," he confessed shyly. "The other—seems harder, somehow."

"Oh, she is; she's taking Arton for everything she can get," Kethry replied.

"To answer your question—yes, I'm still worried. But I also know that all three of us are doing the best that we can, so worrying isn't going to make a great deal of difference, one way or the other." He stood up, with visible reluctance. "I probably should leave you. . . ."

"Why?" Kethry asked, frankly. "Are you expecting anyone tonight?"

"Well, no, but—"

"Neither am I." She glanced at Warrl, who took the hint, padding through the still-open door between their rooms, shutting it behind him with a casual kick. Kethry moved closer to Jadrek before he could move away, not touching him but standing so near that their faces were within inches of each other.

"Jadrek, I want you to know that I find you very, very attractive."

His eyes registered his complete surprise as she deliberately held his gaze.

He licked his lips, nervously, and seemed utterly at a loss for anything to say.

"I also want you to know that I am *not* a virgin, and I'm perfectly capable of dealing with attentions that I don't welcome. You," she finished, "do not come under that category."

"I—you never stop surprising me. I hardly know what to say. . . ."

"Then don't say, do. Unless you don't find *me* attractive—"

Slowly he lifted one hand, and cupped it against her face. "Kethry—" he breathed, "Kethry, I find you very attractive. Almost unbearably attractive. But I'm not a young man—"

She echoed his gesture, his cheek warm beneath her hand. "If I wanted a young man, there's a tavern full downstairs. It's *you* I admire, Jadrek; the mind, the person. You're something special—something those pretty bodies downstairs aren't, and probably never will be."

Very hesitantly, he leaned forward and kissed her. She returned the kiss as passionately as she dared, and suddenly he responded by embracing her and prolonging the kiss until she was breathless.

When they broke apart, his gray eyes were dark with confusion. "Kethry—"

"There are more comfortable places to be doing this," she said, very softly. "Over there, for one." She nodded at the curtained bed, half-hidden in the shadows.

He blushed. He blushed even harder when she led him there by the hand, and all but pushed him down onto it. "I—" he stammered, looking past her, "Kethry, I'm not—very experienced at this sort of—"

"You were doing just fine a moment ago," she interrupted him gently, then prevented further protests by embracing him and resuming the kiss where it had been left off.

He seemed to hesitate for a moment, then seemed to make up his mind all in an instant, and returned her embrace with a fervor that at least equaled her own. He pulled her down beside him; she did not resist in the least, that being exactly what she wanted from him.

For a very long time, all they did was kiss and exchange halting, hesitant caresses, almost like a pair of naive youngsters. But when she returned every tenderness with more of the same, he grew braver, daring to undo the lacings of her dress, daring to touch her with fingers that slowly grew bolder.

He frequently stopped what he was doing for long moments, just to look at her, his eyes full of wonder, as if this was something more magical for him than all the exercising of her powers as a sorceress. As if he couldn't believe that she was returning touch for touch and emotion for emotion. When he did that, she had to fight to keep back the tears of sympathy—the only way she *could* was to keep a little corner of her mind free to concentrate on the hatred she felt for the women who must have treated him with coldness or indifference, so that *this* experience was such an unexpected revelation for him.

He stroked her with hands so gentle that she could hardly credit it. He was by no means the best lover she'd ever had; he was, perhaps, a little clumsy, and as he had confessed, not at all practiced—but his gentleness made up for that, and more.

And besides, she rather figured that she had experience enough for both of them.

When they finally joined together, it was like nothing she'd ever dreamed of, for her heart was as involved in the act as her body.

"Kethry—" he whispered hoarsely as he started to sit up—whispering into the darkness, for the candle had long since burned out. She could hear the beginnings of an apology in his voice, and interrupted him.

"Don't you *dare,*" she replied, reaching up for him and pulling him toward her so that his head rested on her shoulder. "Don't you *dare* spoil this with any of your nonsense about being old!"

"Then I—didn't make a fool of myself?" he asked shyly. "You don't want me to go?"

"You weren't making a fool of yourself any more than I was," she told him. "If showing how you feel is so very foolish. I don't think it is. And no, please, don't go. I *want* you to stay. I've had my fill of nights spent alone."

He sighed, and relaxed into her arms. "Kethry—I care for you, maybe more than I should."

She reached into the darkness, and brushed strands of damp hair from his forehead. "Don't think you're alone in caring more than you should." She let him take that in for a moment, then laughed, softly. "Or did you think I was only after you for your book collection?"

"Gods—Keth—" He who was usually so glib was once again at a loss for words, then he joined in her laughter. "No—I didn't; *Tarma,* on the other hand—"

They held each other for another long moment, until he spoke again. "Kethry, what we've got ahead of us—"

"—makes *promises* foolish," she interrupted him. "We've already made all the promises either of us dare to for now. Let's just enjoy what times we have, and worry about staying alive, shall we?"

"That's probably wise," he replied, with a reluctance that made her heart race.

He raised himself on his elbow for a moment, and cupped her face in both hands, and kissed her—kissed her in a way that made his words about not making promises a lie.

And eventually he fell asleep with his head cradled on her shoulder.

Kethry held him, her heart full of song.

Oh Windborn, this is *the one,* she thought, before she joined him in slumber. *He's—he's like something I've always missed, and never known I missed it until now. But now—I could never be content with anyone but him.*

Not ever again.

Eleven

Kethry sighed, rose from her chair, and went once more to the window. She stood there restlessly, leaning on the sill, with her chin in her hand, watching the street below; a dark silhouette against the oranges and reds of a spectacular sunset.

More than a hint of weariness in that sigh, Jadrek thought sympathetically, rubbing his tired eyes. *Last night was yet another late night, with both of us too exhausted at the end of it to do anything other than sleep. Tonight looks to be the same. There's never a moment to spare for simple things like food and sleep, much less anything else. I want to tell her how I feel—that I —I love her. But there never seems to be* any *time, much less the* right *time.*

He studied the way she was holding herself, the sagging shoulders, the way she kept turning her head a little to ease the stiffness he knew was in her neck because he had loosened those muscles for her far too many times of late. His own neck felt as stiff, and he felt echoes of those same aches in his own shoulders. *Gods. We're both tired, mentally and physically. She's spent more hours cajoling stubborn, suspicious merchants than I care to think about; I've spent almost the same number of hours dancing around the touchy sensibilities of priests and highborn. Not the way I would have chosen to spend our time, and both of us return from meetings so—completely drained. Conspiracy is for the young. Combining it with a love affair is insanity!*

Warrl gave an amused snort from where he lay curled on his chosen spot on the hearth. *:You manage well enough, wise one,:* the rough voice in Jadrek's mind said.

That is solely, I suspect, because our opportunities have numbered far less than our wishes, Jadrek thought at him, feeling a little more revived just by the casual contact with the *kyree*'s lively mind. *I fear that even the supposed wisdom of accumulated years fails to keep my desire from outstripping my capabilities. The only difference between my youth and my age is that now I am not ashamed to admit the fact.*

The *kyree* snorted contemptuously again, but Jadrek ignored him and continued. *Furthermore, I shudder to think what Tarma is likely to say about this liaison when she learns of it.*

:You know less about her than you think,: was the *kyree*'s enigmatic reply. Suddenly the great beast raised his head, and stared in the direction of the palace. *:A message—:*

"What?" Jadrek asked aloud, as Kethry turned to look sharply at the lupine creature.

:Tarma sends her regrets, but Char requires her presence, and she seems to think that the tran-*dust he intends to abuse this evening might make him talkative. Needless to say, she does not intend to miss her opportunity.:* The *kyree* turned warm and glowing eyes on the Archivist. *:She asks me to come to the stable at dark, so that she can return here afterward without worrying about spies on her backtrail. I would suggest, given your earlier plaint about not having any time to yourselves, that you might take advantage of the occasion that has been presented to you . . . unless you have other plans.:*

Jadrek nearly choked on a laugh at Kethry's indignant blush.

"I think we can find some way of filling in the time," he said aloud, as she glared at both of them.

The hour grew late; the candle burned down to a stub, and Kethry replaced it—and still no sign of Tarma. Jadrek regretted—more than once —that his ability to communicate with Warrl was sharply limited by distance.

Kethry suddenly dropped the candle end she was about to discard, and her whole body tensed.

"What?" Jadrek asked, anxiously, wondering if she had sensed some sort of occult probing in their direction.

"It's—anger," she replied, distantly. "Terrible, terrible *anger.* I've never felt anything like this in her before."

"Her? Her who?" She didn't answer him, and he said, a little more sharply, *"Who,* Keth? Keth?"

She shook her head as if to clear it, and resumed her seat at the table, but he could see that her hands were trembling before she clasped them in front of her on the table to conceal the fact.

"Keth?" he repeated gently, but insistently.

"It's—it's the *she'enedran* bond between us," she said at last. "We each can feel things the other does, sometimes. Jadrek, she's in a killing rage; she's just barely keeping herself under control! And I *can't* tell why."

She looked up at him, and he could see fear, the mirror to his own, in her eyes. "I've never felt anything like this out of her; she's usually so controlled, even when *I'm* ready to spit nails. It has to be something Char said or did—but what could bring *her* to the brink like this? There's enough rage resonating down the bond that *I'm* half prepared to go kill something!"

"I don't know," he said slowly. "And I'm almost afraid to find out."

They stared at each other helplessly, until finally he reached out and laid his hand over her clenched ones, offering what little comfort he had to give.

After that, it was just the deadly waiting.

Finally, after both of them had fretted themselves into a state of nervous exhaustion, they heard Warrl's nails clicking on the wooden steps outside. Tarma's presence was revealed only by the creaking of the two trick boards, one in the fifth step, one in the eighth—otherwise she never made a sound. Kethry jumped to her feet, ran to the door and flung it open.

Tarma/Arton stood in the light streaming from the door, so very still that for a moment Jadrek wasn't entirely certain she was breathing. She remained in the doorway for a long, long moment, her face utterly expressionless—except for the eyes, which burned with a rage so fierce Kethry stepped back an involuntary pace or two.

Warrl came up from behind her and nudged Tarma's hand with his nose; only then did she seem to realize where she was, and walk slowly inside, stopping only when she came to the table.

She did not take a seat as she usually did; she continued to stand, half-shrouded in shadows, and looked from Jadrek to Kethry and back again. Finally she spoke.

"I've found out what happened to Idra."

". . . so once Char had downed a full bottle of brandy to enhance the *tran,* he'd gotten himself into a mood where he was talkative, but wasn't really thinking about what he was saying."

Kethry tensed, feeling Tarma's anger burning within *her,* a half-mad fire at the pit of her stomach.

Tarma spoke in a tonelessly deadly voice, still refusing to seat herself. "Alcohol and *tran* have that effect in combination—connecting the mind to the mouth without letting the intellect have any say in what comes out. And as I'd been hoping, his suspicious nature kept him from wanting to confide in any of his courtiers. And there was good old Arton, so sympathetic, so reliable, always dependable. So he threw his rump-kissers out, and began telling me how everybody abused him, everybody turned on him. Especially his sister."

She shifted her weight a little; the floorboard creaked beneath her, and Kethry could feel the anger rising up her spine. *Channel that*—she told herself, locking her will into Adept's discipline. *There's enough pure rage here to burn half the city down, if you channel it. Use the anger*—don't *let it use you!*

With that invocation of familiar discipline came a certain amount of relief; the fires were partially contained, harvested against future need. It wasn't perfect; she was still trembling with emotion, but at least the energy wasn't being all wasted.

And there will be future need—

"Then he told me about how his sister had first supported him, then betrayed him. How he had known from the first that the hunt for the lost sword had been nothing more than a ruse to get her across the border and into contact with Stefan. He carried on about that for long enough to just about put me to sleep; what an ungrateful, cold bitch she was, how she deserved the worst fate anyone could imagine. He was pretty well convinced she was *she'chorne,* too, and you know how they feel about that here—I had just about figured that was all I was going to get out of him, when suddenly he stopped raving."

Kethry felt a prickle of fear when the bond of *she'enedran* between herself and Tarma transmitted another surge of the incredibly cold rage her oathsister was feeling. *I've never known anyone who could sustain that kind of emotion for this long without berserking.* Had Tarma been anything other than Kal'enedral—someone, or several someones, would be long dead by now, hacked into many small pieces. . . .

" 'I *fixed* her,' he said. 'I fixed her properly. I planned it all so beautifully, too. I had Zaras bespell one of his apprentices to look like me, and sent the apprentice off with the rest of the Court on a three-day hunt. Then Zaras and I waited for the bitch in the stables; I distracted her, he hit her from behind with a spell, and when she woke up, her body belonged to Zaras. He had her saddle up and ride out just as if it were any other day, but this time her destination was *my* choice. We took her to the old tower on the edge of Hielmarsh; it's deserted, and the rumors I had spread about hauntings keep the clods away.' "

From there, what Tarma told them horrified even Kethry, inured to the brutality of warfare as she was. And she, of the three of them, had been the least close to the Captain; Tarma's own internal torment was only too plain to her oathsister, who was continuing to share in it—and Jadrek's expression could not be described.

Idra's torture and "punishment" had begun with the expedient most commonly used to break a woman—multiple rape. Rape in which her own brother had been the foremost participant. Char's methods and means when that failed became more exotic. Jadrek excused himself halfway through the toneless recitation to be audibly sick. When he returned, pale, shaking and sweating with reaction, Tarma had nearly finished. Kethry's stomach was churning and her throat was choked with silent weeping.

"His own *sister*—" Kethry shuddered, her eyes burning and blurring with her tears. "No matter *how* much he hated her, she was still his *sister!*"

Tarma came closer, looming over the table like a dark angel. She took the dagger from her belt, and held it out into the light of the table-candle. She held it stiffly, point down, in a fist clenched so tightly on the hilt that her knuckles were white.

"Oathbreaker, I name him," Tarma said, softly, but with all the feeling that she had not given vent to behind the words of the ages-old ritual of Outcasting. "Oathbreaker he, and all who stand by him. Oathbreaker once—by the promises made to kin, then shattered. Oathbreaker twice—by the violation of king-oath to liegeman. Oathbreaker three times—Oathbreaker a *thousand* times—by the violation of every kin-bond known and by the shedding of shared blood."

"Oathbreaker, I name him," Kethry echoed, rising to place her cold hand over Tarma's, taking up the thread of the seldom-used passage from the Mercenaries' Code. She choked out her words around a knot of black anger and bleak mourning, both so thick and dark that she could barely manage to speak the ritual coherently through the chaos of her emotions. She was still channeling, but now she was channeling the emotion through the words of the ritual. Emotion *was* power; that was what made a death-curse so potent, even in the mouth of an untutored peasant. This may well once have *been* a spell—and it was capable of becoming one again. She knew that even though she was no priest, channeling *that* much emotion-energy through it had the potential of making the Outcasting into something more than "mere ritual."

"Oathbreaker I do name him, mage to thy priest. Oathbreaker once—" she choked, hardly able to get the words out, "by the violation of sacred bonds. Oathbreaker twice—by the perversion of power granted him for the common weal to his own ends. Oathbreaker three times—by the invocation of pain and death for pleasure."

Somewhat to her surprise, she saw Jadrek stand, place his trembling, damp hand atop hers, and take up the ritual. She had never guessed that he knew it. "Oathbreaker, I name him, and all who support him," he said, though his voice shook. "Oathbreaker I do name him, who am the common man of good will, making the third for Outcasting. Oathbreaker once—by the lies of his tongue. Oathbreaker twice—by the perversion of his heart. Oathbreaker three times—by the giving of his soul willingly to darkness."

Tarma slammed the dagger they all had been holding into the wood of the table with such force that it sank halfway to the hilt. "Oathbreaker is his name," she snarled. "All oaths to him are null. Let every man's hand be against him; let the gods turn their faces from him; let his darkness rot him from within until he be called to a just accounting. *And may the gods grant that* mine *be the hand!*"

She brought herself back under control with an effort that was visible, and turned a face toward them that was no longer impassive, but was just as tear-streaked as Kethry's own. "This is the end of it: he couldn't break her. She was too tough for him, right up to the last. He didn't get one word out of her, not one—and in the end, when he thought his bullyboys had her restrained, she managed to break free long enough to grab a knife and kill herself with it."

The fire-and-candle light flared up long enough to show that the murderous rage was still burning in her, but still under control. "I damn near killed him myself, then and there. Warrl managed to keep me from painting the room with his blood. It would have been suicide, and while it would have left the throne free for Stefan, I'd have left at least two friends behind who would have been rather unhappy that I'd gone and gotten myself killed by the rest of Char's Guard."

" 'Unhappy' is understating the case," Jadrek replied gently, slowly resuming his seat. "But yes—at least two. Good friend—sister—please sit." Kethry could see tears still glinting in his eyes—but she could also see that he was thinking *past* his grief; something she and Tarma couldn't quite manage yet.

As Tarma lowered herself stiffly into her accustomed chair, he continued. "Our plans have been plagued by the inability to bring a force of trained fighters whose loyalty is unswervingly ours into the city. Now I ask you, who served under Idra—*what would her Sunhawks think to hear this?"*

"Gods!" Kethry brought her fist to her mouth, and bit her knuckles hard enough to break the skin. "They'd want revenge, just like us—and *not* just them, but every man or woman who *ever* served as a Hawk!"

Jadrek nodded. "In short—an army. *Our* army. One that won't swerve from their goal for any reason, or be stopped by anything short of the death of every last one of them."

Now, for a brief time, they fought their battle with pen and paper. Messages, coded, in obscure dialects, or (rarely) in plain tradespeech left the city every day that there was someone that they judged was trustworthy enough to carry them. Tarma, from her position as trusted insider, was able to tell them that the few messages that were intercepted baffled Char's adherents, and were dismissed out of hand as merchant-clan warring. The rest went south and east, following the trade roads, to find the men and women who wore (or had once worn) the symbol of the Sunhawk.

The answers that returned were not of paper and ink, but flesh and blood—and of deadly anger.

The last time Justin Twoblade and his partner had entered Petras, it had been with a feeling of pleasant anticipation. Petras had been the turnaround point for the caravan they'd been guarding, and it was well known for its wines and its wenches. He'd had quite a lively time of it, that season in Petras.

Now he entered the city a second time, again as a caravan guard. Three things differed: he would not be leaving, at least not with the traders he was guarding; his partner was not Ikan Dryvale—

And his mood was not pleasant.

He and his partner parted company with the caravan as soon as their clients had selected a hostelry, taking their pay with them in the form of the square silver coins that served as common currency among the traders of most of this part of the world. Then, looking in no way different than any other mustered-out guards, they collected their small store of belongings, loaded them on their horses, and headed for a district with a more modest selection of inns.

And if they seemed rather heavily armed and armored, well, they *had* been escorting jewel traders; it was only good sense to arm heavily when one escorted such tempting targets.

"What was the name of that inn we're looking for?" Justin asked his new partner, his voice pitched only just loud enough to be heard over the street noise. "I didn't quite catch it from the contact."

"The Fountain of Beer," Kyra replied, just as quietly, her eyes flicking from side to side in a way that told Justin she was watching everything about her without making any great show of doing so.

"I suspect that's it ahead of us." His hands were full; reins of his horse in the left, pack in the right, so he pointed with his chin. The sign did indeed sport a violently yellow fountain that was apparently spouting vast quantities of foam.

"If you'll take care of the lodgings, I'll take care of the stableman," Kyra offered. "We've both got tokens; one of us should hit on a contact if we try both."

"Good," Justin replied shortly; they paused just at the inn gate and made an exchange of packs and reins. Kyra went on into the stableyard with their horses, as he sought the innkeeper behind his bar.

Justin bargained heatedly for several minutes, arriving at a fee of two silver for stabling, room and meals for both; but there was a third coin with the two square ones he handed the innkeeper—a small, round, bronze coin, bearing the image of a rampant hawk on one side and the sun-in-glory on the other. It was, in fact, the smallest denomination of coin used in Hawksnest—used *only* in Hawksnest, and almost never seen outside of the town.

The innkeeper neither commented on the coin, nor returned it—but he *did* ask *"Justice* Twoblade?" when registering them on his rolls.

"Justice" was one of the half-dozen recognition words that had come with Justin's message.

"Justin," the fighter corrected him. "Justin of the Hawk."

That was the appropriate answer. The man nodded, and replied, "Right. *Justice."*

Justin also nodded, then stood at the bar and nursed a small beer while he waited for Kyra to return. The potboy showed them to a small, plain room on the ground floor at the back of the inn.

"Stableman's one contact for certain sure," Kyra told him as soon as the boy had left. "He wished me 'justice,' I gave 'im m'name as Kyra Brighthawk, and then 'e tol' me t' wait fer a visitor."

"Innkeeper's another, gave me the same word. Always provided we aren't in a trap." Justin raised one laconic eyebrow at Kyra's headshake. "My child, you don't grow to be an *old* fighter without learning to be suspicious of your own grandmother. I would suggest to you that we follow 'enemy territory' rules."

Kyra shrugged. "You been the leader; I'll live with whatever ye guess we should be doin'."

Justin felt of the bed, found it satisfactory, and stretched his lanky body on it at full length. "It is a wise child that obeys its elders," he said sententiously, then quirked one corner of his mouth. "It is also a child that *may* live to *become* an elder."

Kyra shrugged good-naturedly.

A few moments later, the boy returned with a surprisingly good dinner for two, which he left. Justin examined it with great care, by smell and by cautious taste.

"Evidently we aren't supposed to leave," Justin guessed, "And if this stuff has been tampered with, *I* can't tell it."

Kyra followed his careful inspection of the food with one of her own. "Nor me, an' my grandy was a wisewoman. I don' know about you, friend, but I could eat raw snake."

"Likewise. My lady?" Justin dug a healthy portion out of the meat pie they'd been served, and handed it to her solemnly.

She accepted it just as solemnly. It might have been noted, had there been anyone else present, that neither partook of anything the other had already tried. If any of the food *had* been 'tampered with,' it would likely be only one or two dishes. If that were the case—*one* of them would still be in shape to deal with the consequences.

When, after an hour, nothing untoward happened to either of them, Justin grinned a little sheepishly.

"Well—"

"Don't apologize," Kyra told him. "I tell ye, I druther eat a cold dinner than find m'self wakin' up lookin' at the wrong end'f somebody's knife."

They demolished the rest of the food in fairly short order—then began another interminable wait. After a candlemark of pacing, Kyra finally dug a long branch of silvery derthenwood out of her pack, as well as a tiny knife with a blade hardly bigger than a pen nib. She sat down on the floor next to the bed and began the slow process of turning the branch into a carved chain. Justin watched her from half-closed eyes, fascinated in spite of himself by the delicate work. The chain had only a few links to it when the wait began; when it ended, there was scarcely a fingerlength of branch remaining.

Then, without warning, a portion of the wall blurred and Kethry stepped through it.

Kethry just held out her arms, welcoming both of them into an embrace which included tears from all three of them.

"Gods, Keth—" Justin finally pulled away, reluctantly. "It has been so damned *hard* keeping this all inside."

"I know; none better—Windborn, I cannot tell you how glad I am to see *you* two! You're the first to come; may the Lady forgive me, but there were times I wondered if this was going to work."

"Oh, it's working all right; better than you could guess." He wiped his eyes and nose on the napkin from their tray and locked his emotions down. "All right, lady-mage, we need information, not waterfalls."

"First—tell me how you got here so fast."

"We weren't *about* t' let anybody beat us here," Kyra replied. "Not after that message. Sewen sent me on ahead t' tell ye that Queen Sursha give us leave t' deal with this soon's we get some of her new army units in t' replace us. The rest of the Hawks'll be here in 'bout a month."

"Ikan's out rounding up all the former Hawks we can track down," Justin continued. "We'll be trickling in the same as the Hawks will—no more than two or three at a time, and disguised. One of the merchant houses is going to let some of us use their colors; Ikan took the liberty of taking your name in vain to old Grumio. We have the support of Sursha's Bards, and half a dozen holy orders. We'll be everything from wandering entertainers to caravan guards. You've got a plan, I take it?"

"Tarma has; she's worked it out with a couple of highborn we can trust," Kethry told him. "All I really know about is my part of it, but generally we're hoping to accomplish the whole thing with a minimum of bloodshed."

"Specific blood," Kyra replied, with a smoldering anger Justin shared.

"Oh, yes. One of the lot we've already taken out—Raschar's Adept. But the others—" Kethry allowed her own anger to show. "—Tarma's identified every person that had a hand in the deed. And they *will* answer to us."

Justin nodded, slowly. "What about arms? There's going to be at least half of us without much, given the disguises."

"Being smuggled in to us from an outside source, so that Char won't be alerted that something's up by activity in forges and smithies. We're getting everything Tarma could think of; bows, arrows with war-points, various kinds of throwing knives, grapnels, climbing spikes, pikes, swords —the last is the hardest, that, and armor, but we're hoping most of you will manage to bring your own. Do either of you have a guess how many there might be that we can count on?"

"Six hundred at an absolute minimum," Justin said with grim satisfaction. "That's four hundred Hawks and the two hundred that either retired to Hawksnest or that Ikan knows for a fact he can get hold of and will want in."

"Gods—that's better than I'd hoped," Kethry said weakly. "There're four hundred regular troops here, about a hundred and fifty assorted militia, and fifty personal guards belonging to Char. There're some other assorted fighters, but Tarma tells me they won't count for much; there're Char's adherents, and their private guards, but we don't know but that they won't turn their coats or hide if things look chancy. That means we'll be going pretty much one-on-one; all the professionals starting the fight even."

"Even with his mages?" Justin asked dubiously.

Kethry raised her chin, her eyes glinting like emerald ice in the light from the window beside her. "He hasn't a mage that can come close to me in ability, and I have more power at my disposal than any of them could hope for."

"Where are you getting *that* kind of power?" Justin asked in surprise. "I mean—you're alone—"

"You—and the Hawks. Your anger. I can't begin to tell you how strong a force I've already tapped off just you two; when I start to think about *six hundred* Hawks, it makes *my* head reel. It's the kind of power a mage sees perhaps once in a lifetime, and if I weren't an Adept I'd never be able to touch it, much less control it."

"You're *Adept* class now?" Justin said incredulously. "Great good gods —no wonder you aren't worried!"

"Not with power like that at my disposal. I can channel all that anger, harvest it, and save it for the hour of striking. *We're* the attackers, this time. I can set up as many spells as it takes as far in advance as I need to, spells specifically designed to take out each mage; and wait until the moment of attack to trigger them. I'm assuming only half of those will work. The rest will probably be deflected. But the mages will be off-balance, and I can take them out one at a time. I know how mages think —when they're under magical attack they tend to ignore anything mundane, and they seldom or never work together. White Winds is one of the few schools that teaches working in concert. I think we can plan that they will be concentrating on *me* and not on anything nonmagical. And that they won't even think to band together against me."

Justin nodded, satisfied. "Sounds like you people have a pretty good notion of what you're about. Now comes the hard part."

"Uh-huh," Kethry nodded. "Waiting."

* * *

Singly, or by twos and threes, the Hawks came, just as Justin had told Kethry they would. Each of them arrived in some disguise, some seeming utterly harmless—a peasant farmer here, a party of minstrels there, a couple of merchant apprentices. Day by day they trickled into Petras, and no one seemed to notice that they never left it again. Each went to one of the dozen inns whose masters had bought into the conspiracy, carrying with them a small bronze coin and a handful of recognition words. Each was met by Kethry, or by one of the other "official greeters"—Justin, Kyra or Ikan, who had arrived within days of the first two.

From there, things got far more complicated than even most of these professional mercenaries were used to.

Beaker coughed, scratched his head, and turned his weary donkey in to what passed for a stableman at the Wheat Sheaf inn. The stableman here was, like most of the clients, of farm stock; and probably had never even seen a warhorse up close, much less handled one. Beaker's dusty donkey was far more in his line of expertise. The "stable" was a packed-earth enclosure with a watering trough and a pile of hay currently being shared by three other mangy little donkeys and a brace of oxen. Beaker had serious second and third thoughts about *this* being the contact point for a rebel force, but the instructions had said the Wheat Sheaf and specified the stableman as the contact.

"Ye wanta watch that one," Beaker drawled, handing the wizened peasant the rough rope of the donkey's halter with one hand, and four coins with the other—three copper pennies and one bronze Hawkpiece. "She'll take *revenge* if she even thinks ye're gonna lay hand to 'er."

"Oh, aye, I know th' type," the fellow replied, grinning, and proving that a good half of his teeth had gone with his lost youth. "Ol' girl like this, she hold a grudge till *judgment* day, eh?" He pocketed all four coins without a comment.

Well, that was the proper sign and counter. Beaker felt some of his misgivings slide away, and ambled on into the dark cave of the rough-brick inn.

Like most of its ilk, it had two floors, each one large room. The upper would have pallets for sleeping; the lower had a huge fireplace at one end where a stout middle-aged woman was tending an enormous pot and a roast of some kind. It was filled with clumsy benches and trestle tables now, but after the inn shut down for the night, those that could not afford a pallet upstairs would be granted leave to sleep on table, bench, or floor beneath for half the price of a pallet. Opposite the fireplace was the "bar"; a stack of beer kegs and a rack of mugs, presided over by the innkeeper.

Beaker debated looking prosperous, when his stomach growled and made the decision for him. He paid the innkeeper for a mug of beer, a bowl of soup and a slice of roast; the man took his money, gave him his drink and a slice of not-too-stale bread. Beaker slid his pack off his back, rummaged his own bowl and spoon out of it, then shrugged it back on before weaving his way through the tables to the monarch of the "kitchen."

Rather to his surprise—the inn staff of places like this one were rather notorious for being surly—the woman gave him a broad smile along with a full bowl, and put a reasonably generous slice of meat on his bread. Juggling all three carefully, he took a seat as near to the door as possible, and sat down to eat.

The food was another pleasant surprise; fresh and tasty and stomach-filling. And the inn was cool after the heat and dust of the road. The beer was doing a respectable job of washing the grit out of his throat. Beaker was about halfway through his meal when he heard someone come up behind him.

"How's the food t'day, sojer?"

Beaker grinned and turned in his seat. "Kyra, when are you gonna get rid of that damn accent?"

"When cows fly, prob'ly. Makes me fit in here, though." She straddled the bench beside him, a mug and bowl of her own in hand. "Eat here ev'ry chance I get. Ma Kemak, she sure can cook. Pa Kemak don' water the beer, neither. Finish that up, boy. We gotta get you off th' street soon's we can." She set him a good example by nearly inhaling her soup.

From the inn Kyra led Beaker on a rambling stroll designed to shake off or bore any pursuit, bringing him at last to the stableyard entrance of a wealthy merchant. A murmured word with the chief stableman got them inside; from there they slipped in the servant's door and climbed a winding staircase to the attic of the house. Normally a room like this was crowded with the accumulated junk of several generations, now it was barren except for a line of pallets. There were only two windows—both shuttered—but there was enough light that Beaker could recognize most of those sprawled about the room.

"Beat you, Birdbrain," Garth mocked from a corner; looking around, Beaker could see that a good half of the pallets were occupied—and that evidently, he was the last of Tarma's scout troop to arrive.

"Well, hell, if they'd given me somethin' besides a half-dead dwarf donkey t' *get* here on—"

"No excuse," Jodi admonished. "Tresti and I were Shayana mendicants; we came here on our own two feet."

"Beaker, what have you got in the way of arms?" asked someone off on the opposite side of the room; peering through the attic gloom, Beaker could make out that the speaker was a skirmisher he knew vaguely, a Hawk called Vasely.

"One short knife, and my sword," he replied. "And I've got my brigandine under this shirt."

"Get over here and pick out what you want, then. Take whatever you think you can use, we aren't short of anything but swords and body-armor."

Beaker crossed the attic, picking his way among the pallets, and sorted through the piles of arms. Shortly thereafter he was being caught up on the developments by his fellow scouts.

He learned that they hid their faces by day, slipping out only at night to meet in the ballrooms and stableyards of the great lords who had also joined the conspiracy. There they would hear whatever news there was to hear, and practice their skills.

Each night, as the Hawks gathered to spar, Kethry would siphon off the incredibly dangerous energy of their anger and hate. Dangerous, because the energy generated by negative emotions was hard to control—and attracted some very undesirable other-planar creatures. But it was a potent force, and one Kethry was not going to let go unused. She channeled what she accumulated each night into the dozen trap-spells she was building, one for each of Char's mages. She was beginning to think that she might well be able to carry this off—for despite her brave words to Justin, she had no idea if what she planned was going to work, nor how well. She was just too new at being Adept to be certain exactly what her capabilities were.

"I wish you'd tell me what you're going to do," Jadrek said plaintively. He'd been watching her as she traced through the last of the parchment diagrams, laying in the power she had acquired that night. There were times his patience astounded her still. . . .

"I didn't realize you'd want to know," she replied, sealing the new layer of power in place, and looking up at him with surprise as she finished. "Come around here behind me and have a look, then."

He rose, moved to her right shoulder, and bent over the table with his expression sharp with curiosity. "Well, you *know* I'm not a mage, but I *do* know some of the mage-books—and Keth, what you've been doing doesn't even look remotely familiar."

"You know what a trap-spell is. That's this part." She leaned over the parchment and pointed out the six tiny diagrams encircling the last mage's Name, as he looked over her shoulder with acute interest she could feel without even seeing his face.

"That's just the part that's like a trigger on a physical trap, right?"

"Exactly, except that what will activate the trigger *won't* be something the mage does, but something *I* do—a kind of a mental twist to release the rest of it."

He examined the elaborately inscribed sheet with care, leaning on the back of Kethry's chair, and not touching the page. "That looks familiar enough from my reading—but what's all the rest of this?"

"That's something new, something I put together. There's a mind-magic technique called a 'mirror-egg' that Roald told me about," she said, sitting back. He responded to her movement by beginning to massage her neck as she talked. "It involves surrounding someone with an egg-shaped shield that is absolutely reflective on the inside. It's something you do, he told me, when you've got a projective that refuses to lock his mind-Gift down, or is using it harmfully. Everything he projects after that gets flung straight back into his face—Roald says it's a pretty effective way of teaching someone when admonishment fails."

"I would think so," Jadrek agreed.

"Ah—" his gentle hands hit a particularly tense spot, and Kethry fell silent until he'd gotten the muscles looser. "I thought about it, and it occurred to me that there was no reason why the same kind of thing couldn't be applied to magical energy. So I found a spell to make a mirrored shield, and another to shape a shield into an egg shape, and combined them. That's this bit." She traced the twisted patterns with her finger above the diagram. "When Jiles got here, he agreed to let me throw one on him as a test."

"It worked?"

"Better than either of us had guessed. Scared him white. You see, with most other trap-spells if you have the patience to work your way through it, you can find the keypoint and get yourself loose by cutting it. Not this one—because everything you do reflects back at you. There're only two ways to break this one—from the outside, or to build up such pressure *inside* that the spell can't contain it."

Jadrek pondered that in silence for a moment, while Kethry let her head sag and reveled in the relaxation his hands were leaving in their wake.

"What's to keep the mages from building up that kind of pressure?" he asked at last.

"Nothing—*if* they can. But if they try—and they don't figure out that they're going to have to shield themselves within the shield—they'll fry themselves before they free themselves."

Jadrek spoke slowly, and very quietly. "That—is *not* a nice spell. . . ."

"These aren't nice people," Kethry replied, recalling all the soul-searching she'd done before deciding that this *was* the thing to do. "Frankly, if I could call lightnings down on all of them, I would, and take the guilt on my soul. I agree, it isn't a thing one should use lightly, and just before I trigger the traps, I intend to burn the papers. I won't need them any more at that point, and I'd rather that the knowledge didn't get into too many hands just yet."

"And later? How do you keep someone else from finding out how you did it? What if—"

"Gods—Jadrek, love, once a thing's been thought of—it gets out, no matter what. So once this is all over with, I'm going to arrange for the information to be sent to every mage school I know of, and spread it as far and wide as I can."

"What?" Jadrek asked, so aghast that he stopped massaging.

"You can't stop knowledge; you shouldn't try. If you do, half the time it's the wrong people that get it first. So I'm doing the best thing you *can* do with something like this—making sure *everybody* knows about it. That way, if it's used, it will be recognized. Mages trapped inside one of these eggs will realize what's happened and get outside help before they hurt themselves, ones outside will know the counter."

"Oh," he said, resuming what he'd broken off. There was silence for a while as he plainly pondered what she'd said.

One more thing to love about him. He doesn't always agree with me, but he hears me out, and he thinks about what I've said before making up his own mind.

"Huh," he said, when she'd begun to drowse a little under his gentle ministrations. "I guess you're right; if you can't guarantee that something harmful stays out of the wrong hands—"

"And I can't; there's no way."

"Then see that all the right hands get it."

"And that they get the antidote. I don't know that this is all that moral, Jadrek, I only know that the alternative—taking the chance that someone like Zaras figures out what I did *first*—is less moral." She sighed. "I never thought that becoming an Adept would bring all these moral predicaments with it."

He kissed the top of her head. "Keth, power brings with it the need to make moral judgments; history proves that. You have no choice but to make those decisions."

She sighed again, and reached up to lay one of her hands across his where it rested on her shoulder. "I just hope that I always have someone around to keep reminding me when something I'm thinking about doing 'isn't nice.' I may still *do* it—but I'd better have good reasons for doing so."

He squeezed her shoulder, gently. "Don't worry. As long as I'm around, you will."

That's what I hoped you'd say, she thought to herself, closing her eyes and leaning back. *That is exactly what I hoped you'd say.*

Twelve

"Tarma—"

Tarma looked up from the maps spread before her to see Jadrek nudging his way into the knot of fighters she was tutoring. She'd had ample time to learn every twist and turn of the maze within the Palace, and she was endeavoring to make sure every person of the secret army knew every corridor and storeroom before the planned coup. She felt a twinge of excitement when she saw that Jadrek's expression was at once tense and anticipatory.

She excused herself and turned her pupils over to Jodi. "What is it?" she asked him quietly, not wanting to raise hopes that might be dashed in the next moment. "You look like you've swallowed a live fish, and you're not certain if you're enjoying the experience."

He raised an eyebrow. "You aren't far wrong; that's about how my stomach is feeling. Stefan's in Petras."

"Warrior's Oath!" She bared her teeth in a feral grin as those nearby glanced at her in startlement. Although they had been planning for this very moment, suddenly *she* felt rather as though the fish was wriggling about in *her* stomach.

"When? How long ago did you make contact? Where is he now?"

"About three candlemarks ago, and he's with Keth at the inn; it seemed the safest place for him."

"All right—this is it. He's here, we're ready. Let me get Sewen and Ikan, and I'll meet you at Kethry's." She turned on her heel and began making her way across the crowded, dimly lit ballroom. She kept sight of

Jadrek as he slipped back out the door, and she noticed that he was slump-shouldered and limping slightly.

Poor devil, he looks like warmed-over death. All this is giving me energy, but it's sapping his. Keth, too. Talk all day, plot all night, spellcast when you aren't plotting—

:Chase one another around the bedroom when you aren't spellcasting—: Warrl broke into her thoughts.

Still at it, are they? Tarma thought at him. *Well, if the liaison has survived this much stress for this long, Keth's right about him being The One. Good. I'd welcome Jadrek as Clanbrother with no reservations. He's the closest thing I've seen since Keth to a Shin'a'in.*

:And he has more sense than both of you put together. You know, he still thinks you don't know about the love affair,: Warrl chuckled. *:Keth hasn't enlightened him. I can't read her as easily as I can him, what with all her mage-shields, so I don't know why she hasn't told him that you knew about it from the first. She might assume he knows you know—or she might be waiting to see how he handles the situation.:*

I suspect the latter, given Keth's devious mind. Hmm. If anyone would know about Jadrek's condition, you would; you're practically in his pocket most of the day. He was limping—how's he doing, physically?

:Extremely well; his bones only bother him when he's very tired, like to-night, or very chilled. Need knows how Kethry worries about him, so Need takes very good care of him.:

Good enough to make the Palace assault with us? We need his knowledge.

:I would judge so. He'll have every fighter of the Hawks watching out for him, after all.:

Hai. He'll probably come out better than the rest of us will. Well—back to business.

She had reached Sewen and Ikan by the end of that mental conversation, which had all taken place in the space of a few heartbeats. They looked up at her approach, and knowing her as well as they did, she reckoned they would have no trouble reading the news in her eyes.

"Time, is it?" Sewen straightened, and rolled up the map they'd been working with.

She nodded. "He's here." No need to say *who* "he" was—not when all they lacked for the past several days to put the plan into motion had been Stefansen's physical presence. "Keth's room. Ready?"

Both nodded; Ikan signaled Justin, who came to take his place, Sewen did the same with the scout Mala. Within moments the three of them, darkly cloaked and moving like shadows through the ill-lit streets, were on their way to Kethry's room.

Warrl, as always, told the others of their approach; Kethry was at the door before they set foot on the staircase, and held it open just enough that they could slip inside.

Jadrek was already there, seated at the table; beside him, looking somehow far more princely than Tarma had remembered, was Stefansen.

It was Stefansen the ruler who rose to greet them; to clasp the hands and shoulders of both Ikan and Sewen with that same ease and frank equality Idra had always shown, and thank them for their presence and help with a sincerity that none of them doubted. The meeting was, in some ways, rather unnerving for Sewen and Ikan; Tarma knew how much like his sister Stefansen looked, but the others hadn't been warned. And in the soft light from their candles the resemblance was even stronger. Tarma could almost hear their thoughts—shock, a touch of chill at the back of the neck—

Then they shook themselves into sense.

Kethry gestured, bringing three more chairs into abrupt existence, as Jadrek unrolled the first of a series of maps on the table. All six of them seated themselves almost simultaneously; Stefansen cleared his throat, and the odd note in the sound caught Tarma's attention—and by the way the other two looked up at him in startlement, Sewen's and Ikan's as well.

"Jadrek has kept me appraised of what's been going on," he said, with a kind of awkward hesitation that he had not displayed before. "So I *know* the reason all you Sunhawks are here. I don't—I don't deal well with emotion, it's hard for me to say things that I feel. But I just want you to know that I—understand. I have half a dozen reasons for wanting to roast Char over a slow fire, and that one is at the top of the list. But I think all of you have a prior claim on his hide. I was never as close to Idra as even the lowliest of her Hawks. So—if it's possible—when this is over, he's yours."

Sewen's eyes lit at those words. "The Hawks thank you for that, Highness—an' I'll tell you true, they'll fight all the better for the knowing of the promise."

"It only seemed fair. . . ." He looked straight into Tarma's eyes, as if asking whether this had been the wise choice. She nodded slightly, and he looked easier.

"Very well, gentlemen, ladies—" he said after a moment of silence. "All the pieces are on the game board. Shall we begin?"

* * *

It was Midsummer's Night, and folk in carnival garb thronged the streets. Among the mob of wildly costumed maskers, who would notice six hundred-odd more celebrants?

Who would notice masks on a night of masking? Who would note six hundred-odd sets of phony weaponry among so many thousand tawdry pieces of junk like them? Who would take alarm from another merchant or peasant playing at warrior?

Except that beneath the cheap gilding and pasted-on glass jewels, beneath the paper and the tinsel, the arms and armor of *this* lot were very real.

This was the night of all nights that the rebels had hoped to be able to use—in part because of the ability to move freely, and in part because of one aspect in particular of the Midsummer's Night celebrations of Rethwellan. Though the folk of Petras were mostly long since severed from any direct ties to the farms that formed a good third of Rethwellan's wealth, Midsummer's Night was *still* the night which ensured the fertility of the land. There would be reveling in the streets right up until the stroke of midnight—but *at* midnight, the streets would be deserted. Every man and woman in Petras would be doing his or her level best to prove to the Goddess in Her aspect as Lover that the people of Rethwellan still worshiped Her in all the appropriate ways. *This* Midsummer's Night they would be trying especially hard, because over the past three months the priests of the city had been doing *their* best to encourage exactly that behavior tonight. Some of them had even unbent themselves enough to admit that—on *this one night*—perhaps it didn't altogether worry Her if your partner did not happen to be your lawfully wedded spouse. And that if one felt guilty after being infected with Her sacred desires and fulfilling same—well, for a case of indulgence after Midsummer's Night, penances would be few and light, and forgiveness easily obtained.

For all but six hundred-odd, who would not be fulfilling Her desires as Lover, but as Avenger.

Tarma picked her way through the thinning crowds, still wearing her guise of Arton. It was that guise that was going to give the Hawks the entry to the Palace grounds. From all directions, she knew, the Hawks were converging on the Palace; she would be one of the last to arrive. Kethry was already in place, waiting to spring her trap-spells. If they didn't work, she would be in a position to guide Hawks to the mages to deal with them physically while she kept them occupied magically. If they *did* work, she would be a most welcome addition to their arsenal.

And just in case Char somehow slipped through their fingers—*Warrl?*

:Here, mindmate.:

Got the horses in place?

Warrl's duty was to work with Horsemaster Tindel; the fastest of the Shin'a'in-bred mounts she'd sold Char the year before were to be saddled and kept at the ready, in a cul-de-sac just outside the Palace gate, with Warrl and Tindel guarding them. If Char got away from them, Tarma and the best riders among the Hawks would be hot on his heels—

:Saddled, bridled, and ready to ride.:

Good. Let's hope we don't have to use them.

:Devoutly.:

Tarma approached one of the side gates, that gave out onto a delivery area. Tonight the gate stood open for the convenience of servants, and the courtyard beyond was dark and deserted. And there was Kethry— still in *her* own disguise, and looking angry enough to bite a board in two. Tarma altered her walk, swaying a little, as if drunk. She was carrying what looked like a jug loosely in her right hand. As it happened, it *wasn't* a jug; it was her sword, magicked with another illusion.

Kethry spotted her; Tarma put a little more of a stagger into her step. "*There* you are, you *beast!* And drunk as a pig!" she shrilled, to the amusement of the two gate guards.

"J-janna?" Tarma slurred uncertainly, coming to a halt just before the gate.

"Of course it's Janna, you brute! You asked me to meet you here, you sot! I've been waiting for *hours!*"

"Don't you believe her, Arton," snickered the right-hand gate guard. "She ain't been here more'n half a candlemark—an' she showed up with a big blond lad on one arm, too. Reckon she's been playin' more'n one game tonight, eh?"

"You—damned—slut!" Tarma snarled, feigning that she had suddenly gone fighting-drunk. She advanced on Kethry, brandishing the jug. Kethry backed up until she was just inside the gate itself, giving every evidence of genuine and absolute fear. "I'm gonna beat you bloody, you fornicating little bitch!"

Kethry whirled, and threw herself on the left-hand guard, begging his protection, distracting both guards for the crucial moment that it took Tarma to get within arm's length of the right-hand guard.

Then Tarma pivoted, and took her guard out with the pommel of her sword, just as Kethry executed a neat right cross to the point of her target's chin. Both went down without a sound. Within heartbeats the Hawks were swarming the gate—as two of their number, already be-spelled into looking like the two guards they were replacing, dragged the bodies into the gatehouse, trussed and gagged them, and took up their stations. The fighters filled the courtyard on the other side, hidden in the dark shadow of the Palace, waiting for Tarma and Kethry to make the next moves.

Kethry stood in frozen immobility for a single moment; sensitized to stirrings of energies by her own status as Kal'enedral, Tarma actually *felt* her spring her trap-spells.

"Well?"

Kethry's eyes met hers with incredulous shock. "They're holding—all of them!"

"Lady with us, then, and let's hope they keep holding. New body, Keth."

"Right," the mage answered, and Tarma waited impatiently as the figure of "Janna" blurred, became a rosy mist, and the mist solidified into a new guise—a very ordinary looking female fighter in the scarlet-and-gold livery of Char's personal guard.

"All right, Hawks," Tarma said, in a low, but carrying voice. "This is it —form up on your leaders—"

She marched up to the unlocked delivery door, Kethry beside her, and pushed it open. The half-drunk guard beyond blinked at her without alarm, and bemusedly; he was one of Char's own personal guards and Tarma (in her guise of Arton) had ordered him to stand duty tonight on this door for a reason. He was one of the men that had participated in the rape and torture of Idra.

She swung once, without a qualm, cutting him down before he had a chance to do more than blink at her. Her only regret was that she had not been able to grant him the lingering death she felt he deserved. She and Kethry hastily dragged his body out of the way; then she waved to the waiting shadows in the court behind her.

And the Sunhawks poured through the door, a flood of vengeance in human shape, a flood which split into many smaller streams—and all of them were deadly.

"No luck," Tarma said flatly, as her group met (as planned) with Stefan's, just outside the corridor leading to the rooms assigned to the unattached ladies of the Court. "He wasn't in his quarters, and he wasn't with the mages."

"Nor with any of his current mistresses," Stefansen reported. "That leaves the throne room."

Their combined group, which included Jadrek (who had accompanied Stefan) and both the other Sunhawk mages, now numbered some fifty strong. The new force surged down the pristine white marble of the Great Hall to their goal of the throne room, all of them caught up in battle-fever. The Hawks had met with opposition from Char's fighters, some of it fierce. The bodies lying in pools of spreading scarlet on the snowy marble of the halls were not all wearing Char's livery. Sewen had been hurt, and Ikan. Garth was dead, and more than fifty others Tarma had known only vaguely. But the Hawks had triumphed, even in the pitched battle with the seasoned troupers of Char's army, and all but a handful of those who had murdered their Captain were now making their atonements to her in person.

But among that handful—and the only one as yet uncaught—was Raschar.

Those in the lead shouted as they reached their goal—the great bronze double doors of the throne room—first in triumph, and then in anger, as they attempted to force those doors open. The sculptured doors to the throne room were locked, from the inside.

Justin and Beaker and a half dozen more battered at them—futilely— as the rest came up. Their efforts did not even make the glittering doors tremble.

"Don't bother," Stefansen shouted over the noise, "Those damned doors are a handspan thick. We'll have to try to get in from the garden."

"No we won't," Kethry snarled, audible in her rage even over the frustrated efforts of those still trying to batter their way in. *"Stand back!"*

She raised her hands high over her head, her face a mask of fury, and Tarma felt the surge of power that could only mean she had summoned some of that terrible anger-energy she had channeled away but not used in the trap-spells. This was the best purpose for such energies, Tarma knew—anything destructive would do—

Kethry called out three piercing words, and a bolt of something very like scarlet lightning lanced from her hands to the meeting point of the double doors. There was a smell of hot metal and scorched air, and a crash that shook every ornament in the hall to the floor. The fighters around her cringed and protected their ears from the thunder-shock; the doors rocked, but did not open.

"Fight it down, girl," Tarma cautioned her, and Kethry visibly wrestled her own temper into control; if she lost to it, she had warned Tarma, she would be prey to the stored anger.

Kethry closed her eyes, took three deep breaths, then faced the obstacle again. "Oh no," she told the doors and the spell that was on them, "you don't stop *me* that easily!"

Again she called the lightning, and a third time—and on the fourth, the doors burst off their hinges, and fell inward with a crash that shook the floor, cracked the marble of the walls of the Great Hall, and rained debris down on all their heads from the ceiling. None of which they particularly noticed, as they stormed into the throne room—

To find it empty.

Jadrek cursed, with a command of invective that astounded Kethry, and pointed to where a scarlet and gold tapestry behind the throne flapped in a current of air. "The tunnel—it was walled off years ago—"

"Figures that the little bastard would have it opened up," Stefan spat. "Think, man—where does it come out?"

Jadrek closed his eyes and clenched both hands at his temples, as Kethry tried to will confidence and calm into him. "If the records I studied are right—*and* I remember them right," he said finally, "it exits in the old temple of Ursa, outside the city walls."

Tarma and her chosen riders had already spun around and were sprinting for the door, and Kethry was right behind them. Because she had already laid most of the spell on them, it was child's play to invoke the guises she'd set for just this eventuality—even while pelting down the hall as fast as her legs could carry her. They were exceedingly simple illusions, anyway—not faces, but livery, the scarlet and gold livery of Char's personal guards, exactly as the guise *she* wore was garbed.

They didn't have far to run; and Hawks now held the main gate and had forced it open, so there was nothing to bar the path to their allies. As they pounded into the torch-lit court behind the main gate, a dozen Shin'a'in-bred horses, driven by Warrl, and led by Tindel, galloped past that portal. Their iron-shod hooves drew sparks from the stones of the paving, and they tossed their heads as they ran, plainly fresh and eager for an all-out run.

Which was exactly what they were going to get.

As the horses swirled past the Palace door, the Hawks ran to meet them, not bothering to give Tindel the time to bring them to a halt. Instead they mounted on the run, as Tarma had taught them. Even Kethry, the worst rider of all, managed somehow, grabbing pommel and cantle and getting herself in the saddle of the still-cantering gelding she'd singled out without really thinking about what she was doing.

"Where?" Tindel shouted, over the pounding of hooves as they thundered out the gates again, leaving a panting Warrl to collapse behind them. This was no race for *him* and he knew it.

"Temple of Ursa—" Tarma yelled in reply, and Tindel cut anything else she was about to say off with a wave of his hand.

"I know a quicker way," he bellowed.

He urged his gray into the fore, and led them in a mad stampede down crazy, twisting alleys Kethry had never seen before, a good half of which were just packed dirt. Festival gewgaws and dying flowers were pounded to powder as they careened through; once a tiny hawker's cart—thankfully unattended—was knocked over and kicked aside; reduced to splinters as it hit a wall. Kethry's nose was filled with the stench of back-alley middens and trampled garbage; she was splashed with stale water and other liquids best left nameless. Her eyes were dazzled by sudden torchlight that alternated with the abyssal dark valleys between buildings. She got only vague impressions of walls flying past, half-seen openings as they dashed by cross streets; and the pounding of hooves surrounding her throbbed like the pounding of the power at her fingertips.

Then, a startled shout, a wall that loomed high against the stars, and an invisible wall of cooler air and absolute blackness that they plunged through—still without a pause—

Then they were outside the city walls, continuing the insane gallop along the road that led to a handful of old, mostly deserted temples, and beyond that, to Hielmarsh.

The moon was full; it was nearly as bright as day, without a single cloud to obscure the light. The fields and trees before them were washed with silver, and the horses, able now to see where they were going, increased their pace.

Kethry urged her beast up to the front of the herd, until she rode just behind Tarma and Tindel. She gripped her horse with aching knees and tried to see up the road. The temple couldn't be far—not if it was to be reached by a tunnel.

It wasn't. The white marble of a building that could only be the temple in question stood out clearly against the dark shadows of the trees behind it—at this pace, hardly more than a breath or two away.

Just as they came within shouting distance of the temple, moonlight reflecting from a cloud of dust on the road ahead of them told them without words that Char had already started the next stage of his flight. This road led almost directly to Hielmarsh, Kethry knew. He was heading for his little stronghold, or perhaps the mazes of the marsh. There would be *no* pulling him out of there.

But Hielmarsh was hours away, and that dust cloud a few furlongs at most. And *their* horses were Shin'a'in, not much exhausted by the race they'd run so far, scarcely sweating, and still on their first wind.

The little party ahead of them knew they were coming, though, they had to; they had to hear the rolling thunder of two dozen pairs of hooves. They also had to know there was no escaping—

But the Hawks didn't want a pitched battle if they could help it.

The dust was settling, which meant the quarry had turned at bay. Kethry saw Tarma give the signal to pull up as they came within sight of Char and his men. The knot of fighters ahead of them huddled together on the moon-drenched road, swords glinting silver as they held them at ready. Kethry and the rest of the Hawks obeyed their leader, and slowed their horses to a walk.

The King's party numbered almost forty—putting the Hawks at a two-to-one disadvantage if they fought. Tarma's contingency plan, as Kethry knew, called for no such fight. That was the reason for the magical disguises.

"Majesty!" Tarma called, knowing Char would see the Arton he trusted. "Your brother's stormed and taken the Palace; he's holding the city against you. I got what men I could and tried to guess which way you'd be heading."

Raschar dug his spurs into his gelding's sides and rode straight to his "faithful retainer." "Arton!" he cried, panic straining his voice, "Hellfire, I heard you'd gone down at the gates! I have never been so glad to see anybody in my life!"

As he pulled up beside Tarma, Kethry could see his skin was pale and he was sweating, and his eyes were hardly more than black holes in his head.

"Rein in, Majesty; I've got you some help. Here—" she called up at the mixed group of guards and common soldiers still milling about uncertainly up ahead. "—you lot! Get back to the temple! Split yourselves up, I don't much care how. Half of you head back down to hold the road for as long as you can, the rest of you lay a false trail off to Lasleric. Come on, move it out, we haven't got all night!"

There hadn't been a single officer among them, and the mixed contingent was obviously only too happy to find someone willing to issue orders that made *sense*—unlike the frantic babbling of their King.

They obeyed Tarma without a murmur, sending their nervous beasts around the clot of Hawks blocking the road. Within moments they were out of sight, returning back toward the temple and beyond.

Tarma waited until they were completely out of sight before giving Kethry a significant *look*.

Kethry nodded, and dropped the spell of illusion she'd been holding on their company.

Char stared, his jaw sagging, as what appeared to be his guard was revealed as something else entirely.

Then he paled, his face going whiter than the moonlight, as he recognized Tindel, Tarma and Kethry.

"What—" He started to stutter, then drew himself up and took on a kind of nervous dignity. "Just what is this supposed to mean? Who are you? What do you want?"

"You probably haven't heard of us before, your Majesty," Tarma drawled, as two of the Hawks closed in on the King from the rear, coming up on either side. "We're just a common mercenary troop. We go by the name of 'Idra's Sunhawks.' "

When she spoke the name, he choked, and rowled his horse savagely. Too late; the Hawks were already within grabbing distance of his reins. He tried to throw himself to the ground, but other hands caught him, and held him in his saddle until he could be tied there.

"Should take us about three candlemarks to get him back—" Tindel began.

A growl from the ranked fighters behind Tarma interrupted him, and he stopped, looking startled.

"Stefan promised him to us, my friend," Tarma said quietly. "He goes back only when we're finished with him."

"But—"

"We called the Oathbreaking on him," Kethry pointed out. "He's ours by the code, no matter how you look at it."

Tindel looked from face to stubbornly set face, and shrugged. "Well, what do we do with him?"

"Huh. Hadn't thought that far—" Tarma began.

"*I* had," Kethry said, firmly.

There was still a vast reservoir of anger-energy for her to draw on, and while the coercion of innocent spirits was strictly forbidden a White Winds sorceress, the opening of the gates of the otherworld to a ghost that had a debt to collect was *not*.

And Idra most certainly had a long, bitter debt owed to her.

"We called Oathbreaking on him—that's a spell, partner. I do believe we ought to see that spell completed."

Tarma looked at her askance; so did the rest of the Hawks. Char, gagged, made choking sounds. "How do you propose to do that? And just what does it mean to see it completed?"

Kethry shifted in her saddle, keeping Char under the tail of her eye. "It only takes the priestess and the mage to complete the spell, and I know how. Jadrek found the rest of it in some of the old histories. As for what it does—it brings all the broken oaths home to roost."

"Does that mean what I *think* it does?"

Kethry nodded, and Tarma smiled, a bloodthirsty grin that sent a chill even up her partner's backbone.

"All right—where?"

"The temple back there will do, I think; all we need is a bit of sanctified ground."

With Char's horse between them, they led the mystified mercenaries toward the white shape of the temple on their backtrail. It was, fortunately, deserted. Kethry did not especially want any witnesses to this besides the principals.

The temple was in a state of extreme disrepair; walls half fallen and crumbling, the pavement beneath their horse's hooves cracked and uneven. Tarma began to look dubious as they penetrated deeper into the complex.

"Are we far enough in, do you think? I don't want to chance one of the horses falling, and maybe breaking a leg if there's any help for it."

"This will do," Kethry judged, reining in her mount, and swinging a little stiffly out of the saddle.

The rest dismounted as well, with several of them swarming the King's mount to pull him roughly to the ground. The horses, eased of their burdens, sighed and stamped a little, pawing at the weathered stone.

"Now what?" Tarma asked.

"Tindel—you and Beaker and Jodi stand here; you three hold Char." She indicated a spot on the pavement in the center of a roughly circular area that was relatively free from debris. "Tarma, you stand South, I'll stand North. The rest of you form a circle with us as the ends."

The Hawks obeyed, still mystified, but willing to trust the judgment of the mage they'd worked so closely with for three years.

"All right—Tarma, just—be Kal'enedral. That's all you need to do. And hold in mind what this bastard has done to our sister and Captain."

"That won't be hard," came the icy voice from across the circle.

Kethry took a deep breath and brought stillness within herself, for everything depended now on creating a channel from herself for the anger of the others. If she let it affect her—it would consume her.

When she thought she was ready, she took a second deep breath, raised her arms, and began.

"Oathbreaker, he stands judged; Oathbreaker to priestess, Oathbreaker to mage, Oathbreaker to true man of his people. Oathbreaker, we found him; Oathbreaker in soul, Oathbreaker in power, Oathbreaker in duty. Oathbreaker, we brought him; Oathbreaker in thought, Oathbreaker in word, Oathbreaker in deed. Oathbreaker, he stands, judged, and condemned—"

She called upon the power she had not yet exhausted, and the rising power within the circle.

"Let the wall of Strength stand between this place and the world—"

As the barrier had been built between herself and the dark mage for the magic duel, so a similar barrier sprang up now; one pole beginning from where she stood, the other from where Tarma was poised. This wall was of a colorless, milky white; it glowed only faintly.

"Let the Pillars of Wisdom stand between this world and the next—"

Mist swirled up out of the ground, just in front of Char and his captors. Kethry could see his eyes bulging in fear, for the mist held a light of its own that augmented the moonlight. The mist formed itself into a column, which then split slowly into two. The two columns moved slowly apart, then solidified into glowing pillars.

"Let the Gate of Judgment open—"

More mist, this time of a strange, bluish cast, billowed in the space between the two Pillars. Kethry felt the energy coursing through her; it was a very strange, almost unnerving feeling. She could see why even an Adept rarely performed this spell more than once in a lifetime—it wasn't just the *amount* of power needed, it was that the mage became only the vessel for the power. It, in a very real sense, was controlling *her*. She spoke aloud the final Word of Opening, then called with thought alone to the mist-shape within the Pillars, and fed it all the last of the Hawks' united anger in a great burst of unleashed power.

The mist swirled, billowed—grew dark, then bright, then dark again. It glowed from within, the color a strange silver-blue. Then the mist condensed around the glow, forming a suggestion of a long road, a road under sunlight—and out of the center of the glowing cloud rode Idra.

Char gave a strangled cry, and fell to his knees before the rider. But for the moment she was not looking at *him*.

She was colorless as moonlight, and as solidly real as any of Tarma's *leshya'e-Kal'enedral.* When Kethry had decided to open the Gate, she had faced this moment of seeing Idra's face with a tinge of fear, wondering what she would see there. She feared no longer. The long, lingering gazes Idra bestowed upon each of her "children" were warm, and full of peace. This was no spirit suffering torment—

But the face she turned upon her brother was full of something colder than hate, and more implacable than anger.

"Hello, Char," she said, her voice echoing as from across a vast canyon. "You have a very great deal to answer for."

Tarma led two dozen bone-weary Hawks back into Petras that morning; they made no attempt to conceal themselves, and word that they were coming—and word of what they carried—preceded them. The streets of Petras cleared before their horses ever set hoof upon them, and they rode through a town that might well have been emptied by some mysterious plague. But eyes were watching them behind closed curtains and sealed shutters; eyes that they could feel on the backs of their necks. There was fear echoing along with the sounds of hoofbeats along those streets. Fear of what the Hawks had done; fear of what else they might do—

By the time they rode in through the gates of the Palace, a nervous crowd had assembled in the court, and Stefansen was waiting on the stairs.

The Hawks pulled up in a semicircle before the new King, still silent but for the sound of their horses' hooves. As the last of the horses moved into place, the last whisper coming from the crowd died, leaving only frightened, ponderous silence, a silence that could almost be weighed and measured.

There was a bloodstained bundle lashed on the back of Raschar's horse, a bundle that Tindel and Tarma removed, carried to the new King's feet, and dropped there without ceremony.

The folds of what had been Char's cloak fell open, revealing what the cloak contained. Stefan, though he had visibly steeled himself, turned pale. There was just about enough left of Raschar to be recognizable.

"This man was sworn Oathbreaker and Outcast," Tarma said harshly, tonelessly. "And he was so sworn by the *full* rites, by a priest, a mage, and an upright man of his own people, all of whom he had wronged, all of whom had suffered irreparable loss at his hands. We claim Mercenary's Justice on him, by the rights of that swearing; we executed that Justice upon him. Who would deny us that right?"

There was only appalled silence from the crowd.

"I confirm it," Stefansen said into the silence, his voice firm, and filling the courtyard. "For not only have I heard from a trusted witness the words of his own mouth, confessing that he dishonored, tortured and slew his own sister, the Lady Idra, Captain of the Sunhawks and Princess of the blood, but I have had the same tale from the servants of his household that we questioned last night. Hear then the tale of Raschar the Oathbreaker."

Tarma stood wearily through the recitation, not really hearing it, although the murmurs and gasps from the crowd behind her told her that Stefan was giving the whole story in all its grimmest details. The mood of the people was shifting to their side, moment by moment.

And now that the whole thing was over, all she wanted to do was rest. The energy that had sustained her all this time was gone.

"Are there *any,*" she heard Stefansen cry at last, his voice breaking a little, "who would deny that true justice has been dispensed this day?"

The thunderous *NO!* that followed his question satisfied even Tarma.

Quite a little family party, Tarma thought wryly, surveying the motley individuals draped in various postures of relaxation around the shabby-comfortable library of Stefansen's private suite.

:Enjoy it while you can,: Warrl laughed in her mind, *:It won't be too often that you can throw cherrystones at both a King and a Crown Prince when they tease you.:*

It was only Roald, and he was asking for it—

Stefansen had been officially crowned two days ago, and Roald had arrived as Valdemar's official representative, complete with silver coronet on his blond head—*and* with a full entourage, as well. The time between the night of the rebellion and the day of the coronation had been so hectic that no one had had a chance to hear the full story of the rebellion from either Tarma, Kethry or Jadrek. So Stefansen had decreed today that he was having a secret Council session, had all but kidnapped his chosen party and locked all of them away. Included in the party were himself and Mertis; and he had taken care that there was a great deal of food and drink and comfortable seats for all. And once everyone was settled in, he had demanded *all* the tales in their proper order.

The entire "Council" was mostly Sunhawks or ex-Hawks; Sewen and Tresti; Justin and Ikan; Kyra, Beaker and Jodi. Tarma herself, and Kethry, of course. Then the "outsiders"—Tindel, Jadrek, and Roald.

It had taken a long time to get through the whole story—and when Kyra had finished the last of the tales, telling in her matter-of-fact way how Idra had ridden out of the cloud of mist and moonlight, you could have heard a mouse sneeze.

"What I don't understand is how you Hawks took that so calmly," Tindel was saying. "I was as petrified as Char, I swear—but you—it was like she was—real."

"Lad," Beaker said in a kindly tone (to a man at least a decade or two his senior!), "We've ridden with Idra through things you can't imagine;

she's stood by us through fear and flood and Hellfire itself. How could we have been afraid of her? She was only dead. It's the *living* we fear."

"And rightly," Justin rumbled into the somber silence that followed Beaker's words. "And speaking of the living, you will never guess who sauntered in two days ago, Shin'a'in."

Tarma shook her head, baffled. She'd been spending most of her free time sleeping.

"Your *dear* friend Leslac."

"Oh *no!*" she choked. "Justin, if I've ever done you any favors, *keep him away from me!*"

"Leslac?" Roald said curiously. "Minstrel, isn't he? Dark hair, swarthy, thin? Popular with women?"

"That's him," groaned Tarma, hiding her face in her hands.

"What's it worth to you," he asked, leaning forward, and wearing a slyly humorous expression, "to get him packed off to Valdemar? Permanently?"

"Choice of Tale'sedrin's herds," she said quickly, "Three mares and a stallion, and anything but battlesteeds."

"Four mares, and one of them sworn to be in-foal."

"Done, done, done!" she replied, waving her hands frantically.

"Stefan, old friend," Roald said, turning to the King, "Is it worth an in-foal Shin'a'in mare to force a swordpoint marriage by royal decree on one motheaten Bard?" Roald's face was sober, but his eyes danced with laughter.

"For that, I'd force a swordpoint marriage on Tindel!" Stefansen chuckled. "Who's the lucky lady?"

"Countess Reine. She's actually a rather sweet old biddy, unlike her harridan sister, who is—thank the gods!—no longer with us. I'm rather fond of her, for all that she hasn't the sense of a new-hatched chick." Roald shook his head, and sighed. "A few years back, her sister went mad during a storm and killed herself. Or so it's said, and nobody wants to find out otherwise. I'm supposed to be keeping an eye on her, to keep her out of trouble."

"How delightful."

"Oh, it isn't too bad; she just has this ability to attract men who want to prey on her sensibilities. They are, of course, all of honorable intent."

"Of course," said Stefan, solemnly.

"Well, Leslac seems to be another of the same sort. It's common knowledge in my entourage that the poor dear is absolutely head over heels with him. *And* his music. He, naturally, has been languishing at her feet, accepting her presents, and swearing undying love when no one else is around, I don't doubt. I can see it coming now; he figures that when I find out, I'll confront him—he'll vow he isn't worthy of her, being low-born and all, I'll agree, and he'll get paid off. But *I* actually have no objection to lowborn-highborn marriages; I expect Reine's family will be only too happy to see the end of the stream of vultures that's been preying on her, and I can see a way of doing two friends a favor here. I'm certain that the threat of royal displeasure if he makes Reine unhappy will keep the wandering fancy in line once I get him back with me."

"I," Tarma said fervently, "will be your devoted slave for the rest of your life. Both of you."

Stefan shook his head at her. "I owe you too much, Tarma, and if this will really make you happy—"

"It will! Trust me, it will!"

"Consider it ordered, Roald. Now I have a question for you two fellow-conspirators over there. What can *I* do for *you?*"

"If you're serious—" Kethry began.

"Totally. Anything short of being crowned; unless the Sword sings for you, even I can't manage that. Titles? Lands? Wealth—I can't quite supply; Char made too many inroads in the Treasury, but—"

"For years we have wanted to found a joint school," Kethry said, slowly. " 'Want' is actually too mild a word. By the edicts of my own mage school, now that I'm an Adept I just about *have* to start a branch of the White Winds school. What we need, really, is a place with a big enough building to house our students and teachers, and enough lands to support it. But that kind of property isn't easily come by."

"Because it's usually in the hands of nobles or clergy. I'm disappointed," Stefan said with a grin, "I thought you'd want something *hard.* One of Char's hereditary holdings was a fine estate down in the south, near the border—a large manorhouse, a village of its own, and an able staff to maintain it. It is, by the by, where I was supposed to end my days in debauchery. It has an indoor riding arena attached to the stable because Char hated to ride when it rained, it has a truly amazing library; why it even has a *professional* salle, because the original builder was a notable fighter. Is that just about what you're looking for?"

Tarma had felt her jaw dropping with every word, until, when Stefan glanced over at her with a sly smile and a broad wink, she was unable to get her voice to work.

Kethry answered for her. "Windborn—gods, *yes!* I—Stefan, would you *really* give it to us?"

"Well, since the property of traitors becomes property of the crown, and since *I* have some very unpleasant memories of the place—Lady

Bright, I'm only too pleased that you want it! Just pay your taxes promptly, that's all I ask!"

Tarma tried to thank him, but her voice still wouldn't work. Kethry made up for her—leaping out of her chair and giving the King a most disrespectful hug and kiss, both of which he seemed to enjoy immensely.

"Furthermore, I'll be sending my offspring of both sexes to you for training," he continued. "If nothing else, I want them to have the discipline of a good swordmaster, something I didn't have. Maybe that will keep them from being the kind of brat I was. This will probably scandalize my nobles—"

"Oh, it will, lover," Mertis laughed, "But I agree with the notion. It will do the children good."

"Then my nobles will have to live with being scandalized. Now, I want the rest of you to decide what you'd like," he said when Kethry had resumed her seat, but not her calm. "Because I'm going to do my best by all of you. But right now I fear I *do* have a Council session, and there are a lot of unpleasant messes Char left behind him that need attending to."

Stefan rose, and gave his hand to Mertis, and the two exited gracefully from the library. The rest clustered around Tarma and her partner, congratulating them—

All but Jadrek, who had inexplicably vanished.

The partners made their weary way to their rooms. It had been a long day, but for Tarma, a very happy one.

But Kethry was preoccupied—and a little disturbed, Tarma could sense it without any special effort.

"Keth?" she asked, finally, "What's stuck in your craw?"

"It's Jadrek. He hasn't said anything or come near me since the night of the rebellion." She turned troubled and unhappy eyes on her partner. "I don't know why; I *thought* he loved me—I *know* I love him. And this afternoon—just disappearing like that—"

"Well, we're official now. He's reverting to courtly manners. You don't go sneaking around to a lady's room; you treat her with respect."

"Courtly manners be hanged!" Kethry snapped. "Dammit Tarma, we'll be gone soon! Doesn't he care? If he doesn't say something—"

"Then you'll hit him over the head and carry him off, like the uncivilized barbarian mercenary I know you are. And I'll help."

Kethry started laughing at that. "I hate to tell you this, but that's exactly what I've been contemplating."

"Go make wish-lists of things you think you'll be needing for this new school of ours," Tarma advised her. "That should keep your mind occupied. I have the feeling this is going to sort itself out before long."

She parted company with her *she'enedra* at Kethry's door. They had rooms inside the royal complex now, not in the visitors area. Stefansen was treating them as *very* honored guests.

She knew she wasn't alone the moment she closed the door behind her. She also knew who it was—*without* Warrl's helpful hint of *:It's Jadrek. I let him in. He wants to talk.:*

"Tarma—"

"Hello, Jadrek," she said calmly, lighting a candle beside the door before turning around to face him. "We haven't been seeing a lot of you; we've missed you."

"I've been thinking," he said awkwardly. "I—"

She crossed her arms, and waited for him to continue. He straightened his back and lifted his chin. "Tarma shena Tale'sedrin," he said, with all the earnest solemnity of a high priest, "Have I your permission to pay my court to your oathsister?"

She raised an eyebrow. "Can you give me a good reason why I should?"

Her question wilted him. He sat down abruptly, obviously struggling for words. "I—Tarma, I *love* her, I really do. I love her too much to just play with her, I want something formal binding us, something—in keeping with her honor. She's lovely, you know that as well as I do, but it isn't just her exterior I care for, it's her *mind*. She challenges me, like nobody I've ever known before. We're equals—I want to be her partner, not— not a—I don't know, I want to have something like Mertis and Stefan have, and I *know* we'll give each other that! I want to help you with your schools, too. I think it's a wonderful dream and I want to make it real, and work alongside of both of you to make it more than a dream."

"We're something more than partners, she and I," Tarma reminded him. "There's certain things between us that will affect any children Kethry may have."

"I took the liberty of asking Warrl about that," he said, blushing. "I don't have any problem with—children. With them being raised Tale'sedrin. Everything I know about the Shin'a'in, everything I've learned in working with you—I would be very, very proud if you considered my blood good enough to flow into the Clans. Tarma, this is probably going to sound stupid, but I've come to—love—you. You've done so much *for* me, more than you guess. What I *really* want is that what we've built with the three of us in the last few months should endure—the friendship, the love, the partnership. I never had that before—and I'd do anything right now to prevent losing either of you."

Tarma looked into his pleading eyes—and much to his evident shock *and* delight, she took both his hands, pulled him up out of his chair into her arms, hugged him just short of breaking his ribs, and planted a kiss squarely in the middle of his forehead before letting him go again.

"Well, outClan *brother,*" she laughed, "while I can't speak for the lady, I would suggest you trot next door and ask her for her hand yourself—because I *do* know that if you don't, you're going to find yourself trussed hand and foot and lying over Hellsbane's rump like so much baggage. You see, *we* happen to be barbarians, and we *will* do anything to prevent losing *you. He shala?*"

His mouth worked for a moment, as he stared at her, his eyes brightening with what Tarma suspected were tears of joy. Then he took her face in both his hands, kissed *her,* and ran out her door as if joy had put wings on his back.

"Better get Stefan to pick your successor," she called after him. "Because we're going to keep you *much* too busy to putter about in his Archives."

And so they did.

Appendix One

Dictionary of Shin'a'in Terms

PRONUNCIATION:

': glottal stop, a pause, but not quite as long a pause as between two
   words
ai: as in air
ay: long "a" as in way
ah: soft "a" as in ah
ee: long "e" as in feet
ear: as in fear
e: as in fend
i: long "i" as in violent
oh: long "o" as in moat
oo: as in boot

corthu: (cohr-thoo)—one being
dester'edre: (destair ay-dhray)—wind(born) sibling
dhon: (dthohn)—very much
du'dera: (doo dearah)—(I) give (you) comfort
for'shava: (fohr shahvah)—very, very good
get'ke: (get kay)—(could you) explain
gestena: (gestaynah)—thank you
hai: (hi)—yes
hai shala: (hi shahlah)—do you understand?
hai'she'li: (hi she lee)—surprised "yes," literally "yes, I swear!"
hai'vetha: (hi vethah)—yes, (be) running
her'y: (hear ee)—(is this not) the truth
isda: (eesdah)—have you (ever) seen (such)
jel'enedra: (jel enaydrah)—little sister
jel'sutho'edrin: (jel soothoh aydthrin)—"forever younger siblings," usually refers to horses
jostumal: (johstoomahl)—enemy, literally, "one desiring (your) blood"

kadessa: (kahdessah)—rodent of the Dhorisha Plains

Kal'enedral: (kahl enaydhrahl)—Her sword-brothers or Her swordchildren

Kal'enel: (kahl enel)—the Warrior aspect of the four-faced Goddess, literally, "Sword of the Stars." Also called Enelve'astre (Star-Eyed) and Da'gretha (Warrior).

kathal: (kahthahl)—go gently

kele: (kaylay)—(go) onward

kestra: (kestrah)—a casual friend

krethes: (kraythes)—speculation

kulath: (koolahth)—go find

leshya'e: (layshee-ah ee)—spirit; *not* a vengeful, earthbound ghost, but a helpful spirit

Liha'irden: (leehah eardhren)—deer-footed

li'ha'eer: (lee hah eeahr)—exclamation, literally, "by the gods"

li'sa'eer: (lee sah eeahr)—exclamation of extreme surprise, literally "by the highest gods!"

nes: (nes)—bad

nos: (nohs)—it is

pretera: (praytearah)—grasscat

sadullos: (sahdoolohs)—safer

se: (sy)—is/are

she'chorne: (shay chornah)—homosexual; does not have negative connotations among the Shin'a'in.

she'enedra: (shay enaydrah)—sister by blood-oathing

sheka: (shaykah)—horse droppings

shena: (shaynah)—of the Clan, literally "of the brotherhood"

shesti: (shestee)—nonsense

Shin'a'in: (shin ay in)—the people of the plains

so'trekoth: (soh traykoth)—fool who will believe anything, literally, "gape-mouthed hatchling"

staven: (stahven)—water

Tal'edras: (tahle aydhrahs)—Hawkbrothers, a race who may or may not be related to the Shin'a'in, living in the Pelagiris Forest

Tale'sedrin: (tahle saydhrin)—children of the hawk

te'sorthene: (tay sohrthayne)—heart-friend, spirit-friend

Vai datha: (vi dahthah)—expression of resignation or agreement, literally "there are many ways."

var'athanda: (vahr ahthahndah)—to be forgetful of

ves'tacha: (ves tahchah)—beloved one

vysaka: (visahkah)—the spiritual bond between the Kal'enedral and the

Warrior; its presence can actually be detected by an Adept, another Kal'enedral, and the Kal'enedral him/herself. It is this bond which creates the "shielding" that makes Kal'enedral celibate/neuter and somewhat immune to magic.

vyusher: (vi-ooshear)—wolf

yai: (yi)—two

yuthi'so'coro: (yoothee soh cohr-oh)—road courtesy; the rules Shin'a'in follow when traveling on a public road.

Appendix Two

Songs and Poems

SUFFER THE CHILDREN
(Tarma: *Oathbreakers*)

These are the hands that wield a sword
With trained and practiced skill;
These are the hands, and this the mind,
Both honed and backed by will.
Death is my partner, blood my trade,
And war my passion wild—
But these are the hands that also ache
To hold a tiny child.

CH: Suffer, they suffer, the children,
    When I see them, gods, how my heart breaks!
    It is ever and always the children
    Who will pay for their parents' mistakes.

Somehow they know that I'm a friend—
I see it in their eyes,
Somehow they sense a kindly heart—
So young, so very wise.
Mine are the hands that maim and kill—
But children never care.
They only know my hands are strong
And comfort is found there.

Little enough that I can do
To shield the young from pain—
Not while their parents fight and die
For land, or goods, or gain.

All I can do is give them love—
All I can do is strive
To teach them enough of my poor skill
To help them stay alive.

OATHBREAKERS

CH: Cursed Oathbreakers, your honor's in pawn
    And worthless the vows you have made—
    Justice shall see you where others have gone,
    Delivered to those you betrayed!

These are the signs of a mage that's forsworn—
The True Gifts gone dead in his hand,
Magic corrupted and discipline torn,
Shifting heart like shifting sand;
Swift to allow any passion to run,
Given to hatred and rage.
Give him wide berth and his company shun—
For darkness devours the Dark Mage.

These are the signs of a traitor in war—
Wealth from no visible source,
Shunning old comrades he welcomed before,
Holding to no steady course.
If you uncover the one who'd betray,
Heed not his words nor his pen.
Give him no second chance—drive him away—
False once will prove false again.

These are the signs of the treacherous priest—
Pleasure in anyone's pain,
Abuse or degrading of man or of beast,
Duty as second to gain,
Preaching belief but with none of his own,
Twisting all that he controls.

Fear him and never face him all alone,
He corrupts innocent souls.

These are the signs of the king honor-broke—
Pride coming first over all,
Treading the backs and the necks of his folk
That he alone might stand tall,
Giving himself to desires that are base,
Tyrannous, cunning, and cruel.
Bring him down—set someone else in his place.
Such men are not fit to rule.

ADVICE TO YOUNG MAGICIANS
(Kethry)

The firebird knows your anger
And the firebird feels your fear,
For your passions will attract her
And your feelings draw her near.
But the negative emotions
Only make her flame and fly.
You must rule your heart, magician,
Or by her bright wings you die.

Now the cold-drake lives in silence
And he feeds on dark despair
Where the shadows fall the bleakest
You will find the cold-drake there.
For he seeks to chill your spirit
And to lure you down to death.
Learn to rule your soul, magician,
Ere you dare the cold-drake's breath.

And the griffon is a proud beast
He's the master of the sky.
And no one forgets the sight
Who has seen the griffon fly.
But his will is formed in magic
And not mortal flesh and bone
And if you would rule the griffon
You must first control your own.

The *kyree* is a creature
With a soul both old and wise
You must never think to fool him
For he sees through all disguise.
If you seek to call a *kyree*
All your secrets he shall plumb—
So be certain you are worthy
Or the *kyree*—will not come.

For your own heart you must conquer
If the firebird you would call
You must know the dark within you
Ere you seek the cold-drake's hall
Here is better rede, magician
Than those books upon your shelf—
If you seek to master others
You must master first yourself.

OATHBOUND
(*The Oathbound*, Tarma & Kethry)

CH: Bonds of blood and bonds of steel
  Bonds of god-fire and of need,
  Bonds that only we two feel
  Bonds of word and bonds of deed,
  Bonds we took—and knew the cost
  Bonds we swore without mistake
  Bonds that give more than we lost,
  Bonds that grant more than they take.

Tarma:

Kal'enedral, Sword-Sworn, I,
To my Star-Eyed Goddess bound,
With my pledge would vengeance buy
But far more than vengeance found.
Now with steel and iron will
Serve my Lady and my Clan
All my pleasure in my skill—
Nevermore with any man.

Kethry:

Bound am I by my own will
Never to misuse my power—
Never to pervert my skill
To the pleasures of an hour.
With this blade that I now wear
Came another bond indeed—

While her arcane gifts I share
I am bound to woman's Need.

Tarma:

And by blood-oath we are bound
Held by more than mortal bands
For the vow we swore was crowned
By god-fires upon our hands.

Kethry:

You are more than shield-sib now
We are bound, and yet are free
So I make one final vow—
That your Clan shall live through me.

ADVICE TO WOULD-BE HEROES
(Tarma)

So you want to go earning your keep with your sword
And you think it cannot be too hard—
And you dream of becoming a hero or lord
With your praises sung out by some bard.
Well now, let me then venture to give you advice
And when all of my lecture is done
We will see if my words have not made you think twice
About whether adventuring's "fun!"

Now before you seek shelter or food for yourself
Go seek first for those things for your beast
For he is worth far more than praises or pelf
Though a fool thinks to value him least.
If you've ever a moment at leisure to spare
Then devote it, as if to your god,
To his grooming, and practice, and weapons-repair
And to seeing you both are well-shod.

Eat you lightly and sparingly—never full-fed—
For a full belly founders your mind.
Ah, but sleep when you can—it is better than bread—
For on night-watch no rest will you find.
Do not boast of your skill, for there's always one more
Who would prove he is better than you.
Treat swordladies like sisters, and not like a whore
Or your wenching days, child, will be few.

When you look for a captain, then look for the man
Who thinks first of his men and their beasts,
And who listens to scouts, and has more than one plan,
And heeds not overmuch to the priests.
And if you become captain, when choosing your men
Do not look at the "heroes" at all.
For a hero dies young—rather choose yourself ten
Or a dozen whose pride's not so tall.

Now your Swordmaster's god—whosoever he be—
When he stands there before you to teach
And don't argue or whine, think to mock foolishly
Or you'll soon be consulting a leech!
Now most booty is taken by generals and kings
And there's little that's left for the low
So it's best that you learn skills, or work at odd things
To keep food in your mouth as you go.

And last, if you should chance to reach equal my years
You must find you a new kind of trade
For the plea that you're still spry will fall on deaf ears—
There's no work for old swords, I'm afraid.
Now if all that I've told you has not changed your mind
Then I'll teach you as best as I can.
For you're stubborn, like me, and like me of the kind
Becomes one *fine* swords-woman or -man!

THE PRICE OF COMMAND
(Captain Idra)

This is the price of commanding—
That you always stand alone,
Letting no one near
To see the fear
That's behind the mask you've grown.
This is the price of commanding.

This is the price of commanding—
That you watch your dearest die,
Sending women and men
To fight again,
And you never tell them why.
This is the price of commanding.

This is the price of commanding,
That mistakes are signed in red—
And that *you* won't pay
But others may,
And your best may wind up dead.
This is the price of commanding.

This is the price of commanding—
All the deaths that haunt your sleep.
And you hope they forgive
And so you live
With your memories buried deep.
This is the price of commanding.

This is the price of commanding—
That if you won't, others will.
So you take your post,
Mindful of each ghost—
You've a debt to them to fill.
This is the price of commanding.

THE ARCHIVIST
(Jadrek)

I sit amid the dusty books. The dust invades my very soul.
It coats my heart with weariness and chokes it with despair.
My life lies beached and withered on a lonely, bleak, uncharted shoal.
There are no kindred spirits here to understand, or care.

When I was young, how often I would feed my hungry mind with tales
And sought the fellowship in books I did not find in kin.
For one does not seek friends when every overture to others fails
So all the company I craved I built from dreams within.

Those dreams—from all my books of lore I plucked the wonders one
    by one
And waited for the day that I was certain was to come
When some new hero would appear whose quest had only now begun
With desperate need of lore and wisdom I alone could plumb.

And then, ah then, I'd ride away to join with legend and with song.
The trusted friend of heroes, figured in their words and deeds.
Until that day, among the books I'd dwell—but I have dwelt too long
And like the books I sit alone, a relic no one needs.

I grow too old, I grow too old, my aching bones have made me lame
And if my futile dream came true, I could not live it now.
The time is past, long past, when I could ride the wings of fleeting
    fame
The dream is dead beneath the dust, as 'neath the dust I bow.

So, unregarded and alone I tend these fragments of the past
Poor fool who bartered life and soul on dreams and useless lore.
And as I watch despair and bitterness enclose my heart at last
Within my soul's dark night I cry out, "Is there nothing more?"

LIZARD DREAMS
(Kethry: *Oathbound*)

Most folk avoid the Pelagir Hills, where ancient wars and battles
Were fought with magic, not with steel, for land and gold and chattels.
Most folk avoid the forest dark for magics still surround it
And change the creatures living there and all that dwell around it.
Within a tree upon a hill that glowed at night with magic
There lived a lizard named Gervase whose life was rather tragic.
His heart was brave, his mind was wise. He longed to be a wizard.
But who would ever think to teach their magic to a lizard?

So poor Gervase would sit and dream, or sigh as sadly rueing
That fate kept him forever barred from good he could be doing.
That he had wit and mind and will it cannot be debated
He also had the kindest heart that ever gods created.
One day as Gervase sighed and dreamed all in the forest sunning
He heard a noise of horse and hound and sounds of two feet running.
A human stumbled to his glade, a human worn and weary
Dressed in a shredded wizard's robe, his eyes past hope and dreary.

The magic of his birthplace gave Gervase the gift of speaking.
He hesitated not at all—ran to the wizard, squeaking,
"Hide human, hide! Hide in my tree!" he danced and pointed madly.
The wizard stared, the wizard gasped, then hid himself right gladly.
Gervase at once lay in the sun until the hunt came by him
Then like a simple lizard now he fled as they came nigh him.
And glowered in the hollow tree and hissed when they came near him
And bit a few dogs' noses so they'd yelp and leap and fear him.

"Thrice damn that wizard!" snarled his foe. "He's slipped our hunters
    neatly.
The hounds have surely been misled. They've lost the trail com-
    pletely."
He whipped the dogs off of the tree and sent them homeward running
And never once suspected it was all Gervase's cunning.
The wizard out of hiding crept. "Thrice blessing I accord you!
And is there somehow any way I can at all reward you?"
"I want to be a man like you!" Gervase replied unthinking.
"A wizard—or a man?" replied the mage who stared, unblinking.

"For I can only grant you one, the form of man, or power.
What will you choose? Choose wisely, I must leave within the hour."
Gervase in silence sat and thought, his mind in turmoil churning.
And first the one choice thinking on, then to the other turning.
Yes, he could have the power he craved, the magic of a wizard
But who'd believe that power lived inside a lowly lizard?
Or he could have the form of man, but what could he do in it?
And all the good he craved to do—how then could he begin it?

Within the Councils of the Wise there sits a welcome stranger
His word is sought by high and low if there is need or danger.
He gives his aid to all who ask, who need one to defend them
And every helpless creature knows he lives but to befriend them.
And though his form is very strange compared to those beside him
The mages care not for the form, but for the mind inside him.
For though he's small, and brightly scaled, they do not see a lizard.
He's called by all, both great and small, "Gervase, the Noble Wizard."
He's known by all, both great and small, Gervase the Lizard Wizard!

LOVERS UNTRUE
(Tarma: "Swordsworn")

"I shall love you till I die!"
Talasar and Dera cry.
He swears "On my life I vow
Only death could part us now!"
She says "You are life and breath
Nothing severs us but Death!"
Lightly taken, lightly spoke,
Easy vows are easy broke.

"Come and ride awhile with me,"
Talasar says to Varee,
"Look, the moon is rising high,
Countless stars bestrew the sky.
Come, or all the hours are flown
It's no night to lie alone."
This the one who lately cried
That he'd love until he died.

"Kevin, do you think me fair?"
Dera smiles, shakes back her hair.
"I have long admired you—
Come, the night is young and new
And the wind is growing cold—
I would see if you are bold—"
Is this she who vowed till death
Talasar was life and breath?

Comes the dawn—beneath a tree
Talasar lies with Varee.
But look—who should now draw near—
Dera and her Kevin-dear
He sees her—and she sees him—
Oh confusion! Silence grim!
Till he sighs, and shakes his head—(pregnant pause)
"Well, I guess we must be dead!"

THE LESLAC VERSION
(Leslac and Tarma)

Leslac: The warrior and the sorceress rode into Viden-town
   For they had heard of evil there and meant to bring it down
   An overlord with iron hand who ruled his folk with fear—
Tarma: Bartender, shut that minstrel up and bring another beer.

L: The warrior and the sorceress went searching high and low
T: That isn't true, I tell you, and I think that I should know!
L: They meant to find the tyrant who'd betrayed his people's trust
 And bring the monster's power and pride to tumble in the dust.

L: They searched through all the town to find and bring him to de-
  feat.
T: Like Hell! What we were looking for was wine and bread and
  meat!
L: They found him in the tavern and they challenged him to fight.
T: We found him holding up the bar, drunk as a pig, that night.

L: The tyrant laughed and mocked at them, with vile words and base.
T: He tripped on Warrl's tail, then took exception to my face.
L: The warrior was too wise for him; his blade clove only air!
T: He swung, I ducked, he lunged—and then he tripped over a chair.

L: With but a single blow the warrior brought him to his doom!
T: About that time he turned around—I got him with a broom.
L: And in a breath the deed was done! The tyrant-lord lay dead!
T: I didn't *mean* for him to hit the fire iron with his head!

L: The wife that he had kept shut up they freed and set on high
And Viden-town beneath her hand contentedly did lie.
T: I went to find his next-of-kin and to the girl confess—
"Your husband wasn't much before, but now he's rather less—"

T: "He was a drunken sot, and I'll be better off," she said.
"And while I can't admit it, I'm not sorry that he's dead.
So here's a little something—but you'd best be on your way—
I'll claim it was an accident if you'll just leave today."

L: In triumph out of Viden-town the partners rode again
To find another tyrant and to clean him from his den—
The scourge of evil and the answer to a desperate prayer!
T: Don't you believe a word of it—I *know*, 'cause I was there!

WIND'S FOUR QUARTERS
(Tarma: "Swordsworn")

CH: Wind's four quarters, air and fire
      Earth and water, hear my desire
      Grant my plea who stands alone—
      Maiden, Warrior, Mother and Crone.

Eastern wind blow clear, blow clean,
Cleanse my body of its pain,
Cleanse my mind of what I've seen,
Cleanse my honor of its stain.
Maid whose love has never ceased
Bring me healing from the East.

Southern wind blow hot, blow hard,
Fan my courage to a flame,
Southern wind be guide and guard,
Add your bravery to my name.
Let my will and yours be twinned,
Warrior of the Southern wind.

Western wind, stark, blow strong,
Grant me arm and mind of steel
On a road both hard and long.
Mother, hear me where I kneel.
Let no weakness on my quest
Hinder me, wind of the West.

Northern wind blow cruel, blow cold,
Sheathe my aching heart in ice,

Armor 'round my soul enfold.
Crone I need not call you twice.
To my foes bring the cold of death!
Chill me, North wind's frozen breath.

THE SWORDLADY, OR: "THAT SONG"

(Leslac)

Swordlady, valiant, no matter the foe,
Into the battle you fearlessly go—
Boldly you ride out beyond map and chart—
Why are you frightened to open your heart?

Swordlady, lady of consummate skill,
Lady of prowess, of strength and of will,
Swordlady, lady of cold ice and steel,
Why will you never admit that you feel?

Swordlady, mistress of all arts of war,
Wise in the ways of all strategic lore,
You fear no creature below or above,
Why do you shrink from the soft touch of love?

Swordlady, brave to endure wounds and pain,
Plunging through lightning, through thunder and rain,
Flinching from nothing, so high is your pride,
Why then pretend you hold nothing inside?

Swordlady, somewhere within you is hid
A creature of feeling that no vow can rid,
A woman—a girl, with a heart soft and warm,
No matter the brutal deeds that you perform.

Swordlady, somewhere inside of you deep,
Cowers the maiden that you think asleep,
Frozen within you, in ice shrouded womb
That you can only pretend is a tomb.

Swordlady, all of the vows you have made
Can never make your heart die as you've bade.
Swordlady, after the winter comes spring;
One day your heart will awaken and sing.

Swordlady, one day there must come a man
Who shall lift from you this self-imposed ban,
Thawing the ice that's enshrouded your soul,
On that day swordlady, you shall be whole.

SHIN'A'IN WARSONG

(The old tradition holds that the Shin'a'in—now forty-odd Clans in all—originally came from four: the Tale'sedrin (Children of the Hawk), the Liha'irden (Deer-sibs), the Vuysher'edras (Brothers of the Wolves), and the Pretera'sedrin (the Children of the Grasscats). Hence the monumental seriousness of the threat of declaring Tale'sedrin a dead Clan in *Oathbound*.)

Gold the dawn-sun spreads his wings—
Follow where the East-wind sings,
Brothers, sisters, side by side,
To defend our home we ride!

Eyes of Hawks the borders see—
Watchers, guard it carefully
Let no stranger pass it by—
Children of the Hawk, now fly!

CH: Maiden, Warrior, Mother, Crone,
     Help us keep this land our own.
     Rover, Guardian, Hunter, Guide,
     With us now forever ride.

Speed of deer, oh grant to these—
Swift to warn of enemies,
Fleeter far than any foe—
Deer-child, to the border go!

Cunning as the Wolf-pack now,
To no overlord we bow!

468

Lest some lord our freedom blight,
Brothers of the Wolves, we fight!

Brave, the great Cat guards his lair,
Teeth to rend and claws to tear.
Lead the battle, first to last,
Children of the Cat, hold fast!

Hawk and Cat, and Wolf and Deer,
Keep the plains now safe from fear,
Brothers, sisters, side by side,
To defend our home, we ride!

SHIN'A'IN SONG
OF THE SEASONS

(Although Tarma seldom mentioned the fact, her people have a four-aspected male deity to compliment the female. This song gives Him equal time with Her.)

The East wind is calling, so come ride away,
Come follow the Rover into the new day,
Come follow the Maiden, the Dark Moon, with me,
The new year's beginning, come ride out and see.

Come follow the Rover out onto the plains,
Come greet the new life under sweet, singing rains,
Come follow the Maiden beneath vernal showers,
For where her feet passed you will find fragrant flowers.

The South wind, oh hear it, we ride to the call
We follow the Guardian, the Lord of us all,
We follow the Warrior, the strong to defend,
The New Moon to fighters is ever a friend.

With summer comes fighting, with summer, our foes;
And how we must thwart them the Guardian knows.
The Warrior will give them no path but retreat,
The Warrior and Guardian will bring their defeat.

Come follow the West wind, the wind of the fall,
The Mother will cast her cloak over us all.
Come follow the Hunter out onto the plain,
Return to the Clan with the prey we have slain.

For now comes the autumn, the time of the West,
The season of Full Moon, of harvest, then rest.
So take from Her hands all the fruits of the fields,
And thank Him for all that the autumn-hunt yields.

The North wind, the cold wind, the wind of the snow,
Tells us, it is time winter pastures to go.
The Guide knows the path, and the Crone shows us how—
The Old Moon, and time for returning is now.

And if, with the winter, should come the last breath,
And riding, we ride out of life into death,
The Wise One, the Old Moon, will ease our last load,
The Guide will be waiting to show the new road.

THREES

(Leslac)

Deep into the stony hills, miles from keep or hold
A troupe of guards comes riding with a lady and her gold—
Riding in the center shrouded in her cloak of fur,
Companioned by a maiden and a toothless, aged cur.
Three things see no end, a flower blighted ere it bloomed,
A message that was wasted, and a journey that is doomed.

One among the guardsmen has a shifting, restless eye,
And as they ride he scans the hills that rise against the sky.
He wears both sword and bracelet worth more than he can afford,
And hidden in his baggage is a heavy, secret hoard.
Of three things be wary, of a feather on a cat,
The shepherd eating mutton and the guardsman that is fat.

From ambush, bandits screaming charge the packtrain and its prize,
And all but four within the train are taken by surprise,
And all but four are cut down as a woodsman fells a log,
The guardsman, and the lady, and the maiden, and the dog,
Three things know a secret—first, the lady in a dream,
The dog that barks no warning and the maid who does not scream.

Then off the lady pulls her cloak, in armor she is clad,
Her sword is out and ready, and her eyes are fierce and glad.
The maiden gestures briefly and the dog's a cur no more—
A wolf, sword-maid and sorceress now face the bandit corps!
Three things never anger or you will not live for long,
A wolf with cubs, a man with power and a woman's sense of wrong.

The bandits growl a challenge and the lady only grins,
The sorceress bows mockingly, and then the fight begins!
When it ends there are but four left standing from that horde
The witch, the wolf, the traitor, and the woman with the sword!
Three things never trust in, the maiden sworn as "pure,"
The vows a king has given and the ambush that is "sure."

They strip the traitor naked and they whip him on his way
Into the barren hillsides like the folks he used to slay.
They take a thorough vengeance for the women he cut down
And then they mount their horses and they journey back to town.
Three things trust and cherish well, the horse on which you ride,
The beast that guards and watches and the sister at your side!

For further information on these songs, send a stamped, self-addressed envelope to:

FIREBIRD ARTS AND MUSIC
(formerly Off-Centaur Publications)
PO Box 424
El Cerrito, CA 94530